continued . . .

W9-AYY-443

Much Ado in the Moonlight

"A pure delight." —*Huntress Book Reviews*

"A consummate storyteller . . . Will keep the reader on the edge of their seat, unable to put the book down until the very last word."
—*ParaNormal Romance Reviews*

"No one melds ghosts and time travel better than the awesome Kurland."
—*Romantic Times*

Dreams of Stardust

"Kurland weaves another fabulous read with just the right amounts of laughter, romance, and fantasy." —*Affaire de Coeur*

"Kurland crafts some of the most ingenious time-travel romances readers can find . . . Wonderfully clever and completely enchanting."
—*Romantic Times*

A Garden in the Rain

"Kurland laces her exquisitely romantic, utterly bewitching blend of contemporary romance and time travel with a delectable touch of tart wit, leaving readers savoring every word of this superbly written romance."
—*Booklist*

"Kurland is clearly one of romance's finest writers—she consistently delivers the kind of stories readers dream about. Don't miss this one."
—*The Oakland Press*

From This Moment On

"A disarming blend of romance, suspense, and heartwarming humor, this book is romantic comedy at its best." —*Publishers Weekly*

"A deftly plotted delight, seasoned with a wonderfully wry sense of humor and graced with endearing, unforgettable characters." —*Booklist*

My Heart Stood Still

"Written with poetic grace and a wickedly subtle sense of humor . . . The essence of pure romance. Sweet, poignant, and truly magical, this is a rare treat: romance with characters readers will come to care about and a love story they will cherish."
—*Booklist*

"A totally enchanting tale, sensual and breathtaking . . . An absolute must-read."
—*Rendezvous*

If I Had You

"Kurland brings history to life . . . in this tender medieval romance."
—*Booklist*

"A passionate story filled with danger, intrigue, and sparkling dialogue."
—*Rendezvous*

The More I See You

"The superlative Ms. Kurland once again wows her readers with her formidable talent as she weaves a tale of enchantment that blends history with spellbinding passion and impressive characterization, not to mention a magnificent plot."
—*Rendezvous*

Another Chance to Dream

"Kurland creates a special romance between a memorable knight and his lady."
—*Publishers Weekly*

The Very Thought of You

"A masterpiece . . . This fabulous tale will enchant anyone who reads it."
—*Painted Rock Reviews*

This Is All I Ask

"An exceptional read."
—*The Atlanta Journal-Constitution*

"Both powerful and sensitive . . . A wonderfully rich and rewarding book."
—Susan Wiggs

A Time FOR Love

LYNN KURLAND

B

BERKLEY SENSATION, NEW YORK

THE BERKLEY PUBLISHING GROUP
Published by the Penguin Group
Penguin Group (USA) Inc.
375 Hudson Street, New York, New York 10014, USA
Penguin Group (Canada), 90 Eglinton Avenue East, Suite 700, Toronto, Ontario M4P 2Y3, Canada
(a division of Pearson Penguin Canada Inc.)
Penguin Books Ltd., 80 Strand, London WC2R 0RL, England
Penguin Group Ireland, 25 St. Stephen's Green, Dublin 2, Ireland (a division of Penguin Books Ltd.)
Penguin Group (Australia), 250 Camberwell Road, Camberwell, Victoria 3124, Australia
(a division of Pearson Australia Group Pty. Ltd.)
Penguin Books India Pvt. Ltd., 11 Community Centre, Panchsheel Park, New Delhi—110 017, India
Penguin Group (NZ), 67 Apollo Drive, Rosedale, North Shore 0632, New Zealand
(a division of Pearson New Zealand Ltd.)
Penguin Books (South Africa) (Pty.) Ltd., 24 Sturdee Avenue, Rosebank, Johannesburg 2196,
South Africa

Penguin Books Ltd., Registered Offices: 80 Strand, London WC2R 0RL, England

This book is an original publication of The Berkley Publishing Group.

PRINTING HISTORY
Berkley Sensation trade paperback edition / September 2010

Library of Congress Cataloging-in-Publication Data

Kurland, Lynn.
   A time for love / Lynn Kurland.—Berkley Sensation trade pbk. ed.
      p.   cm.
   ISBN 978-0-425-23654-3 (trade pbk.)
   I. Title.
   PS3561.U645T57   2010   2010020513
   813'.54—dc22

PRINTED IN THE UNITED STATES OF AMERICA

10 9 8 7 6 5 4 3 2 1

CONTENTS

Another Chance to Dream

To Lynn Rowley, dearest of friends,
whose opinion of my work given
via a gas station pay phone truly
changed the course of my life

ACKNOWLEDGMENTS

No author is an island, as it were, and that was never truer than with the writing of this book. The author most gratefully acknowledges aid from the following exceptional individuals:

Elane Osborn, for such fabulous title inspiration;

Dr. Kirk Lorimer, who never fails to enthusiastically ponder the gruesome possibilities of medieval wounds and their complications;

Gail Fortune, editor extraordinaire, for consistently giving the author the freedom to follow her heart;

and Matthew, who gave up vacations and other precious free time to be the author's hands while those hands were tending to the needs of a little one.

❧ Winter ❧

THE YEAR OF OUR LORD 1200

1

She was going to die.

It was a pity, though, to die so soon, seeing that so much of her life remained before her and that 'twas only now she'd had her first taste of true freedom. But there was no denying the direness of her current plight. Who would have thought it took such skill to ride a horse? Perhaps she should have spent more time in the stables learning of horses and less time loitering in her mother's solar working heroic designs on fine linen. That she could scarce tell one end of a horse from the other should have told her that she knew too little about them to handle one with any skill.

Too late now for regrets. All she could do at present was cling to the saddle with one hand and the horse's mane with the other and watch as both the surrounding countryside and the more noteworthy events of her life rushed past her with dizzying speed. Her sins, too, seemed determined to present themselves to her with all haste—likely before the horse either ran her into a tree or managed to scrape her from his back and leave her in a broken heap on the wild grass.

Stealing. Aye, there was that grievous folly for which she would unfortunately have no time to make a penance. At the time, though, thievery had seemed her only choice. She'd needed a sword to aid her in her new choice of vocation and 'twas a certainty no one would have given her one had she asked for it. It had taken her a pair of days to study the inhabitants of her fiancé's keep intently enough to decide on a likely victim. Fortunately the hall was in enough disrepair and the knights drunken enough for the most part that filching a sword had been an easy task. She half suspected her prey had laid it beside him in the marshy rushes on the great hall floor and then thought he had lost it in the filth. Obviously the like had happened to others, for the lout had only cursed heartily, received condolences from his fellows, and then gotten on with his business.

As far as repenting went, perhaps she also should have done so for the bodily damage she'd done to a pair of knights and a serving wench as she'd struggled to get herself and her newly acquired sword to the stables without being marked as who she truly was. One wouldn't have thought merely walking about with a blade strapped to one's hip would have been so hazardous to others nearby.

Lying. She squirmed in discomfort, but what else could she have done? 'Twas perfectly reasonable to have won booty while dicing—never mind that she'd never thrown a die in her life. And if she were going to win some beast while gambling, why not Alain of Ayre's finest stallion? The stableboy had swallowed her tale readily enough and seemingly been impressed with her wagering skills.

Besides, lying and stealing were perfectly acceptable traits in a mercenary. Indeed, she suspected such talents were more than desirable; they were necessary. Perhaps they would make up for her lack of ability with a sword.

And, of course, with a horse. Her teeth snapped together as she bumped along furiously on the back of her racing steed. A pity the reins were naught but a fond memory as they dangled well out of her reach. They likely would have aided her in controlling the beast.

Her third sin fought mightily for her attention, but she ignored it. Yet the harder the horse's hooves pounded against the earth, the more the very sound of the word seemed to echo in her head: *covetousness.* She coveted a man and that surely was something to repent of. Never mind that his very reputation should have sent any sensible maid fleeing for cover. 'Twas said he wanted nothing to do with wedded bliss, though she believed otherwise. But it had been a handful of years since she'd seen him last, so 'twas possible things had changed. She had cause to wonder. He should have returned from France long ago.

But the man hadn't, so she was left with speculation about not only the state of his feelings for her, but the truth of the tales circulating about him. She had decided to take matters into her own hands and seek him out. And if the rumors were true that he no longer wanted a wife, perhaps he wouldn't be opposed to having another sword to guard his back. And if it took her even as long as a pair of months to hone her skills so she could offer them to him, then so be it. She would have Sir Rhys de Piaget, whether he willed it or not.

His battle prowess was a desirable thing. His foul temper could be ignored. His singlemindedness could eventually be turned from swordplay to her. Convincing him to wed her might entail tidying her person up a bit and unlearning the warrior's skills she currently sought to acquire, but she felt certain she would manage it. No matter the perils of pursuing him, no matter the rigors of living as a mercenary while her swordplay improved, it would be worth the effort if he were the prize.

It certainly was preferable to the hellish future she'd left leagues behind her at Ayre.

She stiffened in fear as a low fence of rocks appeared suddenly before her.

Her mount, however, seemed to find it much to his liking if the equine glee with which he sailed over it was any indication. Gwen was reunited with the saddle, accompanied by a mighty clacking of her teeth. She realized immediately that dwelling on her destination was a dangerous activity, given that all her attentions should have been focused on her mount.

She raced through the countryside, feeling as if an eternity had passed since she'd managed to get herself into the saddle outside Ayre's gates. Perhaps speed was a boon. By the time Alain realized she had fled, she would be well on her way to Dover. Surely it would be a simple thing to sell her betrothal ring and find passage to the continent. If not, more lying and stealing would likely be called for. 'Twas a good thing she'd had her first taste of both while still on familiar ground. She suspected she could do either now without so much as a twitch.

She caught sight of something dark out of the corner of her eye. She hazarded a second glance only to find that a man was riding toward her. She would have stiffened in horror, but she feared to move, so she contented herself with a small squeak which was immediately lost in the rushing of wind around her. Merciful saints above, had Alain noticed her absence this quickly and sent someone to fetch her? Or was it instead another mercenary, bent on stealing her blade and her horse?

Ah, so the first test of her mettle would come sooner than she had thought. Perhaps 'twas just as well. Like her vices, her skill with the sword could be first tried while she was still on English soil.

If she could have stopped her horse long enough to draw her sword, that is.

"Away with you, oaf!" she shouted as the man drew alongside her. Then she realized it was more the tone her mother might have taken with a recalcitrant servant. She immediately attempted something more mercenary-like.

"Leave me be, you . . . you . . ." She racked her poor brains for something appropriately vulgar, but soon found herself distracted by the amazing display of horsemanship going on alongside her.

Without so much as a pucker of concentration marring his brow, the young man leaned over, reached out a gloved hand, and swept up her reins. A sharply spoken word and a healthy tug brought her horse to a gradual, graceful, and quite dignified stop. Gwen was so grateful for the cessation of motion, she couldn't find her tongue to speak. That, and she was too busy running it over her teeth to make certain all of them still resided in their proper places.

Satisfied they had survived the journey thus far, she bared them at the man and held out her hand for her reins. Then she pulled back her hand. Dirty as she might be, she looked passing tidy compared to the man facing her. Touching him was not something she was sure she wanted to do.

He'd been traveling, and for a great amount of time, if the condition of his worn cloak told the tale true. He would have been better off to have shaved his cheeks more often, for his beard was ragged and scruffy. Shaving also might have helped scrape away a bit of the dirt that adorned his features. Indeed, the whole of him could have used a good scouring.

She considered. A mercenary, and obviously a good one by the disreputable look of him. A pity she hadn't the time to sit and have speech with him. He might have offered her advice on how to comport herself.

She sighed regretfully and turned her mind back to the task at hand, namely recapturing her reins so she might be on her way again.

"Release my mount, you fiend," she commanded in her huskiest tone.

"*Your* mount?" the man drawled. "Why is it such an idea stretches the very limits of my imagination?"

"Perhaps you use yours less than I do mine," she said, sending him what she hoped was an intimidating glare.

"Horse thieves are hanged, you know."

"Won him dicing," Gwen returned, finding that this time she hadn't even flinched while spouting that bit of untruth. Indeed, she was beginning to think perhaps learning the skill of dicing would be a good addition to her repertoire. Who knew what sorts of things she might acquire thusly?

"From whom, lad?"

"Alain of Ayre, not that 'tis any of your business. Now, give me those bloody reins!"

The man only shook his head with a smile. "Alain is many things, but so poor a gambler he is not. No boy would have bested him so thoroughly as to have relieved him of this piece of horseflesh."

"Then you know little of me," she said, eyeing her reins and wishing her horse would in his shifting but shift a bit closer so she might make a more successful capture, "for I am most skilled not only with dice, but also with the sword. And," she added, "I am a bloody good horseman!"

She leaned over and snatched the reins from his hand.

And with the next breath, she found that her horse was no longer beneath her.

As she lay with her face in the dirt, she wondered if she might have executed her move with a bit more grace. She was too winded at first to notice that she no longer held on to her horse's reins, or that her horse was no longer close enough to step on her and crush the life from her. She could hear the man shouting at her, but it took her several moments before the ringing in her ears cleared enough for her to understand what he was saying.

"—trampled, you fool! Saints above, since when do the lads in England know so little about horseflesh? Bloody hell, but you're just as much trouble as I suspected you'd be. Damn that chivalry; I should make ignoring it more of a habit. As if I had time to aid some fool youth who'll find himself hanged inside a fortnight just the same!"

The tirade went on as Gwen managed to heave herself to her feet. She looked about her for her mount.

"There!" the man said, gesturing impatiently back the way she had come. The bay was nothing but a speck in the distance. "He's gone home to Ayre, likely to look for someone who has the skill to ride him!"

Gwen considered her situation. Horseless and bruised, she stood little chance of walking all the way to France. She eyed the young man before her, then looked at his very well-behaved mount. There appeared to be only one course of action. She twitched aside her cloak, put her hand on her sword hilt, and planted her feet a manly distance apart.

"You cost me my horse," she said. "I believe I'll have yours in trade."

That, at least, was enough to stop the man's tirade. He blinked at her in astonishment.

"Surely you jest," he said, seemingly overcome by the very thought.

Gwen took courage at his expression. Obviously she presented a more intimidating look than she'd dared hope. Perhaps it had to do with the unruly swing to her shorn locks. She hadn't been half satisfied with the work her eating dagger had done on her tresses, but plainly the raggedness lent her a dangerous air. The soot she had liberally smudged on her face no doubt added to her sinister appearance. Perhaps she would need to do less lying and stealing than she'd feared, if her aspect would daunt those about her. That she should intimidate someone even dirtier than she gave her a fresh surge of courage.

She motioned him down with a wave of her hand. "I'm in earnest. Dismount, if you will, lest you force me to draw my sword."

A corner of the man's mouth began to twitch under his scruffy beard. Fear, Gwen noted with satisfaction. Aye, this was much easier than she'd thought it would be.

"Let me see if I understand you aright," the man said, leaning on the pommel of his saddle. "You wish me to dismount and hand over the reins of my horse. To you."

"Aye."

"To you, who could not control that pitiful beast from Ayre's stables."

Gwen gritted her teeth. "He is a very fine horse. Powerfully spirited. Besides," she added when the man looked less than convinced, "even the most seasoned of mercenaries has the occasional run of ill luck."

The man snorted, then began to cough, his eyes watering madly. Gwen toyed with the idea of felling him while he struggled to regain control, then reluctantly let go of the thought. It wouldn't be sporting to do in a man who was obviously having such trouble breathing.

"By the saints," the man said, gasping.

Gwen folded her arms across her chest and frowned. "You've no need to fear. I'll do you no harm if you'll but dismount *now* and let me be on my way. I've many leagues to travel before the sun sets."

He wiped the tears from his eyes with the back of his glove, smudging a bit of the dirt in the process, snorted yet another time, then seemed to master his fear. "Is the whole of Ayre coming after you, or just Alain?"

"Likely the whole garrison," she said impatiently, "so as you might imagine, I've little time to waste. Now, do you obey me or must I draw my sword?"

The man swung down with another muffled exclamation of fear. At least Gwen thought it was fear. He was still wiping his eyes and his shoulders were shaking. There could be no other explanation for his actions.

He took off his soiled cloak and tossed it over his saddle, then stepped a few paces away from his mount. Gwen took a moment to indulge in envy that he possessed a mount who remained where he'd been left, then turned her mind to other matters—namely the man standing before her wearing a sword that seemingly didn't get in his way when he moved. Then there was that ruby the size of a child's fist in the hilt of his sword. Who was he? How had he come by such a sword and a mount that any knight would have groveled to own?

A pity she wouldn't have answers to those questions. Already she had wasted more time on him than she had to spare. She planted her feet more firmly in the dirt and dragged herself back to the task at hand.

"I can see you wish not to cooperate," she said. "You leave me with no choice but to do you bodily harm."

He lifted one shoulder in a negligent shrug. "'Tis a chance I'll have to take. I have yet need of my horse."

"As you will then. It pains me to do this," she said, gritting her teeth as she struggled to remove her stolen sword from its sheath, "but you are obviously a stubborn"—she huffed as she twisted herself to one side for better control—"soul with perhaps a less developed desire for long life than another." She jerked the sword free triumphantly, then almost went sprawling from the movement. She let the sword rest where it seemed to want to—point down in the dirt—and hunched over it as if she'd meant to be doing the like. "One last chance to spare yourself."

"You are too kind."

"Aye, 'tis a trait I'm seeking to rid myself of," she agreed, grasping the sword and pulling it upright. "It only hampers me in my mercenary endeavors."

"I can see how it might."

Gwen felt a small twinge of unease at the fact that the man had not yet drawn his sword. It seemed passing unfair that she should cut him down where he stood, but surely she had offered him ample opportunity to save himself, hadn't she?

She lifted her blade and brandished it. Saints, but she should have been hefting other things besides sewing needles these past few months. The blade wasn't that heavy, but to untried arms it was very awkward. With a grunt she got the blade upright and pointing in the man's direction. She gave him her most menacing glance and waved her blade meaningfully at him.

He shook his head. "I should have remained abed this morn."

"Too late for regrets now," Gwen said, swinging her sword carefully. It moved more easily than she'd hoped, but it certainly was reluctant to give her any ideas on where she should cut first.

"Go to, would you?" he asked politely. "I am in haste, with much to see accomplished before the sun sets."

"I *am* going to," Gwen said, through gritted teeth. "This sword is heavier than those I am accustomed to."

"Perhaps if you waved it with more enthusiasm, you might manage to nick me here or there."

"I know that," she said, beginning to wonder if he thought her less skilled than he should. She took a swipe at him. It almost sent her sprawling, but she managed to regain her feet before the blade overbalanced her into the dirt. She shoved the remains of her hair out of her eyes and frowned at him. "Are you ready to cry peace yet?"

"Not quite yet."

"Then fight me," she said. She lifted her weapon against him again. "You haven't even drawn your swo—"

Sword, she meant to say. Somehow, though, the word was lost in her astonishment at the feeling of her blade leaving her hand. She stared in fascination as it flipped end over end up into the air and then came back down, flashing in the sunlight. The man caught it neatly with his left hand. He resheathed his own sword—the one she hadn't even seen him draw—then assessed hers with a practiced glance.

"Damascus steel," he noted with admiration. "You've a good eye, at least." He impaled her sword into the dirt next to him. "From whom did you filch it?"

"I won it d—"

"—dicing," he finished with a sigh. "Lying is a sin, you know. As is stealing."

"Desirable traits in any ruthless mercenary," she corrected him. "Now, as you have made off with my sword in such a dishonorable manner, you leave me with no choice but to take my knife to you."

He clapped his hand to his head with a groan. Taking that as a very good sign, Gwen fumbled in her boot for her dagger. She drew it forth with a flourish, hoping it had come out as if she'd planned the whole exercise to come down to this.

The man didn't move, so she took her courage in hand and stabbed the air in front of her with as much fierceness as she could muster.

Stabbing the man before her was, however, quite another matter.

The man shook his head sadly and clucked his tongue.

Perhaps if she merely impaled him in his sword arm it would wound him enough that he would be unable to wield his blade, but it wouldn't finish him off. It occurred to her that she would likely be finishing off a great number of men in her future as a hired sword, but that would perhaps come later when she had more stomach for the deed. For her first conquest, a mere stabbing would have to do.

She lifted her knife and commanded her body to fling itself forward.

Her arm, and her feet for that matter, wouldn't cooperate.

"Too bloody much time at a tapestry frame," she muttered under her breath. She took herself in hand and tried again. She forced the blade to descend and felt a faint satisfaction when she saw it heading directly for the man's upper arm.

And then quite suddenly she found her wrist captured in a firm grip and her knife removed from her hand. And then the man paused. He looked at her and frowned.

"Have we met?"

Saints above, this was all she needed, to be recognized and carried back to Ayre.

"Nay. Never," she said, gritting her teeth and trying to pull her hand from his. "'Tis my fierce mercenary mien that has confused you. I've no doubt you've seen like expressions on many fighting men's faces."

"Nay," he said, staring at her intently.

He looked at her shorn hair, tucked her knife in his belt, then clamped a hand on her shoulder to hold her in place. Before Gwen could protest, he reached out and started to clean her face with the hem of his tunic sleeve. Apparently that didn't satisfy him, for he licked the fingers of one hand and rubbed industriously on her cheeks.

"What do you—" she spluttered.

He whirled her around so the sun shone down on her face. She blinked against the brightness of it. He reached out suddenly and tucked her hair behind her ears. Then he went still and his jaw hung slack.

"Gwen?" he gasped.

Aye, she almost said, then it occurred to her that no one loitering so far from her own keep should have known who she was. She frowned up at him.

"And you would be. . . ?"

He smiled dryly. "Ah, how soon they forget, these fickle maids. Though I will admit," he said, reaching out to tug on her ear, "that though you don't look much cleaner than the first time we met, you smell much more pleasant."

And in that moment she knew.

"Merciful saints above," she breathed. "'Tis you."

"Aye, *chérie*, 'tis I."

Gwen frowned. She hadn't intended to be covered with muck the next time she saw the man before her.

She opened her mouth to begin to ask the scores of questions she had to put to him, then she caught sight behind him of a company of horsemen in the distance. Alain of Ayre's white stallion was easily recognizable in the lead. Gwen closed her mouth around her queries.

"Alain comes," she said simply.

"Damn," he said, looking over his shoulder. He looked back at her. "You've been at Ayre?"

She nodded.

He frowned deeply. "We've much to discuss, I can see. But later," he added, with another look over his shoulder. "Perhaps he won't recognize me in my current state."

"We couldn't be so fortunate." She looked up at him appraisingly. "Obviously we'll have to invent a ruse for why we're together."

The man's eyes widened, then he began to back away. "Nay, not that."

"We must."

"We *mustn't*. I'm not recovered from the last time—"

"What other choice do we have?"

He shook his head firmly. "We have several—"

Gwen knew there was nothing else to be done. With a regretful smile, Gwen drew back her arm and then let fly her fist . . .

Straight into Sir Rhys de Piaget's nose.

2

England, 1190

Rhys rode in the rear of his foster father's company and gaped at the castle that rose up before him. He had seen a great deal of England and France given his tender age of ten-and-four, and considered himself mature and fairly jaded, but all he'd seen as he traveled over Segrave's land had left him almost speechless. He wondered if Segrave looked magnificent simply because of what he'd left behind him at Ayre. Bertram of Ayre was not poor by Rhys's standards, but his modest wealth and small keep paled to insignificance when compared to what Rhys had seen that day.

Segrave's walls were sturdy and in good repair. The land surrounding the outer walls was cleared of all trees and other growth that could have provided shelter to an enemy. And, amazingly enough, the folk here seemed to be using the moat for defense. At Ayre the water was simply a place to fling refuse, leaving the keep's inhabitants suffering as much as any foe who might find himself tripping into the moat. Though as far as defenses went, Ayre might have the advantage when it came to filthy water keeping an army at bay.

The drawbridge came down smoothly and settled gently into a fitting that was seemingly fashioned just for the receiving of it—nothing like the crude bridge that welcomed a body to Ayre's unkempt courtyard. Rhys spared a moment to admire such fine construction, then reined in his mount and looked back over the way he had come. As interesting as the keep might have been, it surely didn't compare to the fields he had just crossed.

By the saints, the land was beautiful.

It had been all he could do to keep himself in the saddle that morn. What he had wanted was to be wandering through those fields, bending to feel the warm earth slide between his fingers, smelling the grasses and flowers. He had wanted to walk over every inch of it, feel it beneath his feet, and lose himself in the dream that such a place might be his.

"Rhys?"

Rhys turned to look at the man who had spoken to him. He jerked to attention out of habit. "Aye?" he asked.

Montgomery of Wyeth, the captain of Bertram's guard, smiled. "Little lad, you're staring the wrong way. The beauty of Segrave finds itself inside the walls, not out."

Rhys shook his head. "Your eyes fail you, Captain. Nothing can compare to what I've already seen."

"Ah, the wisdom of youth," Montgomery said, not unkindly. "Have I not told you enough tales of the maid of Segrave to pique your curiosity?"

"What is a maid but a means to land?" he asked. "Besides, she is very young."

"She has nine summers," Montgomery said with a knowing smile, "and she shows every promise of inheriting her mother's considerable beauty. Come, young one, look on her and see if I don't have it aright."

"As you will," Rhys said reluctantly, and he wanted to add, *What good will such a thing do me?* Gwennelyn of Segrave was so far above him in station he stood little chance of ever being in the same hall with her, much less being allowed to gape at her. Besides, she was a child. He had no interest in children.

Her land, however, was a different tale entirely.

But there was also no sense in lusting after what he could never have, so he followed Montgomery across the drawbridge and into the bailey. Lads came to take their horses. Rhys dismounted and started toward the stable, but then halted when he heard his foster father call to him. He turned to find Bertram approaching.

"Let them, son," Bertram said. "You've no need to see to such things now."

Rhys inclined his head respectfully. "Thank you, my lord, but I prefer to tend my own mount."

Bertram looked at him for a moment in silence, then shook his head with a smile. "As you will, Rhys. Come join us in the hall when you've finished. I'll introduce you to William of Segrave, as he asked specifically to meet you. I suppose he wishes to see for himself how a lad knighted so young carries himself."

Rhys nodded and made his way to the stables. He was accustomed to, if not fairly uncomfortable with, the notice his knighting had garnered him. By the saints, it wasn't as if he'd asked to be knighted at the battle of Marchenoir, especially having just reached his fourteenth summer. But who had he been to say nay to Phillip of France? Especially considering his family's relations with the French monarch. Though he had chosen a different path from his father and grandfather, he was still a de Piaget and Phillip considered him his.

By the time Rhys had tended his horse, he'd ceased thinking of political intrigues and Segrave's soil, and turned his mind to the filling of his belly. Perhaps William would exchange an introduction for a hearty meal. Rumor had it that Joanna of Segrave laid a fine table indeed.

He hadn't taken two paces from the stables when he heard a horrible noise coming from the pigsty. He looked about him, but no one seemed to find it out of the ordinary. Men carried on with their tasks, though some of them were smiling. Rhys shrugged and started across the bailey to the hall, but found himself stopping but a pace or two later.

Those were not sounds that normally came from a piggery.

He found that his curiosity was a more powerful force for once than his desire for a full belly. He turned about and made for what sounded like a beastie from the forests venting its anger. He rounded the corner of the stables and came to a dead halt. There was indeed a body making those horrendous noises, but it wasn't something foul from the forest.

It was a girl.

She sat in the muck and wailed for all she was worth. Rhys suspected that she might have tried to make an escape, for there were smears upon the gate in the shape of hands, and there were indentations in the muck where evidently she had stomped about in frustration. Not being a practiced judge in these matters, Rhys couldn't tell how old she was, though he supposed her to be of a fair age. She was not a girl full grown, though certainly old enough to have escaped the sty on her own. Perhaps there was more to it than what he could see. Rhys approached carefully.

The girl looked up at him and, blessedly, stopped wailing.

Rhys leaned upon the gate and stared back at her. "Trapped?" he asked.

She only blinked, then nodded, her chin beginning to quiver.

"Someone lock you in?"

She nodded again. "Geoffrey of Fenwyck."

Rhys knew of Fenwyck, but nothing of his son. Obviously a lad of little chivalry, but a fair amount of imagination judging by the cleverness of the knots binding the gate closed. Little wonder the girl hadn't been able to let herself out. Why she hadn't climbed the fence he didn't know, but that was a girl for you. The reason she found herself therein, however, was another matter entirely. Rhys leaned on the fence and looked at her speculatively.

"Why'd he do it?"

The girl scowled. "In return for my locking him in the tower chamber I suppose."

Rhys felt one of his eyebrows go up of its own accord. "That took some doing. Is he so foolish then?"

"Nay, 'tis that I have a very practiced imagination. My mother tells me so often." She seemed to take her declaration as simple fact, for there was no look of boasting hiding under all that mud on her face. "I saw him filch a bottle of my sire's finest claret. When he threatened to toss me in the dungeon if I told, I took the empty bottle, put it in the chamber, and sent a messenger to tell him that yet another bottle awaited him there."

Rhys stroked his chin thoughtfully. This was not a normal young girl he faced here. He wondered how many white hairs she had given her sire already.

"I assume you're here," Rhys mused, "because he knew you arranged that. Did you turn the key in the lock yourself?"

"Aye," she said, and there was pride in her face this time. "He deserved it, the wretch. He told me but yester-eve that my ears stick out from my head most unattractively and that no wimple ever stitched would hide them."

Rhys put his hand to his mouth and chewed on his finger to keep from laughing. The child wore no wimple at present, and he couldn't help but agree with Fenwyck's description of her ears. But 'twas passing unchivalrous to say so. And he suspected he would do well not to irritate her. She spoke with the tongue of a woman full grown, and Rhys suspected her schemes were just as ripened. Best to remain in her good graces.

He undid the gate and looked at the captive.

"You'll have to hurry, lest the piglets escape as well."

Said piglets were rooting enthusiastically at her skirts. At least the sow was nowhere to be seen. Credit young Fenwyck with some sense about that.

The girl, however, only sat and looked at him.

"Well, come on," he said, gesturing to her. "You're free now."

She started to rise, then her feet slipped out from under her and she fell back into the muck with a very wet splatting sound. Her chin began to quiver. When tears started to leak from her eyes and forge a trail of cleanness down her cheeks, Rhys knew he had to do something. It was tempting to hasten the other way, but the noise in his head made by his sword kept him where he was. That and the weight of all the lectures he'd heard from his foster father over the years. A chivalrous knight would remain and rescue the maid from her plight. Rhys sighed. He wasn't overly fond of the thought of layering his boots with muck, but there was obviously nothing else he could do if he intended to live up to the standards Bertram of Ayre had set for him.

He stepped into the pigsty. With another sigh he reached down and pulled the girl up and into his arms. He forced himself not to complain when she threw her arms around him and buried her face in his neck. And as he stepped from the pen, he came to a conclusion.

Chivalry was a messy business indeed.

He set the girl down outside the piggery, then shut the gate. Then he turned to her and used the sleeve of his tunic to wipe away some of the mud that was smeared over her face. She looked up at him with pale, tear-filled eyes.

"My gratitude," she sniffed.

"'Twas my pleasure," he said, trying to ignore her smell, which had now become his smell.

She looked down at her gown. "'Tis ruined," she said sadly.

"Perhaps if you let it dry."

"'Twas my finest stitchery," she said, showing him the hem of her sleeve. "See?"

He meant to obey, but made the mistake of looking at her and truly seeing her. And for the first time in the extensive experience fourteen years had given him, Rhys felt himself grow a tiny bit weak in the knees.

The girl had the most beautiful eyes he had ever seen.

"See?" she repeated.

It was with effort that he dragged his eyes down to her sleeve. He looked at the mud-encrusted fabric and nodded gravely, as if he actually could see the stitches worked there.

"Terrible tragedy," he managed. "Truly."

"I should be avenged. The knave should pay for his dishonorable assault upon me."

Well, obviously this one had been listening to too many *chansons*, but Rhys refrained from saying so. 'Twas a simple matter to remain silent, actually. The girl had rendered him speechless.

"I'll need a champion," she said, looking up at him appraisingly.

"Um. . ."

She looked down at his sword. He could feel the metal heat under her gaze. It came close to burning a stripe down his leg even through the sheath.

"You're young to be wearing a sword," she said.

"Well, I—"

Then her eyes widened. "By the saints," she breathed, "you're Rhys de Piaget. My father told me of you. You were knighted but a pair of months ago for saving Lord Ayre's life. Why, you're a knight of *legendary* prowess!"

She wiped unconsciously at her face, leaving a large swath of mud running down her cheek. Then she seemed to remember her ears, for she reached up to rearrange her hair about them. More dung was left behind.

"My mother's minstrels already tell tales of your skill." She looked at him worshipfully. "You could be my champion."

Rhys blinked. *This* was Gwennelyn of Segrave? Lays had been written describing in intimate detail the beauty of her mother's face and her goodness of heart. Bards, players of instruments, and artisans all came to kneel at the feet of the former lady-in-waiting to Queen Eleanor and offer up to her their finest work. Rhys had not been so distracted by his sword-play that he hadn't listened now and then to the rumors of the woman's beauty, or the rumors of how the promise of that beauty rested heavily on Joanna's daughter.

Was everyone blind, or was he himself so distracted by the overwhelming stench of pig manure that clung to the both of them that he couldn't see what others had been raving about?

As he contemplated that, he found himself torn between looking at the muck now in Gwen's hair and squirming under the weight of her assessing gaze.

"Aye," she said with a smile, "I couldn't ask for a more chivalrous knight to restore my honor to me. Already I can imagine how the battle will go."

So could he and it would finish with him trotting off to her father's gibbet. But before he could tell her that Geoffrey of Fenwyck was a baron's son and mere knights did not go about challenging baron's sons, she had taken him by the arm and started back to the hall.

"Challenge him after we sup," she advised. "I'll have a wash so that I might look my best while I watch you dispatch him. You will dispatch him, won't you?"

One thing he would accord her; she had the most stunning pair of aqua eyes he'd ever seen. How could a man, even a young man such as himself, say nay when finding himself lost in them?

He tried to shake himself back to some semblance of reason. He reminded himself that she had no more than nine or ten summers and that it could not matter what she thought of him. He would never have a one such as she, so disappointing her should mean nothing to him. Yet when she turned the full force of her shining eyes on him, he found words rushing out of his mouth he surely hadn't intended.

"Aye, I'll challenge him," he blurted out.

And then he knew that the only course of action left to him would be to draw his sword and fall upon it. As if he could actually dare such cheek. By the saints, he should have clamped his lips shut!

"You will?" she asked with a dazzling smile.

"Ah . . . I'll demand an apology," Rhys amended quickly. Perhaps he could shame the fool into giving Gwen one.

"Will you use your sword?" she asked breathlessly.

"If necessary," Rhys said, feeling the urge to drop to his knees and pray for deliverance from his own wagging tongue. "But first I'll give him a chance to comport himself well without violence."

"If you think it best," she said, sounding somewhat disappointed.

"Though I would surely like to see him poked a time or two for his crimes."

Evidently her disappointment was not so great that she was ready to release him from his errand. She took hold of his hand and dragged him back toward the keep. Rhys searched for a means of escape, but saw none until he happened to glance upon Sir Montgomery. Montgomery stopped the sharpening of his sword to look at them.

"Escorting our lady to the hall, Sir Rhys?" he called.

"He is my champion, Sir Montgomery," Gwen returned promptly. "He's going to avenge my bruised honor. Plans to use his sword if he has to."

Rhys threw Lord Bertram's captain a beseeching glance, but Montgomery only smiled.

"Well done, lad," Montgomery said approvingly. "Trot out that chivalry as often as possible. Keeps your spurs bright, as Lord Ayre always says."

Rhys wondered what Lord Ayre would say when he found out his foster son had been talked into taking to task the son of one of the most powerful barons in the north of England. Likely something along the lines of, "Best of luck to you, you chattering fool," as he headed back to Ayre, leaving Rhys to be carried off to Fenwyck and left to rot in the dungeon. Considering Fenwyck was a good two weeks' travel north from Ayre, Bertram could rest easy knowing he'd never have to hear Rhys's dying screams.

"I'll deserve it," he muttered. "Never should have picked up a sword."

"You said something?" Gwen asked.

Rhys shook his head. "Nothing of import."

"Then let us be about our business," she said enthusiastically.

Rhys sighed and let her pull him toward the great hall. He should have contented himself with the keeping of a field or two instead of lusting after knight's spurs. It would have been safer. It also might have been safer had he paid more attention to filling his belly than to rescuing a fair maid in the mud—only to find himself Gwennelyn of Segrave's champion.

But in his heart of hearts, he found that being chosen as such was quite possibly the sweetest pleasure he had yet had in his fourteen years. Foolish or not, he felt his step, and his heart, lighten. Gwen turned on the threshold to look at him and he gave her his best smile. He suspected that even his mother had never had such a smile from him.

Gwen smiled in return, and the sight of it smote him straight to the soul.

Aye, he found himself feeling that there was much indeed he would do for the girl before him.

"A favor," she said, patting herself.

"Another one?" he asked with a gulp. By the saints, serving this girl could take up a great amount of his time.

"Nay, I meant a favor for you to wear upon your arm. 'Tis how it is done, you know," she informed him.

"Of course," he said, wondering if he should have spent more time paying heed to Bertram's minstrel.

Gwen continued to pat until she pulled forth from some unidentifiable portion of her mud-encrusted gown a thick ribbon. Rhys could only speculate upon the color. He thought it might have been green. It likely still was, under all that dirt.

She tied it around his arm with great ceremony, then smiled up at him again. "Now you are truly mine. Coming?" she asked, taking him again by the hand.

How could he say her nay? He loosened his sword in its sheath and cast one last prayer heavenward before he ducked into the great hall behind his lady.

3

Gwen lay next to her mother in the large, comfortable bed and found, for a change, that the events of the day were far more interesting than the happenings she usually made up in her head to put herself to sleep.

"Gwen, please stop squirming."

"Oh, but, Mama, was he not wonderful today?"

Her mother sighed, but Gwen recognized the sigh. It was her I-wish-this-girl-child-would-fall-asleep-but-even-so-that-won't-stop-me-from-listening sigh. It was a sound Gwen was very familiar with. She'd overheard her mother say that she had only herself to blame, that it was her fault that Gwen's head was so peopled with characters from *chansons* and bardly epics, so she as well as anyone should pay the price. But it had been said gently and followed by a loving laugh from her father, so Gwen knew her parents weren't displeased with her.

But now she had a very live, very brave champion to think on, and that was better than anyone from her imaginings.

"He didn't even have to use his sword," Gwen said, relishing the moment yet again. "Just his reputation and the drawing of his blade was enough to set that Fenwyck demon to trembling."

"Aye, love."

"Would he have bloodied Geoffrey, do you think, Mama?"

"Likely so, if he'd had to."

"Was he so serious then, think you, about avenging my bruised honor, Mama?"

Her mother laughed and hugged her close. "I think he was very serious, my girl. But do you not think you earned a bit of Sir Geoffrey's ire? You did lock him in the tower."

"He told me my ears were overlarge."

"Only after you pointed out to him that he has a gap in his teeth."

"He's vain, Mama, and I couldn't bear him swaggering about. Besides, he tweaked one of my plaits when your back was turned. Sir Rhys would never have done such a thing."

"Likely not."

"Is he not wonderful, Mama?"

"Aye, my Gwen, he is. But do you not recall that you are betrothed to Alain of Ayre? As fine a lad as Sir Rhys may be, he will not be your husband. Perhaps you would do well not to think on him overmuch."

What Gwen didn't want to give thought to was Alain, so she agreed quickly with her mother, turned away, and pretended to go to sleep.

In truth, she dreamed with her eyes open of a gallant lad who had taken his life in his hands to challenge a man at least six years older than he. Gwen could still see the steadiness of Rhys's hands as he rested them upon his sword hilt, telling all who watched that he had the courage of a score of Geoffreys of Fenwyck. She had no trouble recalling the fineness of his dark hair as it fell to his shoulders, or the noble tilt to his chin and the regal shape of his nose.

And he had such marvelous ears.

She sighed in pleasure before she could stop herself, then coughed, lest her mother think she was dreaming instead of sleeping.

If only he could offer for her instead of that foul-tempered, lackwitted Alain of Ayre. Then would the truth of her life be as glorious as what she imagined up in her head.

Was there a way? Rhys was but a knight, true, but would not his glorious deeds count for something? Could her father not be persuaded that Rhys was far more desirable as a son-in-law than Alain? She was discerning enough to know that land and alliances would decide whom she wed—indeed, such things had already decided the matter. But could that not be set aside this once? Her father denied her nothing. Perhaps he would continue the practice with this. She would ask him first thing.

She yawned and closed her eyes, and then she dreamed in truth.

Of a splendidly chivalrous young man with serious gray eyes and a bright, sharp sword.

• • •

Rhys had watched the rest of the keep seek their beds, yet he found himself standing guard near his lord. He wasn't in truth a member of Lord Ayre's guard, but he volunteered for the duty willingly. Bertram had given him much; it seemed the least he could do in return. Being near his lord tonight was especially soothing, given the busy afternoon he'd had. He'd come away the victor, but it hadn't been without price—namely his peace of mind.

No sooner had Gwen washed her face and brushed the mud from her hair than she had reappeared, waiting for him to do something. Rhys had entertained one last hope that perhaps her mother might have talked her into reason, but he had found said mother sitting beside his championed lady, watching just as expectantly. His promise to avenge resting heavily on his shoulders, he had taken his cheek in hand and approached Geoffrey of Fenwyck with as much seriousness as he could muster.

Fenwyck's son had laughed at him at first. It had taken a great deal of courage to stand there and not flinch, but Rhys had done it. Then he'd drawn his sword and rested it point down in the rushes before him. It was but a borrowed sword, as Bertram had only recently ordered another to be fashioned for him, but a sword was a sword when it came to the finer matters of chivalric duty. Evidently Geoffrey had seen that the point was sharp enough and that Rhys's determination was firmly fixed, for he had stopped laughing and started blustering about. His bluster had soon turned to uncomfortable silence when Rhys had invited the older lad to have a go in the lists. Uncomfortable for Geoffrey, that was. By that time Rhys had begun to feel that his reputation for fierceness on the battlefield might indeed serve him well.

It had certainly earned him a look of worship from Gwen after the deed had been done.

By the saints, but it was enough to make him believe there was something to Bertram's lectures on chivalry after all.

William rose, startling Rhys from his reverie. He waited until Lord Bertram had risen as well before he fell in behind them. He stopped outside Segrave's solar and stood with his back to the partially open door. And much as he tried not to, he couldn't avoid hearing the conversation going on inside.

"You missed the excitement this afternoon, my friend," William said. "While you were napping, your foster son was going about correcting injustices."

Bertram laughed uneasily. "He didn't challenge your entire guard, did he?"

"It wasn't my guard he was taking on, 'twas that rascal who locked my Gwen in the piggery."

"Young Fenwyck?"

"Who else? The boy's a menace."

Bertram whistled softly. "A full score of years he has, yet he's still causing the maids to weep. It doesn't surprise me that Rhys took him on."

"Indeed he did. He swaggered up to Fenwyck's get just as boldly as you please and told Geoffrey he'd throw *him* into the piggery if he didn't apologize to Gwen. He added that he would escort him there by way of the lists if necessary."

"Ah, that's my lad," Bertram said, his voice full of pride. "I take it young Fenwyck did as he was bid?"

"Ungraciously, but aye. Young Rhys's reputation is the stuff of legends already."

Rhys stood straighter. He couldn't help himself. That William of Segrave should compliment him was something indeed. He fingered the ribbon he wore on his arm. His first favor, and from a lord's daughter no less. He had lived up not only to her expectations, but her father's as well. 'Twas something to be proud of.

"He'll be a fine man," Bertram said quietly.

"Aye," William agreed. "A pity he'll have no land. He would make a good husband and lord."

There was silence for a goodly while. Then Bertram spoke.

"He would make a fine husband just the same. Especially to a girl whose antics would terrify the bravest of men."

"Bertram," William said with a half laugh, "you insult my sweet Gwen. She's merely adventurous."

"You told me yourself that just a se'nnight ago you found her preparing to scale the outer wall to assure herself that your defenses against such a thing were what they should be. The girl thinks far too much for her own good!"

William's chuckle was enough to make Rhys begin to sweat. If he found that bit of mischief amusing, what other things was Gwen about that he indulged? Saints, the girl would kill herself before she reached a score of years.

And he found, unsurprisingly, that the thought was deeply distressing to him, the saints pity him for an impractical fool. As if anyone would care that he felt the sudden compulsion to make sure she didn't dash her dainty toes against a sharp rock.

"William, she deserves someone who will appreciate that."

"One would think, my friend, that you would rather me give Gwen to him than your son."

"Rhys has many things Alain lacks."

"And he lacks what Alain has, which will be a barony in time. I cannot wed my daughter to a simple knight, Bertram."

Bertram sighed heavily. "I know, William. I know."

And that, it seemed, was that.

Rhys swallowed with difficulty, surprised by how much such simple words pained him. It wasn't as if he hadn't had the same words hurled at him all his life, and by those with certainly purposefully crueler tongues than Segrave's. He should have been used to the sting by now, but he wasn't. For a moment he had actually believed that he might be looked on as more than just a knight.

He should have known better than to allow himself to hope that he might have a baron's daughter, or any other woman of such exalted station. He'd heard the truth of the matter and straight from William's lips.

Rhys sensed eyes upon him and looked up to find Sir Montgomery watching him. He stiffened.

"How long have you been there?" he demanded.

"Long enough," Montgomery said quietly.

"Must you always lurk in dark corners?" Rhys snarled. Montgomery only clapped a hand on Rhys's shoulder and urged him down the passageway.

"I'll remain," he said, and the tone of his voice warned Rhys that he would accept no argument. "Go sleep. You'll want to be in the lists early."

Rhys would have gone to the lists then if he could have, to relieve the feelings of shame that coursed through him. Of course he'd known he could never have someone like Gwennelyn of Segrave. Hadn't he told himself as much as he rode through the gates that morning? He wouldn't have her and he wouldn't have her land. Instead they would be given to Alain of Ayre, a young man whose thoughts ran no deeper than to which falcon to choose for his day's hunt. Gwen's soil would turn into a wasteland under his care. For all Rhys knew, Gwen herself would turn into the same with Alain as her mate. And there wasn't a damned thing he could do to amend either.

A pity that he wanted to.

By the saints, desire was a bloody awful thing.

He set off down the passageway, and as he did so, the ribbon she had given him fluttered with the movement of his striding. He fumbled at it, then found that he couldn't release the knot. By the saints, who had taught the girl to tie things so securely? He worked at it with frantic intensity. He pulled, then yanked, cursing the favor and its giver. Finally it came loose and he cast it to the ground, the stinging in his eyes blinding him to where it had fallen. He walked away, leaving it behind him in the passageway.

He cursed the day he'd ever gazed into those aqua eyes and prayed the day would never come when he had to look in them again.

• • •

It was very much past the wee hours of the morn when Rhys crept back up the steps. The torch had burned low and the passageway was empty. Rhys inched his way along the wall, stopping at the place he thought he'd been before.

The ribbon was no longer there.

He leaned back against the wall and swore softly. Then he gathered his wits about him. It had been a foolish idea, just as foolish as all the hopes he had entertained that day. He made his way back down the great hall to return to his sleeping place. On the morrow he would rise before dawn and train. He felt confident in the lists, secure in his abilities and proud of his performance. He was safe there. It was a far safer place to be than anywhere near Gwennelyn of Segrave.

Aye, deciding to keep as much distance from her as possible might be the most rational decision he'd made all day.

It would likely serve him just as well in the future.

4

England, 1196

Gwen peered into her mother's polished silver goblet, trying to see if the wimple sat properly on her head. Upon closer inspection, she discovered a pair of smudges on the white fabric near her ears.

"By all the bloody saints," she exclaimed, "who dirtied this?"

"Gwen," her mother chided, "such unattractive words to come from your mouth."

"My finest wimple is ruined."

"Perhaps if you wore them more often," Joanna said, "you might become more acquainted with their state of cleanliness, or lack thereof."

"I am endeavoring, Mother," Gwen said with as much patience as she could muster, "to make a good impression."

"On Lord Bertram?"

"Who else?" Gwen lied. Her future father-in-law could have seen her covered in leavings from the cesspit and she wouldn't have cared. Nay, there was only one whose good opinion she craved.

And the bloody lout hadn't looked at her once since he'd arrived.

She couldn't understand it. He had departed the keep with Lord Bertram the day after he'd challenged Geoffrey of Fenwyck those six years ago, which was unexpected, but she had assumed he'd done it not to cause Fenwyck's son further embarrassment. That was far more than Geoffrey deserved, the wretch.

She had been at the gates to watch Rhys ride away. She'd exchanged no words with him, but certainly a good long look. His eyes had been clear and bright and his jaw set strongly as if he sallied forth to do more heroic deeds to delight her. She'd recognized the look that hid all emotion. All fine champions did so, lest prying eyes discover the innermost feelings of their hearts. It was a ruse they put into play, and Gwen had been greatly cheered to know Rhys was doing the like. It could only mean he had given his heart into her keeping. She had nodded to him gravely, then escaped to her mother's solar to imprint upon her memory her last sight of the man she was certain she loved.

It had troubled her occasionally to find Lord Bertram arriving without Rhys in the ensuing years. It had troubled her even more to see Alain arrive with his father from time to time, but she had comforted herself with the knowledge that one day Rhys would come for her and claim her as his own. That made enduring Alain's poor manners and feebleminded conversation less difficult than it would have been otherwise.

And then today had dawned. She'd been loitering on the battlements, observing her father's archers and wondering how difficult it would be to filch a bow from one of them to learn their skills, when what had she seen but Ayre's banner coming toward them. She'd groaned at the sight of it, but remained on her perch that she might see if she were to be burdened with her betrothed's presence or not.

And then she'd seen who rode in Lord Bertram's company.

She'd almost fallen off the walkway in surprise.

Her mother had kept her busy in the solar for the whole of the day. Gwen had sewn tunic sleeves shut, hemmed sheets too short, and stitched a three-footed falcon onto her father's finest surcoat. Her mother had finally put her to playing the lute to entertain Segrave's ladies, but even that had proved too taxing a duty. Gwen couldn't for the life of her remember her notes.

He was below.

She could hardly breathe for the excitement that coursed through her.

Then she'd finally been allowed to go to the great hall and partake of a meal. It had been a very long meal, and Rhys had sat at the table below her father's for a very long time.

Ignoring her.

If she'd dared, she would have walked up to him and demanded an explanation. Concealing his feelings was one thing, yet even that demanded the occasional stolen glance filled with love. What had she had from the champion of her heart?

Not a bloody nod. Nary a wink. Not even a twitch of an eyebrow when she'd accidentally knocked a pitcher of wine over into Lord Bertram's lap.

Events were not progressing as she had planned.

Which was why she found herself on this, the second morning of Sir Rhys's stay in her keep, digging through her trunk for a suitable wimple to cover her ears. Perhaps he had thought better of wanting to champion her because he had spent too much time dwelling on the state of filthiness she'd found herself in the last time they'd met. Not so this time. She fully intended to show him that she could keep her clothes clean, her demeanor demure, and her ears covered. He couldn't fail to be impressed by that.

Only now her plans were dashed by the discovery of dirt on her finest wimple. How was she to make a good impression with a filthy headcovering? She was in mid-contemplation of a selection of curses when she felt her mother's hands on her head.

"Here, my love," Joanna said gently, removing the soiled cloth, "you'll wear one of mine."

"Nay," Gwen protested, "you know I'll only ruin it."

"For such a tidy girl, you do manage to wear a great deal of dirt," Joanna agreed placidly.

Gwen didn't bother to argue. She did find herself smudged quite often, but it came from the places she went and the things she investigated. She needed fodder for her own tales and 'twas a certainty she wouldn't find it in her mother's solar. Women's gossip, no matter how entertaining, was not interesting enough for the elaborate lays she wrote out in her head. But her father's armory was. Never mind that she had never hefted a sword in her life. She needed no hefting for creation.

She stood still as her mother fussed with tying the wimple under her chin and tucking her hair under the cloth. And she found it very difficult to meet her mother's eyes, lest she see the plots and schemes lurking therein.

"Gwen."

Gwen looked at her mother reluctantly. "Aye?"

"Your course is set before you, my girl."

"Would that I could alter it," Gwen muttered.

"I had no choice in the wedding of your father," Joanna reminded her, "and see you how well that has turned out?"

Ah, but her sire was a far different man than the volatile, selfish Alain of Ayre. That his temper was matched only by his stupidity made him a very disagreeable prospect indeed.

But with any luck, he would be searching for a new bride very soon. Sir Rhys would see to that. Gwen had faith in him.

Now, if she could just convince him to agree with her.

"I must go down," Gwen said, feeling the need to escape from her mother's assessing glance. "It will show Lord Bertram that I will be a good chatelaine if I am there to tend to our guests."

Her mother sighed. "Be careful, Gwen."

Gwen fled before she had to hear any more. She had the feeling what her mother didn't know, she'd guessed. Had she been so obvious then, over the past six years? She'd lived for every scrap of news about Sir Rhys and made any bearer of such tidings repeat over and over again what they'd heard. She'd reminded her parents that she was composing heroic lays as a tribute to Queen Eleanor's fondness of them, and it only served her to hear of the gallant Sir Rhys's remarkable adventures. He had gone on many errands for Lord Bertram and somehow always managed to extricate himself in the most glorious of ways from impossible situations, using his sword and his wits with equal skill.

Gwen stopped at the bottom of the steps and hung back in the shadows where she could observe the occupants of the great hall, yet remain unseen herself. It was yet early in the day and the men had returned from their morning business to break their fast. Gwen had given much thought to the timing of her entrance. Sir Rhys would have to acknowledge her as he left the hall after finishing his meal. And if he did not do so then, she had other plans to plant herself in his path and leave him with no choice but to look at her. What she would say to him then, she didn't know. She prayed something would come to her. For now, it was enough to have him look on her and see her.

Even by the light of torches on the walls, she had no trouble finding him. There were many who sat at her father's lower tables, but none who set the very air about them to trembling merely by being there.

He sat with his back to the fire, his helm on the table next to his arm, and a dark cloak pushed back over his shoulders. The torchlight shone on his dark hair and glanced off his perfectly chiseled features. His clothing was simple and unadorned, though as Bertram's favored foster son he likely could have bedecked himself as lavishly as did Alain and his brother Rollan. Gwen decided then that he had no need. Not even the simpleness of his garb could hide the nobility of his bearing and the beauty of his face.

And to think he was a mere knight with nothing to his name but his sword and horse.

By the saints, 'twas no wonder Alain hated him so. He was everything Alain wasn't.

He ate quickly, speaking gravely to those about him only when he was spoken to. Gwen watched him finish long before those around him had satisfied themselves, rise and beg leave of Lord Bertram to depart the hall, and make his way out the door. He was gone before Gwen had realized that her initial plan to put herself in his path before he left the hall had failed miserably. She would have to exert better control over herself. Gaping at the man while he escaped the web she set for him would get her nothing but fodder for her dreams at night. She fully intended to have more. Her parents might have intended her for Alain of Ayre, but she had a different idea.

Even if it entailed wedding only a knight.

But that wouldn't happen until she had speech with him, and that surely wouldn't occur until she had found a way to attract his notice. She certainly wasn't going to roll about in the pigsty again to have it. She was a woman now. Though she'd been but a child the last time she'd encountered him, she'd known then he was what she wanted. Now that she was grown, surely he would take her desire for him to be her champion more seriously.

She walked from the hall as quickly as she dared, hoping her father would think she had ignored his calls to come sit and eat due to a sudden loss of hearing on her part. She breathed a sigh of relief when she found that no one was following her from the great hall. She might succeed after all.

Sir Rhys had gone to the stables. She knew this because it was his habit to check on his mount after the morning meal to assure himself it was being treated well. And after his visit to the stables, he would return again to the lists, where he trained for several hours a day. Surely he wouldn't mind interrupting his habits this once.

She ran toward the entrance to the stables, fearing she might have missed him already. She had almost reached the opening when her toes made contact abruptly with a sharp stone. She greeted the pain with a most unladylike expression and hopped about on one foot, clutching her offended toe with her fist.

She hopped, of course, directly into Rhys de Piaget's substantial chest.

He caught her by the arms. She looked up, her pain forgotten. Indeed, she had to remind herself that breathing, not standing there gaping at him like a halfwit, was the best way to make a favorable impression.

She lowered her foot as casually as she could. She made no move to straighten her garments, for that might have induced him to release her and that she couldn't have.

"Hurt?" he asked.

Ah, but he did have such a rich voice. Surely the stuff of any maid's dreams.

He frowned. "Are you unwell?"

It was all she could do not to fling herself into his arms and blurt out her love for him right on the spot. Instead, she shook her head and prayed she looked even the slightest bit dignified while doing so.

"Well, then," he said, releasing her abruptly and taking a step backward. "Good morrow to you, lady."

He was halfway across the bailey before she managed to gather up enough wits to realize he had once again escaped her clutches.

"Sir Rhys, wait!"

He didn't stop. Gwen couldn't credit him with rudeness, so she assumed perhaps too many victims screaming for mercy had ruined his hearing. She hiked up her skirts and dashed off after him.

"Sir Rhys, wait," she repeated breathlessly when she caught up with him. His ground-eating stride did not slow, which forced her to keep running alongside him. "Won't you stop and have speech—"

"Have things to do," he said curtly, increasing his pace.

"But," she said, breaking into a full run.

"No women in the lists," he threw over his shoulder as he fair sprinted to his destination.

Gwen realized how foolish she must look, so she stopped and frowned. No women in the lists? So *he* thought. He obviously was unacquainted with her determination. She would have the chance to win his heart before his visit was up or perish in the attempt. Surely he couldn't resist her. She was wearing her mother's finest wimple, for pity's sake. Had he no idea what kind of sacrifice that was?

She thought about following him to the lists, then realized that perhaps she might need to rethink her strategy.

But he would succumb in the end. She would give him no other choice.

Rhys leaned on his sword and forced himself to take deep, even breaths. It wasn't that honing his skills against the majority of Segrave's garrison wasn't enough to cause him to pant; indeed, any man might have been forgiven a bit of gasping after the morning's exercise Rhys had just taken.

But not every man had Gwennelyn of Segrave loitering along the walls, watching his every move.

He could feel her gaze on him, just as surely as it had been for the past three days. Relentless, that's what she was, relentless and determined. He'd never felt so scrutinized in his entire life, and to be sure he'd had his share of souls watching him to mark any misstep. But he'd never forced himself not to pant for any of them.

The saints preserve him, he was losing his mind.

He'd done his best to ignore her. He'd even gone so far as to be rude to her on more than one occasion. Once he'd realized she knew his habits, he'd changed them, thinking that she couldn't possibly outwit him. Obviously there was a very clever girl under all that beauty, for she'd discovered him straightway and thereafter taken to shadowing him. She would have made a bloody good spy.

He had no idea what she wanted of him. Likely to talk him into another rescue. He scowled. He'd learned his lesson the last time. It hardly mattered what he did for her, for he would never have her. What was the point in pleasing her?

A pity the thought of pleasing her was the one that had haunted him for six years.

Out of the corner of his eye, he checked to see if she still held her position. Still in place, aye, but seemingly overwhelmed by the taxing nature of her chase. In spite of himself, Rhys began to smile. He walked over to the wall quietly and stopped a few paces away from her. He fussed with his gear, lest he be observed, and surreptitiously drank in the sight of the young woman snoring so peacefully where she sat with her back against the wall.

Six years had done nothing but enhance the promise of beauty he'd seen in her. No wonder Bertram wanted her for his son. She would bring a loveliness to his table no jewel-encrusted goblet could hope to equal, and she would likely do all Alain's thinking for him. It was a wise choice to have made as far as Ayre's future was concerned. Rhys would have done the same thing in his lord's place, only he never would have given such a one as she to his son; he would have taken her for himself.

He sighed, and it felt as if it had come from the marrow of his bones. It had been a mistake to come to Segrave. He'd told himself he would come because Lord Bertram had asked him to come. He'd been asked before, of course, but he'd never dared think he was equal to the task of gazing upon Gwen and remaining unmoved.

Fool, he thought with another sigh. All it had taken was one look at her and his carefully constructed defense against her had crumbled.

He resheathed his sword and cursed softly. He should have gone to France in the spring. He'd planned to. Lord Bertram had been willing to free him from all current obligations in order for him to do so. Rhys had envisioned a few years' tourneying yielding enough gold to purchase some fine bit of soil somewhere. He'd sketched out in his mind the sort of keep he might build and tallied the number of knights he would have about him calling him lord.

He had, of course, studiously avoided peopling his keep with any kind of family, especially a wife, *especially* after his first musings had cast Gwennelyn of Segrave in that role.

France had, in the end, seemed a rather unattractive destination that spring. His duty to Lord Bertram, given of his own free will, was almost over. He'd offered seven years of knightly service and had it accepted willingly. Six had been fulfilled and Bertram hadn't seemed reluctant to collect the seventh at a later time. Still, Rhys had been unable to move himself from Ayre.

And, as he stared at the young woman before him, he wondered if this might have been what he had waited for. Against all reason, he suspected one last glimpse of her had been what had kept him off the continent. Bertram traveled to Segrave often enough. It had certainly been no difficulty to come along.

Now the difficulty would be leaving.

And if he had even a grain of sense in his head, he would have packed up his gear and fled for France that very day.

His feet, however, had a different idea. They seemed to have no intention of responding to his command that they carry him far away from certain heartache.

"Oh, you're finished!"

The sound of her voice startled him so badly, he stumbled backward. Gwen leaped to her feet. The look of delight she gave him slammed into him like a dozen fists and left him gasping more surely than his morning's exercise.

Run, you fool!

His common sense had that aright. He made Gwen a low bow and turned to flee from the field.

"Sir Rhys, wait!"

If he had to hear that phrase one more time from her, he knew he would scream, so he did the only sensible thing he'd done since he'd first clapped eyes on her. He fled to the guardtower and closed himself in the garderobe.

After all, how long could she possibly wait for him to come out?

5

Gwen's feet hurt. Standing outside the guardtower for most of the day had been mightily taxing on them. At least she had the chance to rest them for a bit. She currently did so as she sat at her father's table and scowled at Rhys's profile. Who would have thought the man could be so stubborn? He had escaped every snare she'd set for him, resisted every attempt at polite conversation, and resorted to flight when all other avenues had been closed to him. But the most irritating thing of all had been the length of time he'd remained in the garderobe that morn. Who would have thought a man's business could take him so long? If she'd had a sword, she would have prodded him into an empty corner with it and kept him there with it at his throat until she'd had speech with him.

She nursed the wine in her cup and gave that thought more consideration. She had no sword at her disposal, but she was clever enough for a young woman of her tender years. Perhaps a message, delivered by someone he trusted, would lure him to a private meeting.

After the meal she penned a quick missive, approached Sir Montgomery, and smiled a most innocent smile at him. And bless the man if he didn't do as she intended, which was smile back at her just as foolishly as did anyone her mother chanced to grace with her attentions. Though people told her she resembled her mother, Gwen couldn't see it somehow. Blessedly Montgomery seemed to think so as well, so she without hesitation used what wiles she had.

"A favor, good sir?" she asked him.

"Anything," he said, blinking at her as if he had stared too long at the sun.

She handed him the tiny scrap of parchment. "Might you deliver this to Sir Rhys? Discreetly, of course."

"Of course," he said, though she could see in his eyes that he was wondering about the wisdom of it.

"A few harmless words," she said with a dismissive wave. "Nothing of import." She smiled again for good measure.

He took a step backward as if he'd been struck, nodded, and turned to walk obediently, if not a bit unsteadily, to where Sir Rhys sat at the table.

Gwen escaped the hall and ran for the roof before Rhys could suspect that she might be behind the meeting. She went out onto the battlements and secreted herself in a darkened corner. No sense in having the whole of her father's guard watching her as she was about her business. She had every intention of convincing the gallant Sir Rhys to snatch her away before she was forced to wed with Alain of Ayre, but that was best done in secret.

'Twas but a moment or two later that the door next to her creaked. Rhys slipped from it carefully, as if he expected to be attacked. Even the very sight of him, dark and full of stealth, was enough to set Gwen's heart to racing. Aye, this was surely the man for her, and what a man! Her father could not help but be pleased with his prowess. Gwen tucked that thought away for future use. Perhaps she could suggest to her sire that Rhys would be a far better protector than Alain. Surely he would be swayed by that.

Rhys closed the door behind him softly. Gwen took her courage in hand and reached out to touch his arm.

And before she could even open her mouth to greet him, she found herself slammed back against the wall with a knife at her throat. She would have squeaked, but she didn't have the breath for it.

As suddenly as it had appeared, the knife disappeared into a sheath somewhere up Rhys's sleeve. Rhys hung his head and let out a shaky breath.

"'Tis only me," she managed.

He lifted his head and glared at her. "I could have slain . . ." he began, then he shut his mouth and started to pull away.

"Nay," she said, grasping him by the tunic sleeve more firmly, "don't leave."

He paused.

"Please," she added.

The moonlight shone down on him, casting his face into shadows. There was no smile that she could see, but she had no trouble hearing a sigh of resignation. It was a sound her father made regularly.

"What is it?" he asked.

Gwen feared he would disappear if she released him, so she kept hold of his arm. It was the same arm she had tied her favor around seven years earlier. She wondered if he still had it.

"What is it you want?" he asked again, more roughly this time. "I've things to do."

"Well," she said, wishing this were turning out a bit more like she had dreamed it would, "I thought we could talk."

"I've no time for talking." But he didn't move.

He wasn't declaring undying love, but he wasn't running off either. Gwen rifled through what pitiful wits still remained her for something clever to say to keep him there a bit longer until she could discover for herself if he had tender feelings for her. Then she would present her plan to him.

"'Tis a lovely night, is it not?" she asked.

He growled something unintelligible.

"The moon is quite large," she added.

"Did you lure me here," he said through gritted teeth, "to discuss the contents of the heavens or something more interesting? I pray you, lady, come to a decision quickly for I have little time to waste upon foolishness."

Gwen took a deep breath. Had she been made of lesser stuff, she might have been cowed by his grumbles. Or, worse yet, she might have taken them to mean he cared nothing for her. She wasn't about to believe that. He'd agreed to be her champion once before. She felt certain that, given the chance, he would do so again. And if he wanted her to speak frankly, then frankly she would speak.

"I asked you here to discuss my hand in marriage," she said as calmly as she could.

"Your marriage to whom?" he asked curtly. "Alain of Ayre?"

"Nay," she said plainly. "To you."

He blinked. Then he blinked a bit more. And then his jaw went slack. "You cannot be serious," he managed.

"Oh, but I am."

He shook his head. "You're daft."

"I believe I'm quite in possession of all my wits. Hence the craftiness of my ruse to get you here."

He seemed to give it some thought, then a look of coldness came over his face. "Is Ayre so unappealing," he asked flatly, "that you would lower yourself to wed with a mere knight?"

"Alain is unappealing," she agreed, "but that is not why I chose you."

"How arrogant you are, lady, to think the choice is yours."

It was her turn to stare at him, speechless. That he might not want her had never occurred to her. She had imagined him rescuing her from her current plight so often that she had come to believe that he cared for her as greatly as she cared for him.

She shut her mouth as casually as she could, then gathered her courage about her. She released his arm, though it was done most reluctantly. Then she tried a smile. It wasn't her best effort, but she persevered.

"Could you not," she ventured, "be persuaded to be mine?"

He seemed suddenly to have difficulty swallowing. Supper had been delicious as always, so she couldn't credit the fare for his trouble. Perhaps 'twas that he was suddenly confronted with something he'd tried to deny. She'd seen the condition in other men, and it usually meant they were overcome by some strong emotion. Could it be affection for her? Perhaps he wasn't as unmoved as he seemed.

"Hmmm," he said, looking as if he were giving her proposition serious thought, "I would need to think on it."

"You were my champion once," she said, hoping to spark a bit more enthusiasm from him. "You could perhaps be that again."

"Your champion?" he echoed. "Of course it would be only that. What else could it be?" He started to turn away.

This was not going at all as she had expected.

"Champion, husband, 'tis all the same to me," she said in exasperation. "The point is, 'tis you I love and 'tis you I would wed."

He froze. Then he turned to look back at her. "'Tis me you love," he echoed, blinking at her.

"Aye, and now 'tis your task to accomplish my rescue and carry me off to a priest."

"But . . ."

"I know you can do it. I'm quite familiar with your exploits."

"But," he spluttered, "I cannot wed you."

"Of course you can. You said you might somehow be persuaded to want me."

He waved a hand impatiently. "That isn't what hinders me."

"Then you *do* want me." She smiled. She'd known it. Only a man who wanted a woman badly could have ignored her as thoroughly as Rhys had.

"Of course I want you," he said in an angry whisper. "I've wanted you from the moment I bloody clapped eyes on you."

He sounded none too pleased about it.

She smiled happily. "How lovely—"

"But I can hardly have you," he interrupted. "Or have you forgotten that your father would never give you to me?"

"He would if he could. He said as much to my mother not six months ago."

Rhys pursed his lips. "Words prompted, no doubt, by a visit from your betrothed."

"Alain slipped rather heavily in his cups and vomited upon my father's finest mattress."

"I see."

"'Twas a most unpleasant se'nnight." She shrugged. "My mind, however, was made up long before that. And even though my father's hands are tied, mine are not."

"And you think your sire wouldn't tie your hands and lock you in your mother's solar until the wedding if he knew what you have proposed this night?"

Gwen would have liked to think not, for her father was enormously patient with her antics, but she wondered if Rhys might have it aright. She settled upon another course of action.

"We won't tell him," she said.

He fell silent. Gwen looked up at him and felt hope begin to spring to life in her breast. He was giving it thought, she could see that. He'd said that he wanted her from the moment he'd clapped eyes on her, never mind how irritated he'd sounded over it. 'Twas obviously a powerful love indeed, for she remembered vividly her liberation from the pigsty and how she must have smelled.

He was what she wanted, she was certain of it. Memories of the gallantry and kindness of a fourteen-year-old lad were forever emblazoned upon her memory.

He looked down. Gwen watched as he slowly reached out and took her by the hand. He rubbed his thumb over the back of her hand slowly, as if he sought to memorize how it was shaped.

"You'll see to it, won't you?" she asked.

He said no word, but continued to look at her hand. Gwen would have prodded him further, but she was too distracted. His fingers were callused and warm against her skin. How odd. His touch was far different than she'd imagined it might be. She'd held her father's hand often enough; he had calluses from wielding a sword and his hands were warm.

Rhys, however, was not her father and the touch of his hand on hers was entirely different. Shivers went up her arm and scattered themselves over the rest of her poor form.

She watched, mute, as he lifted her hand and brought it to his lips. The touch of *them* upon her skin sent a rush of something through her she'd never felt before. Not even almost falling down the barbican steps after having snuck up on her father's garrison captain to see if he performed his duties sufficiently well had sent such tingles of fear through her.

Only, somehow, she thought what she was feeling wasn't fear.

"Aye," he said, taking her hand and resting it against his faintly scratchy cheek, "I will."

Gwen blinked at him. "You will?"

"I'll see to it."

"See to it?" She was so overcome by his nearness, by the sheer height and power of the man that she could scarce remember her name, much less what they'd been discussing. He smiled and the sight of that almost sent her pitching backward off the wall. By the saints, he was beautiful.

"I'll see to the rescuing of you from Alain's nefarious marriage designs upon you," he reminded her.

"Oh," she said, nodding. "That."

"Aye," he said, with another smile, "that."

His smile faded. He closed his eyes and sighed. Then he opened his eyes and looked down at her. The longing in his gaze was like nothing she'd ever seen before on any man's face, not even those men who came to look at her mother knowing they would never have her. That a man, much less Rhys de Piaget, should look at her thusly was a marvelous thing indeed. She studied his look intently that she might call it to mind during the next few months while he was conceiving a way to have her as his.

And then before she could ask him to turn a bit more to the left that the moon might light his features the better, he had taken her face in his hands, bent his dark head to hers, and kissed her very sweetly upon the lips.

Gwen was certain the stones had moved beneath her feet.

"Oh," she managed as he lifted his head and looked down at her.

He looked as dazed as she felt.

"Aye," he said hoarsely. He shook his head, as if to clear it. "We should return below, lest someone see us."

But he didn't move.

Neither did she.

All she could do was stand there with his rough hands upon her cheeks, the remembered warmth of his mouth lingering upon hers, and his beloved form standing but a hair's breadth from her, and wonder if any maid in the annals of time had ever had such a man willing to champion her.

Or to kiss her, for that matter.

Before she could ask him if he wouldn't be so kind as to do the like again, he had taken her by the hand and pulled her along behind him down from the roof.

"We must return," he said over his shoulder.

"But—"

"Short of snatching you away in the night, I don't know how I'll manage this," he muttered as they descended the steps.

"But—"

"Bribery, perhaps," he mumbled. "Very expensive, but you're well worth the price, I should think."

"Well, thank—"

"Aye," he said as they reached the bottom of the steps. "I will take up my journey to France and there frequent a tourney or two."

Gwen jumped in before he could interrupt her again. "And then you'll return? Well before I'm to wed with that fool?"

He turned around to face her. "Well before, with bags of gold in hand."

"Then—" *Perhaps another kiss,* she started to say as she leaned up on her toes and aimed for his mouth with hers, but a bellow from down the hall interrupted her.

"Gwen!"

The sound of her father's voice echoed down the passageway. Gwen gasped and pulled her hand from Rhys's. A look of intense alarm fixed itself upon his features.

"Do something," he whispered fiercely, "lest he cast me into the dungeon and then there will be no hope for us at all!"

Another ruse. She sighed. She was destined to be called upon to think them up.

"Why, Sir Knight," she exclaimed, putting her hands on her hips and affecting a look of outrage, "how dare you!" She threw him a look that she hoped said *'Tis the best I could think of,* and pulled back her fist. "Father, I'll dispatch him myself," she called down the passageway, then with an unspoken plea for forgiveness, firmly and with deadly accuracy, let fly her fist.

Very ungently into Rhys's nose.

6

For the second time in all the years he had known Gwennelyn of Segrave, Rhys clutched his nose and cursed. He'd thought that four years ago would be the first and last time he would have to endure such a smacking from her.

"Damn you, Gwen," he exclaimed, "why must you always do that?"

"For the same reason I did it the last time," she said. "That we might not be discovered!"

Rhys felt his nose gingerly and wondered if it was worth it. He couldn't argue that it hadn't been the last time. William of Segrave had stood at the end of the passageway and watched with ill-concealed amusement as the blood dripped down Rhys's face. He'd only nodded to Rhys as Rhys had escaped past him to the safety of the garrison hall. Rhys had fled the next morning after having begged leave of Bertram. His request hadn't been refused and he'd been fortunate enough not to encounter Gwen's sire again.

He hadn't exchanged any words with Gwen, either. She'd only watched him ride out with a look of perfect trust and confidence. It had been enough to send him straight to France with only a brief stop at Ayre to collect his few belongings.

And now, against all odds, he stood staring down at the woman he'd spent the past four years working to buy. It hardly surprised him that he didn't have the peace or privacy to greet her properly. Then again, he was close to having enough coin at his disposal to offer for her, so what should he care what her betrothed thought?

"I wonder if it really matters what you reveal," he said, dabbing at his face with his sleeve, "for in a few more months I'll have plenty of gold—"

"A few more months?" Gwen echoed, whirling on him. She jabbed with her finger toward where Rhys could see Alain's white stallion approaching rapidly. "I'm to wed him within the se'nnight!"

Rhys stopped dabbing and gaped at her. "You aren't. You can't. You weren't to wed him—"

"Until I was a full score and one, aye, I know! But who is to stop him? My sire is dead two years now, and my guardian cannot wait to rid himself of me."

Rhys had known of her sire's passing but hadn't dared return to comfort her. Besides, the news of it had taken half a year to reach him. He'd grieved for her and hoped she would know as much.

But Lord Ayre was still alive, and Rhys knew his foster father wouldn't allow her wedding to happen before the agreed-upon time. Gwen had been convinced incorrectly by her guardian as to the date of her nuptials.

Nuptials which, of course, wouldn't take place with Alain of Ayre.

"Bertram will see to it," he assured her. "He sent for me less than a month ago, which is why I am here and not in France still filling my coffers." He smiled at her. "Fear not, Gwen. He will not allow this to happen yet."

Rhys wasn't sure why, but she seemed not at all reassured by that. She looked over her shoulder, then turned back to him. "This may be the last time we have speech freely together."

"Surely not—"

"You've no idea what has transpired."

Rhys looked at Alain's rapidly approaching figure and cursed the inconvenience. "I'll see to it all," he said confidently. "We'll just tell this fool here to be off—" He stopped at her warning look. "Very well, we'll keep up the ruse a bit longer. Shall I clutch my nose again to please you?"

She opened her mouth to speak, then shut it. Rhys would have been more satisfied with some kind of declaration of affection, but obviously 'twas not to be. Whatever catastrophe had occurred, he felt certain Alain was responsible for it. It could be solved, if they could just avoid displaying before the entire garrison of Ayre their true feelings. Rhys fingered his nose gingerly. It might not be so difficult after all if the alternative was another fist in his nose.

He suddenly had no more time to contemplate the significance of the last few moments of his life, for he was standing surrounded by Alain's men. He watched Alain expertly cut Gwen off from Rhys's own horse. Rhys had never doubted Alain's skill with horseflesh. It was his skill with handling the souls about him that Rhys had never felt sure of. Alain sat there, his chest heaving, and stared down at Gwen for several moments, likely trying to choose the appropriate word to voice his obvious displeasure.

"Bitch," he said finally. Then he bit his lip, looking faintly appalled at what he'd just said.

"Fool," Gwen shot back.

Alain only stared at her, his mouth working a bit. Rhys surmised that Alain's mind was not keeping pace, for no sound came out. Perhaps an impasse between thought and utterance had been reached already.

Alain seemed to gather his wits about him. Then he looked at Gwen in faint disbelief. "You ran from the keep," he managed finally.

"Aye, I did," she said.

He scratched the side of his head with the leather crop he held. "Why?"

"To escape you, you halfwit!"

"Halfwit," he echoed, gaping at her. *"Halfwit?"*

Rhys wondered just what response Alain might find to that insult in the recesses of his overworked brain when to his complete astonishment, Alain leaned over and backhanded Gwen full across the face.

Rhys caught her only because the force of the blow sent her sprawling into his arms. He looked down into her soot-smudged face and felt a white-hot rage well up in him. His sword was halfway from its sheath before he even realized what he was about.

And then a slighter hand came down upon his suddenly. He looked down into Gwen's eyes and saw the pleading there. It was the hardest thing he had ever done, that releasing of his blade. And he suspected, in the back of his mind, that 'twas only the beginning of the things he would have to do to keep his desire for the woman in his arms a secret.

By the saints, this was a difficult path they'd chosen.

Alain glared at him. "I don't know who you are, but you've a manner about you I don't like. Release the wench, for I've yet more blows to deliver."

Rhys was the first to admit his appearance left something to be desired, but surely Alain had seen him often enough in the past to recognize him. Obviously Alain's wits had not increased during Rhys's absence.

"Your sire, my lord," Rhys said, "does not approve of the beating of women."

"And what would you know of my sire, you . . . you . . . ." Alain sputtered furiously. He seemed to be searching again for a term foul enough to express his displeasure, when his gaze fell to Rhys's sword and his mouth dropped open.

Rhys knew then that Alain had finally realized whom he was looking at. Lord Bertram had given Rhys not only his sword, but a fat ruby to put into its hilt. Alain had never forgiven his father for it, for he surely hadn't received the like. Bertram's reasoning was that since Alain would eventually inherit everything else, he had no need of gems adorning his blade. Alain, though, being Alain and not precisely overendowed with logic, had raged over the injustice of it for years. He hadn't, however, raged thoroughly enough to invite Rhys to step into the lists to soothe his bruised feelings.

Rhys wondered, in the back of his mind, if he just might end up paying for his foster father's generosity all the same.

Alain spat at Rhys's feet. "My sire is dead, de Piaget, which means he's not here to disapprove—"

Rhys felt the ground grow unsteady beneath him.

"Dead?" he echoed. "He lived but a month past."

"It came upon him suddenly," Gwen said quietly. "He had but traveled to Segrave most recently—"

"And I was until recently being paid attention to!" Alain interrupted angrily. "By the saints, I hate being ignored!"

Rhys could hardly believe Alain's father was dead and he was now staring at the current lord of Ayre. If he'd known the truth of that, he never would have left France so ill-prepared.

"Now, brother," a voice said from behind Alain. "Surely you should save your irritation for a more private display."

Rhys pulled Gwen behind him while Alain's notice was off her and onto someone else.

Alain looked at the man who had spoken. "She called me lackwit," he complained.

"Actually, she called you halfwit," Rollan said gently, "but who remembers such trivialities?"

Rhys could hear Gwen muttering under her breath behind him, and he wished mightily that she would cease with it. Never mind that Alain was a fool. His younger brother, Rollan, was as crafty as the devil himself, and just as ruthless. Even if Gwen's insults eventually slipped Alain's mind, Rollan would choose the worst time possible to refresh his brother's memory.

"She should be punished," Alain grumbled. He glared at Rhys. "And you should step out of the way so I can be about it."

"Her guardian surely would not approve of such treatment," Rhys said, hoping to spark some small sense of reason in the man.

"Who are you to tell me what to do?" Alain demanded.

"Aye," Rollan agreed. "Who indeed, Sir Rhys? I daresay you forget your place. You have no title, no rank, no lands."

No lands. Well, that was always the heart of the matter, and Rhys felt the sting of it almost as keenly as he had the first time the insult had been hurled at him.

"I am a knight," he said curtly, his bruised pride demanding some kind of assuagement, "and therefore sworn to protect those weaker than myself."

"Indeed," Gwen said, with an approving poke in his back.

"I should have thought these years of battle, mock battle though it was, would have taught you the truth of the matter," Alain said. "The strong rule the weak. Isn't that so, brother?" He looked at Rollan for a nod of approval. "And so I will rule you," he continued. "And I'll rule that headstrong wench once I beat some obedience into her. I think I'll begin now."

When I'm dead, Rhys thought to himself. He would have said as much, but he hadn't earned his reputation by ignoring the odds of success in any given battle. It was him and Gwen against Alain, Rollan, and a score of Alain's guardsmen, several of whom had reason not to care for him overmuch. Better to talk his way out of this one.

"You might want to leave her with her strength of will intact," Rhys offered. While Alain digested that, Rhys spit his next words out with as much haste as possible. "'Tis something she may well pass on to your sons."

"Ha," Gwen said from behind him. "As if I would ever bear a son of his!"

Alain urged his horse forward, and Rhys backed up a pace to avoid being trampled.

"She's bound to wed me," Alain said. "Her father promised."

Gwen snorted. "He was in his cups at the time—"

Rhys looked over his shoulder and spared Gwen a frown. She left the rest of her words unsaid, but scowled at him. Rhys turned back to Alain, ready to move should he need to, but the newly made lord of Ayre only caressed his whip and chewed on his thoughts. Not a substantial meal likely, but seemingly an enjoyable one.

"Perhaps there are more effective ways to drive her cheek from her," Rollan offered smoothly.

Alain looked at his brother. "Are there?"

"On your wedding night, perhaps," Rollan said.

Alain looked faintly perplexed, then shrugged. Obviously uncovering the hidden meaning in Rollan's words was too much for him. Alain looked down at Rhys.

"I see by your nose that she's marked you. I take it you were trying to stop her from fleeing?"

"Of course," Rhys managed. "What else?"

Alain grunted. "Then I suppose you'll serve me well."

"Serve you?" Rhys echoed. "Why would I serve you?"

"You owed my sire one more year."

"Aye, your sire. Not you."

Alain scowled. "Before he died, my sire commanded that you give that year to me. As part of my inheritance."

It wasn't the first time Rhys had heard of the scheme, but he'd always managed to avoid agreeing to it. He found, as he stared up at Ayre's new lord, that he could say nothing in return. How often had Bertram tried to convince Rhys to tend Alain? "Just a year or two, son," Bertram would say. "Stay by him for a year or two after he weds. Perhaps you can be a steadying influence." *With the way he feels toward me?* Rhys would always argue. *I'll be serving out my year in the dungeon.* Bertram had always promised Rhys it would be worth his time, but Rhys had never been able to imagine anything that would have made such a sacrifice bearable.

In return for Segrave perhaps.

Or Gwen.

Damn you, Bertram, he swore silently. *Why did you do this to me?*

"I'm still itching to beat her," Alain announced. "Everyone stand out of my way so I might do so."

And with that, Rhys had his answer. Bertram had obviously wanted Rhys close by to protect Gwen. Rhys snorted to himself. What was he to do, sleep between the pair?

Nay, it would never come to that. Gwen would never wed with Alain. Rhys would see to that personally.

"Perhaps you should wait until you reach home," Rollan suggested. "Beat her in the privacy of your solar with a goblet of wine at the ready. You'll be more comfortable there."

Alain considered, then nodded. "Someone give me a rope," he barked, dismounting. He shoved Rhys out of his way and reached for Gwen. "Perhaps the walk back to Ayre will teach you not to run away again," he said as he jerked a coil away from one of his men.

Rhys clenched his hands at his sides as Alain bound Gwen's hands together. He mounted and turned his horse toward Ayre, holding on to the rope's end. "Mount up, de Piaget. I have important things to see to. A hunt, perhaps, though 'tis certain she's ruined the morning already for that kind of sport."

Rhys hardly had time to fix Gwen's stolen sword to his saddle before Alain had led her a goodly distance away. He grasped his horse's reins and hastened after the company. He fell into step next to Gwen, leading his mount. They walked together for a time in silence before she spoke.

"I was coming to find you," she said quietly.

He sighed. "I wish you had waited at Segrave."

"I was already at Ayre and I couldn't bear the thought of staying there another night. Besides, I thought you might have wanted someone to guard your back."

He almost smiled at that. "Indeed."

She scowled at him. "Think you I could not have done it?"

"Ah . . ."

"Today was my first day as a mercenary. I assure you I would have improved with practice."

The thought of Gwennelyn of Segrave guarding his back was enough to make him break out in a sweat. Saints, but 'twould be enough to get him killed.

"Besides," she said quietly, "I'd heard rumors that you were uninterested in taking a wife." She looked at him from under her eyelashes. "I thought I might appeal more as a mercenary."

"Oh, by the saints," he groaned, wondering what other untruths she'd heard bandied about the garrison hall. He generally kept enough to himself that the only tales people had to tell of him were ones they made up themselves. He turned to ask her just what she'd overheard, but found himself looking at air.

Alain had jerked the rope so hard, he'd tugged Gwen completely off her feet. He was currently dragging her, ignoring her struggles to regain her footing. Rhys dropped his reins and ran forward to pick her up. Alain wheeled around and lashed out at Rhys with his crop. Rhys ducked, pushed Gwen to her feet, and backed up a pace.

"This is most unseemly, my lord," he said sharply.

The riding crop came at him again so quickly, he barely had time to react. He caught it before it struck his face.

"You forget your place," Alain snarled.

"I haven't yet agreed to serve you," Rhys returned before he could think better of his words.

"Such cheek," Rollan said with a shake of his head. "Truly a disturbing trait in him."

Alain looked at his brother. "It is, isn't it?"

Rollan nodded. "I don't know that I wouldn't worry about his lack of humility, given his station."

"True enough," Alain said.

"Perhaps a taste of your displeasure," Rollan suggested.

Alain fingered his crop, then nodded suddenly. "Ten lashes for his disobedience. Guards, come hold him."

Rhys was surprised enough to just stand still and gape at his lord's son.

"I will not be flogged," he managed.

"You will if I command it."

"I will *not* submit willingly," Rhys said, wondering how many of Alain's men he could do in before he was overcome just the same. A full score surrounded him. He could take perhaps half of them if he could mount quickly enough.

"Then I'll whip *her* instead for your cheek," Alain said, jerking on Gwen's rope.

"Nay," Rhys said, aghast. "You cannot mean to—" He didn't bother to finish. It was all too clear that Alain would do whatever he pleased, the consequences be damned.

"Submit, then," Alain said, dismounting. "Kneel at my feet and submit."

'Twill keep her from his wrath, Rhys told his knees, but they weren't listening. It took all his willpower not to draw his sword and use it liberally on the fool standing in front of him.

"Perhaps he needs aid," Rollan suggested.

"Likely so. Guards!" Alain called. "Take him and bend him over something solid."

Rhys considered. If he didn't have to kneel on his own, perhaps he could submit. Besides, ten lashes were a small price to pay for keeping Gwen on her feet and out of Alain's whip arc. Damned annoying chivalry. He was far better off when he ignored its clamorings.

He looked at Alain's guardsmen and recognized most of them. Those were the ones he had met previously in the lists while training. There wasn't a bloody one of them he hadn't left crying peace more than once. They were the ones who were slow to dismount and even slower to draw their swords.

The others bounded down enthusiastically and surrounded Rhys. Rollan, of course, was still safely sitting atop his horse a healthy distance away. Rhys looked at Alain's brother and hoped the man could see the promise of retribution in his eyes. Rollan only lifted one eyebrow and smiled. He didn't, however, come any closer.

Rhys looked at the other handful of Alain's guards who had encircled him. Either they had heard nothing of his skill or had heard it and didn't believe it. Rhys told himself it would do him no good to wipe those smiles off their faces, but the temptation to draw his sword and do just that was almost overpowering.

This will save Gwen from Alain's whip.

That was the only thing that kept his sword in its sheath. He didn't think, however, that he would be condemned overmuch for using his fists a time or two. He bloodied several noses and felt the satisfying crunch of teeth coming loose, but in the end there were simply too many hands for him to avoid. They stripped off his upper garments and bent him over a stump.

"You vicious whoreson!" Gwen exclaimed. "He did but try to protect me from your foul temper!"

"My foul temper?" Alain echoed. "You're the one with the shrewish tongue!"

"At least I don't flog innocent men for my flaw!"

"He's hardly innocent," Rollan said, "and far too cheeky for his place. I'd say that deserved twenty lashes not ten, wouldn't you, brother?"

Rhys fixed his gaze upon Rollan and gave himself over to the contemplation of revenge. That unfortunately didn't last long, for it took all his concentration to keep his own mouth closed.

There were two things Rhys could say for Alain of Ayre: he was very strong and he wielded his crop with great skill. Rhys would have bitten off his own tongue before he cried out, but he did his fair share of grunting. Alain paused in his work, came around, and lifted Rhys's head up by his hair.

"Have you found obedience yet, Sir Rhys?"

Rhys took stock of his strength and measured his fury. Aye, there was a bit more there yet to sustain him. He immediately thought of half a dozen vulgar things he could suggest Alain do to himself, but he had no breath for the voicing of them. So he contented himself with spitting at Alain's feet.

"Another ten!" Alain thundered, stomping off.

After those were accomplished, Rhys decided he'd perhaps had enough of the building of his character for the morning. He could see that Alain was almost beside himself with rage. Rhys suspected if he pushed the man any further, he would be seeing a great deal of Ayre's oubliette. That hardly served his purposes.

It galled him to do it, but he gave Alain the answers he wanted and was deposited none-too-gently back on his feet. He thanked those who helped him back into his clothes, memorizing their faces for future reference, and then imprinted upon his memory every pull, twitch, and drop of blood that his back had produced.

Alain would pay for them all.

And then Rollan would pay as well.

Rhys walked stiffly over to his horse and swung up into the saddle, biting his lip to maintain his silence. And then he found the presence of mind to look for Gwen.

She was watching him with tears streaming down her face.

Rhys looked away before he himself wept. This was not how he had intended their reunion to go. What he wanted to do was snatch her up in his arms and flee with her. All he could do at the moment, however, was concentrate on keeping himself in the saddle. He was hardly in any condition for successful rescuing.

He would repay Alain for that as well.

He would return to Ayre with her. He would see his back tended and take a day or two to shore up his strength. And then perhaps it would come to him just how he intended to see the future come about. If they fled, they would leave behind her mother, which Gwen would not do, and her lands, which he would not do.

He closed his eyes and wondered if his desires were too greedy to merit a heartfelt prayer for deliverance.

He looked at her again as she stumbled along behind Alain's horse, and watched the woman who had kept him on his feet for the past four years. Saints, but she was beautiful. And so full of fire she fair left him gasping for air. To think he'd had her ragged, dirt-smudged self within his grasp and he'd been too stupid to recognize her while they'd had the time.

He should have asked for another ten lashes as repayment.

7

Gwen felt her face flame as she trudged along up the way to the castle. Her mother would have been appalled, her sire incensed at her current plight. She herself was simply mortified. She'd gone off in such a rush of glory. This was not exactly how she would have chosen to return. Given that she'd never intended to return at all, the insult was doubly painful.

"You could release me now," she said distinctly, jerking suddenly on her rope to gain Alain's attention.

He only glared over his shoulder at her. Gwen thought briefly about fighting, then abandoned the notion. Alain would just drag her along as he had before. Considering the wretched condition of Ayre's bailey, she preferred to have her face remain as far away from the ground as her legs could manage.

She did her best to cross the drawbridge without breathing any of the stench wafting up from the moat. It was no wonder Alain employed so few upon his walls. The reek of the water alone was enough to cause his enemies to swoon.

Unfortunately, the smell in the inner bailey was no better. She could hardly believe her father had actually wanted her to pass the rest of her life in this hovel. Surely no political alliance was worth this.

She sighed. She knew she had no cause for complaint. Her sire had made the best match for her he could and trusted her to use her wits to improve her surroundings. Which she would have done, of course, if she'd ever found herself misfortunate enough to be at Ayre for any length of time. As it was, she didn't plan on being there long enough to gather up the rubbish and refuse and carry it well away from the walls. What freedom her attempts at being a mercenary hadn't earned her, Rhys's appearance in England certainly would.

Though she had to admit that she felt the tiniest bit anxious about how he would manage to free her from the wedding Alain had planned for less than a se'nnight hence.

She breathed through her mouth as she trudged over the hard-packed dirt. Alain dismounted before the great hall. He was no taller than she, which afforded her a fine view of his angry eyes as he released her hands from their bonds. Gwen prayed her disdain didn't show. Alain was a bit on the plump side, nigh on to losing the greater part of his hair, and had teeth that would likely rot from his head before spring. And he was bowlegged. She suspected that came from his spending most of his time on horseback, either hunting or using the perch as a means to intimidate those who might have been taller than he.

All in all, not her first choice for a husband.

That soul, whom she could see out of the corner of her eye, was stiffly dismounting his horse. His feet hit the ground with an unsteady thump. He leaned his head briefly against his horse's withers before he suddenly straightened. She suspected that he wished no one to know of his pain.

He looked over his shoulder, and she found herself staring into pale gray eyes. He said no word, nor did his expression reveal anything of what he felt. But in his eyes she could see it.

We will be free of this place.

Then, as if he knew she'd understood him, he nodded. He turned and slowly led his horse toward the stable.

Gwen winced at the stiffness of his gait. Perhaps she had made a mistake by stopping him from drawing his sword. Then again, had he done so Alain likely would have had his guard cut him down where he stood. This was a painful alternative to death, but likely a better one, though she wished she hadn't been privy to it. She had made herself watch Alain take his whip to Rhys's back, partly so she might meet his eyes should he look up and need strength, and partly to imprint on her mind another example of Alain's cruelty. It had taken every smidgen of willpower, though, to remain where she was and not fling herself at Alain and maim him with her hands alone.

"I see you found the gel."

"No thanks to you. You were to watch over her and see she comported herself well!"

Gwen looked up. Alain was currently expressing his displeasure to her guardian, who stood on the steps leading up to the great hall. She indulged briefly in the wish that she could have hied herself off after Rhys to the stables. Listening to Hugh of Leyburn and her betrothed argue over who was responsible for her flight was something she would have been pleased to avoid.

"I am but a simple man," Hugh said, reaching into the pouch at his belt for something else to put into his mouth. He slurped up a fig or two, then chewed diligently. "I am unused to such disobedience. I surely threatened her properly."

"How?" Alain sneered. "By vowing to take away her sewing needle?"

Her guardian shrugged. "It worked for my gels."

Gwen wondered if Hugh's daughters had also been threatened with losing their place at the supper table. Hugh was not a slender man and neither were his girls, or so rumor had it. The only reason Gwen could divine as to

why her father had chosen him to watch over her and her dowry was because
Hugh was more interested in Segrave's larder than he was either in Gwen
or her mother. Tallying up the rents with one hand while stuffing his maw
with the other left no hands free to investigate either of Segrave's ladies.
Gwen was most grateful. She suspected her mother was even more so.

"Might I go now?" Gwen asked, moving past Alain before he could say
her yea or nay.

"To my mother's solar," Alain commanded. "Fitzgeralds! Finish your
duties, then put yourselves at the wench's doorway and see she doesn't go
anywhere else."

Gwen gaped at the two blond giants who stepped from the great hall
and came down the steps as one. Admittedly she hadn't been at Ayre but a
pair of days, and she had pleaded pains in her head at every opportunity that
she might miss the filth of the great hall, but she should have noticed the
two before her.

Twins, they were; identical pillars of ruthlessness, and surely possessed
by foul demons as well. Who knew what was left of the twisted soul who
had been split to make its home in two bodies? Why hadn't someone
drowned them both while they could?

She bolted past them with a squeak. She slipped and slid across the
rushes in the great hall but didn't slow her pace. Once she reached the stairwell, she scraped the bottom of her filched boots on the lowest step, then
climbed the steps as quickly as she dared. She gained the solar, then paused
at the door to look back down the passageway and make certain the demons
weren't following her.

All clear, but she had no idea how long that would last. How many duties did they have? She entered the solar and closed the door behind her. She
didn't envy Rhys the besting of those two, for best them he would need to
if they were to leave Ayre.

Perhaps she should take her courage in hand and find him before the
devils sent to guard her could take up their posts outside her door. It would
certainly save his strength. She suspected he had little enough of it at present to spare.

She thought on the possibilities for a goodly length of time. She had
just decided that perhaps a brief journey to have speech with Rhys would
have been a good thing when the door opened. Too late. She turned, steeling
herself for the worst.

"Oh," she said with a scowl as the other soul entered, "'tis only you."

A lad of no more than fourteen summers made her low bow and then
straightened, grinning. "You overwhelm me with your delight at my arrival."

"I was expecting someone else," she grumbled. "How did you manage
to slip past my guards?"

"None there yet, though it wouldn't have mattered. I would have told them Alain had sent me."

That made sense enough, she supposed. John was Alain's youngest brother and as much unlike Alain as she was. At least he didn't look to have come out of the morning's events any worse for the wear. He'd been the one to find clothes for her. He had also given her much advice on how to walk like a lad. Perhaps she had been too quick a student. If she'd looked more like a girl, Rhys perhaps might have recognized her more quickly and they both could have avoided their encounters with Alain's temper.

"Sir Rhys is here," John announced. "I saw him in the great hall."

He was as enamored of the man as she was, she noted with another scowl. John had fostered with her father, then remained at Segrave at her mother's request, leaving Gwen amply acquainted with John's worship of the gallant Sir Rhys. John had the most amazing talent for ferreting out the most insignificant details about the man. Where he came by all his information was still something of a mystery, but she suspected he acquired most of it by eavesdropping either in the stables or the garrison hall. She hadn't allowed herself to believe that John had exaggerated either Rhys's fierceness or his skill. She was as ready to believe any and all tales of the man as Alain's brother was.

Except, of course, for those rumors that he wanted no wife.

"You'll not believe what has happened to me," John said, fair frothing at the mouth. "Ask me what happened but moments before. Make haste and ask me."

"Did you see Sir Rhys?"

John made a sound of impatience. "I told you I had. This is more glorious even than that. Ask me what could be more glorious than that."

Gwen sighed. "What could be—"

"Well, as you know," John interrupted, "your mother bid me remain by your side that I might report to her your antics—"

"John!" As if she wanted to be reminded that her mother had saddled her with a keeper!

"And once I realized you were to wed Alain so soon and knew I would be continuing on here at Ayre," he continued animatedly, "I found myself at a loss as to what to do with myself. There was the thought of immediately earning my spurs, of course. 'Tisn't unheard of at such a tender age. Sir Rhys himself had earned his at ten-and-four, and by King Phillip's own hand you remember, though was against the wishes of my father, who was his master at the time, but who was he to argue with the king of France—"

"Who indeed?" she muttered as John drew another great breath for more speaking. She knew all of that, of course, but it never hurt to hear it all again. It helped remind her that Rhys was infinitely capable of extricating himself, and her as well, from any impossible situation.

Or so she hoped.

"So, I supposed that it was possible to be knighted so young, but to be sure I haven't Sir Rhys's skill as yet, though 'tisn't because I haven't worked very hard to acquire it, as you know from having watched me in the lists where I spend most of my time—"

"The event, John. The glorious and noteworthy event that just transpired!" Saints, but there were times the lad could babble on more expertly than the giddiest of serving girls.

John took a deep breath and with great ceremony announced his news. "I am to serve him."

"Whom?"

"Sir Rhys," he said, his joy fair exploding from him. "Can you believe my marvelous fortune?"

"And Alain said as much? In those words?" John had certainly wasted no time in realizing his desire. Would that she could do the same.

"He said, 'I don't care what you do, John. Serve the devil for all I care, just stay out from underfoot.' I took that as permission."

"And the chivalrous Sir Rhys? What did he have to say about this?"

For the first time since he'd burst in upon her, John looked the faintest bit unsure. "He seemed rather absorbed with downing a goodly quantity of ale, so I thought it wise to approach him with the glad tidings after supper."

"A sensible choice."

"I thought so, too."

Gwen paced the short distance to her window, then turned and leaned back against it.

"Why is he here?" she asked. She knew the answer from Rhys's own lips, of course, but there was no harm in hearing what tales John had heard.

"Sir Rhys? Why, my father sent for him. Likely to bid Sir Rhys farewell before he passed."

"Perhaps your sire thought Rhys was finished with his business in France."

"Oh, nay," John disagreed. "I daresay Sir Rhys planned on another full year of tourneying, at least. He needs the gold, you see, to buy his land."

His wife, Gwen corrected silently. She cleared her throat. "You told me several months ago that he had gone to France to make a name for himself."

"Aye, and to earn gold to buy the land he wants. He has no title and to be sure his sire's antics have done nothing to aid him in acquiring one by name alone."

"Hmmm." She nodded, as if she understood what John was talking about. This was a tale she knew nothing about. She'd heard rumors about Rhys's sire coming to a bad end, but she had no idea what he'd done to arrive there.

"Why then," she asked carefully, "doesn't he spend his gold on a title for himself and then seek out a rich heiress to wed?" She realized with something of a start that while she was almost certain Rhys would have her or die in the attempt, she had no idea how he planned to accomplish the deed. *'Tis all in the details, my love,* her mother always said. Gwen was beginning to understand what she'd meant by it.

"He's given some thought to doing that," John informed her, as if he'd been privy to Sir Rhys's most intimate deliberations with himself. "Of course he'll have a wife in time, but that isn't what concerns him the most and it surely isn't what concerns him now. He needs land. Unless," he said with a frown, "unless she came with a large dowry. Then he might be persuaded to burden himself with a bride. And I suppose only the richest would suffice."

Gwen thought of her dowry and of the enormous estates it entailed. Aye, Rhys would not suffer by having her. But would he manage it?

As she stood in her small chamber, she began to wonder just what her worth to him might be if she came with just herself.

Nothing?

She shook her head sharply. He'd just bent himself under the rod for her sake. He'd promised her several years ago that he would find a way to have her. Surely he hadn't lied about something so serious.

"I'm certain," she said, prying a bit further, "that if he met the right woman, he would wed her despite her poverty."

John looked at her as if she'd just sprouted horns. "Of course he wouldn't," he said promptly. "What good would she be to him then?"

There was no point in trying to explain to John the finer points of chivalry. He should have spent more time eavesdropping at her mother's solar door.

She turned him around by the shoulders and pointed him toward the door. "*Adieu*, little lad. Go nip at your new master's heels."

"He wouldn't wed a woman with nothing, Gwen. He has to have land. He speaks of nothing else—"

She pushed John out the door and shut it behind him. He couldn't be right. After all, what else would Rhys say? That he only wanted to wed for love?

He'd said as much to her. The size of her dowry was something she had no control over. She wouldn't begrudge him the wanting of it. He had no land of his own. Why not have hers?

They would have to have speech together, and the sooner the better. Perhaps she would do well to have a small wash and become presentable. Her hair was a detriment in its shorn state, especially given how much of her ears it revealed, but she could unearth a wimple from the bottom of her traveling trunk. Surely there would be a clean one lurking there.

Then again, perhaps the tidying of herself could wait yet awhile. The events of the day had caught up with her, and she felt a sudden weariness descend. She sat down on a stool near the window and closed her eyes, giving herself over to contemplation of her gallant champion. It was better to first shore up her courage by imagining how it would be when she and Rhys actually managed to flee from Ayre. She propped her elbow on the edge of the window, rested her chin on her closed fists, and concentrated her considerable powers of imagination on the memory of his kiss.

And to think it could quite possibly happen within hours.

Perhaps her destiny had taken a turn for the better that day.

8

Rhys finished his ale and helped himself to another cup. It was quenching his thirst but hardly dulling the pain in his back. Not even his thoughts, absorbing as they were, were enough to distract him completely from the discomfort. But at least giving them his attention was more interesting than concentrating on the throbbing.

He could hardly believe Bertram of Ayre was dead. Had it been a natural death? He could believe many things of Alain, but murder was not one of them. His lust for the title was not so great. But there was always Rollan to consider. With Rollan, anything was possible.

Rhys frowned. Perhaps he should have left France sooner. Once Bertram's messenger had found him at the tourney, Rhys had collected his ransoms, gathered up the rest of his gold, and deposited it with his mother for safekeeping. That had taken him a se'nnight, then he'd wasted another se'nnight traveling to the shore. After that he'd sacrificed a fortnight to pass through London and leave a bottle of costly claret with the king's steward. He hadn't even paused for a bit of bathing along the way, not that such a thing was fashionable in England. He scratched his cheek in annoyance. Shaving would be the very first thing he would do once his back was seen to.

He sighed. A pity he hadn't known Bertram's true condition, else he would have made more haste. He vowed to discover the truth behind Bertram's demise in time. For now, all he could do was assume Bertram had known he was failing quickly and had called Rhys to his side to inform him how he would exact Rhys's final year of service.

Rhys scowled and took another mighty pull from his cup. By the saints, the very last thing he wanted to do was stand at Alain of Ayre's elbow and steady him before he made a fool of himself. And it was something he *wouldn't* be doing if he had his way. Bertram might look down upon him from heaven and forgive him the lapse. Far better that Gwen should be out of Alain's sights than Rhys fulfill a vow of service to one who was dead and perhaps wouldn't know the difference. In this instance his honor could be damned for all the heed he would pay it.

He put his shoulders back and flinched at the movement. The time for seeking out Ayre's healer had come. He rose carefully and turned, then found his way blocked by two expansive chests with beefy arms folded over them. Rhys looked up, no small feat given his own formidable height, and met the gazes of two men who were even taller than he.

Despite their advanced age of at least five-and-thirty winters, the identical features were as smooth as marble, and just that unyielding. Long blond hair flowed over impossibly broad shoulders and great paws of hands were tucked under arms, hands that easily could have snapped a back in two without any effort.

The Fitzgerald brothers returned his stare with those great, unblinking eyes of theirs and not a flicker of emotion on their faces. Rhys folded his own arms over his chest and stared back at them. It would take a warrior of the most courageous mettle, the surest hand, and the stoutest heart to face these two and come away the victor. Rhys quickly took stock of his weapons and the damage already done to his poor form that day. He cursed silently. Besting these two would only come at great cost, but it might very well turn out to be something he couldn't avoid—

"Told you he wouldn't write."

Rhys blinked. One of the statues had spoken.

"Young ones never do," the other grumbled.

"That is the thanks we get for all our tender care of him," the first added, a small pucker of irritation beginning to form between his eyebrows. "Looking after him when he was a wee lad."

"Tending his cuts and bruises."

"Making sure he ate as he should."

"Spinning yarns of Viking splendor for him every night so he would have glorious dreams of war and bloodshed."

The first's expression had turned very unpleasant. "I vow, Connor, 'tis enough to make a man rethink his desire for seed to carry his sword after he's gone."

"Aye, Jared, you have it aright. Children. Bah."

Rhys smiled weakly. "I was busy," he offered.

"Too busy for a handful of words on a scrap of parchment?" Connor demanded.

"Or scrap of skin," Jared suggested. "I would have been well satisfied with that."

"I was much consumed with traveling about earning the gold I need," Rhys said.

The twins were seemingly unimpressed. Connor's scowl was formidable. By the thoughtful look on Jared's face, Rhys suspected he was still contemplating the possibilities of skin as a missive instrument.

"I was never bested with the sword," Rhys continued. "And I held over a hundred souls for ransom—"

"And the lance?" Connor barked.

Rhys gritted his teeth. "Bested once."

"Once?" Connor fair shouted "Saints above, boy, did I teach you nothing?"

"It was once, Connor—"

"Once?" Connor repeated, in much the same tone. "Once is one time too many! Kill, or slink off in shame. Vanquish, or don a hairshirt for a full year. Humiliate, or forgo the pleasures of the flesh for *two* years—"

Rhys wanted to put his hands over his ears and disappear under a handy table. "I know, I know," he groaned. "Saints, but I've heard the list for what feels like every day of my life! I've too much to see to today for the listening to it yet again."

"See?" Connor grumbled to his brother. "These young ones are always in haste. Never time to sit and speak of their travels to those less fortunate."

"Aye," Jared agreed sadly. "Or to quaff a companionable cup or two with the aged and infirm—"

"Oh, by all the bloody saints!" Rhys exclaimed. "I traveled, I humiliated, I vanquished. Satisfied?"

Connor's expression darkened considerably. "Should I cuff his ears, brother?"

"Turn him over your knee and leave welts on his arse," Jared advised. "Such cheek and disrespect from a little lad deserves no less."

"I'm a score-and-four, if you'll remember," Rhys growled. "And if you'll also remember, you haven't executed either of those threats on my poor form for the last twelve years. Since I was ten and two," he added as he watched Jared begin to count surreptitiously on his fingers. "Not since the day I bested you both, one with each hand."

"Aye, and the proudest day of my life it was," Jared said, reaching up to dab away a bit of moisture from the corner of his eye. "Me with your right and Connor with your left."

"Aye," Connor said, beaming with paternal pride, "and using all my own stratagem on me. That little feint to the left—"

"The forward thrust—"

"The graceful backhand sweep aiming for the knees—"

"The dodge and disembowel parry—"

"The delicate slice across the throat—"

Rhys knew just how long the list was, so he endeavored to refocus his former nursemaids' attentions on the present moment.

"If you'll excuse me, I've a need for Master Socrates."

"In the cellar," Jared said. "Lost his place near the weaver's shed. You can imagine why."

Rhys could. It only made sense that Alain would go through the keep and do his best to make everyone as miserable as possible.

Connor looked at Rhys critically. "You're wobbling."

"An encounter with Ayre's strips of leather."

"Ah," Connor said wisely. "Couldn't guard your tongue, eh?"

"He slapped the lady Gwennelyn."

The twins blinked at him.

"I encountered her this morning," Rhys explained. "I thought she was a he, and that he had stolen a horse. She tried to fight me for my mount."

Jared seemed to be trying to decide whether he approved or not. Connor continued to blink, as if such a thing were simply beyond his comprehension. Or perhaps it was the mere mention of a horse to send him into a stupor of such proportions.

"Who bloodied your nose?" Connor asked, at length.

Rhys gritted his teeth again. "She did."

Two jaws fell open in unison.

"I was taken by surprise," Rhys said defensively.

Two sets of teeth clicked together as jaws were retrieved.

"Well," said Connor.

"Well, indeed," agreed Jared.

Rhys squirmed at the bit of untruth he'd just told. Never mind that he had known what she had intended. That she had actually carried out the threat was surprising enough. Then again, this was Gwennelyn of Segrave. He should have known better.

"I hadn't expected to see her there," Rhys added. "I didn't recognize her."

"You had plenty of opportunity to go to Segrave to look at her," Connor said. "Lord Bertram went often enough."

"You didn't go, either," Rhys pointed out. He'd been to Segrave twice, twice more than he likely should have gone.

The twins paled as one. Then they began to shake their heads.

"Couldn't go."

"Best not to leave the keep."

"Lord Bertram needed us to stay."

"Important tasks for us to see to here."

Rhys knew the reason why they hadn't left the keep and why they kept as much distance between themselves and anything that moved faster than their own two feet, but he chose not to say anything. There were things a body could torment the Fitzgeralds about, and then there were things one didn't dare. Rhys knew very well where to draw the line.

"A pity I recognized her too late," Rhys said with a sigh. "The day might have ended differently otherwise."

Jared sighed as well. "Poor child. I fear we gave her quite a fright when she first saw us."

"How could we help it?" Connor asked. "You give me a fright, and I've looked on you all my life!"

Rhys shook his head, wishing he could stave off the inevitable discussion of who they resembled more: their axe-wielding mother or their dual-broadsword-wielding sire. It was impossible and he knew he wouldn't be noticed even if he tried to interrupt the argument, so he sidestepped them and limped through the hall to the kitchens. Gwen was in good hands. If Alain had sent the Fitzgeralds to watch over her, he had no intention of troubling her again that eve. If there were any bodies who could make the new lord of Ayre nervous, it was these two. They had been Bertram's favorite guardsmen for precisely the effect they had on others.

Rhys gingerly made his way down the stairs to the cellar, pausing often to catch his breath. Alain's crop had taken more out of him than he cared to admit. Perhaps he had been too hasty in submitting to Alain's display of displeasure.

He came to a halt under a torch and leaned his head against the stone. Never had it crossed his mind that Alain would disobey his sire's wishes, though he now wondered why he'd been so stupid. Of course Alain would wed with Gwen as quickly as possible. Her dowry was enormous.

"Who are you mooning over now, or should I guess?"

Rhys peered back upward into the gloom. Montgomery of Wyeth came down the steps, holding a cup of what Rhys assumed to be ale.

Rhys looked at him in surprise. "You're still here?"

"Apparently so."

"I would have thought Alain would have buried you with his sire."

Montgomery raised his cup in salute. "It wasn't for a lack of trying, believe me."

"Fortunately for you, you're harder to do away with than that."

Montgomery only smiled. "Indeed I am. Now, what of you? It took you long enough to come back. Bertram had been anxious to see you."

Likely to give me the details of his command that I serve Alain, Rhys thought with a scowl. "Trust me, I was busy."

"I'll wager you weren't," Montgomery said with a snort. "Just dawdling, as usual."

"I hurried, but I've no time to tell you of it. I'm off to see Master Socrates for something useful. Care to come?"

Montgomery shuddered. "Don't like to watch him make his potions. I like the taste of them even less well."

"You've a weak stomach, my friend. They're always very effective."

"Aye, they work simply because your poor form heals itself to avoid having to down any more of his brews."

Rhys laughed and the movement made him catch his breath.

"Saints, Rhys, what befell you?"

"An encounter with our new lord and his riding crop," Rhys said, pausing to let the pain subside.

"The lash *and* a fist in your face? You must have let your tongue run mightily free at his expense."

Rhys pursed his lips. "He only saw to my back. I earned the other mark from someone else."

"Brawling again, good Sir Rhys? I'm disappointed in you."

"It was Gwen," Rhys muttered, feeling as disgruntled as he had the last time she'd clouted him on the nose and he'd been forced to explain to Montgomery just where he'd gotten the mark.

"Again?" Montgomery asked with a laugh. "By the saints, lad, you'd think you would have been expecting it this time."

"She took me by surprise—"

"I can see that."

"—and bloodied my nose while I was gaping at her, amazed to find the heiress of Segrave traipsing about the countryside pretending to be a mercenary," Rhys finished darkly.

Montgomery shook his head with a fond smile. "The girl has an imagination, I'll give you that."

"And a ready fist," Rhys agreed.

Montgomery stared at him thoughtfully. Rhys wanted to squirm, but he was too old for squirming.

"What?" he asked defensively,

"I was just wondering what it is you keep doing to the girl that causes her to abuse your poor nose thusly."

"'Tis no affair of yours."

"And I was wondering how your tourneying went on the continent and what it was you intended to do with all that gold you no doubt earned."

"Again," Rhys growled, "'tis no affair of yours."

Montgomery scratched the side of his face thoughtfully. "Was it a very large amount of gold you earned? Enough for, say, a bribe?"

Rhys scowled at him.

"And is it possible that he whom you intend to bribe is disposed to accepting your bribe?"

"You think too much."

"Have you thought that perhaps your gold would serve you better in other ways?"

Rhys had no answer for that. His only goal for the past four years had been to earn enough to buy Gwennelyn of Segrave. What other use for his gold could he have?

"Your sword might buy you a better heiress than you think, especially if you could convince King John your allegiance ran more toward the English crown than the French."

As if John would give Gwen to him merely because of his skill with a sword! Rhys almost laughed out loud. "He is uninterested in a blade which has seen the clasp of a French king. Gold, however, could come from the devil himself and John wouldn't care. Besides, he knows I want land here. And surely he knows it was hardly my fault Phillip knighted me."

Not that Rhys could have argued with the French king anyway. His father and grandfather had ties to the crown of France that Rhys certainly hadn't been in a position to break. Even though he had chosen a different path than the other two men of his family, he was still a de Piaget.

"England is my home," Rhys continued. "What greater display of loyalty could John ask of me than that?"

"I daresay he still has fond memories of his brother wearing the English crown and keeping his feet mostly on French soil."

Rhys sighed as he dragged his hand through his hair. "I have few ties to France, Montgomery. My mother is there, true, but she has her own vocation and no interest in political intrigues. My grandsire is old and well past posing any threat to any king." A small lie, but a necessary one. "The land I want is here. I've never kept that a secret."

"Ah, but you have kept secret just what little plot of ground it is you covet so fiercely." Montgomery leaned forward conspiratorially. "Just a hint, Rhys. I vow I won't tell a soul."

"Until you slip into your cups later this evening," Rhys said dryly. "Then the entire keep will know."

"Your doubt cuts me to the very quick. For all you know I might be able to aid you in your quest."

Rhys pursed his lips. "The only thing that might help me in this quest is another few chests of gold."

Unfortunately, he didn't have time to earn any more. What he had already would have to do.

"Go see Socrates," Montgomery said, retreating back toward the stairs. "I'll find you later and pry more of the truth out of you."

Rhys pushed away from the wall and continued down the passageway. Gwen's guardian was a greedy man. Perhaps he could be convinced to hold off the wedding for another pair of months until Rhys could return to London and convince John fully that he intended to remain on English soil, loyal to the English crown. Rhys smiled grimly. Perhaps he would even be able to convince the king that he wasn't interested in following in his father's footsteps.

Or perhaps he would merely snatch Gwen away during the night and flee.

It was tempting, but that would leave them no choice but to go to France. England was her home. England was where he wanted to dwell. He would just do as he intended from the beginning and settle for bribery. And he would see to it first thing in the morning before Alain could do anything else to foul up Rhys's plans.

"Let the gold be enough," he muttered under his breath as he made his way to the healer's chamber.

It would have to be.

He had no other choice.

9

The child sat on a stool near the cooking fire and watched the contents of the kettle boil frantically.

"Nay, not that," a wizened old man muttered to himself, stooping over to peer into the recesses of his collection of pots. He shoved aside what he didn't want and reached in with bony fingers to pull out a leather pouch of some moldering substance. He opened the pouch, sniffed carefully, then smiled in triumph. "Knew I had a bit more left," he said, turning back to the pot. "Keep stirring, child."

"Aye, Grandfather," the child replied, giving the bubbling brew a hearty stir. She watched as the old man dropped a pinch of something into the thick potion. It disappeared under her awkward strokes into a rather unappetizing mass of greenish paste.

"Mmm, something smells wonderful," a voice said from the doorway.

The child looked up without surprise. She'd known the knight would come home today. She'd seen it, though she hadn't said as much to anyone else. Her grandfather would have thought her fanciful, but she knew better. It was a gift she had, this seeing.

"Ah, Sir Rhys," her grandfather said, drawing the young man into the tiny chamber, "you've returned safely! And not a moment too soon, I'd say. Terrible things afoot in the keep, terrible indeed! Knew you'd come put an end to them as quick as you could."

"Master Socrates, your faith in me is, as usual, greater than I deserve."

"Not at all, lad. Here, come and sit. I've something especially tasty on the fire."

"I could smell that from fifty paces, despite the foul odors from the kitchen. How is it you find yourself in this hellhole instead of near the weaver's shed where I left you?" He paused and smiled down at her. "Good to see you as well, *ma petite*."

The child found her hair ruffled gently as the tall knight moved past her to sit himself down with a wince on the stool near the fire. She didn't understand the little words he always called her, but she liked how they sounded against her ear and she knew by his tone that they were good words. Her heart warmed within her as she continued to stir diligently, stopping only long enough for her grandfather to ladle out a cup full of his current combination. It smelled not at all tasty, but the knight sipped, then complimented her grandsire lavishly on not only the strength and texture but the unique flavorings of his brew. When her grandfather turned his back to putter amongst his things, his face aflame with the pleasure of the compliment, the knight winked at her and put a finger to his lips. She nodded, her heart full of love and appreciation. There was not another soul in the keep who tried to save her grandsire's pride.

"I wonder, Master Socrates," the knight said politely, "if you might have something for the soothing of cuts and bruises? I seem to have run afoul of a few stripes this morn."

The knight's back was soon bared to view, and the child watched as her grandfather ran his gnarled fingers over the lash marks. He clucked his tongue in grave disapproval, then turned away to prepare his poultice.

The child stood against the wall and watched the knight. He was digging in the pouch attached to his belt for something, and she wondered if he might be searching for something to rid his mouth of the less than pleasant taste that no doubt lingered there. She loved her grandfather, true, but she would be the first to admit he was not a very skilled cook.

The knight beckoned to her. "I've something for you, *chérie*. They called your name when I saw them."

The child approached, stunned that he should think of so small and insignificant a personage as herself while on his travels. She held out her hand and blinked at the sight of the pieces of colored sea and sky he laid there.

"I happened upon a glassmaker putting in a chapel window," the knight explained. "He assured me these colors were pleasing together, but I've no eye for such things. I thought you might make use of them somehow."

The child ventured only a peep at the three smooth pieces of glass, green, azure, and yellow, but already she saw more in them than she ever had in the still water of her grandfather's wooden cup. She closed her small fist about them and looked at the knight. She could scarce see him for her tears, and she could find no words to express her gratitude.

The knight only laughed softly. "Ah, if only others were so well pleased by so little." Then he turned his face away and sighed. "If only I were so satisfied with so little."

The child watched as the knight bowed his head. She wondered if it might be the wounds he bore that grieved him so, then thought better of it. Though she knew little of men and their sorrows, she suspected this gallant soul was carrying a heavy burden indeed.

She waited until her grandfather had applied his healing salve and turned back to his brew before she approached. Her mother had warned her to use her gifts sparingly, for men would not understand them, but also to use them generously when called upon. If ever there were a time to be unselfish with what little good she could do, now was the time.

The child stepped up to the knight carefully and touched his back with her small hand. Though she could not ease his heart, perhaps she could ease his body.

The knight stiffened in surprise, then looked over his shoulder at her, his eyes wide.

"In return for your gift," she said, lowering her eyes and pulling away.

She saw the knight stretch. She chanced a look in time to see him appear mightily surprised at his pains being taken from him. Then he lifted his hand and ran it over her head gently. "Little one, 'tis I who should thank you, I think." He looked at her grandfather's back, then shook his head as he arose as if he just wasn't sure what had eased him—her touch or her grandfather's brew.

Her grandfather turned and looked at the knight expectantly. "Are you soothed, Sir Rhys?"

"Aye," the knight said with a faintly bemused smile. "'Tis nothing short of a miracle."

"Ah, good," her grandfather said, looking very pleased. "A new recipe, but obviously a good one!"

The knight stretched again as he redonned his tunic, then looked at the child with another glance of wonder. He shook his head with a small smile, bid her grandfather farewell, and then left the chamber.

The child waited until her grandfather had turned back to his pots before she opened her hand and stared down at the glass pieces there. They were so much clearer than the water in her grandfather's cup.

And she told no one of what she saw.

10

Rollan of Ayre was smiling as he sat at the lord's table in the great hall and nursed a cup of ale. It had been a particularly interesting day, what with all the excitement over Gwen's escape and recapture, and that savory flogging of Rhys de Piaget. Rollan had wondered, as he'd wandered about the keep, just what could happen to possibly improve on the day's events.

To his surprise and delight, the day had indeed improved. After returning to the keep, he'd descended to the cellars to visit his favorite ale spigot. He'd just settled down for a fine afternoon of imbibing when he'd heard Rhys and Montgomery begin to speak together. He'd slipped back into the shadows immediately. Uncomfortable, aye, but the rewards had been well worth the trouble. He'd ignored the rats and spiders crawling about him and listened raptly to the discussion going on just in front of him.

Rollan had eavesdropped until he thought he couldn't bear any more. The pair had parted ways with Montgomery ascending the steps and Rhys continuing on to Ayre's pitiful excuse for a healer. Then, feeling as full and satisfied as if he'd just spent hours at the king's table, Rollan made his way back up to the great hall where he could watch the goings-on and give thought to what he'd learned. He'd relished the idea of spending a full evening pondering just what the ever truthful Sir Rhys was about. With Alain still raging in his solar over Gwen's short-lived flight as violently as a pricked boar, Rollan had had ample time to turn over in his mind the possibilities. Never in his most vivid imaginings would he have suspected such a devious notion as bribery of his father's beloved foster son.

Rollan was momentarily tempted to do a bit more lurking to see where Rhys went and to whom he spoke, but he stopped himself. He would speculate a few more hours and decide for himself what sort of scheme de Piaget would try to put into motion. Discovering the details any sooner would be an insult to his own imagination and plotting ability.

Nay, he would give de Piaget ample time to ruin himself, then do the honorable thing and step forward and expose the subterfuge before it went any further.

After all, a knight was bound to tell the truth, wasn't he?

Rollan nodded to himself thoughtfully. It was the least he could do for the cause of chivalry.

11

Gwen stared out the modest window that had earned her chamber the lofty title of solar. It wasn't much of a view, what with the courtyard of Ayre right below her. She'd been studying the piles of filth gathered here and there for an hour since the sun had risen, and devoted much thought to the merits of a sewing needle as a weapon. She'd used them before with good success. It was all she had at her disposal given that Rhys still possessed her filched sword.

Unfortunately she suspected that a small needle, even a sharp one, would be of little use against the Viking demons who guarded her. She'd had two meals brought to her since her imprisonment, and both times her guardsmen had been standing like unmoving trees in front of her door. They looked far too substantial for a good poking to do them any harm.

It was not an encouraging sign.

A frantic pounding on her door almost sent her pitching forward into the window enclosure. She turned and hastened to the door, flinging it open.

"Alain wants you," John panted. "Immediately."

Gwen would have given John an earful of her displeasure over being ordered about, but the look on his face stopped her. "He's furious, obviously. Over what?"

John's eyes were very wide. "I've no idea, but it has something to do with Sir Rhys. He's been commanded to come as well."

The Fitzgerald brothers parted in Red Sea–like fashion, and Gwen slipped out of her chamber behind John before her shadows could decide she shouldn't be allowed any freedom. She heard them fall into step behind her. She suppressed a shudder.

The journey to Alain's private solar was far too short. Gwen entered the chamber and looked about her. Alain, Rollan, and her guardian all sat in chairs as if they'd been royalty and she the lowly servant come to receive instruction. She was sorely tempted to comment on the ridiculousness of the situation, for to be sure if she were a man and owned her property by herself she could buy and sell the three before her several times over, but she knew it would not serve her. The less attention she drew to herself, the better off she would be. Perhaps if Alain thought she was malleable, he would ease his scrutiny of her and she would stand a better chance of escaping his clutches.

And then there was Rhys. He had obviously had a bath. A dangerous activity, but then again here was a man used to risking his life with his sword. Gwen looked up at his face and wished suddenly that someone had provided a chair for her as well. Even a small stool would have served. This was a sight that required something sturdy beneath one's backside.

How four years could have made him more enticing she surely didn't know, but it had. He was beautiful and forbidding and so darkly handsome that she could hardly look at him. She wondered if the men he fought were as overcome by the unyielding strength of his features as she was, or were they merely chilled by the coldness of his pale eyes? She very much suspected the women he met could only stare at him and wonder where their minds had gone. She understood completely.

And then she realized two things: she was gaping at him, and he was returning her look—only he wasn't seeing her.

She dragged her attention back to Alain and his companions.

"You sent for me?" she said, hoping she sounded calmer than she felt. She'd given it thought on her way there and could divine no reason why she and Rhys should find themselves having an audience with Alain at the same time.

Unless he knew of their feelings for each other.

Alain, as usual, merely stared at her as if he rehearsed in his mind all the things he found so objectionable about her person. He frowned and chewed on the inside of his cheek.

"Is it possible then, my lord," Rollan asked hesitantly, "that she knows nothing of this scheme we've discovered this morn?"

Hugh of Leyburn snorted and then smacked his lips. "'Tis a scheme I could easily credit her with dreaming up. Her sire let her run too freely in her youth, I say. I never would have allowed such daydreaming in my household."

Gwen sent a heartfelt prayer of gratitude flying heavenward that her sire hadn't been this corpulent lump of lard. She pitied his daughters.

"I'll rid her of the habit," Alain grumbled. "I've no mind for a headstrong bride."

"But she'll breed well for you," Hugh said, reaching for another fig and slipping it between moist lips. "Got good hips, does this one."

"And what would you know of it?" Gwen demanded.

Hugh's face turned a very unattractive shade of red. Alain's eyes had narrowed, and he looked to be considering something foul. Rollan's eyes had lowered, and she thought he might be judging her hips to see if Hugh's observation had any merit.

Saints, but she could hardly believe she found herself in the same chamber with three such poor specimens of manhood.

She stole another glance at Rhys, just to remind herself what a man could be. Perhaps it was the contrast between him and the other men in the chamber to make her realize just how magnificent he was. Perhaps it was the way he carried himself, as if he had acres of soil under his feet and a powerful title to shield himself and his loved ones behind. Perhaps it was the simplicity of his garb that presented such a pleasing diversion from the baubles, feathers, and gaudy trappings that bedecked the buffoons before her.

Or perhaps it was that fat ruby in his sword that screamed he was not a man to be toyed with, else his victims would be finding themselves covered with a like color.

She sighed. A pity Rhys couldn't just do Alain and the other two in. That would have saved her the trouble of this current foolishness which the three before her seemed determined to drag out as long as possible. Alain was fingering his ever-present riding crop. Hugh, of course, was shoving figs into his furiously working mouth as fast as he seemingly could. Rollan was looking far too contemplative for her peace of mind. It could only mean trouble where she was concerned. At least he wasn't salivating at the very sight of her. She'd cured him of that during his last visit to her keep with his father.

He'd caught her alone in a passageway and proceeded to acquaint her with his kissing. His groin had been impervious to her knees and his skin resistant to her pinches. His belly, however, had seemed a fine place to stick her sharpest needle a time or two. At least her steel had worked well enough for her then. She'd left him howling and quickly retreated to her mother's solar to there spend the duration of Lord Ayre's visit.

She looked at Rollan and rubbed her belly pointedly. He seemed to take the hint well enough and turned his attentions elsewhere.

"Hugh," Alain said, "tell me again what happened this morn, just so this pair hears it clearly."

"Of course," Hugh said. He licked his fingers thoroughly, then wiped them on his tunic front. He pointed a now clean finger at Rhys. "He came to me first thing this morning, before I'd had a chance to break my fast, mind you, and tried to—"

He belched a time or two, then started to choke. Gwen sighed. Not another brush with death. The man ate so much and so swiftly, he spent at least once a day fighting for air. She looked at her love and lifted one eyebrow in question. He wouldn't meet her eyes. She would have been much relieved by a small look in her direction, but perhaps 'twas better this way. After all, she would soon be his and she would have all the looks she wanted. She turned back to the predicament before her.

Both Rollan and Alain were pounding on Hugh's back. Gwen normally would have suggested they cease and leave Hugh to his fate, but she was too curious about what Rhys had done to say anything. Finally Hugh spat forth a great lump of something she had no desire to investigate more closely and sucked in great gasps of air. He wheezed for a moment or two, then pointed again at Rhys.

"—bribe me," he finished with another gasp.

"Bribe you," echoed Rollan, putting his hand over his heart as if it stood ready to fail him at the very thought. "Almost too dastardly a plan to contemplate."

Hugh nodded enthusiastically. Alain looked momentarily perplexed, and Gwen wondered if he were having trouble with Rollan's assessment of Rhys's scheme.

So Rhys had tried to bribe Hugh. For her hand in marriage. Bold indeed.

"He wanted Segrave," Hugh continued. "Said he'd been working for the land for years."

Gwen nodded. A clever ruse. Of course he would have said the like.

Alain snorted. "I can understand that, seeing as how he has no land of his own."

"Just for the land?" Rollan asked. "Nothing else?"

"What else would he want?" Alain returned. "Her? He probably would have tried to bribe Hugh into keeping her if he'd thought she would come with the soil."

Gwen looked at Rhys. She knew she shouldn't. She knew that any look other than bored disinterest would be marked and remembered by Rollan and tucked away for use at the worst possible time, but she couldn't help herself. She began to wonder what the truth was.

"Just the land?" she asked.

He looked at her and his eyes were chilly. Or bleak. She couldn't decide which until he spoke.

"Just the land," he said flatly. "What else?"

What else indeed. She searched his expression for any sign, however small, that perhaps he lied, or that he told less than the truth to cover his true feelings for her.

She saw nothing of the kind.

She could hardly believe what she saw, but there was no sign from Rhys that she should deny it.

She turned back to her tormentors and schooled her expression into one of complete disinterest. Let them speak of her disparagingly. Let them pick and prod at Rhys and hope to force from him some sort of confession. She cared nothing for either.

He didn't want her.

She could hardly believe it, but Rhys's eyes were so cold. Obviously, he'd had a change of heart. Or perhaps he had lied to her all along.

She wasn't sure which thought hurt her more.

Rhys stood in Alain's solar and had but one thought rage through him with the force of an angry gale: Hugh had betrayed him.

He should have known as much. He'd approached Gwen's guardian but two hours before with more naïveté than he'd obviously ever possessed in his entire life. For being as skilled a warrior as he was, he'd been blindingly stupid.

He knew little of the man, but watching him at supper the night before had revealed a soul whose interest lay primarily in his gullet. How was he to know that behind all that belching and burping lay a man devious enough to place a substantial amount of gold in his purse with one hand, continue to throw food into his mouth with the other, and yet still have enough presence of mind to plot another man's ruin? If Rhys had thought he could have gotten his fingers about Hugh's throat to strangle him, he would have. Unfortunately, Gwen's guardian was every bit as corpulent as he was untrustworthy.

By the saints, he had been a fool.

What gold he'd brought with him to England was lost. His chance to have Segrave was lost as well. He could hardly bear to think on what else he had lost in the bargain, but it was hard to avoid as she was standing not three paces from him, her back as straight as a blade. He'd hurt her, he knew, but there had been naught to be done about it. 'Twas bad enough that Alain suspected Rhys wanted Segrave. If Alain suspected Rhys truly wanted Gwen, Rhys knew he would find himself in Ayre's dungeon in truth.

And then *all* hope would be lost.

"Her land alone?" Rollan mused, breaking Rhys's concentration. "I'm surprised, Rhys. One would think your lofty chivalry would have dictated you desire the woman as well."

Saints, but wouldn't the man let the matter drop? Rhys clenched his fists. Strangling Rollan of Ayre would be too swift and easy a death for the man. Rhys wished he had the time and the leisure to think of a more painful way to end his life, but there was no time to spare. Alain was thinking again and that never boded well. Rollan generally did all the contemplating for the pair, but that didn't improve matters, either. Rhys had no doubts Rollan was somehow at the bottom of this catastrophe, but he could afford to spare no thought to how that might have come about. What he had to concentrate on now was how to distract the fools before him until he could think of a way to free both himself and Gwen. Obviously, he would have to go to the king.

"I want land," Rhys said, dragging himself back to the present. The three men were still staring at him waiting for him to say something.

"It must be very hard to have never had any of your own," Rollan said sympathetically.

"And you do?"

A swift flash of loathing swept across Rollan's face, but it was gone as quickly as it had come.

"I am full well content to do nothing but serve my brother," Rollan said humbly. "And should he see fit at some time to gift me with a poor bit of soil, I would only count it graciousness on his part."

Gwen snorted.

Alain ignored her. Rhys felt a shiver of apprehension course through him at that. That the lord of Ayre should overlook such cheek could only mean Alain's attention was fixed upon him.

"Alain," Rollan said quietly, "perhaps you should speak to Sir Rhys about that matter that concerns him so closely."

Alain scowled at his brother. "Don't want to."

"Now, brother, a desire for land is not such a poor thing."

Rhys had no idea where Rollan intended to go with that, but he knew it couldn't be a good place.

"Our sire would have wanted him to have what is due him," Rollan continued.

"Why should he have anything more than what he's already received?" Alain demanded. "Father gave him enough. Besides, 'tis my land now."

Rollan shook his head and gave his brother a patient smile. "How can it be yours, Alain, when our good sire had other plans for it?"

"It wasn't his to give, either!"

"Ah, but it will be once you wed with Segrave's lady." He put his hand on Alain's shoulder. "You must do the right thing in this matter, my lord. 'Tis only fair that Sir Rhys have everything that should be his. Regardless of the cost to you."

Rhys wished desperately for a chair beneath him, for he was beginning to wonder if he would manage to stand through whatever madness these brothers intended to spring upon him.

"Very well then," Alain said, sounding extremely reluctant. He looked at Rhys. "You're to have Wyckham."

Rhys blinked. And then he blinked again. Yet for all that, Alain still sat in the same place and Rollan still stood behind Alain's chair with his hand on his brother's shoulder. Hugh still shoved figs into his mouth at an alarming rate.

"Wyckham?"

"My sire wished for you to have it," Alain said. "And so you shall. When I see fit."

"Alain," Rollan began soothingly, "do not torture poor Sir Rhys thusly. Making him wait yet more time for what he desires so mightily . . . why 'tis nothing short of cruel."

Rhys wouldn't have been any more surprised if Alain had offered him Gwen.

"Wyckham?" he repeated, stunned. "But how . . ."

"'Tis mine upon my marriage to her," Alain said, with a negligent gesture toward Gwen. "My sire commanded me to give it to you afterward."

"When Rhys had reached his score-and-sixth year," Rollan corrected, "for then he felt the lad would be ready for the challenge."

Lad? Rhys ignored the urge to glare at Rollan. He had more important things to keep from reacting to—such as the fact that a piece of land might possibly be within his grasp and all he had to do to win it was stand there and keep his mouth shut.

"So you will serve me until that time," Alain continued.

"That is two years, not one," Rhys replied, somewhat amazed he'd found his wits to say even that. "I was bound to your sire for but one year."

"And *I* say you will serve me two," Alain said angrily, "in whatever capacity I choose."

Cleaning the privies, no doubt, Rhys thought to himself.

"'Twas bloody foolish of him, if you ask me," Alain groused. "Don't want to do this at all."

"But 'tis the honorable thing to do," Rollan said gently. "And no one can argue that you do not always strive to be honorable. Besides, 'tis but a small token of esteem from our father for his beloved foster son."

It wasn't a small token. It wasn't Segrave, but it was land enough. But in return for two years of service to Alain? Rhys found he simply could not voice any sentiment, either of shock or disbelief. Not even the thought of having to serve Alain for an extra year was enough to clear the haze of surprise away.

He could, though, see clearly enough that honoring his father's wishes galled Alain to his depths. Rollan, however, was the mystery. Rhys had never once had anything but venom from Ayre's second son. There had to be something he'd missed. He glanced at Rollan and saw the slight smile. And he knew then there was a great deal more to the proposition than there seemed.

"Where is the deed?" Rhys asked.

Alain glared at him. "I say 'twill be yours. That should be enough."

"It isn't," Rhys said. He listened to the words come out of his mouth and was astonished at his own audacity. Never mind that he would be beholden to Alain of Ayre for another pair of years. It meant land would be his, and he should have been willing to do anything, believe anything to have it.

Then again, this was Alain of Ayre he was bargaining with.

Rhys watched as Alain came up out of his chair, his face a mask of fury. If Rollan hadn't caught his brother by the shoulders and jerked him back, Rhys was certain Alain would have tried to cut him down where he stood.

"'Tis a perfectly reasonable request," Rollan said calmly. "Not very politely stated by our gallant Sir Rhys, but reasonable enough." He kept a hand on Alain's shoulder. "The deed will be drawn up after the wedding."

"Two copies," Rhys said. "One to be held here, the other to be held in London."

Rollan laughed softly. "By the blessed saints, you would think Sir Rhys had been acquiring land the whole of his life. I suppose when one doesn't have the burdens of nobility resting upon him, one has ample time to think on these things."

"Greedy bastard," Alain muttered. He looked at Rhys narrowly. "You'd best serve me well, else I'll rip up the deed."

All the more reason to have another copy in the hands of the king, Rhys thought to himself. Yet even as the distrust of Alain washed over him, he was also overwhelmed by the truth of what he'd just learned.

Bertram had left him land. He could hardly take it in.

"Are you finished with me?"

Rhys blinked at the sound of that voice, then realized just what he'd forgotten.

Gwen.

"Come now, Rhys," Rollan said ignoring her. "Can you not assure my brother that you will serve him well? I vow were it me standing in your place, I would be throwing myself at his feet and kissing his boots."

Which is exactly what I will be doing for the next pair of years, Rhys thought sourly.

"I will serve you well," Rhys heard himself say, and he wondered where the words had come from.

"Ah," Rollan said with a sigh of contentment, "chivalry in the flesh. He possesses it in abundance, wouldn't you say, Gwen?"

"Oh, aye," she said quietly. "There is a veritable glut of it in this chamber this day."

Rhys cleared his throat. "If there is nothing else, my lord? I am certain there are duties I should be about as quickly as possible."

"Duties," Alain repeated. "I must give thought to what those might be."

"Perhaps something else as a reward for his morning's work," Rollan suggested. "I daresay it should be something that only the honorable Sir Rhys could fulfill."

"Aye," Alain said, scratching his head, then looking at his brother. "Perhaps I should think on it later."

"A wise decision, my lord," Rollan said, inclining his head submissively. "And I will be at your disposal to hear anything you might suggest, of course."

The saints preserve me, Rhys thought to himself. Then he shook his head. What duties Alain might decide upon did not matter. Rhys would not be there to fulfill them.

Or would he?

If he could just remove himself from the chamber, he was certain he could think more clearly. Land was within his grasp. And Gwen was within Alain's grasp. And in order for him to have his land, he would have to watch Alain take Gwen to his bed. And if Gwen wed with Alain, her life would be nothing but a misery—if she survived life at the man's hands. Rhys knew that if her sire had known of Alain's true character, he never would have allowed the union.

And if Segrave had never allowed the union, Rhys never would have had Wyckham.

It was a situation more fiendish than the devil himself could have imagined up.

"Now to the wedding," Rollan prompted. "Surely it should be accomplished with all haste? Perhaps on the morrow?"

Alain scowled. "I had a hunt planned for the morrow."

"Ah," Rollan said, sounding immensely regretful, "and I know how you love a good hunt."

"Best tame her as soon as you can," Hugh offered between slurps and gulps. "Can't start too soon with a wench, or so I've always said."

Rhys felt the words sink into him like blades. *Tomorrow. The wedding on the morrow.* It was too soon. He needed more time. He had to speak to the king, to promise the man gold, fealty, his own sweet neck if that was what was required. Tomorrow was too soon.

"Tomorrow, then," Alain said, waving his hand at them. "You both may go. We'll have the ceremony at noon. I might yet get in an hour of falconing beforehand. And remember, de Piaget, obedience in exchange for your land."

"Of course, my lord," Rhys responded, and he said as much because he was too numb to do anything else. Numb and terrified.

He was on the verge of losing the two things he'd spent the last four years paying to have with the price of his own sweat and tears.

Gwen passed out of the chamber before him without looking at him. Rhys was silent until the Fitzgeralds had come out behind him into the passageway and closed the solar door.

"Gwen," Rhys began.

She turned and looked at him and her expression was bleak. "I seem to have misunderstood you."

He shook his head sharply. "You've misunderstood nothing. I've always wanted land, of course—"

"And I possessed an abundance of it," she interrupted. "Thank you, sir knight, but I understood that very well."

"It isn't as it appeared—"

"And to think I thought you were different than the rest of them," she said.

"I—"

Am, he meant to finish, but she had already turned and walked away. The Fitzgerald brothers trailed after her in her wake. Rhys started to go after her when the door behind him opened and Alain appeared, looking at him with irritation.

"Loitering?" Alain demanded. "Lazy already?"

Rhys made the new lord of Ayre a very low bow, ignoring the protests of his damaged back, then turned and walked away before his visage betrayed him. Or his tongue. He already knew what that would win him, and the last thing he could afford was to find himself with a lock between him and Gwen.

Bertram had given him land, and all he had to do to have it was give up the love of his soul.

By the saints, but he'd never expected any of this.

12

A knock sounded on the door.

Gwen ignored it. She was far too busy contemplating the shattering of her dreams to disturb such morose musings by answering what could only be yet another disaster for the day. As if the thought of becoming Alain's bride on the morrow wasn't disaster enough.

The knock came again, more firmly.

"Leave me be, I'm brooding!"

The knock came again and Gwen cursed. Well, at least it couldn't be Alain; he wouldn't bother to accord her the courtesy of a knock. Perhaps it was John with a sharp blade on which she could impale herself. Feeling that such a thing would be a vast improvement on the day's events, she crossed over to the door and opened it.

The Fitzgeralds stood there, looking down at her from their great height.

Gwen, feeling emboldened by her impending doom, stared right back at them without so much as a flinch. A pity she hadn't felt this hopeless when she'd first escaped Ayre. She might have passed more easily for a mercenary. The horror of these two was nothing compared to the terror she would face on the morrow at Alain's hands. Somehow she doubted very much he would woo her to his bed with sweet songs and wine, as did the heroes of her mother's favorites *chansons*.

"Aye?" she said finally, when it became apparent that the twins were bent on doing nothing but staring down at her with those fierce expressions. "One of you knocked?"

The one on the right cleared his throat. "I did."

"Fool," muttered the other.

"She should know of this," whispered the first.

"Babble on then," grumbled the second. "I've no mind to listen to the tale." And with that, the second stuck his fingers in his ears and stared up at the ceiling.

Gwen looked at the first who had spoken and wondered how anyone told them apart, themselves included. The only possible way was that this one on the right seemed to scowl just a bit less than the other.

"He wants you," he said.

Gwen waited. Then she found herself scowling up at the twins. Saints, but it was contagious this foul humor of theirs. "How was that?"

"Him," the first said, inclining his head back down the passageway. "Young Rhys."

"He sent for me?"

"Nay. But the words he spoke today were not the words of his heart."

Gwen wanted desperately to believe that, but she'd heard the words come out of his mouth with her own ears. They were very hard to deny. Despite his expressions of affection yestermorn, it had been four years since she'd seen him. Much could have changed.

The other demon started to tap his foot impatiently.

"Enough, Connor," the first said, elbowing him in the ribs. "'Tis rightly your tale to tell and you won't see to the telling of it, so it falls to me to do it."

The second, apparently Connor by name, unplugged his ears. "I've no mind to relate this to such innocent ears, Jared."

"She deserves to know."

"He won't like it that you've said aught."

"She won't repeat it. Will she?"

Gwen found herself pinned to the spot by bright blue eyes that seemed to demand a response in the affirmative. She wasn't, however, above reserving the right to remember the tale for use in future extortion. But she shook her head, as if the thought of repeating such tidings was simply beyond her.

"Well then," the one named Jared said, looking a bit more comfortable, "this is how it all came about. 'Twas a night several years ago that we were roaming the hall—"

"Looking for makers of mischief," Connor interjected.

"Overenthusiastic revelers—"

"Oppressors of the weak and helpless—"

"Filchers of savories from the kitchens—"

Gwen sighed heavily. "I think I understand what you were about that night."

Connor frowned fiercely at her, but she was too weary in mind and spirit to give him any reaction of fear he might have wanted. She looked at Jared expectantly.

"Well?"

"Well," Jared said, "as we were going about our business, we happened upon the chamber where Rhys was making his bed for the night."

Gwen wondered if this could possibly be something she would want to hear. Jared seemed to think it necessary, for he plunged on ahead.

"Connor, being the inquisitive soul he is, put his ear to the wood to see how young Rhys's labors were progressing."

Gwen snorted before she could stop herself.

"My thoughts exactly," Connor grumbled. "Must the child hear this?"

"Aye, she must," Jared said with another elbow in his brother's ribs. He turned his attentions back to Gwen. "Finding the moans the wench was making little to his liking, Connor opened the door with the purpose of observing Rhys to divine just what it was he was doing so poorly as to wring such inadequate sounds from his companion."

"Well," Gwen said, hardly able to believe her ears. "This is news."

Connor pursed his lips and resumed his contemplation of the ceiling.

"Aye, well to be sure what Connor saw inside was news indeed."

Jared paused in his tale and waited expectantly, as if he desired some sort of response from her. All Gwen could do was return his stare. He frowned at her a bit, as if by so doing he could wring from her the reaction he wanted. Finally he frowned again in exasperation and spoke.

"Well," he asked, "will you not know what was occurring inside?"

Gwen shrugged helplessly, feeling completely at a loss. Did she need to know this? Then again, how could the tidings possibly make her any more wretched than she was at present?

"Um," she began, "well, I don't know—"

"Nothing," he interrupted.

Gwen blinked. "Nothing?"

"Well," Jared said with a thoughtful look, "it wasn't as if nothing at all was happening."

She waited. And when he said nothing more, she prompted him with an "I beg your pardon?"

"Aye, that was what Rhys said at the time, too, as he turned from his game of dice to look at Connor."

"Then he was . . ."

"Dicing," Connor said, shaking his head in disbelief. "And a fine-looking wench she was, too. I could hardly believe my eyes."

"Then he wasn't . . . they weren't . . ." Gwen hardly knew how to voice her question.

"Wasn't," Jared confirmed. "Didn't. Not then."

"Not ever," Connor added in a disgruntled tone. "If you can believe that."

She couldn't. "That isn't the tale I've heard." Rumors of Rhys's prowess in many areas had reached her ears thanks to John's finely honed eavesdropping skills. Men bedded women, and some men bedded as many women as possible. Rhys, by all accounts, fell into that last lot.

"I should hope you hadn't heard differently," Connor said. "Think on the embarrassment for the lad!"

"'Tis highly chivalrous, if you ask me," Jared countered. He looked at Gwen. "He invited the wench to leave, then relented under our questioning—"

"Which was most fierce," Connor said. "Had to rough the little lad up a bit to pry the truth from him."

"In the end," Jared continued, "he told us his true motive."

"Unwillingly enough, though," Connor said. "And to be sure I can understand why he was loth to give voice to such a ridiculous notion."

"It isn't a ridiculous notion," Jared argued. "'Tis most romantic."

"'Tis foolish."

"'Tis not!"

"Please," Gwen interrupted, wishing she had the courage to knock their heads together and stop them from arguing. "Tell me what his motives were!"

Jared looked at her and smiled proudly. "He was saving himself."

"Saving himself?"

"Aye," Jared nodded. "Nary a taste of those pleasures has the lad had in all his years."

"Not that he's a gelded stallion," Connor hastened to add. "He's a man sure enough. Ruthless."

"Fierce," Jared added.

"Merciless."

"And quite the swordsman, if I do say so myself," Jared finished. "Taught him all he knows," he boasted.

"*I* taught him all he knows," Connor said, turning to glare at his brother. "That two-fisted thrust through the ribs and out the back—"

"*My* axe in the thigh with the right hand and dagger across the belly with the left—"

"*My* ferocious swipe with one blade and a delicate slice the other way with the second—"

Gwen had the feeling this kind of argument could go on for more time than she had to spare. Besides, the descriptions were starting to make her more than a little queasy. Perhaps a mercenary's life was not for her.

"Let me understand this," she said, interrupting them. "He has never made any of the conquests he's credited with."

They looked at her as one and nodded.

"Why?"

"Why?" Jared echoed. "Why, for you, my lady."

"Me?" She shook her head. "He doesn't want me. He wants my land."

"Bah," Connor said, "'tis a bad habit he learned from Jared, that lying."

"From me?" Jared gasped. "'Twas from you he learned to deny the feelings of his heart! I taught him to express himself in the most tender of ways. If he'd spent less time listening to you and more time to me, he would have told this girl years ago of his feelings for her!"

"But he did tell me," Gwen said.

Both Jared and Connor turned to look at her, their mouths hanging open.

"He did?" they asked, as one.

She nodded. "It took me a bit to wring them from him, of course."

Jared's ears perked up. "Did you stick him?"

Connor snorted. "She wouldn't stick him. She's a passing sweet girl." He turned his fierce gaze on her. "What'd you do, then? Loosen his tongue with sweetmeats cooked right proper? Well-cured eel smothered in savory sauce? Roasted pheasant with all manner of little nuts and pleasant things surrounding it on a fine platter?"

Obviously Connor had heard of the delicacies produced by her mother's kitchens.

"Nay," she said, "I used my womanly ways to convince Sir Montgomery to deliver a message for me—"

"That Montgomery always was soft," Connor said in disgust.

"And I cornered Rhys on the roof and told him I wished him for my champion."

"And he agreed," Jared stated, as if there could have been no other outcome.

"Of course he agreed," Connor groused. He frowned at her. "He's had tender feelings for you since he was a lad, sadly enough. Ruins him for serious swordplay, I've always said. He spends at least a handful of moments each day mooning over you, and has done for years. That time was better spent honing that little dodge to the groin, or perhaps the blade carving artistically along the jawbone—"

Gwen could hardly bear another listing, so she turned to Jared, who seemed much less inclined to catalog his warriorly moves than his brother.

"Why then do you suppose he said what he did?" she asked.

"What else was he to do?" Jared said with a shrug. "It wasn't as if he could admit the innards of his heart to Lord Ayre. Wouldn't think he thinks on it overmuch himself, though. And that isn't because of any lack on my part, of course."

"Of course," she murmured.

She felt suddenly as if her world had righted itself again. Rhys loved her. He had for years, just as she had him. He couldn't have said as much to Alain or Rollan, and he certainly wouldn't have said the like to her guardian. After all, hadn't he tried to bribe Hugh that morning? Bribery for land was one thing; bribery for a woman was another. It wasn't something Hugh would have understood, so Rhys approached him with something he *could* understand. A pity Rhys hadn't used a few wagons of foodstuffs instead of gold. It might have had a better effect.

But what were they to do now? She stood to marry Alain in the morning. She looked up at the twins.

"Escape," she said distinctly. "'Tis our only hope."

They only blinked at her.

"He lied to distract Alain and Rollan," she said, "so that we might escape." Her heart lightened so greatly and so quickly, she thought she just might be able to fly from the keep. "I'll find him, then we'll flee," she announced. She smiled up at the brothers and then parted them with ease. "My gratitude, twins. You've been a great deal of help to me."

She ran down the passageway and thumped down the circular stairs to the edge of the great hall. Alain would likely be engrossed in his plans for his hunt on the morrow. Rollan's whereabouts were always a mystery, but with any luck she could avoid his notice as well. All she needed to do was find Rhys, tell him she understood his plan, and decide how they would accomplish their flight.

And then she came to an abrupt halt.

Every exit from the great hall was under heavy guard.

She looked to the high table only to find Rollan sitting there with a goblet at his elbow. He smiled pleasantly and raised his cup in salute to her.

And it was at that precise moment that she knew there was no hope of escape.

She could not flee to the kitchen. She certainly couldn't slip out the hall door. There was no other way from the keep besides leaping off the parapet into the moat, but she suspected she wouldn't survive the trip down, and it wasn't as if she could keep herself afloat in the water.

She was doomed.

Her breath came in gasps and she began to see faint specks of light all over the room. She stumbled back into the stairwell and leaned against the wall. There was no leaving Ayre. Not even had she been able to find Rhys and convince him she was for him would she have been able to sneak away from the keep. It was tempting to give in to the fancy that perhaps during the changing of Alain's guard she might slip past them . . . but nay. If Alain had taken this kind of trouble now, he would surely take just as much trouble to ensure the changing of the watch went just as smoothly.

She mounted the steps and walked slowly back to where the Fitzgerald brothers waited. She looked up at them and smiled sadly.

"No escape."

They seemingly had no reply for that, so she entered her chamber and shut the door behind her. What else was she to do? She had no wings to fly off over the walls to freedom. She suspected that not even Rhys could single-handedly take on the entire garrison of Ayre, no matter his reputation. At present she would be of little help to him. There would be no evading her fate: she would marry Alain of Ayre whether she willed it or no.

And after he wedded her, he would most certainly bed her, and she very much suspected that would not be a pleasant experience. She had given him one taste too many of her insolence. Aye, she would pay for her cheek.

And that was enough to make her think that perhaps she *should* throw herself into the moat.

She walked to the window and looked down. Saints, even the barbican was swarming with guardsmen. If she hadn't been so panicked, she might have been flattered at the precautions Alain seemed to be taking to keep her safely within the keep.

Now it only forced her to realize that there was indeed no escaping her fate.

She would sacrifice herself on the morrow to a man who cared nothing at all for her when but a handful of paces away would stand a man who loved her enough to have denied himself his entire life that she might be the one he first took to his bed in truth. A pity she could not somehow find a way to switch bridegrooms at the altar. Or to switch herself. Perhaps there was more advantage to being a twin than she'd suspected at first, though she certainly wouldn't have wished her fate on anyone else.

The knock on the door startled her so badly she almost fainted. She put her hand over her heart to soothe its pounding and turned to the portal.

"Aye?"

The door opened. John stood there, looking as dejected as she felt.

"He doesn't want me now," he said with a long, drawn-out sigh. "Says he has too much to brood about tonight."

"Sir Rhys?"

"Who else?"

Gwen refrained from informing John that while Rhys might not want him, he most certainly wanted her. Her straits were too narrow for such disparaging comments.

"And Alain had no task for you?"

"Too busy planning his hunt on the morrow."

"I'm happy to see he isn't overly consumed with thoughts of his wedding."

John looked at her and she thought she might have detected the hint of tears in his eyes. "I wish you could wed with Rhys, Gwen. Even if he wants you just for your land. I think he might become fond of you eventually."

"With any luck," she agreed, "he just might."

John sighed again and fingered the hem of his tunic. "I even put on clean clothes to present myself to him. And the new helm your mother gifted me. Just so he might see I was ready for battle at any moment." He looked at her. "He was unimpressed."

"Poor lad," she said, unable not to smile. It was difficult to have one's idol take no notice of such efforts.

And then, of a sudden, a flash of brilliance overcame her. She pulled John into her chamber, feeling more grateful than usual that Alain had chosen to put her in a solitary cell, and shut the door behind him.

"I had wished for a twin," she said, shoving aside the nagging thought that this was a very poor idea indeed, "but I think you'll do just as well."

"Uh," he grunted as she released him, "what are you—"

"Strip."

"I beg your pardon!" he said, aghast.

Oh, the finer sensibilities of a lad of ten-and-four. Gwen put her shoulders back and prepared to put forth her arguments for the scheme, which she was sure John would hardly agree with, for 'twould be his neck as well as hers in the noose if they were to be caught. Perhaps she would do well to clout him over the head before she left the chamber. At least that way he wouldn't be completely responsible for her flight.

"What do you want my clothes for?" he asked. "Are you thinking of escaping again?"

"With Sir Rhys," she admitted.

"Not without me," John said stubbornly. "You'll not leave me behind this time."

This was going to be a problem. Maybe she'd have to do damage to him before she relieved him of his clothes. Either that or tell him a falsehood and make off with his garments.

"Gwen . . ." he warned.

Lying and stealing, she thought with resignation, were indeed vices determined to become part of her character.

Not many minutes and the promise of a hefty bribe to John later, Gwen opened the door to her chamber and parted the Fitzgerald brothers in what she hoped was a John-like fashion. She spared no time in trivial speech with them, but immediately set off down the passageway. John had been soothed with the knowledge that he could indeed escape Ayre on his own more easily than she, as no one would likely mark him as he left the gates. Thusly appeased, he had informed her where Rhys was keeping himself and given her directions on how to reach the guardroom in the north tower.

Gwen made her way down the passageway with a confident air. She would reach Rhys, convince him she knew the truth of his heart, then they would set off together for France.

Unfortunately, her journey took her through the great hall once more. She couldn't deny the number of men there, nor the completeness of their weaponry.

No matter. She and Rhys would manage it.

But by the time she'd managed to gain the stairs to the north tower, she was beginning to have her doubts. She had no sword. Would Rhys's sword, lethal though it was, and his formidable skill be enough to win them their freedom?

She hazarded another glance into the bailey on her way up the stairs. Even though the arrowloop was small, she had no trouble marking the number of men crowded into the inner bailey. She paused on a step, finding that more than doubts were assailing her now. They would not manage it, she was almost certain of that. As fierce as Rhys might have been, there was virtually no hope of him subduing all the men in the great hall and still having enough strength left over to see to the men outside.

She leaned against the stone wall. There was no hope. She should have realized it before.

She looked up the stairwell, defeated.

And then a thought occurred to her.

She might not be able to flee, but she wasn't without a choice about one thing. After turning the idea over in her head a time or two, she nodded to herself. Perhaps Rhys would find the idea foolish, but then again, perhaps not.

Alain, if he noticed, would be livid, but that was something she could face on the morrow.

Heartened, she turned and marched purposefully up the stairs.

13

Rhys paced the confines of the small chamber and cursed the walls that surrounded him. And when that gave him no relief, he cursed the circumstances that surrounded him in just as unyielding a fashion. Gwen, or her land. That he was even faced with such a choice was enough to send him straight to the cellars to cozy up to a keg of ale for a fortnight.

Wyckham.

Or the most beautiful, courageous, perfect creature ever to set her dainty foot to English soil.

By the saints, if he'd had but a grain of sense in his head, he would have recognized Gwen the moment he'd seen her, then fled with her then and there to France. Alain would have eventually decided that perhaps some foul fate had befallen her and gone on to wed with some other heiress. Hugh would have savored Gwen's wealth for several more years. Rhys would have bought himself a little piece of ground in France, and he and Gwen would have lived out their lives in perfect bliss. But now where did he find himself?

In a tiny upper guardroom, staring at walls that would imprison him for another two years, and contemplating what tortures Alain and Rollan might invent for him during said two years.

But it was not how his future would come about if he had anything to say about it. To be sure there were guards aplenty, but couldn't he take them? Perhaps he and the Fitzgeralds could fight their way through the press, pulling Gwen along behind them. Even if he were forced to leave Gwen with his mother while he and the twins earned a bit more gold, it would be worth the sacrifice. To be sure, three such hired swords would be enough to set any lord's tongue to lolling.

Assuming, of course, he could convince Gwen her sword was better used as an ornament in the abbey. The saints preserve him if she insisted on guarding his back.

He jerked open the door, ready to storm down the passageway and inform the Fitzgeralds of his plans, only to run bodily into a lithe form standing before him. He cursed silently. Saints, but this lad was persistent. Rhys couldn't deny that he was somewhat flattered by John's blatant worship, and then there was the added pleasure of knowing that at least one of the Ayre brothers held him in esteem and by so doing irritated the other two to no end, but now was not the time to begin the training of his new squire. He had men to slay.

"John," he said, mightily annoyed, "did I or did I not tell you I've no need of you this eve?"

To his complete astonishment, John put his hand in the middle of Rhys's chest and shoved him back inside the chamber. The lad followed him in, then shut the door behind him. Rhys was so shocked, all he could do was just stand there and gape at the lad's cheek.

"I should leave welts on your arse," he exclaimed.

"Wouldn't if I were you," John responded promptly. "It would put a mighty damper on the evening's events, I'm sure."

And with that, John pulled off his helm and before Rhys's very eyes appeared none other than Gwennelyn of Segrave dressed, of course, like a lad. Rhys felt his jaw slip downward.

"By the saints, lady" he managed, "you don't wear gowns all that much, do you?"

"I'm in disguise," she confided.

"Can I assume John is left in your solar in skirts?"

"And none too happy about it, I assure you."

"Well," he said, completely at a loss. "Well," he tried again, wishing that the chamber contained more than just a pair of chairs and a table, for he wished desperately for a bed on which to put himself until his head ceased spinning.

"I couldn't agree more," she said.

Rhys felt for a chair and lowered himself into it, then realized what he had within his grasp. He leaped up and reached for her arm.

"Come," he commanded. "We'll fetch the Fitzgeralds and cut our way from the great hall. The stablemaster will saddle our mounts for us, for he has little love of Alain. You'll ride behind me, aye?"

"But—"

"I know you want your own mount, but 'tis safer this way. I'll teach you what you need to know to have your own once we reach France. I have gold enough to at least see us passage across."

"But—"

He reached for the door, but she put her hand on the wood and shook her head. He shook his head as well, uncomprehending.

"Haste, lady," he informed her, "is of the essence at the moment."

"Have you peeked into the great hall of late and seen the number of men?"

"Perhaps you have had a recent lapse of memory regarding my reputation," he said pointedly. "I can take them."

"I didn't doubt you could as well after I gave it some thought," she agreed, "but then I saw the courtyard filled with the rest of the garrison. I think even you might be outnumbered there."

It occurred to him that she just might be right. And then something else occurred to him.

She had obviously seen through what he'd said in the solar.

"You would come?" he asked.

She leaned back against the door and smiled up at him. "Despite the fact that you want nothing but my land?"

"'Tis good land," he reminded her.

"The best, I should think."

"Without land I am nothing," he reminded himself.

She smiled. "That's a matter of opinion, but 'tis a manly thought and one I can understand."

He sighed. "I've gold enough to buy us a poor bit of soil in France."

"Rhys de Piaget, keeper of a small vineyard?" she mused. She shook her head. "It seems a waste somehow."

"Then we'll travel the world living off my sword."

"Nay, not just your sword. I could learn—"

"My sword," he interrupted.

"But—"

"Trust me. I am capable of protecting us."

"I could be a very dangerous mercenary," she informed him archly.

"Aye," he agreed, with feeling. Dangerous to him, but he didn't dare say as much. She'd planted her hands on her hips, and there was the beginnings of a glare forming on her face.

And then just as suddenly she shook her head and leaned back against the door. Her arms came around her waist, as if she sought to comfort herself.

"Nay, Rhys, 'tis not possible."

"I could take them all," he said desperately.

She looked at him and shook her head again. "There are too many. Besides, 'tis what Alain expects. Either you would finish on the gibbet or in his dungeon, and neither of those things could I bear."

"We have no choice."

"Aye, but we do. I will wed with Alain. You will give him your two years and have your heart's desire."

"The land be damned," he growled. "You know that isn't what matters the most to me."

"But it does matter."

"Of course it does," he retorted sharply, "but only because I need somewhere to build a keep. How will I protect you without walls? How will I protect our children without men to man those walls? I need a place to take you!"

She didn't answer. She merely moved away from the door, slipped her arms around his waist, and gathered herself close. She laid her cheek against his chest.

"Rhys, we cannot leave. It is not possible."

He put his arms around her and rested his chin on the top of her head. It had to be possible. He would accept nothing less. Much as he wanted Wyckham, he wanted Gwen more.

"At least," Gwen said, pulling back, "there is one thing I will not give Alain."

"There are several things you will not give Alain," he managed. It was the most rational thing he could say as the sensation of having Gwennelyn of Segrave in his arms was as distracting as it had been the last time he'd held her. It had taken him almost four years to recover from that. He put his arms around her, lest she think better of her action and try to pull away. She only leaned against him and nestled closer. "You won't give him your hand in marriage, for instance," he said.

"I cannot escape it."

"I'll see that you do—"

"Nay, Rhys." She pulled back only far enough to look up at him. "The land should be yours. The saints only know you will have earned it by then."

"I'll not have it at the expense of you."

"Go carefully, Sir Rhys, for you lead me to believe that perhaps you might begin to value me for something besides my dowry."

He scowled at her. "You shouldn't believe everything you hear."

She only laughed softly and laid her head back against his chest. Rhys closed his eyes and wished with all his heart that the castle would fall down upon him at that very moment. He would have gone to his grave a perfectly contented man.

"Nay," she continued, "Alain will have my hand and you will have your soil. But he will never have what I intend to give you this night."

Rhys felt a frown begin. He looked up at the ceiling for an answer to her riddle, but saw nothing but cobwebs. No aid from that quarter.

"Well," she said, pulling back to look at him. "Will you have it?"

"Have what?"

"My virginity."

"Your *what*?"

She started to smile. He, however, saw nothing amusing at all about the fact that his ears had already started to fail him. Deaf at a score and five. It was a tragedy.

"You heard me. My virginity. My virtue. Call out the mounted knights and let us breach this maidenhead."

He took a step away from her. Then he took a few more steps backward until he found himself with a sturdy chair beneath his backside. He knew he was gaping at her, but he couldn't stop himself.

"Surely you aren't serious."

"Then you don't want me?" She took off John's cloak and dropped it onto the floor. "I apologize that I have no gown, but it seemed a bit imprudent under the circumstances, and I also apologize for my hair, but you know how that tale came about."

And as she continued to describe and apologize for her failings, all Rhys could think was, *The woman I dreamed about for almost half my life has just come and offered herself to me.* And if she'd had any idea just how appealing hose and a tunic were on her, she wouldn't be speaking at all.

"Ah," he managed, "I couldn't. Unchivalrous, I think."

"Don't you want me?"

He crossed his legs in self-defense. "That isn't the point."

"Do my ears trouble you then?" she asked, pulling her hair over what she deemed to be the offending features.

"Of course not."

She considered. "Perhaps, then, a game of dice might soften you to the idea."

"Dice?" he echoed.

"I understand you're an excellent teacher."

He could only stare at her, uncomprehending. And then the light began to dawn. He'd been exposed, and by the most unlikely of sources.

"Damn those Fitzgeralds," he grumbled.

"A talkative pair, indeed."

He scowled at her. The saints only knew what else they had told her. It was obvious he had no more secrets.

"Think of tonight as a chivalric duty," she coaxed.

He groaned and dropped his face into his hands. He was so bewildered he groaned again for good measure.

And then he felt a soft hand against his hair and heard a knee pop as she knelt before him and took his hands.

"Rhys," she began, and there was no light of jest in her eye, "this is not how I would have it."

Nor I, he wanted to say, but no words would come.

"But 'tis the only choice I can make. I cannot escape my fate. And I will not ask you to give up what you have worked your whole life for."

"But you are asking me to give her up."

She blinked very rapidly. "Cease with that romantic foolishness, lest I lose my resolve."

"Gwen, the land means nothing to me."

"Well, it should, for the price is very dear."

"But it would be you to pay the price for it," he argued. "And that I cannot have."

"You haven't asked me to pay anything," she said. "Our course is laid out before us, Rhys. We are both bound to Ayre, and the time for flight is well past. I can make no choice there. But I can choose to whom I will give my virtue. And if doing so means I must spend the rest of my life with Alain of Ayre, then 'tis a price I will gladly pay."

"But, Gwen—"

"Please, Rhys," she said, and for the first time he heard fear in her voice.

And that frightened him.

"He will not be gentle," Gwen added. "I have provoked him one time too many. I can only pray that he will use me quickly and be off to other matters."

He swallowed with great difficulty.

"I would truly prefer it if I had some pleasant memory of what it should be like to concentrate on while enduring the other."

"Oh, Gwen," he said miserably.

She smiled, but it was done too brightly to be believed. "So, let us be about our work while the night lasts. The morrow will take care of itself soon enough, I'll warrant."

He drew her up onto his lap and cradled her against him. He thought he might have managed a solid front until he felt her hot tears on his neck. His own eyes burned and his cheeks were soon wet with his own grief.

Saints, but this wasn't how he had planned things.

And so he rocked the woman in his arms, as much to soothe himself as to soothe her, and wished with all his might that he might somehow bend time to his will and place them both back outside Ayre's gates with her manfully struggling to lift her blade to do him in. He would have caught her hand, hauled her into his arms, and kissed the breath from her, then fled with her to France. Their mutual deflowering would have taken place in the most expensive inn he could have found, preceded by a fine meal, rare wine, and as many *chansons d'amour* as a minstrel could have racked his brains for.

It certainly wouldn't have happened in a filthy guardroom on the night before she was set to marry someone else.

She pulled away, took his face in her hands, and kissed both his cheeks softly. Then she smiled at him.

"Come, my gallant knight, and let no other soul come between us tonight."

"But how can I have you," he asked, "and then never have you again? Live in the same keep with you and know you are forever out of my reach?"

"Perhaps Alain will put you to cleaning the cesspits, and we will see little of each other."

He considered. "There is that."

"I will likely be confined to my tapestry frame in the solar." She brushed his hair back out of his eyes. "We will see each other now and again and know in our hearts that we shared what no one can ever steal from us."

"It isn't enough."

"It will have to be. 'Tis all we are allowed."

"If we are allowed even that."

"If it is a sin, then I will bear the burden of it. Surely I will be forgiven this desire for such a small comfort."

He couldn't help but agree, though he suspected the comfort would certainly not ease either of them over the next pair of years.

And that didn't begin to embrace the rest of his sorry life.

To have Gwennelyn of Segrave, and then to lose her?

"Chivalric duty," she reminded him.

"How you can possibly make that out of what we intend to do this night, I do not know."

"I use my imagination more than you do."

He sighed and dragged a hand through his hair. "Very well, then," he said, feeling somewhat at a loss. "We should begin, I suppose."

"Aye."

But where? Saints, it wasn't as if he had any experience in those matters. He fished about in his almost empty purse, sparing Hugh of Leyburn one last hearty curse for its lightness, then pulled forth a pair of dice. He fingered them nervously.

"Perhaps a brief game," he conceded.

"Time is of the essence," she agreed.

"A very brief game, then," he said.

And as he began to teach her all he knew of dicing, he marveled at the absolute improbability of the situation in which he found himself. Wooing the love of his heart by divulging to her the finer points of a game of chance. His most recent encounter with her had come while she was posing as a mercenary, lying and stealing as enthusiastically as if she'd been doing it all her life. That they were now playing not only with dice but also with their lives shouldn't have surprised him.

And he studiously avoided thinking about the very real possibility of someone, Rollan for instance, stumbling in upon them.

"I'd best bolt the door," he said.

He returned from his errand to find Gwen studying the dice intently. Would that she would study him with like concentration.

And then she looked up at him and smiled.

The sight of it almost felled him where he stood.

"One final game?" he croaked.

She nodded happily, and he knelt down next to her. His hands were shaking, and he wondered if she would respect him less if he indulged in something of a swoon before he indulged in her. He later remembered nothing of their game except the sight of her hands, the warmth of her body next to his, and the sound of her laughter in his ears.

He thought he might just perish from it all.

"I won," she said suddenly, smiling smugly at him. "Didn't I?"

"Aye," he managed, dazed by the sight of her.

"And my prize?"

He felt very self-conscious as he held out his hand to her. "Will I do?"

She put her hand in his. He looked down and remembered the last time he'd reached for her hand. It had been on the roof of her father's keep when she had chosen him for her champion. Champion, husband, 'twas all the same to her. Rhys looked at his lady and wondered if it was sweat running down his cheeks. They were very wet.

"I don't think I can—" he croaked.

She put her finger to his lips and shook her head. Then she brushed the damp from his cheeks, leaned forward, and very gently kissed him on the mouth. And this time her sire was not standing at the end of the passageway to stop her.

At least his nose was in no peril.

He thought, however, that his heart would be much worse for the wear.

"This moment is ours, my love," she whispered against his lips.

He wanted to argue, but her mouth distracted him from his thinking. He wanted to flee, but her hands touched him and left him caring nothing for anything outside their chamber. He wanted more than what they would have that one night, but her arms went around his neck, and he found himself pulling her so closely against him that clothes were stifling.

And so they shed their clothes, layer by layer, with nervous hands and embarrassed smiles, until they had made a nest of them in the corner. Rhys lifted Gwen into his arms, then laid her down carefully on their poor bed. He followed, drawing her tightly against him, praying that the night might last far into eternity.

And then there was no more time for thinking, no more room for arguing, and no more will for fleeing.

They were alone, and no other would intrude upon their bliss.

14

Rollan of Ayre stood behind his brother's chair on the morn of his brother's wedding and observed the two standing next to each other in the midst of Alain's solar. They had been slow to answer Alain's summons and both looked exceedingly weary. Even with their drawn and spent expressions,

Rollan had to admit that they made a fitting pair. De Piaget, damn him anyway, with his commanding height and muscular build made even Gwen look slight and fragile. Not that Rollan cared how mannishly tall she was. He would have taken her against whatever surface was handy at any time, any number of times, and not regretted it once.

And now she was on the verge of becoming his brother's wife.

It had been enough to sour his stomach that morn.

He suspected the only satisfaction he would have out of the day would be watching de Piaget's reaction to what his new duties would be. Rollan had come up with the idea himself, based on a nagging suspicion he'd had for years. He could hardly wait to see if his instincts ran true. Alain hadn't been happy about cutting short his hunting that morn, but Rollan had managed to convince him that getting Rhys settled was best done that day, preferably before the wedding.

"I've come to a decision on your duties," Alain announced.

"Then why am I here?" Gwen demanded.

"Because, you wasp-tongued wench," Alain growled at her, "you're involved as well."

Rollan could have sworn he heard her mutter something about a cesspit, but he could have been imagining it. He watched Rhys raptly, waiting for the reaction he fully intended to savor for many months to come.

Rhys, however, made no move and spoke no word. His face wore a mask of impassivity even Rollan had to admire.

"She's been left to run wild too long," Alain said, pointing at Gwen. "She'll embarrass me at some important moment. Or so Rollan says, and I believe him."

Alain paused. Rollan realized that only he himself seemed to be enjoying the drama of it. Gwen looked as if she might lose the contents of her stomach. Rhys was as still as stone.

Interesting.

"She needs a guard," Alain ground out, "and you are to be its captain."

Rollan could have wished for a much better delivery, but the crack in Rhys's armor was all he could have hoped for. The man flinched as if he'd been struck. Rollan spared Gwen a quick look to find her as pale as an altarcloth.

So, he had been right. There was something between them.

Could it possibly become any more entertaining than this?

"Everywhere she goes, you'll follow. Everything she does, you'll remember and report on. Everything she says, you'll repeat to me when I demand it. Understood?"

Rhys was, to all appearances, speechless.

Gwen looked as if she would faint.

"Excitement over the wedding?" Rollan asked her, unable to resist the question.

She only looked at him with eyes as bleak as a winter sky. In spite of himself, Rollan felt a twinge of regret for her. It wasn't as if he would have looked forward to marriage to his brother, either. The man was a rutting boar, and a stupid one at that.

But, Rollan consoled himself, it would only make her appreciate him all the more when the time came.

"De Piaget, your duties begin immediately," Alain said. "See her safely to the chapel. Then you'll stand guard outside the bedchamber door tonight as well. Don't want to be disturbed in my labors."

Gwen turned and walked from the chamber. Alain pointed a finger at Rhys.

"And see that she stops that. I hate it when she leaves before I can tell her to go!"

Rhys bowed his head. "My lord, if I may?"

"Aye," Alain said, waving his hand dismissively, "go. Two years, de Piaget."

"As you will, my lord."

Rollan watched him leave and leaned against the back of Alain's chair, full well satisfied with the morning's events. Gwen's hell would begin in a few hours. Rollan rubbed his belly with a frown. She would deserve every second of pain.

And Rhys's hell had already begun.

Truly, it was a fine morning's work.

15

The child crept up to the top of the steps, then hastily hid herself at the end of the passageway. It wasn't as if she needed to be there to observe the events, but compassion drew her. The knight and his lady suffered. If only she could have done something to ease it.

Earlier that day she had watched the lady go to the chapel, pale and drawn. As evening shadows fell, the lady had gone to her marriage bed.

The knight had stood guard outside the bedchamber door, his face pale and drawn.

Even the child had paled at the muffled sounds of discomfort.

And then the two Vikings had appeared and led the knight away.

"I must stay," he had protested.

"You've been there long enough," one of the blond ones had growled.

"Aye, and now you can hear him snoring from here," the other had snarled. "He'll not know you've gone."

"But she will."

"'Tis better that way, lad."

"There's wine aplenty downstairs," the other stated.

"I don't want any."

"Best to have some, young one."

"Aye, it will ease you."

The knight seemed not to agree, but the child could see that he was in little position to argue. Never mind the fierceness of the men who escorted him down the steps. His heart was broken and his will bent under the load he carried. He had no strength left for arguing.

She wondered if she could have eased his burden, but she suspected even the touch she had inherited from her mother would have been too small and mean a thing to aid him. All she could do was stare into the glass stones in her hand and watch.

And then even her tears blinded her to that.

16

Gwen stood at the door of her solar with her hand on the bolt and fought with herself. She wanted to leave the chamber. She also wanted to repair immediately to her bed and never emerge again from beneath the coverings.

It was the morn after her wedding, and she suspected that she had passed better nights.

She couldn't hide forever. She would have to face the keep, Alain, and his filthy living conditions. She would also have to face Rhys.

She drew in a deep breath and opened the door. The Fitzgerald brothers stood in their accustomed places. They parted without comment. She stepped between them, then looked up at them. Connor, and she could tell it was he by the intense scowliness he seemed to wear like a fine cloak, would not meet her eyes. She turned to look at Jared. He seemed determined not to look at her, either, but she had come to suspect that he was less resolute about his gruffness than his brother. His lips pursed, tried to form a scowl, and failed. He unbent enough to let his gaze dip down to meet hers. She smiled up at him as best she could, but it was a less than happy smile. He unfolded his arms from across his chest and briefly rested his hand on her shoulder. Connor growled at him, and he hastily reassumed his tree-like pose.

So much for sympathy from the Fitzgeralds.

Gwen started down the passageway only to find them grumbling along behind her after only a few paces. In spite of herself, she felt comforted. At least she would have some sort of companionship.

And then she looked up.

There, standing in the dim light coming in through an arrowloop, was the very person she had hoped with all her heart she could avoid. He leaned negligently against the wall, resting one shoulder on the stone, his arms folded over his chest. The ruby in the hilt of his sword was dull and lifeless in the gloom. His face was cast in shadows.

All hail, captain of my guard, Gwen thought to herself without humor. She should have been flattered. Any number of women would have been overjoyed to be looked after by a man of such a reputation.

But not her. She wanted to weep.

He didn't move. Indeed, he seemed to be waiting for her to come to him.

She came to a stop before him. She couldn't smile. She couldn't even speak.

Rhys, apparently, hadn't much more to say than she did. He stared down at her, his expression grim and forbidding. He looked as if his most recently passed night had been more taxing than hers. His eyes were very red and his hair and tunic damp. She might have suspected that he'd drunk himself into a stupor and then stumbled into the moat, but he did not carry that stench with him. Perhaps he had spent the night pacing, then dunked his head into a rainbarrel to refresh himself.

And then she had no time for speculation, for he straightened and pushed himself away from the wall. He folded his arms over his chest again. She had first thought that it was a posture he so often assumed because it intimidated. Now she thought he might be trying to protect his heart without realizing it.

Rhys cleared his throat.

"Did he h—"

He cleared his throat again.

"Did he hurt you?" he whispered hoarsely.

Gwen shook her head, mute.

"Then he lives another day."

She nodded. She believed him. She suspected that if she ever answered any other way, Alain's time to linger in his mortal frame would be very short indeed.

"It was very impersonal," she began, then came to an abrupt halt as Rhys flung back his head as if she'd struck him.

"I don't want to hear of it," he said through gritted teeth.

"Then we won't speak of it," she agreed. Nothing could have suited her better.

Rhys unfolded his arms and started to reach for her, then he jerked his hands down by his sides. He glared at her instead.

"You are mine," he whispered harshly.

"Rhys—"

"You were mine before you were his."

"But now I am—"

"You are still mine, and I will have you or die in the trying."

She shook her head and reached up to put her hand over his mouth. He backed away sharply, shaking his head.

"I *will* have you."

And with that, he spun on his heel and walked swiftly away.

"Fitzgeralds," he barked over his shoulder, "come with me."

Gwen's keepers trailed after him obediently. Connor's hands were already caressing his sword hilts, so Gwen assumed he anticipated some sort of sport in the lists.

She contemplated what her options were for tasks to keep her busy that day. She could have written to her mother to let her know that she should have been grateful that Hugh hadn't allowed her to come to the wedding. He'd claimed there wasn't enough room in the baggage wains, but Gwen suspected he'd wanted one less wedding guest to stand in the way of his ingesting the finest Ayre's larder had to offer. But writing to her mother would only remind her of what she had lost, and that she couldn't bear. Not even the thought of beginning to make Ayre habitable raised any sort of enthusiasm in her.

All that was left was to make her way stealthily to the lists and see what the men were about. It looked to be a gray day outside. She could put on a cloak and remain unmarked. If nothing else, her day as a mercenary had prepared her for that much.

Without any more thought, she returned to her chamber for her cloak, then made her way to the lists. She'd almost reached them when she ran bodily into Sir Montgomery. He made her a low bow.

"My pardon, lady. I should have been watching for you."

She waved aside his apology. "The fault was mine. Think nothing of it."

"Oh, but I must think on it. I am a member of your personal guard now, and my captain would be mightily displeased to know I'd come close to plowing you over."

Gwen blinked. "But you were captain of Lord Bertram's guard. How is it . . . ?"

He smiled. "The fortunes of fate, my lady."

"Rhys possesses much cheek to think to order you about."

"He possesses more skill with the sword than cheek, and believe me when I say he has the latter in great abundance. Had he not bested me so thoroughly when we discussed the matter, I might not have been so willing to do his bidding."

"Well," she began, unsure if she should feel sorry for him or not, "I am glad to have you, if that matters."

His smile was as sunny as ever. "It matters a great deal, lady, and I am happy to serve you. Where go you now? I will see you safely there."

"I thought to hug the walls of the lists and see the goings-on there."

He lifted one eyebrow. "Your husband is there. As well as Captain Rhys, of course."

"Fighting each other?"

His eyes twinkled merrily. "Now, wouldn't that be something to see. Nay, lady, I daresay Lord Alain has little desire to cross blades with any but those in his own personal guard."

She didn't doubt it. None of them would dare best him.

"But Rhys's back is still not fully healed," she said. *And I would know.*

"Ah, but his mood is powerfully foul. That is more than enough to make up for what strength he lacks."

And likely more than enough reason for Alain to keep a safe distance. It was the first wise choice Gwen had seen the man make.

Within moments she had chosen a handy rock to rest herself upon and turned her attentions to what went on before her. Alain was easily marked. He made more noise with his mouth than his sword, and his ridiculous boasts and comments about his own skill filled the air. Gwen wondered how his men stood training with him. Given the somewhat ineffective way he seemed to be puttering about with his sword, she suspected he didn't spend all that much time in the lists.

Not like the man at the other end of the field.

Gwen watched Rhys facing the Fitzgeralds and wondered which one he intended to fight first. The twins each drew a sword. Rhys drew two himself.

It was then she realized he intended to fight them both at the same time.

Montgomery whistled low under his breath and laughed a huff of a laugh. "What cheek that boy has."

"He'll never manage it."

Montgomery looked down at her and smiled. "Have you never seen him do it?"

"I saw him fight at my sire's keep, but that was several years ago."

"He's improved since then. He must be powerfully irritated this morn. He doesn't usually take them both on at once."

Gwen knew he was angry and she knew exactly why. And she wondered, as she watched Rhys take on those two enormous men, if Alain knew what sort of raging storm was brewing inside his keep. She turned to look for her husband only to find him staring at Rhys. She watched him watch her captain fight and suspected that Alain knew very well what lived beneath his roof. She also suspected he had no desire to admit as much.

Rhys continued to keep the Fitzgeralds at bay. Alain turned back to his own exercise, raising the volume and the arrogance of his boasts.

Rhys had said he would have her. As she watched him work, she decided that if anyone could make good on those words, it was he.

She rose and walked back to the hall before she could think on it any longer. Going out to watch him had been a mistake. Better that she concentrate on something she could control, such as the filth in Alain's keep. She would attack the piles of refuse and see them thrown far beyond the walls where they would trouble her no longer.

A pity she couldn't have done the same thing with the man to whom she now found herself wed.

Rhys came in from his morning's exercise the same way he had for the past two months. Silently. His anger unappeased. He'd worked the Fitzgeralds to the bone, driven Montgomery into the dust, and made his squire John weep with exhaustion.

And yet still the sun rose.

Alain breathed.

Gwen was still wed.

His only comfort was knowing that he was commanded to stay near her at all times. Taking the time to train was probably something he shouldn't have done overmuch, but he felt no guilt over it for Gwen came to the lists frequently to watch him. When she did not come, he left the Fitzgeralds to guard her door.

John and Montgomery did not like those days.

But that was how the days had been passed. He had trained. He had contemplated all the ways he could extricate Gwen from her marriage. He had spoken to her of trying to obtain an annulment.

He had prayed for a miracle.

None had come.

Rhys glanced at the high table to see who was there. Alain reclined in his chair, obviously having enjoyed a fine meal already. Rhys pursed his lips. The current lord of Ayre never spent more time than necessary in the lists when it stood to interfere with his time at the table. Hugh would have been proud.

Rollan sat in his accustomed place next to Alain, as close as possible to his brother. It was likely easier to whisper his venom into Alain's ear thusly.

Gwen sat on Alain's other side, leaning as far out of her chair as she could. Rhys half wondered why she bothered. The one thing he could say for Alain was that the man was determined to ignore his wife. Rhys couldn't have been happier about that. Now if he could just be counted on to ignore her at night as well.

Satisfied that there was no mischief afoot, Rhys retreated to one of the lower tables and sat down to what was left there. He'd had worse. Indeed, there had been times during his first few months in France when he'd gone to earn his gold that he'd had none at all. But he'd definitely had better. Try as she might, Gwen had been unable to improve the kitchens at Ayre. She'd seen the hall and the bailey rid of most of its filth, but she'd been unable to remove Alain's cook from his post, or encourage him to produce better fare. Rhys indulged in a fond memory or two of the meals he'd eaten at Segrave. Well worth the journey. Hopefully he could convince Gwen that a trip home would be good for her. He could use something tasty to eat.

"There's nothing wrong with the fare."

Rhys looked up to see Alain glaring at Gwen. She only blinked at him, obviously surprised at his outburst.

"The fare?" she echoed.

"This is the first time you've managed to stir yourself to come down for a meal in days. You'll not shame me by refusing my food!" he shouted as he shoved back his chair and leaped to his feet.

Rhys didn't think; he leaped. How he managed to cross all that space and clear the high table in so short a time, he couldn't have said. All he knew was Alain's hand was coming toward Gwen's face, and he would be there to stop it.

"Forbearance, my lord," Rhys said, pulling Gwen behind him.

"Insolent cur, stand aside! I'll beat her where all can watch. Perhaps 'twill cure her once and for all of her disobedience."

"I will suffer in her stead," Rhys began, but Gwen poked him sharply in the back.

"Beat me if you will," she said, looking around Rhys's arm and glaring at her husband, "and lose your child in the process."

Rhys turned to look at her. "A babe?"

"A son?" Alain asked, as if the child he'd just learned of could be nothing else.

"Aye, a babe," Gwen said, pushing past Rhys to stand toe-to-toe with her husband. "And you'll drive it right from my body if you take a hand to me."

Alain looked her over critically. "I suppose you could be breeding. You haven't had your courses yet, and we've been wed nigh onto four fortnights."

Rhys looked at Alain and, for the first time ever, saw him smile.

It was, somehow, not a very pretty sight.

"Well," he said, smiling a bit more, "now that's done, I can see to other things. De Piaget, see that she cares for herself well, else you'll answer to me. I'm for Canfield this afternoon. Long overdue for a visit there. I think I'll have a bit of a hunt before I go. Aye, I've missed that."

He walked away, continuing to enlighten those around him as to his immediate plans for the future.

Rhys turned back to Gwen in time to find her nigh onto slipping down to the floor. He caught her by the arms and lowered her into her chair.

"You're feeling poorly?" he asked, bending to peer into her face.

She waved him back. "Not so close."

He straightened, wondering if he should feel as offended as he wanted to.

"Your breath," she said, waving her hand in front of her nose.

Now he *was* truly offended.

"All manner of smells," she continued. "I can scarce bear them."

Well, that left him feeling a bit better.

"I think I can find someone to aid you," he offered. "If you like."

She looked up at him, and he could see something in her eyes. He wasn't sure if it was pain or embarrassment.

"I'm going to bear him a child," she said quietly.

He nodded.

"Now there can be no—"

Annulment, he knew she meant to say, and he coughed loudly to cover it up. He hoped Rollan hadn't seen her mouth move.

"Off to Master Socrates," he said, reaching for her hand and pulling her to her feet. He looked at Rollan and inclined his head. "If you will permit us, my lord?"

He didn't wait for an answer. He pulled Gwen along behind him, felt rather than saw the Fitzgeralds fall into step behind her, and managed to collect Montgomery and John as well as he passed through the kitchens. And all the while he tried not to think about what he'd just learned.

A child.

Aye, there would be no annulment now. Their chance for a miracle had just passed. If he managed to free her, it would be through his own sweat. He wondered if he had enough of it for the deed.

He kept walking because there was nothing else he could do.

17

Gwen followed Rhys through the kitchen, trying to hold her breath as best she could. Damn Alain's cook for being so stubborn. Gwen suspected she likely would have felt better if she'd been able to install someone with a bit more skill and a great deal more tidiness.

"Where are we going?" she managed.

"Master Socrates. Lord Bertram's healer. Out of favor with the current lord, of course, and therefore consigned to the cellars, but a fairly skilled maker of potions just the same."

Anything to settle her stomach. But the closer they drew to their destination, the more certain Gwen was that she wouldn't keep down even the crust of bread she'd managed to ingest that morn, much less any potion.

Her guardsmen wouldn't even come down the passageway with her. She left them loitering by the ale kegs and walked with Rhys into a tiny chamber. She put her hand over her mouth as a precaution. A wizened old man stood over a kettle, stirring intently. A girl-child stood nearby, watching just as intently.

"Master Socrates," Rhys began, "the lady Gwennelyn is feeling poorly this day. Perhaps you have something to help?"

The old man looked up at her from under bushy eyebrows and frowned. "Feeling poorly? Perhaps 'twas something she put in her belly. Sour wine? Overrotted eel?"

"'Tis the babe," the child whispered.

Gwen looked at the girl in surprise. It wasn't as if she'd announced her tidings to anyone as of yet.

"A babe, eh? Then come in, my lady, and I'll fetch you a cup of what's on the fire at present. 'Tis a concoction of my own making with several things that perhaps another might not think of combining."

Gwen came closer, holding her hand even more tightly over her mouth. Then she abruptly used her fingers to pinch her nose closed.

"What are the black spots?" she managed.

"Flakes of dried vermin. Adds a bit of unexpected flavor—"

As did, subsequently, the contents of her stomach. Gwen knew she should have felt more remorse than she did, but there was only one pot to retch into, and it was right there before her.

She heaved until she had no more strength, then felt herself turned around and gathered into strong arms.

"Ah, *chérie*," Rhys whispered, stroking her back gently, "don't you know you should never ask a healer what he puts into his potions?"

"I know it now," she croaked, clutching the front of his tunic to keep herself upright.

"Perhaps a brew of soothing herbs, Master Socrates," Rhys suggested.

"Oh, um, aye," the healer said.

Gwen looked over her shoulder to see him peering down into his kettle with a look of intense regret.

"I suppose I could do that," he said slowly. "I have some extra things I could add to it—"

"Perhaps but a simple herb or two," Rhys interrupted gently.

Master Socrates looked ready to argue, then he looked at Gwen.

"But one or two?" he asked, fingering his wooden spoon.

Gwen belched miserably before she could help herself.

"Just one," Master Socrates said with a sigh.

Gwen soon found herself deposited on a stool with her back against a chilly wall. She wasn't sure what helped her more, the cold or the sitting. Or perhaps it was knowing that Alain would leave the keep and the oppressiveness of his presence would be lifted.

Then perhaps she could see a bit more of Rhys. It wasn't in the best interest of her poor heart, but she could hardly stop herself from wanting the like.

She looked at him as he squatted down before the little girl and spoke to her with soft words and gentle smiles. Envy seized her. Even the luxury of such effortless speech with the man was something she couldn't enjoy. Never mind that he was near her so much of the day. There wasn't a moment that passed that she didn't guard against a gaze that might linger too long upon him, or a smile that might soften overmuch and alert those around her as to her true feelings.

If only she'd had the chance to perfect her mercenary skills, subterfuge would have come much more easily to her and she would have been able to outwit her husband. It wasn't that such a thing required a great deal of effort, but there was always Rollan shadowing his elder brother, pointing out to him what Alain himself missed. Would Alain leave Rollan behind to report on her activities, or would he trust Rhys to do as he was bid and keep his own memories of her behavior? But if not Rollan, then a score of others who would take great pleasure in marking and relating every glance, every smile, every manifestation of her affection for the man not five paces from her.

And the very thought of it was enough to make her want to retch again.

She tucked her clammy hands beneath her arms and leaned back against the stone wall. They'd spoken in snatches of how her freedom might be won. The only solution they could see was an annulment. Not that such a thing was possible now.

What was she to do, flee to France with Rhys, taking Alain's heir with her? Or was she to leave the child behind? It hardly seemed possible that she carried so quickly, but there was no denying the strange illness that coursed through her. Perhaps she would feel nothing for the babe after it was born, but she suspected that wouldn't be the case. She had been undone by every babe she'd ever held. Nay, she could not leave her babe behind, and she could hardly take him with her. She meant nothing to Alain and she suspected he might be somewhat relieved if she were to vanish, but his son?

He would comb the earth looking for him.

Nay, there would be no peace there.

She felt large, warm hands come to rest upon her knees and she opened her eyes. Rhys knelt before her, a small frown on his face.

"You are still feeling poorly?"

"Aye," she managed.

He reached up and brushed away the tears she hadn't realized were coursing down her cheeks.

"Ah, Gwen," he whispered, reaching for her, "come here, my love."

"Nay," she said, with so violent a shake of her head that the entire chamber went spinning.

He blinked in surprise. "But—"

"Nay, Rhys. You cannot touch me."

"I cannot touch you," he repeated.

"Not even an innocent touch."

"But Alain is leaving today. There will be no one here to see anything." He looked at her, then frowned again. "I hardly see the harm in an innocent touch now and then. It isn't as if I'm proposing a little adultery to pass the time."

"I didn't think you were. And it isn't for them; it is for me."

"For you?"

She nodded. "Aye. I cannot bear it."

"You cannot bear it," he repeated.

This wasn't going at all well. She took his hands and gently pushed them away.

"We must forget what happened between us."

"We must—" he spluttered.

"I cannot live in the same keep with you for the next pair of years and have your touch remind me of the night we shared!" she exclaimed, starting to feel rather exasperated that all he could do was repeat what she had said. "We'll survive better if we put it behind us."

That, at least, had seemingly rendered him silent.

"We'll have speech together," she said, feeling as if that might just be the thing to save them both. "You can sing to me, as do the knights in the *chansons d'amor* my mother's minstrels performed." She paused. "You can sing, can't you?"

"Nary a note," he growled.

"Ah," she said, feeling slightly disappointed. "Well, then perhaps you could just relate to me the lays you have no doubt heard on your travels. You have heard lays, haven't you?"

"More of them than I could stomach."

She had the feeling he was less enthusiastic about her plan than she was. But she knew it was the only way, so she forged ahead, ignoring the formidable frown he was now wearing.

"'Tis how it is done," she informed him. "The knight worships his lady from afar, riding off into battle with her favor on his arm, composing lays to her beauty and goodness, and doing all that he does in her name and for the glory of his love for her."

"All from afar?"

"Aye. Or so I've heard."

"And your favor?"

"I think you've already had it," she said, feeling her cheeks grow warm. "And more than once, if memory serves."

He only glared at her.

"'Tis the only way," she pressed on, clutching her hands together to keep from reaching for him. "How can it be otherwise?" Then she had a flash of insight. "Perhaps 'twould be easier if we considered ourselves comrades-at-arms."

His mouth fell open.

"John is at your side constantly and rejoices in it. If we were to attempt the same thing, always speaking of swords and such other knightly endeavors, perhaps it would go easier for us."

"Swords and such," he repeated. "Swords and such?" he said again, in a more enthusiastic tone.

At least she thought it was enthusiasm to prompt him to raise his voice in such a manner.

"See? Already you begin to appreciate the wisdom of my plan. We must put aside whatever passed between us and consider ourselves nothing but comrades from now on. It is a most reasonable scheme."

She looked up to see Master Socrates bearing down on her with a steaming mug of something. She accepted it hesitantly, then sniffed. It smelled passing sweet, and there was a conspicuous lack of dark spots floating along the top, so she took her courage in hand and sipped.

"Very pleasant," she said, smiling at the old man.

"Bland if you ask me," he said with a sigh, "but a mama's belly is nothing to trifle with."

Gwen finished the brew, handed the cup back to the healer, and looked again at Rhys, who had not moved, nor had his expression of intense irritation changed.

"Come, my friend," she said brightly, "and let us be away and leave the good man to his work. Perhaps you might help me improve my swordplay this afternoon. I'm feeling remarkably better all of the sudden."

"My friend?" he repeated in a choked voice.

"Aye," she said with a firm nod.

He looked as if he would have truly liked to throttle her. Gwen saw the idea come into his head, then watched as he contemplated the merits of it. He scowled most fiercely at her and rose to his great height.

"If you think," he began in low, gravelly tones, "that what passed between us can be so easily forgotten—"

"I never said forgotten—"

"Dismissed then!" he hissed. "Set aside as a thing of naught."

"I never said naught, either," she managed as he drew a deep breath.

"I will not be your friend!" he roared. "Saints above, woman, what sort of man do you think me to be?"

"An honorable one surely," a voice drawled from the doorway. "And one whose lord is preparing to depart for another keep. Perhaps you should be there to at least bid him farewell?"

Gwen looked around Rhys's long legs to see Montgomery standing near the doorway wearing a most speculative glance. She rose carefully, found that her feet were steady beneath her, then looked up at Rhys.

"We'd best heed him. Alain will no doubt wish to see us appropriately heartbroken at his leave-taking."

"You are bound for your bedchamber where you will rest," Rhys growled. "And I'll brook no argument from you on that score."

It seemed a more appealing alternative than seeing her husband, so she nodded and moved past him. She thanked Master Socrates again, smiled at the child who stood by the cooking fire watching her, and then left the chamber.

She kept walking even though she was fair to dropping on the spot in a fit of weeping. Though she'd put a bright smile on her face and suggested the most sensible plan she could think of, she was more than a little miserable. By all the saints above, how was she to endure another pair of years with this man always at her side but ever out of her reach?

By thinking of him as a comrade, she reminded herself.

"Friend, my arse," Rhys muttered from behind her.

Gwen almost smiled at that. He would agree with her in time, for she knew she was in the right. They would form their own garrison of two. He would teach her swordplay and other warriorly skills. She had little to offer him, but at least she could sing. And she could read. Perhaps she could teach him that in return for a few lessons with the blade. And perhaps with the dice.

Nay, she thought sharply, not with the dice. It would only bring back other memories she simply couldn't bear to think on anymore. But the other she could manage.

Aye, 'twas a most sensible plan.

18

It was the most ridiculous plan he'd ever heard.

Rhys deposited Gwen inside her bedchamber before he was tempted to give in to the overwhelming impulse that raged inside him—that of strangling her. As he'd tromped up the steps behind her, he'd managed to reacquire the rest of her guard. Said guard was now clustered around him as he stood outside Gwen's door. He fixed John with a steely glare.

"Tend her."

John's expression fell. "Must I?"

"Aye, you must."

"But where are you going?"

"To the lists," he growled. "I've a need of sport to cool my temper."

"I could stay behind as well," Montgomery offered with a small smile.

Rhys considered the Fitzgeralds, how long it would take him to dispatch them and what there would remain of his irritation after that was done. He shook his head.

"I'll have need of you later. You'll come with me."

Montgomery shook his head. "I think I would rather stay here."

"Aye, he should stay," John agreed, "and then I could go with you."

"I assure you, John," Rhys growled, "that you would be much safer guarding your sister by marriage."

He motioned for the twins and Montgomery to follow him as he strode back along the passageway and down the steps to the great hall.

Alain and Rollan stood near the fire, dressed for travel. That boded well.

"Godspeed, my lord," Rhys said to Alain as he passed him.

"Remember your duties," Alain said.

"And remind him not to add to them, brother," Rollan replied.

Rhys made Alain a low bow, then walked briskly for the door. The last thing he wanted was to listen to Rollan's gall by way of Alain's mouth.

He made his way quickly to the lists, trailed by the three members of Gwen's guard. He paused, then contemplated who would give him the least trouble and the most pleasure to dispatch first. Montgomery would be a fine choice if he'd wanted nothing but to stretch his muscles, but he would be of no use in cooling the white-hot irritation that flowed so strongly through his veins. Perhaps he would save Montgomery for later, as a sort of sweet to be enjoyed after a full, hearty meal.

He looked at the twins and decided on Jared first. Connor was smiling, never a good sign, and fingering a pair of swords. Rhys would need to do a bit of warming up before he took on those flashing blades.

Not to say Jared was any less the swordsman than his brother was. Indeed Rhys had to admit, as he fended off Jared's sudden attack, that he couldn't have had two better masters when it came to swordplay. They were overly large, uncommonly strong, and wily as two foxes. But it was also not without reason that Rhys had held over a hundred knights for ransom on the continent. It took a bit of effort, but the time soon came that Jared cried peace. Rhys had but a moment to reach out and take Montgomery's sword, then pull it from the sheath before Connor was coming at him, still smiling.

Saints, but it was enough to give a man the chills.

Connor certainly seemed to be enjoying the two-handed sport, for his smile soon turned into a grin. As he caught Rhys with an especially wicked backhand, he actually chortled. The blades flashed in the sunlight, and Rhys found himself hard-pressed to keep the larger man at bay. It wasn't an everyday occurrence to fight with swords in both hands against a man who wielded either with like skill.

"Come now, my little friend," Connor chided, "surely you have more to show me than that."

My little friend. Well, at least Gwen hadn't added the little. But the reminder of just what she had called him brought to the fore a fresh surge of
annoyance. He wasn't about to become her comrade-at-arms. That she
would no doubt get either herself or him killed with her swordplay was
beside the point. He didn't want her as a comrade, he wanted her as a . . .

Montgomery's sword went flying from Rhys's hand. Rhys looked at his
empty fingers in surprise, then looked at Connor who had chortled yet again.

This was not good.

Rhys put aside his uncomfortable thoughts of just what he wanted from
Gwennelyn of Ayre and concentrated on finding a way of either ridding
Connor of his second sword or regaining Montgomery's that Connor seemed
determined to keep under his heel.

It was the beginning of a very long, unpleasant morning.

By the time Rhys had finally beaten Connor back, it was past noon.
Rhys was dripping with sweat and wished for nothing more than several
mugs of cold ale.

"My turn," Montgomery said brightly. "Come, Rhys, and let me see
what you have yet in reserve for me."

"Go to the devil," Rhys wheezed.

"Before you have a go at me? Surely not."

Jared clapped Rhys on the shoulder. "I'll fetch you something cold, lad.
You deserve it."

"Deserve it?" Connor echoed. "What did he do to deserve ale? I had him
the whole time. If he just hadn't avoided my lethal jab above the knees with
both blades."

"You'll note," Jared said, "that he used my defense against just such a
womanly move. 'Twas my training that won the day for him."

"Your training? Bah, 'tis a wonder he can lift a sword after what you
taught him!"

Rhys suppressed the urge to stick his fingers in his ears until the argument was over. Fortunately, Connor seemed as inclined for something cold
as his brother did, and he and Jared made straightway for the great hall, still
arguing about who had taught whom what. Rhys leaned on his sword and
sucked in great gulps of air.

"If it will soothe you, I doubt I could have stood against them," Montgomery offered. He shuddered. "That Connor frightens me."

"Tame as a bunny once you know where to scratch," Rhys panted. "Distract him with a compliment on his swordplay and he's yours."

"Don't think I want him, thanks just the same. Now, tell me what it is
that has you in such a temper. It can't be the thought of seeing the last of
Alain until he tires of his mistress at Canfield."

"As I'm certain he'll move on from there," Rhys said, "I doubt we'll need endure him again before the babe is born."

"Ah," Montgomery said, looking at him closely, "then 'tis the babe that troubles you?"

"Now why would Alain having an heir trouble me?"

"Ah, Rhys, I am not so great a fool as you think. I know where your heart lies."

Rhys glared at him. "As I always say—you think too much."

"Ah, but when thinking yields such delicious insights, how am I to help myself?"

Rhys would have cut off Montgomery's head to stop him from babbling the more, but he found he was simply too weary to lift his sword at the moment.

"I wonder just what it was you and our sweet Gwen were discussing in the healer's hovel," Montgomery mused. "So many hints, but so few details."

"Eavesdropping is a very unattractive fault, Montgomery."

Montgomery only smiled. "You wound me. I was merely shadowing my captain. Is that not one of my duties?"

"Why do I have the feeling I'll live to regret having asked you to be a part of this foolishness?"

"Come now, Rhys," Montgomery chided. "You chose me for Gwen's guard, which kept me from Alain's clutches, and I am most grateful. I can only assume it was as a reward for past service to you."

"Past service?" Rhys asked. "What past service have you ever done me besides your efforts to corrupt my sweet soul?"

Montgomery waved aside the accusation. "Stretch yourself to remember, Rhys. Who was it who fed you tales of Gwennelyn of Segrave all those years when you wouldn't travel with us to her keep, hmmm? Who was it who laced descriptions of her soil with equally as interesting descriptions of her person as she grew into the beauty she is today?"

Rhys only scowled at him.

"And these are the thanks I receive for such heavy labors? All those hours of being forced to observe her at close range, just so I could bring you tidings of the girl?"

Rhys felt his fingers begin to flex of their own accord.

"Hour upon hour of following after her with my eyes, marking her every movement, seeing how her hair moved as she walked, how the sunlight turned those pale eyes of hers to something the shores of southern France would envy, watching her bloom from a girl into a beautiful, pleasingly proportioned wom—"

Rhys wasn't at all surprised at how well his fingers about Montgomery's throat silenced the man to mere gurgling. He contented himself with but a mere shake or two, for after all, Montgomery had provided him with visions of Gwen he'd been too cowardly to go and obtain for himself. That alone was likely worth sparing the wretch any further punishment.

Montgomery only knocked Rhys's hands away and backed up a pace, grinning like the empty-headed fool he was.

"Saints, lad, but you are smitten."

"As if it served me!"

Montgomery shrugged. "You never know what the future holds—Ah, my lord Ayre," he said, putting on a less open expression, "a pleasant journey to you."

Rhys turned and saw that Alain and Rollan had begun to make their way to the stables. He bowed along with Montgomery and hoped his relief at seeing them gone wasn't as obvious as he feared it was. He had no doubts Alain would have his spies everywhere marking his and Gwen's every move, but that could be borne.

Then he shook his head in wonder at his own conceit. Could Alain possibly care what either of them did? It wasn't as if Alain had any intention of holding to his marriage vows. Canfield was the home of Rachel, Lord Edward of Graundyn's sister. She was unwed and likely to stay that way, for her brother was very loth to give up her lands. She did manage, however, to warm her bed with any number of men, married or not. That Alain believed himself to be the only one loitering there between the sheets merely proved the extent of the man's stupidity. The saints only knew what Rollan would be about for the next while, but Rhys contented himself with knowing he would be about his business in some other keep. At least he and Gwen would have peace from that pair of prying eyes. Though what there would be to see, he surely didn't know.

The truth of it was enough to make him want to sit down and weep. She was Alain's. She was now carrying Alain's babe. The time for an annulment was surely past. The only alternative left them was divorce, and proving that Alain continued to bed his whores would be difficult indeed. Rhys wondered if Alain had even maintained the sanctity of his wedding night before he'd sought out other companionship in the castle.

Rhys couldn't have said, as he remembered so little of the eve thanks to the amount of spirits the Fitzgeralds had poured down him. And should he have by some miracle even marked the events of the night, he would have forgotten them straightway thanks to the awakening he'd had before sunrise the next morn. He'd been snoring in peaceful oblivion one moment, then snorting under the deluge of cold water the next. He had sat bolt upright only to find he was in a makeshift bed in a forgotten corner of the cellar, naked, with no idea how he'd gotten there. The Fitzgeralds had been standing over him, frowning fiercely, both holding empty buckets in their hands.

Such had done nothing to begin a day he'd been sure would be one of the most hellish of his life.

Gwen was wed. And not to him.

"Speak of our angel and suddenly she appears," Montgomery said with a happy sigh. "Just looking at her is enough to break my heart."

Mine as well, Rhys thought with a slow shake of his head. How could anyone possibly expect him to have the keeping of her for the next two years and not want her? Just the sight of her was enough to bring him to his knees.

She was dressed, and by now this came as absolutely no surprise to him, in John's clothes. At least the lad wasn't wearing her skirts. Rhys was just as grateful for that as he was sure John was. She carried her filched sword, and Rhys wondered at whose feet to lay that blame, for he was just certain he'd concealed it well enough with his gear. Someday he would have to take the time to find its rightful owner and pay the poor soul for it. Either that or he would have one made for her strength of arm. She would never learn any swordplay with this blade.

"Is he gone yet?" she asked.

"Aye, lady," Montgomery said with a low bow. "You can be about your sport freely now." He looked at Rhys and raised one eyebrow.

Rhys ignored him. "I thought you were resting."

"I rested," she answered promptly, "and now I am here for my lesson."

He remembered vividly the last lesson he'd given her. He saw by the immediate flush on her face that she remembered it as well.

"In swordplay," she added.

"What else?" he grumbled.

"What else indeed?" Montgomery murmured.

Rhys gave him a healthy shove, then turned back to his would-be apprentice. From all appearances, she seemed ready and eager to learn.

"What will you have me do first?" she asked.

Take off that bloody ring of Alain's and flee to France with me, was on the tip of his tongue, but he refrained from giving voice to the thought. Unfortunately, that was just the beginning of the things he wanted her to do.

He wanted her to look at him again as she'd looked at him the night she came to him. He wanted her to put her arms about him and tell him that she couldn't live without him by her side. He wanted her to fumble hesitantly with his clothes as she had that night, touch his flesh with cold, trembling fingers, and lift her mouth to his for sweet, lingering kisses.

She is not yours.

Rhys scowled at the voice in his head. Surely there was some angel somewhere recording the deeds of his life, and it would be noted that before Alain of Ayre laid a hand upon her, Rhys had taken her as the wife of his heart and the love of his soul. He had bound himself to her just as surely as if he'd stood with her before a priest and spoken the vows aloud.

Now, if only that angel also kept a book of ways to take a woman away from a husband who most certainly did not deserve her. And if they both could but survive the next pair of years, Wyckham would be his, and he would have a place to take her when he managed to free her from Alain.

She is not yours to take.

"Nay, but she will be," he vowed as he looked at her.

"I will be what?" Gwen asked, leaning on her sheathed sword.

Rhys put aside his schemes. There would be ample time to think on them later.

"A damned good swordsman by the time I'm finished with you," he said with a sigh.

"Think you?" she asked with a smile, so bright he almost flinched. She lifted the sword with gusto.

Predictably it overbalanced her, and she stumbled backward into John, who, obviously unused to dealing with these sorts of crises, fell straightway upon his arse. Gwen fell upon him just as directly, and the sword hilt smacked her solidly in the face.

She blinked for a moment or two in silence, then began a most unladylike round of howling and cursing.

Rhys clapped his hand to his forehead and groaned. He would surely have no time at present for plotting and scheming. Keeping Gwen unbruised would take all his attention.

Saints, but it was going to be a long afternoon.

And an even longer summer. There was surely nothing they could do about escape until the babe was born, and by his count that wouldn't happen until early spring, at least. Swordplay would have to occupy their time until then, for at least as long as she could lift one safely.

"John," he said, "you'll be the one to help show her how to hold the blade."

"Me?" John squeaked from where he was still sprawled in the dirt.

He looked as terrified by the prospect as Rhys was.

Heaven help them all.

19

Gwen sat under the lone tree in Ayre's garden, enjoying the spring sunshine and the fact that she'd managed to lower herself to a sitting position with almost no help at all. Given the fact that she was ripe to bursting with her babe, it was a feat to be proud of.

She savored the smell of the herbs and flowers that were clustered in eat, orderly patches about her. Her keepers were clustered about her as well, but not nearly as neatly and certainly not in as orderly a fashion. Montgomery was sitting near a patch of yarrow, rubbing his nose and looking about him in irritation as if he could thereby divine what it was that was making his eyes water so fiercely. The Fitzgeralds stood a few paces off with their arms folded over their chests and their customary frowns adorning their faces. They had declined her invitation to sit and enjoy the day. Gwen supposed when a pair of men seemed less likely to bend than oak trees, standing was preferable to trying to find a place between pasque-flower and Saint-John's-wort.

Rhys was sprawled out next to several hills of lavender, twirling a stalk of it between his fingers and staring off unseeing into the distance. Gwen told herself she was happy with the turn of events. Her lessons in swordplay had progressed for a pair of months' time the previous fall, then abruptly ceased when Rhys decided it was no longer safe for her to practice. Safe for whom was still the question. She hadn't cut John that often, and she'd only bloodied his nose a handful of times as he struggled to show her how to hold the blade. She'd wondered at the time why Rhys had chosen his squire for such a task. Perhaps Rhys had pressed John into such service because he thought it would train his squire at the same time.

Or perhaps he had decided that he truly felt nothing more for her than friendship and therefore had no reason to want to be near her.

"Which is what I wanted, of course," she said.

"Huh?" John asked, looking up from the manuscript on his lap. He sat the closest to her, burdened with the task of reading aloud.

"Nothing," Gwen said.

She could feel Rhys's eyes on her, but she didn't dare look at him.

Comrade-at-arms. By Saint George's crossed eyes, what had she been thinking?

"Gwen, this is too hard," John complained.

"How can you be a great lord if you know nothing of reading?" she asked, then she bit her tongue. For all she knew, Rhys couldn't read. Insulting him was the last thing she had intended.

John sighed heavily and started up the tale again from the beginning.

"'Not so many . . . um . . . years a . . . ago, there lived a lady who . . . who . . .'"

"Whose," Gwen said.

"Aye, 'whose beauty was re . . . renowned through . . . out all the land.'" He rolled his eyes. "Why would anyone care?"

"'Tis a most marvelous story of love and devotion," she informed him.

"I'd rather read of war and slaughter," he said, turning up his nose.

"No war today, though I'm certain I should be apologizing most heartily for it. This was my favorite tale from my mother's finest minstrel. She had it copied down, and I learned to read from it."

"Indeed," Rhys said with a cough.

"Oh, aye," she said, nodding. "I daresay I have it memorized by now."

"All that romance has warped her thinking, if you ask me," Montgomery muttered, looking as if he were on the verge of a mighty sneeze. He gingerly tried to move aside a few flowers that were leaning toward him. "What is this weed here?"

"Yarrow," Rhys said absently, firming up a bit of loose soil near the base of the plant nearest him.

"Yarrow?"

"Bloodwort," Rhys said. "Good for staunching wounds. Don't crush it."

Montgomery put his hands in his lap and looked at the cluster of herbs with new respect.

"'Tis a most romantic tale we are hearing," Gwen said defensively, feeling somewhat slighted by Montgomery's criticism of her favorite story.

Montgomery scowled. "And romance is what is wrong with the world toda . . . ah . . . hachoo!"

"Ignore him," Rhys said, casting Montgomery a dark look. "Press on, John. The lady Gwennelyn has it aright. Learning to read will serve you well in the future."

"But this?" John asked plaintively. "'Tis drivel! I've heard the tale before. The knight does nothing but worship her from afar."

"Ugh," Montgomery said, looking down with intense dislike at the herbs that had somehow migrated onto the front of his tunic.

"'Tis very—" Gwen began.

"Feebleminded," John interrupted. "He sighs, he swoons, he beats upon his breast with his fist, and moons over her for pages. Saints, Sir Rhys, look you how many pages of mooning there are!"

"'Tis highly chivalrous," Gwen said stiffly. "And I find the tale much to my liking."

"All I can say," John grumbled, "is I think the knight's time would be better spent in the lists. At least then he would be seeing to something of value—"

"Oh, by the bloody saints," Rhys growled, "give me that thing."

John blinked at him. "Can you read?"

The look on Rhys's face should have alerted John he was treading in dangerous waters. John, however, as Gwen well knew, was oblivious to such unspoken warnings.

"After all," he said, plunging ahead heedlessly, "your sire was merely a—"

"John."

"Aye, Sir Rhys?"

"Do you wish to continue to be my squire?"

Even John seemed to realize he had perhaps gone too far. He gulped audibly.

"Aye, Sir Rhys."

"Then hand me the manuscript and do it silently."

John handed over the manuscript without another sound, then shifted as far out of Rhys's sights as he could get.

Gwen watched the entire scene with fascination. It was almost more interesting than the tale Rhys held in his hands. Rhys's parents were a mystery, though she knew his grandfather had been a knight of some renown in the French court. It was he who had seen Rhys sent to Bertram of Ayre, though why he had chosen an English lord instead of a French one, she couldn't have said.

Perhaps Rhys's sire was a mere knight. Based on her experience, she had to conclude that being a nobleman did not necessarily guarantee that a man was noble. Perhaps Rhys had been well served by having no nobility flowing through his veins. Gwen could find no fault with his conduct because of it.

"'Not so many years ago, there lived a lady whose beauty was renowned throughout all the land.'"

Gwen caught her breath. Now, there was a voice that any bard would envy—deep and rich. Gwen found herself immediately under his spell. She gave a passing thought to the fact that Rhys could indeed read very well, spared one last question as to where he might have learned such a thing, then gave herself over to the magic he was weaving with his voice alone.

"'Many a knight came to gaze upon her beauty, then depart with a solemn vow on a quest to win her, whatever the cost. The lady knew of none of these vows, of course, for her father kept her sheltered, and the lady herself saw not her true love amongst the men who came to her father's hall.'"

Gwen closed her eyes with a sigh of pleasure. How many times had she heard this tale? Too many to count. Only never had she heard it told in such a fashion, even when it had been put to music and sung by her mother's most skilled minstrels.

And as she continued to listen, she felt the babe begin to stir within her. Obviously he was just as charmed as she by what he was hearing.

And then she realized, with a start, that it wasn't just the beauty of the poetry that moved her babe.

She was on her feet before she knew how she had gotten there.

"Gwen!"

She would have replied, but she found quite suddenly that she couldn't. She held out her hands and immediately found a pair of strong forearms there, ready to support her.

"The babe comes," Rhys announced.

The pain passed and she found that she had the strength to scowl up at him. "And what would you know of it? It could be anything. Supper. The saints only know Cook is incapable of preparing anything edible."

He looked down at her solemnly. "Have the stirrings of your babe come more closely together than before?"

"Aye, but—"

Before she could answer, she found herself off her feet and into his arms.

"Rhys, put me down!" she exclaimed. "What will Alain—"

"I would imagine, given how he's passed his afternoons for the fortnight since his return, that he will be occupied for several hours still."

"Rollan—"

"Is a fool I will see to when the time comes. Why do you not save your energy for the birthing of your babe and leave your other troubles to me?"

He certainly wasn't giving her much choice in the matter. Gwen found herself being carried back into the keep before she could clear her mind enough to voice any more protests.

The afternoon passed slowly. Rhys had cleared her solar of her ladies straightway, which had suited her very well, as most of them had spent ample time in her husband's bed and she cared not for them as a whole. Fewer souls had also meant more room to pace, which she had done for what seemed like hours.

She'd wanted the midwife from the village to come, but Alain had refused. He'd sent instead his surgeon, who had done nothing but lay out the sharp tools of his trade. Gwen had done her best to ignore him. A birthing stool had been brought by one of the serving maids, and Gwen had been tempted to have her stay just for the companionship of another woman, but the surgeon had banned her from the chamber. Gwen would have protested to her husband herself, but evidently he had already been in his cups when he'd learned that his son's arrival was imminent. The tidings had only heralded the opening of another keg of ale.

And still the surgeon sharpened his knives.

And Rhys stood in the corner of the chamber with his arms folded over his chest, glaring at the man. At least Alain had been too drunk to wonder about Rhys's whereabouts. Rhys was no midwife, but he was companionship.

The pains came harder. The surgeon rubbed his hands together as if he itched to be about some business. Rhys glowered all the more. They began to exchange insults. Gwen felt her tongue loosen as well, and she began to use it generously on the other two souls in her chamber.

Somehow, though, that did not help her pass the time anymore easily.

The sun had set and candles had been lit. Rhys stood in the middle of the chamber staring down in satisfaction at Alain's senseless surgeon. At least now the evening could progress without any more threats, blasphemy, or taking of Rhys's name in vain.

At least from the surgeon.

Gwen was still sharpening her tongue on him, but Rhys couldn't blame her. He'd only made the mistake once of telling her that her body was designed to birth babes, which had resulted in another string of aspersions being cast at him. Her having likened labor to his passing a large egg through his . . . well, it had left him crossing his legs in discomfort and racking his brains for something else with which to distract her. Suggesting that perhaps it was due recompense for Eve and the apple—

He still marveled that a woman in labor could move so fast or use her fist so liberally. At least she hadn't had the energy to reach up for his nose. He rubbed it absently, somewhat relieved to find it still unbruised.

With a sigh, he hefted the surgeon and deposited him in a corner, out of the way of Gwen's pacing. Then Rhys leaned back against the wall, half afraid to say anything for fear of saying the wrong thing.

Not that Gwen would have noticed him by now, likely. Where she had gone he didn't know, but her spirit was certainly far away at present. She was pacing the confines of her chamber, pausing frequently to grab hold of whatever sturdy object was handy to lean against until her pains passed. She was making a great deal of noise, and the groans had initially frightened him. He'd made the mistake of interrupting her pacing and paid the price in the blistering of his ears. After that, he'd done his best to stay out of her way and make certain that no one else disturbed her.

Her pacing brought her his way, and he remained perfectly still as she clutched his arms and rested her head on his chest. He didn't dare touch her.

"Gwen?"

His only answer was something of a grunt.

"Shall you have a potion from Master Socrates? It might ease your pains."

She grunted again and pushed away from him to resume her slow, deliberate pacing.

This at least was something he could do. He walked toward the door, wishing his mother had been in attendance at least. Much as he might have wanted to believe that he alone would suffice Gwen in her times of need, he was fast beginning to believe that birthing was women's work. A pity he didn't trust any of Ayre's ladies, else he would have called for them. Perhaps a softer touch would have soothed Gwen.

He opened it to find Rollan leaning against the far wall of the passageway. Rollan's eyes widened as he caught sight of Rhys.

"What are you—"

"Saving her life," Rhys said shortly. He looked about the passageway and espied Master Socrates and his granddaughter. He'd had John fetch them earlier that afternoon, should Gwen need them. "She has need of one of your potions."

"I should be unsurprised to find you here," Rollan said with a snort. "I suppose you would have the skills to do this thing, seeing as how your father's skills lay there. Son of a healer," he sneered. "How you came to earn your spurs is a mystery to m—"

Which just went to show how little Rollan knew of Rhys's family. His father had healing skills, 'twas true, but he'd also earned his spurs. It just hadn't served him to let others know the like.

Rhys retreated inside the chamber with Master Socrates and his granddaughter, then slammed the door shut. The last thing any of them needed that eve was to listen to any more of Rollan's spite.

Rhys turned to Master Socrates, "Can you ease her pain?"

"Aye, Sir Rhys. I have brought with me all things needful."

"And can you birth the babe?"

Master Socrates looked down at his gnarled hands, then met Rhys's eyes. "My wife and daughter were midwives. But I do not know—"

"Better you than me," Rhys said grimly. He intercepted Gwen in the midst of the chamber. He was surely no midwife, but even he could tell there was a change in his lady.

"Gwen?"

"My time is upon me," she said with a gasp.

And so, apparently, it was. Rhys found that now the moment had come, he felt as if he shouldn't be near her. Surely she would be better off in the company of women.

He shook himself. There were no women to be had. He would have to suffice.

He stood behind the birthing stool and put his hands on her shoulders. At least she wasn't cursing him anymore. She was, however, coming close to drawing blood on his hands with every wave of labor that came over her. He didn't care. 'Twas surely the least he could do for her.

Not a handful of moments had passed before the chamber door burst open and Alain himself stood there. He looked at Rhys, his mouth working furiously. Rhys only returned the stare, unruffled.

"Y-you!" Alain managed finally.

"Aye, my lord?"

"Who do you think you are?" Alain bellowed.

"I am the one charged with protecting her life," Rhys said calmly. "And so here I am."

Alain frowned, as if he knew there was something amiss with that, but couldn't divine what. He turned his attentions on Master Socrates. "Him!" he said, pointing furiously. "I told you I wanted nothing to do with that filthy old man!"

'Twas obvious Master Socrates had heard this before, for he took no notice of Ayre, but continued to speak to Gwen in soothing tones.

"The babe comes," Rhys said shortly, "and he can keep both the child and its mother alive."

"Then why are you here?" Rollan said from where he had come up behind his brother. He smiled coldly. "Gazing upon what you can never have?"

"I was protecting my lady from that," Rhys said, jerking his head toward where the surgeon lay in a heap against the wall. "It is my duty."

Alain looked at Rollan for aid. Rollan's returning look was one of grave concern.

"I would worry, my lord," Rollan began, "about Sir Rhys's parentage. You know what a poor reputation his sire had. Never amounted to much, or so I remember."

Alain blinked. "I thought his sire was a healer. Roamed the countryside plying his craft."

Rhys didn't stir himself to comment.

"Or was he a minstrel?" Alain asked, sounding very unsure of his information. "I've heard both tales."

"Does it matter if he was both?" Rollan asked. "The man was burned as a heretic, accused of using witchcraft to heal his victims."

"Ah," Alain said, nodding. He turned to Rhys. "Leave."

Rhys clenched his jaw. "Nay."

Alain's expression darkened. "I'll not have your reputation tainting my son!"

"My sire was unjustly accused."

"Was he?" Alain asked, frowning. He looked at Rollan. "Was he?"

Rollan shrugged. "Who's to say? Perhaps 'tis the truth. And perhaps I spoke out of turn. Considering Sir Rhys's heritage, perhaps this is the place for him."

Alain waited, seemingly for enlightenment.

"Birthing is peasants' work, after all," Rollan said.

"The lady of Ayre is no peasant," Rhys said, wishing he had the right to throw the lot of them off the parapet. "Rollan insults both her and your son."

Alain looked to be working that out in his head. He finally pushed Rollan toward the door.

"You insulted my son," he said sternly. He shot Rhys a final look. "The babe dies and you die, understood?"

Rhys nodded and breathed a sigh of relief when the chamber door closed behind Ayre's lord and his brother.

"Finally," Gwen gasped. "I learn some of the tale. Why—" Another pain shook her and left her breathless. "Why I had to be suffering this before I heard of it I surely do not know."

"Ugly rumors," Rhys said shortly. "My sire was no heretic."

"Healers are ofttimes misunderstood," Master Socrates informed them. "Add a pinch of something unusual to a potion, and one becomes labeled a witch."

"And here I thought . . . your sire . . . was a knight," Gwen said, gasping for air. "Or so . . . I'd heard."

"He was several things," Rhys muttered. "Push, Gwen. Let us have this babe out."

The candle on the hearth had not burned down but another hour before Ayre's son had indeed made his entrance into the world. Rhys watched Gwen weep with relief. He watched Master Socrates pull the babe from beneath Gwen's gown.

Socrates' face drained of all color.

Rhys looked at the babe.

It wasn't breathing.

20

The child stood in the corner of the chamber and watched the babe come into the world. Her grandfather's hands shook as he held the lad. The babe was still.

The knight took the babe in his hands. He rubbed the tiny body, crooning to it in soft tones of command, bidding the child to take his place in the world.

Yet the child did not respond.

And then she watched as the knight leaned over, brushed aside the matter that covered the babe's face, then put his own mouth over the tiny nose and mouth that had not yet moved.

Once.

Twice.

Three times the knight gave the babe his own breath, his own means of life, as if he strove to breathe into the wee one his own will to live.

The tiny chest moved.

And then it moved again.

And then, to the child's relief, the lad set up a weak wail.

The child watched the lady take her firstborn son and cradle him close to her breast. She watched the young woman's tears and felt tears course down her own cheeks at the sight.

Then she looked at the knight kneeling at his lady's feet and saw that he wept as well.

The child looked at his hands and saw that they were full of healing. His heart was full of love for both mother and son, unlike Ayre's lord. The child wished she could have changed things, but that was far beyond her modest arts.

The breath of life. Aye, 'twas what she would have done as well in his place. Her own mother had done it often enough. The knight was powerfully wise to have thought of it.

"Come, granddaughter. Our work is done here."

The child obeyed the whispered command of her grandsire. She cast one last look behind her as she walked to the chamber door, saw the knight lift his lady's hand and kiss it tenderly.

Ah, that she could have changed things!

She suspected the pair behind her likely felt the same.

Gwen lay back against the pillows of the bed, exhausted in body and spirit. Aye, the laboring had been hard, but 'twas almost losing her son that had stretched her to the very limits of her endurance and reason. At least the babe was safe. And she had Rhys to thank for that.

There was a sudden commotion by the doorway. Gwen looked up to see Alain and Rollan entering the chamber, shoving aside Master Socrates and his granddaughter in the process. As tempted as she was to chastise her husband for his ill treatment of the old man, she found she had little energy to do aught but lie where she was and cradle her son close.

"Let me see the babe," Alain said, reaching for him.

Gwen reluctantly allowed Alain to have the boy. Much as she would have liked to deny it, Alain was the father and had every right to at least hold his son.

"Ah," he said, looking at the boy with satisfaction, "a healthy son."

"No thanks to you," Gwen whispered. "'Twas Rhys who saved the babe."

Alain frowned at that, then looked back at his son. "I did my work well with this one," he said, sounding supremely satisfied. "He resembles me, don't you think?" he asked his brother.

"Oh, aye," Rollan said, bobbing his head obediently. "Very strongly."

Alain contemplated the babe in his arms. "Fragile little beast," he said, hefting him. "What if I lose him?"

"Surely you won't," Rollan said gently.

"But if I did," Alain argued. "Damnation, but I had thought not to need to sire any more on her." He sighed heavily. "I suppose I'll need another, in case something happens to this one."

"Perhaps you should make certain nothing happens to this babe," Rollan suggested. "If he were mine, I would give thought to who might best care for the lad."

"Aye," Alain said, seemingly giving that what he thought to be an appropriate amount of thought. He smiled suddenly at his brother. "I'll take him to Canfield to be raised by someone with experience."

Gwen felt a coldness rush over her. "Nay," she croaked. "You'll not take him from me."

"I'll do what I like—"

"I am his mother," Gwen said, sitting up with great effort, "and I will be the one to care for him."

Alain looked at his brother. "What think you?"

Rollan smiled. "Take him to Canfield. That is a most sensible plan. Indeed, I'll find a wet nurse immediately, and perhaps we could take up our journey this afternoon."

"Nay," Gwen said, reaching for the babe.

"Rachel would care well for the child," Rollan continued.

"Aye, my thought as well," Alain said. "Let us be off then—"

Gwen found herself on her feet, reaching for the dagger in Rhys's belt almost before she knew what she had intended. She rushed at her husband with blade bared. And if she hadn't been so enraged at his cheek, she might have found the way he and Rollan both squeaked and stumbled backward to be somewhat amusing.

But there was nothing humorous about their plan.

"Give me the child," she commanded.

Alain hesitated.

Gwen brandished the knife, and Alain promptly handed the swaddled babe over to her.

"I'll kill you if you try," she said hoarsely.

"I doubt very much—" Alain spluttered.

"I'll kill you if you try," she repeated, dropping the dagger and clutching her son to her. "And if you think I won't turn over every stone on the isle to find you and end your life, consider it again, my lord. You will not take my son from me."

Alain looked rather startled. Then he seemed to gather what wits he possessed around himself.

"I'll give it more thought," he promised.

"Begone from my chamber," Gwen rasped. "You have your son, but you'll take him from me at the peril of your own life. And if you slay me, I'll haunt you for the rest of your days until you're driven mad."

Alain was, if nothing else, a superstitious soul. Without another word, he turned on his heel and scurried from the chamber. Rollan, however, was slow to follow his brother. He lingered at the doorway. When he opened his mouth to speak, Gwen pointed her finger at him.

"Don't," she warned. "Say nothing at all, if you value your sorry life."

He shut his lips around the saints only knew what kind of foolishness, then inclined his head.

"Hearty congratulations on the birth of your son," he said simply.

Gwen looked at him narrowly. "That is all? Just congratulations?"

Rollan shrugged. "I could not be happier for you. If there is anything I can do . . . ?"

"You can leave," Gwen said shortly. "I need to rest."

Rollan made her a low bow. "As my lady wishes." He straightened and looked at Rhys. "Surely your presence here is no longer required, Sir Rhys."

Gwen watched Rhys pick up the dagger she had filched from his belt, resheath it carefully, then incline his head to Rollan.

"My place is, as always, outside her door as captain of her guard," he said with a grim smile. "After you, my lord."

Gwen gingerly sat back down on the bed, clutching her son close. Rhys waited until Rollan had departed, then went down on one knee in front of her.

"I know of a trustworthy woman or two from the village," he said quietly. "Perhaps you would care to have them attend you rather than your ladies?"

"I daresay I could use the aid," she admitted.

"Then I will see to it. Once I am returned, if you have need of me, I will be immediately without your chamber. All you must needs do is call."

Gwen nodded and bent over her newborn son. She knew she should have been thinking a score of other more uplifting thoughts, but all she could think was how she wished this child had a different father than Alain.

Rhys, for instance.

A short while later a pair of women appeared at her door, waiting hesitantly for permission to enter. Gwen was grateful for them. The very last thing she wanted was to have any of Alain's whores in attendance.

Once she was made comfortable and had made her first fumbling attempts at nursing the babe, Gwen laid him by her side and watched him sleep. It was a miracle the babe lived. If Rhys hadn't been there, he wouldn't have. The thought of that caught her tight around the heart and wrung grief from her she didn't realize she had.

And then as relentlessly as sleep had claimed her babe, it began to claim her. She fought it, knowing there were things she had to consider before much more time passed. Already ten months of Rhys's service to Alain was fulfilled. What would she do when he left?

It was surely nothing she could bear to think on at present. Perhaps it was best that weariness was so heavy upon her. Rhys would be keeping watch outside her door, and for the moment both she and her son were safe.

It was enough.

Rhys knocked softly upon the door, and one of the women he had fetched opened it hesitantly.

"She sleeps, Sir Knight," the woman whispered.

"And the babe?"

"He sleeps as well."

"You made them both comfortable?"

"Aye, good sir. Will you have us remain?"

"Yet a while, if you will."

The woman nodded and withdrew back into the chamber. Rhys lingered at the doorway, unable to tear himself away.

Gwen slept with her babe cradled in her arms. The sight was such a peaceful one, nay, 'twas a sacred one. Rhys looked at the tiny babe and blessed his father wherever he currently resided—heaven or hell—for having passed on if not his gift for healing, his gift for quick thinking. Rhys had seen life breathed into a body before, but had also watched his father be carried away by furious envoys from the church after having done such a thing. A flimsy excuse to put him to death, of course, but no one had seemed to find it unreasonable. One life had been saved, the other destroyed as a result. At least Rhys, hadn't had to watch his sire die.

And at least he'd avoided the same fate. The saints be praised Alain hadn't seen what he'd done to the boy.

Nay, it had been worth the risk. Gwen was delivered safely, and her son breathed on his own now. Rhys could ask for no better end to the day.

Unless, of course, he were to have the right to shoo the women from the room and lie down next to his lady, wrapping his arms about both mother and child.

It was what he wanted more than anything else. More than land. More than the saving of Gwen's reputation from scandal. More than his own honor, truth be told. He wanted these two as his.

It would take a miracle for that to come to pass.

His vision blurred and he dragged the back of his hand across his eyes. It was then he realized Gwen was watching him. Her own eyes filled with tears, but she made no move to brush them from her cheeks.

It was an intolerable situation.

He made her a low bow and backed from the chamber before he broke down and wept. He closed the door softly, then turned and leaned back against it.

The rest of Gwen's guard was leaning against the opposite wall. They looked at him in silence for several moments, then Montgomery cleared his throat.

"What say you," he said roughly, "to seeking out a full keg in the cellar?"

Rhys shook his head. "Nay."

Montgomery frowned. "A go in the lists?"

Rhys shook his head again. "Nay."

"Well, *I'd* like to go to the lists," Montgomery grumbled. "I'm feeling passing edgy at the moment."

"I'll oblige you," Connor said, fingering the hilt of one of his swords. "With my left, I think."

Montgomery looked at him narrowly. "Think me to be easy sport, do you?"

Connor only shrugged and followed a cursing Montgomery down the passageway. Rhys almost smiled at that. If Montgomery only knew the left was Connor's better hand and he only reserved it for his more challenging sparring partners. Rhys looked at Jared.

"Perhaps you'd best go keep watch. Wouldn't want Connor to truly do him in."

Jared nodded and took John by the neck. "Come, little one. Let us leave your master in peace."

"But," John protested, "he might need me."

"What he needs is quiet," Jared said, pulling him down the passageway. "If you stop digging in your heels, I might even give you a small lesson in swordplay."

John's heels abruptly stopped trying to find holds in the floor. "You taught my master, did you not?"

"Aye, lad. All his most deadly moves."

John was now moving along quite willingly. "Think you you could teach me how to fight with two swords as Sir Rhys does?"

"Why don't we begin with one, young John."

Rhys watched them disappear into the stairwell, then leaned back against the door and closed his eyes. His men were happily engaged in their business. Alain and Rollan had no doubt descended to fill themselves full of drink. Gwen had likely fallen asleep peacefully again with her son.

And there he stood outside her door, acting the proper guardsman, when all he could think about was how badly he wanted to snatch her away.

He shook his head sharply. He couldn't think on it. Alain would never give up his heir, and Gwen would never give up her son. Rhys knew he could never ask it of her. Whether he willed it or no, he would have to take the situation he faced and bear it.

Though how he could, he certainly did not know.

But he would have to. He would have to smile, look content, keep up a façade for Gwen's sake. She would have more than enough to occupy her mind with the raising of her son. Perhaps she had it aright and they could truly think of each other as nothing more than comrades-at-arms. Rhys wasn't sure he would manage it, but he knew he had little choice but to try to pretend it was so. At least for the next few months.

"By the saints," he muttered, "I wish my father had been an actor instead of a knight!"

Fall

THE YEAR OF OUR LORD 1202

21

Two years wasted. Two years of scheming lost. Rollan of Ayre prowled through the passageways in the cellar, seeking for something to soothe his foul humor. He tried a pull at one of the ale kegs. It was sour, almost as sour as his mood.

Saints, but his plans had gone awry. He'd suspected it before the birth of Gwen's son, of course. He remembered well that spring. Spring was such a wonderful time, with all things springing to life. It was his favorite time to hatch plots. He'd spent a pair of months despoiling a pair of noblemen's daughters, then joyfully wreaking some choice havoc at court. He'd looked forward, with his customary gleeful anticipation, to returning home to find Gwen and her captain wallowing in misery.

But, to his dismay, what had he found?

Gwen growing great with child, but still cheerful. Rhys seemingly concerned, understandably, but not frantic.

It had not boded well.

Rollan had been certain the birth of Gwen's babe would be the thing to truly make the pair realize what they wanted yet could never have. He had looked forward to a rich bit of suffering to enjoy. Yet what had occurred?

Gwen had continued to smile.

Rhys had continued to look if not content, almost resigned.

And damn that bloody babe if he hadn't grown into a strong little lad of an age to be walking and looking about as if he already owned Ayre and all in it.

Damnation, but it had been enough to turn Rollan to drink.

He had watched Gwen and Rhys together as often as he could manage since then, but had seen nothing that indicated they were more than lady and loyal knight. No touching. No lingering looks of love. Saints above, not even a stolen kiss to report to Alain. Rollan had been tempted to brew up a fabrication as large as his irritation to spew at Alain the moment his brother came up for air from all his wenching, but it had offended his finer sensibilities, so he had refrained.

And now the son, yet another soul who stood in the way of Rollan's desire. A son, a doting mother, and a protector of both mother and child in the form of Rhys de Piaget. Events had certainly taken a decided turn for the worse since Alain's marriage to Gwen.

Two years had not improved matters any.

Gwen wouldn't flee the keep now, not with her son to consider. Rhys wouldn't leave the keep because he wanted Wyckham and likely Gwen as well. Captain and lady together always and seemingly content with it. The situation Rollan had thought would drive the pair of them straight off the parapet had turned out to be something the two of them couldn't have designed any more pleasingly if they'd been planning it themselves.

And now, most distressingly, Rollan found himself fresh out of ideas for further mayhem.

He stomped back up to the kitchens, latched onto a likely serving wench, and pulled her behind him up the stairs to his bedchamber. Perhaps a fortnight of wenching and drinking would restore his good humor and provide him with a few new ideas for making Rhys and Gwen miserable. It would take a cleverness that only he could muster, however. And he felt certain it would take something that would stretch even his considerable powers of imagination.

He snagged a second wench as he walked down the passageway.

It was going to be that kind of fortnight, he could just tell.

The child stood at her grandfather's elbow and watched as he scratched upon the parchment with his quill dipped in ink. It was easier to see the strange marks now that she had passed almost another pair of years on the earth and was a bit taller, but easier to see did not necessarily mean easier to read. Her grandfather had taught her a few letters, but those few she recognized were so hopelessly intertwined with the others that she couldn't make sense of any of it.

She could, however, make sense of the pots and pouches littering her grandsire's worktable. Indeed, he had always told her that her gift lay more in the making of potions than in the writing down of them. And so she had trained her nose and her eyes and her hands to weave together things that would heal, and she hoped that would be enough skill for the tasks life would send her way.

But still there was a part of her that wished, wistfully, that she, too, could make those graceful sweeping lines on paper.

Her grandfather sat back on his tall stool and smiled in satisfaction. The child peered at the page.

"Very beautiful," she said admiringly.

"Aye," he agreed. "Much like life has been of late, aye, granddaughter?"

He spoke truly. Though they still lived in the damp cellars, a few comforts had come their way, borne of course by souls who swore not to know the identity of the senders. The child knew, but she chose to say nothing.

Sir Rhys visited frequently, as did the lady of the keep. The child still rarely dared speak to the lady, for her beauty was almost painful to look upon, and the child's own lack shamed her. But the lady was gentle and kind and came often bearing little gifts for her alone. With the added joy of a baby to tickle and laugh with from time to time, life was indeed very sweet.

"This page is much like life," her grandsire began. He made a sweeping gesture, the one he always made when telling her something very important.

Only this time his sleeve caught his pot of ink and sent it splashing over his finely wrought words.

The child cried out in distress and used the sleeve of her dress to try to stem the tide. It was, unfortunately, hopeless. The page was ruined, the letters covered by a wash of dark ink.

Her grandfather sighed and looked at her.

"As with life, little one, sometimes one must begin the page again."

The child thought this a very wise, if not exactly pleasant, observation. So much work and patience, all undone with one chance gesture.

How like life indeed.

22

Gwen transferred her squirming son to her other hip and glared at her collection of keepers.

"How am I to eavesdrop with young Robin in tow?" she demanded.

To a man, well, and John of course, the souls facing her gave no answer. They did, however, wear almost identical looks of panic.

"Oh, by the saints, you are the most useless group of warriors I've ever encountered," she groused. "Afeared of such a small lad. You'd think the child was fierce enough to subdue you all with nothing more than a glance."

There was no change in their expressions, unless it was absolute certainty that such a thing was indeed possible.

Obviously humiliation was not going to work, either. There seemed to be no other choice but to take a drastic measure.

Gwen gave Robin a last cuddle, then turned him about and thrust him at the man nearest her. Jared, the soul so selected by default, held up his hands as if to ward off certain doom. Instead of avoiding his fate, he found himself with his hands full of a squirming lad of nigh onto sixteen months of life. Jared held the boy at arm's length as gingerly as he might have a striking snake. Gwen took one last look at her son who, though likely slightly uncomfortable at his precarious position, seemed to find Jared's features to his liking, for he merely stared at the man with as unblinking a stare as Jared possessed. Then he popped his thumb into his mouth and settled back for a substantial contemplation. Satisfied that both would survive the next few moments, Gwen slipped away and hied herself to her husband's solar.

It was only moments later that she stood with her ear pressed against the wood of the door, struggling to hear even the faintest sounds of conversation going on inside. That all was deathly silent could only mean one of two things: Alain was gloating and Rhys had chosen to remain stoic, or Alain had betrayed her captain and Rhys had slain every soul inside the chamber. The latter wouldn't have surprised her overmuch. Rhys was near the breaking point.

How they had managed to survive this long she surely didn't know. She told him often that it was because her powers of imagination were certainly more well exercised than his—she spent a good deal of time pretending that she was living one of her mother's bard's tales. It was far easier to think of Rhys as an unrequited suitor who worshipped her from afar. Of course that was more difficult than she'd anticipated given that he spent so much time at her side. But he'd been true to his word. He hadn't touched her. He hadn't spoken to her of love. He'd treated her with the same comradely affection that he used with John, Montgomery, and the Fitzgeralds.

Damn him anyway.

Only once had she suggested that perhaps even if he didn't commit the acts in truth, giving her an indication that he might have wished deep inside himself to touch her hand or perhaps kiss her fingers wouldn't be such a poor thing.

The look he'd given her had been enough to make her regret her suggestion most sincerely.

And so she had distracted herself with other things. She'd practiced swordplay. Rhys had had a sword fashioned for her and somewhere procured a jewel for the hilt which perfectly matched her eyes. The edges of the blade, however, were most distressingly blunted. And damn the man if he hadn't threatened every blacksmith within a ten-mile radius with death if the blade had any killing powers placed upon it. Gwen might have tried to sharpen it herself but the steel was beautiful as it was, and she feared to mar it with her clumsy attempts. Besides that, it was something Rhys had given her, and she treasured it for that reason alone, despite its lack of ability to do damage to any foe.

And she had doted on her son. Alain had never mentioned again his intent to carry the boy off to some other keep and she had eventually given up sleeping with a blade in her hand and her other arm wrapped around Robin. She had no doubts Robin would be sent away the very hour he reached seven years, but until that time she had the full keeping of him. Alain rarely found himself at home, and even when he did, he never troubled her at night. Even Rollan spent little time at Ayre stirring up mischief. Gwen raised her son in peace, practiced her swordplay, and spent the rest of her time at her tapestry frame.

And she told herself she was content with her life, for she knew no other choice was left to her.

Which made her wonder what she was doing standing pressed against Alain's door like a lover, straining to hear the faintest sound of speech inside. More disturbing was what she hoped to hear. That Rhys had indeed obtained his land as Alain had promised?

Which meant he would be leaving Ayre no doubt as quickly as he could.

The door opened with such suddenness that she almost fell face-first into Alain's solar. She jerked herself back upright, hoping no one had noticed her. Rhys came out of the solar so quickly, she liked to believe no one had.

He slammed the door shut behind him. He glared down at her. "We spoke of Wyckham."

"Of course," she said. It wasn't something she was overly glad to hear about, for it spelled the end of his time there. She had the feeling, however, that things had not gone as well as he might have liked. The fact that he looked fair murderous was a good indication.

"He told me, and I'll repeat exactly what I heard, 'Take it from under my troops if you want it.'"

Gwen blinked. "He said *what?*"

"You heard me," Rhys snarled. "He's bloody encamped his men on it! If I want it, I'll have to take it by force!"

"How many men?"

"Too bloody many to do in myself!" he roared. "Damn the man to hell!"

She sensed a logical conversation about Rhys's options would not be appreciated. She also suspected that bidding him to stop shouting lest her husband hear his words would also not be received well. So she folded her hands sedately in front of her and tried to look soothing.

"Well?" Rhys demanded.

"Well what?" she asked, lifting one eyebrow. "I daresay you don't want any of my suggestions."

He pursed his lips. "I might."

She shrugged. "You could turn your back on the land."

"Turn my back on the land?" he mouthed, but no sound came out. His face turned a rather bright shade of red, and he began to make inarticulate sounds of fury.

"Not an option," Gwen noted. "Then you could perhaps make a visit to court and petition the king."

"Petition the king, my arse!" he exclaimed. He shook his head sharply. "I like neither of those."

"You could stay with me," she said.

His lips tightened. "As what? Captain of your guard?"

"You needn't make it sound as if it has been that great a burden."

"It has," he said shortly.

Gwen felt as if he'd slapped her. "I see."

"Do you?" he demanded. "Do you indeed?"

"I see that it has been a place you would have rather not taken," she said stiffly. "I regret the trouble it has caused you."

"*Merde*," he snarled under his breath.

Gwen found her hand captured in a grip that obviously wasn't going to be broken any time soon.

"Rhys, nay," she attempted.

He ignored her and pulled her along behind him down the passageway, leaving her no choice but to run to keep up with him.

She thought to wonder why no one seemed to glance at them more than once, then she caught sight of the expression on his face and the mystery was solved. Never before had she seen him so angry.

"This isn't my fault," she said.

He ignored her. He strode down the passageway to her solar. He threw open the door and swept her ladies with a look Gwen surmised by their expressions she had been glad not to be the recipient of.

"Out."

One word sent every woman there scurrying for the door. Gwen would have scurried right along with them, but her wrist was still prisoner in his hand. The women rushed past her, then Gwen found herself propelled into the chamber. The door slammed with a resounding bang.

"Do not begin patting yourself for potential weapons," he growled at her.

Gwen realized she had been doing just that, so she clasped her hands behind her back.

"As you wish," she said.

"As I wish," he repeated. "Do you have any idea what it is I wish?"

"To throttle me?" She tried a teasing smile.

"Nay." He did not smile in return.

"Then I vow I have little idea, for one would think by the expression on your face that a throttling appealed to you most."

He gritted his teeth and resorted to merely glaring at her.

Gwen searched frantically for something to say that would cajole him from his foul mood. But what could she say? *Enjoy your land, you've certainly earned it? Find yourself an army and take the soil by force? Leave me behind and never give me another thought?*

It was the last she found that troubled her the most.

She took a deep breath.

"You *could* stay," she said. She'd said it before, but it was a sentiment that bore repeating.

He lifted one eyebrow, but said nothing.

"You make a fine champion," she pressed on. "It has been tolerable, has it not? Reading together, walking in the garden together, having speech together. Could we not go on as before?"

"Nay, we cannot," he bit out.

"But why—"

"Why?" he interrupted. *"Why?"*

He looked as if throttling her had suddenly become a very appealing idea, so she took a pace backward.

He advanced, his expression thunderous.

Gwen found, to her dismay, that she had no more room for retreat. Her back was against the cold stone of the wall, and Rhys was standing toe-to-toe with her. He put his hands against the wall on either side of her head and glared down at her.

"Let me tell you why we cannot," he said in a low growl. "We cannot because I have spent every day of the past two years on fire for you. I have clasped my hands hard enough behind my back to draw blood and leave scars, all in an effort not to touch you. I have worn Connor and Jared down to the bone in the lists in an effort to tire myself so that when I was with you, I would have energy to speak of nothing more interesting than the condition of your damned herbs or the bloody weather."

"Then I wasn't boring you—" She shut her mouth at the look on his face and thought it a very wise move indeed.

"I cannot remain here one more hour when all I am allowed is to look at you."

She could only look up at him, mute.

"I cannot remain another hour near you and have nothing but speech with you."

He was leaving. She should have been prepared for it, but she found she wasn't.

"And above all else, I will not listen to one more bloody word about me being a noble, chivalrous, and unrequited champion!" he exclaimed.

"You made a good one," she offered.

"At the cost of two years of no bloody sleep at night!" he shouted.

She blinked. "You couldn't sleep?"

"I could not."

"But I slept very well."

"Did you?" he demanded.

"Aye," she said hesitantly, "I did indeed. Well, mostly. Surely your bed—"

"It wasn't the bed."

"Then your chamber—"

"It wasn't the chamber."

Gwen frowned. Perhaps lack of sleep had addled his wits. "I do not see—"

Without warning, she found herself enveloped in his embrace. Had there been any space between them before, it was there no longer. He could not have molded her to him any more successfully had she been nothing but the cook's finest pastry dough. Not that Alain's cook made a fine pastry dough, for it was always full of lumps and sand.

"Gwen," Rhys growled.

She blinked up at him. "Aye?"

She wondered what he had meant to say to her, then she realized he had merely been seeking her full attention. As if he didn't have it already. She was all too aware of his unyielding frame and the strength of the arms that held her captive against it . . .

And then he kissed her.

And she thought she just might faint.

Indeed she would have, if he hadn't had such a grip upon her. And it was surely no chaste kiss a champion might give his unattainable lady.

It was a kiss of raw possession.

All she could do was clutch his shoulders and cling to him. It was devastating enough to have his mouth on hers once again after two long years of wondering if she'd imagined how sweet his lips were. Even more unfortunate, however, were the memories his present kiss brought to mind. He had kissed her thusly before, kissed her long and hard and so thoroughly she wondered if there possibly remained a part of her mouth he hadn't investigated. But that had come as a prelude to his claiming the rest of her body.

And her soul.

She felt tears begin to leak from her eyes, but she didn't bother to brush them away. Oh, how much they had missed! How many hours of loving, how many days of simple touches and soul-stirring kisses.

It would have brought her to her knees if she'd been able to get there.

He started to pull away, but she stopped him.

"Nay," she said against his mouth. "Not yet."

"Now do you see?" he rasped.

"Aye," she managed.

"I never forgot," he whispered, pressing gentle kisses against the corners of her eyes, tasting her tears. "Never once. Never for a moment. I don't know how you could have."

"Perhaps my imagination is my downfall."

"You should use it less."

"How else was I to survive?"

His only answer was another kiss, and then another, and then she began to lose track of where his kisses began and ended.

And when she thought she could truly bear no more, he merely rested his forehead against hers and drew in great, ragged breaths.

"I'll leave you Montgomery and the twins," he said quietly.

She pulled back quickly. "You'll *what*?"

"I'm taking John and leaving today."

Her mouth fell open. She was certain it was passing unattractive to gape at him thusly, but the saints preserve her, it was all she could do.

"Think you I can remain?" he asked with a dry smile. "After that?"

"You're *leaving* me?" she demanded.

"Of course—"

"You unfeeling oaf!" she said, shoving him smartly. "You do that"—she gestured helplessly at the space now between them—"then merely walk away?"

He put his hands on her shoulders, ignoring her attempts to shrug them off.

"How else am I to raise an army?" he asked gently.

She frowned. "An army?"

"To take possession of Wyckham."

"Ah," she said, "then it comes down to this again."

"Saints, woman, how am I to care for you properly without soil to build a home on? Without soil to grow crops in? Without soil for our children to roam over?"

She closed her eyes briefly and prayed for strength. "It cannot be, Rhys—"

"You have no faith," he said. "Either in me or in love."

"I have a great deal of faith in both."

"Then you're failing to use your imagination. If you can imagine me content to live as your comrade-in-arms for two years, can you not imagine me capable of taking you for my own?"

She looked up at him. "And Robin?"

He took a deep breath. "Robin as well."

"Impossible."

"Difficult," he conceded. "But not impossible."

She shook her head. "I don't see how."

"Then stop trying to see. Trust me."

"But there are no grounds for consanguinity."

"As if that has ever stopped anyone before," Rhys said with a snort. "Eleanor divorced Phillip of France on those grounds, and she surely had no relation to him."

"But the sanctity of marriage vows . . ." She didn't bother to finish her thought.

She had kept her vows. Alain had not. Indeed, she wondered when he had first returned to his whores—the day after their wedding? A se'nnight later?

"You were mine first," Rhys said quietly. "Does that mean nothing to you?"

She bowed her head.

"A true vow is more than words spoken, Gwen. It must also be made with the heart."

She looked up at him, feeling her heart begin to break. "He'll never let Robin go."

"He might."

"He never will," she repeated, "and you know it well. And I cannot leave my son behind."

He was silent for several moments. "I would not ask you to choose between us, Gwen. I will find a way to free him as well." He cupped her face in his hands. "Will you trust me?"

She sighed. "Aye."

"I can ask no more of you than that."

"You'll leave today?"

"Within the hour. I've no doubts Alain expects it."

"And return when?"

"Within a year—"

"A *year?*" she demanded.

He lifted his shoulders helplessly. "Raising an army takes time, Gwen. I'll have to hire mercenaries, see to their expenses and training, retain men to see to their gear . . ."

"A year," she said in astonishment. "That is such a long time."

"'Tis a far sight shorter than the rest of our lives," he pointed out.

"You'll find something to keep yourself amused, I am certain of it. Perhaps you should take up minstrelsy."

She blinked, then smiled suddenly. "I could train with the twins."

"Absolutely not!"

"Then I can help you fight your war!"

She would have elaborated on her scheme, but he seemed determined not to hear any of it. And the longer he kissed her, the less appealing truly becoming a mercenary seemed.

At least for the moment.

"Lose sleep over me," he said, when he lifted his head. "Think pleasant thoughts of me. Trust me."

And before she could clutch him to her, he had crossed the chamber to the door.

"Rhys," she said, realizing just exactly what she stood to lose.

He turned and looked at her a last time.

"Wait for me," he said.

And then he was gone.

An hour later Gwen stood near the barbican and didn't bother to pretend to have business there. She was flanked by the twins, who stood in their usual poses with arms folded over their chests. Montgomery stood nearby, his shoulders having been pressed into service as a place for Robin to perch.

Rhys and John stood speaking together not far away. Gwen watched as Rhys and his squire mounted their horses and turned them out of the gates.

Gwen fully expected Rhys not even to mark her. He hadn't before in the two times she'd stood at gates and watched him go out to see to his business.

This time, though, he turned his head and looked at her.

No words were necessary.

Wait for me.

And so she would.

She had no other choice.

23

Rhys walked through the abbey's small outer garden, following a plump, slow-moving novice. He did not attempt to invite her to hasten. He had learned, over the course of his long life, that annoying the Lord's brides while at their duties would only earn him a thorough tongue-lashing. At least he only had his own tongue to guard. The saints preserve him had he been forced to guard John's as well. Unfortunately for them both, John seemed determined to prove to himself things that he could have more easily learned had he merely used his ears to their best advantage.

At present, however, the lad was safely ensconced with Rhys's grandfather in a nearby inn with their horses and all their gear. It had left Rhys free to proceed to the abbey unhindered and in disguise. Rhys could only hope his grandsire would be able to keep John free from trouble for as long as was required. He would have been unsurprised by any of either Sir Jean or John's antics. Perhaps it had been less than wise to leave the pair of them together.

Well, there was little he could do about it now. He adjusted his very fragrant cloak as his guide neared their journey's end. Rhys was ushered into a comfortable chamber where three chairs were occupied by three imposing women. There was the abbess, of course, with her assessing gaze fixed upon him. Rhys stared at her, amazed that such a beautiful woman should find herself in such a place. He shook his head. How strange were the twists of fate that drove women to such seclusion.

The abbess was flanked by women who Rhys knew were her second and third in command. They were no less unswerving in their appraisal of his person. He went down on one knee, as it seemed the prudent thing to do.

"My lady," Rhys said, inclining his head to the abbess. "God be with you."

"And with you, my son."

Rhys looked up in time to see the abbess dismiss her companions with a small wave of her hand.

"This one looks none-too-dangerous," she said placidly. "I think I am able to ascertain his business without your aid. There are other things more pressing than speech with a passing traveler."

Obviously the other women were accustomed to not arguing. They departed without sparing Rhys another glance and closed the door behind them. They wouldn't have recognized him anyway. He never came to this abbey twice wearing the same disguise.

"Rhys," the abbess said with a long-suffering sigh, "could you not have chosen a less fragrant pretense?"

"Swine herding is a very reputable calling, Mother."

The abbess rose and beckoned to him with a sigh. "Come give your mother a kiss, my love. But no hug, if you please."

Rhys laughed as he rose and bent to kiss his mother heartily on the cheek. "Surely you are happy enough to see me not to mind my smell."

She wrinkled her nose. "Could you not have chosen a friar as your disguise? Or a minstrel? They at least smell of smoke and ale, not pigsh—"

"Mother!" Rhys laughed. "By the saints, your novices would be appalled could they hear you."

She only smiled as she drew him over to sit down next to her. "They fear me too greatly to trouble themselves over paying me any heed. They scuttle by and pray they don't attract my notice. Especially when it has been months since I've had word from my son, for that puts me in an especially foul humor."

Rhys rolled his eyes. "I would have written—"

"But you feared to reveal my whereabouts. Aye, I've heard that excuse before."

He started to protest, but she waved away his words.

"You protect me well, and I am grateful for it. Now, tell me of your news and why you find yourself in France."

"Well—"

"Your grandsire says you have fallen in love with a girl you cannot have." She leveled him a very piercing look. "I wonder why it is you have not shared this with me."

"I wasn't sure you would approve."

"Is she so shrewish then?"

He shook his head, smiling. "Nay, she is passing sweet."

"Hard to look upon, then? Knock-kneed, cross-eyed, palsied—"

"Nay, nay," he said, staving off any more descriptions, "she is well formed and quite pleasing to the eye. I only feared you would disapprove of my looking above my station."

"Why?" she asked dryly. "Because you are but a knight?"

"Others would find that enough to deny her to me."

"You bear an honorable name, love. There is no shame in your heritage."

"Knight, healer, heretic." He smiled. "My father had an illustrious career, did he not?"

"Your father is a prince among men and braver than most. You have no reason to be ashamed of him. And if you doubt his courage, look to your grandsire. They are very much alike."

Rhys looked at his mother and wondered if she realized her mistake. "*Was*, Mother. My father *was* a prince among men."

"Hmmm," his mother agreed. "Very true."

It wasn't the first time she had made such a slip when speaking about her late husband. Rhys wondered if the solitude of the convent had begun to prey upon her mind. Did she believe Etienne was still alive?

There was reason, he supposed. His father had never received a proper Christian burial. That would be enough to cause some to wonder if he'd truly been laid to rest. Rhys had always assumed that he had no grave marker because of the slanderous label of heretic which had been placed upon him. It was enough to deny him entrance into any church's graveyard.

From time to time, however, Rhys wondered if it was because his father wasn't buried at all.

"Unfortunately, neither your father nor your grandsire bore any noble titles," his mother continued absently.

"Aye," Rhys agreed, pushing aside his foolish thoughts. His sire was dead. He'd been dead for almost twenty years. "A title would have aided me greatly."

"Ah, Rhys," his mother said, fixing her gaze upon him and smiling, "I daresay there is enough nobility in you for any woman. Now, tell me more about this girl. She is beautiful and her eyes are straight. What is the difficulty?"

"She's a baron's daughter."

His mother waited.

"And she's wed."

"Ah," his mother said. "I see."

"Hence my arrival in France."

His mother blinked. "Of course."

"I need gold. For bribes."

"What else?" she said. "You don't intend to steal her away?"

"'Tis a tradition, is it not? Grandfather stole Grandmother."

"And your father stole me."

"I, on the other hand, have been a dismal failure when it comes to this snatching of women."

"All the more reason to remedy it, my love."

Rhys sighed and leaned back against the chair. "I fear my only choice is to pay for what I wish to have." He looked at her and smiled grimly. "I've never succeeded at bribery before."

"Sword strokes are a much more direct way of solving problems," she agreed. "But the slaying of nobles is still frowned upon in England, is it not?"

"It was the last time I asked."

"She has a son, true?"

Obviously his mother was more versed in the events of his life than she admitted to being. He wasn't surprised. How she came by her knowledge of events outside her walls was a mystery, but her spies were thorough.

"Aye," Rhys said, "one she will not leave without."

His mother reached for his hand. "I cannot blame her. It fair broke my heart to let your grandsire take you away when he did, even though I knew I had no other choice."

"What else were you to do? My sire was dead."

His mother didn't argue that. "And it wasn't as if I could have traveled about with your grandsire. I do not regret my choice. It is a peaceful enough existence."

"Is it?" he mused. "Has Grandfather given up his spying for Phillip?"

"How would I know, love?"

"You would know, Mother, for he sends all his information through you. Peaceful existence, my arse," he said with a snort.

She only smiled. "I do what I can to uphold the family tradition."

"One I haven't carried on. Am I such a disappointment to Grandpère, then?"

"I daresay the king is more disappointed than your grandsire, but he will not press you. He knows you intend to make your home in England."

"A pity he cannot help me obtain the bride I want."

"I suppose he might, if you were to make it worth his time. Your father spent his share of time ferreting out details on the isle. Phillip wouldn't hesitate to use you if you were willing."

He shook his head. "I haven't the temperament for deception."

"So one sees by the lack of glee you take in disguising yourself when you come to visit me," his mother said dryly.

"Spying for the French king is something I cannot do, Mother," Rhys said with a sigh. "My lady has her feet firmly planted on English soil. Her land is there. Her mother is there."

"Her son is there," his mother murmured. "I envy her."

Rhys took his mother's hand and raised it to his lips. "At least I am free to see you when I will it, Mother. And I am still alive to do so. I cannot say what would happen should I follow in Father's footsteps."

She squeezed his hand. "True enough, my love. Very well, continue in your quest and may your efforts bear much fruit. I will keep your winnings safe, as always."

"The saints be praised for the crypt beneath your altar," he said with a smile. "I will appreciate it greatly."

"I am always happy to do what I can for the cause of love." She rose gracefully. "I will call for a bit of refreshment, then you will tell me of your journey here. I suppose the crossing was perilous, as always."

Rhys smiled to himself. If there was one thing his mother did not care for, it was setting foot on any kind of seagoing vessel. He half suspected that was why she found herself still in France after all these years.

Or perhaps it was because her vocation suited her. She had ample time to pray, to contemplate life's mysteries in her garden, and to offer succor to passing travelers. Phillip had seen to it all after Rhys's father's death, and Mary had accepted it willingly.

Who would have thought she would have become just as fine a spy as her husband?

Or was it that her husband was still spying and Mary only provided a convenient shield for his activities?

"Oh, by the saints," Rhys muttered in disgust. His lady's overly active imagination had had a ruinous effect on his common sense. His father was dead. His mother was devious, but not so devious as all that.

Rhys watched his mother as she ordered her novices about and wondered, not for the first time, just where it was his mother had been born. She had told him "England, and leave it there, my love" more times than he could begin to count. His father had divulged no more, and his grandsire had been even more tight-lipped than either of them. Had her life been so terrible, then, that the mere mention of it was enough to grieve her so?

Or did she have kin who would likely want her back should they know where to find her?

"Sweet wine from the south," his mother announced, handing him a silver goblet. "Chilled, just as you like it, son."

Rhys almost asked for the entire bottle to silence his questions. His mother had her reasons for secrecy, and they were likely none of his business. That was enough for him. Besides, it wasn't as if he didn't have enough to occupy his mind at present. There was much to be done in preparation for the frequenting of tourneys. He would need to keep his eyes open for possible additions to his as-yet nonexistent army. If that hadn't been enough to keep him occupied, seeing that John remained unscathed would be. Rhys drank deeply of his wine. The saints preserve him from a squire's arrogance.

"Mother, I need to have a message sent," he said. It was past time he wrote Gwen to assure her he'd reached France safely. "You have someone trustworthy?"

"Of course."

"Then might we retire to your chambers? They are, as I remember, much more comfortable than this."

His mother wrinkled her nose. "I believe first of all, my son, that you'll have a bath. While you're about that, I'll fetch the sister's habit you're accustomed to wearing."

Rhys scowled. "I have the feeling you only do this to see me in skirts."

She patted his cheek. "You would have made such a lovely girl."

"But such a tall one," he said.

"The sisters are more likely to look at the length of your feet than your height."

Rhys sighed. The indignities he suffered for a soft bed. But he would suffer them willingly, for he suspected it would be the last time he would feel goosefeathers beneath his back for some time to come. His mother, at least in her private chambers, was not one given to deprivation. The king had been most generous in his gratitude for Mary's continued service to his cause. Rhys had no qualms about enjoying the luxuries himself while he could.

It was several hours later that he sat at his mother's writing table, begarbed in a sister's habit, working industriously on the first of what he hoped were very few letters to his love. With any luck at all, it would take him half a year to earn the gold he needed and only a few weeks to acquire his army. He was counting on his reputation serving him well.

My love, he began, then shook his head and scratched it out. It wouldn't do to reveal too much of his heart. His mother's messengers were trustworthy, true, but one could not always count on a safe journey for any messenger. Better that he confine himself to less emotional matters.

My lady Gwennelyn, he began, *I am safely arrived here in France to find that the skies are passing gray and a continual drizzle falls wherever I go.* Rhys looked at his words with satisfaction. Should his missive be intercepted, no one would be the wiser as to where he currently loitered. There was drizzle aplenty this time of year. *My accoutrements, including my squire, seem to have survived the journey thus far fairly well. My horse only threw one shoe, which caused me grief, but that was remedied soon enough.*

Rhys paused, then sniffed. His mother's cook had obviously been at her work again. After the slop he'd eaten at Ayre for the past two years, almost anything would be an improvement.

He looked down at his letter and considered, then rose abruptly. He would eat first. It would give him something else safe to relate to his lady.

He left his mother's chamber, his mouth watering already. He walked down the passageway, ducking his head to appear less tall, and praying his mother's women wouldn't notice him. He would have to moderate his eating habits as well. It wasn't as if a traveling sister would devour her meal with the gusto of a starving mercenary.

One of his mother's more substantial sisters stood guard near the entrance to the dining hall. Rhys had seen the woman before and marveled not only at her stature, but her height. The woman looked at him, then quickly looked away.

Rhys sighed as he entered the dining hall. Regardless of what his mother said, he knew he did not make an attractive sister of the cloth. He couldn't blame the woman for not having wanted to look at him. Hopefully the rest of his mother's followers would feel the same way and he would pass his visit peacefully.

It would likely be the last time he had such luxury for some time to come.

24

Ayre
December 1202

"Damnation, not another child! How could I have let this happen?"

Gwen listened to the words in astonishment, as they were ones she had been thinking not a handful of moments before. These words, however, were coming out of a mouth she wouldn't have suspected. She pressed herself back into the shadows and looked at the man leaning down to suck a great mouthful of ale straight from the spigot.

"Bloody babe," Rollan snarled, spitting out the ale. "Bloody ale! Will nothing go aright for me this year? One heir was one thing." He took another large slurp of ale, swished it around in his mouth, and spat it out with a passion. "Now *another* one? I had planned that he should leave her be!"

So, Gwen thought to herself with a silent snort, had she. She'd managed to avoid encountering Alain and his bed at the same time for several months at a stretch, but unfortunately she hadn't been completely successful at it.

Now she had at least another four months of puking to look forward to, which was why she found herself currently loitering near Master Socrates's cell, seeking something without specks to ingest. Perhaps this was a happy chance, for how else would she have been nearby to eavesdrop on Rollan's private conversations with himself?

Rollan seemed to be finding the ale more palatable all the time. In between great gulps he spewed forth more of his innermost thoughts.

"Now there's another one who stands in the way of my prize."

Gwen raised one eyebrow.

"I'll rid myself of the both of them. Nay, the three of them. Alain and both his babes. I could push Gwen down the stairs—nay, then I lose her as well, and that is not in my plans."

The saints be praised for that, Gwen thought, with a fair bit of alarm.

"I'll wait until she's birthed the babe, then I'll deal with the three of them. And then *I'll* be known as lord of Ayre," Rollan said, bending for another drink. He straightened, dragged his sleeve across his mouth, and turned himself toward the stairs. "I'll see Alain sent to Canfield this afternoon, then be about my plans. Perhaps that little brat Robin can take a tumble down the stairs. That would see to one of them . . ."

Gwen felt a cold chill go down her spine. Never mind that her fondest wish was to go back to bed and remain there for several more days. She would have to leave the keep. Perhaps Alain could be persuaded to escort her to Segrave on his way to Canfield. If he thought she would be conveniently tucked away with her mother where she could not trouble him, he might think more kindly about it.

Gwen waited until she was certain Rollan had made his way up the stairs before she followed. Her first task would be to seek out Sir Montgomery and tell him of what she'd overheard. Then she would brave Ayre's kitchens to prepare her husband something to sweeten his humor. Though his palate was not overly discriminating—he never seemed certain when something was tastier than something else except to remark that there was something odd about the fare—food was food when such a man's gullet was to be considered.

And then she would soon find herself ensconced in her mother's solar before Rollan could wreak any havoc.

Or so she hoped.

A fortnight later she found herself safely installed in her mother's solar at Segrave with a missive in her hands. It was a missive she had been waiting for nigh on to two months. She'd counted the days since Rhys had departed, allowing amply for the difficulties a messenger might encounter. She had received the anticipated epistle with joy and great relief.

And then she had begun to read it.

She currently reread the blighted scrap of parchment by light of her

mother's finest tallow candles, and wished Robin were more deeply asleep
that she might vent her frustration with a few words she had learned by
frequenting the lists in her youth.

"'A roasted goose with a savoury sauce of quince and onions'?" she
quoted with disgust. "*This* is the drivel he chooses to write to me!"

Her mother only continued to stitch placidly. "What else is Rhys to say,
my sweet?"

"He could say that he loves me! Or that he thinks of me morn
and eve."

"Which he likely does—"

"Instead, I am forced to read in great detail about the mishaps which
have befallen his gear, the dishes presented at his mother's supper table, and
exactly what the elements are producing this time of year in France."

"Well—"

"These are things I do not care about!"

Joanna smiled. "Gwen, these are perilous times we live in. Messengers
are untrustworthy. He has no way of telling who might read his words."

Gwen cursed under her breath. What she had wanted was a letter full
of love. What she had received was a letter full of unimportant details. If
she hadn't known better, she might have suspected Rhys's feelings had
changed.

"He isn't exactly wooing me with his words," Gwen grumbled. "Perhaps he thinks I am already won."

"Perhaps he is trying to save your reputation, Gwen."

"And a simple word or two of love would ruin me?"

"He only thinks on your future, Gwen—"

"Nay, Mother, he's only thinking on his stomach! 'A sweet pudding
accompanied by a delicate wine from the south.'" Gwen snorted in disgust.
"Would that he were drinking the swill Alain's alemaster produces. I might
have a decent bit of sentiment if that were the case."

Joanna shook her head with a smile. "Gwen, love, it would not serve
you if the king thought you had committed adultery with Sir Rhys."

"I have been true to Alain, pox rot the man. Not that he has accorded
me the same courtesy. And what do I care what the king hears? He doesn't
think past the gold in his coffers."

Joanna set aside her stitchery with a heavy sigh. "Gwen, you accomplish
nothing by pacing in my solar and complaining."

"I am not—"

"Aye, you are, and if I must listen to you go on thusly for another ten
months, you will drive me mad." Her mother, however, smiled as she said
as much. "And for all you know, it may take Rhys longer than that to complete his business, and then where will you be?"

"Hoarse," Gwen said shortly. She sat down across from her mother and tried to compose herself. "I am but restless."

"Then find something to do."

"What am I to do, Mother? Scurry off to the king and tell him my tale? Ask him to grant me an annulment?"

"'Tis a bit late for that," Joanna said, looking fondly at Robin, who lay sprawled on the bed, sound asleep.

"I cannot choose divorce, either. I would lose Robin in the bargain. And all my lands." She looked at her mother. "You would lose your home."

Joanna shrugged. "'Tis only by the good grace of Alain that I live here as it is. I can easily take my cook and go elsewhere." She seemed to brush aside any more thought about it. "Just how is it your young Rhys intends to see you become his?"

"The saints only know. I believe he looks toward bribery."

"Bribery for what?"

An annulment, Gwen started to say, then she stopped herself. Could an annulment be granted? Gwen supposed it could, though it would certainly turn Robin and her coming babe into bastards. Not a fate she would wish on them if she had any other choice. But to her, bastardy was far more tolerable than being at Alain's mercy. She shuddered to think the things Robin would learn at his father's hands.

Gwen glanced at her mother to find her regarding her with a searching look. And not for the first time, Gwen wondered how her mother viewed the situation. She hadn't had the courage before to even ask her, fearing what she would hear.

"Does it bother you, then?" Gwen asked. No sense in not having the truth.

Joanna returned her look gravely. "Though I cannot agree with divorce, given the Church's view upon the matter, I cannot deny that Alain was never the choice either your father or I would have made had it not been for his station."

"And what of turning Robin into a bastard?"

"By an annulment?" Joanna shrugged. "'Tis something that would haunt him, Gwen."

"Would it be more grievous than what he would suffer being Alain's son?"

"And in return losing Ayre, Segrave, and everything else he would otherwise inherit? Only he could answer that, and 'tis a question he will not even understand for several years yet."

"Rhys has Wyckham. He could give that to Robin."

"If Rhys can liberate it from Alain's troops, and even then he will still be Alain's vassal."

Gwen sighed and buried her face in her hands. "Wyckham is his and the king holds the deed for him. But when you remind me of who his overlord would be, it sounds passing intolerable."

"'Tis but the truth of the matter, Gwen."

"Would that I had wed with Rhys from the start."

"Aye. Both your sire and I wished it as well. But Rhys had no title and no lands."

Gwen looked at her mother. "There is more to life than land, Mother."

Joanna smiled. "Aye, I have always thought so, my love."

"Rhys has survived well enough without any."

"It does leave a man free to go where he wills," Joanna conceded.

Gwen rose and moved to kneel at her mother's feet. She took her hands. "Better that my children live with a man who loves them than a man who cares nothing for them, Mother."

"Or for you," Joanna agreed.

"Rhys could perhaps claim them as his own."

"Aye, he could," Joanna said carefully. "Though who will recognize that I cannot say. The king might choose not to."

"Then we'll go to France," Gwen said grimly. "If King Phillip knighted Rhys, then he must have a use for him somehow. Life might be kinder to us there."

Gwen's mother squeezed her hands. "Give your Rhys his year, Gwen, and see how events come to pass. You never know what the future will bring."

"Aye," Gwen said, rising, "there is truth in that." She paced to the window. "But I must do something. I cannot remain here for a year merely waiting."

"You could improve your stitchery."

"I could improve my swordplay," Gwen said, feeling the faintest twinge of excitement.

"Not in your current condition. Stitchery is safer. Or perhaps a few new ballads learned on the lute."

"The bow would not be too taxing. . ."

"Gwen," her mother warned. "You carry a babe."

Gwen sighed and resumed her seat. "My belly reminds me of that more often than I care to think about."

If not swordplay, then perhaps preparation for the establishment of Rhys's household at Wyckham. Assuming there would be such a thing.

Nay, she would not doubt. Rhys would manage what her father had not been able to. She and Robin would find safety behind Rhys's strong arm.

As would the new babe. Gwen put her hand over her belly protectively. Oh, how she wished Rollan had never found her puking into her rosebushes.

She likely could have escaped to Segrave and not have had Alain been the wiser about his future second child. She had little doubts Rollan would go to his brother with the tale, if only to lure Alain back to Ayre so he could be pushed down the stairs. Gwen was tempted to entertain that thought a bit longer. If Rollan were left to himself long enough, he just might solve all her problems for her.

But, for all she knew, if Alain met with a mishap, the king would wed her to Rollan before she could get word to Rhys, and then she would find herself in an even more intolerable situation. At least Alain spent most of his time at Canfield, engaging in the saints only knew what kinds of activities with the lady Rachel. For all the time she had passed with him, her husband might have been such in name only. It suited her well enough— and much more satisfactorily than if she'd found herself facing Rollan of Ayre in front of a priest.

Perhaps she would send the Fitzgeralds back to Ayre just to protect Alain. They were to have come with her to Segrave in her own train, but they begged leave to come more slowly that they might scout the surroundings for enemies. One did not argue with such intimidating men, so she had left them to their own stratagem. They should have arrived several days before, but she hadn't caught even a whiff of them as of yet. They could have walked from Ayre more swiftly than the pace they seemed to be traveling. Perhaps scouting was a more involved activity than she'd supposed.

"Gwen," Joanna said, interrupting Gwen's musings, "why do you not work some heroic design on a surcoat?"

Gwen shook her head. "He would not wear it, Mama." She sighed and put aside her worries. It did her no good to try to divine what Rhys's intentions were, for 'twas a certainty that he would do things in a way she wouldn't have chosen. That much she had learned about men in her short lifetime.

"I think," she said, looking about her for an appropriate amount of cloth, "that I will hem sheets."

"Sheets?" Her mother sounded surprised, and rightly so. It had been the last thing Gwen had ever cared to do.

"Sheets," Gwen said with a nod. "For a wedding bed."

And she prayed she would find the desired man in it. Rhys had said a year, and she prayed she would pass that time without incident. She hoped the time would go quickly. There would be the babe to see to, and Robin to tend as well.

Aye, she could pass a year and not mind it. There would be missives exchanged. Perhaps in time she might even convince Rhys that he could express a sentiment or two and not suffer from it.

It was certainly preferable to reading about what he had been eating.

❧ Winter ❧

THE YEAR OF OUR LORD 1206

25

Letters, letters, ah, the joy of a well-received letter! A veritable hill of them lay on the rough wooden table. They had been read and reread scores of times, just for the sheer pleasure of seeing such words of love be put to paper. Indeed, what finer way could there be to pass an afternoon than perusing such correspondence with a flagon of ale at one's elbow?

Said peruser put a finger to his lips, as if he contemplated which pile of missives to attend to first. The decision wasn't truly a difficult one, as he had two new epistles to digest. It hardly mattered which he chose; each would be delicious in its own way. With a shrug, he reached for the missive nearest his cup of ale.

He read and smiled. It was truly astonishing how the passage of time had broken down the formality shown in the earlier letters.

Epiphany, 1206

Beloved Gwen,

The siege is at long last ended, and I have managed to frighten out of the count d'Auber more gold than he intended to spend, but he cost me six more months of my life than I'd intended he should. With it I daresay I have enough to satisfy even John's greedy hands, with ample left over to send to Rome to sweeten the Pope's humor. You will have your freedom and Robin as well, I am sure of it.

Look for me in late spring. I'm bringing a handful of lads home with me to secure Wyckham.

Ever your servant,
Rhys de Piaget

Sir Rhys's letter was set aside carefully. Another sealed missive from a different author was placed atop the table. It bore no stains from hands of anyone but the author and the one messenger. The wax seal was perfectly intact.

But the seal crumbled under the pressure of opening the letter, for such opening was done with unseemly haste. But that was of no import. No one would ever know how carelessly it had been loosened, for the missive would travel no further.

The letter was read.

And the reader began to chuckle. In a few places the words were actually amusing enough to cause him to throw back his head and laugh. If nothing else, the author of this less than pleasant letter had studied her equine anatomy and had used such studies to her best advantage. Very inventive. A pity Sir Rhys would never read the like.

Still smiling, he set aside the letter and reached for a clean sheet of parchment. He sharpened his quill, dipped it into the ink, and tapped the feather a time or two against his forehead to start his thoughts rolling in the appropriate direction. Inspiration flowed through him and he prepared to write.

My beloved Rhys,

How I long for you! How I have lain awake nights dreaming of you and your strong, manly arms about me! Hurry, my love, and free me from this prison. I think of no one but you, I desire no one but you. Bring all your gold with you that you might bribe everyone in England to have me . . .

Rollan paused, pursed his lips, and realized with a curse that perhaps that was less subtle than he might have wished. Gwen wouldn't have spoken of the gold. And he began to wonder also if she would have used the term "manly arms."

Damn. He would have to start this one afresh.

With a sigh, he crumpled up what had been under his quill and tossed it into the fire. He took another piece of parchment and began again, doing his damndest to keep in the forefront of his thoughts just how he'd worded all the other missives he'd sent in Gwen's name over the past three years. Imitating her fair hand had taken him a pair of months to perfect, but it was trying to second-guess how she would have gushed over the gallant Sir Rhys that had given him the most trouble.

He did his best, then reread his latest offering. Satisfied it oozed enough sentiment, he brushed sand over the ink to hasten the drying. He rolled the parchment, tipped his candle to drip upon the edges of the letter, and then pressed a perfect copy of Gwen's seal into the warm wax. He rose and left the inn's best chamber, found his messenger, and sent the lad on his way with a small bag of gold. The sum did not trouble him, as it came directly from Alain's coffers. Rollan smiled pleasantly. His brother was such a trusting soul.

Intercepting the correspondence from both parties had been difficult, what with Gwen having spent so much time with her mother at Segrave, but Rollan had considered that nothing but an added challenge. Where gold hadn't been convincing enough, Rollan had used other means. Every man had his weakness. Susceptibility to bribery, wenches . . . poison. The list, he had discovered, was very long indeed.

He returned to his chamber followed by a serving wench bearing a heaping tray of their best fare. It was, unsurprisingly, better than what he would have found at Ayre. That was Alain's fault. One did not bed the cook's daughter under the cook's nose without finding some sort of retribution in one's bread from that point on. Rollan shook his head as he sat back down at his table. Discretion had never been his brother's strongest characteristic.

Rollan flipped the girl a coin and she scurried from the chamber. He'd been momentarily tempted to have her stay, then discarded the idea. He wanted to savor the final chapter of his finest scheme and such savoring needed to be done alone.

By now surely Gwen's feelings for Rhys had cooled past the point of rekindling. After all, she hadn't heard from the man in almost three years. What would she do when he arrived at the keep with his heart in his hands?

Fell him with an arrow, if Rollan's luck was running true.

He leaned back in his chair and smiled. And there he would be, ready to step in and comfort her.

Ah, but life was indeed very good.

Summer

THE YEAR OF OUR LORD 1206

26

She needed a change.

Gwen stared at the linen under her needle and cursed as she realized she was going to have to unpick half of what she'd done that morn. The pattern had become fouled hours ago, but she hadn't noticed. It was something for her wedding bed, a casing for a goosefeather pillow worked with all manner of flowers and beautiful stitchery. She did not even feel any guilt over not stitching for Ayre's beds. She suspected that if she ever returned to her husband's keep, linens would be the least of her worries. She shuddered to think on how the filth had multiplied in the three years since she'd set foot inside the gates.

It was hard to believe so much time had passed. Three years of stitching. Three years of waiting for word from a certain man. Three years of going from worried to hurt to angry. Nay, not angry.

Bloody furious.

It wasn't as if she hadn't heard of Rhys's escapades. She had, in somewhat surprising detail and from the most unlikely of sources. Every time Rollan paused in his mischief-making to visit Segrave, he seemed to have a new adventure of Rhys's to relate to her. Where he came by his stories she didn't know, but she hardly doubted the truth of them. Rhys was certainly capable of holding scores of knights for ransom in tournaments all across the continent. He was certainly skilled enough to be sought after by any number of French lords to fight their battles for them. He was more than clever enough to spend ample time at the French court wooing whatever nobles found themselves there.

Or their ladies, if Rollan's gossip was to be believed.

What Gwen couldn't understand was why, with all his other skills, Rhys couldn't seem to find the ability to put ink on parchment and tell her of his successes himself. Was it because he was too busy on the battlefield? Or was he too busy in the bedchamber?

Or had he thought better of entangling himself further in the hopelessness of her situation?

She threw her stitchery into the basket at her feet and left her mother's solar, abandoning her mother and her ladies. A pity she couldn't have convinced Master Socrates and his granddaughter to come with her to Segrave. Perhaps she could have spent more time at their cooking fire and learned something of healing. Instead, they remained at Ayre and she was loitering at Segrave, wishing for a mighty change.

Not even her children were awake for her to amuse. Robin was asleep on her mother's bed, having exhausted himself thoroughly by a great deal of parrying that morn with Jared and Connor. The twins seemed convinced the lad couldn't help but profit from beginning his training so early. Gwen had been dubious until she had seen the great care the two men took of her son. Perhaps foisting the lad upon them so often while he was a babe so she could eavesdrop on Alain's conversations had been a boon. Surely there weren't two souls in the keep more willing and able to tend the boy than the Fitzgeralds.

She sighed and made her way down to the great hall. It was empty and that was tempting enough to entice her to stay and appreciate the quiet. But it wouldn't be enough. She needed the feeling of fresh air and perhaps a bit of sunshine.

The moment she opened the door, though, she could see something was amiss. Segrave was a calm place usually, filled with loyal knights who went about their business with a confident air. But now the inner bailey looked as if it were filled with an entire coopful of frantic hens.

Gwen ran merely because everyone else was running and she feared she might be trod asunder otherwise. She dodged mailed knights, half-mailed knights, and knights patting themselves frantically as if they wanted to assure themselves they were carrying all the weaponry they possibly could.

By the saints, were they under attack? She had wanted a change; she hadn't wanted a siege.

She wished desperately that she'd thought to dress more sensibly and perhaps belt her sword about her waist. Not even a knife resided up her sleeve. At least she had a pair of sewing needles in the purse at her belt. They would have to do.

She hastened to the barbican and ran up the steps. She burst out onto the small circular roof only to find Sir Montgomery leaning lazily against the parapet wall. He, at least, seemed none too worried about the goings-on.

"Well?" she demanded. "What by all the saints is the commotion about?"

Montgomery pointed off across the fields. Gwen followed his finger and squinted to make out what he evidently saw so clearly.

"Merchants," she guessed. "I can see the gleam of gems from here."

"What you see, my lady, is not the gleam of gems, 'tis the gleam of sunlight on armor."

She pursed her lips. "You imagine that."

"Think you?"

Indeed, she suspected he likely spoke the truth, for Montgomery had very keen sight. If he said he saw armor, then armor he had seen.

"Friend or foe?" she asked.

"That would be for you to decide."

She frowned at him. "I've no head for riddles today. Is it Alain?"

"He's still in London, or so I've heard."

"Bending the king's ear and bedding the queen's ladies, no doubt," Gwen muttered.

"No doubt."

Gwen shielded her eyes from the sun with her hand and continued to watch the progress of the small group that came over her fields.

"They've a fair amount of haste," she noted.

"Aye, I'd imagine they would."

Gwen wondered where she could stick him to do the most damage. Montgomery only held up his hands in surrender.

"I had nothing to do with this."

"With what?"

"With the arrival of these lads today."

"Which lads?" she demanded.

He blinked. "Why, Rhys's lads, of course."

She wouldn't have been more surprised if he'd announced Saint George had come down to sit at her table and show her his knobby knees himself.

"Impossible," she whispered.

"Nay, 'tis him in truth."

"You can see him?"

"Aye," Montgomery said, backing carefully out of her reach. He smiled cautiously. "I daresay you're pleased by this."

"Pleased?" she gasped. *"Pleased?"* She spun away from him and leaned over to jerk open the door to the stairwell. "Down with the portcullis!" she bellowed. "Raise the drawbridge!"

"My lady!" Montgomery gasped.

She turned and pointed her finger at him threateningly. "You be silent!" she commanded. She turned back to the stairwell. "Well?" she demanded of its interior. "I don't hear any gears grinding!"

All movement in the barbican seemed to have stopped. Slowly a head peeked around the curve of the stairs and wide eyes peered up at her from inside a helm.

"But, my lady," a guardsman ventured, "'tis Rhys de P—"

"I know bloody well who it is!" she exclaimed. "Now, do as I bid and secure the damned castle!"

The guardsman's mouth began to work silently. Gwen rolled her eyes. Was the man coming toward them going to have this affect on every blessed soul in the keep?

"I'll do it myself," she snapped, taking hold of her skirts and setting her foot to the top stair.

"Don't know that you'll make it in time," Montgomery said from behind her. "They've suddenly picked up their pace."

Gwen ran back to the wall and peered into the distance. Unfortunately, even she could see that the company was indeed coming toward the castle at a gallop.

"Oh, by the saints!" she exclaimed.

Montgomery had resumed his indifferent pose and was regarding her with an amused smile.

"No gate will keep him out," Montgomery said.

"This one will," she said confidently.

"Nor any drawbridge, I should think," Montgomery went on thoughtfully, as if he pondered some great truth. "I've heard tell he can scale an outer wall with his bare hands."

Gwen snorted the most derisive snort she could muster.

"And look how he's gone to the trouble of bringing his army with him." Montgomery smiled at her with wide, innocent eyes. "By the saints, lady, there must be something in this keep he wants very much. It would appear that he's come prepared to battle for it."

"What he wants he cannot have," she snapped, feeling the hideous sting of tears begin behind her eyes. "He's too bloody late. Three years too bloody late."

She slammed the door behind her and thumped down the stairs as quickly as she dared. She made her orders clear to the gate guards, then hurried across the courtyard to the keep. The bailey was still a veritable hive of frantic knightly activity. Perhaps the men scurried to make themselves presentable.

Or perhaps they were seeking a hiding place so Rhys didn't run them through should they find themselves in his path.

Gwen gained the great hall, then turned and pushed the huge door to. Well, almost to. There were several pairs of hands preventing her from doing so. Gwen looked around the door and glared at half a dozen of Segrave's more sturdy guardsmen.

"Stand aside," she commanded.

They were all squirming. One brave one spoke up.

"No sense in barring his way, my lady."

"You fool, you would leave me at his mercy?" she demanded. "By the saints, I am your lady!"

"And he is Rhys de Piaget," another said in awe, as if he spoke of Saint Michael himself.

"All the more reason to lock him out. Now, stand aside!"

They didn't even blink.

She contemplated snatching one of their knives to aid her cause, but heaven only knew how that act might turn itself upon her. She grasped the keys on her belt and with the most hefty of them poked the nearest man. It made little impression, so she searched in her purse for her finest sewing needle. Armed with a very sharp needle in one hand and a heavy key in the other, she poked and prodded and bullied until she had said handful of knights flinching out of her way and right out the front door. While they were still twitching from various small and irritating injuries, she slammed the door home and struggled to heave the beam into its brackets.

There was no heaving to be accomplished. Gwen surrendered without a fight and put her back against the door. She braced her feet on an unslippery portion of her floor and prepared herself for the worst.

"My lady," a plaintive male voice pleaded from without, "we beg you to cease—"

"Begone, you coward!" Gwen said in her most commanding tone. "I've no fear of that black-garbed demon. I'll hold the hall against him myself!"

There was no formal reply, but Gwen could hear them conferring amongst themselves in frantic whispers. They were no doubt racking their pitiful brains for some other foolish ploy to secure her cooperation.

"My lady," the spokesman began again, "if you would—"

"I will not! Off with you all!"

"But, my lady, de Piaget is the captain of your personal guard—"

"Not anymore!"

They seemed to chew that one over for a few more moments. Gwen adjusted her back more comfortably and gathered her strength for the task of holding the door firmly closed.

"Perhaps he has been detained these many seasons," one of the men offered.

"Aye, by other more important matters!" another put in enthusiastically.

"Shut up, you fool," yet another guardsman said frantically. "Think you that will please her ears?"

"Aye, 'tis not what a lady wishes to hear," another voice said, obviously delivering some sort of cuff with his words. He cleared his throat. "My lady," he said loudly, "I feel certain Sir Rhys was perhaps held captive, or found himself detained unjustly at the French court . . ."

Gwen shut out the rest of his list of excuses. They were just words and she had long ago decided that words held little weight in matters of the heart. She hadn't always believed so. Indeed, hadn't words been what she had clung to for months after he had left?

Wait for me.

Aye, wait a year. Or, knowing Rhys, perhaps a bit longer than a year until he'd plundered every coffer on the continent to his satisfaction. One year. Not three.

There were several very audible gulps on the other side of the wood. Gwen dug her slippered heels more firmly into the floor. A pity 'twas stone and not dirt. She might have had better control that way.

Absolute silence surrounded her. She fancied she might have heard the echo of horses' hooves, but she couldn't be sure. Her heart was hammering too loudly in her ears to know for certain.

The timid knock against the wood almost sent her into a swoon.

"What?" she demanded in her haughtiest tone, praying it sounded less breathless than her own ears attested.

"My lady," a quavering voice said, "would you be so kind as to open up the door?"

"Nay, I will not."

"But, my lady, he caught hold of the drawbridge 'afore it came all the way up, and flung himself over it—" a knight began.

"Then rolled himself under the portcullis 'afore it could slam home—" another interrupted.

"And he single-handedly raised the portcullis and lowered the drawbridge so as his army could bring itself in behind him!" yet another finished breathlessly, as if this final act indicated beyond doubt Rhys's godlike prowess.

"I couldn't care less!" she exclaimed.

"Oh," yet another knight moaned, sounding as if he thought himself already a dead man. "We beg you, my lady. We've families, my lady. Small children still in need of their sires. I myself have a wife with a belly fair stretched to bursting, and if I weren't to be there to see to the feeding of that child, and my ten others—"

"Oh, by the saints," Gwen grumbled. She would just open the door and bid Rhys be on his way. Coldly. As a great lady of the realm would. She would show no emotion, raise not her voice, shed not a tear. She would remain perfectly in control of herself and the encounter.

She turned and calmly opened the door. With a regal wave of her hand she sent her handful of kneeling knights to their feet and on their way down the steps to the courtyard. She lifted her chin and looked down at the sight that greeted her. And had she not been so in control of herself and her emotions, she might have gone down on her knees herself and begged for mercy.

By the saints, 'twas no wonder her household had been scrambling for cover.

Some thirty-odd, grim-faced warriors stared back at her. Each was clothed in black from head to toe. Each wore armor that had been mended and repaired countless times. Helmets bore scratches and dents; cloaks were patched and travel-stained; saddles were scarred and worn. And then there were the faces themselves: hard, inflexible, seasoned. Mercenaries, the lot of them. A rougher group of ragtag knights she had never seen before in her life.

A terrifying group of men, to be sure.

Oh, and then there was John, of course. He made their tally a score and eleven, but even though he sported black as the rest of them did, his fresh scrubbed face and idiotic grin set him apart from the rest. Gwen glared at her brother-in-law, then turned her attentions back to the more intimidating souls.

One man nudged his great black destrier forward with his knees. He dismounted and thirty hands went to the hilts of their swords. The man who had dismounted held up his hand in peace, and his group of devils relaxed immediately. In spite of herself, Gwen was impressed. It would take a strong man indeed to command such loyalty from men whose loyalty likely could only be bought.

The man put his foot on the bottom step and stopped. Steel gray eyes stared at her from within the battered helm. Then large hands came up, jerked off the helm, and pushed back the mail coif. Tousled black hair fell down around broad shoulders, shoulders that should have bloody well made an appearance long before now. Gray eyes twinkled merrily and a foolish grin graced lips that were the stuff of a giddy maid's dreams.

"Good morrow to you, *chérie*," he said, coming up the steps with a joyous bound and reaching up for her hand. "I came as soon as I could. I had expected to find you at Ayre. Why were you barring your mother's gates? Did you not recognize me?"

She'd promised herself she would not scream at him. She'd vowed she would not shed a tear in his presence. She'd been certain that she could dismiss the lout with a mere flick of her wrist and that would be enough to satisfy her.

But somehow, she found that remaining unmoved was the very last thing she wanted to do. She pulled her hand away from his. It was all she'd meant to do. Truly.

But somehow her fingers found themselves forming a fist.

And then her fist did what it had been longing to do for almost three years.

27

"Bloody hell, Gwen, why must you *always* do that!" Rhys exclaimed, stumbling back down the stairs. Several gasps accompanied his feet reuniting with the dirt of the courtyard. Rhys clutched his nose with both hands and looked around him.

Segrave's pitiful guardsmen who had been clustered about the great hall door all stood looking at him with their mouths agape. John was still atop his horse, gaping just as mightily. Rhys's army wore looks of astonishment, as well they should have. He had bested every last bloody one of them so thoroughly, they never dared gainsay him in anything. The sight of him being vanquished by a woman had likely scattered what wits remained in the company.

Then he looked to his right to find the Fitzgerald twins staring not at him but at Gwen with looks of supreme satisfaction, as if they'd taught her the bloody maneuver themselves. Rhys was faintly surprised to see them there. Evidently they had somehow, in the past pair of years, managed to get themselves to Segrave intact. He had the feeling, based on the throbbing of his nose, that he might have been better off if they'd remained at Ayre.

And then there was the sound of a chuckle.

Rhys looked to the source. It was Montgomery, who stood to Jared's right with a finger or two covering his lips and his eyes watering madly.

Rhys wondered if he had time to humiliate his friend in the lists before finding out what Gwen was about. Montgomery only smiled and held up his hands in surrender.

"I wasn't the one to bloody your nose," he said with another grin.

There was suddenly much murmuring amongst his mercenaries, and Rhys turned and swept them all with a glare. To a man, they clamped their lips shut and suddenly found other things to look at besides him.

Rhys turned back around to face his errant lady and gave her the same glare he'd just dealt his men.

"*This* is the greeting I receive?" he demanded. He mounted the steps. "After three long years of driving myself into the dust, sleeping on my sword, risking my life in war and tourney alike?" He dragged his sleeve across his bleeding nose. "*This* is my greeting?"

"Nay, this is," she said. She looked at him so coldly, he felt as if a chill winter wind had blown through him. "Go to hell," she said distinctly.

And with that, she turned and disappeared into the hall, slamming the door home behind her.

If it hadn't been that he had truly seen Gwen with his own eyes, he would have believed he had just stumbled into the wrong keep.

He stared at the closed door, feeling more bewildered than he had in the whole of his life. By the tone of her missives he'd been led to believe she was anxiously awaiting his arrival. He'd expected tears of joy. He'd expected smiles and looks of love. He *hadn't* expected a fist in his nose.

"At least she didn't have a blade at her disposal," Jared offered suddenly. "Would have done you more harm than a little bruise."

"Especially after what I've taught her," Connor added.

"You? What did *you* teach her? *I'm* the one who taught her to approach coyly and blink her eyelashes rapidly at her opponent while slipping a dagger under his ribs—"

"But *I* taught her to feign a stone in her shoe, then catch him under the chin as he bends to see—"

"And *I* taught her to examine the embroidery on her sleeve as she slips a blade from its sheath strapped to her arm, then to bury it suddenly in his gullet—"

"Aye, a womanly move if ever I encountered one, which is why *I* showed her how to distract an enemy with a great baring of her teeth in a ferocious smile whilst she pulls a sharp stabbing needle from her purse—"

Rhys tried to ignore just what Gwen had been taught in favor of looking the twins over for new scars. Jared had a nick or two on his forehead, a bright red slash down one forearm which appeared to be rather recent, and a bandage wrapped around his hand.

Connor was missing part of his left ear.

"Did you allow her to sharpen that blade?" Rhys demanded.

Connor and Jared stopped their discussion and looked at him, blinking.

"Well?" Rhys asked. "Did you?"

Connor pursed his lips. "Didn't see any harm in it."

"I'd say your ear might have a different view of it," Rhys said.

Connor folded his arms over his chest and frowned at Rhys. "Had to keep the child busy somehow. She's been powerful irritated for these past pair of years."

"And as usual," Jared added with a grumble, "'tis his fault. He never writes."

"I never write?" Rhys echoed. "Of course I write! I wrote! I wrote every bloody fortnight for almost three years and fair beggared myself to see the missives delivered!"

Connor and Jared both blinked several times, sure signs they were having trouble digesting what they'd just learned. Montgomery's mouth had fallen open in surprise.

Rhys frowned. Something foul was afoot.

He turned to his ragtag group of followers and dismissed them with a flick of his wrist. They'd been instructed to set up camp outside the walls and seek what sustenance they could in the village. Rhys waited until they'd gone, then tapped his foot until John had seen to the horses before he turned back to Montgomery.

"I have the feeling there are things we should discuss."

Montgomery continued to look at him in surprise. "You wrote?"

"And a bloody inconvenient thing it was, too. If you knew the places I've been in just the last year—"

"Gwen only received two letters," Montgomery said. "And those just in the pair of months right after you'd gone."

Rhys felt himself to be the one gaping now. "Just two missives?"

"Aye. If it hadn't been for the snatches of gossip we've heard over the past many months, we would have thought you dead."

"But I sent her scores of letters! And she responded!"

Montgomery shook his head. "I think perhaps you misread them. I'm surprised you didn't expect your reception, what with what she's been saying to you."

"*You* read the letters she sent to me?"

"She forced me to. Wanted to see a man's reaction, I suppose."

"But her letters were full of love!"

"Rhys, my friend, either you've lost all sense, or you weren't receiving what she sent to you."

Without another word, Rhys turned and strode off after John. Fortunately his squire seemed to be taking an inordinate amount of time to get to the front gates, likely because he would have rather stayed behind and eavesdropped, and Rhys was able to catch him easily enough. He rummaged about in his saddlebags, drew forth a bundle of missives, and turned to stomp back up to the keep. He entered the hall and stopped, realizing with a start that he had no idea where his lady might be hiding.

He'd been to Segrave, true, but that was many years ago. There was no one at the lord's table to ask where he might find his lady. The first servant he approached took one look at him and fled to parts unknown.

And then he heard the faint sound of cursing.

At least, he thought philosophically, there was something to be said for being out of favor. It certainly made finding the curser a great deal less difficult.

He followed the sound up the steps and down the passageway. He

stopped at a likely door and gathered his wits. Clutching the proof of his
devotion in hand, he pushed open the door.

"And if that pompous horse's arse thinks he can—"

Gwen stopped in mid-curse and glared at him. Rhys looked, about the
solar to see who else had been privy to the slander. A handful of Segrave's
ladies sat near the window, sewing industriously. Gwen was on her feet, and
Rhys suspected she had been pacing just as energetically. Joanna sat in the
largest and finest chair, holding a small child in her lap. Out of the corner
of his eye, Rhys noted that Robin was in the chamber as well, staging a
mock battle with wooden figures. A gift from the Fitzgeralds, no doubt.
Rhys had received his own set to enjoy, though he'd already been wielding
a small sword at the time he'd received them. He'd treasured them just the
same and had plotted battles just as enthusiastically as Robin seemed to be
doing. Rhys lifted an eyebrow in surprise. The boy had grown.

"We will have privacy," Joanna announced. "Ladies, if you will."

Sewing was cast into baskets and five women filed reluctantly past him.
Rhys scowled. They likely were regretting not being able to be privy to more
of the slander they'd no doubt been enjoying those few moments past.

"Close the door if you will, Sir Knight," Joanna said with a smile.

"Why?" Gwen said sharply. "I care not if the entire keep hears what I
have to say about him."

Rhys looked from one woman to the other and made a hasty decision as
to whom to approach first. He shut the door behind him, then walked across
the chamber to kneel at Joanna's feet. He was painfully aware of his travel-
stained clothing and the dust in his hair, but that couldn't be helped. He
gave her his best smile.

"Lady Joanna," he said, bowing his head. "God's blessings upon you and
upon yours. My grandsire and my mother send their greetings to you."

"How is Mary?" Joanna asked. "Still well-satisfied with her vocation?"

Rhys lifted his head and smiled at her. "Aye, my lady, she is."

"And you left your grandsire hale?"

"Stirring up as much mischief as he ever did. His only regret is that he
could not come with me to present himself to you in person. He says you
are the only sight worth making the journey for in the whole of England."

Joanna blushed and Rhys had to stop himself from smiling at the sight.
Beautiful and charming. 'Twas no wonder men made excuses to pass by
Segrave to tarry for a day or two. Joanna was indeed well worth the delay.
She had to have been very young when she bore Gwen, for she was still an
enormously beautiful woman and looked more of a sister to his lady than a
mother. Rhys couldn't help but agree with his grandfather's words, though
he himself would have made the journey merely for Gwen, no matter how
she looked.

And she looked passing furious now. He turned to her and tried a smile to see how things would go for him.

She glared at him in return.

Ah, well, perhaps more conversation with the lady of Segrave would allow his love to cool her temper. Rhys turned his attention back to Gwen's mother. It was then that he had a good look at the girl-child sitting upon Joanna's lap. And then he felt his mouth fall open of its own accord.

The child was Gwen's. She could be no other. Already she resembled her mother as greatly as her mother resembled the lady Joanna. No one could mark those aqua eyes as belonging to any other line of women.

"Who is this?" he asked in a strangled voice.

"She's mine," Gwen snarled.

"Now, Gwen," Joanna said gently, "there's no need for that tone."

"No need?" Gwen echoed. She pointed at Rhys with a shaking finger. "He leaves me alone for *three* years, then comes bounding up my steps as if he had every expectation of me falling right into his arms!"

Joanna sighed. "You see, Sir Rhys, it has been a bit of time since Gwen received—"

"*Three years!*" Gwen bellowed.

"Three years," Joanna conceded, "since Gwen has had word from you. She was understandably worried."

"I wasn't worried," Gwen corrected. "I was bloody furious!"

Joanna sat back, embracing Gwen's daughter in her arms, and shrugged. She obviously had made her efforts toward peace and was now turning the matter over to him.

He sighed, said a quick prayer, and rose to his feet. Maybe if he blurted the truth out as quickly as possible, Gwen would actually hear him and forgive him before she cursed him any further.

Rhys held out the clutch of letters like an offering. "These are your letters to me. I was led to believe by them that you would be happy to see me."

"Then you didn't read very well what I wrote you," she returned. "And I certainly have none of your letters to me to show for the past three years."

"I wrote you every fortnight."

"Then you didn't send them."

"But I did!"

"Too much of whatever you were doing for the past three years has obviously addled your wits, Sir Knight, for I received nothing."

Rhys disentangled Gwen's last letter to him and opened it. " 'Beloved, I await your return anxiously,' " he read. " 'I am pleased to know you will be returning to England in May. My arms ache to hold you once again." He looked at her. "Your words."

Gwen frowned. "I didn't write that. In my last epistle I spent a great amount of ink likening you to a horse's arse. And that was the pleasant part."

Rhys pulled forth another letter and read to her from it. He stopped at the look of confusion on her face. "Not this one, either?" he asked.

She shook her head. "Nay."

Rhys looked down at his fistful of missives. "I believe, my lady," he said, feeling a chill run through him, "that we have been deceived."

"But my messengers were trusted men." Gwen looked at her mother. "Were they not?"

Her mother looked as shocked as Rhys himself felt. "Aye, so I thought," she said slowly. "But both sides of the correspondence were snatched. Who could manage such a thing?"

Rhys met Gwen's eyes.

"Rollan," they said together. There was no doubt in his mind and obviously no doubt in Gwen's.

"Devious," Joanna said quietly. "Aye, that I suspected of him. But to purposely set out to destroy your affection . . ."

"It would not surprise me," Rhys said grimly.

"But how can you be sure?" Joanna asked. "It could have been anyone."

"Who else would care?" Gwen asked. "Especially since we know what his true intentions are."

Rhys looked at her. "What intentions?"

"It was shortly after you departed for France that I overheard Rollan conversing with himself at the ale kegs," Gwen said. "It would seem that his plan is to become lord of Ayre with me as his bride."

"A modest plan," Rhys said dryly.

"Aye," she agreed, "but an unpleasant one. I listened to him consider the merits of pushing everyone in his way down the stairs. I have no idea what he planned to do with you, but I'm certain 'twas equally as dire. Perhaps he planned to become both lord of Ayre and Wyckham."

Lord of Wyckham. Rhys had become that when he reached a score and six, but somehow it had never seemed to mean anything to him—likely because there was a bloody army on his land, and it wasn't as if he'd been able to take possession of it.

"How lovely that I am returned to oblige Rollan in the carrying out of his plans," Rhys said with a snort. He looked at her with a frown. "You could have written me to tell me of what you'd learned."

"I did," she said shortly.

Rhys sighed. He had no answer for that, and no way to change what had transpired.

"Let us hope this is the extent of his treachery," Joanna interrupted. "He hasn't seemed bent on destruction while he has visited me."

"He also had the Fitzgeralds to face at every turn," Gwen said. "I doubt I would have tried anything with them about, either."

Rhys looked at Gwen and frowned. "I wish I had known."

"Would you have returned?"

"Aye," he said briskly. "I would have."

"And lost your time to tourney," Gwen said with a sigh. She looked at him. "At least I assume you were spending your time tourneying."

"Tourneying, hiring out my sword to whoever would pay the most, warring." He shrugged. "Whatever it took."

"And you have earned what you need?"

He looked at her and attempted a smile. "Aye, and I can only hope there is still a need for what I've earned."

She only returned his stare, but he thought he might have seen a softening begin around her mouth.

"I would have come home sooner," he said again, "had I known what Rollan was plotting."

She shook her head. "That wouldn't have served us, Rhys, and no harm came of all Rollan's chattering to himself. Well," she added with a scowl, "no harm save three years of simmering irritation toward you."

"Simmering?" Joanna echoed with a laugh.

Rhys thought it best to distract Gwen from thinking any more on how angry she'd been. At least she appeared to have cooled her temper a bit and was thinking kindly of him. "I did write you," he said, thinking that such a thing could not be said enough times. "And I spent a great deal of gold seeing the missives sent," he added, hoping that would impress her.

"Not gold well spent," Gwen noted.

"Well, nay, it wasn't." He shook his head. "I thought you were perfectly content to wait for me."

"And I thought you were bedding every noblewoman in Phillip's household."

He blinked. "Surely you jest."

"You are the stuff of legends, Sir Rhys. In the bedchamber and on the battlefield."

"You can rest assured half of those rumors are false."

"Which ones?" she grumbled. "Tales of your swordly prowess?"

"Oh, nay," he said, feeling as if he might now have a chance to at least apologize for the fact that he had overpaid his messengers, "those were no doubt greatly underexaggerated. My swordplay is much improved."

She scowled at him. "And your other weapon?"

"Dusty from disuse, no doubt."

Gwen's mother laughed out loud. She rose with the girl in her arms. "I will see to some refreshment for our poor, neglected Sir Rhys. Take the babe, Gwen."

Rhys watched Gwen accept the child and marveled again how much of a resemblance there was even at such a young age. Gwen held the child close and said nothing until her mother had left the solar.

"This is Amanda," Gwen said, lifting her chin as if she dared him to say aught.

"I see," he said, nodding. "A beautiful child."

"She has two years," Gwen added. "And three months. Alain was counting on another lad. He hasn't much use for a girl."

"Ah," he said, merely because he could say nothing else.

"I would not trade her," Gwen said fiercely.

Rhys took a few steps toward her, reached out, and trailed a dirty finger down Amanda's cheek. "Of course you wouldn't. Alain is very shortsighted not to prize her."

He smiled at Amanda and received a sudden smile in return that smote him straight in the heart. Then, to his surprise, Amanda stretched out her arms to him. He took her, ignoring the tightness in his chest and the crumpling of letters in his hand.

This child could have been his, had things been different.

"And Robin you already know," Gwen said, beckoning to her son. "Robin, give greeting to Sir Rhys. He's been off in France these past years, fighting bravely against many knights."

Rhys looked down into huge gray eyes which found home in a solemn little face.

"Robin, a greeting," Gwen prompted.

"Good morrow, Sir Knight," Robin said, ducking his head.

Rhys looked at Gwen. "He resembles you less than Amanda does."

"He has my father's features," Gwen said. "And his eyes." She clutched Robin closer. "I only have him until he's seven," she blurted out. "And then his sire intends to send him to foster at court."

Rhys shook his head slowly. He hardly dared speak in front of the boy, but he vowed then that Robin would be in King John's clutches over his own dead body.

"And he is now almost five years?" Rhys asked.

Gwen nodded, her eyes suddenly swimming with tears.

"Two years is a very long time, lady," Rhys said softly. "And much can happen in that time."

"Men always send their sons off to foster."

"Not all men," Rhys assured her. "If I had a son, I daresay I would keep him home until he had at least twelve summers. 'Tis only then that a lad truly appreciates the adventure of making his own way. I daresay until that time he is better served by learning his craft under his father's hand. Wouldn't you agree?"

She held Robin even more closely to her. "Can it be done?"

He smiled. "I have several chests of gold in France which would agree that it could."

And then before he knew what would come next, Gwen had put her arm around his waist and buried her face against his chest. Rhys had barely the wits about him to put his free arm about her and draw her close before she burst into tears.

Well, a drenching was better than a sticking. Or another fist in his nose.

Or so he thought until Amanda saw her mother's violent weeping and set up a howl of her own. And then Robin began to use quite effective little fists to pummel him about his hips and waist.

"Oof," Rhys gasped as Robin made rather forceful contact with a tender part of his frame. "By the saints, lad, I'm friend, not foe!"

"You've made Mama weep," Robin said with marked disapproval. He did, however, leave off with his assault.

"Well, she bloodied my nose," Rhys offered.

Robin looked up and seemed to be weighing the sight of that against the sight of his sobbing mother.

"I think she's weeping because she's happy to see me," Rhys added, wondering what sort of logic would sway a five-year-old child.

Robin frowned. "How can that be when she struck you?"

"Ah, well, there was something of a misunderstanding between us, lad," Rhys said. "She was telling me of her displeasure, I'd say. I think she's forgiven me now."

Robin appeared to be taking this into account. Rhys had the most ridiculous urge to squirm. By the saints, this lad was too old for his modest years. Perhaps he'd seen more of Alain's mistreatment of his mother than was good for young eyes. His gaze was far too assessing.

"You aren't my sire," Robin announced.

"Nay, lad, I'm not," Rhys said, wishing mightily that he were. "But I was at one time the captain of your mother's guard."

Robin nodded thoughtfully. "The Fitzgerald brothers told me tales of you," he said finally.

"Good ones?"

"Aye," Robin said, starting to look just a bit more interested. "They said you've a ruby the size of an egg in the hilt of your sword."

"I do."

"And that you've taken so many knights for ransom that you've lost count of the gold you've earned."

Lost count? Rhys smiled to himself. Saints, but he was intimately acquainted with every piece of gold he'd laid hands on the past three years.

"I've had my share of successes," he conceded modestly.

"All right, then," Robin said, seemingly approving of Rhys's person.

Gwen drew away, dragging her sleeve across her face.

"Sir Rhys is a very dear friend," she said, smoothing her hand over her son's hair, "and I've missed him sorely these past years."

Robin looked slightly confused. "But you called him 'unfeeling oaf' and 'blighted whoreso—"

"Robin!"

The insults had rolled off Robin's tongue so easily, Rhys could only assume he'd heard them enough to have mastered them. Gwen turned a rather alarming shade of red and put her hand over her son's mouth.

"Aye, lad, I called him those and more," she said. "But there was this misunderstanding—"

"And you bloodied his nose for it," Robin said, escaping her silencing fingers. "But all is well now?"

"Aye, son."

Rhys felt the full impact of Robin's interest then.

"You'll show me your sword?" Robin asked. "And teach me swordplay? I have a wooden sword, you know. I give the twins splinters all the time with it."

"Better that than wounds that need to be sewn," Rhys said, smiling down at the boy before turning to his mother. "Connor seems to be missing pieces of himself."

"Very distractable, that one," Gwen said with a slight frown. "Set him to boasting of his skill and his guard slips completely."

Rhys found his sleeve being tugged on and looked down at the tugger.

"A lesson in swordplay?" Robin asked. "Now?"

"Grandmother has prepared something for him to eat," Gwen said. "And then he will likely want a rest. He's no doubt done many heroic deeds on his way back from France and is weary from them. Perhaps tomorrow."

"Tomorrow." Robin sighed, as if the time required to reach such a place was simply too great for him to fathom.

"Perhaps a short lesson this afternoon," Rhys said. "And then your mother and I have much to discuss."

He disentangled his clutch of letters from Amanda's hands, not exactly sure how they'd gotten there to begin with and thereupon realizing that children took more watching than he'd suspected, and handed them to Gwen.

"You might find these interesting," he said.

"I daresay I would," she agreed. "I only wish I had like number to show you."

He looked down at her and wished greatly that a pair of gray eyes would find something more appealing to observe than him so he could kiss Gwen properly. Painfully conscious of Robin's regard, he could only smile grimly at Gwen.

"I did write."

"I believe you."

Rhys wanted more than life and breath to draw her into his arms and never let her from them again. He had spent three years aching for her, dreaming of her, contenting himself with the thought that she would in the end be his. Every moment apart, every moment of thinking of her as Alain's wife would only add to the sweetness of her being his when he could manage it. He was tired of warring, tired of racking his pitiful brain for ways to see her freed from her marriage to Ayre, to see that she took her son with her, to appease whatever clergy and royalty necessary to see his ends accomplished.

And now he stood a hand's breadth from the creature he'd dreamed about every waking moment for three years, and all he could do was hold on to her daughter and submit to her son's investigation of his person for possible warriorly accoutrements.

And look at the woman he loved more than life itself.

"Food now?" Robin prompted.

Rhys felt Robin slip his hand into his and Amanda's arm tighten around his neck.

"Aye," he managed, "food first. Then speech."

And he vowed in that moment to never let these three go.

No matter the cost.

28

Gwen wondered, as she chewed thoughtfully on a bit of roasted fowl, how it was that she could be so angry with a man one moment, then have such a rush of friendly feelings for him not a pair of hours later.

Such, she supposed, was the course of true love.

They sat together at her mother's table, sharing a trencher and a goblet. It had been her mother's doing to seat them thusly, and Gwen wasn't sure if she should be grateful for it or not. She'd wanted time to think on what she'd learned that afternoon. The thought of Rollan having possibly read all her missives left her torn between wanting to blush and wanting to murder him. Along with anger and embarrassment, she felt a chill. That Rollan should go to such great lengths to cool her feelings for Rhys only spoke of his determination and cunning. She had underestimated him.

How could she have been so blind? Rollan had visited Segrave many times over the past three years, and though Gwen had made certain never to be without a goodly portion of her mother's household nearby, she had never once suspected that he might be doing something so calculating. She had been waiting for him to push someone down the stairs, and he had instead been reading her letters. Always he came from a direction she didn't suspect. She would do well to be more on her guard. Perhaps with her and Rhys both watching him, he would succeed in making no more mischief.

"Shall we retire again to my solar?" Joanna asked, leaning in front of Rhys to look at Gwen. "We would be more comfortable resting there."

Gwen looked at Rhys. "Does that suit, or would you rather have speech with my guard?"

"To find out just how it is you damaged the Fitzgeralds so thoroughly?" he asked with a smile. He threw a look at the lower table, where Montgomery and the twins sat with John, indulging the young man by listening politely to his stirring retelling of his adventures. Either that, or John was retelling Rhys's glorious adventures. He shook his head. "I'm better off not knowing. And I would imagine that John would be slow to forgive me for robbing him of his audience."

Gwen nodded to her mother. "Aye, Mother. We'll be along presently."

Rhys looked at Gwen as her mother rose and made her way to the stairs. "Her will is still followed here?"

"Aye, my father commanded it."

"And Alain agreed to this?"

"We have, if you can stomach it, Rollan to thank for it," Gwen admitted grudgingly. "Whatever else his faults, he knows how to appreciate a fine meal. I imagine he feared Alain would offend the cook somehow, so he managed to convince his brother that Segrave was better left to itself."

"Kind of him."

"My mother had a hand in it as well, of course. Do you not remember the first time you and I came to Segrave after the wedding?"

Rhys shook his head, a small smile on his face. "I remember nothing save you, lady. I paid no heed to my surroundings."

She couldn't help but feel the pleasure of the compliment, though she would be the first to admit she remembered little of the visit as well. It had been a brief stay and Gwen had been mostly concerned with wondering how she might avoid Alain's bed as often as possible.

"Then you may not have noticed," she said, passing on those less than pleasant memories, "but my mother hid her comeliest serving wenches in the village and installed a stable lad as head cook."

Rhys laughed. "She didn't."

"Aye, she did. Even Alain noticed there was something amiss with the fare. I daresay it wasn't hard for Rollan to convince him that Segrave as a residence was not a desirable place. Collecting the rents is something, of course, that he hasn't failed to do, but visiting seemingly doesn't appeal."

Rhys looked at her thoughtfully. "Then Alain has not troubled you in recent months?"

"I haven't seen him since Amanda was conceived."

"A blessing, to be sure."

"He fears my mother, I think," Gwen said. "And, of course, he has no interest in a daughter. He sends Rollan to investigate and bring him back tidings." She frowned. "I have been a fool not to watch that one more closely. Had I known what he was about, I would have added something foul to his wine."

"Better to leave him trusting," Rhys said. "At least that way the enemy is known."

Gwen sighed and rose with him. "Let us speak of something else for the night. I have no more stomach for thinking on Rollan's schemes."

As her mother had seen to putting the children to bed, Gwen had nothing else to do but lead Rhys to the solar. She was acutely aware of him following her up the steps and down the passageway. She'd grown far too accustomed to the light step of her mother's feet, or the ever rushing patter of Robin's as he ran here and there. Rhys's solid footfall behind her was a pleasing sound indeed.

It was but moments later that she found herself sitting next to her love in her mother's solar. Perhaps she should have occupied her hands with some sort of stitchery, but the saints only knew what sorts of abnormal appendages would result on any kind of animal she embroidered.

"So, Sir Rhys," Joanna said, obviously feeling that stitchery was not beyond her, for she had intricate work under her needle, "why do you not tell us a tale or two of your travels. Since, of course," she added with a small smile directed her daughter's way, "we've had no word of them from you directly."

Gwen grunted in agreement, but said nothing. She'd said too much as it was. Rhys's ears were likely still burning from her curses.

"Well," Rhys said, settling back in his chair with a cup of wine, "I could perhaps begin with the tourney at Toulouse."

Gwen hardly cared where he began, for where he had ended was in the chair next to her. She leaned back and watched him as he spoke of his travels and felt for the first time in years that she might actually enjoy the evening, surrounded by those she loved.

Three years of warring had changed him—that and bearing the weight of almost a score and ten years on his shoulders. Gone were any of the soft lines of his youth. In his face were signs of the sorrows he had carried, but they showed mostly in the creases between his brow when he frowned while remembering this detail or that.

He looked at her now and then as he spun his tale and then he would smile. Gwen memorized the way the skin about his eyes crinkled and how the little dimple in his cheek appeared as if to celebrate his merriment. And the more she looked at him, the more she thought her heart just might break.

Ah, that he could be hers in truth.

"Gwen?"

She looked at him and couldn't stop the words from leaving her mouth. "I love you," she said.

He blinked, then another sunny smile burst forth from him. "By the saints, *chérie*," he said, reaching for her hand, "I think I should go away more often—"

"Do not," Joanna interrupted with a laugh, "lest you force me to take drastic measures. You did not have to endure her rampages for the past three years."

"I did not rampage," Gwen said archly. "I did but give vent to a bout or two of displeasure."

Joanna snorted delicately. "I cannot even speak of it, for the very thought gives me pains in my head yet again. Gwen, love, why do you not make your nightly rounds. Perhaps Sir Rhys would accompany you tonight."

Rhys looked at her and lifted an eyebrow in question. Gwen shrugged.

"I walk upon the roof to see that all is well." *And to see if anyone comes toward the keep in the evening when he might not be marked.* She should have known Rhys would come in the middle of the day, and anyone who thought to deny him entrance be damned.

His smile said that he guessed a bit of what she hadn't admitted. "You go alone?" he asked.

"Montgomery comes now and then. Usually the twins accompany me. It gives them a chance to intimidate my mother's guardsmen yet another time before retiring."

"I'm certain that pleases them," Rhys said dryly. He stood and held out his hand to her. "If I might have the pleasure this evening?"

"Don't be long, children," Joanna said as they walked out into the passageway.

"Aye, Mother," Gwen said, pulling the door shut behind her. "I've never heard that before."

"Perhaps she fears I will ravish you upon the roof."

Gwen looked at him. "Will you?"

"What else are battlements for," he asked with a smile, "if not for the ravishment of future brides?"

Just one night, Gwen thought. *Let me believe 'tis truly possible for just one night*. The roof limited greatly what sorts of things they could engage in, which was likely just as well, but at least she might feel his arms about her and imagine that she was to be his.

He took her hand and drew her along behind him up the steps. Gwen did not even make the pretense of walking the walls. She stopped in her accustomed spot and looked out over her father's land. It was Alain's land now, but she rarely thought of it that way.

"Do you always look south?"

Gwen put her hands on the rock and let the chill of it seep into her fingers. "Aye."

"Any particular reason?"

She looked up at him. "I was looking for someone to come."

He covered her hand with his own and looked down at her seriously. "There was no purpose in earning only a fraction of what I needed."

"Three years is a very long time, Rhys."

"We will have the rest of our lives together."

"And if something should happen to you, and we have no future together?"

"I am invincible, or hadn't you heard?"

"This is not a matter for jesting—"

He put a finger to her lips and shook his head. "I will make light of it no more, Gwen. But I will not think on giving you up before I can even call you mine. Trust me, my love. We will have many happy years together, and then what we have endured will seem but a small moment. Do not the past three years seem but a blink of an eye now we are together yet again?"

"Nay," she said shortly, "they do not."

He only laughed softly. "Ah, sweet Gwen, but I have missed having someone about me who is unwilling to humor me."

"I take it you have your army appropriately cowed, then?"

"Aye, they fear my temper."

"Which I do not, of course."

He reached out and tucked her hair behind her ear. "Is there nothing you fear, lady?"

"Losing my children," she said promptly. "And," she added, almost unwilling to say it lest it somehow come back to haunt her, "losing you. Or, even worse, never having you at all."

"I will see to it, Gwen."

How, she did not know, and the thought of it was enough to sour her humor. It was impossible. Even if she managed to free herself, how would she keep her children? Even Eleanor of Aquitaine, as powerful as she was, had been obliged to leave her children behind with her first husband. Gwen could not bear the thought of it.

"I don't see how," she said with a sigh.

"Then don't look. At least not now."

"But . . ."

He shook his head, then reached out and put his hands on her shoulders. Gwen immediately conceded the battle, deciding that speech was unnecessary, yea even undesirable, at the moment. Let the future see to itself—

Rhys bent his head and very softly, very tenderly kissed her on the mouth.

And the touch of his lips upon hers sent shivers down through her to the soles of her feet. By the saints, she had forgotten what a mere kiss from the man could do to her.

He wasn't wearing mail. She discovered that almost immediately, for he enveloped her in a formidable embrace from which she suspected there was very little hope of escape. Not that escape was uppermost on her mind. Never mind that 'twas passing chilly outside, or that her mother's guardsmen were likely all gawking at her—

"Gwen."

Gwen blinked and looked up at him. "Aye?"

"Stop indulging in so many thoughts."

"How do you know I'm thinking—"

"Your brow furrows. 'Tis quite attractive, of course, but leaves me wondering how well you are concentrating upon my kisses."

She sighed and closed her eyes. Let the morrow see to itself. Tonight was perhaps the only night for some time to come that she would have Rhys to herself, and she would not ruin that time.

And so she gave herself over to the sweetness of his kiss. She sighed at the pleasure of having his hands sliding softly over her hair. And when he cradled her close, merely running the flat of his hand over her back time and time again, she closed her eyes and rested her cheek against his chest. Ah, that such comfort could be hers in truth.

"I will see to it," he murmured.

Gwen sighed, too content to argue with him. She concentrated instead on how it felt to be in Rhys's arms again. She listened to his breathing, felt the warmth of his body seep through his clothes and warm her, and heard the echo of his voice rumbling deep in his chest. And she realized in that instant how much more she had missed him than she'd been willing to admit. Even though they had not shared such embraces while he was her captain, at least he had been ever near her.

Three years had been a very long time.

"Would you care to hear an item of interest?"

"Hmmm," she agreed, settling more comfortably into his arms. "As you will."

"It would seem," he said conversationally, as if he discussed nothing more important than what they stood to eat for supper the next day, "that Lord Ayre is out of favor with our good Lackland."

"Is he?" Gwen asked. She almost smiled. Standing there as she was in Rhys's arms, feeling as if it were the one place she truly belonged, it was easy enough to speak of Alain. Where she was at present, he could not touch her.

"Aye, he is," Rhys continued, as easily as if he somehow shared the same feeling. "It would seem he made the grave mistake of deflowering the king's cook's daughter."

"Poor girl."

"And, as usual, he was caught while at his work."

"How inconvenient for him," she remarked. "I would say he spends far too much time in the kitchens."

"I couldn't agree more. Unfortunately, this is the cause of John's understandable irritation. Having caught wind of the turn of events while I was still in France, I managed to procure His Majesty a fine new creator of delicacies, so I am, oddly enough, in the king's good graces."

That was enough to make her look at him. "How in the world did you manage to unearth that tidbit?"

He smiled modestly. "I can take no credit for it. My grandfather had been talking with an old friend who had quite recently been in London listening to the king rage on. My grandsire met me at the dock with a new cook saddled and prepared to venture forth from France."

"And this man was willing to come to England?"

"My grandsire can be very persuasive when he wants to be."

Gwen felt her contentment begin to slip away. She rested her head against Rhys's chest and looked out over the fields. "Even if you manage to convince John, Rhys, how can you hope to convince any clergy? I have two children I will likely lose."

"Nay, love, you will not. If they will have me, I will claim them as well."

"They would have you, but how will you convince Alain to give them up? He will want his heir. He cares nothing for Robin save that."

"He can sire another on Rachel. Or acknowledge one of the handful of bastards he has scampering about here and there."

She stiffened, then pulled away. "He has bastards?"

"Aye, Gwen," Rhys said patiently, "he has bastards. Robin would likely be better off as my son, for he will have no one crowding his hall to fight him for his inheritance."

"You uncover too many things," she said slowly. "I think I would rather know less about Alain's activities."

"'Tis all done to aid me in my goal, which is to have you. Now, come," he said, bending to kiss one, then the other ear that seemed to have escaped with his help from their covering of hair, "and let us descend before you grow chilled. I don't wish to ride off to Wyckham knowing I've left you here ailing from the ague."

"Ride off to Wyckham," she repeated. "Without me?"

"Well—"

"You will *not*," she said distinctly, "leave me behind again. The saints only know when I'd see you next."

"Gwen—"

"Nay," she said. So much for any more kissing. For all she knew, Rhys intended to distract her so thoroughly that she would forget what he was about until he'd already ridden out from her gates. She took his hand and pulled him toward the tower door. "I'll come along."

"It would mean stopping at Fenwyck."

She stopped and considered. Passing any time whatsoever with Geoffrey of Fenwyck was enough to make her rethink her choice. He would look at her ears. She'd only seen him a handful of times since her imprisonment in the piggery, and each time he had stared most rudely and thereafter favored her with a smirk she couldn't help but interpret as slanderous.

She had always returned the favor by looking quite pointedly at the gap in his front teeth.

But her alternative was watching Rhys ride off again. Humiliation, or letting her love out of her sights. Saints, but it was a difficult choice.

She turned toward the door, her decision made. "We'll start off tomorrow that the journey might end that much sooner," she said grimly. "I'll bear it."

He laughed softly from behind her. "I'll need a day or two to rest and prepare the men, Gwen."

"A day or two?" The thought of putting off the torture even that long was tremendously unappealing.

"We're heading toward possible war."

"With Fenwyck?" she asked darkly.

He tugged on her hair gently, then reached over her and pulled the door to the stairwell open. "Of course not. A mere glare from you will subdue Geoffrey. I am thinking on Wyckham."

"Then perhaps we should talk a bit and enjoy some quiet, what with both of us heading into battle."

"My thought exactly," he said dryly.

"Besides," she said, starting down the steps, "'twill give me time to sharpen my sword."

She only managed to reach the bottom of the stairs before Rhys pulled her into his arms again. She shook her head.

"No more."

"Aye, more," he said, smiling.

"You think to distract me—"

"Actually, I was just thinking about kissing you, but if distraction happens as well . . ."

Let him try, Gwen thought to herself as his mouth came down on hers. And then as he kissed her, she suspected that he might very well succeed, at least for that night. There was no harm in that, she supposed. The morrow would bring a return to her concentration, and then she would prepare for their journey north. A new wimple would perhaps distract Geoffrey from his observation of her e—

"Gwen," Rhys said in exasperation.

She blinked at him. "What?"

He took her by the shoulders and turned her away from him. "Do all your thinking now, lady, for I vow I will not share you once we are wed!"

He sounded as if he expected it to come about. Gwen nodded and let him direct her down the passageway.

If he believed it so fully, how could she do anything else?

29

Rhys walked along the dusty path into the village, praying he wasn't being foolhardy in taking Gwen from the keep with only Montgomery, the twins, and John as guardsmen. It wasn't as if he was expecting any mischief, but then again he had no idea of Rollan's whereabouts. Joanna seemed to think Alain's brother to be harmless, but Rhys knew better. That he should voice his schemes aloud, even if he thought it was in private, indicated to Rhys how certain Rollan was that he would find success. It was enough to make a man look behind him before he considered descending any steps.

"—Don't you agree, Sir Rhys?"

Rhys looked down at the small boy who walked next to him. "Forgive me, lad, I didn't hear you."

"An arrow through the eye," Robin said patiently. "That would fell a dragon, wouldn't it?"

"Well," Rhys said slowly, "I suppose an arrow through the eye would be as effective as anything, but it doesn't seem very sporting, does it?"

"But the fire," argued Robin. "The beastie'd burn my fingers should I try to get closer than that!"

"And I suppose chain mail would be little protection against such heat," Rhys agreed solemnly. "Passing warm, I should think."

"Two-fisted thrust through the underbelly," a voice grumbled from behind them.

"Nay, brother, better a slash made to lop off the head. Solves the problem of fire from the nostrils."

"Dodge *under* the fire," Connor insisted, "and come up under the belly."

"And be squashed in the process?" Jared demanded. "Have you lost all sense?"

Rhys heard Gwen sigh lightly next to him, and he wondered if she'd been privy to these kinds of arguments for the past three years. He met her gaze and saw the amusement lurking there.

"A day of leisure?" she asked dryly.

"Matters of war, Mama," Robin said importantly, "are always a ripe subject for glorious discussion."

Rhys looked over his shoulder at Connor. "Did you teach him that?"

"Nay, *I* did," Jared said proudly. "A quick study, that young one. As eager as you were."

"Aye," Connor agreed, "he'll make a fine warrior, he will."

"So," Robin continued, "I think it must be an arrow through the eye." He looked back at Connor and Jared, seemingly to check to see if they approved of his line of thinking. "'Tis the only way."

"Thinks for himself," Jared noted.

"*I* taught him that," Connor boasted.

Rhys began to wonder if he'd brought too many guardsmen with him that day. John would have likely been enough. At least he was watching his surroundings instead of chattering them to death.

Gwen cleared her throat pointedly. "And what of the maiden? Shouldn't you be giving consideration to her rescue?"

"She *is* the point of the entire exercise," Montgomery agreed from where he walked in front of Rhys. "Not that you'd know it in this company."

Gwen snorted and looked up at Rhys. "This is the company you left me with. You can imagine the reaction I've had to whatever lays I've struggled to compose."

"Not nearly enough blood," Connor complained, "though 'twasn't for a lack of my trying to aid her."

"Her accounts of battle have improved, though," Jared conceded. "That was *my* doing."

"The dragon, Sir Rhys," Robin said, tugging on Rhys's hand. "*He* is the interesting part."

"The saints preserve me from the child," Gwen muttered under her breath. "And to think I spent all these years spinning him tales of bold rescues. I had no idea what part he was listening to the more!"

Rhys listened to the confusion going on around him and found the sound of it sweet indeed. The feeling of a small boy's hand in his and the sight of his lady's daughter riding in Montgomery's arms was delightful as well.

But the most wonderful thing of all was knowing that his love was by his side. Every time he caught sight of her, he smiled. Every time he heard her laugh, he wanted to laugh as well. And every time he thought about what it would take to have her as his own, he wanted to drop to his knees and pray for success. Gold he had. Determination he possessed in abundance. But a plan that would guarantee victory?

It was the one thing he needed, and the one thing he lacked.

"You, there! Cease!"

Montgomery's shout startled Rhys from his uncomfortable thoughts. And almost before Rhys could think about what he needed to do, he found himself leaping ahead of the company. He caught the strap before it came down another time.

A young boy lay in the dirt at Rhys's feet, cowering. A very large man held the leather strap in his beefy fist. He jerked it free of Rhys's hand and glared at him.

"'E's mine," a man snarled, "and I'll beat 'im as I see fit."

Rhys pursed his lips in disgust. "And what could a child of such tender years have done to merit this?"

"Didn't work 'ard enough," the man said. "There's no place for a sluggard at my board."

Rhys looked at the man, noted the substantial arms and broad chest. A blacksmith, perhaps, or a mason. Not a pleasant soul, if the coldness in his eyes was any indication. Certainly not a man Rhys would want anywhere near any of his children.

Rhys ignored the man's growling and reached down to pick up the boy where he had fallen in the dirt. There was blood on the back of his ragged tunic. Rhys pulled the boy behind him.

"How much do you want for him?" he asked bluntly.

The man's eyes took on a calculating look. "More than you're willing to pay, likely."

"Think you?" Rhys asked. "Shall it be a piece of gold or two, or would you rather barter with my fists?"

"Or my sword!" John interjected, bouncing on the balls of his feet as if he itched to show his prowess.

"Or his sword," Rhys agreed, folding his arms over his chest.

"Take more than a piece of gold to replace the labor I'll lose," the man said. "Not that I ever wanted him anyway, but 'e's a strong lad."

"For a sluggard," Rhys agreed dryly.

"What was I to do with 'im?" the man demanded. "Ayre's young lord came through 'ere one day and took me sister home for his pleasure. Damn 'er if she didn't return a'carryin' this whelp. Was I to turn 'er out, I ask ye?"

"How kind," Rhys remarked.

"Someone had to work for their keep," the man continued. "And it weren't to be 'er. Lazy wench."

"She's sick," the boy whispered. "Not lazy."

Rhys found himself pushed aside by Gwen before she knelt down before the child.

"Your mother is ill, lad?"

His eyes filled with tears. "Aye, lady. Near to dying, I'd say."

She took his hand. "Where is she?"

He nodded toward the hut.

"Show me."

Rhys watched her go inside and wondered at the wisdom of it, but he suspected there was little he could do to stop her. When his lady was determined about something, the saints preserve any soul who thought to stand in her way.

He found that he had nothing to say to the man, so he merely stood there and stared, his arms folded over his chest, and waited.

Gwen returned in time, bringing the boy along behind her. Rhys opened his mouth to ask her what had transpired, but she seemingly had no desire for speech with him.

"His mother is gone," she said shortly to the boy's uncle. "How much for the boy?"

"Three pieces of gold," the man said promptly. "'E is me nephew, after all, and dear to me—"

"By all the saints," Rhys exclaimed, "you were nigh onto driving the life from the lad!"

Gwen removed Rhys's purse from his belt before he could protest, rummaged around in it, then handed the man four pieces of gold.

"Gwen—" Rhys gasped.

"Here is an extra piece to make certain you do not change your mind. The boy is mine now," Gwen said to the blacksmith. "If you come within ten paces of him again, I will kill you."

The man looked at his gold, then at her. And his eyes took on a calculating look she didn't care for in the slightest.

"Or perhaps Sir Rhys will merely use you as sport," she conceded. "You've no doubt seen his band of mercenaries camped yonder. He is, of course, the fiercest of the lot and more merciless than the rest. I doubt his finishing of you would be nearly as swift as mine would be."

The man looked at Rhys appraisingly. Rhys mustered up his fiercest look. No sense in not living up to Gwen's boasts.

"You know," she continued, lowering her voice as if she had a delicious secret to share, "I've heard the sound of screaming soothes him." She smiled pleasantly. "I wouldn't want to know the truth of the matter myself, but perhaps you're made of sterner stock than I am."

Rhys smiled at the man. The man took one last look at Rhys, then immediately turned and went inside his hovel.

"Montgomery," Gwen said softly, "if you would be so good as to see to the mother's remains?"

"Aye, lady," Montgomery agreed.

"Twins, you will see to my children?"

Amanda and Robin were summarily deposited upon broad, Viking shoulders and carried back toward the keep.

"John, go after them and inform my mother we come and we've a lad in need of tending."

John looked at Rhys as if to ask if he should be obeying his sister-in-law.

"I wouldn't argue," Rhys advised.

John trotted off obediently.

Gwen drew the boy alongside her. "Rhys, this is Nicholas. Nicholas, this is Sir Rhys."

Rhys looked down into a dirty little face belonging to a lad who could be no older than Robin, or so Rhys guessed. His hair was filthy enough that Rhys could not divine its color, but the boy's eyes were pale. And filled with tears.

"Oh," Rhys said, his heart breaking a little within him. "Poor lad." He looked at Gwen. "Are we keeping him?"

"Aye," she said, and he was almost surprised by the vehemence in her voice, "we are."

Rhys had another look at the lad. Though the child's uncle claimed the

boy had been sired by Alain, Rhys could not see it. The child looked nothing like Ayre, and that was likely why Gwen wanted him so badly. Then
again, his lady had a tender heart where children were concerned.

"Well," Rhys said, "if you wish to have him."

"Don't you?"

Rhys met those pale gray eyes and saw the despair there. If humoring
his lady hadn't inspired him to acceptance, the sight of a half-starved, sor-
rowful little one certainly did.

"Aye, I will take him gladly," Rhys said firmly.

"I suspect," Gwen said, "that that isn't the last time you'll say that."

Rhys looked at her in surprise, but there seemed to be no hidden message in her gaze. He surmised that she was pleased with him for his choice,
and he accepted that with a smile. Then he looked at Nicholas.

"Do you care to come with us?"

Nicholas looked as if the very thought and the hope it engendered
might break him into pieces.

Rhys smiled and took the lad's small grubby hand in his own. "Answer
enough, I suppose. Let us seek out something for you to eat. I suspect you
could use something substantial."

Rhys found his other hand taken by his lady. So much for their leisurely
walk. Perhaps 'twas just as well. He needed to make final preparations for
their journey north. Joanna seemed determined to come with them, and he
welcomed not only the protection from scandal she would provide, but the
handful of men she intended to bring along. He was glad of the aid. Perhaps
he might even have a bit of help from Fenwyck.

Assuming, of course, he could keep Gwen and Geoffrey from killing
each other.

The saints preserve him from the pair of them long enough for him to
battle what he truly needed to.

Gwen stood at the doorway of the kitchens and smiled at the sight before
her. By his words, Rhys had seemingly intended to go straight to the lists
after they had returned to the keep. Somehow, though, he had found himself
seated at a table in the kitchens with Robin at one elbow, Nicholas at the
other, and Amanda on his lap. Robin was talking as quickly as his chewing
would allow, Amanda was investigating Rhys's purse for anything interesting, and Nicholas was staring at the three of them as if he couldn't believe
where he was.

It was where he belonged, though. Gwen thought back to what she'd
learned that afternoon and had to shake her head.

She'd had but a handful of words with Nicholas's mother, but they were enough to identify Nicholas's father and how the event had come about. The poor girl had found herself carried back to Ayre from Segrave to be used for Alain's pleasure. The thought of that had set Gwen's teeth to grinding, but she knew she shouldn't have been surprised. It had been on the day of Lord Alain's nuptials, very late that evening, the girl had found herself meeting her fate, as it were. The man had been, however, so into his cups that he could hardly manage to keep his feet.

As Gwen had bent to hear the man's name whispered in her ear, she had fully expected for it to be Alain's.

It hadn't been.

Gwen looked at Rhys, then at Nicholas, searching for the similarity of features. It was there, but only if one looked very closely and if one knew what to look for. Perhaps things would change as the lad grew.

Gwen wondered if she should perhaps have been jealous of Nicholas's mother. To have Rhys in her arms for even a night . . .

But nay, Gwen had had him as well, and she had been his first. With any luck at all, she would be his last.

It was enough that Nicholas was found and rescued. Perhaps she would tell Rhys in time, for she very much suspected he wouldn't notice it himself. For all his skill, he was powerfully unobservant about some things.

"We go Fenwyck?" Amanda was asking Rhys.

"Well . . ." Rhys began slowly.

"We come," she said firmly, seeming to sense Rhys's hesitation.

"But—"

"We *come!*" she announced, her chin jutting out stubbornly. She turned a sunny smile on Nicholas. "And bring *him.*"

Gwen put her hand over her mouth to hide her smile. Rhys might have bested the most formidable knights France had to offer, but he stood not a chance against Amanda of Ayre.

Rhys sighed, defeated already. "If you wish."

Gwen left the kitchen and made her way up to her mother's solar to begin her own preparations. Perhaps she would take an extra wimple or two. Tight ones that would bind her ears more closely to her head. There was no reason to give Geoffrey more to mock her about than he would find on his own. She also packed her sharpest sewing needle and strapped her knife to her forearm. No sense in not being prepared.

She had little desire to halt at Fenwyck, but she could see the wisdom of it. Her father and Geoffrey's father had been comrades, if not friends, and her mother was certainly still in Geoffrey's good graces. It would give them a chance to rest before they continued on to the inevitable skirmish at

Wyckham. And for all Gwen knew, Geoffrey might find Rhys a more tolerable neighbor than Alain's troops and be willing to help with the removal of her husband's men.

She also knew that Rhys had hopes that Geoffrey might speak kindly of him to the king. Gwen had little confidence in such a thing, but perhaps in this case Rhys was using his imagination more than she did. All she could imagine up in her heart was a score of ways to humiliate Geoffrey before he returned the favor.

By the saints, she did not relish the thought of the journey. And to think she had considered three years of waiting for Rhys to be disturbing.

She put her hands over her ears in one last attempt to train them, and continued on her way to her mother's solar.

30

Rhys thought he actually might have to use his sword on Geoffrey of Fenwyck this time.

Assuming, of course, that Gwen didn't get to the man first.

Rhys sat on his horse just inside Fenwyck's gates—and he knew he was damned fortunate to even have gotten that far—and struggled to remind himself of all the reasons why taking his sword and heaving it through Fenwyck's heart would be ill-advised. He would be killing one of John's favorite, if not double-crossing, barons. He would be killing one of Gwen's childhood acquaintances— though he was certain they all still remembered her time in the piggery and Gwen would feel no regret at all if she never had to look Geoffrey in the face again. Unfortunately Rhys had to admit that he would also be killing a potential ally who could very possibly help him convince John that gold in his coffers was reason enough to aid Rhys in further bribing the necessary clergy to see Gwen's liberation accomplished.

But at the moment, all Rhys could do was stare at the way Fenwyck was slobbering over Gwen's hand and imagine up in his heart a score of very painful ways to end the man's life.

Gwen looked about her in a panic. Her mother only shrugged and smiled. Gwen searched for Rhys. She met his eyes and he could hear her thoughts as clearly as if she'd been shouting them at him: *Get him away from me!* She had vowed she would do all in her power not to offend, that Rhys might fare better with Geoffrey, but Rhys could tell she was using every smidgen of control she possessed not to draw her sword and do damage with it.

Unfortunately, he felt the same compulsion. In truth he couldn't blame Geoffrey for the less than friendly welcome. One did not travel with thirty ill-mannered mercenaries and expect to find gates flung open in welcome. But by the saints, it wasn't as if Gwen's mother hadn't brought several of her own guardsmen wearing her late husband's colors. She had even sent a man ahead with tidings of their impending arrival. Geoffrey had known who had come knocking. It had been a discourtesy directed at him personally, and Rhys was swallowing a great lump of pride to ignore it. Never mind that he would have left his men outside the gates in any case. That Geoffrey had come close to denying him entrance as well was the true insult.

But there he sat, contemplating his next action—and that action would have to come quickly, before Gwen had a good look at Geoffrey and his pleasing face. Rhys knew Gwen's heart was true, but 'twas rumored that the sight of Geoffrey had made more than one strong-minded maid lose her resolve. At least that was the rumor, and it was one Rhys couldn't be completely sure that Geoffrey hadn't started himself.

Of course none of Geoffrey's supposed charm would have mattered had the man been every day of fifty and as corpulent as Gwen's former guardian. Unfortunately, Geoffrey was fair-haired and fair featured and damn him if he didn't look as fit as if he trained regularly with his men—which Rhys suspected he did. He was also a widower and surely the most sought-after of nobles in the realm. Why some clever father hadn't ensnared the man for a son-in-law before now was surely a mystery. Rhys could only regret the oversight as it surely left him with trouble he didn't need.

Such as all that slobber on the back of Gwen's hand.

And now on her palm!

"Ahem," Rhys said pointedly.

Geoffrey looked up narrowly. "Something stuck in your throat, friend?"

There was little warmth coming from Fenwyck, and Rhys understood why completely, as he had little to return. Geoffrey obviously still had very vivid memories of their last encounter. Rhys dismounted in the muddy courtyard and in the next heartbeat had Gwen's hand disentangled from Geoffrey's. He congratulated himself on limiting his actions to that when he would have rather been clouting the randy whoreson on the nose.

"I daresay the lady Gwennelyn needs a cup as well," Rhys said, pointedly tucking Gwen's hand into her own belt. "Long ride, you know."

Geoffrey deftly untucked Gwen's hand and slipped it into the crook of his arm. "How right you are, *Sir* Rhys."

The emphasis was, of course, on Rhys's lack of station. Rhys had to remind himself that he was indeed lord of Wyckham. Never mind that he was no baron as Geoffrey was with numerous holdings to his name. He was a lord and would inform Geoffrey of it at his earliest convenience. It would do little to impress Fenwyck, but Rhys suspected he himself would have his pride eased a bit.

"Here I have kept our lady outside when I could have been looking after her more carefully inside the house," Geoffrey continued. He looked at Rhys coolly. "I'm certain you'll want to take your ease in the garrison hall. After," he added with a look at Gwen's guard, "you see to your men."

Rhys gritted his teeth. It wasn't as if he was Fenwyck's equal in station, but he was certainly above the garrison hall.

"Rhys," Gwen began.

"Never fear, lady," Geoffrey said smoothly. "I will see to you. And to your lovely mother. Lady Joanna, 'tis ever a pleasure to see you."

"But—" Gwen protested.

"You will come to no harm in my care."

Gwen was still spluttering as Geoffrey led her and her mother away.

"Montgomery!" Rhys shouted, spinning to look for his friend. The sooner his business was seen to, the sooner Gwen could be rescued. "Montgomery," he said again, "see to the men!"

Montgomery had already swung down and seemed to be preparing to do just that. He stopped and stared at Rhys. "All but them," he said, pointing to the Fitzgeralds. "I'm not going near that pair."

Rhys supposed he couldn't actually blame him. He wasn't looking forward to it overmuch himself, but the twins would have to be tended eventually.

Rhys walked over to where the Fitzgeralds lay strapped to their horses, completely oblivious to their surroundings. He could only assume they were still exhausted from all the puking upon flora and fauna they'd done during the first few days of the journey.

The Fitzgeralds did not travel well by horse.

In fact, he suspected the Fitzgeralds did not travel well by any means other than their own two feet.

He approached Jared's horse, then laid a hand on the man and shook him gently.

"Jared," he called softly.

Jared lifted his head, moaned, then vomited down the front of Rhys's tunic.

Well, at least one of them was awake. Rhys loosened the ropes binding Jared to his horse and made a token effort of catching the larger man as he fell face-first down into the mud. Satisfied Jared would eventually find his feet now said feet were on solid ground, Rhys turned his attentions to Connor. At least with this twin he managed to avoid finding himself in Connor's sights, as it were. Connor fell off his horse into Rhys's arms. Rhys let him slip down gently into the muck.

"I imagine there's supper inside when you're up to it," he announced to both fallen warriors.

Groans were his only answer.

Rhys looked about him for his squire only to find John standing a healthy distance away. It was, to be sure, the first time the lad hadn't been within arm's length for years.

"See to their mounts and ours," Rhys instructed.

"And them?" John asked, looking powerfully afraid he might be asked to act as nursemaid.

"You could help them up when you've tended their horseflesh. I'd leave them be until then."

John didn't have to hear that twice. He was heading toward the stables with four horses in tow before Rhys could give him any more instructions. Rhys turned back to his fallen comrades and wondered if he shouldn't perhaps at least remain with them a bit longer. Then he noticed that Jared was feeling the mud tentatively with one hand. A bleary blue eye opened and stared at the soil closest to it with something akin to astonishment, as if the man couldn't quite believe he was on the ground and it wasn't moving. He gurgled something that Rhys could only assume was some sort of prayer of gratitude.

Connor seemed to be making the same patting motions with his hand and Rhys relaxed. They would realize soon enough that they were no longer atop their steeds. As he was certain they hadn't eaten in days, or rather they had but they hadn't enjoyed the benefits of the food for days, there was no doubt they would be seeking Fenwyck's table soon enough. All that remained was for him to put on less fragrant clothing and find his own place at Fenwyck's table.

Sitting in between, of course, Fenwyck's lord and his quarry.

"I need him alive," Rhys repeated to himself as he crossed the courtyard. "Unmaimed. Coherent."

He had the feeling he would be reminding himself of those things quite often in the near future.

It took him longer to clean himself up than he would have liked. At least an hour had passed before he entered the great hall, let his eyes adjust to the gloom, and saw what he'd feared he might.

Geoffrey sat between Gwen and her mother looking as smug as if he'd just, well, managed to seat himself between the two most beautiful women in the realm. Joanna was lovely, as always, and Gwen was so fair Rhys thought he might expire on the spot just from the sight of her. Expiring, however, seemed to be the last thing on Fenwyck's mind. Fawning and petting seemed to be more in his thoughts. He had obviously matured when it came to how he chose to treat women. Rhys had liked him better before.

And he hadn't liked him very much then.

"Swordplay?" Geoffrey's gasp of surprise echoed in the great hall. "With these soft fingers? Lady, you jest with me! Lady Joanna, tell me your daughter—and I can hardly believe that she is actually your daughter, for you are far too young for such a thing to be true—"

Rhys rolled his eyes in disgust.

"Tell me that the lady Gwennelyn jests about wielding a blade. Such a delicate maid about such an ugly business!"

Rhys saw more finger fondleage than he would have liked as he looked at the table. He was half tempted to vault over it and land in Geoffrey's lap. With any luck a weapon of some sort might come loose in the vaulting and Geoffrey would find himself accidentally, and surely regrettably, impaled in some strategic spot. Not a fatal wound, though. Rhys did have a use for the man eventually.

He cleared his throat purposefully as he approached the table.

Geoffrey looked up and a dark scowl came over his features. "I believe, Sir Knight, that you—"

"Were captain of my lady's guard," Rhys said as he rounded the end of the table, "and am now lord of Wyckham. If I am not welcome at your table, I will at least stand behind it and offer my lady the security of my presence."

Geoffrey looked at him in surprise. "Wyckham?"

"As of his twenty-sixth year," Joanna said smoothly, "which is a wonderful thing, is it not?"

Rhys suspected Geoffrey was thinking it to be anything but that.

"Surely he can sit with us," Joanna said, giving Geoffrey a smile that would have knocked any breathing man to his knees, "don't you think, my lord Fenwyck?"

Geoffrey was not unaffected. He blinked as if he'd been stunned by a sharp blow to the head. Rhys took the opportunity to slip into a chair next to Gwen before Geoffrey could gainsay him. Geoffrey finally roused himself from his stupor and turned back to Gwen. "Ah," he said, "swords . . . wasn't it?" he asked, blinking stupidly.

"She's quite the swordsman," Rhys said, leaning over Gwen to look at Geoffrey. "Perhaps you would care to face her over blades." *And perhaps she will cut off something important, and it will distract you enough to keep your mind off licking her fingers for a bloody heartbeat or two!*

"Tempting," Geoffrey managed. He looked at Gwen and seemed to focus again on her. "What an afternoon that could turn out to be."

Gwen was looking more tempted by the thought of skewering Geoffrey on her sword than was good for her, so Rhys distracted her by removing the trencher she was sharing with Geoffrey and placing it between himself and his lady. He took his own freshly dressed slab of bread and tossed it in front of Fenwyck's lord.

"You look to have a hearty appetite," Rhys said shortly.

"Aye, I do," Geoffrey said, seemingly finding the energy to dredge up an appreciative glance for Gwen. "For many things."

Gwen was beginning to look as nauseated as the Fitzgerald brothers.

"I do as well," Rhys said. "But since the lady Gwennelyn is in *my* care, I am careful not to overindulge. I would suggest, my lord, that perhaps you follow my example."

Fenwyck looked at him and apparently finally realized Rhys had taken a place at the table. He glared. "I think I can choose my own meal well enough, friend."

"In this instance, I think you would be wise to take my advice on the matter."

"And who are you—"

"I am her—"

"Oh, by the saints," Gwen exclaimed, "will you both cease!"

"Please do," Joanna agreed.

"We need him alive and unirritated," Gwen muttered under her breath. "The saints help me remember it!"

"I think you both should keep yourselves to your own trenchers," Joanna continued, obviously striving for a lighter tone. "Perhaps Gwen and I would be safer eating directly off the table."

"Best wash that hand first, Gwen," Rhys grumbled.

Fenwyck scowled. "Our good Sir Rhys is powerfully protective for being just the captain of your guard, my lady Gwennelyn."

"As I said before, I am no longer captain of her guard," Rhys said, resurrecting thoughts of a sharp weapon through some part of Geoffrey's form.

"Then what interest do you have in the girl?" Geoffrey demanded. "A simple knight does not—"

Gwen slapped her hand down on the table so forcefully that Rhys, as well as Geoffrey, jumped. She glared at Geoffrey.

"He is my love," she began angrily.

"Your *what?*" Geoffrey gasped.

Rhys watched as Gwen reached for his hand and clasped it between both her own. At least 'twas better that both her hands rest there than be free to be captured by Geoffrey's.

"I love him," Gwen said distinctly, "and he loves me."

Geoffrey's mouth worked, but no sound issued forth. Rhys thought, however, that Geoffrey's eyes might fall from his head at any moment.

"We plan to wed."

"You plan to wed," Geoffrey echoed in disbelief.

"And then we'll likely need your aid, though I've no mind to beg you for it. Perhaps Rhys isn't a baron with your lands and power, but he is a good man . . ."

Rhys listened to her list his virtues and watched the realizations enter Geoffrey's eyes. Rhys was now, whether he liked it or not, the lord of land that bordered Fenwyck. Rhys would be, whether Geoffrey cared for it or not, Gwen's husband.

Geoffrey seemed to be having a great deal of trouble swallowing it all.

"And you would actually have this," Geoffrey pointed at Rhys and looked at Gwen in disbelief, "this . . ."

Later Rhys knew that if Fenwyck had finished that thought, he would have been recovering from a potentially fatal wound, but the man was spared by a commotion at the door. Rhys turned his attentions there, fully expecting to see the Fitzgerald twins stumbling inside, perhaps covering others with the contents of their poor bellies.

Instead what he saw was a man so exhausted, Rhys marveled that he was still moving. The man fell to his knees in the rushes, panting. Rhys found himself on his feet and walking around the table almost before the thought of doing so took shape in his mind. Geoffrey had obviously had the same idea, for they collided on their way to the door. Rhys growled at Fenwyck, received a growl in return, then continued on his way, Geoffrey keeping pace with him. They approached the man together.

"My lord," the man said, panting, "there is a fire. *Was* a fire."

"Fire?" Geoffrey demanded. "Where?"

The man bowed his head and continued to suck in great gulps of air. "A fire," he gasped. "Too great to stem."

"Where?" Geoffrey asked again. "Fenwyck?"

"Aye," the man rasped, "there, too."

"Damnation!" Geoffrey bellowed.

"The rain quenched it," the man wheezed, "but not before it burned a field or two of yours, my lord. I saw the fires from a distance and rode to see. A great amount of smoke."

"Aye, well, that's a fire for you," Geoffrey said impatiently. "Who set the bloody blaze?"

"Didn't recognize them," the man answered. "But there were a handful of them riding hard away from the keep. There's nothing left of that now."

Geoffrey frowned. "The keep? What keep?"

"Nothing left of any of the fields surrounding the castle, either," the man continued. "The fire burned itself out there."

"By all the sweet saints above," Rhys exclaimed, unable to help himself. "Where is the bloody fire?"

The man looked at him and blinked.

"Why, Wyckham, of course."

31

Wyckham.

Gwen heard the man's words, saw Rhys reel as if he'd been struck, then watched as he began to weave. She thought he just might faint.

"Wyckham?" he repeated, but the man didn't answer him. He turned to look around him, as if he searched for aid. His gaze fell upon Gwen. "Wyckham?" he asked again, as if he simply could not take in what he'd heard.

Geoffrey waved him aside. "Your problem, friend, not mine. Now, Edlred, what is this of damage to my fields?"

Rhys stumbled toward the door. Gwen leaped up from the table and rushed after him. Geoffrey caught her by the arm and stopped her.

"I daresay it may rain again, lady. Perhaps you would be better served—"

"Let me go," she said, jerking her arm from his. "He's going to go see the ruin. I can't let him go alone."

"Of course you can—"

"You fool, that is his land!"

"I know, but—"

"The fire was purposely set. The saints only know who has been left behind to harm him!"

"Now, Lady Gwennelyn . . ." Geoffrey began.

"Mother," Gwen called, "please rescue me from this imbecile! I must go after Rhys."

She managed to get out the door and into the courtyard before Geoffrey caught up with her again. Gwen ignored him and looked about her for the stables. She watched in consternation as Rhys ran from the stables, pulling his mount along behind him. He vaulted into the saddle and spurred his horse through the gates. It took her no time at all to confirm her decision. He couldn't go alone. If he did, the saints only knew what might happen to him.

Gwen ran across the courtyard and was almost plowed over by John, who didn't wait to leave the stables before he had mounted his own horse. She caught her breath, then made her way down to the proper stall. Fortunately three years at Segrave had done more than just provide her with sheets for another marriage bed. Though the twins had been of no use when it came to equine endeavors—and now she understood why—Montgomery had been susceptible to bullying and had therefore taught her a great deal about horses. She'd even come to the point of being able to saddle one with moderate skill.

She put all her skills to good use now. It took her longer than she would have liked, but Geoffrey was of no help— not that she would have asked him anyway. He was far too busy ordering his lads to see to the saddling of mounts for himself and several guardsmen. The only thing that remotely cheered her was the sight of Montgomery retrieving his horse. At least she would have companionship she could bear.

"How far is Wyckham still, do you think?" she asked him as they left the stables together.

"A good day's ride," Montgomery said grimly. "Far enough that we should take along provisions."

Gwen found her way blocked again by Geoffrey. He frowned at her.

"This is very ill-advised, lady," he said. "He will likely collect his mercenaries on his way, and I think it imprudent that you be amongst such company."

"And yours is any safer?" she demanded.

He seemed to be searching for some return for that. Gwen was certain it would take more time than she had at her disposal, so she tried to push him aside.

"Out of my way," she commanded. "I've things to do."

He remained stubbornly in front of her. "I don't understand how the land came to be his," he said.

"It was my sire's," Gwen said shortly. "It became Alain's upon my marriage to him. Alain's father Bertram commanded that Alain give it to Rhys upon Rhys's twenty-sixth year as reward for his faithful service."

Geoffrey grunted. "Then I suppose 'tis more than simply Sir Rhys boasting to impress you."

"Get out of my way," she said distinctly, "lest you force me to draw my blade and use it upon your sorry form."

"The saints preserve me from that," he said as he hastily stepped aside. He cleared his throat. "I'll come as well."

She paused and looked at him. She didn't want to converse any more with him, but she would be the first to admit that he was, after all, a powerful man with many knights at his disposal. And she had promised Rhys she would be agreeable to the wretch.

"Why would you come?" she asked reluctantly.

"I'll need to see what's been done to my fields."

Of course. It wasn't as if he would come along to help Rhys. "Do as you like," Gwen said, tugging on her horse. "I could not care less."

"Of course you couldn't. Provisions!" Geoffrey bellowed at one of his men as he halted in the courtyard. "See to them and follow us as quickly as may be."

Gwen found her mother in the small group gathered near the keep and wasn't surprised to see the children there with her. Robin looked to be itching to go, that much Gwen could surmise by the firm hold Joanna had upon his small person. Amanda was clutching her grandmother's skirts. Nicholas stood a few paces back, looking very uncertain. Gwen spared a brief moment to hug all three little ones, then thank her mother for their care.

"Back soon?" Amanda asked, looking worried that such might not be the case.

"Aye, love," Gwen said, bending to kiss the small, plump cheek. "Very soon. We must fetch Sir Rhys, then we'll be right back. Watch after the boys until then, aye?"

Amanda looked at Robin and turned her nose up. She espied Nicholas and immediately released Joanna's skirts and advanced upon her prey. Satisfied that the children would survive her absence, Gwen mounted her horse and left the bailey.

She soon found that Geoffrey seemed determined to ride beside her, so she did her best to concentrate on the view before her. It was either ignore him or say something she would regret. With the morning Rhys had had already, she knew he wouldn't appreciate her damaging his chances for flattering Fenwyck.

"How odd that someone should set fire to the land."

"Odd?" she echoed. "You fool, 'twas deliberate!"

He looked at her narrowly. "I am no fool, lady—"

"You misunderstood what your man said, then, and if that doesn't make you a fool, I don't know what does." She looked pointedly at the gap in his teeth for good measure. By Saint Michael's crossed eyes, what had possessed Rhys to think this oaf could possibly be of any aid to them? He was rumored to know of all that passed in England. How could he not know of the business at Wyckham?

Geoffrey scowled. "Very well then, lady, if you are so wise, who was it who set the fire? Alain?"

"His troops were upon the land, daring Rhys to take it from under them."

That, at least, seemingly captured Geoffrey's attention. "In truth?"

"Alain said as much to Rhys three years ago. Hence his long journeying in France to obtain an army."

"Surely Alain would not do such a thing," Geoffrey said, though Gwen suspected by the hesitation with which he spoke that he believed it readily enough.

"I doubt 'twas his idea, either to encamp upon it, or to burn it. He hasn't the imagination for something this foul."

"Who then?"

"Rollan, of course."

Geoffrey did not look at all surprised. "I am always amazed by the depth of Rollan's spite. How Bertram sired such a knave is a mystery. Alain is almost as disagreeable."

"I thought you found Alain's company quite to your liking." She glared at him. "You never spared any breath on my behalf at Segrave when he would disparage me."

He shrugged. "You were insufferably smug. Why would I have wanted to defend you?"

"Me?" she gasped. "Smug?"

"Aye. Forever were you about some mischief at my expense."

"I only reported upon the mischief you combined."

"Smugly," he agreed.

"At least I had a large enough store of wits to warrant such arrogance."

"And large enough ears," he said with a nasty smile that reminded her of all the reasons she truly did not care for the man riding next to her.

"At least my ears do not show when I open my mouth," she countered. "I can hide them with a wimple."

He glared at her and she returned his glare. She would have truly given him full measure of her irritation, but the smell of smoke was faint in the air and the sight of it was clear on the horizon. That was enough to persuade her to cease her journey down this path of insults. Best to do so anyway before she completely humiliated Geoffrey. He would, of course, never best her. She had imagined up in her mind countless encounters with the man and in every one, she had come away the victor. It would be no different this time and that would only serve to perhaps convince him that Rhys did not deserve his help. Gwen gathered all her strength of will and held her tongue.

"What does he think to do?" Geoffrey asked, obviously having come to the same conclusion that fighting was pointless. "Stand on his soil and stamp out the remaining flames himself?"

"He'll grieve," Gwen returned shortly. "What else can he do?"

"Retaliate?"

"How? By attacking Ayre?"

Geoffrey chewed on that, but said nothing.

Gwen turned away and concentrated on the smoke in the distance. She should have known Geoffrey would be of little aid. They would have to invent a new scheme. Perhaps there would be something left behind, something that would point to who had done this thing. Then they would go to the king and give him the tale. Perhaps it would be enough to convince him that Alain was an unfit lord for all her lands and that they should be given to another.

Rhys, for instance.

It was dusk when she finally caught up with him, though they had left Fenwyck in the late morning. Gwen had hated to use her mount thusly, but it was either that or lose Rhys's trail.

She dismounted and left Montgomery to deal with their small company. Rhys stood some paces away, alone and unmoving. She approached quietly. Rhys continued to stand as still as stone. Gwen half wondered if he'd even marked her arrival. Then she stopped at his side and looked up at his face.

His cheeks were wet with tears.

She slipped her hand into his. When he gave no sign of noticing even that, she took his hand in both of hers and merely stood next to him silently, wishing she could take away his grief.

"Oh, Rhys," she said softly. "I'm so sorry."

Without warning, he pulled her in front of him, wrapped his arms around her, and buried his face in her hair.

His shoulders shook, but only once.

Gwen put her arms around him and held him tightly.

"I'm so sorry," she repeated. It was all she could think of to say.

She wasn't certain how long they stood there thusly, with his silent tears slipping across her temple and down her neck. It could have been hours. Finally, though, he lifted his head and looked down at her. She could scarce see him for the lack of light, but what she could see was the bleakness in his gray eyes.

"Will you know what frightens me the most?" he whispered.

She waited, mute.

"If they—Alain and Rollan—can do that to land that I loved a great deal, what might they do to what I love the most?"

She swallowed, hard. "I've thought on that as well."

He gripped her by the shoulders. "You will not leave my sight, do you hear me? Not for a moment. The saints only know what either of them will think to do next."

"As you will, Rhys."

"And the children," he continued. "You'll keep them near, and I'll see to you all."

"Of course, Rhys."

He dragged his sleeve across his eyes and swept the landscape with a disbelieving glance.

"Am I the only one here who cannot believe what I'm looking at?" he asked. He looked down at her. "Alain did this, don't you think? Have I lost what little wits still remain me? Could someone else have wrought this to spite me?"

She shook her head. "You know it was Alain and Rollan together, Rhys."

"I wish I had proof."

"They might confess it, given enough incentive."

Rhys laughed shortly, without humor. "What am I to do? Use hot irons?"

She shrugged. "Perhaps Geoffrey will offer his aid."

Rhys sighed, and it sounded as if it had come straight from his soul. "We couldn't be that fortunate. Besides, it doesn't help us now. Gwen, I don't see how we can survive here. We've nothing left of the crops and 'tis too late to replant this year. And we would have to rebuild the keep." He looked at her bleakly. "I don't have the gold for this."

"We'll live in a tent, then."

He laughed bitterly. "Oh, aye, and freeze our sorry arses off in the winter. What kind of protection can I offer you in a tent, my love? I want walls about you so strong that not even John and his armies can breach them. I want no thief coming in to steal you away, or to make off with Robin or Amanda."

"Or Nicholas," she added.

He smiled faintly. "You've become fond of that lad."

"Aye," she agreed, "I have."

"The three of them, then," Rhys said. "And most important, you. I'll not leave you unprotected."

Gwen looked around her and could see that indeed restoring Wyckham to anything livable would be an undertaking of immense proportions. And it would only be done at great expense. But how much less dear would improving the land she was thinking of be?

"Rhys," she said slowly, "there is another choice."

"Another choice? What?"

"I never thought to speak of this before, as my sire always told me the land was worth nothing."

He waited.

"I have land that is mine," she continued. "It remained mine even after wedding Alain."

He started to frown. "And?"

"And I never thought it was of any value. It is another week's hard ride north of here—at least so I've been told. My sire thought that perhaps I might will it to an abbey at some point in my life, so he left its disposal in my hands. I think it must be quite a barren and wild place, for it borders those barbaric northern lands."

"Barren?" he asked with a dry smile. "Can it possibly be any more desolate than this?"

"The saints only know." She sighed. "I should have perhaps told you sooner. I just never thought it would be of any use to either of us."

"Land is land."

"Is it?" she asked, nodding to the scorched field next to her. "This may look rather inviting after your first view of Artane."

"Artane," he mused. "'Tis a good name, I suppose."

"Sounds a bit on the bleak side to me, but 'tis perhaps worth a look."

"Perhaps it will be so bleak no one will trouble us." He laughed suddenly. "John, Alain, and the whole of England on one hand and barbarians from the north on the other. By the saints, lady, our life together is destined to be a troubled one."

"I was actually thinking it might be just the place for us. Perhaps we will go north and everyone will forget of our existence."

He looked down at her and pursed his lips. "When I have snatched the most beautiful woman in England and carried her north to some bleak wasteland to ensconce her in a keep I cannot afford to build? Somehow, Gwen, I think forgetting about us is the last thing anyone will do."

"If the king thought you might be willing to defend his borders, perhaps he would build you a keep."

"And likely install a permanent garrison there to keep me in check. Many thanks, but I'll find a way to build it myself."

She shook her head. "Not another handful of years on the continent warring, Rhys. I cannot bear that."

"There may be no other way."

"We'll find one," she insisted. "Either that or you will take me with you and I will be the one to guard your back."

He looked as panicked as if she'd suggested she would be the one to single-handedly defend the English border.

"We'll find another way," he agreed promptly. "Wonderful idea. Wish I'd been the one to think of it."

She patted him on the back and smiled up at him. "Then let us see to our journey north. We'll likely want to return to Fenwyck for stores before we go."

He nodded with a smile, then she saw him look at his land again. His expression sobered.

"This is still mine," he said softly.

"Aye, and you've earned it. It will recover, Rhys. I've always heard there was good soil here. You'll see the day when it's well planted and the keep rebuilt."

He sighed, bent his head, and rested his forehead against hers.

"Thank you."

"For what?"

He smiled at her. "For the hope." He raised his head. "Come, lady, and let us see what bleak bit of ground your wily sire left to you. And let us hope Alain hasn't been there before us."

Gwen watched him for the rest of that day, and then the pair of days that followed after they returned to Fenwyck to prepare for their journey. And despite the size of his loss, he seemed to be taking it remarkably well.

When he thought people were watching him, of course.

It was those unguarded moments that broke her heart, those moments when he seemed to think he was unobserved. It was then that she saw how deeply Alain's desecration had wounded him. It was hard enough to have been denied Bertram's gift for so many years, but to watch that gift so senselessly destroyed was surely another matter entirely.

It was at just such a time that he caught her watching him from behind a tree in Geoffrey's garden. He had been sitting in the sunshine on a bench, his hands dangling between his knees and his head bowed. Gwen had been sure she'd made no noise, but evidently his hearing was better than she credited it for being, for he lifted his head and looked straight at her. His expression of grief didn't change, but he did hold out his hand for her.

She emerged from her hiding place and came to sit next to him on the bench.

"I'm sorry," she said. "I can't seem to say anything else."

"I wasn't thinking on the land."

She blinked. "Then what?"

"You," he said simply. "And how much worse it would hurt if something happened to you." He smiled sadly. "I thought I knew how much I loved you, Gwen, until this happened. All I could think about as I stared at those ravaged fields was how much worse I would feel had it been you to suffer such an injury."

"I won't."

"Aye, you won't," he said calmly, "because you will never be in a position to be harmed thusly. I cannot believe I left you for three years in the company of those puking Vikings."

"The Fitzgeralds are remarkably skilled when they've both feet on *terra firma*."

He looked unconvinced. "We will also make do with the gold we have," he continued, "that I need not tourney in France again. If I must kneel and lick John's boots for a keep of my own, then I will do so. I daresay he won't be coming north that often to see how his garrison fares."

"With any luck, he won't."

He rose and pulled her up with him. "Why don't you go rest for the afternoon. We've a long ride before us on the morrow."

"I feel fine—"

"And cease with your spying upon me, Gwen."

"I haven't been spying."

He lifted one eyebrow as he pursed his lips. "Yesterday you had cobwebs in your hair, and today you've enough twigs therein for a bird's nest."

She would have argued, but he suddenly took her face in his hands, bent his head, and kissed her. It was a sweet, gentle kiss that completely distracted her from what she'd been intending to say.

He lifted his head and smiled down at her. "Agreed?"

"Agreed," she said, hoping that he didn't realize she would have agreed to near anything at that moment.

"Then come, my love, and let us be about the rest of our day. I, for one, am actually relishing a small journey north. We never know what we'll find."

They started back to the keep only to find Geoffrey in their way. Gwen glared at him and he glared back at her before he turned his attentions to Rhys.

"I'll help," he said shortly.

Gwen almost fell down in shock. Even Rhys seemed greatly surprised by the offer.

"You will?" he asked.

"I have little love for Alain."

"And that is your reason for helping?" Gwen demanded. "What if it wasn't Alain who did the deed?"

"I am willing to at least consider the notion that he was behind it. And if I discover that 'tis the truth, indeed, I will not hold him guiltless."

Rhys seemingly had no hesitation about Geoffrey's motives. "Good," he said shortly. "I'll need all the aid I can have."

Gwen was still unconvinced. "That is all?" she asked. "You've no other reason to aid us?"

He looked at her and for the first time ever she had a small smile of camaraderie from him. "He bedded my cook's daughter the last time he was here. Haven't had a decent meal since."

Rhys laughed shortly. "Poor Fenwyck. 'Tis nothing more than you deserve for inviting him to visit."

"I *didn't* invite him," Geoffrey grumbled. "He caught me in a hospitable moment. I should have listened to my first instinct, which was to raise the drawbridge against him."

"And yet you let us in," Gwen said suspiciously.

He smiled. "You and your mother both at my table? Only a fool would deny himself such beauty."

He'd made no more mention of her ears, and he didn't seem to be looking at them overmuch. Gwen felt Rhys elbow her in the ribs and decided that perhaps 'twas time to call the battle a standoff and leave it at that. It was likely as close as Geoffrey would ever come to an apology for his slandering of her while she was young. She could perhaps forgive a little. Besides, Geoffrey had seemingly cast in his lot with Rhys.

Perhaps things had begun to turn their way at last.

32

A se'nnight later Rhys sat atop his horse and shook his head, unable to believe what he was looking at.

Artane was not at all what Rhys had been expecting.

For one thing, the only thing that could even remotely be termed empty was the remnants of a keep that rested atop a ridge that had a commanding view of both ocean and land. The keep was nothing more than a wooden shell that consumed only a fraction of the space that could have been allotted to such a dwelling.

What a crafty old whoreson William of Segrave had been.

He looked to his right to see Gwen wearing a look of complete astonishment. It was the same look she had worn for the past three days, the three days during which they had traveled only partway over her land. She'd been certain they would arrive to find it nothing but wasteland. She had apologized in advance scores of times while they had made their preparations to come north. While Rhys had been organizing his men, Gwen had been interrogating her mother—with no success. Either Joanna had not been able or hadn't wanted to divulge any details. Now Rhys understood why. What a surprise it had been, and an exceedingly pleasant one at that.

"You were so right," Rhys drawled. "Pitiful, barren bit of soil this is."

She looked at him, still gaping. "I had no idea!"

"I imagine your sire did," Rhys said, feeling his smile turn into a grin. "By the saints, Gwen, the man had a fine instinct for a good jest."

"It is *enormous*," she managed.

"Aye," he said in wonder, "such vastness I've never seen outside the Aquitaine. Not quite as lush, of course, but the soil seems workable enough."

"We can only hope Alain went straight home and didn't see this."

"He wouldn't have bothered."

"Rollan might have made the effort."

Rhys shook his head. "My scouts have seen nothing, and believe me they would love to capture him. And then Alain would have spent the rest of his life wondering what had happened to his brother, for he never would have seen him again."

Gwen shuddered. "I wonder about the company you keep, Rhys. How does your mother feel about this?"

"She's praying mightily for their souls and mine, believe me."

"I don't doubt it." She looked toward the shore. "Shall we go up the hill and see the view?"

"Aye, gladly."

It was a perfect place for a keep. Rhys had known it from the moment he'd seen the bluff, but setting foot on the crest of the hill reconfirmed it. The knoll stretched down to the sea in hills of sand that no army would be able to wade through with less than great difficulty. Behind them, a rocky cliff separated the top of the hill from the floor of the land. Beyond that was land that had lain fallow for the saints only knew how long. Rhys suspected it would yield plentifully when it was finally planted.

"Listen," Gwen breathed.

At first it was hard to hear anything but Robin's and Nicholas's shouts of delight as they rolled themselves down the hillside. Rhys spared a brief moment to be glad that Joanna had kept Amanda behind. He had visions of cleaning sand out from behind her ears for days. At least the boys he could merely dunk in a barrel of rainwater and consider them washed.

Once the boys had rolled away far enough, Rhys found he could listen in peace. And it was then that he noticed the sound of the waves against the shore.

Gwen slipped her hand into his and stared out over the sea.

"Bliss," she whispered. "Surely my father must have come here and known it would please me."

"I suspect he did, my love," Rhys said quietly. "And if not him, surely your mother knew."

She looked up at him and her eyes were full of wonder. "Will you build us a keep here? Right on this spot where we may hear the sound of the sea?"

He smiled and reached over to push strands of hair back out of her face. "If you do not mind my building a castle on your land."

"Count it as my dowry. That will soothe the wagging tongues on both sides of the sea. Think on your reputation should you marry me merely for love."

"It would ruin me, certainly," he agreed.

"Then will this suit?"

"Aye, love," he said, "it will suit very well indeed."

"Then let us wander our land a bit and plan where the keep should go. Two baileys, don't you think? It should be much larger than Segrave, and we certainly should make Ayre look like a hovel. And then we must have a garden. I wonder what will grow this far north. We must needs question the friars at that abbey we passed on our way here."

"Seakirk," he supplied.

"Aye, there," she said, pulling him along with her as she walked the top of the hill. "They will surely know what we can grow successfully in this wasteland."

Rhys heard what she said and had to smile at her plots and schemes for growing this herb and that, but at the same time he could hardly concentrate. It was so much more than he had expected. By the saints, it made Wyckham seem as large as a modest abbey pleasure garden. To think this all belonged to Gwen. No matter if she held it in her name for the rest of her life. If she would just be kind enough not to flinch when he built the most modern keep England had ever seen on her soil, he would be content.

"What do you think?"

Rhys realized she had stopped and was looking to him for some kind of response.

"Ah," he stalled, "very nice. Truly."

Her eyes narrowed. "You were not attending me."

"I was—"

"You were not. Roses, Rhys. We must see if roses will grow here. I've seen the ones brought back from the Crusades. Aye, I will have them here to please the eye as well as serve their medicinal purpose."

And off she went again, listing in detail the herbs she would need planted and then the flowers she would have for their beauty alone. But all Rhys could think about was stone, and a great amount of it. He would construct walls so thick, they would never be torn down. Gwen would be safe here, safe from Alain and safe from Rollan.

Rhys wondered just how much William of Segrave had known about his future son-in-law's character. Had he kept this whole plot of land secret for a specific purpose?

"—trees, don't you think?"

Rhys blinked. Then he winced at her glare. "My apologies, lady. I was thinking of stone."

"As in a wall around the garden? A fine idea, Rhys. You'll see to it, won't you?"

He bent his head and stole a brief kiss. "I'll see to it all, my love."

Gwen groaned suddenly. "Those lads will drive me daft. Robin! Nicholas! Do *not* go out into the sea thusly! Know you nothing of the beasties therein?" She stalked off to where she could no doubt be better heard bellowing her displeasure, casting an "I'll be back presently" at Rhys.

He watched her go, then turned his attentions back to the soil under his feet and the vastness surrounding him. He could see for miles. No army would come upon him unawares. No ships could attack without him having marked them well in advance. It was, undoubtedly, the perfect place to build a keep, and Rhys could only shake his head in wonder that John had not appropriated the land for the crown already.

And if the land was to be inherited by Gwen only, perhaps Rhys could go down on both knees, kiss John's crooked toes, and beg for fealty straight to the crown for it. As appealing as Wyckham was, it came with Alain as liege-lord, something Rhys was not relishing. Perhaps John would accept his sword, and his loyalty, for Artane and count himself fortunate to have someone trustworthy guarding his northern border.

Rhys stood with his feet firmly planted on goodly soil, heard the crash of the waves against the shore and the screaming of gulls as they wheeled in the air, and thought he just might weep from the wonder of it all.

This land could be his. And all he had to do to have it was win the one thing he wanted more than life itself.

Gwen.

And though there was no time like the present to begin, he found that he couldn't force himself to go confer with his mercenaries quite yet. Nor could he chase after his lady and join in the scolding of the two very wet lads who cavorted happily along the shore. All he could do was stand where he was and breathe deeply of the salt air and listen to the rumbling roar of the sea.

Land.

And Gwen to share it with.

Now all he had to do was see that it happened.

•   •   •

They camped on top of the hill for two days. Rhys could have stayed there forever, and so could the boys if their moans of frustration at leaving were any indication. Well, perhaps calling it two sets of moans wasn't exactly the way of it. Robin complained quite loudly. Nicholas bore up stoically under the burden of loss, though Rhys suspected he was every bit as disappointed as Robin was. As Rhys watched them have a final run down the hill, he vowed again that he would make certain Gwen kept her son.

Robin could be claimed as his. So could Nicholas. Considering that Gwen's annulment would make Robin a bastard as well, what was the difference between the two lads? Besides, Gwen had taken a great liking to Nicholas, and Rhys had to admit that he was growing fond of the lad as well. A man could do worse than to acquire a bride and two sons at the same time.

They returned as quickly as the horses could manage. Rhys could have traveled more quickly with just his mercenaries, but he didn't mind the slowness of the pace, for it gave him ample time to observe his surroundings and discover the lay of Gwen's land.

But he was relieved nonetheless to see Fenwyck in the distance. The sooner Gwen was free, the sooner the keep could be started. Rhys knew there was a wedding that would take place also in that time, but he'd spent so many years not thinking about it that it had become a habit. He would give it some thought after he'd secured John's and the archbishop's blessing.

He prayed he had enough gold for the like.

After seeing to the men and spending a few moments in the garden submitting to young Anne of Fenwyck's and Amanda's demands that he serve as a horse for their pleasure, Rhys finally made his way into Fenwyck's hall for a cold cup of ale and a bit of peace for thinking. He was unsurprised to see Fenwyck's lord hovering over Gwen like a persistent cloud.

"What I wouldn't give for a substantial gust of wind," he muttered as he accepted a cup from a servant. He carried it to the high table and made Geoffrey a small bow. "If I may sit?" he asked.

Asking permission would be another thing he would be bloody happy never to do again.

Geoffrey looked at him with something akin to reluctance. "I suppose if you must."

"Now, Geoffrey," Joanna chided gently from where she sat on his left hand. "You've behaved so nicely the past fortnight."

While I was away, Rhys noted wryly. He reached over and pulled Gwen's hand from Geoffrey's. No traces of spittle. So it would seem that Geoffrey of Fenwyck would keep his head for another few days.

Geoffrey tried to pull her hand back, but Rhys held on to it more firmly.

With a disgusted snort, Gwen retrieved both hands and tucked them under her arms.

"You would think I was a roast fowl," she said.

"Give me your hand," Geoffrey said, "and I'll nibble it to see—"

"Do and your life will end." Rhys couldn't believe the words had come out of his own mouth, but there they were and there was no taking them back now. Perhaps he'd exhausted his store of patience more quickly than he'd thought.

Joanna laughed. "Oh, by the saints, cease." It was the same exasperated tone Rhys had heard her use with Robin and Nicholas several times already that day. "If you cannot treat each other with kindness and respect, then please take yourselves out to the lists and solve your differences there."

Gwen looked as disgusted as her mother sounded, and Rhys began to feel as immature as Robin himself. He felt somewhat better, however, when she turned the same look of disgust on Geoffrey.

"Harumph," Rhys said. "Well, then."

"Indeed," Geoffrey said, sounding equally as disgruntled.

"Rhys," Joanna said, leaning forward to look at him, "what are your plans now, love? Are we for Segrave, or will you have us remain here?"

Rhys felt, unaccountably, a rush of pleasure go through him. Never mind that he was not Gwen's husband, nor Joanna's son-in-law. That she should accord him such a courtesy despite his lack of rights was a sweet thing indeed.

"Well, my lady," he said, "I plan to send a messenger to my grandfather today. I must needs travel to London to meet him there and grovel before the king, but I daresay 'tis best neither you nor my lady accompany me there."

"In case you lose your head?" Gwen asked grimly.

He smiled briefly. "I will lose nothing and will instead come away the victor, you'll see. All you must do is trust me."

"And remain here?" Gwen shot Geoffrey a frown.

He held up his hands innocently. "I have said nothing to you, my lady Gwennelyn, neither about your ears or your height."

"My height?" Gwen echoed. "What is amiss with my height?"

Geoffrey very quickly, and very wisely, took hold of a leg of roast fowl and began to chew industriously upon it.

Gwen turned to Rhys and glared. "Are you to leave me here then to face this?"

"I will travel more quickly alone," Rhys offered.

"Best be quick about it," Geoffrey said from behind his joint. "I may need a rescue." He shook his head. "I cannot believe you intend to make off with this girl."

"'Tis a family tradition," Gwen said, "though you would have to admit that he's been a failure at it so far." She looked at Rhys with one eyebrow raised. "You said so yourself."

"Do you hear me gainsaying you?" he groused. "My sire would be appalled. My grandsire *was* appalled. He snatched his lady as she was being garbed for a wedding to another. He thought I'd had more than ample opportunity to make off with you before you made your vows."

"Did you remind him how many guardsmen filled Ayre's courtyard?" she asked.

"He remained quite unimpressed. Something about spending several se'nnights recovering from wounds inflicted by a score of sewing needles. Fair ruined his nuptials, or so he claimed." Rhys grimaced. "I think my grandmère's ladies were aiming for a most strategic target."

"By the saints," Geoffrey gasped, crossing his legs quickly. "I marvel at your grandsire's courage."

"Well, since you're here sitting with us," Gwen said to Rhys, "we can assume that he recovered."

"Aye," Joanna agreed, "and now tell us how it is you intend to proceed. It concerns me that you go to London with gold and no guard to speak of. Do you not fear John will take your offering and give you nothing in return?"

Rhys had very unpleasant memories of Hugh of Leyburn accepting his purse and then laughing in his face. Short of heaving a chest of gold at King John's head and hoping it knocked the man so senseless he could do nothing but say aye to whatever question was put to him when he awoke, Rhys wasn't sure how to proceed.

Rhys looked at Geoffrey. "You have the king's ear."

Geoffrey frowned. "From time to time."

"Perhaps you might be persuaded somehow to suggest a few ways it could be bent my way."

Geoffrey scowled. "Now, why would I want to do that? Especially when the one you intend to steal away is the one woman in all of England I would choose to wed were she free?"

Rhys turned over in his mind all the reasons why Geoffrey would want to help him, the most important being that if he didn't, Rhys would do him bodily harm. Gwen saved him from having to admit that.

"You should do it because I love him," Gwen said.

Geoffrey pursed his lips. "I suppose I can think of worse justifications for sedition."

"Especially since I wouldn't wed with you if you were the only male left in England," Gwen muttered.

Rhys watched Geoffrey scowl at her, then return his attentions to his leg of fowl.

"Alain is a powerful man," he said between chews.

"And you are no less powerful?" Joanna asked. "Come, my lord Fenwyck, you are too modest."

Rhys would have snorted loudly at her flattery, but Geoffrey actually seemed to believe what she said. He sat back, not about to ruin the spell his lady's mother was weaving. Joanna spent a goodly amount of time pointing out to Geoffrey all his good points while at the same time listing all Alain's bad points so thoroughly that even Rhys began to believe that perhaps Geoffrey could succeed where Alain never could have.

"So true, so true," Geoffrey agreed finally when Joanna had seemingly exhausted a very deep well of flattery. He stretched like a satisfied cat. "I suppose that along with alerting the king to Alain's damage to my land, I might also speak kindly of you, Rhys. I feel quite certain he will listen to me."

Rhys felt nothing of the kind, but he supposed a little help was better than no help at all. Perhaps Geoffrey could distract John while Rhys snuck up behind him and clouted him over the head with several bags of gold. Perhaps the clouting would render the king's reason a bit unusable, but not affect his hands so much that they couldn't sign a handful of documents Rhys would have prepared.

"I'll think on it more," Geoffrey announced, "and let you know my plans within the se'nnight."

Rhys sighed. It was longer than he wanted to wait, but when he'd already been waiting for Gwen half his lifetime, what was another week?

But as it happened, his decision was made for him much sooner than that. He and Gwen hadn't been returned to Fenwyck but two days when a messenger came running across the lists to him, a missive clutched in his dirty hands. There was no seal, which aroused his suspicions immediately, but seals were certainly no guarantee of authenticity. If anyone would know that, it would be him. How many letters had he received under Gwen's seal only to learn later that they were forgeries?

I, Jean de Piaget, write this by mine own hand this last day of June, the Year of Our Lord 1206, to Rhys de Piaget. Greetings to you, Grandson, and may the good graces of our Lord be upon you.

There is trouble afoot and I fear it travels to your mother's doorstep. Meet me there, if you will, and come with all haste. You know the swiftest way there, though I would not think it strange if you were to pause in London and obtain some trinket to sweeten her humor. You know how foul-tempered she will be otherwise.

Let not all you've worked for be snatched away from you whilst you sleep, Grandson.

Jean de Piaget

Rhys pursed his lips and handed the letter to Montgomery. "What think you?"

Montgomery read it and looked up. "I think your grandsire wastes ink overmuch worrying about your mother's temper."

"You don't know my mother."

Montgomery smiled. "I know what you've told me, and she doesn't seem a woman given overmuch to bouts of ill humor."

Rhys folded the missive. "I'll leave before dawn on the morrow."

"But, Rhys," Montgomery said, aghast, "you cannot believe this is genuine. There was no seal, no guarantee—"

"It was from my grandfather," Rhys said, knowing it could be from no other. Not even his mother knew the combination of items and cities he and his grandfather had discussed between themselves. Trinkets from London, cloth from Paris, and fresh fish from Calais. Simple, foolish things, but a guarantee of authenticity.

As much as anything could be guaranteed.

"I'll leave the twins behind with you," Rhys continued.

"I'm certain they will be grateful for that," Montgomery said dryly.

Rhys couldn't smile. That his grandfather should have investigated enough not to only find him but to send a missive along as well could only mean there was serious trouble afoot indeed. Was the abbey near to being overrun?

"Fenwyck's garrison should be enough to keep Gwen safe, and I'll make certain Geoffrey knows you have the keeping of my lady," Rhys said, pushing aside his worry. He could only ride so fast, and it wasn't as if he made for France from Ayre. He had a good fortnight before he would even reach London, then another fortnight to reach his mother's. This was not how he intended to pass his fall.

"Go freely, my friend," Montgomery said. "I will keep watch over your lady."

"I fear Geoffrey more than any ruffians."

"As well you likely should."

"I want you to mark every drop of spittle he leaves on her hands," Rhys growled. "The saints preserve him should he place any in other locations."

Montgomery laughed. "Poor man. I suspect he knows that already and is appropriately cowed. I suspect you'll return to find your lady safely un-molested."

"For his sake," Rhys said with a sigh, "I certainly hope so."

It took him all of that day to arrange matters to his liking. Gwen had demanded to come along, and it was only by threatening to bind her to a chair and leave Geoffrey with any tools of liberation that she relented and reluctantly agreed to stay behind. Rhys didn't trust her word, and he sus-pected he had good reason not to based on the glint in her eye, but a quickly exchanged look with Joanna at least allowed him to rest easier knowing that Gwen's mother would do her best to stop Gwen from following him.

He planned to take fifteen of his most ill-tempered mercenaries and leave the others behind to guard his lady. Where Joanna and the Fitzgeralds failed in convincing Gwen to remain at Fenwyck, perhaps the lads would succeed.

It was near dawn when he and his company were finally prepared and waiting in the courtyard. He surveyed whom he was leaving behind that he might call up the memory to give him courage when he needed it.

Geoffrey seemed to think that remaining at Fenwyck with Gwen might be more than his frail powers of restraint could bear. He promised to meet Rhys in London in six weeks' time to have speech with the king. By then Rhys hoped he would have finished his business in France, rescued his mother and his gold, and returned to London prepared to haggle with the king over Gwen's hand. Perhaps Geoffrey would have reached the king first and filled his ears full of Alain's treachery. Rhys suspected he would need all the aid he could muster.

Joanna wished him godspeed and good fortune. Geoffrey stood next to Gwen's mother, his hands in plain sight in front of him and a look of in-nocence on his face. Gwen's guard, augmented by grim mercenaries, looked equal to the task of keeping her in line. Nicholas stood near Gwen with his hand on the hilt of the dagger Rhys had gifted him earlier. Rhys had bid him look after Gwen, and Nicholas had taken the instruction to heart, though Rhys suspected the lad knew nothing more about wielding the blade than what Robin had showed him. He would remedy that when he returned.

Of Robin there was nothing to be seen. He'd asked to come along, been flatly refused, and gone off in a temper. Rhys tucked away a thought to re-mind himself to glance up at the walls before he left them, just to make certain Robin wasn't about to fling something at him in retaliation. Rhys sighed. He would bring the lad back something from London to sweeten his humor. He could do no more than that.

Amanda wept and clung to him, begging him not to leave. By the time Rhys had hugged her to her satisfaction, the neck of his cloak was drenched and he was near to weeping himself. By the saints, no one had warned him children could have such a detrimental affect on his heart.

He started to bid farewell to his lady only to find that she had flung her arms around his neck as well. She kissed him full on the mouth before the entire company, then stepped back and shooed him away.

"Off with you then," she said with a frown. "Why are you dawdling here when there is gold to be fetched?"

He laughed and kissed her for good measure, grateful for confidence shown when she could have been continuing the berating she'd given him earlier for going without her. He mounted quickly and set off before she could change her mind and curse him yet more.

If they rode hard, they could make Dover in less than a pair of fortnights. He started to worry about how long it would take to accomplish everything else, then stopped himself. It would take as long as it took; there was little he could do to hasten things along unless he sprouted wings.

Gwen would be his before the chill of winter had fallen, surely.

Or so he prayed.

33

"Where is Robin?"

Amanda looked up from where she was digging enthusiastically in Geoffrey's garden with Anne and smiled a toothy smile. "Gone," she said cheerfully.

Gwen looked about frantically. She could hardly believe she'd been preoccupied enough with Rhys's having left not to have made a more continual effort to ascertain her son's whereabouts. She'd seen Nicholas several times the day before and assumed that he was alone only because he and Robin had had another fight. The two scrapped like puppies one moment, then were inseparable the next. Nicholas had been often out of her sight, which had led her to suppose that he'd been with Robin. It was hardly unusual for her not to have seen her son for a day or two, especially when he was at his training with the twins. He had of late gone through periods when he liked to pretend he was already a knight and that had precluded, she had come to learn, many unmanly things—such as visits with one's mother. She trusted the twins with her life, so she had reasoned within herself that she had no need for concern.

It was, however, that morn that she realized she hadn't seen Robin with either the twins or Nicholas in quite some time.

Gwen spotted a blond head peeking out from between a cluster of bushes and she strode over immediately.

"Nicholas?"

The blond head lifted and she was greeted by the sight of two very guilty-looking pale eyes.

"Aye, milady?" he said, his voice but a whisper.

"Where is Robin?"

He swallowed, but not very well. He looked as if he were trying to ingest a large boot.

"Is he here in the keep?"

He blinked at her and looked horribly uncomfortable, but he couldn't seem to form words.

Gwen took him by the hand and led him over to a bench. There was trouble afoot, and she had the feeling her son was at the bottom of it. She had a fairly good idea that if she managed to catch him, she would be more than tempted to acquaint his bottom with the flat of her hand a time or two. She doubted she would do it, but it would be tempting. How Robin managed it she wasn't sure, but the lad could talk his way out of a scolding with nothing more than a few contrite looks and a solemn promise never to commit mischief again.

"I didn't want to lie," Nicholas blurted out suddenly.

Gwen looked at the lad. Obviously he had a more developed sense of guilt than her son did.

"You lied?" she asked sternly. No sense in letting him believe such behavior was permissible.

And then Nicholas broke down into such heartwrenching sobs that Gwen immediately regretted her frown. She drew the boy onto her lap and rocked him while he wept as if he'd never stop. Soon Amanda and Anne had joined the little group. Amanda kept patting Nicholas soothingly. Anne merely stood by, clutching her hands together and watching with wide eyes.

"Oh, Nicholas," Gwen said gently, "it can't be as bad as all that."

"He's gone to France!" Nicholas wailed.

Gwen realized then that it certainly could be as bad as all that. She felt a chill steal over her.

"Did he go alone?"

"Nay," Nicholas wept, "he went in Sir Rhys's company!"

"Well, that isn't as bad as it could be." As if the thought of her son traipsing about with almost a score of mercenaries wasn't bad enough. "Does Sir Rhys know of it?"

Nicholas stopped wailing long enough to look at her, aghast.

"Of course not, milady! He would never have agreed to such a thing."

"True enough."

She almost set Nicholas aside to run to the keep and send someone after Rhys to fetch Robin, then she thought better of it. He was already a day out, more than that if he'd started at dawn that morning. The company could be caught, true, but was that the best thing? The thought of Robin riding into possible war with Rhys was enough to make her wish to ride out herself to catch them, but was war what Rhys would find waiting for him? For all she knew, Rollan was behind the entire scheme and Rhys was riding off on a chase that would lead nowhere. Should Alain and his brother decide to visit Fenwyck, wouldn't the best place for Robin be anywhere else?

The more she contemplated that, the more she began to think that might be the best plan. Rhys would care for Robin as if he'd been his own son. It wasn't where she would have chosen to have her firstborn, but the choice apparently wasn't hers.

"How did Robin manage this?" she asked Nicholas with a sigh.

"He bribed one of the mercenaries."

Unsurprising. "With what?"

"Your cloak brooch, milady. I begged him not to, but he wouldn't listen."

"Of course not," Gwen said, pursing her lips. Stealing and bribery. Where, by all the saints, had he come by such unwholesome ideas? Too much time listening to her mother's minstrels, obviously.

"He made me swear I wouldn't tell, swear it by the Holy Rood, lady," Nicholas said. "Then he told me if I kept his secret, he would pretend we were brothers."

Gwen watched Nicholas's eyes well up with tears, and her heart broke at the sight of it.

"I suppose he won't want to now," Nicholas said, dragging his sleeve across his eyes.

Gwen gathered him close and hugged him. "Nicholas, love, by the time Rhys is through shouting at him, he will have so few wits left he will have forgotten about what he made you promise."

"Think you, my lady?"

"Aye, lad, I do. But surely he doesn't think to travel all the way to France undiscovered."

"He's very clever," Nicholas said, his tone tinged with awe.

"*Devious* and *disobedient* are words I would more readily choose, but I suppose you have it aright." She patted him on the back. "Come, lad, and let us seek out the shelter of the hall. Rhys will see to Robin well enough after he's done scolding him. No doubt it will be a grand adventure for him and he'll have many tales to tell you when he returns."

And the first one would likely be how loudly Rhys had shouted at him

for his stupidity, but that was one Gwen would gladly listen to. She knew she
likely should have been sick with worry, but if there were anyone who could
keep Robin safe, it would be Rhys—if he survived the pains in his chest just
seeing the lad attached to some mercenary's saddle would give him.

Gwen started to shepherd her little group back to the hall, but the girls
had a different idea. Nicholas was pressed into service as a horse and he
submitted willingly. Gwen suspected by the long-suffering look on his face
that he thought it a just penance for the grievous sins he'd committed.

She closed her eyes and sent a prayer flying heavenward that her son
would be safe and that Rhys wouldn't strangle him when he'd found out
what Robin had done.

And then she said one for herself that sometime in the near future her
life would arrange itself as it should. No wars. No fighting. Nothing more
to do than sit in her solar with a bit of cloth under her needle and worry
about what might find its way into the stew at supper.

It was over a month later that she had finally managed to at least make
herself a place in Fenwyck's solar. The day was fine, the light was bright,
and the children played at her feet. Her mother had somehow managed to
unearth a minstrel from the surrounding countryside, and the lad sang
skillfully. Sweet music, fine wine at her elbow, and those she loved surrounding her. The only things lacking were her son fingering his wooden
sword purposefully and her love himself sitting across from her, snoring in
the sunlight.

The vision was so powerful, and so disturbing, that she set aside her
embroidery and rose.

"My lady?" Nicholas asked, looking up immediately.

She smiled as best she could. "I'm just a bit restless, lad."

"A walk in the garden, love?" Joanna asked, looking up with a smile.

"Aye, Mother. It will do me good."

"I'll watch over the girls," Nicholas volunteered.

"What a patient lad you are," Joanna said with approval. "A fine,
knightly virtue that is, to look after those weaker than yourself."

Nicholas looked as if he'd just been recognized by the king himself.
"Think you, my lady?"

Joanna nodded at him, then looked at Gwen. "A good lad, this one. You
were fortunate to find him. I wonder if Rhys understands how fortunate."

Gwen pursed her lips. "He's a man, Mother, and as unobservant as they
come. He'll realize his good fortune in time. For now, though," she said,
laying her hand gently on Nicholas's head, "I am merely grateful for a good
lad who is so patient with the ladies about him."

Nicholas smiled gamely. "The girls think of new animals for me to be each day, you know," he admitted. "I learn to be one kind well enough to make them happy, then they change their minds." He considered for a moment, then looked up at her. "Are all women thusly, my lady?"

Joanna laughed. "You've spent too much time with Robin, love. The girls are merely clever, not fickle."

Nicholas appeared to be digesting that. Gwen smiled and bent to kiss the top of his head.

"I thank you for your goodness to the little ones. They love you for it."

By the way he straightened his shoulders and took on a more purposeful expression, Gwen assumed that comment was enough to make him happy. She suspected he would have crawled to London and back on his hands and knees if Amanda and Anne had asked it of him. The lad was starved for any kind of affection, and Gwen was only too happy to see it given to him.

She made her way down to the great hall, wondering if perhaps the twins might be found and persuaded to train with her a bit. Rhys had absconded with her sword and replaced it with a completely useless blunted piece of steel. Fortunately the Fitzgeralds had recovered from their *mal de cheval* in time to discover with whom Rhys had hidden the blade and exerted their considerable charm to take possession of it. Gwen couldn't decide if they thought she should have her sword because it was a challenge to avoid being nicked, or if it was because they thought her skill was improving enough that they no longer needed to worry about their tender skins. She liked to believe it was the latter.

Hisses and angry gestures drew her attention. She looked to the hearth to find Geoffrey and Montgomery quarreling fiercely, albeit quietly. The moment they saw her, they both assumed such false looks of innocence that she knew whatever they discussed involved her intimately. It was definitely something to be investigated.

She strode over to them, stopped a pace away, and put her hands on her hips. That posture always intimidated Robin. Perhaps it would work here just as well.

"What is it?" she demanded.

"Nothing," they answered in unison.

Gwen saw a hint of parchment poking up from the neck of Geoffrey's tunic. Without giving it further thought, she leaped upon him, wrenched it free of his clothing, and stuffed it down the front of her gown. Both men turned on her as one, their fingers flexing and their mouths working soundlessly.

"Good morrow to you," she said, turning to walk away.

"My lady," Geoffrey pleaded, "I beg you return that."

She turned back around. "I think not."

"'Tis a small thing, truly."

"Then what does it matter if I know of it?"

Montgomery took a step backward and shook his head. "I hereby remove myself from this disaster." He looked at Geoffrey. "The full weight of Rhys's displeasure will rest upon you, my lord."

Gwen didn't wait to hear more. She pulled the missive free and managed to read the entire thing save the signature before Geoffrey ripped it from her hands.

I, Jean de Piaget, write this by mine own hand this last day of July, the Year of Our Lord, 1206, to Rhys de Piaget. Greetings to you, Grandson, and may the good graces of our Lord be upon you.

There is trouble afoot and I fear it travels about France at will. I have gathered up your treasure and will bring it to Ayre. Meet me there with all haste.

Let not all you've worked for be snatched away from you whilst you sleep, Grandson.

Jean de Piaget

"We must go at once to Ayre," Gwen announced.

Montgomery held up his hands. "I will have nothing to do with this—"

"Of course you won't go to Ayre," Geoffrey said firmly. "This could be a forgery."

"You fool, the first missive was obviously a forgery!" Gwen exclaimed. "It begins as the last with Rhys's grandfather smelling trouble. It is perfectly logical that he would bring all Rhys's gold to Ayre to keep it from being snatched in France."

"Now, lady—" Geoffrey began.

"And so we must be away for Ayre," she said, glaring at him. "What would you have—Rhys's grandfather delivering the gold straightway into Alain's hands? Or Rollan's? Come, Montgomery. We will see to the gathering of the men and be on our way immediately."

"Oh, nay," Montgomery moaned. "My lady, I beg of you, nay."

"Then I'll go myself—"

"You will not," Geoffrey announced. He folded his arms over his chest and looked at her sternly. It would have worked a bit better, perhaps, if he had been as tall as Rhys. Gwen hardly had to tilt her head backward much at all to meet his eyes, though she did concede that his breadth was somewhat intimidating, as was his steely expression.

And then there were those uncomfortable memories of her time wallowing in pig manure thanks to Geoffrey's ingenuity.

"You have no business traipsing across England to rescue Rhys's gold for him," Geoffrey continued firmly. "I can easily send men to do the deed in Rhys's stead."

"But—"

"I will go myself," he added, then he stopped and frowned. "Saints above, what possesses me to say the like is something I'm certain I'll never understand. I'm equally as certain I'll regret it."

"But it must be done soon—"

"In a day or two," Geoffrey said. "I had planned to meet Rhys in London in a fortnight just the same."

"But you must meet him in London as promised," Gwen argued, "else he won't know what has transpired. He would return here to Fenwyck and find us gone."

Geoffrey sighed heavily. "Very well, I will go to Ayre and send someone else to London to alert him as to what has transpired. He will come to Ayre instead of Fenwyck, and we will have this tale finished with Alain."

"And another messenger sent to Dover."

"But—" Geoffrey protested.

"Lest your messenger in London miss him!"

"Very well," Geoffrey said with a heavy sigh. "Two messengers in two places. And let us hope Rhys does not slip past the both of them. I will have the lads set out in a day or two. Now I will have to see to the running of the keep in my absence." He looked at her. "You would be a good choice for that."

Two days? Rhys's grandfather could already be a handful of miles away from Ayre and nigh onto walking into a trap in that time. Two days was too long to wait.

"Chasing after Amanda and Anne together will occupy your time quite nicely," Geoffrey added. "And perhaps seeing to a bit of my mending."

It was an enormous effort not to wallop him strongly on the head. It was, however, tempting to make several alterations to his clothes.

Perhaps if she filched a horse and left at dusk she could be well on her way before anyone discovered her absence. The twins could be left in charge of seeing to the children. They were as much under Amanda's sway as Nicholas was, but perhaps with a stern lecture from her they might realize how necessary it was to keep the children in check. Nicholas would be there to entertain her. Her mother would oversee the care of the children and Gwen's guard both. Indeed, Gwen suspected she likely wouldn't be missed overmuch.

"And a day or two overseeing the kitchens as well," Geoffrey said, obviously captivated by the thought of all the things a woman could do for him that hadn't been done since his lady had passed.

It was obvious what she had to do. Fortunately she had given much thought, if not practice, to her mercenary attributes over the past few years. One never knew when a vice might come in handy.

"Of course, I'll stay behind and see to all those tasks," she lied enthusiastically.

Geoffrey blinked. "You agree?"

"Geoffrey, 'tis obvious you have given this much thought and I must submit to your superior wisdom in the matter. What good would I be as a mere woman?"

"What indeed?" Montgomery muttered.

Gwen shot him a warning look, then turned a bright smile on Geoffrey. "My place is at the tapestry frame and cooking fire, my lord, as you suggested."

Montgomery began to choke. Indeed, he seemed determined to cough the life out of himself. Gwen pounded him very forcefully on the back until he held up his hands for mercy.

"Rest assured," Gwen said to Geoffrey, "that your keep will be in capable hands while you trot off on the rescue. Rhys will be most grateful to you."

"Well," Geoffrey said, sounding quite frankly amazed, "I'm happy to see your good sense."

"I'm quite certain you are."

Geoffrey looked at Montgomery, then back at Gwen. "I should perhaps begin preparations," he said.

"I couldn't agree more," Gwen said pleasantly. She shooed him away. "Take no more thought for your keep, my lord. I'll see to it all."

Geoffrey walked away, still looking the faintest bit unsure.

"I remain unconvinced," Montgomery said hoarsely.

"Silence, or I'll let you choke the next time."

Montgomery frowned at her. "Lady Gwennelyn, Rhys left me with specific instructions to keep you here."

"And what makes you think I intend to leave the keep, good sir?"

"Have you any idea how long I've known you, lady?"

"I've matured."

He snorted. "You've grown more cunning. Now, to assure myself that you truly intend to do as you should, I think I will require some sort of swearing from you."

"My father taught me never to swear."

"Vow it," he said in exasperation. "Vow by the Rood you will not go to Ayre to get Rhys's gold."

"Need I remind you that I am your lady and 'tis your duty to obey me in all things?"

His frown turned into a glare. "And need I remind you what will happen to *me* if aught happens to *you*? You could be the bloody queen of the whole realm, and I'd still say as much to save my sorry neck. Saints, lady, whom do you think I fear more?"

She couldn't blame him, actually, though it galled her to do so.

"He isn't my lord yet," she groused.

"I'll leave you to convince him of that when he returns. Now, for my own sweet soul's salvation, please swear by the Rood that you will not leave Fenwyck to attempt this foolishness."

Her dilemma was clear. If Rhys lost his gold, he would never be able to bribe John, they would never marry, and she would take a blade to her breast; her soul would be consigned to hell. If she swore by the cross that she wouldn't leave Fenwyck when she fully intended to do so, her soul would be consigned to hell.

Her choice was singularly simple.

Surely God wouldn't hold a little lie against her when it meant so much to a man who had served Him so faithfully for so many years.

She met Montgomery's eyes unflinchingly and gave him the most innocent look she could muster. She'd convinced him to help her do several things he hadn't approved of over the years; there was no reason she couldn't convince him now of her sincerity. "I vow," she said solemnly, "by the Rood that I will not leave Fenwyck to attempt this foolishness."

He looked at her closely. "Are you lying?"

She did her best to gasp in outrage. "Sir Montgomery, you doubt me?" It obviously hadn't been as believable as she might have liked, for he didn't look convinced.

"May heaven have mercy on my soul." He looked at her once more before he walked away. "Assuming that's where I go after Rhys is finished with me. Saint Michael, please let it be a quick and painless death . . ."

Gwen dismissed the future location of Montgomery's soul and concentrated on what she would need to accomplish before the day was through.

Dawn was rapidly approaching. Gwen knew that because she hadn't slept for the whole of the night. She'd wondered repeatedly if she might have been better off having brought someone with her, but whom could she have trusted? Montgomery had threatened at the evening meal to tie her to a chair, and such a plan was heartily seconded by Geoffrey. Nay, leaving alone had been her only choice.

She had just resaddled her mount when she heard the unmistakable sound of footsteps coming from the woods to her left. So soon? In the back of her mind she sincerely hoped it was someone from Fenwyck and not one ruffian in a band of many. The saints preserve her from that kind of test of her mettle.

She loosened her sword in its sheath and moved back into the shadow of the trees. The footsteps continued to approach stealthily, and she was impressed by the lightness of the footfall. For a man to move that silently took concentration and skill. At least her visitor wasn't Geoffrey. He ever moved through the undergrowth with the grace of a wounded boar.

The moonlight glinted off blond hair.

"Nicholas!" she exclaimed, putting up her sword.

"My lady," he said, running to her and throwing his arms around her. "I feared for your safety!"

She lifted his face up. "Did anyone see you?"

He shook his head.

"How did you reach me so quickly? Did you make off with a horse?"

"Nay, my lady. You haven't traveled very far. Indeed, I think you may have gone in a very large circle. Fenwyck is quite close."

Damn. Gwen took his hand and pulled him to her horse. "We'll have to ride doubly hard now, lad. I wish I'd brought some kind of map."

"I can help," he offered as she pulled him up behind her. "Sir Rhys taught me how to tell the direction from the sun. And I remember that we came north to Fenwyck, so we must needs go south to Ayre."

She couldn't argue with the logic of that, and she certainly wasn't about to send a perfectly capable navigator back to Fenwyck. She put her heels to her mount's side and followed Nicholas's directions.

And she sincerely hoped her rescue finished more successfully than it had started.

34

Rhys stood in the clearing, waiting until his breath returned. It had been an exhausting morning, what with the shouting he'd done and the subsequent necessity of having to plant his fist in Jacques de Conyer's face so many times. Damned hard on a man's knuckles.

And now this. Rhys folded his arms over his chest and frowned at the second culprit. He also wondered, in passing, why it was he hadn't realized until now that he'd had an additional member in his company. No wonder Jacques had volunteered to ride behind the company the entire way to France.

Rhys looked down, wondering just what it would take to convince the little fiend of the seriousness of what he'd done. And damned that Robin of Ayre if he didn't fold his own scrawny arms over his chest and frown right back at Rhys as if he'd been the one wronged.

"You stole," Rhys growled, deciding that to be a fine place to begin. "You stole your mother's brooch."

"Mama says mercenaries always steal," Robin informed him.

Rhys scowled, momentarily stymied. Robin had a point with that one. Rhys wondered if he perhaps should save his shouting for Gwen. What was she doing teaching this lad such things?

"You lied, then," Rhys said, grasping for another of Gwen's mercenary vices.

"I did not!" Robin argued hotly. "I bribed Sir Jacques forthrightly."

Rhys could hardly believe the lad before him hadn't yet reached his sixth year. The saints preserve him once Robin truly found his tongue.

"Then," Rhys said, scrambling for something to chastise him for, "you didn't tell your mother where you were going."

"She wouldn't have let me come."

"Neither would I!" Rhys exclaimed.

Robin thrust out his chin. "You may have need of me."

"What I have need of is a handy stump where I might sit comfortably when I turn you over my knee and blister your arse!"

Robin looked properly horrified by the prospect. He gulped, then put his shoulders back. "If you must," he said, his voice only quavering the slightest bit. "Or perhaps you could just bloody my nose and call it good."

Rhys stared down into the earnest little face and tried not to laugh. Saints, but this lad was cheeky. And Rhys had to admire the boy's determination to help. It reminded him so sharply of Gwen, he almost caught his breath. And with the next heartbeat he wanted more than anything to hug Robin fiercely and thank him for the loyalty.

But the saints only knew what sorts of antics that might encourage, so Rhys put on his best frown and tried to think of a suitable punishment.

"You disobeyed me," Rhys said, "and surely that merits some sort of penalty."

"You didn't say that I *couldn't* come," Robin pointed out.

"What I *did* say was that I expected you to stay behind and look after your mother."

Robin looked down at his feet. "You aren't my father." He ducked his head even harder. "I don't have to obey you."

Rhys was surprised by how much the words hurt. In truth, he wasn't Robin's sire. But he would have given much to have been the like.

"I see," he managed finally. "I suppose, then, 'tis good to know what you think—"

And then he suddenly found himself clutched about the hips by a small boy who had broken down into sobs.

"I wish you were!" Robin cried. "I wish it more than anything!"

If the former hadn't left him with tears in his eyes, the latter certainly did. Rhys hefted Robin in his arms and hugged him fiercely. He suspected most, if not all of his company watched him, but he cared not what they thought. He patted Robin on the back and said a few of those soothing words Gwen always said to Amanda when she was weepy. And when Robin had stopped wailing loudly enough to alert everyone in France to their arrival, Rhys set the boy down, took him by the hand, and led him out of the middle of the clearing.

He squatted down in front of Robin and used his sleeve to briskly dry away the boy's tears.

And he fought his smile when Robin reached out and did the same for him.

"Father and son we aren't," Rhys began, "but perhaps we would choose differently if we could. In any case, I think you are a good lad, and I would certainly be proud to call you mine."

Robin looked as if Rhys had handed him two dozen new blades of the finest Damascus steel and the skill with which to wield them all.

"Would you?" Robin breathed.

"Aye," Rhys said simply. "But I fear then that I would expect certain things from you."

The glow dimmed a bit. "You would?"

"Aye. I should hope that you wouldn't steal again. 'Tisn't an honorable thing for a knight to do."

"But a mercenary—"

"I speak of knights, Robin. An honorable knight does not steal. Neither does he lie."

Robin chewed on that.

"He protects women and little ones and he most certainly doesn't put worms down his sister's gown." Rhys knew he was making an impression on the boy; no sense in not clearing up a few other things while he was about the task.

Robin looked crushed. "He doesn't?"

"'Tisn't chivalrous, Robin."

"Oh," the lad said, seemingly considering the consequences of committing to a life of such goodness. Evidently he found it not too taxing a burden, for he put his shoulders back and sighed. "No more worms. No more snakes. No more spiders."

Poor Amanda, Rhys thought to himself.

"But about the other," Robin said, looking up suddenly.

"You plan to steal my mother, do you not?"

Rhys found he had no answer for that.

"And you didn't tell my father, did you?"

Rhys shook his head, still speechless.

Robin regarded him for several moments in silence, then shrugged. "Perhaps it is because you are protecting women and little ones. Is that the most important part of being a knight?"

No lying and stealing, my arse. How did one explain to a five-year-old boy the finer points of life? Or love? Rhys shook his head. Perhaps he was committing the same crimes he'd forbidden Robin to indulge in. Lying and stealing were acceptable mercenary traits, and they certainly were serving him well in his present endeavor. But he was also almost a score and ten and pressed to use whatever he could to have his dreams.

Saints, but children were greatly skilled at making a man question his own actions.

"Robin," he said, taking a deep breath, "I am not going to steal your mother."

"You aren't?" Robin looked crestfallen.

"Nay, lad. I'm going to win her fairly."

"By bribing the king?"

"Knights also do not eavesdrop, lad."

Robin frowned and fell silent.

"I will do what I must, for she needs to be rescued from your sire. Perhaps in this case I will be forced to use bribery, but 'tis not a thing I do lightly, nor do I do it often. Neither should you."

"I did not bribe Sir Jacques lightly," Robin pointed out. "'Twas necessary that I be here with you. To guard your back. But," he added with a sigh, "I suppose I won't escape a bloodying of my nose just the same." He stepped back, clenched his fists down by his sides, and closed his eyes. "I am ready, Sir Rhys."

Rhys put his hands on Robin's shoulders, turned him around, and pointed him to the horses. "A better punishment is seeing to the horses for a se'nnight. Your nose is safe."

Robin threw him a grateful look, then bolted for the other side of the camp. Rhys suspected the joy would only last a pair of hours until he'd had his fill of shoveling horse manure, then the lad would return and beg for a boxing of his nose.

That gave him at least another pair of hours to decide how he would keep

Robin out of harm's way. They hadn't had any trouble thus far, but they'd also been riding hard since they'd landed. The saints only knew what they would find when they met his grandsire at Rhys's mother's abbey. Rhys couldn't credit Alain with stirring up mischief in France, so that left Rollan. And Rhys knew he couldn't put anything past Ayre's younger brother.

Well, all they could do was make for Marechal, where he knew his grandfather currently loitered, and hope to find all well there.

Rhys took a final look about camp and, satisfied that all was going according to plan, took himself off for a walk in the woods. It wasn't to say that he didn't trust the men he paid so dearly for. He told himself he would ease through the surrounding forest simply because it soothed him to do so. He was a good scout, and three years of warring had certainly improved that skill. He'd never once been caught unawares, though he'd certainly run afoot of many others during their naps.

He waved off his guard and made his way carefully through the trees. After all, what need had he for someone to watch his back? He could watch it well enough himself.

He contemplated his well-earned prowess for perhaps another quarter hour. Aye, he was a fine tracker indeed.

And that was the last thought he had before his world unexpectedly went black.

"Ye fool, ye were supposed to wait till *after* the gold was fetched!"

"Ouch! Quit yer wackin' of me!"

"Aye, leave off, François, before I takes to wackin' the both of ye! We wasn't supposed to touch the bugger a'tall!"

Rhys opened one eye a slit. He would have liked to believe it was because he was being stealthy, but in truth it was because of the blinding pain in his head. By the saints, what had they felled him with, a boulder?

"If Jean-Luc wasn't so bloody greedy—"

"If François wasn't so bloody violent—"

"And if the both of you wasn't so bloody stupid, we wouldn't find ourselves in this fix!"

Rhys opened both eyes, certain the argument was heating up enough that he wouldn't be noticed. He found himself tied to a tree, watching three characters of less than sterling quality standing toe-to-toe, shouting and clouting each other. Taking in the dirty hands and faces, torn clothing, blackened eyes and teeth led him to one conclusion: Rollan was behind this.

That led him to another conclusion which was even more startling than the first: Rollan knew at least one of the secrets Rhys and his grandfather shared. And if he knew about their agreed-upon signals to be used in missives, what else did he know about?

The thought was enough to chill Rhys to the bone.

"We *was* just supposed to watch him," the third of the group reminded the others. "And keep our ears open to his mama's whereabouts."

"Aye," said François, giving who Rhys assumed was Jean-Luc another substantial blow to the side of the head. "That's what we was supposed to do, idiot."

Jean-Luc rubbed his ear in annoyance. "Pierre, tell him to stop a'cloutin' me. I'm having pains in me head."

Pierre, the obvious leader of the trio, rolled his eyes in exasperation. "François, leave off. We needs Jean-Luc to do the navigatin' for us. Remember, he's to remember where we's been so we can tell Lord Rollan."

The saints preserve you, Rollan, Rhys thought dryly, *if this is the one you've put your trust in.* Jean-Luc was still rubbing his ear and shaking his head. Perhaps he was afraid François had jarred something loose.

There was a crash in the undergrowth behind Rhys, and he quickly closed his eyes as all three swung about to look at him, their mouths agape.

"A beastie," François whispered in horror.

"Aye, run!" Jean-Luc gasped. "Run for our lives!"

The sound of two forceful slaps echoed in the little clearing.

"Oof," François said. "Thanks be to ye, Pierre."

"Aye," Jean-Luc agreed, "most needful. I'm feeling much better now."

Rhys leaned his head back against the tree and listened to the three resume their discussion of just what it was they were supposed to have been doing. Other than capturing him, of course. It seemed to entail a great deal of instruction from their employer, the mighty Rollan of Ayre. Then they spent ample time discussing what he'd promised to do to them if they failed. The more they discussed that, the more panicked François and Jean-Luc became, which necessitated a handful of slaps which Rhys could only assume had been delivered by Pierre.

Rhys wondered if his mercenaries were clustered about in the underbrush, stuffing their cloaks in their mouths to stifle their giggles.

He had just determined to open his eyes to see if that were the case when he felt the ropes binding his hands begin to be sawed asunder. Once that was accomplished, the hilt of a knife was pressed into his palm. And immediately after that, a small body launched itself into the clearing and dived for Rhys's sword.

Rhys watched in horror as Robin drew the blade and brandished it. He came close to severing Pierre's arm off above the elbow.

Like mother, like son, Rhys supposed.

Fortunately the three in the clearing were so appalled by the sight of a small boy waving about a blade he obviously couldn't control, they could only stand there and gape, which gave Rhys time to get to his feet, clear his head, and take the sword from Robin. He glared at his captors.

François and Jean-Luc dropped to their knees and clasped their hands before them.

"Nay," Jean-Luc pleaded, "don't take me life, Sir Rhys!"

"Aye," François said, bobbing his head in agreement. "We've heard tales of ye!"

"Fierce."

"Merciless."

"And do ye know," Jean-Luc said, turning to François suddenly, "that he bathes quite regular. Heard the rumor meself at that inn near Conyers—"

A muffled laugh or two from the trees made Rhys grit his teeth. Once his head stopped paining him thusly, he would knock a few other heads together for their trouble.

"Yield!" Robin shouted suddenly to Pierre, brandishing his own wooden sword as if it were a mighty weapon of death.

Pierre clutched his bloody forearm and glared down at Robin. "I should cut ye to ribbons, ye little demon—"

Well, there was no excuse for that kind of talk. Rhys leaned over and planted his fist in Pierre's face. Pierre crumpled like a handful of fine silk.

"I could have taken him," Robin pointed out.

"You had him, lad," Rhys assured him. "Distracted him very well. Kind of you to allow me to finish him off."

"Harumph," Robin said, resheathing his own sword with gusto. "Perhaps my mama will make up a tale about it."

"I'll be certain to relate to her all the important points," Rhys said. "Now, let's tie up these other two and see what kind of tidings we can have further from them. I daresay you'll want to remain for the questioning."

"Of course," Robin said, folding his arms over his chest and looking at the two culprits. "Perhaps we could use worms. Or a handful of spiders down their tunics."

Almost six summers. Rhys suppressed his smile as he did the honors of securing Robin's prisoners. So Rollan was spying on him to ascertain his mother's whereabouts. Interesting. Rhys could hardly see what good that would do the man, short of a kidnapping. Did he have no idea of Rhys's mother's secure haven? Or the lengths to which her women would go to see her protected? There was surely some benefit to being Jean de Piaget's daughter-in-law, and, no doubt, another soul following in the de Piaget tradition of spying for the king. Nay, there had to be more to the tale than was being told.

And he would have it all, just as soon as he'd discovered which of his men had been lurking in the bushes, chuckling. After they'd been properly rewarded for their humor, he would turn his mind to the other riddle. He hoped it didn't have as poor an ending as he suspected it might.

With Rollan of Ayre, one could just never be sure.

35

It had been four days. Four days was long enough to wait. And it wasn't just that to annoy him. He'd been loitering about the countryside for well over a month before that, waiting for the effects of his work to come to the fore. The missives had been sent and the journeys begun. Now the time for action had come and where did he find himself?

Waiting for his brother. For four days, no less. Rollan grumbled under his breath as he mounted the steps, narrowly missing being trampled by a pair of foul-smelling knights on their way down to the great hall. Had he not been so adept at hugging walls while eavesdropping, he likely would have tumbled to his death.

By the saints, he hated Canfield. He couldn't understand how Alain bore the place. Rachel wasn't even in attendance, but that hadn't stopped Alain from being entertained nonetheless. Why Alain couldn't have entertained himself thusly at home, Rollan didn't know. What he did know was that he himself had been mightily inconvenienced, and he was less than happy about it.

Of course those four days had given him ample time to contemplate his finest bit of mischief. He'd spent several cups savoring the fact that he had actually sent Rhys to France thanks to a perfectly crafted forgery using the password known only to Sir Jean and Rhys himself.

Or so they thought.

Then he'd enjoyed the knowledge that Gwen had gone dashing off from Fenwyck after she'd received the other forgery Rollan had so carefully concocted. And bless the girl if she didn't do just as Rollan suspected she would by sending messengers to both Dover and London to instruct Rhys to come straightway to Ayre upon his return to England.

Rollan couldn't have planned that better himself if he'd been the one to do so.

Which, of course, he had.

Now the last task that lay before him was to convince Alain that returning to Ayre as quickly as possible was the only course of action left to him. Rollan could almost envision the scene that he was certain would greet his eyes eventually. Alain, comfortable at home and determined to act on the thoughts Rollan had placed in his head. Gwen full of fervor, determined to rescue Rhys's gold. And Rhys himself, likely purple with rage over having been duped.

It could, Rollan conceded modestly, quite possibly be the most ingenious scheme he had ever set in motion.

Now to see to Alain's part in it. Rollan walked down the passageway to the chamber he knew his brother occupied during all his stays here and threw open the door. He was hardly surprised by the sight that greeted him, so he walked to the footpost of the bed and looked down at his brother who lay sprawled in a tangle of sheets.

"Perhaps you didn't receive the messages I sent up," Rollan said.

Alain looked at him blankly. "Messages?"

"I've been waiting to speak to you for several days, brother," Rollan said, dredging up what little patience he still possessed after days of drinking the swill that passed for ale at this keep. To think he might have been dining so deliciously at Segrave. Gwen and Rhys were no longer there to see him denied entrance. Even though Joanna also had gone with them, her seneschal wasn't overly opposed to Rollan. Rollan was, after all, the one who kept Alain far from their doors. Surely that would have earned him a meal or two.

Alain frowned. "What about?"

"I have tidings I'm certain you'll be interested in."

Alain waved with a kingly gesture. "Give them to me now."

Rollan would have preferred to speak to his brother in private, but 'twas obvious Alain had no intention of moving.

"Very well," Rollan began slowly, wanting to make sure his brother didn't miss anything. "It would seem that the lady Gwennelyn is returning to Ayre."

"Thought she was still in the north. Likely trying to get the stench of smoke out of her clothes." Alain smiled widely, obviously waiting for some response to his cleverness.

Rollan would have preferred also to have their activities at Wyckham remain secret, but it wasn't as if a simple castle whore or two would have made sense of it. Rollan laughed to soothe his brother's ego, then recaptured his sober look.

"Gwen is returning to meet Sir Rhys."

Alain looked more perplexed than usual. He sat up and rearranged a pillow or two behind his back. "Meet him at Ayre? I thought they were together at Fenwyck."

"Our gallant Sir Rhys has been in France, collecting his gold."

"He'll need it," Alain said. "It will take every last bloody piece to re-build Wyckham."

"I daresay he doesn't intend to rebuild it," Rollan corrected. "He in-tends to use it to buy Gwen's freedom."

Alain looked as if he'd been plowed over by a team of horses. "Her free-dom? From me?"

Rollan suppressed the urge to clap his hand to his forehead and groan. Truly, the depths of his brother's stupidity amazed even him at times, and he'd lived with the fool his entire life.

"A new scheme," Rollan lied. "I just learned of it myself."

"But how?" Alain asked. "Divorce?"

Rollan shook his head. "More likely an annulment."

"But," Alain protested, "that would say that I had never bedded her."

"But we know you have," Rollan said.

"But others would think I hadn't!"

"You have two children, Alain."

Alain thumped the pillow in frustration. "What does that matter? An annulment means I have not bedded her!"

Rollan sighed lightly. "A blow to your pride, of course."

"Annulment," Alain said in disbelief, as if he hadn't heard anything Rollan had said. "I can hardly believe it."

"Seeking to obtain such a thing would be gold wasted if you ask me," Rollan said. "I thought perhaps you might find a better use for it than see-ing it wind up in some London coffer."

"Always could use more," Alain conceded.

"My thought as well," Rollan said. "Which is why I suspected you would want to make for Ayre as soon as possible. They should be there to-gether by the time you reach the keep. Catching one's wife in the act of adultery should surely be enough to see her disgraced."

Alain blinked. "Will I lose her lands?"

"With the love the king bears you?" Rollan said soothingly. "Surely not, my lord. And think on this: you would be free to wed where you will." Rol-lan looked at the three very voluptuous serving wenches curled up in Alain's bed like so many puppies and smiled faintly. "Or perhaps not. You have an heir. You would simply be ridding yourself of an annoying wife."

"Rid myself of Gwen," Alain said, obviously finding the idea to his lik-ing. He smiled brightly. "I'll do it."

"Now?" one of the women complained.

Alain frowned, distracted by the ample flesh on display. "Hmmm," he said, scratching his head thoughtfully, "perhaps later."

"Ah, but it must be now," Rollan interjected. "Immediately. Before de Piaget and the lady Gwennelyn flee the keep. Why, they could be romping betwixt the sheets even as we speak. You'll want to catch them at it."

Alain shuddered. "Don't know why he'd want the acid-tongued wench."

"Who can explain a man's tastes?" Rollan asked pointedly.

"Who indeed. Let's be off," Alain said as he threw off the sheets, scattering his collection of bedmates. "The sooner, the better."

Rollan leaned against the footpost and watched his brother dress.

"You'll want to insult de Piaget, of course," Rollan remarked casually. "Enough to make him challenge you."

Alain froze. "Challenge me?"

"Can you not see the wisdom in it? A mere knight attacking a lord of the realm?"

"Ah," Alain said, nodding. Then he frowned. "But he will best me."

Rollan laughed softly. "Brother, you give yourself too little credit. The tales of his prowess are greatly exaggerated. Besides, you'll catch him fully sated from being abed with your wife. I daresay he'll have little strength to stand against you."

"You've quite the head for strategy," Alain said.

"That I do."

Alain paused. "Should I have my sword sharpened before we go?"

"Use the crop instead," Rollan advised. "Then finish him with a dull blade. More entertaining that way."

"I believe you're right, brother."

Rollan turned away and left the chamber before he had to watch his brother give very thorough kisses of parting to his afternoon's entertainment. Alain did not deserve Gwennelyn of Ayre. Rollan suspected that he should be very grateful that his brother had found her so unpalatable. The thought of anyone touching her set his teeth on edge.

He descended the steps to the great hall and contemplated the feelings coursing through him. He was surprised to find that amid the rage, there was actually a bit of something soft. He thought again about Gwen and the softness increased.

By all the bloody saints above, could that be love?

He came to a halt, fair frozen in place by the horror of the thought. He'd felt many things over the course of his life for Gwennelyn of Ayre, but love had certainly never been among them. He put his hand to his head. He wasn't feverish. He'd just celebrated the anniversary of his birth, so 'twas possible that the aftereffects of that celebration had wrought this unpleasant change in him.

"Murder," he said, rolling the word on his tongue. "Mayhem. Mutilation." His three favorites.

Ah, there were the stirrings of ruthlessness he felt so comfortable with. That softness had been but a moment's weakness. He would have Gwen, to be sure. And he would find ways to make her suffer while he took her. After all, she had spurned him once, leaving her bloody needle marks in his belly. She should pay for that.

But first Alain. The current lord of Ayre should surely make a stand at his own keep—the keep should have been his, Rollan of Ayre's, by birth. It would be his by death. If that death happened to be his brother's, what could he do but grieve over the deed?

And when his brother was killed by a mere knight, what else could Rollan do but take up a sword to defend his fallen brother's honor? And if that sword happened to end Rhys de Piaget's life, what could anyone do but count it a meet revenge?

Rollan planned, of course, to use a crossbow. There was no sense in getting any closer to de Piaget's sword than necessary.

And when Alain was dead and Rhys slain in recompense for the deed, there would be Gwen, alone and in dire need of a protector.

And who better than Rollan of Ayre to be that protector?

He continued on his way to the hall door, whistling cheerfully. Ah, but familial mayhem was enough to brighten any man's day.

36

"Sir Rhys says thievery isn't a proper knightly activity."

Gwen clutched the stall door and gritted her teeth. Much as she had grown fond of Nicholas over the past fortnight, she thought that if she had to hear one more quote from that unwritten tome *De Piaget's Knightly Wisdom*, she would go mad. How Nicholas had memorized so many entries she wasn't sure, but obviously he'd made good use of his short acquaintance with the gallant Sir Rhys. She took a deep breath.

"So true," she agreed. "But at the moment, neither of us is a knight and both of us are very hungry."

Nicholas considered that for a moment before looking up at her with a small pucker forming on his brow.

"We could not merely beg a meal?"

"From Ayre's cook?" She shook her head. "Nay, lad, 'tis better that no one know we've managed to breach the defenses of the keep. I fear a snatching is what we must resort to. Besides, they would expect nothing less of us dressed as we are in our mercenary garb."

Nicholas looked less than convinced. "My lady," he said slowly, "they cut off hands of thieves. What if they mistake us for thieves instead of fierce mercenaries?"

He had tucked his hands under his arms protectively, as if he could already feel the knife severing hand from arm. She looked down at her own disguise, then at his. They were both liberally smudged with soot and other unmentionable substances and to be sure the clothing Nicholas wore would have done any ragtag mercenary's lad credit. Her own clothing was something she'd filched at Fenwyck, and she felt confident that almost three weeks' worth of travel had added authenticity to her own appearance. Surely they would be taken for what they pretended to be. Besides, she was hungry enough not to care. She'd packed only enough food for herself. To be sure Nicholas was a slight lad, but he was a lad after all and seemingly trying to make up for nigh onto six winters of poor fare at his uncle's cooking fire. As far as she could see, she had no choice but to take her chances at pilfery. Though she anticipated that Rhys would arrive at any moment, thanks to the messengers Geoffrey had sent, she was certain she would be in a better state to greet him having had something to fill her belly.

"Come, Nicholas," she said, reaching for his hand. "No harm will come to us. We're far more likely to starve to death than to be branded as thieves."

Nicholas smiled gamely and took her hand. "I'll protect you, my lady, should it come to that." He patted the spare knife Rhys had given him and put his shoulders back. "Sir Rhys would wish it of me."

Gwen shook her head as she crept with Nicholas from the stall. It was no wonder Rhys had such a following of mercenaries. If he hadn't beaten them all into submission, he surely would have charmed them into following him. It was certain he had made a loyal follower out of Nicholas. She could only hope Robin was being so obedient. She had no doubt her son had been discovered long before now, and she wished mightily she could have seen Rhys's reaction to it. Robin must have hidden himself all the way to France. Gwen didn't doubt Rhys would have turned around and brought the lad home had they still been on English soil.

And turn around he would, once he discovered the falseness of the missive he'd received. It had to have been Rollan behind it. She was certain he had lured Rhys to the continent so he could be at Ayre to receive the gold. She hadn't seen him as yet, but she hadn't ventured out of the stables either, preferring to wait a day or so before making the attempt. Just getting inside the gates had been hard enough on her heart.

"Bloody hell!"

Gwen paused. That sounded uncomfortably like Geoffrey of Fenwyck. That did not bode well.

"Turn the other way, you puking fool!"

Gwen came to a dead stop at the entrance to the stables and looked out into the courtyard. There stood Geoffrey of Fenwyck, his guard, Montgomery, and fifteen grim-faced mercenaries.

Oh, and the twins strapped, as usual, to their horses.

"Oh," she said.

"Nay, Connor, not you, too! And do not fall upon me!"

Gwen would have laughed, but Geoffrey of Fenwyck had just caught sight of her, and she thought better of her reaction.

"You!" he said, shaking the more substantial items off his very damp sleeve and pointing at her. "This is all your fault!"

Evidently the twins had braved the journey south, but not survived it any better than their trip north. Geoffrey looked to have not weathered the ensuing results very well.

"Told you not to stand between them," Montgomery remarked.

Geoffrey snarled a curse at Montgomery, then removed himself from between the two fallen Vikings.

"You could at least roll them over so they don't choke," Montgomery said. "Then again, maybe I'll do it," he added at Geoffrey's look.

Gwen folded her arms over her chest and waited for the inevitable eruption.

"You *swore* you would stay behind!" Geoffrey shouted at her.

"Swore by the Rood, too," Montgomery said with a grunt as he heaved a Fitzgerald onto his belly in the dirt.

"I've never been tempted to beat a woman before," Geoffrey growled, "but I vow that the thought grows more appealing by the moment. Especially now. Look at me!"

Gwen looked. And she suppressed the urge to hold her nose closed.

"What did you feed them last eve?" she asked.

"Does it matter? They bloody can't look at a horse that they aren't puking!" He flexed his fingers. "Yet another thing to hold you accountable for—"

Gwen found herself suddenly standing behind a bristling, knife-wielding six-year-old.

"N-not while I l-live," Nicholas said, brandishing his blade. "You'll n-not t-touch her!"

Gwen realized then that Nicholas wasn't bristling, he was shaking with terror. She couldn't help but smile at his bravery. Even Geoffrey seemed impressed. He folded his arms behind his back and looked down gravely at the boy.

"Think I should leave her be?" he asked.

"If you v-value your 1-life," Nicholas said, stabbing the air in front of him meaningfully with his knife.

"And what think you of her lying her way from Fenwyck to come here?" Geoffrey asked.

Nicholas stopped stabbing and merely pointed his knife at Geoffrey. "Sir Rhys wouldn't have approved—"

Geoffrey looked at Gwen with one eyebrow raised.

"—but since we're posing as mercenaries and not knights, it's all right."

"Mercenaries," Geoffrey repeated.

Montgomery laughed. "Lady, isn't such a thing what got you into trouble initially?"

Gwen scowled at the two of them. "I did what I had to. And now I'll thank you both to leave me in peace to continue my labors. I can only pray you haven't spoiled my ruse beyond repair."

Geoffrey clapped a hand to his head. "By the saints, I think I should let Rhys have you. I don't think I've the stamina for your schemes."

"As if the choice were yours," she said tartly. She put her hand on Nicholas's shoulder. "Come, lad, and let us see if we can filch supper, then we'll return to our post and wait for the proper moment to recover Rhys's gold."

"Oh, nay," Geoffrey said, shaking his head. "You'll not continue along this path. Montgomery and I will see to the unraveling of this mystery."

"Rollan will never reveal himself with you here," Gwen argued. "'Tis better that I see to it."

"How, by holding a handful of sewing needles to his throat?"

"I can wield a blade well enough," she said through gritted teeth. "Shall I demonstrate on your sorry form?"

"If I might venture an opinion," Montgomery began.

Gwen threw a curt "Nay, you may not" at him only to realize Geoffrey had said the same thing.

"My lord, my lady," Montgomery continued, "surely we can settle this amicably."

"He has insulted my skill," Gwen said stiffly.

Nicholas patted her hand that still clutched his shoulder.

"My thanks, lad," Gwen said, "but I think I'd like to repay him myself. There are several other things I should like to avenge myself for as well."

"What?" Geoffrey demanded.

"Numerous tweakings of my plaited hair while I was a child," Gwen said, drawing her blade.

Geoffrey snorted in disgust. "What a pitiful reason."

"Very well, then," Gwen said, pulling Nicholas behind her, "there are other things I might seek satisfaction for."

Geoffrey only glared at her.

Gwen took a deep breath. "The locking of me in the piggery."

"Ha," Geoffrey said, "I *knew* you hadn't forgiven me for that."

"I could have been trampled to death!"

"Snuffled thoroughly, more likely," Geoffrey returned. "Besides, the sow was away from her piglets at the time. You were perfectly safe."

"What about threatening to toss me in the dungeon?"

He smiled just as wickedly as he had when he'd threatened it. "Many thanks for the reminder. Perhaps you would care to see the inside of Ayre's."

Gwen glared at him and fingered the hilt of her sword. Geoffrey folded his arms and looked at her with what she could only term a smirk, as if her skill was too paltry to cause him any distress or concern.

"Make way for the lord of Ayre!"

Gwen jumped. The announcement even produced something of a start in Geoffrey. He whipped around to look at the gate guard who had bellowed those words. Gwen contemplated a quick duck back into the stables to protect what anonymity she still had, then found she was far too late.

She had counted on Rollan. She hadn't anticipated having to face her husband as well. She put her shoulders back. Perhaps 'twas best she confront Alain and Rollan together. At least she would have the support of her small army, though she had to admit Geoffrey looked none-too-enthusiastic about the prospect. At least Rhys's mercenaries were looking appropriately fierce.

The herald's words had hardly died away before Alain himself rode through the gates and came to a halt. He was surrounded by a handful of guards and trailed by his brother.

"Well, this is interesting," Rollan drawled. "Sister, are you felling your guardsmen again?"

Gwen wished desperately that the Fitzgeralds were doing something besides moaning in the muck. They surely would have added to her air of invincibility.

Alain was looking at her and blinking. "You're not abed," he said.

"Nay, my lord, I am not," she agreed.

Alain looked at Rollan. "I certainly wouldn't want to bed her now. She smells."

Gwen wished she'd thought of her disguise on her wedding night.

"Where's de Piaget?" Alain asked.

"Ask your brother," Gwen said. "I imagine he knows."

Alain scratched his head. "Rollan said he would be—"

"Ah, aye," Rollan agreed. "Off doing some chivalrous deed, no doubt."

"But he's supposed to be here," Alain argued. "Bedding *her*. Though why he'd want to, I don't know."

Gwen smiled at her husband. "Oh, you won't have to wait long for him. I imagine he's on his way here by now. I don't know that I'd want to meet him, though. I doubt he'll be all that happy when he arrives."

Alain looked faintly panicked. "Then perhaps we should raise the drawbridge. Just in case."

"Riders approaching!" another guard shouted.

"It can't be him," Alain said, fingering his crop nervously. "I didn't see him on the road."

"I did," Montgomery offered.

"And you know what fine eyes Sir Montgomery has," Gwen added, finding that a great sense of relief had already begun to wash over her. Though she was certain she could have bested Alain on her own, having Rhys there beside her would be a boon indeed.

"No device on them!" the guard shouted down. "But dressed in black they all are!"

Alain gulped audibly. "Raise the drawbridge," he called nervously.

"That won't do any good," Gwen said confidently. "I tried that before."

"He won't scale *my* walls," Alain boasted, but he didn't look all that convinced.

Gwen raised one eyebrow, then shrugged and positioned herself where she could see the barbican. And as the drawbridge began to rise, she began to wonder if Rhys actually would manage the feat.

But then she saw a leg swing over the end, followed by the rest of a black-swathed body which rolled swiftly down the span toward the gatehouse.

"Down with the portcullis!" Alain squeaked.

It was too late. Rhys was standing inside the gates before Alain's command had reached the gatehouse. Rhys looked at the guards and snarled, "Lower the drawbridge."

The men began to crank furiously, in direct disobedience to Alain's direction.

"Traitors," Alain complained as Rhys's men swarmed into the bailey. Gwen smiled pleasantly at Alain.

"Told you so."

Gwen turned back to look at Rhys. He spared her a glare, and she suspected that he was less than pleased to see her there. She searched through the ranks of his men and felt an almost overwhelming sense of relief to see Robin waving merrily at her from where he sat before John on John's horse.

One loved one safe. Now if Rhys could just manage to avoid any stray arrows from Alain's guardsmen.

Another man had seemingly joined Rhys's company, and Gwen marveled at the white in his hair. The resemblance to Rhys was very strong and Gwen wondered if that might perhaps be his grandfather. She smiled at the man and received a sunny smile in return. At least Rhys's gold was safe. Or so she supposed.

She looked back at her love and wondered, by the fierceness of his expression, if she might have relaxed too soon.

Or perhaps he was reserving his stern look for Alain and his brother.

Gwen took a firmer grip on her sword. She'd sought Rhys out at one time in her life, ready to offer her sword to guard his back.

Perhaps that promise would be called upon after all.

37

Rhys knew he shouldn't have been surprised by what he was seeing, but he was. He distinctly remembered a very serious discussion he had had with his lady about the importance of remaining safely at Fenwyck. When he'd encountered Fenwyck's messenger at Dover, however, he'd begun to worry that perhaps Gwen might have decided that a quick journey to Ayre was called for. He couldn't have been so fortunate as to have had her not read the second missive. Rhys shot Rollan a look of promise before he turned back to his lady. Obviously she had as much regard for the sanctity of his word as did her son. He sighed. He was doomed never to be taken seriously. He looked at Gwen and frowned, just to let her know where his thoughts were leading him.

She was dressed, and this came as no surprise to him, either, in what she deemed mercenary garb. She was brandishing her sword as if she fully intended to use it. Well, at least she hadn't done any damage to any of her keepers yet. Nicholas had also been subjected to a liberal sooting and held his knife in front of him as if he expected to be attacked at any moment.

Rhys looked at the men in whose care he'd left his lady and had no doubts of their inability to control her. Geoffrey didn't look overly happy to see him, though Rhys suspected that look came more from wanting Gwen for himself than any remorse for a failure to keep her at Fenwyck. Montgomery was only shaking his head, smiling dryly. Rhys could hardly wait to hear what he had to say about the situation.

And the Fitzgeralds, of course, were lying facedown in the muck, conveniently senseless.

And then there was Alain watching the group just as Rhys was, with his entourage of guardsmen and Rollan slinking along behind him as usual. Rhys wondered how long Ayre's lord had been facing off with his wife.

And he shuddered to think what would have befallen Gwen had Geoffrey's messenger not found him. He would have traipsed back merrily up to Fenwyck, fully expecting to find things as he had left them, only to realize he should have stopped at Ayre.

"You were to be here already," Alain said pointedly.

Rhys blinked, then realized he was the one being spoken to. "Was I?"

Alain shot Rollan a look of irritation. "This isn't working out as you planned."

"Keep to your path, my lord," Rollan advised.

The saints preserve us all, Rhys thought. He found that Alain was looking at him with his customary look of disdain. Alain scowled and huffed and seemed to be searching for something to blurt out. Evidently he stumbled upon something, for his frown was replaced with a look of triumph.

"Can you not choose some sort of device?" he demanded.

"I plan to," Rhys answered calmly. "When my hall is built." Indeed, he'd already given it much thought. It would be a black lion rampant in deference to his own pride in his skill. And there must needs be something to honor his lady. He had not decided finally upon that as yet.

"Well," Alain said, obviously struggling for something else to say, "you look foolish without a device." He looked at his brother for approval.

Rhys watched as Rollan rolled his eyes. What mischief were these two about? Rhys looked back at Alain. He was obviously waiting for some kind of reaction.

"Foolish?" Rhys asked.

"Aye," Alain said. "Quite foolish."

"I think he looks sinister," Gwen put in.

Alain glared at her. "I didn't ask for your opinion." He turned back to Rhys. "And look at your hair. Unfashionably long."

"Oh, by the saints," Rollan groaned.

Alain turned a glare on his brother. "I'm doing well enough on my own, without *your* aid. I've just begun to point out his flaws."

Rhys folded his arms over his chest and tried to maintain a serious expression. He could hardly believe what he was hearing. "Are you trying to insult me?"

"See?" Alain said smugly to his brother. "*He* caught on readily enough."

Rhys wasn't sure if he should laugh or truly be offended that Alain couldn't think up anything more clever. He shook his head.

"Why would you want to offend me?"

"So you'll challenge me," Alain answered promptly. He looked him over critically. "I suppose you're just as weary from your travels as you would be from spending a fortnight in my wife's bed."

Rhys shook his head, certain he was hearing things.

Alain waited expectantly. "Well? Are you going to challenge me?"

"Why would I want to do that?"

Alain looked at him as if Rhys had just lost his mind. "Surely several reasons would be readily apparent."

"Oh," Rhys said, nodding. "The complete destruction of my land, perhaps?"

"That would do for a start."

Rhys smiled. "Somehow I think I'll leave our beloved monarch to take his revenge for that. He was none too pleased to learn of it."

"You told the king?" Alain demanded. "When?"

"When I was in London on my way back from being ambushed in France." Rhys smiled at Rollan. "Hire less greedy thugs the next time, my friend. These could hardly wait to get their hands on my gold."

Alain threw his crop at his brother. "Fool!" Then he looked down at his empty hand. "Damn," he said, looking rather stunned. "Now what am I to use upon him?"

Rollan sighed deeply and gently threw Alain's crop back to him. "Here, my lord. Now you are fully prepared for the task at hand."

"Oh, by the saints!" Gwen exclaimed. "Will someone fetch me a chair of some kind that I might sit through the rest of this absurdity?"

Rhys shared her sentiments fully.

"Aye"—Alain nodded—"the challenge. Well, Sir Rhys, get on with it. A good thing you've already dismounted before you deliver it."

"Easier for you to wield your crop that way?" Rhys asked, amused.

"Aye," Alain said. "And then to finish you with a very dull blade."

"It doesn't seem quite sporting, does it, for me to be on my feet and you on your horse?" Rhys asked. "Perhaps you should dismount as well."

Alain swung down, obviously before he realized what he was doing. He looked so appalled at his own actions, Rhys almost felt sorry for him. He could hardly believe he pitied the man who had caused him so much grief, but then again, Alain was only the figurehead. Rhys felt certain if he dragged the entire affair out long enough, Alain would reveal all of Rollan's machinations.

"So I am to challenge you," Rhys said conversationally. "First for insulting me, then for Wyckham? Or is it the other way around?"

Alain blinked in confusion, then suddenly nodded. "Aye," he said, weighing the crop in his hand.

"And then you'll kill me."

"A knight doesn't insult a lord and come away unscathed."

"Why do you care if I live or die?" Rhys asked. "Surely Wyckham isn't that important to you."

"Isn't Wyckham," Alain said, waving off the guardsmen who had begun to cluster around him. "It's all of her lands."

"All of them, hmmm?" Rhys asked, exchanging a pointed look with the captain of his mercenary company. Robin was safely taken care of by John and the rest of his men had taken up positions behind Gwen and Nicholas. His grandfather was sitting apart watching the proceedings with a smirk. Rhys shot him a warning look, but Sir Jean only lifted a shoulder in a half shrug as if to say he did not feel himself in any danger.

"Aye, all her lands," Alain said. "You see, if you live and manage to buy an annulment—"

"Or a divorce," Rollan interrupted.

Alain shot him a look of displeasure, then turned back to Rhys. "If you have an annulment from the king," Alain continued, "I might lose her lands. But if you're dead, then she'll have nowhere else to go." He looked at Rollan and he frowned. "That can't be right, for that leaves her still with me. How do I marry where I will if I'm still shackled to her?"

"Perhaps *you* could divorce *her*," Rhys suggested. "Consanguinity, or some other such rot."

Alain looked at him in surprise. "Aye, that would work well enough. And then surely the king would allow me to keep her soil."

"After your work at Wyckham?" Rhys asked doubtfully. "I wonder."

"'Twas Rollan's idea," Alain answered promptly. "I'll tell that to John myself."

Rhys looked at Rollan to find him staring intently at his brother, as if he willed him to close his mouth. So, it was as they had suspected. Rollan was behind the treachery. Rhys spared Rollan a brief glance filled with promise of retribution, then turned back to Alain.

"You realize," Rhys said slowly, "that no matter whose idea it was, John will hold you responsible."

"He will not," Alain disagreed.

"Won't he?" Rhys asked. "You are lord of Ayre, not Rollan, and he will surely blame the damage to Wyckham and Fenwyck upon you." He looked at Alain thoughtfully. "I wonder what other ideas of Rollan's John will hold you accountable for."

A look of panic began to descend on Alain's features.

"Indeed," Rhys continued, "I suspect that might be Rollan's plan." He looked at Rollan to see his reaction to that statement. And if he'd been made of less stern stock, he might have stepped back a pace at the look of pure hatred Rollan was sending his way.

"My lord," Rollan said, still glaring at Rhys, "he spouts nonsense. You know my loyalties are to you—"

Alain cut him off with an impatient motion of his hand. "I don't think I understand," Alain said to Rhys. "His plans only include you."

"Do they?" Rhys asked.

"Aye. You are the one who wants all my land."

Rhys shook his head. "I don't want your land. I want your wife."

Alain blinked, as if he wasn't quite sure to what to do with such a blatant admission. "You must want the land."

"I have enough."

The lord of Ayre was obviously becoming more confused by the moment. "But I must kill you, or so Rollan says. And you must challenge me that I might kill you fairly. That is the only way to keep Gwen's lands and rid myself of her as well."

"My lord," Rollan put in.

"Silence!" Alain commanded. He slapped his crop into his hand and frowned at Rhys. "I suppose if all you wanted was the wench, that would still be enough reason to challenge me."

"I would think it would just be easier for me to buy a divorce," Rhys said, "but no doubt Rollan has other ideas about that as well. You might want to think on what those could be."

Rollan laughed, but even Rhys could tell it was somewhat strained. "He babbles foolishness, brother. Have at him and let us be done with this."

Alain fingered his crop nervously. "He doesn't look all that weary to me. He was to be much wearier before I fought him."

"And even if I were," Rhys added, "do you truly think you could best me?"

"Boastful whoreson," Rollan hissed. "Take him, Alain, and repay him for his cheek."

"Rollan knows you won't come away the victor," Rhys said. "I daresay he expects you to suffer a fatal wound as well. I wonder just how long he's been envisioning himself as lord of Ayre."

"'Tis a lie," Rollan said. "I have no other purpose than to serve . . . my brother," he finished with an audible swallow.

Rhys could understand why. Perhaps the light had been slow in dawning on Alain, but apparently he'd finally seen it. He turned to his brother, his mouth hanging open.

"You want what I have," Alain said, sounding stunned.

"Now, brother—"

"You want my land!"

"And your title," Rhys suggested.

"Gwen, too, I'd say," Geoffrey interjected from behind Rhys. "I've seen the way he looks at her."

Alain strode over to where Rollan still sat atop his horse. "You intended to see me slain!" he roared, striking what he could reach of his brother with the riding crop.

"Or at least out of favor with the king," Rhys prodded. "That would likely be a worse fate—"

"Aye, 'tis true," Rollan spat, lashing out at Alain with his foot. "I wanted you dead."

"You traitor!"

"You imbecile!" Rollan returned. "Saints, Alain, you've not even a pair of wits to mate and produce enough intelligence to govern Ayre! Who do you think has seen to everything until now? You?"

"Traitor," Alain said, continuing to beat at his brother with the crop. "You liar! You led me to believe you wanted naught but my glory!"

Rhys watched as Rollan's mount began to buck, having received the brunt of perhaps one too many of Alain's blows. Rollan fought to maintain his seat, jerking back on the reins to try to control his stallion. The more the beast reared, the closer in Alain moved. Rhys would have called out a warning, but it was obvious the current lord of Ayre was beyond reason. He seemed to be viewing the mount as an extension of his brother, for he lashed it savagely.

And then whether by fortune or design, Rollan caught his brother in the head with his foot and sent him down to his knees. Before any in the company could move to pull Alain out of the way, the stallion had taken his own revenge with his hooves, slashing and then stamping until Alain was no longer moving. It was only then that Rollan regained control of his horse and urged him away a few paces.

"Merciful saints above," Gwen whispered from behind Rhys. "Is he dead?"

"Only if he's fortunate," Rhys said quietly. There wasn't enough left intact of Alain for life to have been a possibility. Rhys looked up at Rollan.

Rollan looked more shocked than Rhys had ever seen him. He stared in horror at his brother, then looked about him at the gathered company.

"I never meant—" he began, his hands fumbling nervously with the reins. "I mean, I never meant to be the one—"

"Seize him!" Geoffrey exclaimed.

Rollan seemed to gather his wits about him. "Nay," he shouted suddenly, gesturing furiously at Rhys, "seize *him*!" He looked for the captain of Alain's guard. "He is the one who has caused this tragedy!"

Rhys felt his mouth drop open. "Me?" he gasped.

"Aye," Rollan said, recapturing his coolness. "Captain, bind him and put him into the dungeon. I will see to the lady Gwennelyn until the king can be told—"

Alain's captain, Osbert, did not need to be told more than once that he could have a go at Rhys. Rhys had faced the man numerous times in the lists, merely as exercise of course, but even so the encounters had never been friendly. Rhys suspected Osbert was relishing the thought of doing him harm with a clear conscience.

Rhys held up his hand. "Osbert, you saw with your own eyes—"

"—You goading my lord," Osbert finished with a snarl, drawing his blade with a flourish. "'Tis as Lord Rollan says. All your fault."

Rhys groaned silently. Alain's captain was no brighter than Alain himself had been. There was no point in trying to reason with the man, especially since Osbert's blade was already coming his way with a goodly amount of enthusiasm.

At least Osbert was the only one of Alain's guard who had drawn his weapon. Perhaps the afternoon's events could be sorted out sooner than Rhys had hoped.

And then he found himself with no choice but to draw his own blade and concentrate on the man who came at him, salivating at the prospect of doing him in. It took three strokes to disarm Alain's captain and a fist under the chin to send him slumping to the ground, senseless. Rhys looked at the rest of Alain's guard. Not a one moved. Indeed, they seemed to be finding many things more interesting than him to look at.

Such as the rump of Rollan of Ayre's horse as it galloped out the gates.

"Someone should go after him!" Geoffrey exclaimed.

Rhys shook his head. "Let him go. We'll send word to John and let him see to the matter. Perhaps 'tis best that Rollan live with what he's done for a bit."

"A fine new lord of Ayre in that one," Geoffrey muttered. "Escaping across the countryside."

"The title is Robin's, my lord," Rhys said with a sigh, "as you would realize if you thought about it long enough. We can only be grateful Gwen's lands will go to someone with the sense to see to them."

"Why, thank you so very much," John said, lowering Robin to the ground. "I could have taken them over. And I daresay I would have dowered my sister-in-law very well that she might make a fine match of some nobleman."

Rhys shot his squire a dark look, then turned to look at the freshly made widow of Alain of Ayre.

She was staring at Alain as if she could hardly believe her eyes. Then she walked over, took off her mercenary's cloak, and covered him with it. She turned to look at Rhys.

"This isn't how I would have had it finish."

He nodded grimly. "Nor I. But 'tis done and we must make the best of it. The king will have to be informed."

"I'll see to it," Geoffrey volunteered.

"Later, if you will. I have need of you presently."

Geoffrey looked a bit surprised at Rhys's tone, but Rhys didn't spare that much thought. He had two things to accomplish, and the sooner they were done, the better he would like it.

And once those were done, they would ride like demons for Artane and pray John was too lazy to come after them. Rhys hadn't spared Rollan out of the goodness of his heart. A good chase would keep the king busy, and Rhys could only hope a murderer would interest the king more than a disobedient vassal.

For he fully intended to do exactly what the king had expressly forbidden him.

He looked at his lady and fingered the hilt of his sword. "We have business together, lady."

And it was business best seen to while they still had the freedom to do so.

38

Gwen wondered if Rhys now planned to use his sword on her. The way he'd said *business* had left her wondering just what he intended. With the severity of his frown, it could have been anything from a lengthy kiss to an encounter in the lists. She took a firm grasp on the hilt of her sword and pointed the blade at him.

"I don't know that I care for your tone," she said, mustering up all the haughtiness she could.

"We don't have time to argue about it," he said shortly. He thrust out his hand. "Come with me."

"Where?"

He looked at her as if she'd lost all sense. "Well, to the priest, of course."

"Priest?"

"So we can be wed," he said impatiently. "Saints, Gwen, why else would we need one?"

"To bury Alain?"

"He's not going anywhere. My head, however, *will* be if we don't get on with this business before something else disastrous happens—such as the king arriving and finding out what I'm about."

Gwen found her hand in his and her feet trotting to keep up with him as he strode across the courtyard to the tiny chapel. He hadn't bothered to sheath his sword, and she hadn't had the time. She looked at Alain's priest and watched his eyes roll back in his head at their approach. Unfortunately they didn't approach quickly enough to catch him before he slumped to the ground.

"Damnation," Rhys grumbled. "What else can happen to us this day?"

"A visit from the king?" John asked from behind them.

"A downpour?" Montgomery suggested.

"Ahem," Geoffrey said, trying to insert himself bodily between Gwen and her love, "I believe now that Alain—may his dim soul rest in peace—is gone, *I* should be the one to care for Gwen and what is hers. I am, after all, a powerful baron in my own right—"

Gwen watched as Rhys elbowed Geoffrey out of the way and took a firmer grip on her arm.

"Montgomery," Rhys said shortly, "rouse the priest. And find my grandsire, would you?"

"I am here, Rhys lad," came the crusty response. "Rude you are, young one, not to take into consideration an old man's sore knees." He clucked his tongue. "Such unseemly haste."

Gwen looked to her left to find Rhys's grandfather standing there. He looked anything but decrepit, and she could tell by the twinkle in his eye that he mightily enjoyed giving his grandson as much grief as possible. She found her chin grasped in surprisingly gentle fingers.

"Let me have a look at the girl," he said. He turned Gwen's face this way and that. "Aye, she'll do."

"Thank you," Gwen said dryly.

"Nicely fashioned ears," Sir Jean added, lifting her hair to peer at the appendages in question.

"Your grandfather, Rhys," Gwen said, never taking her gaze from Sir Jean's, "is a man of discriminating taste."

"He's as blind as a bat if you ask me," Geoffrey grumbled from behind her. "Not even a wimple of the stiffest fabric could pin those enormous flaps to the sides of her hea—"

Sir Jean threw him a steely look that had no doubt quelled many a braver soul. Geoffrey apparently found other things to do besides speak, for he said no more. Gwen's affection for Sir Jean grew tenfold.

"We need the priest propped up," Rhys interrupted. "John, go over and help Montgomery."

Gwen turned her attention back to the matter at hand and found that though the priest had regained his senses, he didn't seem to have the strength to stand on his own. She took pity on him and resheathed her sword. She thought to suggest the same to Rhys, but she could tell by the way he was clutching the hilt that he had no intentions of releasing the weapon any time soon.

"By the saints," John complained, "is there aught this man does save eat?"

The priest was rotund, and he seemingly had little interest in helping himself stay afoot, as it were.

"Where are those damned Vikings?" Sir Jean muttered. "If I'd known what weak-stomached women they were, Rhys, I never would have left you in their care. 'Tis a wonder you turned out tolerably well at all."

Gwen found, quite suddenly, that the impossibility of the situation in which she found herself was finally beginning to sink in. Rhys planned to wed her. Their priest either was too lazy or too terrified to stiffen his knees and stand on his own. Geoffrey was muttering under his breath behind her, Sir Jean was stalking off to rouse the Fitzgerald brothers, and Montgomery and John were arguing over whom the priest should be foisted upon. Nicholas and Robin were fighting with their wooden swords, and the whole of Ayre's garrison had gathered in a group behind them, all watching with wide, incredulous eyes. Rhys's mercenaries, the ones he had taken with him and the ones who had followed Geoffrey from Fenwyck, had all gathered themselves into a fierce little group of thirty, their hands on their swords as if they intended to seriously injure any soul who sought to thwart the plans of their paymaster. Rhys was fingering his own sword as if he prepared to fling himself into the midst of a battle, not matrimony.

Oh, and then there was Alain, who lay dead not fifty paces from them, victim of his own fury.

"Am I the only one," she asked no one in particular, "who finds this odd?"

"You think this is odd?" Rhys asked grimly. "Just wait, Gwen."

She looked up at him. "What more could happen to improve upon these events?"

He pursed his lips. "The king could arrive and discover what I'm about. You could find yourself widowed twice in one day."

Gwen blinked. "Then he did not give you leave—"

"He gave me many things, but you were not among them."

"Rhys!"

"Do you love me?"

She swallowed, hard. "Desperately."

"Then it is enough."

"Did you give him all your gold?" she demanded. "Did he take it all and merely thank you kindly?"

Rhys shook his head. "I gave him a bit to sweeten his humor and a bit more for his tax coffers. There is still enough yet in France to fund our escape should we need to leave England in a rush. For now, though, let us be about our business. The king's temper will see to itself eventually."

She sighed. "I suppose this means we will be riding very swiftly north."

"We'll have to pause long enough to consummate the marriage, my lady. You can rest then."

"The very romance of the thought leaves me breathless," she said dryly.

He spared her a scowl before he turned back to the priest. "Up on your feet, man! We've a wedding to hasten through."

"Here," Sir Jean said, shepherding the twins in front of him, "be of some use, you great mewling babes."

Rhys waited until the twins had settled themselves on either side of the priest, who suddenly found that his feet were sturdy enough to keep him upright and therefore there was no need to lean on either of the rather crusty and noisome-smelling men flanking him, then cleared his throat.

"Wed us," he commanded.

"But—" the priest spluttered.

"Robin," Rhys called. "Come name your mother's dowry."

Robin sighed as he put up his sword. He came to stand in front of Rhys, who turned him around to face the priest.

"Artane," Rhys supplied, "is hers alone."

Robin looked at the priest. "She has Artane, Father." He looked back up at Rhys. "Is that enough, do you think?"

"'Tis more than enough for me," Rhys said.

"Perhaps she should have what she had before she married Alain of Ayre," Robin said, as if he talked about someone besides his father. Gwen listened to him discuss the advantages of such a thing with Rhys as if he'd been managing such vast holdings his entire young life. Evidently his journey to France had been instructive.

"All she brought with her before," Robin decided, turning to the priest. "It can go to Lord Rhys. I'll keep Lord Alain's lands. Lord Rhys can see to them for me until I'm of age."

Gwen blinked. She wasn't sure what surprised her more, Robin's tone of authority or his mistake in Rhys's title. She put her hand on his shoulder gently.

"Robin," she said softly, "much as you might like to call Rhys lord, he is but—"

"The newly made earl of Artane," John supplied cheerfully. He smiled at Gwen. "A successful chat with the king and all, you know."

"Do not forget your lands in France," Sir Jean added with a grunt.

Gwen looked at him in surprise. "Land there as well?" She turned to stare at Rhys. "Did you know of it?"

"Not a bloody thing 'til a se'nnight past," he said, sounding none-too-happy about the delay in receiving the tidings.

Sir Jean shrugged. "Could have told him about it sooner, I suppose—"

"Aye, you could have," Rhys agreed with a growl.

"But I wanted to see what he'd make of himself," Sir Jean finished with a wicked smile sent his grandson's way. "Nothing like a little lust for land to make a man into a man."

"Grandpère, had I time, I would take you to the lists and show you what a man I've become."

Sir Jean looked greatly tempted. "Unfortunately you haven't the time, whelp, but don't think I'll forget the offer. In a fortnight or two after we've reached your wasteland in the north and you've recovered from your saddle-sores, we'll see who is the man in truth."

"Earl?" Gwen said, looking up at Rhys.

"Gift from the king for valiant service and bravery," John said.

"As well as for a chest of gold," Rhys muttered.

"Earl?" Gwen repeated.

"It was a very large chest."

"Yet still he would not give me to you?" Gwen asked.

"He said he would think on it," Rhys said shortly, "which left me wondering if I would do better to return to France for more funds or merely tempt him with a barrel or two of peaches."

"You could have threatened to make off with his cook," Sir Jean suggested.

"I had considered that, believe me," Rhys said dryly.

"Rhys, what will we do!" Gwen exclaimed. "If he has said you nay—"

"That was before he knew you were a widow," Rhys said, reaching down to take her hand, "and I'm sorry I've left you no time to grieve—"

The one who possibly would need it was Robin, but he seemed more preoccupied with standing as close as possible to Rhys. And it wasn't as if he'd spent more than what amounted to several days with his sire. Perhaps grief would be the last thing on his mind.

"But haste is of the essence," Rhys finished. "I hope the king will be too busy chasing Rollan to pay us much heed until we're safely ensconced at Fenwyck, where I am certain Geoffrey intends to offer us hospitality."

"Hospitality," Geoffrey snorted. "Think again! I *always* have regrets when I indulge in it."

Rhys ignored him and looked down at Gwen. "John reappropriated Artane and gave it to me. I told him not to, but he insisted I should have something for my trouble since I wasn't to have you."

"And now that you'll have me?"

"I'll keep it, if you don't mind, and build you a very fine hall upon it."

It mattered, she found, very little to her whom the land belonged to on the king's rolls. All that mattered was that she and Rhys now seemed destined to live in the same place, hopefully as man and wife. Assuming the king didn't reach them first and deny them what they'd waited so long to have. Gwen turned to the priest.

"Wed us," she commanded. "Now."

"Um," the priest began.

"Scribe!" Rhys bellowed.

A rather thin, sickly-looking soul was thrust into their midst, endeavoring to balance parchment, ink, and quill. The scribe was instructed to record what had transpired, under the watchful eye and drawn sword of the newly made earl of Artane.

The contract was signed by all parties involved, then the priest was sent on his way to see to the less pressing matter of arranging the former baron of Ayre's burial.

Gwen thought Rhys might find it an appropriate time to kiss her to seal their marriage, so she turned toward him, closed her eyes, and lifted her face up accordingly. But instead of kissing her, Rhys took her by the shoulders and set her aside.

Then he hit Geoffrey of Fenwyck full in the face.

"*That*," he said, "is for slobbering upon *my* wife's hand." He looked down at the baron of Fenwyck, who lay sprawled in the dust. "Never do it again."

Geoffrey could only gape at him, speechless.

Rhys looked about him, flexing his fingers. "Who should be next? I daresay I have many scores to settle this afternoon, especially with those who couldn't seem to follow my simplest command." He frowned at the Fitzgeralds. "Don't know that I'd want to touch them in their current condition."

"Montgomery?" John suggested politely.

Rhys shook his head. "That would leave me having to prop up the twins. He should be repaid as well, though. I left him with instructions to see Gwen remained at Fenwyck."

Gwen winced at the glare Montgomery threw her way.

"She vowed by the Rood," Montgomery said. "How could I doubt her word?"

Rhys snorted. "You know her as well as I do."

"If someone would care to hear my side of the tale," Gwen interjected. "I came to save your gold," she said to Rhys before he could open his mouth. "We received another missive at Fenwyck, you know."

"I know all about it, as I had the pleasure of intercepting your messenger in Dover," Rhys said. "That changes nothing. Fenwyck could have come in your stead."

"I am better at disguise."

"And very vulnerable should Rollan have caught you unawares."

"I've been working on my swordplay," she argued,

"You promised me you would stay behind."

"My plans changed."

"You know," John put in, "we should likely gather our gear and be on our way. Should the king decide to come to Ayre in the near future, I daresay we don't want to be here to entertain him."

Gwen looked at her former brother-in-law. "There are many who will attest to Rollan's murdering of Alain. You've no need to fear."

John smiled. "Oh, I have no fear for myself. 'Tis Lord Rhys who must worry about his sweet neck."

"There is that," Sir Jean agreed. "Powerfully fickle is that king of yours. Never know what he's intending."

"By the saints, Grandpère," Rhys grumbled, "I wish you had told me of the lands before we left London."

"Wanted to see what—"

"—I'd make of myself, aye, I know," Rhys finished sourly. "Have you any suggestions on what I might do to secure my bride?"

"Well, you've already wed the girl. Best bed her as quick as may be. Johnny Lackland can't argue with that much."

Rhys nodded. "Very well. Won't take but a moment or two."

"It will if you value your ability to sire any children," Gwen warned.

"I'll woo you later—"

"You'll woo me now."

"I've no need to woo you now—I've just wed you!"

"Too long out of polite company," John said, shaking his head sadly.

"I could give you a courting idea or two," Geoffrey offered, leaning up on his elbows in the dirt.

"Let the boy work it out himself," Sir Jean said. "We'll see what sort of imagination he has. 'Tis the last test I have before I tell him the last of the family secrets."

Rhys opened his mouth to say something, then shut it and shook his head. "I don't want to know any more. I've learned too much today as it is."

"I have something that might aid you."

Gwen looked at Montgomery to find him fishing about in the purse attached to his belt. He pulled forth a very faded green ribbon and handed it to Gwen with a smile.

"Oh," Rhys said, his breath catching on the word. "Then you had it?"

"Thought you might want it eventually," Montgomery said with a smile.

Gwen took the ribbon she had once given Rhys and gingerly tied it about his arm again. "I don't suppose," she said softly, "that this counts for you wooing me, but it is a most romantic thing just the same."

He drew her into his arms and smiled down at her. His eyes were very bright and seemingly filled with a stray tear or two.

"If you only knew how long I've waited for this moment," he said softly. "If you only knew what I felt the first time you tied this ribbon about my arm, and how desperately I prayed that some day you would be mine."

"You can tell me of it . . . um . . ."

"During?"

"After."

And with that, he closed his eyes, bent his head, and kissed her softly and sweetly on the lips. Gwen felt the world about her fade until there was only the man with his arms about her. No king, no gold, and no others. He angled his head and kissed her more deeply. His hands began to roam over her back and up into her hair. Her plait was loosened and her hair soon flowed freely over her shoulders.

"Oh, by the saints," a crusty voice said in faint disgust, "find a chamber, won't you?"

Rhys spared his grandfather a glare before he smiled down at Gwen again. "Should we?"

She blinked to clear away the haze and gave the matter serious thought. She suddenly felt the eyes of every man in the company turned upon her. Even Ayre's guardsmen were looking upon the scene with great interest, as if they each were counting on her to make the correct decision.

Gwen looked at Rhys.

"I know just the place."

It was only a short time later that she stopped in front of a vaguely familiar door. She smiled at her newly made husband.

"This might be appropriate."

Rhys pushed it open, then pulled a torch from the passageway and found a place for it inside. "I believe, however," he said as he drew her in behind him, "that you were wearing John's clothes the last time we were here. And you were not so liberally smudged."

Gwen felt her mouth fall open. She had completely forgotten about her condition. She had just been wed in garments covered with horse manure and three weeks' worth of travel.

Rhys laughed, as if he understood what she'd been thinking. "Not even that detracts from your beauty, my love."

"As if flattery comforts me!"

"Flattery?" He shook his head. "A knight never lies, so you must believe I speak the truth. Besides, smudged or not, the very sight of you leaves me weak in the knees." He shifted. "I can scarce believe you are mine."

She sighed and looked down at her filthy clothes. "This isn't exactly how I'd envisioned our nuptials."

"Nor I. I had thought even to attempt a song or two."

"The saints preserve me," she said with a laugh. "Perhaps my ears should be grateful for your haste."

He scowled. "'Tis hardly my fault that I cannot hear the notes aright. My skills simply lie in a different area."

"Dicing."

He smiled at that. "Perhaps later."

She looked around her. Not even a blanket or two to throw upon the floor. She looked at Rhys.

"Well?" she asked.

He took a pair of steps toward her, reached over her, and shoved the bolt home. "That should assure us privacy."

"For a moment or two," she agreed.

He looked down at her and smiled faintly. "If you had any idea how badly I want you, you'd realize a brief moment or two may be all you'll have from me at present."

She wasn't exactly sure what he meant by that, but she had the feeling she was soon to find out.

"I will woo you properly," he said as he pulled her into his arms. "Soon."

"The very thought is almost enough to induce me to bathe," she said as he kissed her.

And then she found that the condition of her clothing and her person mattered not at all, except as it served for a bed.

The floor was just as uncomfortable as she remembered it being. At least this time she had no fear of being interrupted. There was something to be said for a band of mercenaries to do her husband's bidding.

Her husband. Gwen could hardly believe it. Widowed and wed within moments. And what a ceremony it had been—

"Gwen," Rhys said with a sigh of resignation.

She winced. "Forgive me. No more thoughts."

He took her face in his hands and kissed her thoroughly. And then kissing led to touching and that led to all clothes being used as a bed, which led to Rhys promising between more long, sweet kisses that he would filch Fenwyck's finest goosefeather mattress at his earliest opportunity. Gwen started to say that it mattered not, then she realized she was several years older and the birth of two children more mature than the last time they'd lain upon such scant padding, and a goosefeather mattress was beginning to sound very pleasant.

And then thoughts of goosefeathers and children and uncomfortable floors began to fade and all she was left with was the man in her arms she'd never thought to have there again. And the thing that fair brought tears to her eyes in truth was the realization that his touch was no more practiced, his loving no more skilled than it had been the last time they'd lain together. He was all enthusiasm and unschooled passion—certainly not a lover who had spent countless hours lazing in his mistress's bed.

The saints be praised for that.

And if his hands trembled now and again when he touched her and he seemed not to know what to do with his knees or elbows on occasion, it did nothing but make her smile and clutch him to her the tighter.

He made her his with a positively mercenary-like laugh of triumphant possession.

And when he managed to breathe again, he rolled away with a groan. He sat up and gingerly planted his backside against the cold stone of the floor, rubbed his elbows and knees simultaneously as best he could, and smiled happily at her.

"That was exceedingly uncomfortable," he said cheerfully.

Gwen was quite certain she would never walk quite as easily again, but she had to agree just as merrily. "I don't know that I can manage that again here."

He paused. "We could filch a few more garments and things from about the castle."

"That would necessitate leaving the chamber. Dressing. Combing our hair."

"Enduring a thorough teasing from my grandsire."

She met his gaze and found herself nodding along with him.

"Best to stay here," he stated.

"We might manage with what we have."

And, unsurprisingly to either of them, they did.

39

Rollan of Ayre wished desperately he'd somehow managed to snatch Alain's crop before he fled the keep. Merely kicking his stallion in the sides was not producing the desired speed.

He looked behind him, but saw no riders following. He knew that reprieve wouldn't last long. They would send men after him, and then he would find himself languishing in some hellhole. He doubted that even he, with his superior charm, could talk himself out of such visible familial murder. John had never had much use for Alain, 'twas true, but the king would likely have preferred something a bit more subtle.

Where to go now? What to do? Whom to blame for his current condition?

The last was the easiest. This was de Piaget's fault. Rollan had counted on the gallant Sir Rhys to slay Alain in defense of Gwen's honor. Things would have been so much simpler that way. Rollan would have slain Rhys, then disposed of Robin and Amanda soon enough, and thereafter found himself lord of Ayre with a beautiful aqua-eyed bride at his side. Gwen would have found herself tamed in time. Indeed, he was certain she would have enjoyed the taming.

And now his scheme was completely ruined because of de Piaget's wagging tongue.

He would have to pay for his words, of course.

Rollan found himself heading west. And once he realized where he was heading, he smiled. Perhaps his plans could be salvaged. He hadn't killed Alain outright, had he? If anyone could it would be John who could understand the frustration of having an elder brother possess what should have rightfully come to him. Alain's death was an accident, an accident precipitated by de Piaget's rash goading of the former lord of Ayre.

Perhaps his schemes weren't for naught after all. Rhys could be finished off. Robin could meet with an unfortunate accident. Lads were always dying of one thing or another.

And Gwen could be convinced in time that they had always been destined to be together.

But first the greatest obstacle must be removed. And Rollan knew just who would be most helpful in doing so. Rhys's true parentage wasn't widely known. Indeed, Rollan suspected that there were only two people on the entire island who knew of it—and Bertram of Ayre had carried the secret to his grave.

And Rollan of Ayre had held the knowledge close to his heart since the moment he'd overheard his sire discussing the matter with Rhys's grandfather.

Ah, but eavesdropping was such a useful skill.

He altered his course and set his mind on his goal.

Sedgwick.

40

Rhys pulled the hall door shut behind him and was glad to do it. Though he had fond memories indeed of a certain tower chamber inside the keep, he would not be sorry never to see it again. He knew he would have to come to Ayre with Robin occasionally to assure himself that the lad's holdings weren't being overrun, but he was more than happy to be leaving the place behind him at present. He'd imagined up in his mind scores of times just how it might feel to walk through Ayre's doors with Gwen as his.

The reality of it was almost more than he could bear.

His company was waiting for him in the courtyard. His mercenaries looked appropriately fierce, not hesitating to send Ayre's guardsmen intimidating looks whenever possible. Rhys hadn't yet decided what he would do with the lads. Perhaps he could be forgiven for having had more on his mind than their futures for the past few days. Matters hadn't improved for his poor head—especially after having passed a long night of intimate deliberations with his beloved. Perhaps 'twas for the best that he keep them about for a bit longer until he could again concentrate on something besides thoughts of where and when he might have his lady alone again.

He gestured for the company to mount up. That much he could do with the small portion of his wits left him. He looked at Gwen and found that she was smiling shyly at him. He grinned back, then heard his grandfather begin to chuckle. A blush came from nowhere and applied itself industriously to his cheeks. He turned away before the entire company, and more particularly his grandfather, could see it and humiliate him with their teasing.

He turned to check the straps that held the Fitzgerald brothers to their mounts and gave them both an encouraging smile.

"One last time, my friends. I promise no more traveling."

"The travails we go through for you," Jared groaned. "Tending your hurts and sorrows—"

"Riding from one end of this barren wasteland to the other—" Connor added.

"Puking 'til there's naught left to puke—"

"I ask you, brother," Connor said, turning his head to look at his twin, "is this worth the pain?"

"Nay, it is not."

"I say we let him go north on his own."

"Aye, brother. You have that aright."

"Too late," Rhys said cheerfully, firmly cinching the rope that bound Jared to his horse.

"I'd rather walk," Connor groused.

"I'd rather stay *here*," Jared complained.

"You would miss me overmuch," Rhys assured them. "Courage, friends. The journey will be swift."

He walked away before more Viking curses could be heaped upon his head.

Gwen was mounted already, as was Nicholas. Rhys looked to find Robin holding Rhys's mount's reins. He looked sick with apprehension. Rhys walked over and ruffled his hair.

"Not to worry."

"But what if the king comes after us?"

Rhys squatted down and looked at Robin seriously.

"Think you I would let you go?"

"But the king—"

"Will be perfectly happy for me to claim you when the time comes. He values my sword, Robin, just as he will value yours in time—should he manage not to eat himself to death. I daresay he would rather keep us here on the isle than see us all go to France."

"But we've properties there, haven't we?" Robin asked anxiously. "Just in case?"

Rhys threw his grandfather a dark look. "Aye, and they're large enough to keep us traveling over them for quite some time."

"Perhaps we should go to France and look at them," Robin suggested, sounding as if he would have sold his soul to do the like. "Then we won't lose our heads."

Rhys smiled. "We won't lose our heads anyway, Robin. We'll hasten north and begin the building of our keep."

And with luck what you won't see is your soon-to-be-adopted father's head on a pike outside those yet-to-be-built gates, Rhys thought to himself.

"Besides, your uncle John has been pressed into service as keeper of Ayre until such time as we return to visit your inheritance. He will be the one to face the king's wrath."

Said keeper was none too happy about the duty, but Rhys had promised to return and knight him before the new year. John was nothing if not practical about such things.

Of course, there would be a great amount of groveling on his own part in the future, but hopefully by then the king would see the wisdom of what Rhys had done. He would be there to keep watch over the northern borders. With any luck, John wouldn't become so angry that he reappropriated Gwen's lands for the crown's pleasure. In his wildest dreams Rhys had never dreamed he would be lord over so much. He was loth to give any of it up.

Though if it came to that, he would take Gwen and the children and hasten to France. It wasn't as if they couldn't have lived quite comfortably there as well.

But all that would come later. First would come a swift journey north, then preparations for building. He could at least start the construction with the gold he had left. He would manage to finish it somehow. All he knew for a certainty was that the fashioning of his home couldn't happen quickly enough.

He could almost see his banner, flying merrily in the breeze.

And what a beautiful sight it was.

The child stood on the side of the road and watched the company pass by her. She would have to go north with them, that much she knew. But her grief was still heavy upon her, and that made it hard to muster up the courage to stop one of the knight's fierce companions and beg for a ride.

Her tears had finally blinded her completely when she felt rather than saw a horse stop. A man dismounted and soon she found herself staring into pale gray eyes.

"*Chérie*," the knight said, "what do you here, dressed for travel? Where is your grandsire?"

"He's gone," she whispered.

Then she wept in earnest.

The knight drew her into his arms and cradled her close. The child then felt the hands of the knight's new lady wife and found herself soon sheltered in soft arms.

"Rhys," the lady said, "we must take her with us if she will come. She cannot remain here."

"*Chérie*," the knight said, laying his hand atop the child's head gently, "will you come?"

The child nodded, unable to speak.

"And your grandfather's things. Surely you should bring them along?"

The child patted the manuscript that she had bound to her small self with strips of cloth. It was the most important thing, and her grandfather had labored long over the scribbling of his potions. But having his pots and pouches would be a comfort as well.

"I'll see to it," the knight said, and then he walked away, calling out orders as he went.

The child soon found herself riding in her knight's company behind an old man who reminded her not at all of her grandsire, but who had a gentle smile just the same. It was enough to ease her.

She clutched her pieces of glass in her hand and rode into her future, dry-eyed.

Gwen thought bathing just might be a fatal activity—for the five girls ignoring their work in the kitchens, that was. She sat on a stool near the tub and glared at the daughters of Fenwyck's cook. They took no notice of her. They had even ceased their chopping, mixing, and stirring to admire the man who currently tarried in the water, seemingly oblivious to the commotion he was causing.

Rhys was, unfortunately, too large to fit into the tub, so his arms were dangling over the sides, and his knees bent over the sides as well. There was *far* too much of him exposed for her peace of mind.

She suspected, as she threw the handful of drooling wenches another warning look they paid no heed to, that she was even less enthusiastic about this visit to Fenwyck than she had been about the last one.

Though even she had to admit that loitering in bed with her love was much more pleasant when they had a goosefeather mattress beneath them. Said goosefeather mattress of Geoffrey's had been relinquished promptly after Rhys had invited Fenwyck's lord to decide the matter in the lists. Geoffrey's attachment to his bed had been clearly shown by his willingness even to set foot on the dirt. Unfortunately for him, said attachment had been summarily severed. He'd gulped most audibly when Rhys had drawn two swords, then snarled out a curse straight from his bruised pride when Rhys put one of the blades away with mock dismay over Geoffrey's agitated state.

Matters had not improved much from there for the lord of Fenwyck.

Gwen had watched Rhys enough in the lists that she knew when he was toying with an opponent and when he wasn't. She could hardly believe her eyes when she saw that Rhys was dragging the entire affair out much longer than he needed to, but then she supposed that since it was Geoffrey's finest mattress that she would be sleeping upon for a pair of fortnights, saving what was left of Geoffrey's pride was the least Rhys could do.

"By the saints, you are a lazy pup, Grandson."

Gwen shifted on her small stool that she might have a better look at Rhys's grandsire. Rhys didn't even open his eyes.

"I've earned the rest, Grandpère," Rhys said, sounding just as lazy as his grandfather claimed he was. "An exhausting fortnight, to be sure."

Sir Jean looked appraisingly at Gwen, and she found herself blushing in spite of her best efforts to look indifferent. Then he turned his attentions to the kitchen's maids and gave them a stern look from beneath his bushy eyebrows.

"Someone stands to lose fingers," he said pointedly, "if she does not attend better to what she is doing."

Evidently the wenches were better impressed with Sir Jean's growls than they had been with Gwen's glares, for they turned back to their work promptly.

Sir Jean pulled up a stool and sat next to Gwen. "Guarding your treasure, lady?"

"I thought it wise."

He laughed at her, and Gwen saw where Rhys had come by some of his charm. Never mind that the man was old enough to be—oddly enough—her grandsire, he was exceedingly charming. She found herself returning his smile and feeling as if she had known him far longer than a month.

"Was he worth the wait?" Jean asked, inclining his head toward Rhys.

Gwen found that even Rhys had opened one eye to see her answer.

"Aye," she said. "Well worth it."

"A good lover then?"

"Grandpère!" That at least seemingly had Rhys fully awake.

Jean only shrugged. "Want to make certain you aren't tainting your name." He looked at Gwen and winked. "Fine lovers, all those de Piaget men are."

"And how would you know?" Rhys asked with a scowl. "It isn't as if you've been with scores of women for them to tell you."

"I had my share before I met your grandmother."

"And after she died?" Rhys prodded.

"I have a very fine memory of former praise," Jean said haughtily. "And who are you, whelp, to question my prowess?"

"You questioned mine," Rhys replied.

Sir Jean began to finger his sword hilt. "I daresay I should plan on seeing you in the lists shortly. You're far too cheeky for my taste."

Gwen suspected, and she had the feeling she had it aright, that Sir Jean would have used any reason to face his grandson over blades. They didn't cross swords a single time that the man wasn't grinning madly, as if he'd been the one to teach Rhys everything he knew about swordplay. Such was a grandfather's pride, she supposed.

"Later," Rhys said, leaning his head back and closing his eyes again. "Perhaps tomorrow."

Jean shook his head. "Lazy," he said, clucking his tongue. "Lazy and soft. Your sire would be appalled were he here to see this."

"I am newly wed but a pair of fortnights," Rhys said, sounding not at all troubled by his idleness.

"You should be wielding your sword daily," Sir Jean instructed, "and that does *not*—forgive me Gwen for saying so for only a fool would rather be in the lists than with you—that does *not* mean the sword you wield in bed!"

Rhys opened one eye and looked balefully at his grandfather. "When do I appear in the lists?"

"Just after sunrise."

"And leave them when?"

Sir Jean chewed on the inside of his cheek before he pursed his lips and answered. "Late in the day."

"And then spend my time how?"

"Plotting and scheming how to leave the table early," Sir Jean groused.

"Today is the first day of leisure I've taken, and you'll not goad me into being sorry for it. For all you know, I'll crawl from this tub and pass the rest of my day in bed."

Gwen jumped at the frown Sir Jean threw her way. "Disobedient pup. Did you teach him that?"

She held up her hands in surrender. "It wasn't me. He was already grown by the time I had the keeping of him."

"Things are progressing as they should," Rhys assured his grandfather. "I've sent to Mother for the rest of my gold, and you know 'twas one of your own men who is seeing to the message. Montgomery is readying the men for our journey on the morrow to Artane. The children are tearing Fenwyck's hall to bits without my having to encourage them, and Lady Joanna—"

"Ah," Sir Jean said, stroking his chin, "now there is a handsome enough woman." He looked at Gwen. "Would she want me, do you think?"

"Well. . ."

Rhys threw a handful of water at his grandsire. "She has no interest in a lover your age."

"I'll have you know my sword is as mighty as it always was—"

"No doubt—" Rhys interrupted dryly.

"And I've still a pleasing visage—"

"Never said you didn't. . . ."

Sir Jean jumped to his feet and drew his sword with relish, sending most of the kitchen maids and lads scurrying for cover. "Out to the lists with you, insolent whelp!" he bellowed. "I'll not be disparaged thusly!" He took Gwen by the arm and pulled her from the kitchen. "You'll come with me and judge the victor. And bring your mother."

Gwen looked over her shoulder to find Rhys crawling from the tub with a resigned sigh. Half a dozen young women hastened to help him dry himself off, which was almost enough to make Gwen reach for Sir Jean's sword.

He stopped once they reached the great hall, sheathed his sword, and smiled at her. "Got him out of the tub, so now I might enter it. Shall we have a cup of ale first, do you think?"

She could only stare at him, unsure if she should laugh or not.

"You'll come sit on the stool in the kitchen and keep the little wenches at bay for me as well, will you not?" he asked, a twinkle in his eye.

"Well—"

"Better yet, send your mother. A passing handsome woman, that one."

Gwen let him lead her over to the table. She hadn't indulged in but half her cup before her husband arrived, dressed and grumbling. He spared his grandfather an irritated look before he tugged Gwen to her feet.

"Come with me."

"Don't forget your mother," Jean called as Rhys dragged Gwen from the hall. "Send her to the kitchens."

"The saints preserve her," Rhys muttered under his breath.

Gwen laughed as he led her to the bedchamber Rhys had appropriated for them. He pulled her inside, shut the door, and shoved the bolt home.

"You don't think I should call my mother—"

"I do not," Rhys said, backing her up against the door.

"But your grandfather—"

"Can fend for himself. He's been doing it for years. I, however, am perfectly helpless and will need much watching over for the rest of this day."

"You pitiful man," she said, clucking her tongue sadly. "I suppose you'll need my full attention?"

"I fear that is the case."

Gwen wrapped her arms around his neck. "How have you managed all these years without me?"

His mouth came down on hers. She suspected, as he soon lifted her up and carried her to the bed, that such a question was not one he cared to answer. Indeed, he seemed determined to make up for all the years that she hadn't had him to watch over, if the tenacity with which he kept her in his bed was any indication.

Evening fell and Gwen managed to escape long enough to light a candle or two. She returned to her husband's arms and sighed in contentment as she rested her head against his shoulder. He ran callused fingers over her back, and she remembered idly the first time he had touched her hand and how even then such a touch had affected her. Things had not changed.

"Gwen?"

"Aye, love," she said.

"I wish this day would never end."

He sounded so wistful, she lifted her head and looked down at him. "We'll have many more such days, surely."

He smiled, a pensive smile that touched her heart. "I hope so, my love. I do."

"We will," she said. "I am convinced of it."

"Then convince me," he asked. "And take your time at it."

She saw the twinkle in his eye and laughed.

Then she bent her head and kissed him, determined to do just that.

41

"Have patience with an old man," the old man said, "and explain to me once again why it is I shouldn't run you through for interrupting my supper."

Rollan admired Patrick of Sedgwick's callousness. Indeed, he understood it well and had no fears for the continuation of his head resting atop his neck. The old man was naught but bluster. Rollan knew he was intrigued, and he also knew Patrick would have slit his own throat before showing it. This was the kind of man he could reason with.

It had taken him a fortnight to reach Sedgwick after his flight from Ayre, then another fortnight to manage to get himself inside the gates. These were not trusting souls.

"I know where your niece is," Rollan repeated. *Or at least the general vicinity—that vicinity being the whole of France.* There was no need for specifics with this man. "And I know who her son is." There was no one else in the solar, so there was no need for secrecy anymore.

Patrick snorted. "I have no niece. She was stolen by ruffians and murdered."

"She was snatched away by a wandering healer. She bore him a son before he was burned as a heretic in France."

Patrick regarded him narrowly. "Foolishness."

"The healer was Jean de Piaget's son, Etienne," Rollan pressed on. "Etienne met Mary of Sedgwick in this very hall and fled with her in the dead of night."

"She was snatched—"

"She wanted to go," Rollan corrected. "To escape a very violent household, or so I've heard."

He wondered, idly, if that was more truth than Patrick wanted to hear. The man had begun to finger his sword hilt. No matter. Rollan knew Patrick was more than ready to listen now. He would live until the full tale was told, and hopefully by then he would have convinced Patrick of his further usefulness. After all, there were some details even he wasn't prepared to share as of yet.

"Go on," Patrick growled.

Rollan suppressed his smile. "Mary wed with Etienne and they returned to France."

"And then what happened?"

"Etienne was not just a wandering healer and a sometime minstrel. He was a highly skilled knight with a gift for taking on the mores of many vocations. He had, as you might imagine, his share of enemies, and most of them were very powerful. One of them paid clergy to accuse him of heresy. Or perhaps he truly was in league with the devil." Rollan shrugged. "His get certainly has prowess that might be seen as unnatural."

Rollan watched closely for Patrick's reaction. His hand moved from his sword to rub distractedly at his knee. Old battle wound, Rollan surmised. A sure sign of some kind of discomfort.

Interesting.

"Etienne was put to death, or so the story goes."

"And their child? How would I know him?"

Rollan wanted to roll his eyes. By the bloody saints, was he doomed to be surrounded by imbeciles?

"De Piaget?" he prompted. "Rhys de Piaget?"

"Oh." Patrick's mouth shaped the word, but no sound came out. The realization of just who stood to claim Sedgwick and all it entailed dawned, and it was followed hard on the heels by what appeared to be no small measure of consternation. Patrick only held Sedgwick by virtue of his brother having died without issue. That his brother's daughter should have had a son, and such a son indeed . . . obviously Patrick had just divined who might come knocking at his gates, demanding his inheritance.

"Now you see the necessity of paying him a small visit."

"Aye."

"He, oddly enough, knows nothing of his parentage, but who knows how long that might last?"

Patrick didn't seem to have any trouble understanding precisely what Rollan meant by that.

"There is no sense taking the risk of him finding out," Rollan continued. Patrick nodded.

"His mother, however, is of no consequence."

Patrick nodded again, and Rollan heaved a silent sigh of relief. In truth there was little Mary de Piaget could do to wrest control of Sedgwick from her uncle, but it galled Rollan deeply that he could not discover her whereabouts. Much as he tried, he'd been unsuccessful in trying to wring that out of his father on his deathbed. He had no one but himself to blame for that. He'd been unskilled with poisons in those days. But how was he to have known too much too quickly would leave a man in agony, yet unable to voice it?

"He will be going north," Rollan continued. "Traveling with a woman and a lad. I will see to those two."

"And I will see to him," Patrick said, standing up suddenly. "We'll leave as soon as I can gather enough men for war."

"Unprovoked?" Rollan mused. "I wonder about the wisdom of that."

"You said he's responsible for your brother's death. That's reason enough to see him repaid."

Rollan smiled faintly. He'd only implicated Rhys slightly in the deed, so he could hardly hold himself responsible for Patrick's incorrect assumption. Besides, someone should pay for Alain's untimely demise.

Why not Rhys?

42

Rhys sat at the base of a partially completed wall and stared out over the sea. The stone was cold against his back, the sun was warm on his face, and the breeze smelled sharply of brine.

He thought he just might die from the pleasure of it.

The keep was progressing slowly, though he suspected that any progress that didn't have his hall up and livable overnight would seem slow to him. They'd been at Artane for almost three months, and what they'd accomplished was truly remarkable.

They had the beginnings of outer walls. The great hall and chapel already had foundation stones laid. The outbuildings and such were to be made of wood and some of them had already been started. Even winter grain had been planted in hopes that they actually might have something more to eat than what they'd brought with them from Fenwyck. Rhys didn't relish having to spend the winter traveling from one of Gwen's keeps to the next to avail themselves of the larders. Even though Gwen's mother had returned to Segrave and offered to see things sent to them, Rhys had little wish to accept of her generosity. If they could finish enough of a temporary hall, they could winter there and keep working.

"We have to train if we want to earn our spurs. And to train together we *both* have to be knights."

"But, Robin—"

"Don't you want to be a knight?"

Rhys heard the voices coming from the other side of the wall and found that he was somewhat grateful that at least this part of the defenses had been built up far enough to hide him. Robin had seemed pleased enough with his new home, but one never truly knew what went on in that young lad's head. No sense in not knowing what was going on. Whatever scheme Robin was about, Nicholas was sure to be dragged into. Nicholas had turned out to be too much the peacemaker to go against Robin's wishes. Poor lad. He would have to find his own footing eventually, or find himself in scrapes he no doubt would have preferred to avoid.

"I would be a better mercenary," Nicholas offered hesitantly. "Much better than a knight."

"You *can't* be a mercenary," Robin insisted. "We both have to be knights, *good* knights. *He* expects it."

Nicholas was quiet for so long, Rhys was tempted to peek over the wall and see what was going on.

"He doesn't expect it of me," Nicholas said finally. "I'm not really—"

"Of course you are," Robin interrupted.

"He's just being kind—"

"A proper knightly virtue," Robin said promptly.

"But he didn't really mean—"

"A knight never lies. He said he wanted you, and he wouldn't lie about it."

"But my blood isn't noble."

Rhys wondered if Robin's ensuing sigh hadn't blown Nicholas over. He found himself smiling in spite of his faint dismay. Hadn't he claimed both boys before the envoy King John had sent north? By the saints, he'd done nothing but congratulate himself for the se'nnight following for the cheek he'd displayed. The envoy had expressed in few, but pointed, words the king's displeasure. Rhys had responded calmly and clearly, stating his position and enlightening the envoy as to why the king should leave him be—with Gwen and her children. He hadn't mentioned Nicholas then, but Gwen had elbowed him firmly later when he'd put his wishes down on paper. Robin, Nicholas, and Amanda. She would accept nothing less.

"Nicholas, he claimed us both before the king," Robin said, seemingly trying to muster up the patience to go through something he obviously had said before. "Maybe we aren't his in truth, but he's acting as if we are. He wouldn't do it if he didn't mean it."

There was another lengthy silence. Then Nicholas spoke.

"If you're sure," he began.

"I'm sure," Robin said firmly. "And we'll prove to him that he didn't choose poorly. Now, are you going to be a knight, or not?"

"All right," came the answer.

"I'll wager I reach the lists first!" was Robin's enthusiastic reply.

Rhys managed to heave himself to his feet and peek over the wall in time to see Robin and Nicholas racing to what would eventually be the lists. 'Twas a good place for them. At least there Robin could work no trouble for Nicholas to follow him into.

That left him with only the three girl children in his care to wonder about. Amanda had acquired a foster sister in the person of Anne of Fenwyck, and the two were forever trying to escape some piece of Robin's mischief. Geoffrey had seemingly sent his daughter to Artane with a sense of relief. Rhys wondered if Geoffrey thought himself unskilled with women unless they were over a score in years. Whatever the case, it had provided Amanda with a companion, and Rhys was pleased about that.

The other little one he seemed to have acquired was Socrates's granddaughter. The child had ridden north with them yet asked nothing in return. Gwen had fussed over the girl and tried to include her in the family, but the girl had accepted only a small tent of her own where she could live amongst her grandfather's pots and pouches. The only other thing she had accepted from Gwen was the promise that Gwen would teach her how to read, that the girl might finish her grandfather's book of potion recipes. Rhys could not deny her skill as a healer, despite her tender years. He was glad to have her about for as long as she contented herself to remain with them.

Rhys saw a movement to his left and realized then that his lady was coming toward him. And, as he usually found himself doing, he sighed in sheer relief that she was his. He leaned his elbows gingerly on the uneven wall and waited for her to arrive. By the saints, he did not deserve this boon, but he wasn't about to refuse it.

"Lazing about again?" she asked when she reached the opposite side of the wall.

"What else?" he asked.

"Your grandfather is searching the lists for you."

"I don't doubt it. You would think I'd never lifted a sword with the way he is ever nagging at me about it."

She smiled and leaned over to kiss him firmly on the mouth. "He's trying to make up for all the years he was unable to watch you work."

Rhys only snorted.

"He is," she insisted. "I pried the truth out of him."

"Did you resort to torture?"

"Nay, I had a go at him myself in the lists," Gwen said.

Rhys felt his mouth fall open. "You did? When?"

"When you were off with Montgomery, scouting out the borders. Your grandfather was endeavoring to induce me to reveal all my secrets, so I thought to distract him with a bit of swordplay."

"Leave any scars?"

She reached out and tugged sharply on his ear. "I did not—and what little faith you have in my skill. Perhaps 'tis just as well I never offered myself to you as a mercenary."

"It would have been the end of me," he said, with fervor, then reached out and managed to snag a bit of her sleeve before she had, in her irritation, pulled completely out of his reach. "Not for any lack on your part, of course."

She paused and waited. "Aye?"

"I would not have managed to concentrate on anything save you," he said.

"Well," she said, sounding somewhat appeased. "That sheds a different light upon the matter."

He smiled, then held out his hand. "Care to join me?"

"Are you surveying your domain?"

He shook his head with another smile. "Staring out over the ocean and dreaming of glorious things in the future."

"Your keep?" she asked.

"You naked for the afternoon?" he suggested.

She laughed and didn't argue when he invited her to step over the wall and join him. He resumed his perch with his lady sitting next to him. He put his arm around her and drew her close to his side.

"Do I dream," he asked, "or are you really mine?"

She nestled more closely to him. "I can scarce believe it myself."

He closed his eyes and leaned his head back against the stone. He'd thought, when he made his lady his, that he could not be more content, nor more satisfied with his life. He'd imagined, after they'd reached Fenwyck without having the king come after them, that his life could not be any better. When the work was begun on his keep and he saw the walls even outlined in stone, he was certain he could not be happier.

But as he sat with his lady and enjoyed both the chill of the breeze and the warmth of the sunshine, he began to realize that thinking his life had reached its crowning moment was futile. He suspected that things could only improve.

Assuming, of course, that the king did not choose to travel to Artane, sever Rhys's head from his shoulders, and carry his head back to London without the rest of his form.

"I am certain, Connor, that I saw her come this way."

"And I tell *you*, Jared, that there is nothing save a steep descent to the sea on the other side of this wall. Why would she heave herself over it?"

Rhys sighed. It looked as if his moment of reflection was passed. At least the twins couldn't see him. Perhaps they would tire of speculating about Gwen's whereabouts and be on their way shortly.

"You don't think," Jared began slowly, "that she heaved herself over the wall apurpose. Do you?"

Connor's gasp of horror was clearly audible. "Whyever for?"

"Perhaps young Rhys—"

"Impossible."

"The children then—"

"Fling herself over the wall to escape them?" Connor demanded. "Have you lost your wits, brother?"

There was a long bit of silence during which time Rhys exchanged a look of amusement with Gwen.

"You look," Jared whispered.

"I will not," Connor returned. "*You* look."

"I will *not*. For all I know you'd heave *me* over the side!"

"Me? I wouldn't. But I wouldn't trust you not to do the same."

"I wouldn't," Jared protested. He paused, then cleared his throat. "We could both look at the same time. Then there would be no heaving of either of us."

"Save our stomachs," Connor groused, "and I've no mind for any more of that. For all we know, they've snuck off the other side of the hill where 'tis less steep and gone off for a bit of—" He paused, then coughed. "Well, *you* know."

"Without us?" Jared demanded, outraged.

"I know," Connor agreed darkly. "Difficult to believe, but there you have it."

"Such gratitude."

"You'd think she would think of us—" Connor said.

"Or at least he might give us a bit of consideration—" Jared agreed.

"I say we take them *both* to the lists," Connor said sternly, "and—"

"Oh, not our little Gwen," Jared interrupted. "Never her. 'Tis likely all Rhys's fault anyway. *She* would never think to leave without us. But he—"

"Very well, then, we'll take *him* to the lists. Once we find him, that is—"

As their voices faded, Rhys was spared the knowledge of what the twins intended to do with him for his cheek. He suspected he was far better off not knowing, but there was something to be said for being prepared. He promised to remind himself to continue to carry both swords for the next little while.

Gwen leaned up suddenly and kissed him.

"What?" he whispered with a smile.

"We could sneak off," she suggested, lifting her head from his shoulder. "No sense in disappointing the twins."

"As if you could," Rhys grumbled. "You, my love, are seemingly firmly ensconced in their good graces. Though I cannot blame them, for I am just as enamored."

"Are you?"

"I am."

"Perhaps you could show me," Gwen said, resettling her head against his shoulder, "later. 'Tis too peaceful here right now to move."

Rhys couldn't have agreed more. He gathered his lady more closely and closed his eyes.

Bliss.

It was, however, bliss he never suspected would last overlong. His life had been too easy for the past few months, and he knew something would have to go awry sooner or later.

He rolled over and put his fist repeatedly into a stubborn clump of feathers. He could hardly believe he hadn't bothered to check what sort of mattress Geoffrey had sent along as a wedding present. Obviously it had been his worst one. Rhys put that away in his mind as something he would have to repay Fenwyck for the next time he saw him.

Rhys looked at the woman lying so peacefully next to him. She didn't look uncomfortable. He frowned. Was it possible that the mattress had been constructed so only his side was so lumpy?

Such a thing wouldn't have surprised him in the slightest.

"Rhys?"

Rhys sat up at the sound of Montgomery's voice. Then Montgomery himself put his head inside the tent.

"Did you not think you might be interrupting something?" Rhys asked with a scowl.

Montgomery's teeth were a flash of white in the predawn gloom. "Your children are scattered all over you like puppies. And your lady was snoring."

"I do not snore," Gwen said distinctly as she burrowed deeper into the blankets.

"What is it?" Rhys asked, already rising. "Something I should see?"

"Nothing of import," Montgomery said. "I was actually just looking for a bit of company on my watch."

Liar, Rhys thought to himself as he kissed his lady and then watched Nicholas immediately gravitate into the warm spot he'd just vacated. He left the tent and walked several paces away with Montgomery.

"We have company," Montgomery said bluntly, "and I daresay it isn't company we want."

"Your eyesight is not a blessing at times, is it?" Rhys asked.

"You can decide that," Montgomery said, "once you've seen this for yourself."

Rhys followed him to the outer walls, or what existed of the outer walls. And once he'd seen what was gathering below them on the plain, he wished the walls were finished. The keep sat on the only knoll for miles, true, but what good did it do them to sit perched up on a hill when they couldn't defend the hill?

Especially against the number of men he was seeing camped on the ground below.

"I would guess they want us to know they're there, else they would have just come up and attacked by now," Montgomery mused. "What think you?"

Rhys nodded in agreement. "Any idea who our guests might be?"

Montgomery sniffed. "I smell Rollan. The stench is unmistakable."

Rhys laughed in spite of himself. "Ah, but there is no love between the two of you, is there?"

"He killed my liege-lord, who was also a friend. Nay, there is no love between us."

"Did he in truth?"

Montgomery shrugged, though the movement was far from indifferent. "I have no proof, but my heart tells me 'tis so. There was no need for Bertram to fail as he did. He wasted away as if from some inner poison. If that doesn't describe his second son, I know not what does."

"All the more reason to see him captured. Perhaps we should see him escorted to London, where the king might see to him at his leisure."

Montgomery frowned. "I wonder where it is he acquired so many men." He looked at Rhys. "And why does he need them?"

"To kill me?"

"Surely, but for what reason? He never does anything without a reason, especially a reason that leaves him looking pure and innocent."

Rhys strove to count the number of tents spread out below, but he was the first to admit he had not Montgomery's eyes. Obviously he had no choice but to wait and see what the daylight would show him.

"We should prepare the men just the same," he said finally. "And place them as best we can to make up for our lack of numbers."

"Our position is a boon," Montgomery offered.

"At least this," Rhys said with a wave at what lay before them, "is our only concern."

Montgomery clasped his hands behind his back. "Care for a walk along the seaward wall?"

Rhys felt his heart sink. "You jest."

Montgomery laughed. "I can do nothing but laugh, for our straits are dire indeed."

"By sea as well?" Rhys asked incredulously.

"A single ship only, if that eases your mind any."

Rhys clapped a hand to his forehead. "What else can this day bring?"

"Rhys, my friend," Montgomery said, putting his hand on Rhys's shoulder and smiling, "that is not a question a man in your position asks."

"At least I don't have Fenwyck coming at me as well." He paused and looked at Montgomery. "Do I?"

"It doesn't appear so. You might perhaps wish for aid from him, though."

"Aye, let us see if a message cannot be sent." Rhys left Montgomery to see to the sending for aid and returned to his tent to rouse his lady. Already his mind was far ahead of his feet, wondering just where he might put those that were dearest to him that they might not be overrun. And he began to wonder if his troubles wouldn't include two small boys who seemed to think their wooden swords were quite powerful indeed.

And the saints preserve him if Gwen took up her own blade. Damnation, but he knew he should have forgotten it at Fenwyck. He strode back through the predawn light, cursing under his breath.

Rollan had best pray he wasn't behind this foolishness.

The saints alone could help him if he was.

43

Rollan stood in front of his tent and stared up at the half-finished walls silhouetted against the early-morning sky. He cursed heartily. Things were not working out as he had planned. He'd tried to convince Patrick to attack under cover of darkness, but Patrick had refused. Rollan suspected that Patrick was indulging in an old man's curiosity to see his posterity in the flesh, never mind that Rhys was not his direct descendant.

A pity the king hadn't been a likely one to choose for an ally. Rollan had contemplated it seriously, once he'd seen for himself that Patrick of Sedgwick was not the warrior he purported being. Attacking mid-morn. What kind of plan was that? By the saints, not even Alain would have attempted something so stupid.

The sky began to lighten and Rollan scowled. He much preferred the darkness for his deeds, and 'twas obvious his own plans would have to be put off yet another day. It was best that Gwen not know he was nearby. He had told Patrick to keep silent about his whereabouts, though considering Sedgwick's inability to hold a thought past the duration of a meal, Rollan did not hold out much hope that he would remain anonymous.

He put his shoulders back. Let them know he was near. It might make the game even more interesting. Sedgwick had brought many men with him. It was quite possible that de Piaget and his mercenaries would be overcome, but that would surely not be before night fell. If that came to pass, Rollan would snatch Gwen away before Patrick had the chance to lay eyes on her.

Of course, things could happen quite differently. Rollan was well acquainted—from a safe distance, of course—with de Piaget's skill. And he'd had an eyeful of the mercenaries. It wasn't inconceivable that Rhys could come away the victor, though Rollan suspected that, too, would not come before night had fallen. And while Rhys was about the long, unpleasant business of deciding by torchlight just who the dead were, Rollan would snatch Gwen away before Rhys had the chance to lay eyes on her again.

Either way, Rollan knew he would have Gwen before another dawn. He had lost Ayre, true, but he would have the true prize. He could earn bread enough through his wits, if not his sword. She would not starve. He would give her other children. He suspected, and this had troubled him at first, that he might even be happy with her at his side.

Unsettling a thought if ever there were one, but he'd become almost accustomed to the idea.

He saw Patrick sharpening his sword and rolled his eyes in disgust. Imbecile. One old fool leading a camp of younger fools to their deaths, no doubt.

Rollan pulled his cloak more closely about him and turned away, knowing he was doomed to spend another day waiting.

But when night fell . . .

44

He would need her to guard his back. Gwen had decided that the moment Rhys had ducked back into their tent. He hadn't said aught, instead merely beckoned to her. She had known immediately that something was amiss.

She had stood shivering in the faint light of dawn and listened calmly as he'd told her what he'd seen. Men on the plain below them. A ship anchored off their coast. And only unfinished walls to protect them.

She hadn't been surprised.

He'd told her where he intended for her and the children to shelter while he fought the battle. He'd reminded her that the twins would be standing guard. He had absolutely forbidden her to do aught but wait until the battle was won. But she wondered, as she'd heard him sigh as he turned away to plan his strategy, if he could possibly believe she would do as he'd asked.

She had immediately retrieved her blade and donned a concealing cloak. She'd been tempted to relieve Robin and Nicholas of their wooden swords, lest they think them adequate protection, then she'd thought better of it. They had knives to use, should worse come to worst and they stand in need of defending themselves. And the swords would make them feel more confident.

She'd pacified the twins with soothing words about her need to wear hose and a tunic just in case she needed to flee. Indeed, she had made such a long and thorough argument for the scheme that she almost convinced herself 'twas more sensible to wear hose than a gown. The Fitzgeralds had merely blinked at her, either overwhelmed by her logic or the sheer number of words she had spewed at them.

Now 'twas midday and the only thing that had come to pass was the discovery that the ship off their coast contained Rhys's mother and a collection of nuns. There was no movement on the plain. The council of war, however, was proceeding in the center of what would eventually be the inner bailey. She approached confidently. Better that than slinking up and hoping to eavesdrop. Montgomery, Rhys, and Sir Jean were huddled together, obviously plotting their strategy.

"He wants to *what?*" Rhys was asking Montgomery incredulously.

"Who?" Gwen asked.

Montgomery ignored her. "He wants to parley. Says he has aught to discuss with you."

"Such as why the hell he's chosen to encamp his men under my keep?" Rhys asked in exasperation. "What is this old fool about?"

"Who?" Gwen asked again.

"Patrick of Sedgwick," Rhys answered, then realized who had asked the question. Gwen felt the intense heat of his glare, but she ignored it. It was best she know what he was up against so she knew how best to defend him.

She looked at Sir Jean, who had shifted. He didn't look uncomfortable. He didn't even look afraid. He had merely shifted his weight from one foot to another, but she had never seen him do that before. She contemplated his action and wondered if it indicated something she should be aware of.

Rhys shot his grandfather a look of irritation. "Do you know aught of this you haven't cared to share with me as of yet?"

"What would he know?" Montgomery asked.

"Aye," Gwen put in, "what would your grandfather know?"

Sir Jean looked about him as if he searched for something else to stare at besides his companions. Then he smiled suddenly. "Oh, look, Rhys. There's your mother finally arrived off her little boat. Isn't it a relief to know that 'twas her come to visit and not Johnny?" He pointed right before Rhys's nose, giving his grandson no alternative than to look where he indicated. "And it would appear she has brought aid with her."

Gwen looked over her shoulder to see a woman who was obviously a nun of some sort coming their way. She was followed by several more nuns of varying shapes and sizes. There was, however, a sister of such great height that Gwen almost winced. What trouble they must have had fitting her with the proper garments.

"Aid?" Rhys snorted, looking thoroughly displeased to see his mother. "She brought herself, a herd of helpless women, and no doubt a great amount of my gold. Why should I consider this aid? What I need is aid from Fenwyck, who has not bothered to show his sorry face in my hall yet!"

Sir Jean looked unimpressed by Rhys's outburst. "Your good mother can care for herself."

"Grandfather, she may spy well enough for Phillip, but she cannot wield a sword, and what I need at the moment is swordsmen, not nuns!"

Gwen looked at Rhys in surprise. "Your mother is a spy?"

"As is my grandfather," Rhys said shortly, "which is why I am wondering what he is doing standing here instead of loitering with the lads below, discovering their true intentions."

"Your grandfather is a spy?" Gwen looked at Sir Jean, who only smiled uncomfortably and shrugged. Then Gwen looked at Montgomery, who looked as surprised as she did. Then she finally fixed her gaze upon her husband and frowned. "And you could not see fit to trust me with this?"

"Well—" Rhys began.

"For whom does he work?" Gwen demanded.

"Ah," Sir Jean said slowly, "well, love, that would take a great deal of explaining—"

"Phillip," Rhys said briskly. "Phillip of France, to whom I am a great disappointment, for I have no lust for subterfuge. All I want"—and he encompassed them all with his glare—"is to know what in the bloody hell Patrick of Sedgwick wants from me so badly that he's willing to march his men across the whole of England to have it!"

Gwen wished she had something to sit down upon. Jean was a spy for the French king? Rhys's mother was a spy as well? Somehow it made the fact that Rhys's father had been burned as a heretic seem a mild thing indeed. Gwen couldn't decide if she should be horrified by the family she'd married into, or incensed by the fact that Rhys hadn't trusted her with the truth. She decided on the latter, as the former was not something she could change.

"You could have told me," she said to her husband, hoping it had come out as coldly as she'd intended.

"I've been trying to forget it," Rhys said with a sigh. He looked at her and attempted a smile. "It isn't much, truly."

"It isn't much?" she echoed. She found herself with the intense urge to throttle him. "It isn't much?" she said again, much louder this time. "Your family is full of spies!"

"Good ones," Jean offered, "if that matters."

"And you couldn't tell me?" Gwen bellowed. She was tempted to draw her sword and use it not on the men below, but on the man across from her. "Why didn't you tell me?"

"I didn't think—"

"Obviously!"

"Gwen . . ."

She folded her arms over her chest and glared at him. "What else haven't you told me?"

"Nothing," he began slowly. "You know it all."

"Do I?"

"You do."

"She doesn't," Sir Jean said.

Gwen looked at Sir Jean. So did Rhys, for that matter. She caught sight of her husband's face and found that his glare was much more intimidating than hers. She would have to work to improve her expression, for 'twas a certainty that she would have need of it if the day's events were any indication of events to come. It would be very handy to have the skill of causing the kind of trembles in others that Rhys did.

There was a thunk to Gwen's right. That overly large sister had set down a chest. Rhys's mother, and Gwen could only assume that such was she, stepped around the chest and gave Rhys a kiss.

"Sorry we're a bit behind, love," she said, smiling. "You likely could have used your gold to aid you in your little war."

"Mother," Rhys said shortly, "I do not remember asking you to come."

She reached up and patted his cheek. "Once I heard you had begun work on your keep, I knew you would want the rest of your funds. I made as much haste as possible."

"Many thanks," Rhys grumbled.

"Now, love"—his mother laughed—"no need to be so ill-tempered." She patted him again on the cheek, then turned to Sir Jean and leaned up to kiss his wrinkled cheek as well. "Father."

"Daughter," Jean said, embracing her heartily. "You look to have survived the crossing well enough."

"Curiosity over my new daughter," Rhys's mother said. "Rhys, introduce me to your bride."

"Mother, Gwen. Gwen, my mother, Mary." Rhys scowled at the both of them. "Why do you not remove yourselves to a safe place so I might return to the business of planning my war?"

Gwen found her hands taken by Mary de Piaget. "God's blessings upon you, daughter," Mary said, leaning forward to brush Gwen's cheek with her own. "I can only wish I had arrived at a more auspicious time. It would seem there is a bit of a misunderstanding to clear up on the plain before we can relax and chat in peace."

Gwen couldn't help but smile. Rhys looked very little like his mother, but they shared the same smile.

"Hopefully it won't take long," Gwen said. "And I fear I have little to offer you. We are a bit on the thin side here as far as our larder goes—"

"Oh, by the saints," Rhys exclaimed, "we're at war!"

"I'll sit on the chest," Mary said, promptly doing so, "and bide my time until you finish up with your business. Go ahead, Rhys, love. I'll wait."

Gwen watched her husband gather his patience about him like a cloak. Then he very calmly turned to his grandsire and managed something akin to a smile. It looked more like a great baring of teeth, but Sir Jean seemed disinclined to quibble.

"Grandpère," Rhys began slowly, "you seemed to know what Sedgwick is about."

Mary stiffened. Rhys noted it immediately and turned to her.

"What?" he demanded.

The large nun came up behind Mary and put a hand on her shoulder. Mary looked at Sir Jean.

"You didn't tell me Sedgwick would be here."

Sir Jean shrugged. "Didn't know it."

"What—" She took a deep breath and then spoke again more calmly. "What do they want?"

"That," Rhys said, through gritted teeth, "is what I am trying to ascertain if someone would just go down and find out!"

There was silence. Gwen looked at those gathered in the small circle and wondered why no one seemed inclined to volunteer to go. Montgomery was still too busy gaping at Sir Jean, likely trying to decide if he looked the part of a spy. Sir Jean was shifting again, more uneasily this time, and looking anywhere but at Rhys. Mary sat on the chest of gold with her head bowed. And the very tall nun with the very large feet still rested a hand on Mary's shoulder.

It was, oddly enough, a very hairy hand.

Gwen looked up and met that sister's eyes.

And she saw, to her complete astonishment, a pair of gray eyes peeping out at her from inside a hood, a pair of gray eyes that she had definitely seen somewhere before.

Or, rather, a pair like them.

She looked at Rhys. Nay, it couldn't be.

She looked the nun over and saw what could have been mistaken for the lump of a sword hilt hiding beneath the woman's habit.

Woman? Gwen shook her head. That was no woman. She wondered why she was the only one who had seen it.

She looked at her husband. He had turned to look out toward the plain, his face scrunched up in a formidable scowl. Then she looked at Sir Jean only to find him staring at her. He shifted again.

"I haven't enough men," Rhys said with another curse. "And I *definitely* haven't got one willing to go down and find out what the bloody hell Sedgwick wants!"

Gwen turned the puzzle over in her mind. Mary seemed somewhat overcome by the knowledge of who stood to attack them. She was comforted by one who could only be Rhys's father—who even Rhys assumed was dead. But what had that to do with what was happening down upon the plain? It wasn't as if those below would have known Mary and her husband were arriving.

Did they?

Nay, not even Rollan could be so clever—assuming Rollan was behind the mischief.

Gwen looked at Sir Jean. Of any of them, he most likely knew what was behind the day's events. It was obvious Rhys was having no answers from him. Gwen suspected she might be the best one to wring the truth from him, given that she had already intimidated the old man in the lists quite thoroughly.

"Sir Jean," she said clearly.

He looked at her, apparently saw her intention in her eyes, and swallowed. Uncomfortably.

"Aye?" he said, looking about him for some avenue of escape.

Gwen put her hand on the hilt of her sword and gave Sir Jean a look of promise. "Where is your son buried?" she asked bluntly.

"Ah . . ."

"The location, good sir," Gwen said. "Where exactly is the location of his grave?"

"Ah . . ."

"And is he in it?"

Rhys turned around at that. He looked first at Gwen, then at his grandfather. Sir Jean looked supremely uncomfortable. Gwen sincerely hoped he was a better spy than that when he was facing those who weren't his family.

The large sister with the hairy hand had even shifted. Gwen decided that before they could plan their war, they needed to know at least who the players were upon the hilltop. She leaned up on her toes and pulled back the hood from, and this came as no surprise to her, Etienne de Piaget's dark head.

He was, she had to admit, a very handsome man still. It was no wonder Rhys was so pleasing to look at. She looked at her husband to find that his jaw had gone slack.

"Father?" he whispered.

Gwen pushed Montgomery out of the way and put her arm around Rhys's waist to hold him up, lest he feel the need to faint.

Etienne was seemingly as affected as his son was, so Gwen turned her attentions to other matters. Why was Mary so overcome by the thought of Patrick of Sedgwick lying in wait below them? Gwen had never cared much for anyone from Sedgwick, and she had suffered through a supper or two with Henry of Sedgwick at her father's supper table. Not a pleasant man. The only thing noteworthy about him had been the rumor that his daughter had disappeared one night and no one had seen her thereafter.

His daughter, Mary.

And Henry had died not a year after that. Some said he had died of his grief. Others said he had died of wounds his brother's knife impaling itself between his ribs had given him. However it had come about, he had left a daughter behind whose whereabouts were a mystery.

Gwen looked at Mary and frowned. It couldn't be. She transferred her gaze to Jean and found that he was, amazingly enough, licking his lips. As if he were nervous. She gave him the sternest look she could muster.

"You know why Sedgwick is here, don't you?" Gwen asked.

"Ah," Jean stalled.

Gwen adjusted her husband's weight. "Well," she said impatiently, "tell Rhys. Tell him why Patrick of Sedgwick has come pounding on his gates."

"We don't have any gates," Rhys whispered, still gaping at his father.

"Well," Jean said, shifting uncomfortably again.

Gwen sighed in exasperation. She opened her mouth to speak only to find Rhys's mother had already begun to do so.

"Henry of Sedgwick was my father," Mary said, looking at Rhys wearily. "And that would make you, love," she continued, "heir to Sedgwick and all that entails. And I suppose Patrick of Sedgwick has come pounding on gates you have yet to build so that you might not come pounding upon his."

Gwen felt Rhys stiffen, then begin to sway. And then she decided that perhaps there was more of him than she could hold up alone, so she didn't protest when Sir Jean offered his aid. 'Twas the least he could do. She had the feeling it was the beginning of the favors he would be doing his grandson to make up for the startling revelations of the day.

45

Rhys found himself sitting upon a portion of his great hall wall with his head between his knees and his grandfather holding it there.

"Breathe, whelp," Jean said gruffly. "And keep your head down. No need to faint in front of your lady."

Rhys didn't want to faint, he wanted to retch. For the first time, he thought he might have sympathy for the Fitzgeralds and what they endured on horseback.

"Father?" Rhys croaked.

"Aye, son."

Rhys managed to lift his head far enough to look at the sister who had always guarded his mother's dining hall.

"You're a nun," he wheezed.

Etienne smiled weakly. "When it suits me."

"I could kill you for this," Rhys managed, "if I could just get to my bloody feet without puking."

"How could I tell you?" his father said softly. "I have too many enemies for that, Rhys. They thought I was dead and you ignorant of my doings. They would have killed you otherwise."

Rhys didn't want to weep, though he was damned close to it. His father was alive. His mother had known. His grandfather had known.

And they had let him suffer anyway.

"It was better that way," Etienne said firmly. "You were safe, Rhys, and that was worth any price." He smiled. "Besides, I've watched you over the years when I could manage it."

"That eases me greatly," Rhys snapped. "It would have been a comfort to have watched *you*!"

"You did often enough."

"In skirts!"

Etienne shrugged. "One does what one must."

Rhys managed to sit up straight. He realized Gwen was standing nearby, and he jerked her onto his lap and wrapped his arms around her.

"Forgive me, my love," he said, "for not telling you what kind of family you stood to ally yourself with. Allow me to make proper introductions. That is my grandfather, the spy. That is my mother, the abbess and sometime spy. And this is my father, the sister of the cloth."

Rhys watched his father take Gwen's hand, bend low over it, and kiss it politely. "How fortunate my son is to have wed a woman who is beautiful and yet deadly. I understand you have a wicked manner with a blade."

Rhys had no idea where his father had heard such drivel, but it certainly served him well, for Gwen immediately seemed to soften toward his father.

And Rhys found he wished he could do the same. But, by the saints, he'd been a lad of seven when he'd last seen his sire! How could he be happy when he was so bloody furious?

Etienne reached out and ruffled Rhys's hair as if he'd been that lad of such tender years. "We'll talk, my son. I will do what I can to make recompense for the years we've lost. But now we must decide what you will do about your uncle."

"I've acquired an entirely new family this day," Rhys said in disgust, "and I've yet to decide if it pleases me or not. I knew I should have stayed abed this morn!"

"At least Patrick wishes to talk," Sir Jean said calmly. "He could merely wish to stick you."

"And you think he does not?" Etienne laughed. "Father, you've obviously led too comfortable a life the past month and it has softened you. Of course he wishes to slay Rhys. Patrick has no desire to lose his keep."

"Why would young Rhys want it?" Jean returned. "Pitiful place."

"Whether or not Rhys wants it matters little," Etienne said firmly.

"I know," Jean grumbled. "'Tis that Rhys could come take it from him if he chose. I'm not so old as all that, whelp," he said, with a glare thrown his son's way, "that I cannot divine that."

Rhys looked at Gwen. She at least was no longer grumbling at him, or about him. In fact, he thought he just might have detected a bit of softness in her expression.

"How fair you look today, my love," he said, tucking her hair behind her ears. She had ears made for just such a thing, but he chose not to tell her as much. "Shall we go for a walk along the shore later?"

She smiled and put her arms around his neck. "I love you."

"As do I," he returned. He kissed her, then pushed her gently to her feet. "Well, let us be about our business and have an end to it. Then perhaps we can return our lives to something somewhat normal."

Then he looked about him and sighed.

His wife was dressed as a mercenary, his father was in skirts, and his mother sat upon a fat chest of gold as if she were a chicken determined to defend her eggs to the death.

Rhys sighed again and put his arm around his wife. "You stay here."

She agreed far too readily, but he could do nothing about it. He looked at his grandfather.

"You come with me."

He nodded. "Of course."

Rhys looked at his father, opened his mouth to speak, then shut it again and shook his head. "You do what you like."

"I always do."

"So I see," Rhys said. "Since I cannot seem to find anyone willing to see just what it is Sedgwick wants, I suppose I'll have to go myself."

By the saints, the day could just not worsen from there. He was sure of it.

Gwen pulled the hood of her cloak close around her face, grateful for the darkening sky and arrival of more inclement weather. The hood also kept her from having to smudge soot on her face to complete her disguise, for which she was most thankful. She would have less to explain if Rhys were

to catch her. He thought her safely tucked away up on the hill, being protected along with the children, his mother, and his chest of gold.

Evening shadows had fallen and with them had come a face-to-face
meeting with Patrick of Sedgwick. Gwen had wondered at the wisdom of
it, but Rhys hadn't hesitated. He had taken with him his father, grandfather, Montgomery, and the Fitzgerald brothers. Evidently he considered
them protection enough.

She didn't.

Hence her intention to take up her position outside the tent that contained her husband and his uncle.

She swaggered her way toward the appropriate tent, her hand on the hilt
of her sword. Obviously she had improved her mercenary mien, for no one
stopped her to question her having business in the area. She came to a stop
near the tent and sat down casually, as if this had been her goal all the while.
With one last look about her to make sure she wasn't being overly observed,
she put her ear to the cloth and strained to hear the voices inside.

And she heard nothing. This was not helping her in her cause. With a
curse, she rose to her feet and looked about her for a better solution. She
walked around the tent, only to find the entrance under heavy guard. The
Fitzgerald brothers stood to one side of the flap with Montgomery pacing
in front of them, while the other side was guarded by men she did not recognize. She pulled back, but not before Montgomery had caught sight
of her.

Obviously her disguise needed more work.

"Well, lad," he said, coming around the tent and looking at her pointedly, "don't you have duties that require you to remain atop the hill?"

She scowled at him and remained silent.

"I'd be about them were I you," he warned.

She shooed him away with her hand, but he only folded his arms over
his chest and frowned at her. With a sigh she turned and walked back
behind the tent, hoping he would think she had relented and returned to
the keep. Obviously, she would have to make do with her current position.
She stretched out on the ground and lifted the bottom edge of the tent a
fraction. With any luck, in the dark, anyone who passed by would just think
she had imbibed too much, and leave her in peace.

"Let me understand this," a deep voice said. "My niece is an abbess?"

"Aye," Rhys answered, "and very happily engaged in her vocation."

With her husband standing guard at her door, Gwen thought to herself.
She wondered in the back of her mind if Mary and Etienne still lived as
husband and wife.

Patrick grunted.

"No intention of returning to England?" Patrick asked sharply.

"None," Rhys assured him. "And, more particularly, no intention of returning to Sedgwick."

"And what of you?" Patrick demanded.

"Well," Rhys drawled, "I suppose that depends."

"Upon what?"

"Upon whether or not you remove your men from my land before sundown tomorrow."

"And if I do?"

"Then you may remain upon my inheritance," Rhys said pleasantly.

Patrick gasped in outrage. "Why, you insolent pup—"

"Insolent and fully capable of lopping off your head where you sit," Rhys assured him. "And if you think I will not do it, think again."

"And I am to remain there by your good graces?" Patrick was, by the sound of him, not happy at all with the idea.

"You should be grateful that I allow you to remain at all," Rhys retorted. "You and your heirs may have the keeping of Sedgwick, but you will have it as my vassals. If this is not acceptable, you are free to find yourself another keep to inhabit."

Gwen wished desperately that she could have seen Patrick's face. There was a great amount of snorting and swearing, as if Patrick strove to reconcile himself to his fate. Then there was the sound of a final, hearty curse.

"Damn you," Patrick snarled. "I don't want to do this."

"Nor do you wish to move your bed," Rhys finished dryly. "I accept your fealty."

There was the sound of more cursing from Patrick, but no further threats. She could have sworn she heard Patrick grumble something about Rollan and his foolish ideas, but then again she might have been imagining it. She put the tent flap back down and crawled to her feet, feeling somewhat relieved.

She started to walk back toward the path up the hill, then paused. The feeling she'd had of needing to protect her husband had not dissipated. Patrick's words might have been well-spoken, but that didn't guarantee that his men felt the same way. And who knew how many men Rollan had been able to sway to his twisted way of thinking.

She had her sword. There was no reason not to shadow her husband and be prepared to use it.

46

Rollan stood a safe distance away from Patrick's tent and waited for the outcome of the meeting. It had taken all the daylight hours for the negotiations to reach the point where a face-to-face meeting had happened. At least now Rollan had the cover of darkness under which to work.

That a meeting between Rhys and Patrick had actually taken place was a most disastrous turn of events. Patrick should have been planning his assault on the hill, not exchanging pleasantries with his niece's son. It showed a serious lack of commitment on Patrick's part, one Rollan was certain he would have to compensate for.

He fingered the crossbow and handful of quarrels he had brought with him for just such an emergency. If Patrick lacked the ballocks to slay Rhys, Rollan would do it in his stead.

He might even do Patrick in as well. Ayre was out of his grasp, but Sedgwick might be his as a reward for exposing to the king the clandestine activities of the de Piaget men.

He stiffened in anticipation as Rhys and Patrick came from the tent. He searched their bearings, hoping the torchlight would reveal whether anger or friendship was written there.

They weren't laughing. But they weren't snarling, either. And then he watched Rhys extend his hand. It wasn't a friendly gesture, but it was one of agreement. Patrick took it.

And then he knew what he would have to do.

He loaded the crossbow and lifted it. He sighted down the arrow, allowing himself the time to relish the thought of ending the life of the man he had hated from the moment he'd clapped eyes on him and realized Rhys de Piaget was everything he himself would never be.

Rhys and Patrick stepped away from the tent. Rollan allowed it. It would be more of a challenge to put his arrow through Rhys's heart without the light of the torches to aid him.

He watched Montgomery of Wyeth and the Fitzgerald brothers fall into step, saw Rhys's grandfather take up his place on Rhys's side, then saw a nun move to Rhys's other side.

A nun?

The mystery of it was almost enough to make Rollan stop, for he wondered if that could possibly be Rhys's mother. But so tall? Impossible.

It was a mystery he would have to leave unsolved. Rollan watched as another of Rhys's followers stepped directly behind Rhys. Rollan snorted to himself. How had the man acquired such a following? Didn't they realize that Rhys came from a long line of spies? Didn't they realize that Rhys himself hadn't had the courage to follow in his father's spying footsteps? It had to have been a lack of courage—that and that annoying desire for chivalry.

It was best he rid the world of the fool. King John would likely thank him for the service. Rollan found himself smiling. He would gather Gwen up and take her to London. The king would be pleased to see her freed of de Piaget's lecherous hands. Perhaps Rollan would find himself master of all her lands. It would be just recompense for having lost Ayre.

And then he would find himself master of Gwen herself.

The thought was enough to make his hand unsteady on the bow.

He clamped down upon his passions and took aim again. The little mercenary had stepped aside, leaving him a clear view of de Piaget's back. He let out his breath, then held it as he depressed the trigger.

"Damn," he said viciously.

The bloody mercenary had moved again behind Rhys's back and taken the arrow himself. Rollan quickly cranked the bow back again and fitted another arrow to the string. Then he watched Rhys turn and bend, then heard a scream.

"Gwen!"

Rollan shook his head. Surely he was hearing things.

"Merciful saints above, 'tis Gwen!" Rhys cried out.

Rollan found himself moving toward the fallen mercenary. It couldn't be. It was just a fool who had chosen to follow Rhys. It was just a boy, a dispensable soul who would likely have died in battle just the same.

Someone fetched a torch. The circle was parted enough that Rollan could see inside it.

He saw the arrow protruding from the dark cloak.

He saw the face of the mercenary as it lay turned on Rhys's knee.

It was Gwen.

Rollan stumbled back. The quarrels fell from his hand to the ground. The sound seemed to explode in the night.

He looked up and found himself staring into Rhys's tortured face. He met his enemy's eyes and saw the tears there. And, to his great surprise, Rollan found that his own eyes were swimming with tears.

"I never meant—" he began, but he couldn't finish.

He'd never meant to harm Gwen. He would have cared for her. He was certain he was the only one who loved her as she deserved.

And now he'd destroyed the one thing he ever could have loved.

Rhys didn't move, but his men rose and started toward him. They could have been running. Their faces were full of rage and hate. Rollan couldn't blame them.

But they moved slowly.

And he moved more quickly.

He turned the bow on himself.

And with one last look of agony at Rhys, he squeezed the trigger.

47

The child stood at the edge of what would in time be the great hall of Artane and looked on the tragedy.

Artane's lady had been laid softly on a bed of hastily arranged cloaks. Those who loved her were gathered about her, some with tears on their cheeks, some with heads bowed in prayer.

"The arrow must come out, Rhys."

The child looked up to find Lord Rhys's mother standing next to her son with her hand laid lightly upon his arm.

"Shall I do it?" she asked gently.

The child looked to Lord Rhys.

"Nay," he said hoarsely. "I will see to it."

"Rhys, 'tis a less grievous wound than you fear." This came from a nun who knelt at the lady Gwennelyn's side—though the child surmised by the large feet and powerful hands that this was no sister of the cloth. It took no gift of seeing to mark that man as Lord Rhys's father. The resemblance was uncanny.

"You'll need a poultice," Lord Rhys's father said. The way he gently examined the injury convinced the child that he had much experience in the healing arts.

"Yarrow," Lord Rhys said absently, his face full of grief and disbelief. "'Tis good for staunching wounds."

"Aye, son," his father said softly, "'tis good for that indeed."

"Someone add to the fire," the mother instructed. "She needs warmth."

"Someone go see to the children," the grandfather added. "Tell them 'tis but a simple wound that will heal quickly enough."

The child listened to all the voices, caught up in grief and anger that filled them, and wished she had foreseen what had been about to befall her lady. Her gift was a fickle one for now, and again the future was dark to her.

She felt the weight of someone's gaze upon her, and she looked up to find Lord Rhys staring at her. He beckoned and she approached the circle cautiously. She'd thought to have stood fully in the shadows so as not to disturb, but evidently he'd seen her just the same.

"Have y—" He cleared his throat and swallowed with difficulty. "Have you," he said carefully, "any yarrow about you?"

The child nodded. She'd brought what was needful from her tent, that luxurious place where she lived blissfully amongst her grandfather's things.

"And can you . . . can you . . ." He didn't finish.

He didn't need to. She knew what he asked. He wished her to ease his lady's pain. She knelt down next to his lady and bent close so only he could hear. She took a deep breath, hoping that her mother's gift might not fail her.

"Her pain I can ease," she whispered. "But her life is in your hands."

And so it was. There were many things beyond the power of her modest art. But she would do what she could.

The knight, now a lord, nodded with a jerky motion, then prepared to do what he must. The child grieved only for what he suffered, for she had seen the end of the night and knew what would transpire before dawn. But he would think her fanciful, so she kept what she'd seen close to her heart and gave him the aid he asked of her.

The lord put his hand on the arrow and made ready to pull. The child could feel the weight of the love and concern bear down upon the lady of Artane and ease her, though she knew it not.

The lord pulled and the arrow came free.

The lady breathed out the smallest of sighs, and those about her wept. But she did not open her eyes and she spoke no word.

The child knelt with her small hand covering her lady's and did what she could with her modest art. But, as she had told her lord, there was only so much she could do.

The lady Gwennelyn's life was in other hands besides hers.

She turned away to gather the things she had brought and be about the work of mixing her poultice.

Rhys sat with his head hanging between his knees, his hands dangling limp beside him. It occurred to him that he'd found himself in that position more than once over the past se'nnight. The first had been after realizing that his father lived still. He had yet to repay his father for the shock of that. He would have to do so eventually. Perhaps he would, when he could move himself from his present position. It had been four days since he'd last stirred himself to leave the tent, so the likelihood of moving in the future was rather slim.

"Rhys?"

That rough, low voice came from the door of the tent. Rhys managed to lift his head to stare at his grandfather. Even that effort was considerable. "Aye?" he croaked.

Jean entered the tent that had been hastily erected to shelter Gwen from the elements. "How fares our lady?"

"She breathes still, though she has not spoken," Rhys whispered.

"Your mother prays for her," Jean said, kneeling down beside Gwen and resting his hand against her cheek. "Her fever has abated at least."

Rhys nodded, but found that a small comfort.

Jean smiled gravely. "Your sire's skill continues in you."

"For all the good that does my lady."

"The little wench's potions have not eased her?"

"Socrates's granddaughter is a fine healer," Rhys said with a sigh, "and I feel certain she has eased Gwen's pain. But she can work no miracles. None of us can."

His grandfather gently smoothed Gwen's hair back from her face with his age-spotted hand. Rhys watched him continue to do so for several moments and knew that his grandfather had no answer for him. What could Jean tell him that he didn't know already?

The arrow had struck bone and remained fixed there until Rhys had removed it. The only stroke of good fortune had been realizing that it hadn't pierced heart or lung. Either Rollan was a poorer shot than they had thought, or he had been aiming for Rhys's heart and the true-flying arrow had found Gwen's shoulder in its way instead. Rhys suspected it was the latter, and he was relieved somewhat by the thought of it. At least Rollan had not been training his sights on Gwen's back. How could he have known? Rhys remembered vividly the horror in Rollan's eyes, horror he could only assume had come by virtue of whom he had struck.

Rhys pushed aside thoughts of that night. The only thing good to have come of the whole encounter was that Rollan had but wounded Gwen and not killed her. But even that bit of good fortune had not caused Gwen to open her eyes any sooner. Rhys could only pray that she would do so in time.

Jean cleared his throat. "The family is settled, if you're curious."

Rhys nodded, mute.

"Borrowed a few tents from Sedgwick," Jean said, sounding as if such a thing would have amused him greatly another time. "Your mother and father are safely tucked away with your gold and your children. The men patrol your walls. Montgomery and your Viking keepers pace about with expressions of great concern upon their faces."

"The children? How do they fare?"

"We've told them that Gwen merely rests. Seeing her sleeping has eased them, though I suspect Robin and Nicholas fear the worst. Amanda only knows she cannot have her mother, and I fear she finds Mary a poor substitute."

"A pity we do not have Joanna with us," Rhys said absently. "Amanda is very fond of her." He looked at his grandfather. "Word should be sent to her, I suppose."

"What word?" Jean asked in a sharp whisper. "That her daughter is recovering nicely?"

Rhys couldn't answer. He didn't dare. He was too afraid that when Gwen did wake in truth, she wouldn't wake to herself. Her fever had been hard upon her, despite their best efforts. If he hadn't known better, he might have suspected the arrow had been poisoned. Knowing Rollan, it likely had been.

"There is no need to tell Joanna that, not that I wouldn't mind looking on her again. Let her come for a visit in a few weeks. Gwen can show her the scar herself then."

Rhys nodded in agreement, simply because he could do nothing else. *Please let her awake whole. We've had such a short time together.*

Jean rose to his feet. "Do you need aught?"

Rhys shook his head. "Nay."

"I could remain—"

"Nay," Rhys interrupted. "I'll stay."

"You do her little good in this state—"

"I'll stay," Rhys repeated. He looked up at his grandfather and attempted a smile. His face was too stiff with worry for any success at it. "My thanks just the same."

Jean nodded and rested his hand briefly on Rhys's head before he ducked out of the tent.

Rhys was once again alone with his lady, with naught but his love and prayers to aid her. He could only hope it would be enough.

He found himself speaking to her before he realized what he was about. He reminded her of all the reasons she had for remaining by his side. He told her of his visions of a magnificent keep to shelter her and her children from elements and enemies alike. He reminded her of the sounds of the sea and the sea birds, of the smell of the air and the chill of the wind. He spoke of his parents and how they currently both prayed for her recovery. He knew he babbled, but he could do nothing but continue, recalling for her every scratch and bruise Nicholas had earned while finding himself caught up in Robin's mischief, every tear and stomping of feet Amanda had indulged in thanks to worms and snakes down her dress.

And when he had exhausted that list, and it was a very long list indeed, he spoke of his love for her, of how he had spent so many hours over the course of his long life dreaming of her, longing for her, hoping that one day she would be his. When that provoked no response, he reminded her that she had said on more than one occasion that they would have a long and happy life together.

But still she spoke no word, gave no sign that she had heard any of his heart poured out so fully.

Rhys bent his head again upon his knees and let his hands rest limply at his sides. Perhaps they had been too confident that merely removing the arrow and packing the wound would be enough to cure her.

Perhaps he would spend the rest of his days with only her children to remind him of her. Much as he loved them, the very thought of that was almost enough to break his heart.

So many dreams yet to be grasped and turned into life. Rhys would have wept, had he the energy for it. They could not end thusly, those dreams that they had dreamed. They could not end on a barren rock on the northern coast with the wind howling and the waves crashing against the shore. Rhys simply could not bring himself to believe that their chance was already past and that his life would stretch out before him with Gwen not in it.

Nay, he would not even allow himself to think it. Gwen would awaken in time. She had to.

He knew he would not survive if she did not.

He felt something skitter across his foot and he cursed. That was all he needed, rats now to plague him.

The rat was bold enough to try again, and Rhys seized it by the tail.

Only it was no tail he held. It was a finger.

He whipped his head up. The motion almost sent him toppling forward onto his lady. It might have, had she not tightened her grip upon his hand.

"Rhys," she whispered, stretching, then catching her breath at the pain. "The arrow?"

He almost shuddered with relief. She was speaking. She remembered what had befallen her.

"The arrow is out, my love," he said, feeling the tears stream down his face.

She smiled and the sight of it broke what heart he had left.

"I've been . . . napping?" She yawned, as if she'd been doing nothing more than just that. She looked at him and frowned. "You need . . . one."

"A rest? Aye, my love, I suppose I could."

She shifted, but flinched at the movement of her injured shoulder. "It pains me."

Rhys stretched himself out and carefully placed his arm over his lady. "Rest then, my love," he said. "I'll not leave your side."

"Pleasant dreams," she whispered.

"If you only knew," he said with feeling. That they would have another chance to dream was not a gift he would take lightly.

He waited until his lady had drifted back off to sleep before he allowed himself to relax. She held his hand still and her grip was strong and sure. He knew he would have to rise soon and inform those without that Gwen had awoken, seemingly sound of mind and body, but for the moment he could do nothing but lie beside her and fair drown in the wave of gratitude that washed over him.

Gwen stirred, murmured his name, then slept again.

Rhys closed his own eyes and sighed in relief.

48

Six months later . . .

Gwen worked steadily upon the parchment, copying carefully the ingredients and amounts she had been given And once she was finished, she sat back and smiled at the child standing next to her chair.

"There," she said, satisfied. "A proper addition to your grandsire's manuscript." She smiled at the girl. "This is a potion of your own making, is it not?"

"Aye, my lady," the child answered.

"'Tis very palatable," Gwen said with a smile. "And I should know as I have ingested enough of it over the past few fortnights."

The child blushed and Gwen smiled. The girl was never boastful of her skill, but Gwen knew from her own experience that it was great. They were blessed to have such a healer there with them. And, most important, the child could brew a potion that contained no specks of unmentionable substances—or at least none that Gwen could see. That was enough to convince her that this was a healer they would wish to keep about them as long as they could.

"We should sign your name, child," Gwen said. She realized, with a start, that she had never asked it. She had referred to the child as "Socrates's granddaughter" to those about her, and used the name "wondrous healer" on the girl herself. "How are you called?"

The child bowed her head. "Berengaria," she answered softly.

"Berengaria," Gwen said, laying her hand upon the girl's head. "A beautiful name. Berengaria of Artane. Will that suit you for the moment?"

"Aye, my lady. It will."

Gwen suspected the girl would not remain there always, but perhaps for the foreseeable future it would be enough. Gwen carefully gathered up the manuscript pages she had written out that day and handed them to Berengaria.

"Will you not sup with us tonight?"

Berengaria shook her head. "When your hall is built, perhaps, if it pleases my lady."

"So that then you might be less noticed?" Gwen asked with a dry smile. "Aye, my girl, if that suits you better. I'll see you have something proper in your tent."

"You always do, my lady."

And with that, the girl kissed Gwen's hand as if she'd been the queen and scampered from the small building that served as great hall at present.

Gwen rose and drew on her cloak. Even though it was almost spring, it was still chilly so near the sea. She winced at the ache in her shoulder. It had been six months since Rollan's arrow had felled her, and still she had pain when she put on her clothes. At least she lived. It was something she was grateful for each morn she awoke. Montgomery had told her that Rollan had seemed devastated enough by the thought that he might have killed her, but none of them would know the truth now. She wanted to believe that it had been a mistake, but if that were the case, then it meant that he had been attempting to kill Rhys.

It was a puzzle she didn't dwell on much.

She stepped out into the bailey and shivered. Winter was hard upon them, but still the work went on. Rhys's gold was building an impressive keep. It hadn't hurt that his father and grandfather had done their share of contributing as well. It would likely take a pair of years yet to finish the castle completely, but she felt certain 'twould be worth the wait and the expense. Rhys was determined to build something not even John could take by force.

Messages had flown from Artane to London and back, with the king growing less irritated with each one. Finally John had tersely informed Rhys that he had intended all along that Rhys should take Ayre's widow as his wife. Gwen smiled at the memory of Rhys's reaction to that. He had, however, quickly agreed with the king that his superior wisdom and foresight had indeed provided Rhys with a fine bride in the end.

A bride and children, that was. Robin, Nicholas, and Amanda had been officially claimed and duly recorded to Gwen's satisfaction. Robin was determined to live worthily of his newly made sire's name. Nicholas seemed still to be stunned by the turn of events and spent most of his time trailing after Robin with a dazed look upon his face.

Amanda, however, seemed to think her father had never been other than Rhys, and Gwen understood perfectly. It wasn't as if Alain had done more than hear the babe was a girl and promptly forget about her. Rhys, on the other hand, was lavish with his affections for all three children, though he would be the first to admit that he held a particularly soft spot for his only girl.

Gwen wondered what Rhys would do when she informed him that in a few months he might just have another babe competing for his affections.

She tucked that tidbit away to share later, tucked her hands under her arms, and went in search of her love.

She found him, unsurprisingly, standing atop his walls, staring out over the sea. She made her way to him, then leaned against the wall and slipped her hand into his.

"Staring into the future again?" she teased.

He squeezed her hand. "For all you know, I might be."

"More than likely, you're imagining how it will be to finally have the hall finished where we might retreat to our place before the fire and be warm for a change."

He put his arm around her and snuggled her close. "There is that as well," he said with a smile. Then he shook his head and looked back out over the sea. "I was just standing here, marveling over my life and the gifts I've been given and wondering what I have done to deserve them."

"Well, for a start," she said, "you saved Lord Bertram's life."

"A happy bit of luck," he said modestly.

"Well," she said, "you rescued me from a piggery."

"Now that," he said with a thoughtful nod, "did surely earn me all that I have now."

"I should think it did. It was a horrible stench you endured to save me."

His rich laugh washed over her. "Ah, sweet Gwen, the prize was well worth the effort." He hugged her to him. "It was indeed a most fortuitous bit of chivalry."

Gwen closed her eyes and sighed in contentment. She could indeed do nothing but agree with him and it amazed her that such a simple thing as wading through pig manure to liberate a child from her prison could have led to such happiness. Rhys once again enjoyed the company of his father from time to time when Etienne, Mary, and Jean ventured northward. Her children were blessed with a father who loved and cared for them. Her own mother had full control of Segrave without worrying that she might lose her home at someone's whim.

And there Gwen herself stood with the walls of a magnificent keep beneath her feet, her children safe within those walls, and the love of her heart standing next to her with his strong arms about her. She'd imagined so often how it might be, but the truth of it made her realize just what a poor imagination she had.

"I love you," she whispered, looking up at Rhys.

He smiled down at her. "What brought that on?"

"Just your nearness," she answered with a smile of her own. "I will never forget how fortunate I am."

"You?" he asked with a laugh. "Why, lady, I am the fortunate one. I have obtained the dream of my youth."

As had she, though she didn't say the like. It would have interrupted one of the most overwhelming kisses of her life and she prided herself on knowing when to speak and when to remain silent.

And so she closed her eyes, held her words, and gave herself up to the magic of her husband's mouth upon hers. It was a sweet kiss full of love, passion, and promise. Her life had become the stuff of dreams.

She was content.

If I Had You

To Matthew,
who is my comfort, my joy, and my forever home.

And to Elizabeth,
who says the word home *with all*
the feeling in her baby heart.

Prologue

England, 1215
Artane

The young girl stood at the door of the healer's quarters and looked out over the courtyard, eyeing the dirt and flat-laid stone that separated her from the great hall. Judging the distance to be not unmanageable, she released the doorframe she had been clinging to and eased herself down the three steps to the dirt. And then she grasped more firmly the stick she leaned upon and slowly and painfully began to make her way across the courtyard.

Sunlight glinted off her pale golden hair and off the gold embroidery on her heavy velvet gown. Though it was much too hot for such a garment, the child had insisted. It hid the unsightly splint that bound her leg from hip to foot.

She looked up and saw that the hall door was closer than it had been. No smile of relief crossed her strained features; she had yet far to go.

"Ugly Anne of Fenwyck!"

"Thorn in Artane's garden!"

The voices caught her off guard and she stumbled. She caught herself heavily on her injured leg. Biting back a cry of pain, she put her head down and quickened her pace.

They surrounded her, not close enough to hurt her with anything but their words, though those were surely painful enough. Pages they were, for the most part, with one notable exception. A young man joined in the torment, a freshly knighted soul who should have known better. They circled her as she hobbled across the smooth stone path leading to the great hall, taunting her mercilessly. The knight folded his arms and laughed as she struggled up the stairs.

"Why the haste, gimp?"

The maid had no time for tears. Safety was but four steps away. She ignored the laughter that followed her and forced herself to continue her climb.

The door opened and the lord of the hall caught her up in his arms and held her close. Her stick clattered down the stairs but she had no stomach for the fetching of it. She clung to her foster father and let his deep voice wash over her soothingly as she was pulled inside the hall. The lord reached out to close the door, paused, then frowned deeply before he pushed the wood to.

Had the girl looked out before the door was closed, she would have seen a dark-haired, gray-eyed lad of ten-and-four standing on the front step of the healer's house, having come to take his own exercise for the day. And she would have seen the rage on his face and the clenching of his hands at his sides; he had witnessed the last of the tortures she'd endured.

And had she been watching, she would have been privy to the events that followed. The lad shrugged off his brother's supporting arm and called to the young knight in angry tones. The knight sauntered over, his mocking snort turning into a hearty laugh when he heard the lad's challenge.

There was no equity in the fight. The boy still recovered from a fever that had kept him abed for half a year. The knight was five years his senior. And the knight had no qualms about humiliating the lord's son each and every chance he had.

It was over before it had begun. The dark-haired lad went facedown in the mud and muck. The last shreds of his strength deserted him, leaving him wallowing helplessly. His brother stepped forward to defend him and earned a pair of broken fingers for his trouble. The knight sneered at them both, then walked away, the older lads in his entourage snickering behind their hands as they followed him, and the younger ones slinking away full of shame and embarrassment for the lad who had no strength to rise to his feet.

The girl witnessed none of this. She was gently deposited inside the chamber she shared with her foster sisters, and had the luxury of shedding her tears of humiliation in private.

Her young champion shed his tears in the mud.

1

England, 1225

The young woman sat atop her mount and looked down the road that separated her from the castle. She had traversed its length many times over the course of her ten-and-nine years and felt reasonably acquainted with its dips and swellings. She was, however, eager to be free of its confines and, as a result, off her horse, so she viewed it with a keen eye. Judging the distance separating her from her goal to be not unmanageable, she took a firmer grip on her reins and urged her horse forward.

Her destination could not be reached quickly enough, to her mind. Behind her rode her matchmaking father, his head likely full of thoughts of the half dozen men he had left behind *him* at Fenwyck, men desperate enough for his wealth to take his daughter in the bargain. Before her lay her foster home, the home of her heart, the home she had left almost half a year earlier only because her father had dragged her bodily from it. She had despaired of ever seeing it again.

But now she was released from her father's hall, if only briefly, and Artane was but a short distance away. That was enough. It would have to be. It might be all she was allowed to have.

"By the saints, I'm eager to be out of this bloody rain," her sire complained as he pulled up alongside her. "How is it, mistress Anne, that I allowed you to enlist me in this fool's errand in this blighted weather? My business with you is at Fenwyck, not here!"

Anne looked at her sire. A weak shaft of autumn sunlight fell down upon his fair hair and glinted on the gold embroidery adorning his heavy surcoat.

"You look well, Father," she said, praying she might distract him and knowing a compliment could not go astray.

"As if it served me to look well, given the circumstances!"

"It was kind of you to bring me to Artane," she said, keeping to her course. "I very much wished to bid Sir Montgomery a final farewell."

"It will be too late for that, I should think," her sire muttered. "He'll be dead by the time we arrive."

But Anne could only assume by the way he began to straighten his clothing and comb his hair with his fingers that he was seeking to present the best appearance possible, even if such an appearance was only to be made at a burying.

She turned her mind back to more important matters, namely staying in the saddle until she could reach the castle. Her leg had not borne the rigors of traveling well. Though but four days' slow travel separated Fenwyck from Artane, she suspected she might have been better served to have walked the distance. She wondered if she would manage to stand once she was released from the tortures of her journey.

Despite that very real concern, Anne felt her heart lift with every jarring clomp of her horse's hooves. The stark stone of the castle rose up against the gray sky, a bulwark of safety and security. By the saints, she was glad of the sight. Though her sire continued to curse a variety of objects and souls, Anne let his words wash over her and continue on their way to more attentive ears. She was far too lost in her memories to pay him any heed.

She remembered the first time she had come to Artane. The castle had been little more than branches marking the place for the outer walls and twigs outlining the inner buildings. The construction had seemed to take but a short time, likely because she'd been passing her days so happily in the company of the family she'd come to foster with. There had been a sister for her, just her age, and brothers too, though she'd paid them little heed at the time. The lord and lady of the yet-to-be-finished keep had treated her as one of their own and for that she had been very grateful.

And then had come the time when she had first noticed the lord's eldest son.

He'd been hard to ignore.

He had announced his presence by putting a worm down her dress.

A particularly jarring misstep by her mount almost made her bite off her tongue. Anne gritted her teeth and forced herself to pay heed to her horse. Perhaps her memories did her more disservice than she cared to admit, especially when they went in that particular direction, for indeed there was no purpose in thinking on the lord's eldest son.

She looked up and realized she was almost in the inner courtyard. She had rarely been more grateful for a sight than she was for the view of the keep before her. She had the captain of Artane's guard to thank for the like, as the summons to Montgomery of Wyeth's deathbed had been the only thing which could have freed her from Fenwyck's suffocating walls.

Anne wended her way carefully through the crowded courtyard. Artane was a busy place with much commerce, many fosterlings, and numerous lordlings continually looking to curry Artane's favor. She supposed it was pleasing to Lord Rhys to find himself in such demand, but she herself would have been happier had the castle been a little less populated. It certainly would have made the negotiation of her way toward the great hall a good deal easier.

She suppressed a grimace when her horse finally came to a halt. The beast was well trained, thankfully, and spent no more energies moving about. Anne stared down at the ground below her mount's hooves and wondered how best to reach it without landing ungracefully on her nose. She took a deep breath, twisted herself around so as to keep hold of her saddle, then slid slowly to the ground.

"Anne!" Geoffrey exclaimed with an accompanying curse. "I told you I would aid you."

"I am well, Father," she said, forcing herself to remain upright instead of giving in to the urge to lean her head against her horse's withers and weep. The pain in her leg was blinding, but she supposed she had no one to blame for that but herself. She had been the one to shun the cart her father had wished her to ride in. She had also been the one who had declined the numerous halts her father had tried to force upon her.

"I begin to wonder why I ever sent you here," Geoffrey said curtly. "I vow they bred a stubbornness in you that I surely do not possess. Mayhap you had been better off to remain at Fenwyck."

Anne had no acceptable answer for that, though her first thought was "the saints be praised you sent me away." She was too old at ten-and-nine for such childish responses, but there hadn't been a day she hadn't been grateful for her fostering at Rhys de Piaget's keep. She suspected, however, that she had best keep such observations to herself.

"We may as well go inside," her father said, sounding as if it were the very last thing he wanted to do. "He'll come to fetch us if we tarry here."

"The lady Gwennelyn will be glad to see you," Anne offered.

"Aye, but that objectionable husband of hers will be there as well. What joy is there in that for me? It only serves to remind me that she chose him over me."

"As you say," Anne said, wincing at the protests her leg was making as she put weight on it.

"Gwen did want me," Geoffrey said. "And sorely indeed."

"Of course, Father," Anne agreed, but her mind was on other things— namely trying not to sprawl face-first into the dirt.

She looked at the great hall. The distance separating them was greater than she would have liked, but not unmanageable. She took a deep breath, then pushed away from her horse. She carefully crossed the flat stones she'd walked over for the greater part of her life and let the familiarity of them soothe her. By the saints, she had missed this place. How had she survived Fenwyck the previous half year? How would she have endured her childhood there? The saints be praised she had never been forced to have the answer to the latter. She suspected that 'twas only recently that she truly understood how fortunate she had been. Gwennelyn of Artane had lavished love and attention on her that she never would have had at her father's hall.

Of course, none of it would have come about had the lady Gwennelyn not had such a long acquaintance with Anne's sire. It had never become more than that, for there had been little love lost between them—despite Geoffrey's boasts to the contrary.

There had been even less affection between Geoffrey and Rhys de Piaget, though Anne knew the two men counted each other as staunch allies. Anne had heard tales enough of their early encounters to know how things were between them, though neither the lord nor lady of Artane had disparaged her father. Her father, however, had certainly never been so polite in return. Fortunately, his relationship with Artane had continued to be amicable enough for Anne to have found herself deposited inside Artane's then-unfinished walls, and for that she was grateful.

"Come on then," Geoffrey said, taking her by the arm and starting toward the hall. "We may as well go inside."

Anne felt her leg tighten with each step she took and she came close to begging her sire to stop. But that would have led to a recounting of her childhood follies, Rhys's lack of attentiveness in allowing them to happen, and a host of other things she knew she could not bear to listen to. She looked up the steps and cursed silently at the number of people coming and going. Well, she had no choice but to make her way through the press if she wanted to find herself a chair. So she gritted her teeth and counted the steps that remained her until she could enter the great hall and sit in peace.

And then a form blocked her path. She looked up and flinched before she could stop herself.

"Why the haste, lady?" the knight asked. "Surely your journey here has been arduous."

Anne suppressed a grimace. Of all the souls she could have encountered in this crowd, it had to be the lout before her.

"Well, here's a man with a goodly bit of chivalry," Geoffrey said, pushing Anne out of the way in his haste to clasp hands with the man. "I believe I should know you, shouldn't I?"

The knight bowed politely. "Baldwin of Sedgwick, my lord. I am well acquainted with your daughter."

Aye, there was truth in that. His acquaintance with her included naught but torment and she had no stomach for any more of it. Anne knew he wouldn't dare insult her before her sire, but that hardly made being in his presence any less unappealing.

Her sire turned to look at her pointedly and she could just imagine what he wished to say. *Look you here, you stubborn baggage. Yet another man who might be induced to wedding you for enough gold in his purse.* Anne looked past her father to Baldwin. She was unsurprised to see him wearing his customary look of disdain. Perhaps he would be bold enough to mock her within earshot of her father.

But when her sire turned again to face Baldwin, there was naught but a polite smile there to greet him.

"Are you wed?" Geoffrey asked bluntly. "You are heir to Sedgwick, are you not?"

"Nay, my lord," Baldwin said, shaking his head, "my brother is. And he has just recently been blessed with a son, William. So as you can see, I am well removed from any chance of inheriting."

Geoffrey grunted. "Well, there's much to be said for a little hunger for something better. My daughter's not wed, you know. She has her flaws—"

"A weak leg," Baldwin supplied.

"Aye, that," Geoffrey agreed.

Anne could hardly believe they were discussing her so openly, and she had no desire to hear more. The saints only knew how blunt her father had been with all the other men he had invited to his keep for a viewing of her and her dowry. And as far as Baldwin went, she knew he would only become nastier in his discourse regarding her, for she knew with exactness what he thought of her. Hadn't she heard the like for as long as she had known him?

She pushed past her father and walked away, though it cost her much to do so without limping overmuch.

The hall door opened before she reached it and Rhys himself stepped out into the crisp autumn air. Before Anne could say aught, Rhys had descended the handful of steps and pulled her into a sure embrace. The relief she felt was almost enough to make her knees give way beneath her. She was safely home. Perhaps beyond all hope she would manage to stay.

She heard her father's complaining long before he came to stand behind her.

"It was foolish to come," Geoffrey said, "but she insisted. She shouldn't be traveling about with that leg of hers."

Anne gritted her teeth. Rhys never would have continued to remind her of her frailty, nor would he have hourly warned her to have a care. Nay, he would have let her push herself to the limits of her pride, then merely picked her up and put her in a chair. Rhys was the only reason she had spent months learning to walk again after her accident; his approval was the reason she struggled each day past the limits of her endurance.

Or so she told herself. Her true reason for wanting to overcome her limp was something so painful she rarely allowed herself to think on it. The approval she sought was from someone who never looked at her twice when he could help it, who had earned his spurs early, then gone off to war. Nay, his was approval she would never have.

A pity his was what mattered the most to her.

Anne felt Rhys give her a gentle squeeze before he pulled away. Anne suspected that she'd never been gladder to see a soul than she was to see the one man who might possibly be able to save her from her sire's ruthless marital schemes.

"A long journey, my girl," Rhys said. "But the sacrifice means much. It grieves me, though, to give you the tidings I must."

"See?" Geoffrey said pointedly. "I told her 'twould be for naught." He snorted in disgust. "All this way for but a burying."

Anne felt the noose begin to tighten about her neck.

"And not even for that," Rhys said grimly. "We couldn't wait any longer."

"Then we surely won't be staying long," Geoffrey said. "I have plans for her at home, Rhys."

Anne closed her eyes and prayed with all her strength. Would that some saint would take pity on her and provide her with some means of staying at Artane. Her fondest wish was to be watching her father ride back to Fenwyck from the security of Artane's battlements. To be sure, she had packed an extra gown or two for just such a happening.

"Montgomery was very fond of Anne," Rhys said. "I've no doubt it would have comforted him to see her again."

"I don't think—" Geoffrey began.

"Aye, well, ofttimes you don't," Rhys said shortly. "Go inside, Geoffrey. Gwen will want to see you."

Anne watched her father hesitate, then consider. Apparently the lure of the lady Gwennelyn's beauty was still a powerful one, for he grumbled something else under his breath, but went inside the hall without further argument. Anne took a deep breath, then looked up at her foster father.

"Are you well, my lord?" she asked.

Rhys smiled gravely. "Well enough. Montgomery was a good friend and he will be missed. He would have been pleased you came home, though."

She was relieved to see he was bearing the loss well. Sir Montgomery was the last of Rhys's original guardsmen to have succumbed to death's grasp. He'd lost twins named Fitzgerald not two years earlier and that had been a grievous blow to him. To lose Montgomery as well had to have grieved him deeply.

"I am sorry to come so late," she said.

"You couldn't have known." He tucked her hand under his arm and turned toward the stairs. "Now, what foolishness did your sire press upon you to keep you so long from your true home?"

"Suitors," Anne said with a shudder.

"Poor girl. I can't imagine he presented you with much of a selection."

"He didn't."

"Leave him to me," he said. "I know how to redirect his thoughts."

Aye, to scores of bruises won during a wrestle, she thought, followed closely by *Ah, that you could*. But she said nothing aloud. She was but three steps from the warmth and comfort of the hall and that was task enough for her at present.

Once the last step was gained, the hall entered, and the door closed behind her, Anne could only stand and shake. She looked at the distance separating her from the hearth with its cluster of comfortable chairs and stools and thought she just might weep. Her pride was the only thing keeping her from falling to her knees. Rhys didn't move from her side. She knew he would merely wait patiently by her side until she regained her will—and from that she drew strength.

But before she could muster up any more energy or courage, a whirlwind of skirts and dark hair descended into the great hall and ran across the rushes. Anne braced herself for the embrace she knew would likely knock her rather indelicately onto her backside.

"By the saints, *finally*," were the words that accompanied the clasp and kiss. "Anne, I vow I feared your sire would never let you from Fenwyck!"

Anne held on to her foster sister and sighed in relief. "To be sure, 'twas nothing short of a miracle that I am here," she agreed.

Amanda of Artane pulled back and rolled her eyes passionately. "What dotards did he have lined up for you to select from?" she demanded. "None worthy of you, I would imagine."

"And that sort of imagination," Geoffrey said from where he appeared suddenly behind Amanda, "was, and no doubt continues to be, your mother's undoing. You might be well to curb the impulse in yourself."

As Amanda turned to face him, Anne suppressed the urge to duck behind her, lest the inevitable argument come to include her. Amanda was painfully frank and had no sense of her own peril. Anne was torn between telling her to be silent, and urging her on. Perhaps Amanda could convince Geoffrey that Anne was of no mind to wed as yet—especially to any man of his choosing.

"My lord Fenwyck," Amanda said, inclining her head, "'tis a pleasure to see you, as always."

"You've your mother's beauty," Geoffrey grumbled. "Unfortunately, you've her loose tongue as well."

"Gifts, the both of them," Amanda conceded. "Now, about these suitors . . ."

"I have chosen several fine men—"

"Likely twice her age—"

"You know nothing of it," Geoffrey returned sharply. "And you, mistress, are well past the age when any sensible man would have taken you and tamed you."

"As if any could—"

Anne waited for blows to ensue, but she was spared the sight by Rhys stepping between his daughter and Anne's father.

"Enough," he said sternly. "Amanda, see Anne to the fire. Fenwyck, come with me. You've had a long journey and I've warm drink in my solar. You can take your ease there."

"He could better take his ease at Fenwyck," Amanda muttered.

Anne bit her lip to stifle her smile as she watched Rhys lead her father off, but she couldn't stop her a small laugh when Amanda turned and scowled at her.

"Oh, Amanda," she said with a gasp, "one day you will truly say too much and find yourself in deep waters indeed."

Amanda flicked away her words as she would have an annoying fly. "Did you but know all the things I think but do not say, you would find me to be restrained indeed. Now, come and sit by the fire. You'll tell me all your sorry tales and I'll weep with you. Then Mother will come, we'll tell them to her again, and she'll speak to your sire. You know she can convince him he's a fool."

Anne suspected that such a thing was even beyond the lady Gwennelyn's powers, but a maid could still hope. At the moment, though, she sorely needed warmth and to sit, so she leaned on her companion, hobbled over to the fire, and sat with deep gratitude on something that didn't move.

As Amanda had ordered, Anne's tale was first told for her ears alone, then others joined to hear the horrors she had endured. The murmurs of displeasure, the cries of outrage, and the threats directed at her father were sweet to her ears and she found herself smiling for the first time in weeks.

She was with those dearest to her and, for the moment, she was free from undesirable suitors. The morrow would see to itself. After all, she had been released from her father's hall and that was something she had been certain would only happen should she find herself leaving it thanks to an unwanted husband. Yet there she was, sitting comfortably by the fire in the company of those souls dearest to her heart.

It was as sweet as she'd known it would be.

The evening passed most uneventfully, with the family having moved to gather about the fire in Rhys's solar as was oft their custom. Anne went with them and counted that a privilege indeed. Though others fostered at Artane, Anne found herself the only one of those so drawn into Artane's intimate family circle. That was just another of the reasons Baldwin of Sedgwick loathed her, of that she was certain. He was Rhys's kin, yet he remained without the solar door. Baldwin was, however, not the soul that took it the hardest. His sister, Edith, also had come to live at Artane and Anne suspected that such denial into the lord's confidences and pleasures ate at her the most deeply.

But for now Anne need worry neither about Baldwin nor his sister, nor anyone else for that matter. She was home, for the moment, and that was enough. She sat in a chair next to Amanda and looked about her in pleasure.

Her foster parents sat close together, hands clasped, seemingly as content as they had been the first time Anne had seen them together. Their happiness was plain to the eye, as was their pride in their children. And why not? Between those they had laid claim to through adoption and those of their own flesh, they had a brood to be envied.

Anne looked at their eldest girl-child, Amanda, and felt her customary flash of envy. But by now, it was a gentle sort of yearning that somehow she herself might have been born with the beauty Amanda possessed. And it wasn't only Amanda's beauty that Anne couldn't help but wish for herself; Amanda had a fire and spirit that Anne knew few women could hope to call their own. But long years of watching her foster sister had shown Anne that such spirit did not come without a price—namely Amanda's rather vigorous disagreements with Rhys about how her life should progress. It was not an easy path Amanda trod, but Anne loved her just the same and was grateful for her friendship.

Miles was next to Amanda not only in terms of age, but where he sat. He looked very much like his sire, which meant he was powerfully handsome indeed. Where they differed, though, was that where Rhys was generally cheery in his outlook, Miles was brooding. Anne, however, found Miles very much to her liking for though his moods might have been gloomy, his wit was fine. She was happy he was home now that he'd won his spurs. She suspected he wouldn't remain long, but she would enjoy him while she could.

Miles's younger sister, Isabelle, was Amanda's likeness in visage, but not in temperament. She was very sweet and as tractable as could be expected from having passed all her time in Amanda's company.

The youngest children were twins, male-children. Fortunately for the rest of Rhys and Gwen's children they had come last, else Anne suspected none of the other children would have been conceived. Their mischief was nothing short of breathtaking and she suspected that they had given Rhys most of the gray in his hair.

But even with the children there, the scene before her was incomplete. Missing were Artane's two eldest sons, but that was nothing unusual. Robin and Nicholas had squired at another keep, then come home briefly after earning their spurs at the tender age of ten-and-nine. Then had come the decision to join the crusade. Nicholas had never truly wished to, but Robin had convinced him 'twas their duty. The time spent had been fruitless as they had arrived just in time to find the defeated knights returning home. Robin's exact reasons for having wished to go were still a mystery. All Anne knew was that she hadn't seen Artane's heir in over five years.

Though that could change at any time. Anne knew Rhys had sent for his son three months earlier. The saints only knew what was keeping him away. Anne had heard the servants speculating that afternoon about the like; the reasons bandied about were everything from him being prisoner in some angry father's dungeon—for having despoiled his daughter, no less—to his having traveled to the Holy Land to collect himself a harem. Anne cared for none of the speculation, so she had quickly retreated from the kitchens.

All she knew was she probably wouldn't have one last sight of Robin before her father sold her to some man likely twice her age who cared nothing for her.

Anne shifted as her leg began to pain her. At least here no one gaped at her as she did the like. At Fenwyck, sharp eyes marked her slight limp, men stared at her, as if they couldn't believe her ugliness was so apparent, her father's wife and her daughter treated her as if she were helpless, far too helpless to do anything but sit in the solar and sew. Coming to Artane was a relief, even though it meant coming back to the site of former disgraces and back to stones that whispered childish taunts as she passed. She could ignore those well enough, especially if she managed to avoid Baldwin of Sedgwick. What was more difficult was not being able to go anywhere inside the walls without knowing that Robin had been there before her. His ghost haunted her, awake or dreaming.

She wanted it to stop.

Or did she?

At present, she wasn't sure what would be worse. But what she did know was that even if she were forced to spend the rest of her days with memories of Robin tormenting her, it would be a more tolerable fate than to find herself packed off with her trunks to some unknown lord.

But that would come later. For now it was enough to be home and to listen to the familiar sounds of the family with whom she had grown to womanhood. Far better to think on what was happening around her than to speculate on what might be happening in France. The saints only knew what mischief Robin was combining at present. It likely entailed some woman or another and the sounds that would result from that were ones Anne had no desire to hear.

She opened her eyes to find her father staring at her. He pursed his lips and shook his head meaningfully. Anne had no trouble understanding the unspoken message.

Do not accustom yourself to this, my girl.

Anne felt Amanda's hand on her arm. Her foster sister leaned over and whispered in her ear.

"I vow we'll see him thwarted before a fortnight is out."

Anne nodded, grateful for the distraction. She knew that not even Amanda could manage such a feat, but at least thinking on it allowed her to turn her thoughts away from Robin.

But she hoped in whatever bed he found himself at present, he loitered with several handfuls of happy, persistent bedbugs who would cause him to cry out with anything but pleasure.

2

Robin of Artane was not a man to take the enjoyment of his pleasure lightly.

So as he wallowed in the aftermath of a well-earned bit of the same, he savored it as fiercely as he had the first time he'd felt the like. He closed his eyes and relished the sweat pouring down his face, his limbs trembling, and his heart beating so hard in his chest, he thought it might burst free. The mighty sense of victory won, of challenge vanquished, of his considerable skill used to its fullest; truly, could there be anything more satisfying? Could he have but fallen asleep at that moment, he might have found a decent rest for a change.

A pity he found himself but standing in the middle of the lists with three layers of mud and dung on his boots, and not abed with a handsome wench.

Unfortunately, such a sorry state seemed to be the extent of his good fortune of late.

But Robin wasn't a man to shun what fortune came his way, so he kept his eyes closed and enjoyed the smell of sweat, leather, and dung. Things could have been much worse.

The savoring, though, never lasted as long as he might have liked, for there was always another conquest to be made and his pride would not let him rest idle. He dragged his sleeve across his eyes to wipe away the sweat, then looked at the cluster of men standing near him. At least he had a clutch of them where they couldn't scamper off across the fields. Such, he supposed, was the happy part of loitering at his brother's keep in France. The less-than-pleasing ingredient in that stew was that since Nicholas found himself comfortably ensconced in one of his own halls, he was reluctant to leave it to seek out the pleasures of warring. Robin had given that his best efforts cajoling, bullying, and brandishing his sword—but to no avail. Nicholas had his feet up before the fire inside, several handsome wenches attending his every need and a soft chair beneath his backside. Robin suspected he might have more success prying an entire complement of nunnery inhabitants from their clothes than managing to separate his brother from his comforts.

Damn him anyway.

Robin knew he could have made his own way at any time, but Nicholas was, after all, his family and there was something to be said for having family about.

Even if it came at the price of a good battle or two.

He scowled. There was no sense in complaining, for it would serve him not at all. He turned his mind back to the matter at hand and hoped it might be enough to soothe his foul mood.

"Another," he said hoarsely. Perhaps he had spent too much of the afternoon shouting at the fools in his brother's garrison. His own men had been exhausted much earlier in the day. As a result, there were few men left to stand against him. It did not bode well for a successful evening. "Sir Guy, come face me and let us see if you are as womanly as your fallen comrade."

Sir Guy drew his sword and came at Robin with a curse. His skill was great, but Robin kept him at bay easily. Years of fighting, either for his king or for himself, had honed his instincts until he likely could have fought with his eyes closed and his mind numb from drink. He countered each of Guy's strokes without thinking, watching his opponent closely, waiting for the first show of weakness or hesitancy. He waited longer with Guy than he had with Guy's predecessor, but the moment came eventually and Robin took full advantage of it, knocking Guy's sword from his hand and putting the point of his own sword over Guy's heart.

"Peace," Guy said heavily.

Robin stepped back. "Another."

And so it went until there was no one left for Robin to fight. He looked about him and swore in frustration. It looked as if he might be finished for the day. But at least he had aught to hope for on the morrow. Despite his chafing at his confinement, he did enjoy the luxury of constant training more than the uncertain sport of war. Battles were never as consistent as he would have liked. There was too much time spent traveling from place to place, waiting for the sieges to flush the quarry out, listening to his men celebrate afterwards, and not having the stomach to celebrate with them.

Robin resheathed his sword and turned his thoughts toward supper. Perhaps a quick meal would give at least one or two garrison knights time to recover. He might have a bit more sport yet before he sought his bed—alone, as seemed to be his lot.

It was truly a pathetic state of affairs.

He strode back to his brother's hall. He realized he'd flattened his squire only when he stepped on him by mistake.

"Mindless babe," Robin said, hauling the lad of ten-and-six to his feet. "Watch where you're going."

"Aye, my lord." His young cousin, Jason of Ayre, backed up a pace and bowed hastily. "Forgive me, my lord. Lord Nicholas waits within with a message from Artane. I believe 'tis from your mother and the tidings are evil—"

"Evil?" Robin echoed. He pushed Jason out of the way, unwilling to wait for his squire to divulge more. He ran to the hall, leaving Jason to follow or not, as he would. His heart tightened within his chest painfully. The saints only knew what sort of disaster had befallen his family. He never should have stayed away so long. There was no good reason for him to have remained in France.

Actually, there were two good reasons for the like, but those were things he never thought on if he could avoid it.

Robin slammed the hall door behind him and looked for his brother. Nicholas stood near the fire with a piece of parchment in his hands. Robin strode over to his fair-haired sibling and took the letter away.

"I wasn't finished," Nicholas protested.

"You are now," Robin muttered.

He read the epistle only far enough to learn that Montgomery was grievously ill before Nicholas snatched it back from his hands. Robin didn't fight his brother. Whatever else was to be read there was likely concerning the family and those were tidings Robin had no stomach for at present.

It was guilt, he knew, that pricked at him so fiercely so as to keep him from reading about home. After all, it would have behooved him to have made the occasional appearance at Artane so that the villagers might recognize him if something were to happen to his sire. Even worse was that his father had been sending for him repeatedly over the past few months. He should have gone back before now.

But return he hadn't and that left him with little heart for tales of home. He preferred to let Nicholas pass on what news he deemed important.

He had heard, through Nicholas's reading of their mother's previous letters, that Montgomery had been wounded. Robin had assumed the men would recover, but apparently he'd been mistaken. Though his parents would likely survive the loss well enough on their own, perhaps it was time he returned home for a small visit. He would pass a bit of time with his father and see how his family's keep had withstood the wear of the past few years. He could also see to his own holdings. Aye, there were several things he could do whilst he tarried for a few days in England. Perhaps the sooner he went, the sooner he could leave.

"We should go," Robin said with a sigh. "And likely within the fortnight."

Nicholas didn't look up from his reading.

"Oh, make haste with the bloody thing, would you?" Robin demanded. Nicholas ignored him.

Robin clasped his hands behind his back and stood with his backside to the fire. At least he might be warm for a moment or two whilst he contemplated the many mysteries of life and how he seemed to be caught up in a goodly portion of them.

There was, for instance, the mystery of his brother. Robin looked at his sibling and scowled. How sweet it must be to have so little weighing upon one's mind. Robin watched as his brother stretched his legs out and sprawled in his chair, looking as if he hadn't a care in the world. And just what cares could he possibly have? He wasn't the eldest son.

Nor did Nicholas's parentage seem to trouble him. If he fretted over the fact that his father was heaven-knew-who and his mother a servant girl, he never showed it. And why should he? He was the beloved adopted second son of one of the most powerful lords in England. He had his own keep in France and other holdings in England that had made him a very rich man indeed. Women panted after him by the score and Nicholas somehow managed to avoid leaving any bastards behind him. Robin couldn't understand it and couldn't help but be irritated by it.

Robin's worries were so many, he couldn't bring them all to mind in a single sitting. Even though he had been adopted by Rhys de Piaget just as Nicholas had been, he was heir to Artane and all that came with it. It was no secret that his sire was actually the late baron of Ayre. After Ayre's death, Robin's mother had married the captain of her guard, Rhys of Artane. For Robin there had been no question whether or not he would accept Rhys as his sire. From the time he could remember, he had wanted to belong to Rhys de Piaget in truth. Even so, with that claiming had come heavy responsibilities, responsibilities Robin hadn't shunned.

He was constantly being watched by his men, other nobles, whatever royalty happened to be about—all waiting for his first misstep, his first sign of weakness, his first failure in the lists. It had always been that way and would likely continue to be that way far into the future. Not only did his own honor rest upon his performance, his father's honor rested there too.

It was a burden Nicholas felt not at all. If Nicholas didn't show well in a tournament, which rarely happened, he shrugged it off and contented himself with a handsome wench. Robin could never be so casual about it. Every confrontation, every encounter meant the difference between success and shame. He couldn't fail. He wouldn't fail. He would die before he was laughed at again.

"Now," Nicholas drawled, "this is interesting."

"What?" Robin asked, wondering just what his empty-headed sibling might find to be noteworthy.

"Mother sent word to Fenwyck."

Robin frowned. "Fenwyck? Why? It isn't as if Fenwyck had any love for Montgomery."

"I doubt it was Fenwyck himself she was giving the tidings to."

"Who else there could possibly care?" In truth, Robin as well couldn't have possibly cared, but Nicholas seemed determined to pursue this course to its end.

"Why," Nicholas said, looking up at Robin and blinking, "Anne, of course."

"Anne? What about Anne?"

Nicholas continued to blink owlishly, as if he just couldn't muster up the wits to speak with any intelligence at all. "I'm sure Mother sent word to Anne at Fenwyck."

Robin felt his belly begin to clench of its own accord. Hunger, obviously. He should have eaten something before he began to listen to his brother's foolishness.

Anne at Fenwyck? She must have returned for her yearly fortnight. Odd, though, that she would have left if Montgomery had been failing. She was fond of the old man.

"Didn't I tell you?"

"Didn't you tell me what?" Robin asked. Odder still that his mother would have had to send word that Montgomery was failing. Anne would have been returning shortly just the same.

"Anne's been at Fenwyck since before spring."

Robin looked at Nicholas. It was all he could do to manage to smother his look of surprise. "Spring?"

"Didn't I tell you?"

It was an enormous effort to keep breathing as if the tidings were fair to putting him to sleep.

"Spring?" he repeated, cursing himself weakly for being able to say nothing else.

Nicholas nodded, then turned back to his letter. "Her father is seeking a husband for her. He's likely been showing her about like a mare at market, knowing him. Mother says that even if Anne is released to bid Montgomery a final *adieu*, she likely won't be allowed to stay long. Fenwyck fair forced her from Artane with a sword at her back before—"

Spring? Then Anne had been captive at Fenwyck for nigh onto half a year. 'Twas nothing short of a miracle that she hadn't been wed already.

And then another thought came at him with the force of a broadside.

Anne had been at Fenwyck for half a year and Nicholas had said nothing.

Robin tore the parchment from his brother's hands, flung it aside, then hauled the dolt up and shook him.

"When did you plan to tell me?" he shouted.

"Tell you what?" Nicholas asked calmly.

"I thought she was at home, you fool!"

"I suppose," Nicholas said slowly, "that I didn't think it mattered to you."

Robin suppressed the urge to slap himself. By the saints, what was he doing? The last thing he needed was to provide his lackwit brother with fodder for his romantic notions! He forced himself to unclench the fistfuls of his brother's tunic he'd grasped, then took great care to smooth the fabric back into something resembling the flat business it had been before it had been assaulted. Robin stepped back and took a deep breath.

"It doesn't," he said. "It doesn't matter at all."

"Doesn't it?" Nicholas asked.

"It doesn't matter to me where she is," Robin continued. "It merely angers me that you haven't told me all that Mother put in her letters."

There, that sounded more reasonable.

"Well," Nicholas said with a slight smile, "I suppose there is aught else I have neglected to tell you."

Robin braced himself for the worst. "Aye?"

"I haven't been as detailed as Mother has been in her demands to have us come home."

"No doubt," Robin muttered.

"She's threatened to come to France herself and prod you from the lists with her blade."

Robin shuddered at the thought. His mother could heft a blade, 'twas true, and at times she managed to get it pointing in the right direction, but inevitably she came close to dismembering anyone she so hoisted a blade against. But Robin knew his mother very well, and knew her threats were not idle. Perhaps 'twas time he returned home, lest he force her hand.

Indeed, there was no sense in not making every effort to return to England as quickly as possible and see how things progressed at Artane. Aye, no sense in not doing that as quickly as possible. Who knew what sorts of adventures he might stop his mother from having? His sire would surely thank him for it. 'Twas yet another reason to leave with all haste.

Nicholas started to sit back down, but Robin snagged him by the tunic before he managed it.

"Pack your gear. We'll leave immediately."

"Why the hurry?"

"Mother will have need of us."

The corner of Nicholas's mouth began to twitch. "Thinking to rescue Anne from her unsavoury suitors, brother?"

"Father will likely have need of us as well," Robin continued, ignoring his brother's grin. "And I don't like to dawdle whilst I travel."

"We'll likely return home too late to see her, you know," Nicholas said. "Unless we make great haste. And look you what great haste you seem determined to make."

Robin would have thrown his brother to the rushes and stomped that bloody smirk from his face, but that would have only added fuel to Nicholas's pitiful blaze. "Hurry," Robin commanded, then he strode across the great hall, ignoring what he was certain was naught but more witless babbling.

Robin took hold of his squire on his way through the doorway. "Bid the men ready themselves. We leave within the hour."

"Aye, my lord," Jason said, nodding with wide eyes. "As you will."

Robin went back to the lists. Jason would see to their gear and Robin suspected he might be better served to stay out of the way. He began to run. He liked the way his body burned as he loped along the outer bailey wall. The blood thundering in his ears pleased him as well, as it almost succeeded in drowning out all his troubling thoughts. The saints only knew he would have little luck finding any wench to aid him in the task; his temper seemed to drive them all into Nicholas's arms.

He ran until he couldn't catch his breath. Then he stopped and stood hunched over with his hands on his thighs, and sucked in great gulps of air. He didn't want to go home, but he knew he had to. His mother would have need of him, his father too. Montgomery had been dear to them both. He hadn't managed to get himself home to see anyone else buried in the past five years; perhaps it was time he made the effort now.

Besides, the sooner he arrived, the sooner he would be of service to them both. A ship could be convinced to deposit him and his brother as far north as possible. That would save them the time of trying to ride north from Dover. Aye, that was sensible enough. If he decided to stay longer in England, his gear could be sent for.

But he suspected he would only stay a fortnight or two, long enough to assure himself all was well, then hie himself off to court. Perhaps he would be exceptionally fortunate and avoid having to clap eyes on Baldwin of Sedgwick, who was no doubt still strutting about Artane with the same arrogance that had irritated Robin when Robin had been but a lad of ten-and-four. Aye, Baldwin would likely be wearing the same smile Robin had seen him wear when he'd reached out and broken two of Nicholas's fingers. Robin could remember the smile surprisingly well, given the fact that he'd seen it through the mud dripping down his face and into his eyes.

He consciously unclenched his fists, trying to ignore the fact that he'd tightened them in the first place. He could hardly help himself. He didn't think on that afternoon when he could help it, but at times it caught him unawares.

Unfortunately, his feud with Baldwin of Sedgwick had lasted much longer than a single afternoon, and he suspected that was why it pricked at him so. Baldwin had arrived at his father's gates almost at the very moment those gates had been finished. Baldwin's uncle had sent him along to foster, though at the time Robin couldn't understand why he'd bothered, as Baldwin had been nigh onto winning his spurs. But come he had, and he'd been as unhappy to arrive as Robin had been to see him at the gates.

There had been instant animosity between the two of them and in his more logical moments, Robin had realized that Baldwin hated him for his birthright. Robin would be, after all, Baldwin's liege-lord in time. Rhys had no use for Sedgwick, or its inhabitants, so their cousins had little need to worry about losing their beds at the moment. Robin had never seen the place, but he'd heard tales enough of its wretched condition to have wished to avoid it as well.

But even had he possessed the glibness to say as much, he suspected Baldwin wouldn't have heard it. The miserable brute had taken every opportunity to goad and annoy Robin until Robin had been relieved to escape his home and go off to squire with another lord. He'd gone off, glad to be free of torment and determined to acquire skill with the sword that would leave Baldwin stumbling in surprise the next time they met.

Robin straightened and sighed deeply. He'd trained himself well, he'd become a man and now perhaps 'twas time he put his childish memories to rest. Baldwin would not best him. He could avenge himself easily of any slight. Perhaps he would go home, walk the paths of his youth, and do his damndest not to think on memories that still afflicted him. He could avoid Baldwin easily enough.

And perhaps he could also avoid that other soul that continually haunted the edges of his thoughts.

He didn't want to think on her. He didn't want to see her in his mind's eye. And he surely didn't want his pulse to quicken at the thought of being in the same keep with her.

Anne.

By the saints, he'd never expected that her father would snatch her away so unexpectedly.

Though why it should have come as a surprise, he didn't know. She was ten-and-nine, surely old enough to have been wed a time or two already. He should have done something about that, but he hadn't. He couldn't have— for more reasons than he cared to admit.

He began to run again, forcing his legs to pump hard against the dirt.

He shoved away his thoughts, praying the exercise would tire him enough to escape them until the business of travel could consume him. Home he would have to go, but the less he thought about it ahead of time, the easier it would be for him.

Or so he hoped.

3

Anne made her way carefully down Artane's passageway, doing her best to avoid her father. She hadn't seen him about that morning and for that she was grateful. Perhaps he would become distracted by other issues, forget about her, and leave. Perhaps Rhys would persuade him that he would do better to spend his energies training his stepdaughter's husband in how to look after Fenwyck's holdings than seeking an already-trained lord for Anne to wed. Perhaps a handsome nobleman would stumble through Artane's gates, look on her, and profess undying love.

Perhaps she would grow a new leg and enough beauty to hold such a man.

She sighed and paused before Rhys's solar. With any luck Artane's lord was within and hoping for a bit of conversation. There wasn't a queue of souls waiting without to see him, so perhaps she might have her desire. There was much she could discuss with him. 'Twas possible he might have knowledge of a place in which she could hide herself until her sire forgot he had a daughter for sale.

But she hadn't put her hand up to knock before Rhys's angry words cut through the wood as if it hadn't been there.

"Why?" Rhys demanded. "Why do you persist in this, Geoffrey?"

"Persist in what?" Geoffrey answered. "Finally finding a husband for her?"

"Aye," Rhys said. "Her future is here!"

"With whom?" Geoffrey asked shortly. "Robin?"

"Aye, Robin—"

"Then where is he?" Geoffrey demanded. "Where was he when she was twelve and of a marriageable age? Where has he been the past seven years when he could have made her his bride? Where is he today?"

"He is off—"

"Aye, off," Geoffrey snarled. "Off doing the saints only know what whilst my daughter grows older by the hour."

"She belongs here," Rhys insisted.

"As what? Dowager aunt to Robin's score of children sired on anyone but her? I will not give her to a second son, Rhys, nor a third or fourth. The heir she will have, and 'tis obvious yours is uninterested!"

"If you would but give the matter more time—"

"She must marry, Rhys, and the duty falls to me to find someone who will have her."

"Many would take her, and gladly," Rhys said angrily. "If you could just see past—"

"See past what? A crippled girl with little beauty and a youth that fades with each passing day—"

Geoffrey's words were abruptly silenced. Anne suspected Rhys had just planted his fist in her father's mouth, for there was a bit of garbled noise, then a great amount of cursing from both parties. Furnishings made great sounds of protest as they were apparently trodden asunder. Anne knew that such unruly behavior would bring along the lady of the house, and Anne could not bear to see Gwen at present.

She turned and fled back down the passageway as quickly as she could manage. What she wanted to do was walk along the seashore until her hurt receded. Unfortunately such a journey was far beyond her capabilities after the rigors of travel, so she settled for the battlements. The climb there would be taxing enough.

No guard stopped her as she slowly mounted the steps, nor did anyone deny her access to the walls. She crept along the parapet, clinging to the stone. Her balance was less than perfect on the ground; being that far above the earth was greatly unnerving. But it was much less unnerving than being below and listening to others discuss her, so she suffered the unease.

She stopped at a likely spot and turned her face toward the sea. The wind blew her hair back over her shoulders and whipped itself against her cheeks. It was only then that she realized her face was wet. She hadn't meant to weep. Indeed, there was little to weep over. She knew her father hadn't meant to be cruel. She suspected that his concern for her warred with his desire to see his holdings pass to a suitable son-in-law. But it was never pleasant to have her flaws noted and considered so openly.

What hurt the most was knowing that he likely spoke the truth about Robin. She knew he did not love her, despite what his father might have wanted him to do. Fool that she was, she couldn't help but wish things were different. Perhaps if she had been beautiful. Perhaps if she had two straight, serviceable legs. Perhaps if she had looked more like Amanda than she did herself. The only thing she could say in her favor was that she didn't possess the gap in her front teeth that her father sported. But that was small comfort when faced with the truth of things.

Robin could have wed her years ago if he'd wanted to.

But he hadn't.

And that left her with a path before her that grew more intolerable by the footstep.

She drew her sleeve across her eyes and stared out over the water. The wind blew fiercely, but the chill was a welcome one, for it brought some semblance of calmness to her soul. Perhaps her sire had no choice but to look beyond Artane. 'Twas a certainty he had to find someone to manage his holdings. The man to whom his wife's daughter was wed could not manage his gear, much less any lands. She was the only hope of holding Fenwyck and perhaps her sire was only doing what he must.

Ah, but the foolish dreams of her heart. It was the letting go of those that pained her the most. Anne stared out over the sea, watching it wash in against the shore ceaselessly. She wondered if her heart's desire watched the same thing and what the thoughts were that consumed him. Was it possible he spared her even a brief thought now and then?

Nay, she decided grimly, it was not. His thoughts were of war, bloodshed, and bedding as many women as possible. She'd heard more tales than she could stomach of the swaths he cut through not only England but Normandy and the whole of France. He likely spared her no thought unless it was one of relief that he must needs not endure her presence.

"The dreams of my heart," she whispered, "are too foolish even for me—"

"Anne!"

That shout almost sent her toppling. The curses that followed left her with no doubt that her father had found her.

"What do you here?" Geoffrey demanded. "And talking to yourself as if you were mad? Bloody hell, girl, think! Would you have that gossip preceding you to every hall in the north?"

"But—"

"Come below," Geoffrey said curtly, but his hand on her arm was gentle. "We've aught to discuss."

Anne waited until she'd reached the upper passageway before she put the only ruse into play she could.

"I feel faint," she lied. "Might I hie myself to Amanda and Isabelle's bedchamber for a time, Father? I will join you once I've recovered."

Her father looked momentarily confused, as if she had upset his finely laid plans. Anne took advantage of it and put her hand to her forehead, hoping to affect a look of true suffering.

"Very well," Geoffrey said reluctantly. "We'll talk later." He walked her down the passageway, then deposited her in front of the bedchamber. "Come to me when you've recovered."

And that will require at least a fortnight, Anne thought to herself as she sought refuge behind a closed door. She put her ear to the wood and listened to her father's footsteps recede. Once she knew she was safely sequestered, at least for the moment, she rested her forehead against the door and sighed deeply.

Perhaps it was time she had a good look at her plight and resigned herself to the truth of it. The desires of her heart made little difference when she could no longer deny that Robin wasn't going to thunder up on his black steed and rescue her from a clutch of greedy suitors. Her choices seemed to be either to wed where her father willed it, or find a way to remain at Artane as something other than a daughter-in-law.

She pushed away from the door with a deep sigh and hobbled over to the bed. She sat, then lay back and stared up at the canopy. She would have to wed. There was no other choice. Her father's lands were too many and her dowry too rich a prize for her to escape her fate. The only thing she might possibly control was the timing of her journey to her matrimonial prison. Her father had had her at his mercy for nigh onto half a year with no success in finding her a mate, for she had done her best to discourage the lot of them. Perhaps she could barter with her sire for a remaining half year at Artane if in turn she gave him her most cooperative self when she returned to Fenwyck.

She suspected her sire could care less about her willingness to behave, or lack thereof.

But it was worth a try. And until she thought of a way to persuade him to her way of thinking, she would avoid him.

And she would pray for a miracle.

It was well past sunset before she forced herself to leave the chamber. She shunned supper and company below, and made her way to the lady of Artane's solar. She had passed innumerable hours there and the memories were warm and pleasant ones. Surely a new idea or two would occur to her there. Her sire likely wouldn't look for her there either and that added reward was too powerful a lure to resist. And with any luck, she would find that chamber empty as well. Unfortunately, Gwen had a number of ladies and foster daughters who lingered there, so the chances of it were slim.

Gwen's ladies Anne could have borne, as well as any number of other maids, but she had to admit as she made her way upstairs that she would be less than pleased to see Edith of Sedgwick. It wasn't that Edith was particularly unpleasant. It was that Anne felt sure Edith envied her her place in Artane's family. As Anne wasn't certain how much longer she would enjoy that place, she couldn't bear the thought of having it frowned upon.

The passageway and stairwell were dark as Anne passed through them, but that was not so unusual. The keep was a drafty place at times with the winds from the sea assaulting the walls continually. Torches often went out. Anne made her way down the passageway from memory and stopped before the solar door. She frowned. It was usually kept closed yet it stood ajar.

And then she heard a faint jingling sound.

The hair on the back of her neck stood up and she stifled the urge to bolt. She quickly entered the solar. It was empty, but somehow that didn't please her as much as she'd thought it would. Then again, perhaps quiet was just what she needed. She turned to shut the door.

Then she paused, her hand on the latch. Best to leave it open, perhaps, while she brought the fire back to life. Then she would make certain the chamber and passageway were empty.

She took a deep breath and let it out slowly. She was home. No harm would come to her. She walked to the hearth where embers still burned weakly. Kneeling on the floor, she leaned over and blew, trying to bring the fire back to life. She sat back after a moment or two, looking about for a bit of wood or peat to toss on the flicker of fire she'd coaxed out.

The door slammed shut. Anne heaved herself to her feet, then spun around, wishing frantically she had a sword and the skill to use it. What had she been thinking to come here alone?

"Who's there?" she called, cursing the tremble in her voice.

No one answered. She let out her breath slowly. As if she should have expected an answer.

Then reason returned to her. The torches had been out, hadn't they? 'Twas naught but the breeze. Doors closing with vigor was a common thing in the keep.

She brushed her hands on her dress. Coming here had been a mistake. What she needed was to be abed, not wandering about the keep like a restless spirit. She took her courage in hand and crossed the chamber with as sedate a pace as she could manage. She left the solar and started down the passageway.

And she could have sworn she heard the same tinkling sound.

Perhaps 'twas nothing, but her imagination more than made up for it. She gasped, pulled up her skirts, and limped for the stairway as quickly as she could. Voices coming up from below were like a light beckoning at the end of a tunnel. Anne stumbled down the stairs, wincing each time she had to put her weight on her leg. How she hated autumn with its chill!

She tripped over the last step and would have gone sprawling had strong arms not been there to catch her fall. Rhys set her back on her feet, then frowned as he saw her face.

"Anne," he said, "what ails you, daughter?"

"Nothing," she said weakly. "I think I'm overtired."

Rhys hesitated, then nodded and bent to kiss her forehead. "Off with you then, girl. A good night's sleep will serve you well."

She nodded and limped down the corridor to the chamber she had always shared with Amanda and Isabelle. She closed the door behind her, leaned back against it, and sighed. What she wanted to do was lay abed for the next fortnight. Unfortunately, she knew that would only make matters worse. As unappealing a task as it seemed, she would have to rise each day. If she didn't, her leg would tighten and take her days to have it be useful again. She walked across the chamber and sat down carefully on the bed.

And all her troubles had come about because she, at the tender age of nine, had been dared to ride an unbroken stallion and she'd done it, just to silence Baldwin who had called her uncomely. The memory of being flung down in the lists was still very fresh in her mind. She could still see the horse stumbling and stepping on her leg, shattering the bone in her thigh. Ah, the agony of not being able to faint . . .

"Anne?"

The door opening startled her. Anne turned around to look at Amanda. "Aye?"

"Merciful saints, what befell you?"

"Nothing," Anne said. "I'm merely weary."

Amanda came and sat next to her. "'Twas a hard day for you, Anne. Come, let me put you to bed."

Anne didn't protest. She allowed Amanda to help her into bed and tuck the blankets up to her chin as if she'd been a small child.

"I'm glad you're home," Amanda said with feeling. "These have been the longest months of my life."

Anne smiled dryly. "I'm sure they haven't been. The race for your hand is on, Amanda. Even the men my father has brought to inspect me can do nothing but babble about your beauty."

"Then they are fools," Amanda said. "They view me as naught but a necessary evil they must endure simply to have my dowry. Guy of York was here a month ago and I vow I thought him ready to check my teeth and ask Father how much feed I would require each day."

Anne laughed. "He did not."

"Aye, he did. I called him a horse's arse and bid him look for a mare in some other stable. They tell me they do not care about the lands and gold, but I can see them counting in their heads even as they cut my meat for me at the board. I'll not be considered a mere bargaining piece."

"At least you have the luxury of thinking thusly," Anne said with a sigh. "I daresay even the vastness of my father's holdings doesn't compensate for my ugliness—"

"Cease," Amanda exclaimed. "Anne, the last time you peeped into a polished mirror was when you were but ten-and-three. That was six years ago, sister. No one is fetching at ten-and-three."

"Oh, Amanda, you know that isn't true. You were as beautiful then as you are now. And look at Isabelle. The garrison knights can hardly breathe when she walks by them."

Amanda looked at her helplessly. "Anne . . ."

Anne blinked back tears of humiliation. "I beg you not to speak of this more."

"Foolishness," Amanda said, but her tone was gentle. "Anne, I grew up envying your pale hair and green eyes, thinking you the most lovely creature I ever saw. Time has only increased your fairness. Your features are nothing short of angelic, your humor is ever sweet, and your goodness shines from you like a beacon. And if you'll know the reason men have not offered for you in the past, I'll tell you. Father has ever demanded the right of choosing your husband and your sire has always refused to grant it to him. Still they argue over this—"

"I am ten-and-nine," Anne exclaimed. "Old enough to be wed years already!"

Amanda leaned over and kissed Anne's cheek. "Sleep, sister, and think no more on it. Father had new stone laid in the garden this summer and 'tis smooth and fine. We'll walk there tomorrow."

Anne nodded as Amanda rose. Perhaps she had it aright and it was best not to think more on such matters. What sense was there in it? She had learned much at Gwen's hand and had at least a few bits of knowledge and skill to offer a husband. She still had not mastered her temper, but perhaps she would be lucky enough to find a man who would not provoke her and would not expect a woman who was beautiful.

It was unfortunate that the only man she had ever wanted did not fit that description at all.

She sighed and rolled over, tired of chewing on her troubling thoughts. Movement didn't help. Amanda and Isabelle making ready for bed didn't distract her either. There was something nagging at her and she could not seem to discover it nor ignore it.

When it came to her, her heart pounded in her chest so loudly and so rapidly, she was sure Amanda would wake up and bid her be silent. All hope of sleep fled. She was lucky to be alive. Bloody lucky. She was not so big a fool that she did not realize that a door would only slam shut when wind from an open window forced it shut.

There had been no open window in the solar that evening.

4

Edith of Sedgwick stood in the northeast tower chamber at Artane and watched deepening twilight through the arrowloop. It took little time for the darkness to envelope the sky over the sea, so she waited patiently until the gloom had descended truly. Waiting was never a burden for her, for patience, she had to admit modestly to herself, was her second greatest virtue. Indeed, could anyone doubt it, should they but examine her circumstances? Hadn't patience been what had won her a place at all at Rhys de Piaget's hall? She'd planted the seed in her father's mind that she really should be going north with her brother. It had taken years until the seed had borne fruit, but she had enjoyed the fruits of her waiting.

Of course, she hadn't been welcomed with particularly open arms, for she was, after all, of Sedgwick and there was no love lost between Artane and her kin. But even that would change, of that she was certain. Weren't her present straits a perfect example of the lengths she was willing to go to in order to have her desire? Instead of the comfort of Artane's solar, she conducted her business in a drafty guard tower.

Patiently.

But did a body but know the truth, he would have to agree that while patience was something she possessed in abundance, her greatest virtue was her ability to plan an intrigue. Unfortunately, her plots of late stood to be ruined by the silly child standing before her. Edith looked at her and struggled to smother her annoyance. She was greatly tempted to slap the girl— and several times at that. Her fear, however, was that by so doing, she might dislodge whatever wits remained the wench. And Maude of Canfield had few enough as it was. Edith took a deep breath to regain her composure.

"Surely," she said calmly, "I heard you awrong. You did what?"

"I slammed the solar door. Scared the piss from her." She laughed gleefully. Her bracelet flashed in the candlelight as she flapped her hands animatedly. "She bolted like a rabbit. Or as well as a lame rabbit might manage."

Edith looked at the girl and wondered mightily if she might not have made a fatal mistake in choosing this one. But what other choice could she have made? Maude was perfect for her needs—assuming she could be controlled. Edith folded her hands sedately in front of her. It was better that way; at least she wouldn't be tempted to use them.

"In the future," Edith said, "you will restrict yourself to taking on the tasks I give you."

The mercurial change in Maude's mood was almost unsettling to watch.

"You'll tell me nothing," she snapped. "I've a stake in this as well."

"We've discussed this, Maude."

"And I'll not be told what to do by you! I am a baron's daughter!"

"Aye, the youngest of a large brood sired by a very minor and unimportant lord," Edith said.

"More important than yours," Maude returned hotly. "Sedgwick is a cesspit and I vow I wonder how you managed to crawl . . . ah, crawl from . . ."

Edith watched as Maude realized that she had said too much. Apparently Maude's pride warred with her fear; Edith watched the emotions cross her face in rapid succession. It was fascinating, truly, to see the progression. And then Maude seemed to gather her courage about her.

"I don't fear you," she blurted out.

Edith inclined her head. "Why would you?"

Maude looked passing unsure of herself. "Well, I don't."

"Of course not. But in the future, you will leave off with your own plans. The lady Anne is not the prey."

"I don't like her," Maude said with a scowl.

Edith smiled. "She hasn't harmed you—"

"And you weren't abed with him when he called out her name instead of mine!" Maude exclaimed.

The tower chamber door slammed shut and Edith looked to see her brother standing there. Baldwin glared at Maude.

"Begone, you silly twit. Hide yourself in the kitchens until you're needed."

Edith pursed her lips as Maude fled, then she looked on her brother with disfavor. "She's useful."

"She's addle-pated. Whence did you dredge her up?" he asked, drawing up a chair, producing his dagger and beginning to pick his teeth with it.

Edith allowed herself a moment of silent disgust over her brother's lack of manners, then gave him the shortest answer she could think of.

"A chance meeting in a solar full of ladies," she said. "Where else?"

"I thought as much," Baldwin said with a grunt.

Actually, nothing could have been further from the truth. Edith had learned various useful skills during her childhood and the most useful had been the ferreting out of information from whatever seedy source was handy. She smiled grimly to herself. At least her torturous youth at Sedgwick had not been completely wasted. It had taken Edith only a handful of months to unearth various items of interest that one soul in particular would have wished to remain buried.

And once she'd obtained a name or two, she'd taken up her journey south on the pretext of going on a pilgrimage. Her first halt at Berkhamshire had proved fruitless, but her destination of Canfield had yielded more than she could have hoped for. Maude had been spurned, seething and distinctly out of favor with her formerly adoring sire who could not understand her repeated refusal to wed with anyone of his choosing. Edith knew who Maude pined for, knew the last time they had lain together, and marveled greatly at the girl's tenacity and patience.

It had reminded her, she thought a bit wistfully, of her own.

A shorn head, a covering of cloth for the remaining blond hair and Maude had become a servant looking desperately for a bit of charity. The few questions asked had been answered promptly and accepted for truth. For Edith, unlike her older brother, had found favor in Lord Artane's eyes from the moment she'd been deposited inside his gates like unwanted refuse. She knew very well how the game was played and she played it well. The favors she asked were few, and those were usually granted graciously.

But that graciousness never made up for what she was denied.

"Mindless twit," Baldwin groused. "She'll befoul the plans, sister. Mark my words."

Edith was much more concerned about Baldwin than she was Maude. Maude might have been stupid, but she was, after all, merely a woman. Baldwin was just as witless, but he possessed a cruelty she had seen only in men. Had she not been convinced she could control him as well, she might have feared him.

"Maude believes herself fated to have him, Baldwin," she said patiently. "A woman will do much for that kind of love."

"Poor sister," Baldwin sneered. "Jealous of her? Or are you jealous of Anne? Will you have Robin for yourself?"

Edith only remained silent. There was no sense in allowing him to bait her. Her brother was ever ready to fight; she had better ways to spend her energy. Besides, he was a fool if he thought she concerned herself with either Maude or Anne of Fenwyck. They were merely obstacles to be removed in time.

"You need to control her," Baldwin grumbled. "I'll not have her ruining my scheme."

His scheme? Edith bit her lip to keep from pointing out to him that his thoughts couldn't possibly rise to the level of a scheme. Baldwin never thought further than the bottom of his cup or the end of his blade.

He had risen and was pacing. "He'll return home soon enough, I'll warrant. Damn him to hell anyway. I should have done him in years ago, while I had the chance . . ."

Edith leaned back against the wall and braced herself for the tirade. Her brother's shortsightedness would be his undoing someday. But for now at least his anger was steady and that would serve her well.

As long as his plans were in accord with hers, of course.

And that was something she could control for now. Robin of Artane would return soon enough and Baldwin could do with him what he willed.

To a certain point.

"I'll kill him this time," Baldwin growled, his pacing growing more agitated.

"If you're here."

Baldwin scowled at her. "Did you hear, then? Artane has sent me off to do his business at a handful of his bloody fiefs. Mayhap he knows I'll kill his son if I'm here."

Edith suspected Rhys had sent Baldwin away just to be free of his presence. What she did know for a certainty, though, was that Baldwin was going along as the guard to one of Rhys's vassals, not as Rhys's agent. She suspected that was a fact her brother preferred to ignore.

"I would be afraid if I were him," Baldwin said darkly. "I'd be afraid for Robin's sorry neck."

Edith pushed away from the wall. "Brother," she said quietly, "how could killing him possibly avenge you?"

"He'll be dead!" Baldwin said, his chest heaving. "Have you no wits left you?"

Edith frowned, as if she truly had to struggle to concentrate. Baldwin thought her empty-headed, as he did all women, and Edith never disappointed him. It was better that way.

"But," she said slowly, "if he's dead, you'll no longer have the sport of tormenting him."

"Ha," Baldwin said scornfully. "You want him for yourself and it grieves you to think of him lying rotting in the ground."

Edith smiled, and she made certain it was a tremulous, hopeful smile. "Aye, well that is part of it."

"I knew it," he said with disgust. He spat at her feet. "He has what should have been mine. I'll have Sedgwick and I'll have it without him as my overlord."

Edith struggled not to sigh. She'd been listening to the same litany for as long as she'd been at Artane and those were ten very long years. Baldwin raged about like a stuck boar, but his rages had been in vain. Robin had been gone much of that time, leaving Anne to bear the brunt of Baldwin's wrath. And even Edith had to admit that Anne had been a poor substitute. There had never been any equity in that fight.

Not that Edith cared overmuch for equity. She'd certainly never enjoyed the fruits of it.

"The bastard," Baldwin spat.

Well, that was something else to be discussed, but Edith decided that now was not the time. Baldwin was beginning to rant and that usually led to his descending to the ale kegs in cellars and that never produced anything besides staggering pains in his head the next day. Best distract him while she could.

"But kill Robin," she said, "and you're left with four other brothers."

"I'll kill them too."

There was a certain appeal to that, but that was something to be savored later. She hadn't dragged Maude away from Canfield only to stand idly by and watch Baldwin slay the entire de Piaget clan. The others could be seen to in time. Robin was her prey now and for other reasons than Baldwin could imagine up in his heart.

And she didn't want him dead before she could put him through a choice bit of agony.

And who better to start with than his love?

Never mind that he hadn't returned for her yet. He would. Edith had watched the pair of them carefully over the years. He would return and he would claim Anne for his own.

And then Edith's revenge would begin.

Baldwin stopped dead in the middle of the chamber. It was sudden enough that Edith looked at him. His expression was one of surprise. And then he broke out into a smile.

And the sight of that, his being her brother aside, was enough to send shivers down her spine.

"I'll kill all the lads, then marry Amanda," he said in wonder. "*That* would give me control of Sedgwick."

"But Amanda is not the daughter of Rhys's flesh," Edith pointed out. "Her sire was the baron of Ayre."

Baldwin looked momentarily perplexed.

"The lady Gwennelyn was wed to Alain of Ayre," Edith reminded him. "Amanda is not of de Piaget's flesh."

"But he's claimed her as his own," Baldwin argued.

"But is that claim enough?"

Baldwin shook his head, as if he shook aside an annoying fly. "I'll think on that later. First the others must be seen to."

He could think on Amanda's inheritance, or potential lack thereof, all he liked, so long as he didn't kill anyone before their time. Edith wasn't about to have her brother foul her plans.

"Humiliate Robin first," she said gently. "You need your revenge."

Baldwin paused and considered, stroking his chin. Then apparently the thought of Amanda was more temptation than he could resist, for he smiled again and chortled.

"Aye, she's a beauty," he said.

"Revenge," Edith reminded him.

He frowned, then cursed. "I'll think on it more when I return. And don't you do anything while I'm away."

"Of course not," Edith agreed, but Baldwin was on his way out of the chamber. The door slammed shut behind him.

Edith sighed and retreated to the alcove. She put her candle on the opposite bench and sat. At least Baldwin would be distracted for a bit and that would leave her free to pursue her own plan.

Baldwin had seen at least some of her heart and that distressed her. That she should be that transparent about anything was unsettling.

For she did want Robin.

But she only wanted him after everything he loved had been methodically destroyed before his eyes. Baldwin could have the satisfaction of dispatching Robin's kin. Edith had the stomach for the doing of it, but there was no sense in denying her brother a bit of enjoyment as well. Aye, all Robin loved would be gone and he would be left alone to suffer.

And then once he was kneeling at her feet in agony, she would see the end of her scheme brought about and she would be avenged for the hurts done her.

She closed her eyes. Aye, she would be avenged, he would die in misery, and then she would be at peace.

But she could wait for that. Now was the time to reconsider her plans and make certain she had forgotten nothing. Artane's heir would arrive within days, she was sure of that, and then it would begin. There were so many things she could do to afflict him, it was hard to choose.

There would be time for that decision later. For now, she would sit and think and enjoy the quiet.

A woman of great patience needed to do that now and then. It was good for her soul.

5

Robin stood at the prow of the ship, glad of the chill of the predawn wind. His thoughts had kept him awake for most of the night. Saints, he was in a sorry state. It had to be the confinement. The captain had forbidden him to pace above deck and the hold below had been completely inadequate for his pacing needs. But now the captain was abed and the first mate had been glared into submission. Unfortunately, even the full run of the ship seemed not to be enough. Robin dragged his hand through his hair, then leaned against the railing, conceding the battle. Let the thoughts come. Perhaps if he paid them heed, they would lose their power over him.

He could hardly believe Anne had been at Fenwyck for the past half year. By the saints, she must have been miserable. He was certain her journey there had indeed been against her will. Why would she go, when her home was at Artane? He sometimes wondered what she truly felt for her sire; she certainly didn't know him very well. In her youth, she had gone to her sire for a required fortnight each year, weeping as she left Artane and frantic to return once she'd reached Fenwyck.

Did not his parents treat her as just another daughter? Did not his father scold her just as he would have any of the rest of his children? The times had been very few, though, as the crestfallen look on Anne's face had been enough to consign him to a hell of guilt for days afterwards.

One of the worst times, save the time her leg had been crushed, had been when Anne was ten-and-two. One of the pages had dared her to ride Rhys's mighty destrier. She had and ridden it well, until Baldwin had approached and sent the stallion into a frenzy. Robin had been home at the time and likely should have stopped her, but he'd been training like a madman and she had been up and riding before he'd come to his senses. He'd then watched, open-mouthed and horrified, as she'd clung to that bucking stallion with a tenacity any knight would have wished for his own. Before he'd found his wits to move, his father had plucked Anne from the saddle, then shaken her until her teeth rattled. After he'd shaken her, he'd given her a tongue-lashing that had raised the hackles on Robin's neck. Rhys had been especially furious at the deed in light of Anne's weak leg and what could have happened had it failed her. Anne had sobbed for hours, grief-stricken that she had disappointed the foster father she adored.

Robin had wanted to go to her, to explain that Rhys was angry because he loved her, because he had come so close to losing her. Somehow the words had never made it past his throat. He had wanted to be gentle with her, to be tender and kind. It had been impossible. How could he have comforted Anne when all he wanted to do was throttle her?

And for precisely the same reason his father had?

"Can't sleep?"

Robin almost fell overboard in surprise. "By the saints, you startled me," he said weakly.

Nicholas leaned on the railing. "Mooning, Rob?"

"Feel like a swim, Nick?" Robin snapped.

Nicholas only smiled pleasantly, his gray eyes twinkling with amusement. Robin blinked his own gray eyes and wondered, not for the first time, just how it was he and Nicholas had come to look so much alike. Perhaps it was that they had spent so much time together. At least Nicholas wasn't repulsive to look at—or so Robin supposed, not being much of a judge in such matters. Robin suspected that if he'd had to look like someone, 'twas better to look like his brother than someone far uglier.

"Mayhap that swim would serve you better than me," Nicholas remarked. "You look positively bewildered."

"Damn you, Nick, leave me be," Robin grumbled. "I cannot stomach your foolish words. I've had almost a se'nnight of them already."

"Stop being so prickly, Robin."

"I am not being prickly!" Robin exclaimed, giving Nicholas a heated glare. "I just needed some fresh air. And some *peace*," he stressed.

Nicholas sighed and turned his face forward. "You've been in a foul mood for months," he said. "In fact, you've been impossible since we left England. I don't know if you'll remember this, but except for a miserable trip or two to court and that disastrous journey to Canfield for the fortnight which we won't discuss in detail, we haven't been back in almost five years. How is it possible you've been so testy for so long?"

Robin scowled. "I've had much weighing on my mind."

"Such as?"

"Hard to believe as it is, Nicholas, even I give myself over to the contemplation of life and its mysteries now and then."

Nicholas laughed. "Ah, Rob, I know you're not truly as shallow and uncaring as you seem to be."

"Do you *want* me to toss you overboard? Or do you take your life in your hands simply because you are destroyed that you could no longer satisfy your mistress and she pitched you?"

"That was not the reason she left," Nicholas growled.

Robin almost smiled. Ah, how sweet it was to know at least one thing that could disturb his brother's enviable calm. It was difficult to ruffle Nicholas, but always immensely entertaining.

But before Nicholas could either retort or retaliate, Robin held up his hand in surrender. He had the feeling his brother's revenge would cause him a goodly amount of discomfort and he had no more stomach for that than he did for Nicholas's words.

"I know that wasn't the reason," he sighed. He turned again to stare out over the moonlit water. "I won't provoke you further."

"No doubt very wise," Nicholas agreed. "The saints only know what I would be tempted to do to your pretty visage otherwise."

Robin only grunted.

"Why don't we speak of your vats of troubles instead of mine?" Nicholas asked. "Surely that will entertain us for quite some time."

As tempting as it was to unbend far enough to speak his heart truly, Robin was too much in the habit of keeping that poor heart protected. He rarely admitted the truth of his feelings to himself in the stillest part of the night. How could he possibly admit anything aloud? He felt his brother's gaze boring into the side of his head, but he ignored it. The last thing he needed was to discuss his innermost secrets with his dreamy-eyed sibling and hear the laughter that was sure to follow.

"Very well," Nicholas said pleasantly. "If you've no mind to bring them up, I'll aid you. Let us speak of Anne."

Robin gritted his teeth, but said nothing.

"Why do you think she stayed away for so long?" Nicholas asked.

"I don't know and I couldn't care less."

"Don't you have any feelings for her at all?"

As if he would babble the like to his brother! "Anne of Fenwyck is feisty, opinionated, and contrary," Robin said. That at least was truth. "When I do take a wife— and the saints pity me when that unhappy day arrives— I'll have a woman who'll obey me, not give me her opinion at every turn."

"I see," Nicholas said wisely. "Then you haven't the stomach for Anne's fire."

Robin could only grunt in answer.

"A meek, obedient woman is the one for you," Nicholas continued.

"Aye."

"Just like Mother."

"Aye."

Robin regretted the word the instant it left his lips. His mother was anything but obedient and his father loved her all the more for her spirit. But he'd be damned if he'd let Nicholas trap him so easily.

"You're nigh onto pushing me too far," Robin said, mustering up what irritation he could—and that was never difficult when it came to Nicholas poking and prodding him. "I don't need your opinions and I don't want your advice. When I feel the need of a legitimate heir, I'll saddle myself with a quiet woman who won't vex me when I take a mistress, nor trouble me when I ignore her for years on end, which I fully intend to do."

"And Anne is not lovely," Nicholas said, slowly. "I suppose that is something you also consider."

"Beauty does not matter to me."

"And, to be sure, Anne does not possess any of it—"

Robin glared at his brother. "There is naught amiss with her face and if you tell her differently, you'll answer to me."

"And her temper," Nicholas continued with a shudder. "Passing unpleasant."

"There is naught amiss with her temper either!"

Nicholas looked at him appraisingly. "Why, Robin, I think you love the girl."

Robin's lunge almost sent them both overboard. Nicholas laughed weakly as he lay on the deck with Robin sprawled over him, his hands at his throat.

"That was close," he said.

"And you are as giddy as a mindless milkmaid," Robin snapped.

"Am I?" Nicholas asked, still grinning like the idiot Robin knew him to be.

But it was a knowing grin and somehow just that much more terrifying for the knowledge behind it. That was all he bloody needed—to have Nicholas babbling what he supposed to be Robin's heart to anyone who would listen. Best disabuse the fool of his idiotic notions whilst he had the chance.

"I give Anne less thought than I do what color tunic to wear each day. She's as skinny as a boy and about that handsome," Robin growled. He was lying, of course, but it sounded convincing so he kept to his tack. "If I wanted a woman, I'd choose someone with a bit of meat on her and a face that I could look at without wincing."

A blinding pain in his face made him instantly release his loose grasp on Nicholas's throat. He was dumped onto his back and banged his head smartly against the deck. Before he could think to start cursing his brother, he was hauled to his feet.

"Don't say anything else," Nicholas bit out softly. "Think what you like about her, but don't say it out loud. And for pity's sake, don't say it to her. If you do, I'll make you regret it."

"I never would," Robin grumbled, shoving his brother away from him.

He rubbed the back of his head in annoyance. "Go to bed, Nick. Mother will see those dark circles under your eyes, think my fist caused them, and take a switch to my behind for my trouble."

Nicholas paused. "And leave you here to stew alone?"

"Begone, dolt. I need not your aid."

Nicholas pursed his lips. "Don't pace all night. Anne will worry if you look too haggard."

"Just go, would you?" Robin ordered crossly. He heard his brother's retreating footsteps and leaned against the rail with a sigh.

Of course Anne wasn't uncomely. And Nicholas was a fool if he thought Robin would ever say anything to hurt her. He might have possessed but a little chivalry, but he knew when to trot it out. Besides, he would never comment on Anne's appearance because he would never have the chance. How could he when he never planned to be in the same chamber with her, much less speak to her?

Aye, that was the wisest course of action. He bloody didn't care for her. He never had. She was obstinate, and disagreeable and she had a perverse fondness for doing exactly the opposite of what he told her to do. How could anyone expect him to endure that for the rest of his life?

Anne wasn't the cause of his problems, but she certainly wasn't the solution either. It was best he stay completely away from her.

He did not love her.

And he certainly wasn't going to wed with her.

And he wasn't going to dream about her ever again.

Five days later, Robin reined in his mount and stared at the castle in the distance. He could have likely coerced the captain into sailing farther north, which would have saved him a grueling pair of days on horseback, but he hadn't wanted to alert his family to his arrival. Better to have it seem as if he had just come in from the lists. His family would be about their various daily tasks and he would walk in and feel as if he'd never left.

Except that five years had passed since he had last seen his home. How much had it changed? How much had his loved ones changed?

Nicholas cleared his throat. "Ready?"

"Aye."

"Mother likely won't be expecting us for at least another se'nnight."

Robin nodded, then looked at his brother. "She won't recognize you. You've filled out a bit whilst we've been away."

"So have you," Nicholas replied solemnly. "Save that empty space between your ears."

Nicholas was away before Robin could reconcile himself to the fact that he had reached out and grasped a fistful of air, not his brother's tunic. He spurred his mount into a gallop, trying to catch up to Nicholas.

By the time they reached the outer gate, Robin had forgotten why he had his brother's death on his mind. His heart lifted with every stride his horse took toward home. He had been away too long. Perhaps he would stay longer than a fortnight. After all, Artane would eventually be his. It might behoove him to remain a bit closer to home for awhile. He did have other fiefs in England to where he could escape if necessity warranted it. But to France? Not again quite so soon.

Perhaps it was a weakness, but he loved his home. Artane was a magical place and he greatly suspected it was his family that made it so.

He raced Nicholas up the long road from the outer gate, laughing at the direness and variety of curses he received from his father's men as they hastily moved out of his way. He slowed as he neared the inner walls and then walked his horse into the courtyard. Robin sat back and breathed deeply. Ah, to actually sleep a night in a bed that was his, eat at his father's table, relax in front of the hearth in the great hall without having to keep one eye over his shoulder.

Just as he was contemplating how best to enter the house and achieve the desired results, the front door opened and his father stepped out, rubbing his arms and stomping his feet to ward off the chill. Rhys blinked a time or two, then began to smile.

Robin dismounted and watched Nicholas walk by their sire with naught but a negligent wave. Rhys was just as busy paying him little heed. Perhaps to an outsider it would have seemed strange indeed, but he and Nicholas had decided upon the like long ago. Nicholas greeted their mother first and their father last; Robin the opposite. It had worked out so well after the first try they had kept to it. Robin walked up the steps and was immediately enveloped in a fierce hug. Robin gave his father a hearty kiss and slapped him on the back.

"Good to see you, Papa. What's for supper?"

Rhys scowled. "And to think I actually told your mother that I missed you . . ."

"Can we carry on this tender reunion inside? It's brutally cold out. I'd forgotten what a bloody frigid place England is."

"You swear too much," Rhys grumbled, pulling Robin inside. Once there, he hugged Robin again, until Robin thought his ribs just might pop. "Damn you, Robin," Rhys said hoarsely, "you didn't have to stay away so long."

"I had to," Robin said, feeling his eyes burn with an unwelcome kind of fire. "I had things to prove to myself. Things I couldn't prove here at home."

Rhys didn't answer, but Robin flinched at the affectionate slaps he received on his back. Rhys pulled away finally, blinking rapidly.

"Looks like you've grown a bit," he said.

"You saw me last year at court," Robin said dryly. "How much could I have grown since then?"

"Well," Rhys said, "it seems as if you have. Don't contradict me while I'm feeling so sentimental."

Robin straightened his cloak over his shoulders. "Care for a wrestle now so you can determine the true extent of the change, or shall we wait until I've had something to eat?"

Rhys took him by the back of the neck and shook him. "After supper. You'll enjoy your meal much more before your thrashing than after."

"No doubt," Robin said. He would indeed take his father on after supper and show him that five years of warring had turned his son into a man to be reckoned with.

The hall was deliciously warm compared to the air outside. Massive logs were burning in the hearth and various members of the family were gathered close, fussing over Nicholas at the moment. Robin felt his palms begin to sweat and cursed himself. By the saints, he had no reason to be nervous.

But that didn't stop him from glancing about likely more than he should have. There were many souls coming and going in the great hall. There was surely no sense in not taking a look at them to see who they were. He looked back at the hall door, then turned and blinked in surprise. A young woman was rushing across the hall toward him. He thought she just might be his sister.

"Oof," he grunted as she launched herself at him.

"Oh, Robby!"

Robin gasped for air. "By the saints, Isabelle, you weigh more than my horse!"

Isabelle clung to him. "I've missed you so much, Robin. What'd you bring me from France?"

Robin let her slip down to the ground and looked at her in astonishment. When had his youngest sister grown up? She had been ten-and-one the year he left. He hardly recognized the slender girl who was certainly no longer a child. Had she been betrothed already?

"Presents, Robby," Isabelle reminded him.

What had he missed by not having watched her grow? The regret that washed over him, for he suspected this was not the first thing he had missed that he shouldn't have, was almost enough to make him weep. Then his sister began checking him over for baubles.

"Isabelle," he managed, "I watched Nick spend a fortune on presents for you and another fortune sending them home."

"A most generous brother," she said, industriously investigating the depths of his cloak.

"Why in the world would I have watched all that, then found myself fool enough to see more gold spent on you by me?"

She smiled up at him and the sweetness of her smile almost brought him to tears in truth. "You did bring me something," she said with a happy sigh.

"I brought you nothing, you greedy wretch," he said, giving her a fierce hug. He closed his eyes and prayed he wouldn't embarrass himself by an unmanly display of emotion.

"Robin . . ." she complained.

He lifted her face and kissed her quickly. "Did you miss me truly?"

"Aye."

"Come, you can do better than that."

She considered. "Desperately?"

"I may have brought you a trinket or two."

"Robin, I hardly slept a wink for missing you all this time. See the lines of worry on my face?" she said earnestly.

"Very well, I brought you several things, none of which you will see until I'm ready to show them to you." He was prepared to give her a further lecture on greed—for indeed he could see how else his guiding influence had been missed—but he saw another sight that deserved attention. "We'll discuss this further when I have time. Now I see that my favorite little slaves are waiting impatiently for their audience."

Isabelle moved just in time to avoid being trampled by Montgomery and John. The twins hugged Robin until he pretended to gasp for breath. Now these were children who had changed. They had to be at least ten-and-three by now. Robin remembered vividly holding both boys up over his head, one with each hand, countless times and their howls of laughter from the like. How he loved his youngest brothers. They were little imps, stirring up mischief even he had to admire. Now he wondered if he could possibly hoist them both any distance at all off the floor. Five years had done a goodly work upon them both.

"Move, little lads." The deep voice was accompanied by two arms that took the boys by the backs of their tunics and hoisted them away.

Well, apparently someone was still equal to that task. Robin felt his jaw slide down.

"Miles?" he asked.

"Who else?" Miles said, setting the twins aside and making Robin a low bow. "At your service, spurs in hand."

Robin laughed. "Saints, but you've grown. I seem to remember picking *you* up when last we met."

"I doubt you would succeed now," Miles said, flexing an arm for Robin's benefit. "If you'd care to try?"

Robin caught sight of his mother. She was coming toward him purposefully, though he could already see the tears streaming down her face. "Later," he said, pushing his brother aside.

He reached her just as she had launched into a thorough scolding of him, and pulled her over to the hearth. No sense in not having the rest of him be warm while his ears were being blistered.

"I vow, Robin de Piaget," she said, frowning up at him with her fiercest frown, "that if another month had passed without some scratch on parchment from you, I would have finished your battles myself, then taken a switch to your backside for your lack of consideration!"

Robin pulled his mother into his arms and rested his chin on her head where she couldn't see his smile over her words. She continued enumerating in great detail the lengths she had planned to go to in instilling in him the smallest smidgen of manners, punctuating her reproof with various and sundry tugs on his hair. Robin closed his eyes and smiled at the novelty of using his mother as a resting place for his jaw. Though he'd outgrown her quickly, it never failed to surprise him that he was taller than she.

Then next he knew, she was sobbing. She shook with her weeping and Robin soon found that tears were coursing down his own cheeks. Perhaps it was unmanly to miss a mother so, but he didn't care. He loved her and damn anyone who wanted to mock him for it.

Gwen pulled back and began to check him over for injuries. He laughed as he submitted to her poking and prodding.

"I am unscathed, Mama," he said with a gentle smile.

"You've grown so much," she said, with a frown. "Making it, of course, very difficult to take you to task. Mayhap I should seek out my blade when I've serious business with you."

"The saints preserve me," he said with a laugh. "I promise, my lady, that I will fetch you a stool, that you might scold me from a like height."

She shook her head with a sigh. "I vow I scarce recognize my sweet little lad whom I used to intimidate by looking down at him."

"Aye, I know," he said. "That lad went off to war to become a man."

"You were a man before you left, son."

Ah, how he wished he could agree with her! He sat her down in a chair, drawing up a stool and sitting before her. He gave her a brief recounting of his recent travels, leaving out the more unsavory parts, though he had the feeling she knew what he'd neglected to tell her. And while he talked, he kept one eye on the stairs leading up to the upper floors of the keep. There was no sense in not knowing just who was coming down to the great hall, was there?

His mother's questions distracted him for a time and when he looked again at the stairs, it was to see a young woman coming down them. He blinked a time or two, wondering if that were his sister or a ghost of his mother. He heard his mother laugh softly.

"Uncanny, isn't it?"

"Frightening is more the word I'd choose," Robin said, drawing his hand over his eyes. "She has certainly inherited your beauty, but 'tis a pity she hasn't inherited your sweetness."

Robin felt a sharp slap to the back of his head and scowled up at Nicholas who strode across the room and picked Amanda up to spin her around. Robin's frown deepened as Nicholas brought Amanda over to the fire. She was weeping. Well, let her weep. She had always loved Nicholas the best anyway and that was just as well, as Robin couldn't abide her sharp tongue or lack of manners.

"I see you haven't forgotten how to scowl," Amanda said, making him a deep, mocking curtsey.

"I'm not home ten heartbeats and already you're irritating me," Robin snapped. "Do you lie awake nights dreaming of how to torment me?"

"I wouldn't spare you the effort, Robin."

Nicholas laughed and pulled Amanda behind him as Robin rose with a growl. "Rob, you're pitifully easy sport. Don't let her rile you. She's already told me I'm hopelessly soft and need a few more hours in the lists each day. Now, give the lass a kiss of peace and let us have harmony for once between you two. Five years have passed and I would hope you would have matured. Come from your hiding place, Amanda, and don't plunge anything sharp into Robby's belly while he's trying to behave."

Robin gave Amanda a quick hug, fierce enough to silence her for a time, then kissed her briefly on both cheeks. "Now, begone, wench, lest I remember the insults I must needs repay you for."

"Nick," Gwen said, reaching up to take his hand, "run fetch Anne from the chapel, would you? She's been out there for some time now. 'Tis far too cold for her."

"I'll go," Robin said, rising and pushing his brother aside before there could be any argument. "Nick would only fuss over her and that would irritate her."

"Don't you hurt her feelings," Amanda warned, poking him sharply in the arm on his way by. "You'll answer to me if you do."

Robin toyed with the idea of strangling his sister, then thought better of it. For one thing, his hands were so slippery with nervous sweat, they likely wouldn't have been able to get a good grip on her neck. Perhaps later, when he was calmer.

Though why he was so bloody nervous was something he couldn't answer. It wasn't as if he were seeking an audience with the queen. This was merely Anne of Fenwyck, the pale-haired girl who had grown to maturity in his home, who had been so painfully shy that he'd hardly noticed her.

He groaned as he slammed the hall door shut behind him.

When had he become such a liar?

He strode across the courtyard, pulling his cloak more closely around him. Bloody frigid country, this England of his. Why had he been fool enough to come back? He should have rather gone south to Spain. He had previously passed many months there quite happily. Indeed, he could have found himself spending his days lazing in bed with the countess who had once taken a fancy to him, strolling along the shore at night, enjoying the cool ocean breezes.

But those shores were a world away and it didn't serve him to think on them. He stepped up to the chapel, put his hand on the door, and took a deep breath. Would she be pleased to see him? Or would she ignore him, brush past him, and leave him standing there like a fool?

Wondering about it was almost enough to make him wish he'd had a bit of a wash before he presented himself to her.

He opened the door before his thoughts turned him in any more circles. He slipped inside the dimly lit structure, then closed the door behind him silently. He'd forgotten what a small place this was, but perhaps 'twas large enough to serve his family's needs. Robin stood still until his eyes adjusted to the gloom. At least his years of moving quietly would serve him now. He would have a look at mistress Anne before she was even aware of him, and see if his memory had served him well or ill.

He found her immediately. One of his greatest strengths in battle was his sharp eyes, eyes that could distinguish the color of a man's eyes at fifty paces. And those eyes were currently riveted on the figure kneeling at one of the side altars, before St. Christopher, protector of those who went to war.

Robin didn't allow himself to ponder the significance of her choice.

He took a pair of steps forward, then stopped, finding himself rendered immobile. He held his breath, wondering if he were seeing a vision or if the sight of the beautiful woman in the deep green gown before him were real.

It could only be Anne. He would never mistake that cloak of pale golden hair for anyone else's. The candlelight flickered over it as it fell over her shoulders and down her back like a waterfall of spun gold. Her slender hands were clasped and resting on the altar before her. Her head was bowed, her lips moved soundlessly. Robin almost went down on his knees himself. Never in his life had he seen such a picture of tranquility, of goodness, of purity. Gone was the homely little girl with freckles, too-large eyes, and ears that didn't seem to fit her face. In her place was a serene, lovely young woman.

He slowly walked to the front of the chapel and felt his way down onto a bench near her. He struggled to think of something clever to say—or at least something that wouldn't leave him sounding as witless as he felt.

By the saints, he'd never expected just the sight of her to leave him breathless.

He couldn't tear his gaze from her. Just looking at her seemed to ease his heart. For the first time in five years, he felt the tension ease out of him.

And it was because of the very woman he had promised himself he would avoid.

6

Anne felt a breeze blow over her hands as she knelt at St. Christopher's shrine, but she ignored it. For all she knew, 'twas her father come to fetch her and she wanted to put that moment off as long as possible. So she held her breath, kept her hands clasped before her, and waited for the inevitable, impatient clearing of a male throat.

The footsteps halted far from her, though, and she sighed in relief. Her fear of discovery was a foolish one anyway. Her sire never would have come to look for her here; it was her sanctuary alone. The other soul who had joined her was likely someone come to look for a little quiet as she had. With any luck, they wouldn't even mark her.

She bowed her head and continued with her prayer. It brought her peace, this ritual of hers. It was her daily trek to the saint's shrine to offer prayers at his feet, prayers that Robin would be kept safe, that he would return well and sound. She did not dare pray for the true desire of her heart. It was a miracle no saint could bring about, no matter his power.

Her leg trembled as she knelt on the hard wooden floor, but she didn't move. For all she knew, her sacrifice might mean the difference between Robin's life and his death. Though he would never know of it, and likely wouldn't care if he did, Anne made her offering willingly.

And when she was finished with Robin's needs, she spared a moment or two for her own.

Let me stay at Artane. Let me stay but another day or two.

She didn't dare pray for anything more. No saint could deter her father any longer than that.

She heard the footsteps begin again and come toward her, but she ignored them. It was likely Miles come to fetch her, or one of the twins. They could wait for another moment or two while she finished a few more supplications.

When she could truly bear the strain of kneeling no more, she crossed herself and opened her eyes. Getting to her feet would be difficult, but not impossible. Perhaps a bit of aid wasn't too much to ask for.

"Miles, if you please—" she began, turning her head to look at her visitor.

Only it wasn't Miles she saw.

It was Robin.

She couldn't have been more surprised if St. Christopher himself had been made flesh from her most fervent prayers. She gaped at the very man she had been praying for. It was impossible to look away. She could only hope she didn't look as foolish as she was certain she did. She made a small effort to close her mouth, but that was all she could manage.

By the saints, he was the last person she had expected to see that morn.

He sat on the long bench nearby, crushing her cloak beneath his heavy thigh. Anne took in the sight of him, marking the changes. His dark hair was long and unruly, falling over his forehead and into his eyes. His face was no longer the face of a boy, round with softness and charm. Five years had changed a young knight into a hardened warrior. His features were tanned, weathered, and very grim. His shoulders were broad, his empty hands wide and strong. His boots were caked with mud and his clothes were travel-stained.

She suspected she had never seen a more beautiful sight in her life.

She met his eyes but could read nothing in his gaze. He merely stared at her. She could readily imagine what he might be thinking, though, for she had been long in the chapel and the place was very cold. Her nose was likely red and her hands pale as death. It wasn't a sight guaranteed to bring a man to his knees pledging his body and soul.

Anne knew she had no choice but to rise. Perhaps in the effort, she might find some bit of wit remaining her. She turned away and put her hands on the shrine, praying she could manage to gain her feet. Robin was the last person she wanted to have see her weakness. She clenched her teeth together and tried to lever herself up using her good leg and her hands to push herself away from the altar. The action served her little but to force the blood of shame to her cheeks. If she wasn't careful, she would be sprawled at his feet.

This was not exactly how she had envisioned her next meeting with the young lord of Artane proceeding.

The altar was not the steadiest of crutches and her leg trembled so badly that Anne felt herself begin to waver dangerously. Instantly strong hands were at her waist, steadying her, lifting her.

Her mortification complete, Anne jerked away. The motion almost sent her stumbling in truth.

"By the saints," she gasped, "I don't need aid!"

Robin cleared his throat. "Well, I just—"

Anne straightened and looked at him with as much dignity as she could muster. It wasn't much, but her pride was all she had left at the moment.

"I was perfectly capable of rising on my own, thank you," she said as tartly as she could manage. This was the very last thing she needed—to have Robin look at her as if she were incapable of standing without aid.

Robin was beginning to scowl. It wasn't a good sign, but Anne was too embarrassed to care.

"Fool that I am, I thought to ply a bit of chivalry on you," he said gruffly.

"I already said I didn't need your help."

"I wasn't trying to help you," Robin returned shortly. "I was trying to maul you. Does that improve your humor any?"

Anne blinked furiously. She'd be damned before she'd let his ill-concealed pity cause her more humiliation. She pointed toward the door. "Your disrespect damns us both, so begone."

"I'll leave when I bloody well please—"

"Now," she snapped. "For the last time, I don't need your help, nor do I want it."

"I never suspected you did," he returned just as hotly. He brushed past her and strode away with a curse that left her ears burning. She waited until he was gone before she picked up her cloak and pulled it around her, willing herself not to break down and weep. Her leg was throbbing and her heart felt as if it had broken in uncountable pieces.

That was not how she had planned it, the reunion with the man she loved. She was to have been elegant and regal, bestowing her best smiles upon him as she sat gracefully arranged in a comfortable chair. He would have knelt at her feet, apologized profusely for having stayed away so long, then showered her with praises about qualities she hadn't even imagined she possessed.

Now, with but a few harsh words spoken, she had ruined everything. Perhaps it was just as well. If she shunned Robin, he wouldn't have the chance to shun her.

She walked stiffly to the chapel door, trying to work the cramp out of her leg. It was impossible. The chapel had been colder than usual and she would pay the price in agony for the rest of the day and far into the evening.

She stepped out into the frigid air and closed the door behind her. She jumped when she saw Robin standing next to the door. He merely glared at her. She ignored him and started for the steps. Damn, who was the imbecile who had decided there should be all these steps up to the chapel door? Then she had at least eight wider ones to face before she would gain the great hall. She suppressed the urge to sit down and weep.

She saw Robin move toward her and quickly held up her hand.

"I do not need—"

"Stubborn baggage," he muttered under his breath as he put his cloak around her shoulders. "At least now you will not freeze as you take all afternoon to cross the courtyard."

Anne blinked back tears. "You needn't wait. I never asked you to."

He didn't reply, he merely descended the steps in time to her painful movements. Once she reached the ground, he stepped in front of her and took his sweet time adjusting his cloak over her own. Anne might have thanked him for the chance to catch her breath had she not been so embarrassed. She pushed him away and started across the courtyard, her eyes fixed to the ground before her. A single false step and she would sprawl face-first in front of the only man whose opinion mattered to her.

She looked up to judge the distance and saw Nicholas come striding out of the great hall. He loped down the stairs with his easy gait. It was a lazy stroll that was so completely him that Anne felt herself begin to smile. How different Robin and Nicholas were. Robin was all fire and fury, roughness and strength; Nicholas was as serene and lethal as a finely polished steel blade.

And to be sure Nicholas possessed charm Robin never had, and likely never would. Even in his youth, Nicholas had been able to produce a look that had entranced every female from his mother down to the crustiest keeper of the larder. Anne had benefitted more than once from Nicholas's ability to beg an apple or two and succeed. Robin could have begged for cloth to staunch a life-threatening wound and Cook would have just kicked him out of her way as if he'd been an unsavoury tablescrap. Robin did not possess Nicholas's pleasing ways.

"You fool," Nicholas exclaimed, casting a baleful glance his brother's way. "Can't you see she's in pain? Here, Anne, let me carry you back to the hall. You shouldn't be out in this chill."

"Leave her be," Robin growled. "She's not a cripple."

"She's a woman, dolt," Nicholas said, pushing Robin aside. "Women need to be cared for; something you never have learned." Nicholas put his hands on Anne's shoulders and smiled down at her. "By the saints, 'tis a pleasure to see you again. It makes me wonder what possessed me to go away when I could have remained at home and gaped at you."

Anne felt an unaccustomed blush apply itself liberally to her cheeks. It was a very unsettling feeling, one she didn't experience very often.

"Nicholas," she said at length, at a loss, "what a flatterer you've become on your travels."

"Flattery? Nay, 'tis but the truth." He lifted his hand and smoothed it over her hair. "Anne, you steal my breath."

And then Anne watched, open-mouthed, as Nicholas smiled at her again, a dazzling smile that fair knocked her to her knees. He put his hands on her shoulders, bent his head, and then, to her complete astonishment, he took a liberty she never would have anticipated.

He kissed her.

And then he kissed her again.

By the third time his lips had come down on hers so softly, she had almost regained her wits enough to breathe. She stood there in his embrace, feeling exceedingly foolish, and examined the feel of Nicholas's lips as they pressed against hers.

They were warm.

They were soft.

And then they were quite suddenly no longer there.

She opened her eyes in time to see Robin jerk Nicholas away and send him sprawling by means of a fist in the face. She stared at Nicholas as he rolled over and sat up, putting his finger to the corner of his mouth and looking at it as it came away bloody.

"Don't do that again," Robin growled.

Nicholas paused for a moment and then leaned back on his hands, slowly crossing his feet at the ankles. His lazy movements were geared, Anne knew, to irritate Robin as much as possible. Nicholas looked up at his brother tranquilly, a smile playing around the corners of his mouth. Anne had to admire his calm in the face of Robin's considerable wrath.

"Why not?" Nicholas asked. "Does it bother you?"

Anne wished she had something heavy and damaging on hand to throw at Rhys's second son.

Robin leaned down and jerked Nicholas up by the front of his tunic. "She's not yours to kiss, damn you. Now, keep away from her." He gave Nicholas a shove toward the hall. "I'll see her inside."

"She doesn't need to walk any more, Robin," Nicholas said, his gray eyes taking on the same glint Anne saw in Robin's.

"She doesn't want any help. She already told me so."

Nicholas snorted. "Knowing you, you didn't ask her the right way."

"She bloody didn't give me a chance to ask before she was telling me to go to hell!" Robin exclaimed.

Nicholas pushed Robin aside. Before Anne realized what he intended, he had scooped her up into his arms.

"She's had enough, Robin," Nicholas said firmly. "Go open the door."

"Damn you, Nick—"

"The door, Robin."

Anne watched Robin stomp up the steps, swearing furiously. He opened the door and left it open, disappearing inside the hall.

"Nicholas, I'm fine—"

"Be quiet," Nicholas said with a smile. "Anne, you didn't used to be this stubborn. Where in the world did you learn this unladylike trait?"

Anne smiled faintly. "From Amanda."

Nicholas laughed. "I don't doubt it for a moment. That girl is a terrible influence on you. I suppose it leaves me with no choice but to take on the task of rooting it from you."

She looked at his mouth as he carried her up the steps. He had kissed her. Why wasn't she trembling from head to toe? Nicholas was one of the most sought-after young knights in the realm. Not even Robin had so many women pursuing him, though that number interested her not at all. She should have been faint with joy that Nicholas had taken note of her. She looked at his face and studied the cut on his mouth.

"Does it hurt, Nicky?" she asked.

Nicholas winked at her as he shut the hall door with his foot. "Why? Thinking to ease my pain with another kiss?"

His head suddenly snapped back. Anne looked over his shoulder to see Robin with a fistful of his brother's hair.

"Put her down," he growled.

Nicholas jerked his head away. "You're sounding rather possessive, brother."

"Put her down."

"Once I'm by the fire, I will."

"Now, Nick."

Nicholas sighed and gently set Anne on her feet. Then he whirled and took Robin down to the floor. Anne didn't bother to watch them scuffle. If there was one thing in this world that could be counted on, it was that Robin and Nicholas would fight at least once a day. She had never seen two brothers closer, nor more ready to let fly a fist. Not even the youngest de Piaget brothers battled so often. She knew it wouldn't last long. An hour from now, Robin and Nicholas would be laughing together, as if nothing had happened.

She avoided the battle now being waged in the rushes and made her way across the floor. She smiled when young Montgomery bounded over and hugged her.

"Put your arm around me, Anne, and let's go over to the fire. How did you come by Robin's cloak? 'Tis powerfully dirty, don't you think? And it smells. I'll wager you can't wait to have it off you."

Anne leaned on Montgomery as he helped her across the floor, grateful for his aid. But she couldn't agree with him about Robin's cloak. It might have been dirty and it might have not smelled terribly fresh, but it was something he'd given her for her comfort.

The ring of swords startled her and she turned around to see what they augured. Robin and Nicholas were now taking blades to each other with great enthusiasm. Anne sincerely hoped Robin didn't cut his brother to ribbons.

"By the saints, take your quarrel outside, you fools!" Amanda shouted from where she sat near the hearth. "You're giving me pains in my head with your idiocy!"

Much cursing and many foul insults accompanied the pair out the hall door. Anne sat down before the fire, swathed in Robin's cloak, and wondered if she had the intellect equal to ferreting out the truth of what had just happened.

Nicholas had just kissed her.

Robin was furious over the fact.

And now they had departed outside to settle the matter with swords.

Anne put her face in her hands and started to laugh. It was the very last thing she would have anticipated for the middle of her day. She could hardly wait to see what the evening would bring.

It likely couldn't equal what she'd just experienced.

7

Robin sat back in his chair and fingered his goblet of wine. The family had sought refuge in the lord's solar, as was often their custom in the evenings. Robin was glad of it, for he was unsettled in his mind and he wanted none of the garrison knights watching to see what ailed him. At least he wouldn't have to confront Baldwin of Sedgwick. Rhys had sent Sedgwick off on an errand a few days earlier and he wasn't expected back for at least a se'nnight. Robin couldn't help but be relieved. Now, at least, the first meeting after so many years would come when he was prepared for it. He fully intended for it to end badly for his enemy.

Robin drank deeply and tried to let the wine soothe him. Tonight, unlike other nights, there was no minstrel to entertain them, nor any visiting noblemen to bring news from other corners of the isle. The entertaining of the family fell to Robin. He had begun the tale of his travels, but had found it difficult to keep to the thread of the story. His mood was fouled and he had finally bid Nicholas in curt tones to take over the exercise.

He knew the precise reason for his foulness. Damn Nicholas for being the first to steal a sweet kiss from Anne's lips! Robin was passing certain she'd never been kissed before, if the look on her face had been any indication. Robin had been so stunned by his brother's boldness, he'd merely stood there and gaped. He couldn't tell if the kiss had pleased Anne or not.

It wasn't actually something he was interested in learning the truth of.

He stole a look at Anne and forced himself to breathe normally. Saints, she had changed! His first sight of her in the chapel had not shown him the extent of the transformation. When he had left five years earlier, Anne had been a plain, unlovely waif of ten-and-four. The Anne who sat across the circle from him was not the same girl.

Robin took a long draught of wine and then put the cup away. He leaned back in the shadows and let his eyes feast on the beauty before him. His father had always said one day Anne would blossom, but he had never believed it. Obviously his father had been right.

She sat in the chair next to Nicholas with her good leg tucked up under her. Robin could conjure up hundreds of memories of Anne in the same position, listening to the Fitzgerald brothers tell their gory tales of battle, minstrels singing praises to his mother's beauty, jongleurs performing their antics to amuse the family.

Gone was the homely little girl who had hugged her knee and watched the goings-on with bright green eyes. In her place was a woman full grown. Her head was uncovered and the firelight flickered over her pale hair. One slender hand rested on her knee, her long fingers absently worrying the fold of her gown. Her left hand rested on the arm of the chair and Robin frowned. Her hand was too damn close to Nicholas's. His eyes flicked to his brother's and his scowl only earned him a grin in return before Nicholas continued on with his story.

Anne shifted in her chair and Robin's gaze was drawn to the way her long hair fell over her shoulder and down. With an effort he forced his eyes up past her flawless throat to her lips. They were slightly parted and he had the most overpowering desire to jerk her out of her chair and capture her lips with his own, just to see if they tasted as sweet as they looked.

She began to chew on her lip and the movement startled him into meeting her eyes. He stiffened as he realized he had been caught staring. She didn't smile, which made him think that perhaps she thought him as big a fool as he was. He rose abruptly, giving her the fiercest frown he was capable of. Damn her if she thought to laugh at him.

He bid his family a curt good-night and strode stiffly up the stairs. He walked all the way up to the battlements, feeling the need of a great amount of fresh air to clear his head. He never should have come home. If he'd just had the good sense to remain on the continent, he would have been perfectly content and happy. And now look. He was letting a slip of a girl ruin his night and make mincemeat of his heart.

As he leaned against the wall, the stiff wind blowing in from the sea cooled his passions. He shivered and then shook his head in disbelief. What was he doing? What did he care what Anne of Fenwyck thought? She could laugh at him all she liked. She was too prickly and disagreeable for his taste. And though she might have filled out a bit, she was still too frail. He liked a woman with a bit more to her, a woman who was lusty in bed and who made herself scarce out of it.

It was several minutes later that he finally made his way back down the stairs. What he needed was a good tumble. Perhaps he'd hie himself down to the kitchens, find himself the first attractive serving wench available, and take her right there. Maybe he'd line up five or six of them and find relief from his torment. Relief from Anne.

But it wasn't to the kitchens that his feet led him so unerringly. He found himself in front of the chamber he shared with his brothers, and he relented with a sigh. So he was going to be as incapable of taking a woman tonight as he had been for months. It was hardly surprising.

He entered the chamber and lit a candle. He had a brief moment alone and there was little reason not to take advantage of it. He rummaged through his gear until he found what he was looking for. Taking his candle and his treasure, he retreated to the alcove and made himself comfortable on one of the stone benches there. He set the candle down, then took the box on his lap.

It contained his most precious possessions and there was not a time that he did not have it nearby. He opened it and examined what was contained therein.

There was the letter his mother had written him before he had been knighted, the crested ring his father had given him as he went off to war, and a gem which had been handed down from father to son for generations in the de Piaget family. Rhys had wanted Robin to bind the stone into a sword but Robin had never been able to bring himself to do it. He suspected there would come a time when he would wish to give the gem to his firstborn son. The thought of such a time gave him pause. A son. Now, that would be a thing to be proud of.

He fingered the four ribbons embroidered with his crest and then pushed them aside. They were dear to him, but not what he sought that night. From the depths of the box he pulled what he was looking for. He unwrapped the cloth surrounding it and held it up to the light.

The gold was so pale as to almost be white. It reminded him sharply of her hair. The paleness of the emerald did not do justice to her eyes, but it came damn close. He slid the ring onto the tip of his little finger and put his hand over his heart. Had Nicholas known of this foolishness, he would have laughed himself to death.

Then again, perhaps not. Nicholas was giddy enough to find the idea romantic. Robin was practical enough to find the idea idiotic. She would never wear his ring. She would laugh in his face.

Or perhaps she would accept him.

At the moment, he wasn't sure what would be worse.

Nay, the laughter would be worse. In his youth, he wouldn't have given that another thought. But that was before being laughed at became something he avoided at all costs. After the first time, he swore he would never be humiliated like that again. It was amazing how such a simple event in childhood could become such a heaviness in the heart of a man full grown.

Nay, she would have no chance to scorn him because he wouldn't come within twenty paces of her.

Besides, he had no tender feelings for her anyway. She was trouble embodied, trouble for his heart, and trouble for his peace of mind. He had never loved her and he never would.

The door opened suddenly and Robin jerked in surprise. Damn, this was all he needed to make his evening of misery complete.

"Robin, are you in here?" Nicholas asked. "Mother feared you were unwell."

Robin shoved everything back in the wooden box and slammed the lid shut before Nicholas could see. He glared at his brother who stood near the doorway.

"There is nothing amiss with me," he said tightly. "I did but need a bit of peace from your witless babbling."

Nicholas bowed. "Of course, my lord. Now I can happily inform Mother that you are not ill, but merely mooning."

"I am not mooning!"

Nicholas only laughed as he turned and left the chamber. Robin would have followed his brother to beat him senseless, but he'd already taken his exercise of Nicholas that afternoon. That added to the weariness of traveling was likely enough for the day.

One thing was for certain, he wasn't about to expose his poor heart to the torments that might await it in his father's solar. He was momentarily tempted to see if any of his lads might be willing to visit the lists with him, then he discarded that idea as well. 'Twas late and what would serve him best was to be abed.

A pity he already could imagine his tossings and turnings and how those might lead to speculation by his brothers.

He leaned back against the wall and stared into the dimly lit chamber. He'd suspected coming home would be difficult. He'd never imagined what would await him here.

Though wasn't that why he'd had the ring made for her?

He closed his eyes and gritted his teeth. And he thought Nicholas was the one awash in romance!

Robin rose, put his treasure away, then put himself to bed. What he needed was a satisfying night's sleep and then a goodly bit of training on the morn. Perhaps he would inspect his father's garrison and see if he couldn't dispatch them all before noon. It was a worthy goal and one easily within his power to accomplish.

And it was something he could understand. This business of love and romance and a heart that pounded uncomfortably at the merest thought of a certain woman was not for him. If he were to find himself swooning, it would be because of a full day's labor in the hot sun, not because Anne had deigned to glance his way. Should his stomach be unsettled, better it be from a questionable bit of fowl than fear she would wed with someone else. And should he weep, better that it be tears of victory over a foe well vanquished. He had no intention of shedding any over a girl who had suffered one of the worst injuries he'd ever been privy to, yet pressed on with the courage any of his men would have been proud to call his own.

He snorted. Courage? Nay, 'twas stubbornness that drove her, and a perverse desire to see him miserable. Aye, that he was certain of.

How she managed to do the like with so little effort on her part was something of a mystery, but one he had no desire to investigate further.

Nay, the lists were the place for him and he would be there as soon as the sun cooperated in the morn and his father's men could be persuaded to indulge him. Far better to face things he could understand and best than to try to unravel the mysteries of womanhood.

Robin rolled over, pulled the blankets over his head, and prepared to dream of war and bloodshed. It was much safer than the alternative.

8

Anne woke to find a very dim light trying to push its way through the bed curtains. Movement was beyond her at the moment so she simply snuggled deeper into the covers and put off the moment when she would have to leave the comforting warmth. There was no other sound in the chamber, so she assumed Amanda and Isabelle had already braved the chill to begin their days. For once, Anne didn't take issue with having been let sleep. Who knew how many more such mornings she might have to dawdle at her leisure? Soon enough she would rise and cloister herself in Gwen's solar with her ladies. There was sewing to be done, fine stitches for decoration to be wrought, and many other things with which to occupy her mind. At least she would have no trouble from her father that day and she had Rhys to thank for that.

Just the night before, when Geoffrey had arrived in Rhys's solar and begun speaking loudly of their impending return to Fenwyck, Rhys had begun tempting him with thoughts of a hunt. Miles amused himself by raising a kennel of hounds, and Anne knew their lure would be a powerful one for her father. Rhys had declared firmly that it would take at least a se'nnight to prepare and who knew how long to enjoy the outing. When she'd realized she had perhaps a fortnight's more grace, she had retired to her chamber and fair jumped for the joy of it. It wasn't as long as she would have liked, but perhaps Rhys could convince her sire of something else in time. This reprieve was enough.

But that didn't mean she was going to take unnecessary risks in encountering her father. Nay, 'twas best she seek something to eat, then retire to Gwen's solar. That might also spare her any unsavoury encounters with the other soul she fully intended to avoid—though she imagined he would be just as busy avoiding her.

She sighed, past fathoming why he did anything. One moment the night before he'd been looking at her as if she'd been a particularly appealing leg of mutton, then the next as if she'd been directly responsible for handfuls of dung set carefully inside his boots. What she had done to deserve either was anyone's guess. She'd simply been looking at him.

But simple things had long been beyond Robin's capabilities of enjoyment. Nay, all had become either life or death with him. He could never go to the lists for the sheer sport of it; with him it was either humiliate or perish in the attempt. Even chess was something he now turned into a full-scale battle. It hadn't always been so. They had played often during his illness and he had actually laughed the first time she had bested him. Gone was that mischievous boy who had spent so much time with her.

One day he had been laughing and the next cursing bitterly. She had never been quite clear on what had happened to change him so and he absolutely refused to talk about it. From that time on, he had shunned her. It had pained her greatly at the time. She liked to believe she had now moved past the hurt, but even thinking on it grieved her afresh. By the saints, what had happened to change him so?

He had not always been so troubled. She could remember much of the mischief he had combined when they had all been together while Artane was being finished. One night she had retired to the tent she had shared with Amanda to find a snake in her blankets—a dead one fortunately. She had retaliated by putting a dead rat under his pillow. It had taken her and Amanda all day to find one and then Amanda had been the one to kill it, as Anne had not had the courage. How Robin had howled when he had found it. The memory still made her smile.

But even with his boyish antics, he had possessed a sweetness she had come to treasure. He'd been just as likely to present her with a fistful of sweet-smelling flowers as he had some creature of dubious origins. She had adored him.

Then the fever had come. It had left half the village near Artane dead in its wake. Robin had been the only one of the family taken sick and for a time she had wondered if he would die too. He had been ten-and-four at the time and already very strong, else he might have lost his life. She had her own convalescence to endure, but she had spent as much time with him as allowed. They had played chess for hours when he felt strong enough. When he had become weary, she had read to him haltingly, and made up stories to amuse him.

It had taken him almost a year to regain his strength. And sometime during that year, he had changed. She had been up and hobbling about, amusing him as she could. Then one day her attempts to tend him had been harshly rejected. She would enter his room to entertain him only to find herself summarily ejected. Even if he spoke to her, he would not look at her, and his words were always clipped and curt.

He had thrown himself into his training. When others were inside the hall taking their ease, Robin had been out in the lists working. He became so ferocious in his sparring that the only ones who would tolerate his aggressiveness were his father and Nicholas, and Nicholas usually found himself vanquished in a matter of minutes.

Soon there had been no one to stand against him save Rhys. Robin had earned his spurs just before his nineteenth birthday and earned them he had. The lord he had gone to squire with was forever complaining to Rhys about how Robin ground his men to powder.

And then Robin had gone off to war. She had thought at the time that it was so that he might need not look at her anymore. Then she had come to suspect that it might have been to prove himself. There was no way of knowing, for 'twas a certainty he would not tell her of his own accord and she certainly wouldn't be asking him.

She sat up slowly, wincing at the protest her leg set up. There would be no vigils in the chapel today. Perhaps it was well that Robin was home. Her body needed a rest.

She rose stiffly and hobbled over to the window. She opened the shutters and leaned on the stone surrounding the opening. The sky was gray outside, which came as little surprise. Though she was passing fond of the rain, her father had done nothing but complain about the drizzle from the moment they had arrived. Anne breathed deeply, relishing both the smell of rainy sea air and no complaints to listen to. And with that lightness of heart and mind came feelings she couldn't deny.

Kind feelings.

Toward that very complicated soul she couldn't seem to put from her mind.

How could she harden her heart against that sweet dimple that appeared in his left cheek on those rare occasions when he grinned, or the wicked gleam in his eye when he was about some devilry? He was just as handsome as Rhys was, and that was something to marvel over for Robin's true sire was Alain of Ayre. Indeed, though Anne had never known Lord Ayre, she couldn't help but think that Robin looked a great deal like Rhys.

And she wondered just how such a thing could have come about.

Anne looked down from the rain-laden sky and turned her attentions to the courtyard. Perhaps she would see aught there that would distract her from her contemplation of things she would never know. With any luck what she wouldn't see would be her sire waiting for her to rise so he could tell her that he'd changed his mind and they were returning to Fenwyck forthwith.

But it wasn't her sire who stared up at her.

It was Robin.

She was just as surprised by the sight of him as she had been in the chapel. She jumped away from the window and banged the shutters closed. It was well past time that she was up and doing. There wouldn't be anything left of breakfast if she didn't hurry downstairs.

She dressed quickly and ran a comb through her long hair. She contemplated donning a head covering, then discarded the idea. No one ever looked at her anyway. She would offend no soul she could think of. Perhaps she might break her fast then retreat to the sanctuary of Gwen's solar before her father managed to lay hands upon her person.

She soon found that the great hall, however, was not as empty as she had hoped it would be. One table was still set up near the hearth and men flanked it. Rhys sat at the head of the table with Nicholas to his left. Robin was just sitting down on his right. Members of Rhys's personal guard were there, as well as men Anne assumed belonged to Robin and Nicholas, for she recognized none of them. They looked to be deep in talk.

Then throaty laughter erupted and Anne doubted very much the talk was all that serious. At least her father was nowhere to be seen. But Anne wasn't about to invite herself to sit in council with the warriors before her. Yet before she could make her escape, Rhys had turned and beckoned to her. Though it was tempting to flee, she would have looked more foolish had she done that than if she continued on her course.

All the men at the table rose as she approached and she found herself for the second time in as many days blushing furiously. Nicholas gaped at her with his mouth open. Anne looked at the other men and they stared at her in much the same manner.

Robin, however, seemed to be clenching his jaw.

She was unsurprised.

But the collective interest she was faced with caused her serious anxiety. And then a horrible thought occurred to her and she looked down hastily, fully expecting to see her clothes falling off in some embarrassing manner.

She frowned. She was laced in all the right places. She looked up again and was amazed to find that several of the men were giving her roguish grins. It flustered her so badly that she almost stumbled. Immediately one of the men jumped up and hastened to her side, offering her his arm.

"Sir Richard of Moncrief at your service," he said with a low bow.

She looked at him, knowing her mouth was hanging open most unattractively, but unable to help herself. Why was this fool being so polite? And why by the saints was he wearing that ridiculous smile? She knew very well who he was for he was one of Rhys's men. Why was he presenting himself to her as if she'd been a great lady?

"I need no aid," she managed, with as much dignity as she could muster.

"Then perhaps you would at least allow me to escort you to the table?"

A flurry of activity ensued as several men made a dash for one of the chairs put up next to the wall. The seat was brought and set down next to Rhys. Anne had the overwhelming urge to crawl into the rushes and disappear. She used every ounce of pride at her disposal to walk across the floor without displaying her limp overmuch, then sat as gracefully as she could.

And still she was the focus of attention.

"Anne," Nicholas said, reaching over his father and taking her hand, "you are a beauty. Don't you agree, lads?"

A chorus of male voices assented with vigorous ayes. Anne pulled her hand away and looked at Rhys.

"My lord," she began and her voice cracked.

Rhys put his arm around her. "What is it, daughter?"

She leaned over toward him. "They're all staring at me," she whispered frantically.

"Ah, but the lads only find you lovely," Rhys whispered in return. "Perhaps 'tis that their manners need improving."

"I'll see to it," Robin growled from where he sat next to her.

"Ah, a bit of bloodshed," Nicholas said, rubbing his hands together enthusiastically. "How I love it when Robin pursues a righteous cause."

"Nay," Rhys said, thrusting out his hand and stopping what Anne was certain would have been Robin's leap over the table. "None of that, if you please, Anne, I would have a cup of wine if you felt so inclined."

Anne was grateful for the excuse to leave, and she recognized the request as such. "At once, my lord."

Half the table rose to their feet. There were equally as many offers to help with any such endeavor. Anne would have turned and fled if she'd been able.

"She can get the bloody wine herself," Robin snarled. "Sit down, the lot of you."

The men resumed their seats slowly, all save Nicholas.

"Nick, don't even think it."

Anne left before she had to watch Robin and Nicholas go at each other again. And she tried not to put more behind word or action than had been there to start. Perhaps Robin merely had a need to speak with the men and didn't want them going off on a foolish errand. Perhaps Nicholas only sought to annoy his brother and had found a way to do so completely.

Perhaps she would be better served by retreating to bed.

She shook her head and made her way to the kitchen. She procured a bottle of wine and a wooden plate piled high with sweetmeats, knowing Rhys's fondness for them. She returned to the hall, praying she would gain the table and then escape without anyone noticing her.

And then before she truly realized what was happening, she felt her foot slip from beneath her. She tried desperately to keep bottle, plate, and her person upright, but it was hopeless. The bottle slipped from her hands, plate and sweetmeats went flying, and she closed her eyes, prepared to meet the rushes with an ungraceful thump.

But she never touched the ground.

She found herself cradled in strong arms and lifted up. She looked into Robin's face, which was only a hand's breadth from hers. She wanted to throw her arms around him, bury her face in his shoulder, and hide. Making a complete fool out of herself had not been in her plans that morning.

But instead, all she could do was stare into his gray eyes and hope he could see that she was grateful for the rescue.

He didn't move. Considering the fact that he could have dropped her where he stood, lack of movement was, to her mind, not an ill omen.

"Thank you," she managed.

That seemed to spark some sense of time and place in him. He set her on her feet with surprising gentleness, then stepped back. "The bottle can be replaced," he said gruffly, walking away.

Anne stood there in the middle of the great hall, shards of pottery, spilt wine, and soggy sweetmeats at her feet and found she could do nothing else but stand and shake. She toyed with the idea of bursting into tears, but that wasn't very appealing. What she wished was that she had time to consider what had just happened.

Robin had rescued her. And to have done so, he had to have been watching her come across the hall. The bottle could be replaced? Did he mean, then, that she couldn't?

She shook her head, hoping that her foolish thoughts would spill from her ear and join the refuse on the floor.

Nicholas appeared before her, looking at her with concern. He was followed closely by several other of Rhys's personal guardsmen. One of the younger ones knelt before her.

"My lady, forgive me. I tossed one of the dogs a bone at supper last night and saw him carry it over here. 'Tis my fault you slipped."

"I'll see him repaid," Nicholas said briskly, "if you like, Anne."

"Could we please return to the business of the day?" Robin exclaimed from his place at the table. "We've manly matters to discuss!"

Nicholas pursed his lips, dismissed the guardsman with a flick of his wrist, then smiled at Anne. "Manly matters be damned. What say you to a walk in the garden?"

"'Tis chilly outside, Nicky," Anne said, wanting nothing more than to escape upstairs.

"I know."

She looked at him in surprise. "You know?"

"A perfect excuse to use all my efforts to keep you warm."

She laughed. She couldn't help herself. It was the most ridiculous thing she'd heard all morning. "Perhaps I would be better served to fetch a cloak."

"Now you insult my chivalry," Nicholas said, with a frown approaching one of Robin's milder ones. "My honor is besmirched and I demand satisfaction."

"Shall we do so with blades?" she asked, finding a smile came readily when induced by such charm. "Or should we settle for something less messy?"

"I'll think on it," he said. "Wait for me and I'll fetch my cloak for you."

Anne watched him make her a low bow, kiss her hand, then trot off to fetch something appropriate for her to wear. She snuck a glance at the table to find the men all dutifully discussing matters of war and training. Robin most pointedly gave her his back. But it was what she was accustomed to, so she didn't begrudge him the like.

Besides, Nicholas of Artane planned to take her for a walk in the garden. What need had she of anything more spectacular to pass the morn?

It was much later in the day that Anne found herself in her accustomed place in Gwen's solar. The fire was warm, the company fine, and Anne had something especially lovely under her needle. She set down her stitchery and let the pleasure of being home wash over her. She closed her eyes and imagined how it would be should such contentment be hers for the rest of her life.

It was with a start that she woke to find that conversation had waned and it was nigh onto time for supper. She sincerely hoped no one had noticed her napping, but no one seemed to be paying her any heed. Anne looked carefully about her at the women who were finished with their day's work.

Three of the women were wives of Rhys's personal guardsmen. Anne's stepmother never would have associated with women below her station and Anne had always admired Gwen's disregard of convention. The women were pleasant and witty and Anne enjoyed their company very much.

Amanda and Isabelle were there, of course, though Anne knew Amanda would have rather been out in the lists wreaking havoc with a bow or something equally as perilous—though Anne sometimes wondered if she shouldn't have learned a bit of that kind of thing herself. It would have served her well if she'd found herself attacked.

The remaining occupant of the chamber, save Gwen herself, was Edith of Sedgwick. Anne looked at her from under her eyelashes and wondered about her. She'd come to Artane when she'd been a girl of ten summers.

Anne had been eight at the time, but she remembered vividly her first sight of the girl. She'd looked as if she'd been wearing the same clothes for years, for her skirts were well above her ankles and the cloth had been riddled with holes and rents. She'd smelled passing foul and her eyes had been full of a wild light.

Gwen and Rhys had taken her in, more because she was in need of aid than that she was Rhys's kin. Rhys's mother had been of Sedgwick and Rhys should have been lord of that keep, though Anne knew he had no desire for it. Rhys's cousin was lord there, at Rhys's behest, and Anne suspected that being Rhys's vassal didn't sit well with the man.

Baldwin was Lord Sedgwick's nephew and likely very much underfoot there, which was no doubt why he'd found himself packed off to Artane at the first possible moment. Rhys had taken the boy willingly enough, though only so he might always know what Baldwin was combining. Anne knew his reasoning well, though she couldn't say she'd been overfond of the logic. She had complained bitterly to Rhys about the torment through which Baldwin put not only her, but anyone weaker than he. Rhys had always remained firm. Baldwin would stay, but he would be watched closely. Apparently such scrutiny didn't bother Baldwin, for he had never seemed overly anxious to leave the comfort of Artane's supper tables.

Edith was much different from her brother, though, for she never complained and never wrought any mischief.

Anne looked at her dark head bent over her stitchery, then smiled faintly in acknowledgment when Edith lifted her head and caught her staring. The woman was fair enough, Anne thought, and passing pleasant when compared to her brother. Gwen was fond enough of her.

But Anne was, as she had been the first time she'd laid eyes on the girl, torn between compassion and fear, for despite her pretty manners, to Anne's mind the wildness had never quite faded from Edith's eyes.

"Ladies, let us be off," Gwen said, rising. "Anne, love, are you coming?"

"In a moment, Mother," Anne said, wanting nothing more than a moment or two of peace in which to think on events much more interesting than stitchery and women's gossip.

The women left and Anne remained in her chair, staring into the flames. It had been a most remarkable day. She was loth to let anything—supper, her father, or other souls in the keep—disturb her contemplation of it.

Nicholas had entertained her the whole of the afternoon.

Robin had rescued her from a tumble on the floor.

There had to be a good reason for both, but she had no stomach for divining what it was. Likely Robin was feeling some sort of fraternal sentiment toward her and Nicholas saw an opportunity to irritate his brother by thwarting the same as often as possible. She could hardly credit Nicholas for true interest and it was even more foolish to think Robin might have any but the most indifferent of feelings toward her.

With a sigh, she threw her sewing into a basket at her feet and rose. It was dark and she was hungry. It was past time she descended to the warmth of the fire in the great hall.

She stepped out into the passageway. The torches were out again. It wasn't unusual, but it was unnerving. Anne peered into the dim passageway, but there was nothing to be seen. She turned and limped quickly to the stairwell, then started down the steps. She saw a glimmer of light around the corner and let out a sigh of relief.

And then she heard a faint sound.

It was the sound keys made when brushed together, or a chain of some sort.

Before she could truly be frightened by the realization that she'd heard a like sound before, she lost her footing and stumbled, her hands flying out to catch her balance. It was hopeless. Her weak leg gave out from underneath her and she tumbled down the remaining stairs, crying out as the edges of them slammed into her body. She rolled to a heap at the bottom and remained motionless, almost afraid to move.

"Anne!"

She heard Nicholas's shout and then the sound of his boots thumping down the passageway. Within moments he was kneeling next to her, gently running his hand over her arms and legs.

"Don't move," he commanded as she started to sit up.

"I'm fine," she insisted, pushing his hands away. It was only then that she noticed the pain in her wrist, pain that intensified as she moved it.

Nicholas took her wrist in his hand and gently ran his fingers over it. "It isn't broken," he said, frowning over it. "We'll bind it with stiff cloths and keep it immobile—"

"By the bloody saints, what is happening here?" Robin bellowed from down the passageway. Anne lay back with a groan. The last thing she needed was to have Robin see her in such an undignified sprawl. She made a half-hearted attempt to toss her skirts back down over her knees.

"Nick, you fool, move out of my way," Robin growled, shoving his brother aside. "Anne, what's befallen you? When will you learn to be more careful? These stairs are steep, much too steep for you to walk down them in the dark. Must I watch over your every move to see you do not kill yourself?"

Anne could have borne his tirade in silence, but his strong hands roaming over her limbs, checking gently for further injuries was something she could not bear.

And then she felt his hand on her ruined thigh. She shoved it away and sat up, backing away from him.

"Don't," she gasped.

"Anne—"

She could hardly believe his actions. Had no one ever told him there were parts of a woman a man simply didn't touch?

"Leave me be," she managed. "I'm perfectly sound."

"I see," he said stiffly. "Nicholas can see to your injuries, but I cannot."

"He wasn't pawing my leg!" she exclaimed.

"Believe me," Robin snapped. "I meant nothing by it."

She expected nothing less, but his words hurt her just the same. "My only injury is to my wrist and I can bind that well enough myself," she said. "Favor some other wench with your impersonal touch."

Robin's eyes flashed in the torchlight. "There are many who long for it, I can assure you of that."

"Then find one and avail yourself of her," Anne said, turning her face away. "I can see to myself."

"Then see to yourself and trouble me no further with your accidents."

There was a grunt from Nicholas and Anne could only assume Robin had elbowed him out of his way. Robin's curses trailed behind him as he left, then finally died away. Anne lay in silence, grateful for the pain in her wrist that numbed the pain in her soul. Robin would never want her. Why had she ever allowed such a dream to have a place in her heart?

The most sensible thing to do would be to stay out of his way and pray he decided to return to the continent quickly. Perhaps once he was gone, she would rid herself once and for all of the foolish notions she had entertained. Even a simple man wouldn't have wanted a maimed wife. Robin wasn't a simple man, he was the future lord of Artane. He had little patience and even less heart. She would likely be better off with a man of her father's choosing. At least she would know she was wanted for her dowry.

The sound of cloth being torn distracted her and she looked up. Nicholas had stripped off his tunic and was currently tearing the latter into shreds. Anne averted her eyes from his bare chest. She continued to look away from him as he bound her wrist securely. Then he helped her to her feet.

"I'll have to feed you while you rest that wing for a bit," he said with a smile. "Will you oblige me? It has been many months since I last had the honor of serving a maid so very fetching and sweet."

She sighed. "Nicholas, stop, please."

Nicholas put his arm around her shoulders and led her down the final set of stairs to the great hall. He sat her down and smiled at her. "I'll run and clothe myself. Save my place. Or I'll be forced to kill anyone who's taken my seat," he said with a mock frown. "Father wouldn't approve of bloodshed at his dinner table."

Anne nodded absently, then frowned when Nicholas squatted down next to her chair.

"Do you feel unwell, Anne?"

She shook her head. "Nay. Why?"

"I just wondered if you'd felt dizzy and lost your balance. You did lose your balance, didn't you?"

She nodded, forcing a smile to her lips. "Of course, Nicholas. I'm just clumsy. I'll be more careful in the future."

He nodded and rose, seemingly content with her answer. Anne sighed in relief once he had gone. At least Nicholas wouldn't ask any more questions she'd have to answer with a lie.

Nay, she hadn't lost her balance.

She'd been pushed.

9

Edith stood in the alcove of the tower chamber and stared out the window. It soothed her to do the like. There was no sea near Sedgwick, and very little wind to take away the stenches of castle life. The sea here was so many things.

Savage.

Violent.

Beautiful.

It was the thing she loved best about Artane. It was also one of the reasons she never wanted to leave the place.

Not that she had any intention of ever leaving, of course.

The argument behind her increased enough in volume that she could no longer concentrate on her contemplation of the waves. The dispute had been going on for some time, far longer than Edith would have permitted. Perhaps 'twas that her brother and Maude were so ill-suited to a battle of words. 'Twas a certainty they were not equal to a battle of wits. Edith turned and listened to them scream at each other things that made little sense at all.

"Enough!" she said loudly.

Both Baldwin and Maude looked at her in surprise.

"The entire keep can no doubt hear you," Edith said in a quieter tone. "Perhaps you might consider that as you shout yourselves hoarse."

The other two settled for glares to express their displeasure. Edith looked at Maude first. The girl was wild-eyed and disheveled from her hasty flight up to the tower chamber. Baldwin looked just as disheveled, but that was from his recent return to the keep. Apparently his errands for Lord Rhys had been unsatisfying, for he had only been gone a pair of days. Edith suspected that her brother was relieved to be back. He was consumed by the thought of slaying Robin; any time away from the keep had no doubt been a burden.

"And *I* say," Baldwin said, "that you should leave her be. Don't give him a reason not to come to the lists."

"He doesn't love her!" Maude exclaimed.

"And he does you?" Baldwin said.

Unkind, Edith mused, but true. She watched Maude's temper flush across her face and knew that the time for silence was over.

"Leave Anne to us," Edith said, turning to her brother. "She won't be a distraction."

"See that she isn't," Baldwin said. "And keep *her*," he said, gesturing with his head toward Maude, "far from me. I can't bear her screeching."

"And you'll be in the lists?" Edith asked. "Honing your skills?"

"Waiting for him to come timidly from the great hall to face me," Baldwin said, starting for the door. "I'll humiliate him immediately, of course."

"Better that than killing him too soon," Edith agreed.

Baldwin only grunted and left the chamber.

Once he was gone, Edith turned to Maude.

"Pushing her was foolish," she said bluntly.

Maude shrugged and pouted. "She was there. I was there. It seemed the best thing to do."

"You could have killed her."

"And if I had?" Maude challenged.

"You are better off not knowing what would have become of you had you done so," Edith said pleasantly. "Now, let us turn our minds to something of a happier nature. I think we should torment her, aye, but not kill her. Understood?"

Maude looked unconvinced. Edith sighed. One more chance would she give the girl before she took action against her. She could afford no more disobedience. Her plans were carefully laid and she would allow no deviations.

Edith handed Maude a leather envelope. "Put this in wine and see that she drinks it. But use it sparingly."

Maude blinked. "Poison?"

"Very deadly. Use it sparingly," she reminded her.

Maude looked happier than she had in days. She clutched her treasure and departed the chamber without another word.

Edith turned away and resumed her position at the window. The sea rolled in ceaselessly, patiently, with a roar that was ever just on the edge of what she could hear. She loved the sea. Odd how she'd never known of it until she'd come to Artane.

Aye, 'twas right that now she'd found it, she never be forced to leave it. This pleasure would be hers for the rest of her life.

That also was included in her carefully laid plans.

10

Robin strode purposefully from the great hall, his squire trotting along dutifully behind him. Robin's mail shirt likely should have hampered his striding, but he was accustomed to the weight. What he wasn't accustomed to, however, was the intense irritation and stung pride that threatened to sap all his powers of concentration.

He strode to the lists, needing distraction more than he'd ever needed it before in his life. Though, in truth, how he could be more distracted than he was at present, he surely didn't know. He couldn't remember the last time he'd slept well, and his appetite was failing. If he hadn't known better, he would have thought himself suffering from some slow, lingering illness.

Unfortunately, he knew exactly whence his frustration sprang and he fully intended to seek refuge in the lists and drive all thoughts of her from his mind. He would not think about her, nor about the fact that she had shunned him for the past two days, preferring the company of his lackwit younger brother. Anne's preference in men was a sharp sting to his pride. Nicholas's visage was no more pleasing than his!

Nicholas's skill in healing was nothing to sing praises over either. Robin would have sooner trusted his precious flesh to a scullery maid than to his bumbling younger brother. Nor was Nicholas's disposition that tolerable. Fluff and prettiness was all his brother possessed. If Anne found that more appealing than a real man, then she was welcome to her folly and he sincerely hoped she earned stomach pains as reward from the sweetness.

Robin stopped in the outer bailey and looked about him to see what sort of sport would appeal to him most at present. There was the quintain, as usual, as well as hand-to-hand combat. Robin wasn't overfond of the bow, so he found himself not at all tempted by that.

And then he spotted him. Baldwin of Sedgwick. His nemesis, the one man he hated with all his soul. So, the wretch had returned from whatever errand he'd been sent on. Robin had no doubt the lout had been lurking about in the countryside, robbing unwary travelers and stirring up like mischief wherever he could. But now he was home, and Robin was in the mood for sport. He smiled. The morn was shaping up nicely indeed.

In the past, he'd cursed his father for keeping Baldwin at Artane, but Rhys had insisted. His theory was that it was far easier to watch an enemy at close range than it was to let him go and wonder where he would strike next. Patrick of Sedgwick was actually Rhys's uncle, though no one at Artane would have any dealings with the whoreson. Rhys's mother had fled Sedgwick to escape harsh treatment and 'twas very late in life that Rhys had even discovered he was kin with them.

The hatred between Artane and Sedgwick ran deep, and truly nowhere did it run deeper than in Robin. Robin had the nagging suspicion it might be his undoing someday, but for now he was young and strong and Baldwin was nowhere near his equal. It was past time to repay Baldwin for a few of his insults.

He strode over to the near end of the jousting field and took the reins of a horse away from a squire. He swung up into the saddle, snatched a shield out of the poor lad's hands, and picked up a lance. Baldwin was at the opposite end of the field, leaning casually against the outer bailey wall. Robin stood up in the stirrups.

"Sedgwick!" he shouted. "Are you man enough to come against me, or will you remain clinging to the wall like a woman?"

Baldwin's response was immediate. Robin settled himself in the saddle and smiled grimly, already planning his strategy.

"Rob, your helmet!" Nicholas bellowed from near the wall.

Robin waved his brother's words away—foolishly no doubt, but he was past reason. Besides, Baldwin hadn't the spine to put a lance through his eye, not with so many witnesses about. Robin waited until Baldwin was prepared, then put his spurs to the warhorse's side. He guided the mount with naught but his knees as he positioned both the shield and his lance. He struck Baldwin full in the center of his chest, sending him toppling backward. Robin wheeled his mount around and dropped to the ground. Aye, this was the sport he longed for. He waited impatiently until Baldwin had risen, then waited for Baldwin's attack.

"Whoreson," Baldwin spat, lashing out viciously.

"That is *my lord whoreson* to you, Sir Baldwin. Ever you forget your manners. Perhaps I should teach you a few this morning."

Baldwin's largest flaw, and a fatal one it was, was his temper. Robin had been too young to take advantage of it in his youth, but he had studied Baldwin long, marking all his weaknesses for future use. Now he was older and the future had come.

"I'll kill you this time," Baldwin snarled, his eyes blazing.

"Indeed," Robin drawled. "And find yourself dangling from the end of a rope come nightfall, I'd imagine. But I wouldn't worry over that possibility, Baldwin. My sisters could best you in a sword fight. I daresay I can manage the feat as well."

Robin heard Nicholas's hearty laughter from behind him and knew that his brother and likely his father were looking on. Five years ago, having his father watch him would have unnerved him completely. Five years of warring had done much to work that unsurety out of him. He was confident in his skill and had no doubts that he could best anyone on the field. Except perhaps his sire. Even at two score and five, Rhys of Artane was still a master.

But Robin was his father's son and had learned well his craft. He continued to toy with Baldwin, pretending to fall back only to attack with parries that left Baldwin stumbling in surprise.

And when Baldwin let his guard slip, Robin shunned his sword, stepped in, and caught the man under the chin with his fist. His foe slumped to the ground, senseless.

Robin felt wonderful. It was the first time in months he'd felt a genuine smile come to his face. He shoved his sword into the ground, cracked his knuckles with a happy snap, and came close to beating on his chest in a most victorious fashion.

"A wrestle!" a young voice cried.

"Aye, a wrestle!"

Robin looked about to find his youngest brothers racing toward him. He smiled indulgently as he motioned for his squire to come relieve him of his mail shirt. Let the children come. It was the least he could do when he'd had such success already.

So he took them on, two on one, and allowed them to win. Of course, it was a lengthy battle. No sense in giving the lads less than a full sense of victory.

"We have you!" Montgomery cried, sitting on Robin's chest and waving his fist over his head triumphantly.

"And so easily done," John agreed with a war cry that set Robin's ears to ringing.

Robin only lay in the mud with them sitting upon him, and laughed at their boasts. His own pride had been mightily assuaged and he was ready to concede almost any other battle. Robin put his hands behind his head and sighed in contentment.

He suspected that life simply could not improve.

His brothers were eventually pulled off him and a hand extended. Robin allowed his father to pull him to his feet.

"Tolerable, for a whelp of your size," Rhys said gruffly.

Robin laughed and clapped his father on the shoulder. "Ah, such high praise, Papa. I think I might blush."

"Let us go sup, then perhaps you'll indulge me this afternoon. I've yet to find a lad to stand against me and I find my swordplay has suffered because of it." He grabbed Robin around the back of the neck and shook him. "I'm glad to have you home. Perhaps now I'll have some decent sport."

There was simply no compliment higher than that. Robin had to cough to cover his grin of pleasure. Nicholas groaned.

"Father, his arrogance is excessive as it is. I pray you, do not add to it more than necessary."

Rhys pursed his lips. "You both have more arrogance than is good for you, but I'll not complain. I will complain, however, about your short stays in the lists, Nick. I daresay you and I are the only sport for Robin, yet you will find yourself unable to stand against him if you do not train harder."

Nicholas waved a dismissive hand as he started back to the hall. "I've been tending Anne, Father. 'Tis a much more important task than tending Robin, believe me."

Robin stiffened and would have gone after his brother immediately had his father's heavy hand on his shoulder not kept him in place.

"He's baiting you, Rob," Rhys said quietly.

"I could not care less what he does with Anne," Robin said, trying mightily to sound more uninterested than he was. "Let him wed her if he wills it." He looked behind him for his squire. "See to my gear, Jason. I will be within."

"As you will, my lord."

Robin turned and walked with his sire across the lists. Rhys refrained from speech until they had reached the steps leading up to the great hall. Then he paused. Robin steeled himself. He knew something of great import was about to be distilled on his pitiful ears. His father was wearing that look. It wasn't often that he wore it, but Robin had learned to pay heed when he did. Robin could only hope it was something he could bear to hear.

"Anne is a very special woman, Robin," Rhys said slowly, "and she will require a sure hand and a loyal heart to win her trust."

Robin felt as if he should say something, but there was naught to say. His father had it aright. If Anne needed anything, 'twas a loyal heart.

"Nicholas coddles her overmuch and I daresay she doesn't care for it."

"I've told him that," Robin muttered.

"That isn't the way to win her," Rhys continued.

Robin waited, but apparently no more wisdom was forthcoming without some prompting on his part. Somehow, though, he wasn't sure he wanted to hear the remainder. He turned his face away and scowled as he looked out over the courtyard. It was filled with ghosts, shadows of him and Anne when they were growing to maturity, teasing and playing together. Robin could still remember how she had seemed to worship him and how it had empowered yet humbled him at the same time. Ah, the fervent vows he had made as a callow youth, vows to become a man she would be proud of, a man worthy of her goodness.

And then she had been trampled and he had been humiliated. She had withdrawn and he had let anger and bitterness fill his soul. Had he been a fool? Was it truly possible to undo the past and have her?

Robin took a deep breath and let it out carefully. He put his shoulders back. Best have the question over with and the answer received before he lost what courage he had remaining him.

"And how would a man win her?" he asked carefully.

Rhys clapped him on the shoulder. "Why would you care?"

Robin watched, open-mouthed, as his father entered the hall, leaving him standing outside on the step. He doubted he would have been more surprised if his father had clouted him on the nose.

But there was some truth in what Rhys had said. What did he care?

The problem was, he did.

The hall door opened and Robin fully expected his father to come back out and finish what he'd started. Unfortunately, the soul who stepped outside was none other than Geoffrey of Fenwyck. Robin tried a weak smile.

"My lord."

Geoffrey looked at him with intense dislike. "Oh. 'Tis you."

Robin made Geoffrey a bow. Surely a bow couldn't go wrong.

But when he straightened, it was to see Geoffrey give him a look he might have given a plump and steaming pile of dung he'd narrowly avoided plunging his foot into. Fenwyck then grunted and brushed past Robin without further comment.

Apparently the girl was not to be won through her sire.

Then Robin clapped his hand to his head, hard enough to make himself flinch, though likely not hard enough to rid himself of his unwise thoughts. He was beginning to wonder what would be worse for him—winning Anne or not. If this was the state he was to be left in by the deed, perhaps he was better off without her.

He entered the hall to find Nicholas and Anne sitting close to the fire.

Nicholas was hovering over her as if she'd been a plate of sweets he intended to devour as quickly as possible whilst allowing no other a taste.

Robin was momentarily tempted to move his brother by force, but thought better of it. Then again, there was no sense in leaving Nicholas free to accustom himself to Anne's nearness.

"Nick, a word!" he called as neutrally as if he had nothing more important to discuss than what might stand to arrive upon the supper table within the hour.

"I'm busy," his brother returned, not looking away from Anne.

Robin decided then that perhaps familial murder wasn't such a poor idea. He gritted his teeth as he crossed the room, trying to keep his fingers loose and not clenched into a purposeful fist. He stopped directly beside his brother.

"Your horse, I believe, has thrown a shoe," Robin said. "You should see to it."

Nicholas only looked at him and raised an eyebrow. "I believe Father has a blacksmith for that kind of thing. Why don't you take the beast yourself? As you can see, I am much occupied at the moment."

"I believe this is something that requires your personal overseeing. You wouldn't want to have your horse lamed by your inattentions, would you?"

"I'm sure my horse will keep for a few more moments."

Robin looked at his brother and hoped the lad could see his own death in Robin's eyes. Nicholas merely smiled serenely. Robin knew his brother was enjoying himself immensely and that irritated him further.

"You should go," Robin growled. *"Now."*

"Can't," Nicholas said cheerfully. "Have things to do here."

Robin seethed silently. Well, short of taking the oaf by the ear and hauling him out of the hall bodily, there was nothing more he could do to distract Nicholas from his purpose.

And then Robin espied the empty stool next to Anne.

Robin planted himself upon it with all the alacrity of a pig leaping upon fresh slops. He looked at his brother archly, daring him to issue a challenge—any sort of challenge which would allow Robin the opportunity to justifiably beat him senseless.

"You've mud in your hair," Nicholas remarked. "And something else that smells rather foul. Perhaps you should go have a wash?"

Robin was halfway to his feet, his fists at the ready, when the import of his brother's words struck him.

Did he smell foul?

Unchivalrous and unrefined as he might have been, even he knew that a man did not leave a favorable impression on a maid if he reeked of manure. Robin found himself crouched uncomfortably between standing and sitting and could do nothing but surreptitiously sniff, on the off chance that Nicholas had things aright.

He smelled dung, but that could have been on his boots. It was acceptable on one's boots, of that he was certain.

And then, just as he was trying to decide whether he should continue on to a stand or gracefully return to a sit, he felt the lightest of touches on his arm.

"'Tis but a bit of mud, Nicky."

It was the voice of an angel and Robin felt the import of it wash over him like a soothing wave. He hardly dared look at her, lest he see laughter lurking in her eyes, but he found himself powerless to stop. Her face was turned away from him so he couldn't divine her expression, but her hand was still upon his arm. Before he could truly unravel the mystery of her touch and what it might mean, she had removed her hand and clasped them both in her lap again.

That was enough for him.

Robin sat.

And he glared up at his brother.

"'Tis but a bit of mud, idiot," he said with a growl.

"It doesn't smell of mud," Nicholas said, sniffing enthusiastically. "'Tis definitely dung. Anne, have a care lest the stench leave you faint."

Robin suddenly found himself staring into pale green eyes and he could do nothing but blink stupidly in return. Then she smiled a bit and the sight almost felled him where he sat.

"Montgomery and John boasted of their victory," she said. "It was kind of you to give it to them, even if it left you the one lolling in the dirt."

"Dung," Nicholas repeated. "Dung. Possibly something even more foul. Is that possible, do you think, Anne? Something fouler than dung? Whatever it is, Robin seems to have rolled himself liberally in it."

Anne turned her head to look at a small commotion near the hall door. Robin looked at Nicholas and glared.

"Death," he mouthed.

Nicholas's returning look was full of meaning Robin couldn't mistake.

His brother intended to woo Anne. And he wanted Robin out of his way.

Before Robin could rise and throttle him, Nicholas had taken his leave of Anne and crossed the floor to greet Fenwyck as he entered the hall.

"Perfect," Robin muttered. He turned to Anne, intent on asking her if she cared to escape the hall before they had to watch what would surely be one of the more nauseating events in history—namely Nicholas flattering Anne's father—but Anne was already pushing herself to her feet.

"Best see to supper," she said.

And then she was gone.

Robin was tempted to offer her his aid, but that would have removed him from earshot of Nicholas and Geoffrey and he had no intentions of missing out on any of that conversation—should he be able to stomach it. There was no sense in not knowing exactly what his brother was about.

It would give him something to say when he eulogized the fool.

For there was not a means conceived in either Heaven or Hell by which Nicholas de Piaget would woo and win the lady Anne. Robin wondered why he had begun the morn with such confusion clouding his brain. Anne was his. She had always been his. And if Nicholas thought differently, it was past time Robin disabused him of that notion. Then he would turn his own thoughts to how Anne might be won.

Then he caught a whiff of himself. Perhaps Nicholas had it aright. Well, there was no sense in giving either Fenwyck or his daughter a reason to think poorly of him.

Robin left the hall at a run, planning on a quick wash, then a return for eavesdropping.

11

Anne stood near the hearth and watched several things that currently un-folded before her.

There were the preparations for supper, of course. That was nothing unusual. Anne had made a visit to the kitchen, assured herself that every-thing was proceeding as Gwen would want it, then returned and watched the hall be laid for supper. That was an appealing enough sight, for she was hungry, but it was not what held her attention.

Her father was currently holding court with Nicholas. Anne couldn't help but feel a bit grateful for that, for it saved her the bother of having to dodge her sire's meaningful glances. Indeed, since he'd begun to speak with Nicholas an hour ago, he seemed to have forgotten that he had meaningful glances to send her way.

And then Robin entered the hall. His hair was dripping wet, as was the majority of his tunic. Anne suspected that perhaps his brother's words had spurred him to action after all. She watched as he walked up to his brother and her father. Nicholas elbowed him aside and stood before him, apparently blocking Robin's access to her father. Robin merely made himself a place on Nicholas's other side.

Her father pushed him out of the circle that time.

Anne continued to watch their little dance with astonishment. By the saints, what were they about?

"It looks, sister, as if you might be here longer than you think," Amanda said.

Anne looked at her foster sister, who had suddenly appeared at her side. "What do you mean?"

"They're trying to woo your sire," Amanda said wisely. "I've seen it dozens of times. Doesn't look as if Robin's having much success."

"My father doesn't like him, I don't think."

Amanda snorted. "It pains me to tell you this, Anne, but I can understand completely. Robin's impossible. Intolerable. I can't imagine what you see in him."

The sigh escaped her before she could stop it. And once it was out, there was no sense in not following it up with the words.

"He's beautiful," she said.

Amanda grunted in a most unladylike manner. "I'll give you that, but his manners more than make up for that."

"He can be very sweet," Anne protested.

Amanda turned and looked at her with an open mouth. "Sweet?" she echoed.

"Occasionally," Anne clarified.

"I don't think your father agrees."

Anne looked at the dance in progress to find Nicholas and her sire making every effort to keep Robin outside their conversings.

"Mayhap Nicky offers for you," Amanda said quietly.

Anne shook her head. "He only does it because he thinks, for what reason I cannot fathom, that the doing of it will irritate Robin."

"Men," Amanda said grimly. "Why can they not confine their games to the battlefield?"

"The thrill of conquest," Anne said. "Why else?"

"Ugh," Amanda said. "Here they come. I will slap them both if I stay."

And Anne's last hope of a pleasant dinner walked away. She looked to find both Robin and Nicholas coming her way, fierce frowns adorning both their faces.

Anne couldn't help but wonder why Nicholas of Artane seemed determined to fair stitch himself into her clothes. She couldn't believe he was interested in her. And she couldn't imagine that her father would give her to him. He was the second son and Fenwyck would never settle for that.

Besides, Nicholas would be fortunate indeed to last the evening, what with the glares Robin had been casting his way. Perhaps the battle would be conceded before it was fought. Not that it would have done him any good to fight it anyway, Robin had her heart in his keeping, whether he knew it or not, and whether he wanted it or not. She watched him walk toward her and wondered how it was she could watch him from a distance and understand him so well, yet when she drew to within ten paces of him, her logic fled. When he glared down at her with flashing eyes, her temper immediately rose to the surface and found voice. Or she retreated and wept. She'd done that often enough in the past. Her feigned cheerfulness served her only until she reached the safety of her chamber.

She jumped slightly as she realized Nicholas was standing in front of her, looking down at her with a smile.

"Green becomes you," he said, raising her hand to his lips. "But so do all the other colors you wear. Anne, you are nothing short of stunning."

"Nick, stop slobbering on her." Robin pushed his brother aside and took her hand. "Come and sit, Anne. I want to look at your wrist."

Anne pulled her hand away so sharply, she fell against Nicholas. She pushed away from him just as quickly.

"My wrist is fine. By the saints, stop hounding me. The both of you."

Nicholas pushed Robin out of the way and offered his arm. "Will my lady permit me to escort her to the table?"

"Nay, I will—"

Anne turned and walked away before she clacked their heads together. Perhaps they were amused by their game, but she was beginning to find it intolerable.

She took her seat and immediately found herself flanked by the eldest Artane lads. Robin couldn't have pulled his chair any closer; neither could Nicholas. Anne surrendered for the evening since there was indeed little hope of escape, unless she hiked up her skirts and climbed over the table. She sat back and sincerely hoped Robin and his brother would not begin a war with her as the main battlefield.

A servant leaned over and poured wine into the large cup she shared with Nicholas. The girl's elbow caught Anne sharply on the shoulder and Anne turned and looked up at the girl with faint annoyance.

But her annoyance changed to surprise when she saw the glare the maid was giving her.

She blinked. By that time, the girl's expression had become one of a long-suffering sort of sullenness that Anne had become well acquainted with at her father's hall. It was an unusual thing to see here. At Artane the servants were treated well; Fenwyck could not boast the same fairness.

The girl pulled away and retreated behind the table. Anne turned back to her meal and shrugged off her bewilderment. She'd been imagining things. Perhaps the girl had thought Anne at fault for being in her way.

And then she heard a sound that set the hairs on the back of her neck to standing:

The unmistakable jangle of a bracelet.

Anne looked behind her in surprise, but the girl was gone. She looked around at the table and wondered if she nigh on to driving herself daft. Tankards were clanking as they were thrust together, spoons rattled, daggers clanked as they met with spoons. Then Anne looked down the table to see Isabelle holding her arm aloft. A bracelet gleamed in the firelight.

Anne blew out her breath in relief. Her relief was magnified by the fact that she hadn't been fool enough to tell anyone of her fears. The saints only knew what sort of rumors that would start—about her state of mind this time.

Nicholas tasted the wine, then turned the cup and held it for Anne. She looked down at the golden goblet, knowing that if she put her lips in the most convenient place, it would be the same place Nicholas's lips had been. It was a lover's custom. Anne lifted her eyes and looked into Nicholas's gentle expression.

"Drink, my love."

Anne began to do just that when her movement was stopped abruptly by a brawny arm in her way. Robin snatched the cup away and poured the contents into the pitcher a page standing behind him was carrying.

"Drink it all yourself, lad," Robin growled.

"Thank you, my lord!"

Anne opened her mouth to retort when she caught sight of his thunderous expression, which was directed over her head at his brother. She shut her mouth and leaned back against her chair.

"If you two are going to do battle," she said with a sigh, "please do it outside."

"Robin is a bit testy, love," Nicholas said cheerfully. "I don't think he's been sleeping well."

"She is not your *love*," Robin growled.

"Look, Anne, at the fine meats before us tonight," Nicholas said, closing his fingers gently over her wounded wrist. "What will you have? The fowl looks particularly fine this eve. Or perhaps the eel. Nay, I think we'll start with the boar. I can smell the fine sauce from here."

Anne watched as Nicholas's fingers were removed from her arm and Robin's placed there. He pulled her right arm gently toward him until she had no choice but to shift in her chair so she faced him.

"I'm trying to eat," she said pointedly. "And with your brother, if you don't mind."

"Nick can feed you whilst I look at this," Robin said gruffly. "I don't trust his methods of healing."

Anne forced herself not to tremble at his touch. Impersonal or not, it was gentle. She stared at his long, tanned fingers as they unwrapped the binding on her wrist, then she felt his calluses as he trailed his fingers gently over the bruised flesh. He lifted his head and looked at her.

"Does it pain you still?"

Anne had difficulty finding her wits to speak. It had been years since she had been this close to Robin. Or, more accurately, been this close to Robin and not been either shouting at him or giving him a false smile before she fled to weep in private over his harshness.

And he was no longer the hot-tempered lad of ten-and-nine. He was a man, not a boy, and being so close to him and having his hands on her skin made her want to bolt. Or faint. She couldn't decide which.

"Anne?"

She blinked. "It still hurts a bit when I move it."

"Has it occurred to you, then, to keep it still?"

She started to snap out a retort, then she caught sight of the faint twinkle in his eye. She blinked a time or two, certain her eyes were deceiving her. He couldn't be teasing her. Robin had forgotten how to jest years ago.

"I don't think the cloths are stiff enough," she managed.

"Then you should have let me tend it to start with," he said, sitting back and recapturing his brisk tone. "I'll have to splint it now. After supper. And I suppose I'll have to serve myself since you're unable to do it."

Anne pursed her lips. Apparently his lack of manners had robbed him of a supper companion, for he had no one with which to share his trencher.

Nicholas put his arm around Anne's shoulders. "Pay him no heed, Anne. He forgets he is now in a civilized hall, not out in his tent with his men. Here, I've chosen all the best pieces of meat for you. Shall I feed you, or can you manage?"

"By the saints, Nick, she isn't helpless. Stop hovering over her."

"I'll hover as much as I like, Rob. You aren't her lord and master. If she doesn't want me hovering, she can tell me so herself."

"She doesn't like to be fussed over, you fool."

Anne sat back and listened to them talk about her as if she weren't there. Robin was annoyed and Nicholas was fast becoming that way. She suppressed the urge to crawl under the table.

"And I say a woman needs to be fussed over. 'Tis nothing but the chivalrous thing to do."

"And I say you're treating her like a cripple. Her leg is weak, not useless, and her hands are perfectly capable of bringing food to her mouth. Don't pity her."

"I'm trying to woo her," Nicholas growled.

"She's *not* yours to woo," Robin returned, just as darkly.

"And just who are you to determine whom she belongs to?"

Robin rose so quickly, his chair almost toppled over. "Outside."

"Gladly."

Anne sighed as they both strode angrily across the rushes. It was another peaceful night in the de Piaget household.

But apparently they were fighting over her and that was something to be examined. Anne wondered if anyone would notice if she left the table to savor the miracle. She looked about her carefully.

Her father was deep in discussion with Gwen, which boded very well for her being allowed to escape the hall. The rest of the family and garrison were applying themselves industriously to their supper and the noise in the hall was formidable. Anne slipped out of her chair and made her way up the stairs. Perhaps a bit of fresh air would help her see more clearly.

Though she wasn't sure what it was she was supposed to see. Nicholas was flattering her, but it couldn't be more than that. Robin was doing the saints only knew what. Perhaps he lusted after her wealth. Perhaps he was merely trying to thwart his brother.

Perhaps he had lost his mind somewhere in his travels over the past five years.

She clapped her hand to her head, and then turned her attentions to getting herself up to the battlements without getting killed. The memory of being pushed down the steps was almost enough to make her turn around and go back down to the light and comfort of the great hall.

But then she would have to face Artane's eldest lads when they returned from their brawl and she didn't think she was equal to that task. Besides, there were guards aplenty on the roof.

She would certainly be safer alone than finding herself squeezed between two Artane brothers who seemed bent on killing each other.

12

Robin whirled on his brother the moment they were outside, and slammed him back up against the hall door.

"Leave her be," Robin snarled. "She's not yours and she never will be."

"Let Fenwyck determine that," Nicholas said stubbornly.

"Damn you," Robin shouted, "she is *not* a mare at market! She is not available for you to look over and decide that a tryst with her would be amusing sport for the winter. She does not want a husband and even if she did want one, that man would not be you!"

Nicholas leaned back against the door and folded his arms over his chest. A lazy smile formed on his face.

"Is that so," Nicholas drawled.

Robin snagged his brother by the front of his tunic and dragged him down the stairs, feeling that the dirt would be more suited to beating Nicholas senseless than the top of the steps.

"She is not for sale," Robin growled, releasing Nicholas.

"Then you'd best pass those tidings to the garrison for I know of several who think she just might be."

"Who?" Robin demanded.

"Careful, brother," Nicholas said with a grin. "If I didn't know you so well, I would think you were jealous."

Robin grabbed Nicholas by the tunic and shook him. "Names!"

Nicholas only grinned again. "I wouldn't presume to sentence any lads to a thrashing from you, my lord. I suppose you'll have to discover their identities on your own."

"I know the identity of one man already," Robin said pointedly, "and that man would be wise to turn his attentions elsewhere."

"Why should I?" Nicholas asked pleasantly. "You've made no claim on her."

Robin had absolutely nothing to say to contradict that, so he contented himself with plowing a fist into his brother's belly and stomping back up the steps. Perhaps he would do well to keep a closer eye on mistress Anne, just to keep her safe. The first lad to look at her with lust in his eye would die a slow and painful death. It was a perfect reason not to let her out of his sight.

He strode back into the hall and immediately noted that Anne was not in her place. He fixed Amanda with a glare.

"Where is she?"

Amanda smiled serenely. "Gone."

"Where?"

"I daresay she thought to escape your foul temper by hiding on the battlements. She often goes there—"

Robin vaulted over the table and jogged to the stairs. He wanted to sprint there but didn't want anyone to think him anxious. By the saints, she could fall and kill herself and no one would be the wiser until they saw her body on the ground! What had possessed his father to allow her to wander up there without an escort?

He ran up the various flights of stairs to the battlements and burst through the door onto the walkway. He spotted her immediately and walked over to her without hesitation. He turned her away from the wall and began to pull her toward the door.

"What are you doing?" she gasped.

"Taking you downstairs."

"But—"

"Leading you along is the only thing which keeps me from wringing your neck here on the walkway, Anne. Do not argue with me."

She didn't. She wasn't exactly coming with him enthusiastically, but she wasn't fighting him either. Robin wasn't sure if he should be pleased or terrified by that.

He led her down to his mother's solar and shut the door behind them with his foot.

"Light a fire, won't you?" she asked quickly.

He looked at her, and felt himself grow weak under her gaze. By the saints, she had become a beauty. And it wasn't all just the fairness of her face. The quiet inner beauty she had always possessed had somehow found its way to the outside. It was no wonder half the garrison wanted to offer for her. The saints be praised that her father wouldn't give her to any less than a lord's heir. At least he had no reason to fear a mere knight stealing her away from under his nose.

"Robin?"

"The fire," he said, "aye, I remember. Do not start your harping on me already, mistress Anne."

She turned her face away. Robin led her to a chair near the hearth and cursed under his breath. He hadn't meant to hurt her feelings. In truth, he had no idea what he was about. He'd been fuming for a se'nnight that he couldn't seem to get Anne away from Nicholas, and now that he had her, he wanted to flee.

It was enough to make him want to throw up his hands and surrender.

He built up the fire, then sat back on his heels and looked at his lady. The moment he met her eyes, she averted her gaze. So she cared nothing for him. He couldn't blame her. He didn't care much for himself of late either.

He sat down and reached for a piece of kindling. She'd need a splint on her wrist. Nicholas knew better than to leave an injury such as that alone. Robin cursed under his breath as he worked. It should have been splinted and wrapped immediately. It would likely take her twice as long to recover from it now.

The rustle of fabric drew his attention and he looked up to see Anne rising.

"Where are you off to? Sit back down."

"I'm not going to stay any longer and listen to you curse me," she said stiffly.

"I was cursing Nicholas, not you. He should have splinted your wrist. Sit back down. I won't chase you the next time."

She hesitated, then she slowly sank back down to her chair.

And for some reason, that hurt him—likely because he knew he was hurting her. Didn't she know he would chase her as many times as she wanted? Didn't she have any idea that she was the reason he hadn't come home in five years? Didn't she have any idea that she was one of the reasons he trained until he dropped each day? He never, *ever* wanted to see her look at him and find him lacking.

Her insecurity broke his heart. Sweet, lovely Anne who should have had nothing but smiles filling her days, who deserved a gallant knight to court her, and a body that was perfect and didn't pain her.

Yet what did she have instead? A leg that was lame and a surly knight who couldn't string two words together to form a decent compliment.

Robin bent again to his whittling, not liking in the least the emotions that raged inside him. He could never give Anne what she needed, be what she deserved, and he was a fool to want to. He finished with the thin strips of wood and tucked his knife back into his belt. Then he looked around him for the cloth that had initially bound Anne's wrist.

She held it out and he took it. He laid the cloth on her lap and placed her wrist on it.

"Hold the splints, Anne girl, while I wrap it," he said, placing the wood where he wanted it.

"What did you call me?"

He looked up and met her pale eyes. "I don't remember," he lied. It had been a slip, an unwitting indication of his thoughts. He hadn't called her that since before his humiliation at Baldwin's hands. It had been his pet name for her, his alone. He'd broken Nicholas's nose the first time Nick had taken up calling her that. He resumed his work, feeling acutely uncomfortable. Gentleness was not in his nature. Soft words and silly endearments were not in his vocabulary. He was a warrior, not a woman, and he had no time for foolishness.

"I don't want you using this arm," he said as he tied the two ends of the cloth together. "No sewing, no cooking, no carrying. If I see you doing the like, you will regret it, and rest assured I will be watching you closely for the next se'nnight to see that you obey me."

"I am not one of your men, Robin."

He slipped his fingers under hers and rubbed his thumb over her knuckles. "I know that, Anne." He lifted her hand to his lips and kissed it roughly. He didn't dare meet her eyes.

And then he realized how foolish a thing it had been. He released her hand quickly and stood. "'Tis time you were abed. Let me bank the fire and I'll see you downstairs. I don't want you tripping again." He carefully tended the fire, then brushed off his hands and turned to look at Anne. She hadn't moved. She was looking at her hand as if she'd never seen it before.

Robin wiped off his hands again and crossed the two steps that separated him from her. He held down his hand and called her name quietly. She looked up at him and her eyes were full of tears.

Robin suppressed the urge to run.

Anne put her hand into his and he gently pulled her to her feet.

"You're overly tired," he said gruffly. "Rest is what you need."

She nodded, but she didn't move. Robin hesitated, wondering what he dared do. What he wanted to do was pull her into his arms; what he dreaded was having her push away in disgust. Or would she laugh at him? That he couldn't have borne—

The door burst open and Nicholas stood there, disheveled. He met Robin's eyes.

"The page," he said, holding on to the doorframe for support. "The one you gave my wine to. That was Stephen of Hardwiche, wasn't it?"

"Aye. What has befallen the lad?"

Nicholas looked at him, his gray eyes wide with shock and horror. "I think he's dead."

13

Edith walked sedately down the passageway, doing her damndest to appear calm. She nodded regally to whatever servant she passed and slipped by members of Artane's guard with as little notice as possible. She reached the base of the tower steps, took a deep breath, and climbed them slowly. After she reached the landing, she took another deep, calming breath, opened the door, and stepped inside the chamber. Once the door was closed behind her, she gathered all her reserves of control and asked the question she could not believe she was forced to utter.

"Dead?" she queried politely.

Maude was naught but a huddled mass against the wall, quivering and sniveling. Baldwin loomed over her with his fist raised. He turned to glare at Edith.

"Aye, dead," he snarled. "And this silly twit here was the one to do it."

And then he did something that forever damned him in Edith's eyes. He reached out and kicked Maude with all his strength.

It was one thing to kill a man. Even torturing a man was acceptable in several circumstances. Tormenting a woman could also be done, should the offense be grave enough. But beating a woman who was already cowering on the floor, who had no defenses, who was unable to fight back . . .

Edith knew that somehow she would have to reconcile that with what she was doing to Anne, but for now all she could see was herself in Maude's place, trying to avoid the battering fists and flailing feet of her own sire.

Then again, Baldwin was Sedgwick's get. What else could she expect?

"Cease," she said, striding across the chamber and pushing her brother away. She stood between him and Maude. "I'll see to her."

Baldwin drew his hand back, likely to slap her, but she stood her ground. She was certain he could see the hate in her eyes. When his own anger faltered and he lowered his hand, she knew she had won at least that battle.

"I should punish you as well for this," he growled.

"Do, and you'll regret it," she said calmly.

"You wouldn't dare."

"The only way to be sure would be to kill me now."

He looked to be contemplating it, then he cursed most foully and turned away. "That sport is too easy."

Of course. She pursed her lips at his contemptuous tone, but said nothing further. There was no point in trying to humiliate him. Robin had done that well enough that morn. She had watched them earlier and seen Artane dispatch him with barely an effort. Her brother's bluster was a great deal of wounded pride, surely, and perhaps encouraging him to assuage that pride would keep him out from underfoot until she could decide further how to proceed.

"Perhaps you'd find better sport in the lists," she suggested.

He glowered at her. "'Twas a moment's misstep this morn," he said.

"Doubtless." She smiled at him sympathetically. "I suppose we all have them." Some fewer than others, but she didn't bother to point that out to him.

Baldwin pointed a shaking finger at Maude. "See to her. If you don't, I will, and rest assured, they won't find her to bury her."

Edith watched him leave the chamber and wondered if he actually had the spine for such a deed. He boasted of it often, but she'd never seen the fruits of his foul labors. She very much suspected that he didn't have the bollocks for the like. She wondered if he would even be capable of seeing through any of the tasks she intended to assign him.

Good assassins were always in such short supply.

Edith sighed and turned to kneel down next to Maude. She lifted the blubbering girl's face up and looked dispassionately at the swelling already apparent. There was one thing she could say for her brother: he knew how to use his fists to their best advantage.

"I told you but a little, Maude," Edith said quietly.

Maude only whimpered.

"The temptation was too strong, wasn't it?" Edith asked.

Maude nodded and sniveled.

Edith sighed. It looked as if Maude's usefulness had come to an end, at least for the immediate future.

"You'll rest now," Edith said. "No more schemes until you've rested. Indeed, I think it best that you do nothing more until I tell you otherwise. Understood?"

Maude nodded jerkily.

"I think beating a woman is despicable," Edith continued. "I would never do it."

"You w-wouldn't?" Maude asked.

Edith shook her head. "A clean death is much more dignified, don't you think? And in this intrigue we're engaged in, disobedience would merit the like."

Maude looked at her with wide eyes.

"You won't disobey again, will you, Maude?"

"Nay, Lady Edith," Maude whispered.

"Good," Edith said, smiling. "Stay here until you've recovered. If anyone asks you about your bruises, say you fell down the stairs. They won't ask any more."

"Aye, my lady."

"You'll do nothing until I tell you otherwise."

"Aye, my lady."

Edith nodded, rose, and brushed off her hands. She left the tower chamber. Supper was over, the keep in an uproar and there would be no peace for her that night to sit and think on her plans. That likely wouldn't have served her anyway. Now it was best that she show herself to the family and express the appropriate horror and outrage. She could think on the morrow about how best to proceed.

Perhaps 'twas time she haunted the lists and watched Baldwin at his work. The saints only knew what kind of mischief she might find to stir up there. If nothing else, the fresh air might give her a new idea or two.

She shook her head as she descended to the great hall. Too much poison. By the saints, was she required to do all this herself?

14

Anne stood on the steps leading up to the great hall and watched the scene before her in the courtyard. There was the wagon, of course, bearing young Stephen of Hardwiche's body. The lady Gwennelyn was already mounted. Rhys's men were preparing to go, checking their gear and such.

Rhys stood apart with Robin, no doubt giving him last minute instructions. Anne watched Robin listen and marveled at his patience. He certainly hadn't shown any with her the night before. He'd been gruff in his mother's solar as he splinted her wrist and she very much suspected that he had been cursing her right along with his brother. Once Nicholas had arrived with the grim tidings, Robin had dragged her down the steps behind him, put her in a chair in the great hall, then ignored her for the rest of the evening.

Then again, he had kissed her hand.

In a rough, unpolished sort of way.

She looked down at that hand, then clasped it with the other and hid it back beneath her cloak. Her hands were white and they were shaking. She knew the reason why. It had come to her as she'd sat in the great hall the night before, looking at young Stephen's body laid out before the hearth. The solar door slamming she could have understood. Losing her footing on the stairs she also could have understood. She could have imagined being pushed.

But almost drinking wine that had killed a child?

That she could not ignore and the realization the night before had almost left her faint.

Someone was trying to kill her.

She'd sat in her chair the night before and trembled. She'd watched the goings-on around her and shaken with the horror of it all. She'd said nothing of it to anyone. It had seemed almost too foolish a notion to give voice to. After all, who was to say the wine hadn't been meant for someone else?

Cook had found the lad slumped in a corner of the kitchen, an empty jug at his elbow. It could have been drunk by anyone, though Anne remembered vividly Robin's rudeness in snatching the cup from her and giving it to Stephen. Had he not done so, she would have found herself in that baggage wain, dead and not minding at all the journey back to Fenwyck.

It was enough to weaken her knees.

She found herself sitting on the steps before she knew she intended to do so. Then before she could understand how she had gotten there, she felt hands on her arms. She was shaken so forcefully, her teeth began to clack together.

"Are you unwell?" Robin demanded urgently.

"Stop shaking me," she said. Her head was starting to spin uncomfortably. "Robin, please stop."

He knelt down on the step beneath her and looked at her with clouded eyes. "Why did you sit?"

"My head pained me," she lied. There was no sense in telling him the truth. He likely wouldn't believe her anyway.

A long shape sat on the step next to her. Anne looked to her left to find Miles there. His customary grave look was even graver than usual. He put his arm around her, then looked at his brother.

"Rob, think you 'twas poison?"

"What else could it be?"

"Bad eel?"

Robin glared at his brother.

Miles shrugged apologetically.

"Well," Robin said, "I know of no malady but strong poison that could kill so quickly. It could be nothing else."

"But why?" Miles asked. "Who would want to kill a hapless child?"

"I don't know. And I don't envy Father the trip to Hardwiche."

"Stephen was the favored son," Anne whispered. "The youngest, but the most well beloved."

"At least your sire goes with him," Miles offered. "That may help. They are related, aren't they?"

"Aye," she said. "My stepsister's husband is Hardwiche's youngest brother."

"Well, then," Robin said with pursed lips, "perhaps your sire will be of some use after all."

Anne looked up to see her father standing behind Robin. He was less than gentle in pushing Robin aside.

"Anne, a word," he said curtly.

Robin regained his balance, stood, and offered Anne his hand. Between that and Miles's arm still around her shoulders, Anne found herself on her feet.

"Shall I stay?" Miles asked with a slight frown.

Anne watched her father push Robin and send him stumbling down the stairs. Miles was hauled away by his tunic and sent on his way with much the same results. Anne looked at her sire.

"That was unnecessary," she said simply.

"And that is the last I'll hear of that kind of disrespect from you," he said angrily. "I can see that being here breeds that in you and I'll not have it any longer. I'll return within the month. Be prepared to leave when I arrive."

There was nothing else she could do to delay her day of reckoning and she knew it well. She swallowed with difficulty. "As you will, Father."

"No more reprieves, Anne. Rhys fair talked himself into a faint trying to convince me I should leave you here until winter. I'll not do it, do you understand?"

"Aye, Father."

Geoffrey grunted, then turned and walked down the stairs. She caught a side view of the glare he gave Robin before he continued to his horse. Anne watched him mount and ride through the gates without a backward glance. Well, at least he was leaving, though she suspected it was under protest and with a great deal of reluctance. Her freedom would last another pair of fortnights. It was the best she could ask for.

The rest of the company followed suit, followed by the wagon bearing the boy's body. Anne didn't breathe easily until the gates were shut.

Once the dust had settled, Robin strode off to the lists, likely to reduce whatever lads he could find there to nothing. Miles made her a low bow, then disappeared after his brother, likely to clean up whatever bodies were sure to be littering the lists after Robin's work was finished.

Anne sat back down on the steps and watched until the courtyard was completely empty. She tortured herself with visions of her being the one to be leaving, riding down the way to the outer gates, looking back for a final sight of the home she loved so much. It was enough to bring tears to her eyes.

And it was such a ridiculous thing to do, she could hardly believe she was wallowing in her misery so fully— and so unnecessarily. There was no sense in ruining her last few days of freedom with grim thoughts about the future. The future would arrive in its own good time. The best thing she could do would be to enjoy what time remained her.

She stood, stretched, and carefully made her way down the steps. One of the pleasures she enjoyed at Artane that she didn't at Fenwyck was the freedom to walk where she willed it. She hugged the walls of the lists as a general rule, for the distance was manageable and aid was ever near her should she need it.

She steadfastly refused to think about the fact that this morn she might also have the pleasure of watching Robin while she took her own exercise.

It took her longer than she would have liked to reach the lists, but even so she couldn't complain. The day was fine, the sun shining, and her cloak protected her from the chill. It couldn't last, the weather and her freedom, so she savoured it fully while she could.

She walked along near the wall, trying to keep out of anyone's way. The lists were never empty, but since Robin and Nicholas's return, they were a busier place than usual. Apparently Robin had surrounded himself with men who were as driven as he—either that or his handpicked guard feared he would truly do them in if they didn't train as hard as he did.

As usual, she set herself a goal, for there was no sense in not pushing herself while she could. She would make one circuit of the lists before she allowed herself to look for Robin. Her second trek could be made while stealing glances at him every few paces. The third time, should she have the means of managing it, she would look at him fully and not be shamed by it. If she managed to walk that much in one morn, she would deserve whatever pleasure she could take for herself.

She continued on her way slowly, forcing her leg to straighten with each step she took, to accept her weight, to work the muscles that would have rather remained idle. As the pains shot up through her leg into her hip, she cursed herself soundly for having been so inactive. Sitting and sewing peacefully came with a heavy price she had paid often enough in the past. She should have known better this time—

"Anne!"

A man's scream made her jerk her head up in surprise, then she shrieked as she was knocked to the ground. Her breath had been completely driven from her. If that had been the worst of it, she would have been relieved. But having a mailed man sprawled atop her was fast crushing the life from her.

"Move," she mouthed, trying to suck in air.

A mail coif was shoved back from the wearer's head and Anne had a mouthful of dark hair as the man turned his head to look back over his shoulder.

"Robin," she gasped, "I cannot breathe." Unbidden tears of pain sprang to her eyes. He was pinning her leg under his thighs and she thought he just might break it soon. "Please!"

Robin heaved himself off her and rose, leaving her lying in the dirt. Anne tried to sit up, but found she couldn't. All she could do was stare up at the sky and wonder if by some miracle her form would ever again draw breath.

It returned slowly, but moving was still beyond her. She looked above her and saw that Robin was holding the head of a mace in his hand.

"Whose is this?" he bellowed.

A knight fell to his knees. "My lord, it was an accident!"

"You bloody whoreson, you almost killed her!" Robin thundered. He jerked the knight to his feet and shoved him. "Did your master never teach you to check your weapons? A bloody good thing you're my father's man, else I'd kill you where you stand!"

"I'd sooner kill myself than harm the lady Anne," the knight said fervently. "I vow it, my lord. I checked it before I wielded it."

"And I say you didn't," Robin snarled. "If the lady Anne's life is so precious to you, why is it she almost found herself without a head on her shoulders thanks to you?"

The knight looked as devastated as Anne felt. She knew him to be one of Rhys's guardsmen and a goodly warrior. She couldn't believe he would actually try to harm her.

Then again, she never would have believed anyone would try to poison her, either.

Robin looked about him, cursing loudly and fiercely. "Miles!" he shouted.

Anne realized that Miles was kneeling at her head only because he grasped her briefly by the shoulders before he stood and faced his brother.

"Aye?"

"Take this fool and put him in the dungeon."

The knight protested his innocence, but evidently Miles's reputation was not far behind Robin's, for all it took was a drawing of his blade to have the man falling suddenly silent. Anne couldn't twist her head to see what the outcome of that would be, but she assumed Miles had prodded the poor man toward the great hall.

"Sir Richard," Robin snapped, "see that all these weapons are checked again. By you personally."

"Aye, my lord."

"You will find yourself in the dungeon with Sir Edward if you fail me."

Anne lifted her eyebrow at that. Richard of Moncrief was Rhys's man and she was half surprised he took the insult from Robin. Then again, she'd never seen Robin quite so fierce before. She was almost flattered at his concern.

Then she found herself in his sights.

And she sincerely wished she were capable of getting up and hastening away.

He stomped over and glared down at her for a goodly moment before he took her by the arms and hauled her to her feet.

"And you!" he shouted. "What in hell's name were you thinking to come out here?"

Her breath had returned enough for some speech, though she suspected it wouldn't be enough to cool Robin's temper. "Well, I walk here often—"

"This is no place for a woman," Robin bellowed, "especially one who hasn't the sense to watch where she's going. I never want to see you out here again by yourself, is that clear?"

Had she actually had pleasant feelings toward this man? She was a fool.

"I'll go where I please—" she began haughtily.

"You'll be locked in your chamber if you don't obey me! Mindless wench, what were you thinking?" He shook her. "You could have been killed! Do your daydreaming somewhere besides the lists."

Anne had never been so embarrassed in her life. The garrison was standing not fifty paces away and she knew she couldn't have been fortunate enough not to have had them hear Robin's chastisement. She jerked herself away from Robin and turned to go back to the hall. She took only a pair of steps before her leg gave way and she fell to her hands and knees. Her mortification was complete.

Robin came to stand before her. "Pick yourself up and hie yourself back to the house," he growled. "You have no place here, Anne."

Anne watched his booted feet retreat and knew deep inside her that she had never hated Robin of Artane as much as she did in that moment.

Richard of Moncrief squatted down before her and held out his hands.

"Let me assist you, my lady," he said quietly.

"Get away from me, you baseborn wretch," she spat, her grief and shame crashing over her in a fierce wave. "I need no aid." She lifted her head and swept the rest of the men with a glare. "Begone! I'm no cripple, damn you all! Go!"

Anne knew she should rise, but she couldn't. All she could do was remain on her hands and knees and bow her head. At least that way she didn't have to look at the cluster of men that no doubt still watched her. Though they had retreated, she knew they were still there. And what a sight she must have made!

And it was a sight she would no longer provide for them. She lifted her head long enough to look for something by which she could lever herself to her feet. There was a bench pushed up against the wall, but it was a goodly distance away. It would have to do, for she could see nothing else useful.

She began to crawl.

15

Robin put his hands against the bailey wall and leaned against it, trying to catch his breath and ease the pain in his chest. He closed his eyes and prayed he was imagining things. With the handful of days he'd just endured, perhaps 'twas understandable that his wits were not at their sharpest. There was much of coincidence in this life. Perhaps he had just experienced a greater share of it of late than a normal man might.

Then again another man might not have seen the woman he loved in a crumpled heap at the bottom of the stairs.

Another man might not have recently stopped that same woman from drinking wine that would have poisoned her to death.

Another man surely wouldn't have watched the heavy spiked ball of a mace go flying through the air toward that woman's head. That was the most unsettling of all. 'Twas naught but chance that had left him walking toward her. He'd scarce turned in time to save her.

He couldn't shake the feeling that this had gone far past happenstance.

He pushed back from the wall, dragged his hands through his hair, and blew out his breath. He would go back to the hall and apologize to Anne. She would likely think he had spoken to her harshly. If she knew he'd done it out of fear and not malice, perhaps she would forgive him.

He turned, but before he could begin to walk, he saw a sight that was almost as terrible as the one he had almost been privy to.

Anne on her hands and knees, crawling.

He looked at her in dismay. By the saints, he'd never meant to reduce her to this!

She was making her way toward a bench. Just that effort looked to be costing her much. He spared the garrison a brief glance and saw a variety of emotions on their faces. Pity for the most part. Even Sedgwick's expression was a serious one. That was just as well for him. Robin would have likely killed him for anything else.

And then a handful of the men turned to look at him and Robin was faintly surprised to see anger in their faces and a goodly amount of accusation—as if he had been the one to put Anne in that position!

But hard on the heels of that came the realization that indeed he had. He could only speculate on the humiliation she felt and that he could certainly take credit for. That surely wasn't the worst. The saints only knew what kind of damage he had done to her by crushing her as he had.

Well, better crushed than dead. He met those damning looks with a glare of his own, then strode over and stopped in front of Anne.

"Anne—"

"Move," she said in a raspy whisper.

Robin's mail voiced a loud protest as he bent, took her by the arms, and lifted her to her feet. She swayed drunkenly and he clasped her to him. His hoped his mail would not pinch her—though he doubted it could be any more painful than what he'd already done to her.

"Release me," she said, trying to push away.

That was the last thing he would do. He could not stomach the sight of her on her hands and knees again. He put one arm under her knees, one arm behind her back, and swept her up.

"Put me down, you blighted bugger," she gasped.

Robin ignored her slander, knowing that he had been the one to teach her to curse in her youth.

He also ignored the flat of her hand across his face. He supposed he deserved it. He had humiliated her, but damnation, what did she expect? Was he to let her be killed without any effort made to stop it?

He continued to ignore her steady stream of curses as he carried her back to the hall. Had he ever thought of Anne as shy and retiring? Why, the woman could make a hardened warrior blush with her foulness.

"Anne, please," Robin said, exasperated. "I believe I've been left with little doubt about what you think of me."

Her curses gave way to tears. Robin felt his own eyes begin to sting. That he had been the one to wring such weeping from her was almost his undoing. He gritted his teeth and climbed the steps to the hall door. Damnation, what else was he to have done?

The great hall was empty save Amanda sitting by the fire. Robin paused, then scowled. His sister was staring off into nothingness as if she had naught but maidenly dreams as her most pressing occupation. He glared at her as he passed and was faintly gratified to find she had obviously felt the like, for she looked up in surprise.

"What happened?" she asked.

"I'll tell you later," Robin said shortly. "Fetch Nicholas to Father's bedchamber and don't eat or drink anything until we've had a chance to talk."

She blinked, then looked at Anne in his arms. "What is he babbling about, Anne?"

"By all the bloody saints, Amanda, will you for once just obey me?" he demanded. "Fetch Nick and do it now!"

His sister rose with a sigh he was certain she had intended should blow him over, but at least she was on her feet.

Robin paused, then another thought occurred to him. "After you've sent Nick, fetch Miles, the twins, and Isabelle as well," he called after her. "Bring them upstairs."

Amanda waved him away and left the great hall. Robin continued on his way up the stairs and down the passageway to his parents' bedchamber. No sense in not appropriating the finest for his lady while he was lord of Artane. He kicked open the door and then set Anne down on her feet in the passageway.

"Stay here," he commanded, taking a torch off the wall. He drew his sword and entered the chamber, pushing the firelight into each corner and checking under the bed. By the saints, a body wasn't even safe in his own home anymore.

He returned to find Anne leaning heavily against the doorframe. He put his arm around her shoulders, led her into the chamber, and placed her in a chair near the hearth. He built up the fire, taking more time than he needed to, but he knew he had things to say to his lady and he wasn't all that certain how to begin. It was time enough to gather at least a few of his thoughts. Once he was finished with his task, he remained on his knees and turned to look at her.

Her cheeks were smudged with dirt. Except, of course, for those trails of cleanliness her tears had left in their wake. Robin couldn't bear to see what might be revealed in her eyes, so he turned back to the fire. He took a deep breath for enough courage to put to her the questions he had to.

"You didn't fall down the stairs, did you?" he asked quietly.

She was silent for a moment or two. "Nay."

He dragged his hand through his hair and looked up at the ceiling as he let his breath out slowly. So it was as he feared. But who could possibly want to hurt her?

"Merciful saints above, Anne," he said with a sigh. "Who have you irritated lately besides me?"

He looked at her. She was looking at him, but her expression was not what he had expected. The hatred in her glance chilled him to the bone. He had been accustomed to looks of ill-disguised affection and undisguised annoyance, but hatred?

"Anne . . ." he began slowly.

She turned her face away and remained silent.

Robin would have cheerfully handed over all his teeth to have possessed a bit of Nicholas's glibness at that moment. The only looks of hatred he was accustomed to receiving were from those he prepared to put to the sword. He'd never had such a chilling glance from a woman.

Then again, he'd never left a woman trampled in the dirt before, either.

Perhaps Anne was angry with him over that. She had reason to be, he supposed. Perhaps she did but need a few moments to regain her composure and realize he hadn't done it out of malice. Perhaps if he turned her mind to other things, such as their current problem, she might forget that he had been the one to crush her. He cleared his throat purposefully.

"I could have believed you were clumsy enough to fall down the stairs," he began.

Anne didn't move.

Robin frowned at her lack of response, but continued on. "I also could have believed that Stephen had eaten something that made him feel poorly," he continued, "but Nick was up all night retching and mace heads do not simply fly off without some kind of aid. There is more to this than simple coincidence."

Still she made no move, gave no indication that she had heard him. Robin sighed heavily and rose.

"Very well," he said. "Perhaps rest is what you need. Let's have your boots off, then I'll carry you to bed. You'll be perfectly safe here for the present."

"Do not touch me."

Robin stopped before he did just that. "'Tis nothing I wouldn't do for Amanda," he said stiffly, "though with likely less care than I'll use now."

"Go away, Robin."

Robin stared down at her, his anger warring with his concern. Her pale hair was coming loose from her braid and strands of it fell around her face. She breathed poorly, as if it pained her to do so. He paused. Had he broken anything, falling on her as he had? He reached out and touched her hair as gently as he could.

"Anne, do you have pain anywhere?"

She ignored him. He watched as she slowly and with a good deal of effort turned herself away from him.

Robin sighed and stepped back. Well, 'twas obvious he would have none of her thoughts at present. Perhaps later, when her temper had cooled.

He was momentarily tempted to ask Nicholas to pry the tale from her, then he thought better of it. The last thing he wanted was Nicholas and Anne alone in the same chamber together. Nicholas would be charming and gallant and say just the right things. Robin would return to find Anne having swooned directly into his brother's arms. Nay, far better that she be forced to talk to him.

He would, however, reserve the right to talk to his brother himself. Despite Nicholas's flaws, which were indeed many and mainly sprang from his great love of the fairer species, he had a head for strategy. Robin had benefitted more than once from discussing tactics with his brother.

"I'll return as soon as I may," Robin said.

Anne said nothing. Indeed, she made no move to even indicate that she had heard him.

Robin was unsurprised, and in spite of everything, that almost cheered him. He'd known she wouldn't speak to him. At least he was learning to predict her reactions.

He left the bedchamber and closed the door behind him. The passageway was well lit, but even so there were patches of gloom along the corridor. Robin peered into them, but saw nothing amiss. He decided then that a guard would have to be posted outside the door. More than one set, likely. Indeed, the best thing to do was likely to have someone inside with Anne to protect her.

He paused.

Who better than he to be that guard?

He turned the thought over in his head until he saw his brother coming down the passageway. It was a thought worth pursuing, but later, when he had determined just how dire circumstances were. Perhaps Nicholas would be more able than he to judge if events were accidental, or if Robin had discovered something more sinister.

For once, Robin hoped his imagination had overpowered his good sense.

Nicholas came down the passageway, then stopped across the passageway from Robin. Robin looked at his brother and was momentarily chilled by the thought of how close he had come to losing not only Anne, but Nicholas too. Irritating though he might have been, Nicholas was his brother, after all, and Robin loved him dearly. It had been a passing unpleasant night, what with Nicholas being violently ill for the whole of it. He didn't look much better now.

"What?" Nicholas rasped. He swayed, then leaned heavily against the wall. "I've no stomach for riddles today."

"A mace head flew off a weapon today," Robin said.

"And?"

"If I hadn't thrown Anne to the ground, it would have struck her in the face."

Nicholas's jaw slipped down. "Nay."

"Am I imagining things," Robin asked, "or does there seem to be a pattern here?"

"No one else nearby? No other possible targets?"

Robin shook his head. "I was walking toward her, but it wasn't aimed at me."

Nicholas looked even paler, if that was possible. "It would seem," he said weakly, "there is something foul afoot."

"I thought so as well."

"Could we sit to discuss it?" Nicholas asked. "I vow I'll fall to my knees if I must stand any longer."

Robin moved to aid his brother only to find Amanda already there. She moved silently enough, when she wasn't screeching her complaints at him. She put Nicholas's arm over her shoulders and helped him into the bedchamber. Robin waited for the rest of his siblings, who were coming down the passageway. And as he watched the souls he loved coming toward him, he realized that perhaps keeping them all protected was a more serious concern for him than he had realized before. Though these attacks seemed to be directed at Anne, who knew who the true target was?

Robin herded his family into the bedchamber, then shut the door and bolted it. He watched them take places near the fire. Nicholas sat near Anne, but even Robin had to concede that he looked too ill to take advantage of his position. Amanda first fussed over Anne, then drew up a stool at Nicholas's feet and sat. Montgomery and John sat on the floor flanking her. They leaned against her on either side and wrapped their arms about her as if she'd been a kind of bolster put there especially for their comfort. Isabelle and Miles fought over the remaining chair. Perhaps Miles's chivalry was in full bloom that day, for he conceded the battle quickly and sat at her feet.

"Rub my shoulders, will you, Iz?" he asked.

Robin watched the normal goings-on in his family and wished heartily that he could do naught but enjoy them. But he was responsible for his kin. Not only was he answerable for his own actions, and theirs as well, he was answerable for their safety. He was beginning to wonder if his sire had made a mistake in entrusting him with these souls.

He shook aside his thoughts. The responsibility was his and he would not shrink from it. He had no choice but to bring something very foul into their midst, so best be about it while he could. But once he found the culprit, this loss of their innocence was something else he would make the fiend pay for.

He took a deep breath. He could keep them alive and unharmed. After all, warring was what he did best. Perhaps his sire hadn't chosen amiss. He stood behind Anne's chair and prepared to give them the tidings.

"Would someone care to enlighten us as to why we've been dragged here?" Amanda asked tartly.

Robin pursed his lips. Not even a chance to start before she was at him. Perhaps Amanda could be left to the wolves whilst he concentrated on the rest of his family. At least then he might have a bit of peace.

"We are here," he said briskly, "because there is something afoot in the keep and 'tis my task to see it discovered and rooted out."

"And you know this because . . ." Amanda asked slowly.

"Because Anne has almost lost her life three times in the past fortnight," Robin said. "I cannot credit it to coincidence."

"Perhaps the fiend was targeting you," Amanda said, "and missed."

Miles laughed, but quickly covered it up with a cough. "Sorry, Rob," he said. "I know this is no matter for jesting."

"Aye, how do you know 'twas for Anne?" John asked.

"Aye, maybe 'twas a garrison knight Rob wore down to his bones," Montgomery offered enthusiastically. "'Tis a surety there would be several of those."

And then they were off, those souls Robin had just recently vowed to protect, apparently having no lack of names to suggest as to who might be such a likely lad. Robin listened to them list his victims and was torn between a bit of pride that the list was so long and annoyance that his siblings seemed not to realize their peril.

All except Nicholas who sat behind Amanda, sprawled wearily in his chair, drumming his fingers on the arm as if he hadn't a care in that empty head of his. But at least the dolt wasn't smiling. He was too sick for it and Robin couldn't help but find a bit of comfort in that.

And then there was Anne. Robin moved slightly so he could see her face—then he wished he hadn't. He'd never seen her look more weary or grieved. And when he caught her gaze, she favored him with a look of such ill-disguised ill-will that he flinched. He opened his mouth to defend himself, but she looked away so purposefully that he shut his mouth with a snap. It would do him no good to plead his case now, not with all the rampant speculation that was going on about him.

Amanda rose suddenly and held down her hands for Anne. "Come, sister," she said quietly. "Let me put you to bed. You look as if you need rest."

Miles was instantly on his feet to aid them. Robin moved to help, but Anne pushed his hand away. His first instinct was to blister her with a caustic remark, then he bit his tongue. In truth, he couldn't blame her for her actions. She was likely afeared for her life, bruised mightily from his protection, and angry that he hadn't helped her up in the first place. Perhaps sleep was what she needed to restore her to her good sense.

He watched Miles and Amanda care for her, and as he did so, his earlier thought came back to him.

He could sequester his siblings in the lads' bedchamber. Nicholas could keep watch over them. And when Nick had to be about some other business, Miles could take over the duty. The girls and the twins would be perfectly safe. Nicholas was infinitely capable of seeing to them. Miles was hard on his brother's heels when it came to swordplay and he was devious enough to anticipate any foul intent from a murderer.

But even Nicholas would have to admit that such an arrangement left mistress Anne to be watched over.

And who better to do that than him?

Alone. Where she could not escape him. And then perhaps for once in their sorry lives, they might have speech together that did not involve insults and shouting, and then Robin might discover the lay of her heart once and for all.

He was, after all, the best warrior in the keep. 'Twas only fitting that he be the one to guard her. She was Fenwyck's heir. She needed to be protected at all costs.

"Well," he announced, "that's enough discussion. I'll look into the matter. Until it's solved, everyone will hie themselves to the lads' chamber. Lads, leave only in pairs. Girls, don't go out without either Nick or Miles."

Nicholas frowned at him. "I think it best we remain all in the same chamber, brother. If we have a war within our own keep, far better that we remain in a single body."

As if Robin would allow his brother and Anne to be in a chamber together! Nicholas had already fair draped himself over Anne for the past fortnight. Best get him as far away from her as possible. Robin turned to Amanda and gave her the sternest look he could muster.

"Take the little ones to my chamber."

Amanda pursed her lips, but nodded readily enough.

"But," Nicholas spluttered, "you can't mean—"

Robin turned to Miles.

"Nick and I have aught to discuss. 'Tis your task to protect the family until we've arranged our strategy."

Miles rose without comment or question. It was, though, a goodly while before he managed to get everyone out the door. Robin listened to his siblings suppose and surmise until he was near to screaming at them to get themselves gone. They had no useful suggestions and if he had to listen to the little lads discuss once again what kind of poison could be put in wine to kill so quickly, he would have silenced them himself.

But Miles was successful in the end and Robin couldn't help but feel faintly satisfied about it. At least there was someone in the keep who would obey him.

Once the door was closed, Robin looked over at the bed. There was no movement there. It was possible Anne was asleep, and Robin prayed the like was true. At least she wouldn't have to hear the argument that was to come. Nicholas was still lazing in his chair, but Robin knew that such a display of tranquillity couldn't last for long.

He put his shoulders back, took a deep breath, and prepared for battle. He would have loosened his sword in its sheath, but that might have alerted his brother to what he was about. Besides, a sword fight would awaken Anne and that was something Robin wanted to avoid. His plan would be put into action before she awoke and could add her voice to Nicholas's.

And he hoped he wasn't about to make a colossal mistake.

16

"You're *what?*"

Anne winced at the force of that thunderous shout.

"Be silent, you fool! Say nothing else until I've made certain you haven't woken Anne."

Anne held her breath. It was very difficult to feign sleep with Robin coming over to stare at her and muttering under his breath loudly enough for the entire chamber to hear. One day she would have to tell him he did that when he thought too hard. She suspected he didn't know, and would likely have been highly irritated to learn of it. It gave away far too many of his secret thoughts.

Robin cursed as he stomped away.

"I've already decided this," he whispered sharply.

"Robin, you cannot be serious!"

Anne wished she had heard Robin's initial declaration, but damn him if he hadn't found it in him to whisper then. She had a feeling without hearing anything else that Nicholas had it aright. Whatever new strategy Robin had proposed could be nothing but madness.

She shifted on the bed and her body set up a clamor that fair left her gasping. And with that renewed wash of pain came back all the ill feelings she had acquired for the acting lord of Artane.

She despised him. She loathed him. She never wanted to feel his hands on her again. And she especially never wanted to be crushed beneath his heel again, as if she'd been a particularly noisome species of insect he was bent on destroying.

"'Tis the only way." Robin's deep voice was firm.

"Have you gone mad?" Nicholas continued, sounding as if he fully believed that his brother had accomplished the like. "Her father will slay you if he learns. Not to mention what ours will do!"

"By St. George's throat, Nick, I'm not about to bed her," Robin retorted.

"I should hope not. She's a virgin, for pity's sake—"

"She's the same as a sister to me—"

"*Merde*," Nicholas snapped. "She is not your sister and keeping her prisoner in this chamber is equal to fornication, you fool! Do you for one moment believe anyone will think her virtue unmarred once they discover she's spent the night in your bed?"

"Saints, Nick, it isn't as if I'll be joining her," Robin growled. "I'll sleep here before the fire. Her precious virtue will remain unsullied by my filthy hands."

"Let her sleep with us—"

"Nay! She'll stay with me. I'm the only one here who can protect her."

"Ha," Nicholas said scornfully. "I'm perfectly capable of doing it. Indeed, I think I might be a better choice."

"When I'm dead," Robin snarled. "And not a moment before. Your task is to see that Amanda and Isabelle are kept safe. Give the girls the bed. The lads can sleep on the floor."

"I still say we should all remain together!"

"And I say we shouldn't!"

There was silence for a goodly amount of time and Anne began to wonder if Nicholas and Robin were looking at each other, trying to decide where to cut first. And then Nicholas spoke.

"I see," he said quietly.

"You see nothing."

"You'll not see this end as you wish it, Robin."

"Won't I?"

"You will not. I fully intend to woo her."

"And as I continue to tell you, Nick, she isn't yours to woo."

"Why not? Think you she's yours?"

When the sun falls from the sky and turns us all to ashes, Anne thought sourly. Robin of Artane was the very last person she intended to be wooed by—as if he would make the effort to do the like!

"Post a guard outside where you sleep," Robin said. "Should anyone attempt an attack, they'll find themselves facing a sword, not a sleeping idiot. You can manage that, can't you?"

"Your confidence in my skill is nothing short of staggering, my lord."

"Saints, Nick, someone tried to kill Anne not once but thrice! This is not a matter for jest."

Nicholas grunted. "I was not making it such. And as far as this other business is concerned, I like it not at all."

Anne didn't either, but saying as much would tell the men that she'd heard everything they'd said and she had no intentions of that.

"It matters not to me what you like."

"I have not given up my fight," Nicholas said. "Her father certainly prefers me to you."

"He doesn't know you very well," Robin snapped.

"I'll make it a point to see that he does—"

"Oh, by the saints, will you cease!" Robin exclaimed. "Go do something useful, such as finding us a meal. I daresay Anne will be hungry when she wakes and doubtless too weary to move. Feed a taste of everything to the dogs first. Who knows who this cur will choose as his next victim."

Nicholas sighed deeply. "Aye, you have that aright."

"And help me off with this mail before you go."

"Ah, demoted to his little lordship's squire. Rob, how I do love being your brother."

Anne heard Nicholas lose his breath with a *whoosh* and prayed he wouldn't retaliate. Truly, pretending she was sleeping through a brawl would have been more than she could have managed.

There was a muffled thump and a sigh. "Better."

"Must I help you with your boots also? And need I mention that strutting about Father's bedchamber naked would be something I would certainly have to take a blade to you for?"

"I'll endeavor not to offend Anne with my sorry form. I would appreciate something to eat. Now."

"I'll return with a meal and stay to see if it agrees with Anne."

"You'll deliver it, then go. I do not need your aid in seeing her fed."

There was a goodly bit of silence after that and Anne wondered if they were trying to glare each other into submission. Well, at least there was no ringing of blades as of yet.

And then Nicholas sighed heavily. "I think you're making a mistake."

"I've no doubt you do."

"You'll not have her, Robin."

Robin only grunted. Anne listened to them both cross to the door, then heard the footsteps pause.

"And be forewarned," Nicholas said. "You'll repay me for my serving you thusly. Fetching meals," he grumbled. "Acting the squire. Saints, I'm past all that!"

The door opened, then closed softly. Anne remained motionless, listening to Robin rustle about the chamber. There was the sound of steel against wood as she assumed he had laid his mail shirt over a chair perhaps, or a trunk. Then she heard two distinct thumps—his boots coming off perhaps. Muted footsteps crossed the room, then she heard the rustling and popping of a fire being brought back to life. The scrape of a stool across the floor sounded overloud to her ears and she took advantage of the following sigh to roll over so she faced the fire. She waited until silence had descended again before she opened one eye a slit and looked to see what Robin was about.

He sat facing the fire, with his back to her. His head hung down, leaving only the thick hair flowing over his neck exposed to her view. His broad, bare shoulders were hunched, his long, muscled back bowed. He looked enormously weary. And, for a small moment, she had the urge to go to him, to put her hands on his shoulders and work the stiffness out of them, to drag her fingers through his hair and soothe him.

But nay, Robin wouldn't care for that. Even in his youth, he'd never cared for it. Nicholas, on the other hand, had dropped everything at even a hint that she or Amanda might be willing to scratch any part of his person. Robin had shunned anything like such petting, calling it a most unmanly pursuit. Nicholas had always called him a fool for missing out on such lazy delights. Anne had wondered if Robin secretly longed for such affection, but he had never relented.

And he wouldn't relent tonight. He would likely shrug off her hands and bark some unfeeling curse at her. And it would wound her, as it always did.

Or as it would have in the past, she corrected herself. Now, it wouldn't bother her. Since she had protected herself with this newfound dislike for the young lord of Artane, his derision and shunning of her wouldn't hurt her in the slightest. Indeed, it would only confirm the opinion she should have had of him from the first. He was an unfeeling worm of a man with no heart and no chivalry. A gallant knight did not crush his lady in the dirt, then leave her there to pick herself up. Nay, she would have no part of a man who possessed such poor manners.

Then why did the fact that he had saved her life, albeit roughly, make her want to weep?

Another knock sounded on the door and Anne immediately closed her eyes. She remained perfectly still as Robin answered the door.

"Guards?" Robin asked.

"Your own men," Nicholas said quietly. "At this door, and the lads' chamber down the passageway. Jason will come here as well."

"What of Sir Edward?"

"Weeping in the dungeon," Nicholas said, with disgust. "A pitiful excuse for a knight if ever I saw one."

"Leave him there," Robin said curtly. "Perhaps it will loosen his tongue."

"He swears he had nothing to do with this."

"Do you believe him?" Robin asked.

"He's one of Father's men. I can't imagine this kind of disloyalty."

"Well," Robin said with a heavy sigh, "leave him there for a day or two and let us see if aught else happens. Now, if you don't mind, I've a lady to protect and I don't need your aid."

"Robin, I still don't know about this——"

"I know what I'm doing. Your task is to see to the rest of the ruse. And have a care with Amanda. Wouldn't want the wench to die before I have a few more goes at her backside."

Nicholas snorted. "I'll be sure and give her your best, brother."

"You fed some of this meal to the dogs?"

"Aye, and all are still breathing."

"Good enough."

Anne heard the door close, then watched him walk over to the hearth and set down a basket full of food she could smell from where she was. It had been hours since she had last eaten and her belly protested the delay rather loudly.

"Anne?"

She realized he was looking at her and she knew feigning sleep was foolish. "Aye?"

"Come eat," he said, turning his back on her and sitting on the floor.

Ah, such a paragon of chivalry. She sat up, wincing at the way her body protested such a simple act. She felt as if she'd been beaten. Or flattened by a very heavy, mailed knight. Perhaps being struck by the mace would have been less agony than this. She pushed herself up from the mattress, swayed, then regained her balance with a quick step forward, one that rattled her teeth. She shuffled across the floor carefully, too angry at Robin's rudeness to be embarrassed by her ungainly walk. The least he could have done was rise off his slothful backside and offer her his arm!

He didn't even look up as she stood next to him, trying to decide the best way to reach the floor short of falling. Robin made a sound of impatience.

"Sit down, Anne."

She gritted her teeth. "I'm trying."

"You're dawdling."

"Damn you, Robin, you could help me!"

He looked up at her and his eyes were dark, so dark she couldn't tell their color. "You don't like to be coddled, so I'm not coddling you. Sit down and eat, Anne, while there's aught to spare."

She wanted to strike him. Aye, she didn't want to be coddled, but she wouldn't have scorned a gallantly offered hand now and then. She blinked back tears of frustration and looked for something with which to lower herself. If she bent her leg without something to hold on to, it would have collapsed under her. Her body was sore enough without any new bruises. She took hold of the heavy stone of the hearth and used it as a crutch, holding herself up with it while she knelt on her good leg, her lame leg stretched out in front of her. She scraped her hands on the stone, but at least she made it to the floor without mishap.

Other than losing her pride on the way down.

She scooted back to where Robin was sitting and glared at him. He averted his face hastily.

So she sickened him. At the moment, she couldn't have cared less. She hated him. She repeated that over and over in her head as she helped herself to roast fowl and bread, washing it down with wine contained in a bottle she took right out of Robin's hands. And when she was finished, she moved to her right a bit, so she could face her captor.

"I don't want to stay here with you."

He looked into the flames. "You needn't fear for your virtue."

Anne laughed bitterly. "Ah, as if that mattered. You know as well as I that my virtue or lack thereof will never come to light. No man would have me anyway."

"Daft wench," Robin muttered.

"Men do not purchase lame wives for themselves."

"Silence," he said sharply, fixing his gaze to hers. "You speak foolishness."

Anne lifted her chin. "The truth is, I do not wish to stay here, because I can't stomach being in the same chamber with you."

"Your alternative is likely death. I daresay you can endure me if the other is your choice."

"I would prefer death," she said haughtily.

He dashed the contents of his cup into the flames, setting up a sharp hiss. "Somehow, that doesn't surprise me," he said. He jumped to his feet, jerked on his boots, and snagged a tunic from off the back of a chair.

The door banged shut behind him.

Anne turned back and looked into the fire dispassionately, pointedly ignoring the sting behind her eyes. Robin's every movement, his every breath spoke of his distaste, his revulsion for her. And why not? Why would he ever feel anything else where she was concerned? Though he certainly had frightened off the more timid heiresses in England, the bold ones hadn't been fearful.

Tales of his mischief had reached her ears, tales from court, tales from the continent. Rhys had been furious over the bastards Robin had sired, though he was certain the number had been exaggerated. What did it matter if it had? She had seen some of the women who had bragged of having Robin in their beds. Beautiful, elegant women who were perfectly formed, perfectly coiffed, perfectly mannered. And not a one of them had walked with a limp. Why would he ever have looked at her, when those were the choices offered him?

Besides, Nicholas wanted her. Hadn't he said as much? Hadn't he courted her father with more enthusiasm than Robin had likely ever used for anything but a pitched battle?

It made it all the more unfortunate that Nicholas was not the brother she loved.

She closed her eyes, ignoring the tears that crept from beneath her eyelids.

17

Robin leaned back against the door and let his breath out slowly. Then he realized there were guards leaning against the opposite wall. Perfect. That was all he needed to add to his irritation—tidings of his bewildered state being bandied about the garrison hall. He straightened and gave them his most lordly look.

"No one enters," he commanded.

"My lord?" Jason asked from where he appeared at Robin's side.

"Stay here," Robin said. "Watch over the lady Anne."

Jason nodded with wide eyes. Robin turned to his guard, received more nods, then turned off down the passageway before he did anything else foolish. At least the guards were his own men so they could be intimidated if necessary. And they were men he trusted. Anne would be safe enough by herself. Indeed, now that he'd had more chance to think about it, he suspected that she might be safer without him. The only thing he knew with certainty was that he would be rotting in Hell before Nicholas was alone with Anne in that chamber.

Robin stomped down the steps, wishing he could unclench his jaw but knowing it was useless to try. His anger was too near the surface for that. By all the bloody saints, what was Nicholas about? He didn't love Anne, of that Robin was sure. But Nicholas wasn't cruel, so Robin also had to concede that his brother wouldn't be toying with her for his own sport. And he wouldn't use Anne to torment Robin.

It was a damned perplexing snarl.

Well, at least there were a few things Robin could understand. One was that his sire would be away for at least a month and that meant Geoffrey of Fenwyck would be gone for at least that long as well. Perhaps in that time he could invent a strategy to improve his standing with Anne's sire.

The other problem was who to watch over Anne while Robin saw to the business of the keep. His earlier vows aside, he knew it would be impossible for him to remain with her every moment of each day. Someone would have to be recruited to take on the duty whilst Robin was about his affairs.

But 'twas for damned sure it wouldn't be Nicholas. Robin suspected Miles might be equal to the task, so that was something to think on. Miles would likely find Anne more amenable to his company anyway.

And that reminded him of Anne's last words and he found himself scowling. So she couldn't bear his company. She might change her mind when she came face-to-face with a sword. Indeed, she might discover that she needed him after all. But for himself, what he needed was a goodly amount of ale. Perhaps that would drown out her slanders.

He found his brother sitting alone in front of the hearth, a cup in his own hands. Robin sat down across from him and reached for the jug. He assumed by the way his brother continued to breathe that the brew was safe enough.

Only once he had a cup of ale in his hands, he found that his taste for it had disappeared. He stared into the fire and didn't fight the realizations that seemed determined to catch up with him.

Someone was trying to kill Anne.

Anne would have rather died than stay in the same chamber with him.

And Nicholas was likely in higher favor with Anne's sire than he was.

It had been, Robin decided grimly, a decidedly unpleasant day.

"I would suggest you go to bed," Nicholas said, "but I know where that would lead you and I vow that won't happen."

Robin looked at his brother and couldn't even muster up enough irritation to thrash him as he might have another time.

"You needn't fear for her," Robin said wearily. "She cares nothing for me."

"Oh?" Nicholas said, his ears perking up. "Think you?"

"Aye, I know it. She cannot abide my presence."

"How perfectly lovely," his brother said, sounding as if nothing could have pleased him more.

It was that tone that woke Robin from his stupor. He eyed his sibling with disfavor.

"I daresay she wouldn't have the stomach for you either, if you'd been the one to bury her in the dirt this afternoon. At least I saved her precious skin. What have you done for her of late, save leaving a goodly amount of slobber on her hands?"

"I would make a fine husband for her."

Robin didn't even bother to reach for his sword. He shook his head slowly and prayed he wasn't making a mistake by speaking with seriousness to Nicholas.

"You might," he agreed, "but you do not love her truly. Do you?"

Nicholas, for a blessed moment Robin wished had gone on for the rest of eternity, was silent. Then he sighed. "I could learn easily enough."

"She's mine, Nick," Robin said, plunging ahead before he lost his courage. "And she has been from the moment I clapped eyes on her."

"You put a worm down the front of her gown, Rob. I doubt she remembers that with fondness."

"What was I to do?" Robin asked crossly. "Go down on bended knee and profess my love? I was but a lad! Lads do things that only lads would do."

Nicholas stared at him for several moments in silence, then turned and looked into the fire for a like amount of time. Robin suspected he was trying to decide if the fight were truly worth it. Robin hoped he chose well. He would have hated to have run his brother through, but Anne's hand was at stake here.

Assuming she would have him.

But he would stand a far better chance if he didn't have Nicholas underfoot. Besides, he had spoken the truth. Nicholas might have loved her, but it was a brotherly affection. Robin could not possibly imagine the two together. Nicholas would pamper her overmuch, she would grow restive under his care, and they would be unhappy within months.

But that was beside the point. She was *his*, not his brother's. She had always been his.

Assuming, of course, that he could convince her of that.

Nicholas sat back suddenly and sighed. He raised his cup. "Very well, I concede the battle."

"Wisely done," Robin said, feeling a rather unhealthy sense of relief.

"I still say I would have made a fine husband for her."

Robin suppressed a shudder at the thought of Anne's sweetness coupled with his brother's. Too much for one family, to his manner of thinking.

"Find your heart's desire elsewhere," Robin said. "Far away from Anne, if you please."

"I could have loved her. I do love her."

"As a sister," Robin said, hoping the glint he knew to be in his eye left a deep impression upon his brother. "Your feelings for her are of a fraternal nature, nothing more."

"Her sire prefers me," Nicholas said, a small smile beginning to play around his mouth.

"He'll accustom himself to me in time. And if not to me, then to my inheritance."

"You have that aright, at least. I can see the advantages of being the firstborn."

And for once, Robin could too. He put his shoulders back. "See to the keep, will you? I go to keep watch over Anne."

"Watch your back."

"I fear no one," Robin said confidently.

"Anne might stick you while you sleep."

Robin grunted as he rose. There was truth in that. Perhaps he would do well to redon his mail before he took his rest. "Come to me first thing on the morrow," he said. "We'll plan how best to see the day's tasks accomplished between the two of us."

Nicholas nodded. "As you will. Oh, and Rob?"

Robin stopped. "Aye?"

"Sleep on the floor," Nicholas suggested.

As if he dared sleep on the bed! Anne would do him in for a certainty then. Robin gave his brother a flick on the ear for the sheer sport of it, then retreated up to his sire's chamber.

And as he walked down the passageway, he felt a shiver go down his spine. One day he would walk the same passageway, only he would be lord of Artane.

Assuming Anne didn't slay him before he could outlive his father.

He shook aside his thoughts and approached the door. After confirming with his men that no murderers had entered and no stubborn wenches had escaped, he entered and bolted the door behind him.

He saw Anne immediately, lying before the fire in her cloak. He scowled. Didn't she know she would catch her death from a chill? He crossed the room quietly and squatted down next to her, grateful for the time to gaze at her in peace.

It was a miracle she hadn't been betrothed already. Indeed, she should have been. He remembered very well the year she had turned ten-and-five and her sire had arrived with what he deemed to be a suitable mate: a lad of a score-and-five. Robin had been beside himself with jealousy but completely unwilling to show it. Fortunately his father had had more sense than Anne's and talked Fenwick out of the plan.

After her accident, there had been no more offers of marriage. Robin couldn't have been happier about it. Men could not see her for her leg and he was perfectly content to let them be blind.

Aye, she was a beautiful creature. Vexing, but beautiful. How could any man look down at those angelic features and not be moved to lyricism? Unless he was Robin of Artane and found himself tongue-tied in her presence. Robin smiled grimly to himself. Perhaps it was his thoughts running amok in his brain that confused his tongue so. He'd done his damndest never to think of her while he was away.

But since his return to Artane, he'd thought of nothing else. Especially whilst he'd watched his lackwit brother try to woo her. Saints, but he wanted to strangle Nick for the deed! In the past few days, he'd been reduced to staring at her from the shadows in the evening, watching the way the firelight played over her hair and fair skin, the way her hands tortured her gown or smoothed it down, depending on her mood. And he'd wanted to sweep her up in his arms and stalk off with her, never to release her again. But he hadn't. Anne didn't like stalking and she didn't care for him either. She wanted a chivalrous, gallant knight with fine court manners and pleasing ways.

Which was precisely what he wasn't. A man had no use for fine manners and minstrelsy when he was tromping across blood-soaked ground and trying to keep his head on his shoulders. You bloody well didn't ask permission before you cleaved a man's skull in twain!

He sincerely doubted he could remember how to play the fine lord and didn't know if he cared to stir himself to try. After all, he had acquired a reputation for ruthlessness. It would be a pity to lose it simply because his men saw him trailing after Anne like a moonstruck calf. Nay, it was best he remain hard and cold. It would save his good standing with the men, and it would also save his pride, as he had no doubts Anne would spurn him at every turn.

He frowned down at his charge, noting the dark shadows under her eyes and the creases that didn't leave her brow, even in sleep. Sleeping on the floor had been foolish. Her muscles would stiffen up and leave her in pain the next day. What the girl needed was a few lessons in how to care for herself.

Robin paused. That wasn't such a poor idea after all. He'd known a man who had had his leg crushed, in much the same way as Anne's. And now the man was fit and hale, claiming that hot baths and the rubbing of his muscles with oil were what had cured him of his stiffness. And he had forced himself to strengthen the muscles each day. That was surely what Anne needed to do. Taking her for walks outside would give him relief from being prisoner inside his own chamber and it would aid her as well. And though he was certain she wouldn't allow him to touch her leg, he could show her what she needed to do.

And it would give him one more reason to be near her. Even gruff, surly knights longed for the company of their ladies.

He put his hand on her arm. "Anne, wake up. You cannot sleep here before the fire."

"Go away," she muttered, pulling her arm away.

Robin paused and reconsidered. Perhaps this would be more difficult than he thought. Fortunately he was a man of action, so he heeded her words not at all. He lifted her up into his arms.

"You're hurting me!"

"I'm hardly touching you," he retorted. "I'm just carrying you to bed. You needn't sound as if I'm beating you."

She bit her lip and said no more. Robin gently deposited her on the bed and pulled a blanket over her.

"Will you be warm enough?"

She nodded, not meeting his eyes. Well, the girl was half asleep. He couldn't blame her for not showing him any gratitude.

He pulled his cloak off the back of a chair and sat down before the fire. After putting more wood on the blaze, he rolled up in his cloak and tried to make himself comfortable on the hard wood. It was no easy task, and he was certain that come morning he would regret his actions. But it was a small bit of chivalry and perhaps in time Anne would come to appreciate it.

Robin tossed and turned on the floor for a goodly while before he gave up and sought the comfort of a chair. He sat with his chin resting on his steepled fingers and gave thought to the mystery with which he'd been presented.

It was a surety that Stephen of Hardwiche had not been the killer's true target. The accident that morn in the lists had left him with no doubts about that. But why would anyone want to hurt Anne? And who in the keep could possibly have anything to gain by it?

Robin's first suspect was Baldwin, of course, but even that made no sense. Baldwin's quarrel was with Robin, not Anne. And Baldwin couldn't possibly know of Robin's feelings for the girl. Why would he hurt Anne, if Robin were the one he hated? Besides, Robin couldn't credit Baldwin with the imagination to think up such a scheme. Nay, it had to be someone else and for a reason none of them had seen yet.

Robin sighed and pushed away those thoughts. He would begin his training before sunrise and hopefully something would occur to him then. Perhaps Amanda and Isabelle could be deposited inside the chamber; they would be company enough for Anne. Miles could be left with them. Nicholas was no longer a problem, which left Robin free to think on other things.

And first among those was helping Anne recover from the crushing he'd subjected her to. Perhaps that would induce her to think more kindly of him, though he suspected that she would have less than genial feelings toward him after what he planned to do to her leg.

He rested his head back against the chair and closed his eyes. On the morrow. He would see to it all on the morrow.

18

Maude of Canfield stood at the end of the passageway with folded linens clutched in her arms. She had just watched Robin go into the lord's chamber. She shook. Indeed, she trembled so badly, she had to clutch the cloth to her to keep from dropping it. But it wasn't from fear.

It was from anger.

She could scarce believe her eyes. He had gone inside that chamber to be with *her*! It was all she could do not to run screaming down the hall and pound on the wood to bid them cease.

But she couldn't do that. There were guards aplenty in the passageway, guards likely put there to protect *her*. And Maude had seen the dogs downstairs, tasting all that came from the kitchen.

She would have to find another way. And soon. Before anything happened between them. She had to stop Robin before he made a terrible mistake. And *she* would pay dearly for the pain she had already caused Maude.

Maude leaned back against the passageway wall and indulged in her memories. She'd had Robin to herself for almost a fortnight. Of course, she'd only had him in her bed one night, and that after a solid fortnight spent working to get him there. And once she'd had him, who had come between them?

She had.

Maude pushed away from the wall, turned, and retreated back down the passageway. She would have to wait, but she wouldn't wait long. Edith might have had a plan, but it required too much waiting. To be sure, Maude wanted to avoid Baldwin's fists again, but perhaps he could be dodged as well. Besides, she didn't trust either of them. She'd been promised that she would have Robin and she had yet to be allowed to speak to him. Not only that, her most glorious beauty had been shorn straight from her head, leaving her with ragged locks that would attract no simple man, much less Artane's heir.

Nay, she would wait no longer. *She* would have to leave the chamber eventually. And when she did, Maude would be waiting.

A pity, though, that she didn't have Edith's skill with weapons. Maude had watched her on the journey to Artane. She'd dispatched a ruffian or two with blades she seemed to produce from some hidden place on her person. She'd killed without noise, or apparent pleasure.

It had been frightening to watch.

Maude put her shoulders back before she entered the kitchens. Never mind that she didn't have such skill herself. Edith might have been handy with a blade, but Maude was handy with her wits. And she had far more than she'd ever been given credit for. She would just have to use them. Because once *she* was dispatched, then Robin would be free.

And then Maude would have what she'd been promised.

19

Anne woke to an empty bed. It took her a moment or two of panic to realize that she wasn't in her lone bed at Fenwyck; she was at Artane. But she wasn't in her usual chamber. She was in Rhys and Gwen's bedchamber.

With Robin.

There was a hearty bit of snoring going on so she could only assume that he still resided within the walls. She had vague memories of him carrying her to the bed and laying her down. She quickly determined that she was still wearing all her clothing, save her shoes, and she couldn't decide if she should be disappointed by that or not. Had she been naked, at least she could have taken a blade to him in good conscience.

A pressing need presented itself almost immediately and she groaned as she struggled to sit up. How was she to take care of such a thing with Robin loitering about? Perhaps she could leave and seek out a garderobe before he was alerted to her plan. She bit her lip as she swung her legs to the floor. By the saints, she felt as if every bit of flesh she possessed had been bruised. At least now, though, her wrist was the least of her pain. She was heartily tempted to crawl back beneath the blankets until she felt better.

"Anne?"

Damn, but the wretch had finely tuned ears.

"Go back to sleep," she said firmly, hoping he would recognize the tone and obey without question. She waited until she thought Robin might have fallen back asleep before she shifted her weight and put her feet on the floor.

The bed curtains were jerked back to reveal Robin standing there rubbing his face sleepily.

"What in heaven's name are you doing?" he rumbled. "Escaping?"

"I've needs to attend to."

He yawned widely, then pointed to a corner. "There's the chamber pot. Make use of it."

"Robin!"

He blinked. "What? What have I done now?"

"I will not do this with you here!"

"Anne, we're going to be together in this chamber for several days. You may as well accustom yourself to it now."

"I will not," she said. "You'll have to leave."

"I brought in a privy screen yestereve. Surely that's sufficient to protect your modesty."

She gritted her teeth. It wasn't just her modesty she was worried about, but she was hardly going to admit that she doubted her legs would hold her up long enough for her to finish the deed.

"It isn't that," she muttered.

"Ah," he said, wisely. "Foolish of me not to think on that. You'll require aid."

Anne glared at him. "If you think for one moment that I'll ever allow you close enough to me to aid me in this, then you're a bigger fool than I thought. Get out of my way. I'll use the garderobe."

He began to frown. "You'll not leave this chamber."

"I am not your prisoner." She forced herself to her feet.

"Aye, you are. Until this mystery is solved, you'll go where I tell you and stay when I command it."

"What difference does it make to you?" she asked hotly. "Whether I live or die?"

"It doesn't matter to me," he said, through gritted teeth. "That's why I almost took a spiked ball in my head yesterday and that's also why I didn't get a wink of sleep last night from sleeping in that bloody chair!" His voice had risen with every word until it had become a shout. "I'm a lackwitted fool and you're a shrew! Now, use the bloody pot and get you back in bed."

She was momentarily tempted to burst into tears, but she would be damned before she gave him that satisfaction. So she folded her arms over her chest and gave him what she hoped was a formidable glare.

"Get out," she said through clenched teeth.

"Nay."

Almost before the thought had taken shape in her head, she watched her hand reach out and snatch the dagger from his belt. She watched with faint admiration as that same brave hand pointed the little blade at Robin's chest.

"Move," she said.

Robin looked down at the knife, then snorted. "You wouldn't use that on me."

"The temptation is almost overwhelming," she said.

Damn the man if he didn't stand there without making a hint of a move to protect himself. Anne wished she had the spine to stick him firmly between the ribs, hopefully in a place that would pain him greatly. Perhaps it would be a slow, agonizing death. Nothing would have pleased her more than to sit at his bedside and watch him linger on for several weeks before expiring in a great, painful rush.

"You, my lady," he said, continuing to stand there as if he hadn't anything more pressing to do than argue with her, "will use the pot."

"Robin, you great oaf," she said in exasperation, "I am *not* one of your men to be ordered about!"

"Would that you were! 'Twould make this all much simpler!"

She poked at him with the dagger. "Move and do it now. I've no more time nor breath to waste on you. Even you should be able to recognize the difference between your father's bedchamber and your tent on a battlefield."

"Aye," he returned in irritation, "my father's chamber has a pot! Were you in my army, you'd be standing behind a tree!"

Robin of Artane was gruff, irritating, hopelessly rude. And he was lacking in the most basic principles of chivalry. Anne decided that it was futile to waste any more breath on him. She tossed his dagger at him point first and pushed past him while he was trying to fend it off. She crossed the chamber as quickly as her battered form would allow only to find Robin blocking the door before her. She glared at him.

"Robin—"

He looked at her, then slowly held up his hand in surrender. "I have no liking for this—"

"I care nothing for what you do or do not like."

"But if you are determined—"

"Very."

He sighed. "You are the most stubborn woman I have ever had the misfortune of—"

She pushed him aside before he could finish. He pushed readily enough, which made her realize that it had no doubt been something he'd allowed. Had he planned to thwart her, he would have been as immovable as stone.

He caught the door with his hand and stopped her before she could open it fully.

"At least let me come with you and keep watch," he said quietly. "Then should someone attack, you will be safe."

She looked up at him.

And then she wished she hadn't.

His expression was grave, but it wasn't the gravity a man wore like a shield when he faced a distasteful business or considered an unpleasant turn of events. His concern was plain to the eye—even her eye. His gray eyes seemed almost black in the torchlight and his weariness was easily seen. It would have been easy enough for him to send her on her way and abscond with her place on the bed.

Yet there he stood, ready to guard her on her journey to the garderobe.

"Robin, it isn't as if we're walking into a pitched battle," she said, beginning to feel slightly ridiculous.

"And if we are, Lady Anne, 'tis my privilege to protect you."

And with that, he took her hand and pulled her out the door behind him.

Anne followed him, trying to dredge up the loathing she'd felt for him the night before. She dug deep for any shred of anger or irritation she'd felt over the past fortnight. Fortunately, as her body protested each and every movement she made, she had no trouble rediscovering any of those feelings.

But struggling mightily to fight its way through the press of hurt and anger was a tiny feeling of something very quiet and very precious.

It was his privilege to protect her.

The words softened her heart and his actions warmed her soul.

It was rather unsettling, on the whole.

And then there was the feeling of his hand holding hers so securely behind his back. Mayhap he wanted no one to see what he did. 'Twas also likely that perhaps he feared being seen doing the like with her would shame him. But he didn't release her until he had seen her safely inside her destination. And he took hold of her hand again the moment she had come back out into the passageway.

"My lord Robin!"

Anne found herself crushed between the passageway wall and Robin's substantial self so quickly, she lost her breath. She heard Robin's sword come from its sheath with a purposeful hiss. Then she felt him relax.

"Jason, by the saints," Robin snapped, "do not steal up thusly!"

"Forgive me, my lord, but the lady Amanda sends word that she is weary of her confinement."

Robin sighed deeply, then resheathed his sword. He turned and looked at Anne.

"Still breathing?" he asked.

"Barely," she wheezed.

He sighed, and put his arm around her. "Jason, fetch Amanda and Isabelle to my father's chamber. Have Miles come too."

Anne found herself escorted carefully back to Artane's bedchamber where she was made comfortable in a chair while Robin saw to the fire. He said nothing, and he apologized not at all for squeezing her yet again between himself and an unyielding surface. Perhaps he was becoming too accustomed to doing the like. Anne watched him as he worked, his strong hands steady and sure as they tended the fire. Whatever else his flaws, she couldn't deny that he was infinitely capable of protecting her.

He finished with his task, brushed his hands off, and sat back on his heels. He looked at her.

"I need to train," he said, "and I have the business of the keep to see to."

"I know."

He frowned. "I hadn't planned to leave you at all, but I can see now that isn't possible."

"Of course."

"I will return, Anne."

She found that she could do nothing but nod. She knew she should have been telling him to keep himself gone as long as possible, that she had no desire to see him again, nor did she need his protection.

But that little feeling of softness toward him was beginning to work a foul work upon her common sense. She was almost swayed enough by it to thank him for his efforts.

"I'll see food sent," he continued. "Need you something to occupy your hands?"

"I suppose so," she said. "Since you won't be here to throttle."

But she found that she couldn't even manage any venom to deliver with that last sting. Robin looked unimpressed and rose with a half-hearted snort.

"I'll find you your sewing," he said. "And if that doesn't distract you, you'll have my sister to listen to for the morn. By the saints, you can hear her complaining already!"

There was truth in that. Anne had no trouble hearing nor understanding Amanda, likely because Robin figured so prominently in her slander and those were words Anne had used more than once herself.

The door burst open and Amanda swept inside. "I will not be kept prisoner in my own house!" she exclaimed. She stomped over to Robin and poked him in the chest. "And you'll not keep Anne here either, you fool! Have you no thought for the gossip you've caused already?"

Anne watched Robin grit his teeth. She looked down. His hands were clenched as well—never a good sign.

"My duty is to protect her," he said tightly. "And if that means keeping her prisoner in my chamber, then that is what I shall do."

"I could likely protect her with more skill than you—"

"Amanda," Anne interrupted with a gasp.

"Well," Amanda said, with an amazing amount of bluster, considering whom she had just insulted. "I could."

Anne looked at Robin, wondering if he would take a blade to his sister and prove her wrong. There was one thing a body didn't do and live to tell of it and that was insult Robin of Artane's skill with a blade. Rumors of his bastards might have reached her ears with questionable accuracy. Tales of his defending his abused honor rang true with every word.

But Robin was either weary from his night in the chair, or he was trying to impress them all with his calm. He merely unclenched his hands, wriggled his jaw a time or two as if he sought to relieve a cramp there, then took a deep breath.

"Sister," he said with admirable restraint, "I have sworn to keep Anne safe. I will not have her blood on my hands when there is aught I can do to save her life. And if that means keeping her in my chamber from matins to lauds and every hour of prayer in between, then that is what I will do!"

"Ha," Amanda said, with a scowl. "But my blood you would likely wash off those hands readily enough."

"Would I?"

"Aye, you likely would!"

Anne watched the exchange with fascination. Robin and Amanda had ever been at each other with words and pokes of stiff fingers, and she had oft wondered if it might come to bloodshed some day. But somehow this time the game had turned entirely more serious and she couldn't help but wonder about the outcome.

"Then, sister, you know me not at all," Robin said quietly, "for I would not have your blood on my hands either if there were aught I could do to protect you."

And with that, he grasped Amanda by the shoulders, pulled her close, and kissed her gently on the forehead.

And then he strode from the chamber.

Anne looked at Amanda. Her foster sister's jaw fair rested upon her chest. Anne couldn't help the laugh that seemed to come from a very tender portion of her heart. By the saints, Robin could be sweet when he willed it. And to leave Amanda speechless? Now, *that* was a feat worthy of a minstrel's best efforts.

"The oaf," Amanda managed finally. She looked at Anne. "Did you see what he did?"

Anne smiled. "I did."

Amanda scowled. "Bloody wretch. He's a fool if he thinks that will keep me in this chamber for the whole of the day."

But Anne noted that Amanda sat without further comment and she didn't complain about her confinement. And when Miles arrived with food and stitchery, Amanda accepted the both with no disparaging remarks about her eldest sibling.

Anne took up her stitchery but her heart wasn't in it. She finally put it in her lap and stared blindly into the chamber, reliving the morning's events and wondering mightily over them.

It had been, she decided finally, a most exceptional morn.

She could scarce wait to see what the evening might bring.

It was very late in the day when Robin returned and shooed his siblings out of the chamber. Anne rose with difficulty only to find herself almost plowed over by men bringing in a large wooden tub. Water followed and she was treated to several looks of frank speculation that she had trouble ignoring. She could feel her face flaming and she lifted her chin in answer to their challenge. She had done nothing amiss. Besides, 'twas no affair of anyone's what she did or where she slept. As if Artane's servants would actually believe she had shared Robin's bed!

She was, however, very relieved when the men were gone and Robin had bolted the door behind him. She shook her head regretfully at the sorry state of her life. She was locked inside a chamber with one of the realm's fiercest warriors, a tub of bathing water sat not five paces from her, yet she was relieved to be free of potential rescuers?

By the saints, she was losing her mind.

"Make haste while the water is hot," Robin said, startling her.

"I beg your pardon?"

"Get in," Robin said, gesturing toward the tub.

She could only gape at him, speechless.

Robin rolled his eyes. "I want you to bathe, Anne. You're stiff and sore; your muscles will benefit from it."

Anne had taken her share of baths, under protest of course until she had seen the benefit of it for her leg, but bathe in front of Robin of Artane?

Not even should the Fires of Hell themselves be warming the water from beneath the tub and several demons be prodding her toward the bath with their forked tails.

Anne looked for a place of refuge. Well, the bed had served her well enough the night before. She set her sights on that haven and made her way toward it. She soon found, however, that Robin had somehow gotten in her way. She moved ungracefully to one side only to find him again before her. He reached for her and she slapped his hands away.

"What do you?" she demanded.

"I am endeavoring to aid you. Can you lift your arms? Nay? Bend over, then, and I'll pull your dress off you as gently as I can."

Anne could hardly believe what she was hearing. "I am *not* bathing in front of you, you imbecile!"

"I can tell you are stiff, Anne. 'Tis nothing I wouldn't do for one of my men."

"I am not one of your men!" She had the overwhelming urge to clout him on the head and bring sense back to him. "You are not removing my clothes," she spluttered. "Especially in front of yourself!"

He sighed and dragged his hand through his hair. "I'll turn my back and you can do it."

"I don't trust you!"

He flinched, as surely as if she'd slapped him. Anne felt a sudden surge of regret, but that left quickly enough at his next words.

"Why would I stir myself to gape at you, Anne?" he said angrily. "You said yourself that no man would want you."

Tears sprang to her eyes at the words that felt more like a blow. But before she could decide if she should walk or run from the chamber, she found herself with Robin's hands on her shoulders.

"Anne," he said, "by the saints . . ."

Anne held herself stiffly away from him. Mayhap 'twas better that there be no mystery regarding his feelings for her. If he truly found her so revolting—

But if that were the case, then why was he trying to pull her into his arms?

She watched as he took her hands from off his chest, opened her arms, and stepped closer to her. He gently released her hands, then with a tenderness she could hardly credit him with, put his arms around her and drew her close. Anne was so surprised by it all, she couldn't find her wits to move.

And then she felt his hand skim hesitantly over her hair.

It was her undoing.

She knew she should have still been angry with him. She knew she had just cause to keep the fires of her hurt burning long into the rest of her life.

But she also couldn't deny that she had likely hurt him just as intensely.

She wondered if there would ever be a time in their lives when they might have speech together without some kind of altercation marring it. And hard on the heels of that thought came the one that troubled her most: was there even a point in worrying about that? For all she knew, she would be packed off to some uncaring lord and never see Robin again.

The feeling of Robin's hand on her hair slowly and surely caught her attention through her miserable thoughts. She sighed lightly. There was no use in fretting over her future. Perhaps she would be far better served to think on her present. Besides, how often did she find herself in Robin of Artane's arms, with both of them silent?

And then there was the hesitancy of his touch.

As if he truly sought to be gentle with her.

She very slowly, and very carefully, turned her head and laid her ear against his chest. Robin gathered her more securely to him and she felt him sigh. His cheek came to rest on top of her head. He made no move, said no word. He simply stroked her hair and held her close. Anne closed her eyes against the sting there. Even so, she couldn't stop a tear or two from leaking out.

And then a feeling washed over her so strongly that she could scarce stand through it once she realized what it was.

She had come home.

She stood for several minutes with him exactly thusly, until she knew that the feeling of being in Robin's arms was forever burned into her soul.

And then she felt him stir and knew the moment was gone. But that mattered not; she could recall it now at any time.

She pulled back and looked up at him. For the first time in years, gone was the roughness in his expression, gone was the mask he wore, the one he likely believed protected his heart. She looked at a man who returned her look with an expression that though it might not have been considered gentle by some, was gentle enough for her.

"I didn't mean . . ." he began, then he shut his mouth and tightened his lips, as if he had already said more than he intended.

"Nor did I," she said quietly.

He pursed his lips, but a hint of a smile escaped just the same. "Perhaps you shouldn't trust me, Anne. Many a beautiful woman has been ravished in her bath."

"But I'm not—"

A large hand was suddenly over her mouth.

"Enough," he said simply. "Go soak before the water cools so much that it no longer serves you."

She escaped his hand. "And you'll be outside, I take it?"

"You may need my help—"

"Robin!"

"Anne, I give you my most solemn word of honor that I will not look at you whilst you bathe."

She scowled at him.

He sighed. "I'll hide within the bed curtains. Will that soothe your maidenly reserve?"

She folded her arms over her chest.

"Bloody hell, I'll tie a cloth over my eyes!"

"Well," she said slowly, "that might suffice me."

"I've given you my word," he reminded her.

And Robin was as good as his word. That much she could never doubt of him.

Besides, hadn't she said she trusted him? She had to have meant it or she wouldn't have said it. Or so she told herself as she watched Robin cloister himself inside the bed hangings. She watched the bed for several minutes, just to assure herself that he wouldn't pop out to see how she fared. Once she was convinced he would remain where he was supposed to, she turned and limped over to the tub. He was right about the benefits of a good soak. With any luck at all, she might have a bit of time to contemplate what had just transpired between them.

It felt like a bit of a truce.

She stripped off her clothes, biting her lip to keep from groaning as she did so. She sighed as she saw the bruises covering her body. It was a wonder Robin hadn't broken half her bones with the way he had thrown himself atop her. She couldn't deny, though, that he surely hadn't meant to hurt her, nor could she deny that he certainly had saved her life. That was worth, perhaps, a bit of forgiveness. She eased herself down into the tub and a groan escaped her before she could stop it.

"Anne, are you hurt?"

"Nay," she said quickly. "I am well."

Robin's gasp was harsh in the stillness of the chamber. "Merciful saints above, what have you done to yourself?"

"Robin, nay!" she exclaimed, frantically trying to cover herself with her arms as she heard the bed curtains snap back and his feet hit the floor. "You vowed you would not look—"

"That was until I saw this!" he exclaimed, his footsteps approaching rapidly. "Lean up, Anne."

"Oh, Robin, please," she begged. "Please leave me in peace."

He was silent for some time and she might have thought him returned to his place if it hadn't been for the little mutters he was making under his breath. And then he cleared his throat.

"Anne, you're bruised terribly."

She felt his fingers trail over her upper back, then his hand stopped.

"I did this yesterday, didn't I?"

"Of course you did!"

"The rest of you is likely just as bruised, isn't it?"

"If I say aye, will you go?"

He was silent for so long, she almost turned to look at him to see what he was thinking. She could hear him shift hesitantly.

"Should I, um, wash your hair?" he asked gruffly. "As my penance?"

"Nay. I'll manage."

"I wouldn't hurt you."

"I know," she said, wishing mightily that he would choose a more opportune time to beg her pardon. "Now, will you please go? Make your penance later."

"I fear I was too frightened yesterday for gentleness."

Anne gritted her teeth. By the saints, she was naked in her bath and he was continuing to carry on as if they'd been strolling in the garden!

"Anne, did I break anything, do you think? Do your ribs pain you? By the saints, your leg!" He reached around and put his hand on her bare knee. "'Tis no wonder you're stiff—"

"Robin!" she shrieked. "Get away from me!"

"Anne, I was just trying to help—"

"I'm naked, you fool!"

He jerked his hand back instantly. "Of course."

"Go back to bed," she commanded.

He immediately padded back over to the bed.

"Close the bed curtains," she commanded.

He got back onto the bed and jerked the curtains closed.

"Don't open them."

His sigh likely came close to blowing the curtains from their moorings.

"Promise?" she prompted.

"Aye!"

Well, at least he was shouting at her again instead of trying to tend her. Anne waited until Robin had stopped shifting on the bed, then quickly washed her hair and bathed.

And then she merely sat in the water and let it ease the stiffness from her. She hadn't been at all sure of the practice before her wounding, but

Gwen had put her into so many tubs of hot water over the months following that she'd acquired a taste for it.

It was agony to lift the buckets of rinse water, but she wasn't about to ask Robin for help. It was bad enough that he had seen what she hadn't been able to cover with her hair and arms. Not only had Robin seen, he'd touched!

She wondered if such a thing might count as a loss of virtue.

She dressed quickly, then sat down in front of the fire on a stool to comb out her hair. She heard Robin rustle about the chamber, but she didn't look at him. She didn't dare. By the saints, he'd seen parts of her that no one had in years!

Before long, she felt his hand on her back.

"The men come to take out the tub. Nick is bringing us something to eat."

Anne nodded and didn't look at the lads who came to take away the remains of her bath. She could only speculate about what their glances would say now. Best not to know.

"Surviving the lion's den?" ·

Anne looked up at the sound of Nicholas's voice. He stood next to her, looking much improved from the day before.

"We haven't killed each other yet," she said with a smile.

"Anne," Nicholas began, "you needn't stay here if you don't wish it—"

"She stays and you go," Robin growled, taking hold of Nicholas by the back of his tunic. "See that the garrisons are put to bed."

"And just what is it you plan to do this eve?" Nicholas asked.

"Don't worry," he said as he propelled Nicholas toward the door. "We'll find some way to amuse ourselves."

"Keep your hands off her."

"Leaving me free to put them on you repeatedly if you don't cease with your babbling. Go protect the babes."

Anne listened to the door shut and then looked up at Robin as he came back to the fire. "You needn't stay—"

"If you wish me to go, I will," he said briskly.

But he wasn't moving.

And neither was she.

She could easily remember the feeling of his arms around her and the tenderness with which he had touched her hair. She took a deep breath. No sense in not keeping her part of the truce.

"Stay," she said, "if you like. I won't argue with you."

"For once," he grumbled. He picked her up, stool and all, and moved her closer to the fire. "You'll chill."

Well, perhaps it wasn't as gallantly spoken as Nicholas might have done it. Anne couldn't deny that it was chivalry all the same.

Robin's interpretation of it, of course.

And as she watched him mutter under his breath as he laid their supper out, she couldn't help a small smile. Mayhap he grumbled about her, but then again, perhaps not. All she knew was that they were little grumbles she was growing accustomed to and had begun to look on with a small bit of fondness.

Perhaps there was hope for them after all.

20

It was well into the next morning that Robin found himself lingering at the lord's table in the great hall. He stared blindly into the distance. Another day gone by and he was no closer to solving his mystery. He had looked over the lads carefully in the lists that morning, searching for the slightest hesitation when meeting his eyes, or the slightest shifting uncomfortably when he spoke to them.

There had been nothing.

Not even Baldwin had flinched when Robin had glared at him. He'd received his customary sneer in return, but no offer to cross blades. Robin had watched Sedgwick train and suspected that the fury behind it had to do with a desire to redeem himself from his previous humiliation at Robin's hands. Robin couldn't have been happier about it.

How lovely it was to be the victor for a change in that fight.

But no one else had looked at him askance. His own men, he trusted. Nicholas's lads, which were only a handful anyway, were equally as known to Robin, and there was surely no murderer amongst them.

That left only his father's men as possibilities, and Robin had methodically dispatched them that morn in hand-to-hand combat and found not a one of them either lacking in skill or moving about in a suspicious manner. Sir Edward had been interrogated and released from the dungeon when Robin had determined his innocence. It had left the knight free, but Robin without a culprit.

He was beginning to wonder if he might not be unequal to the task of unraveling the tangle.

Of course some of that trouble he could certainly lay at Anne's feet. Who could have possibly foreseen that holding her in his arms could have worked such a foul work upon his good sense? He could remember with perfect clarity the very moment she had ceased to fight him and had come willingly into his poor embrace. He'd felt a peace descend upon him softly and surely until it reached into his heart and stilled all but his gentlest feelings.

Had he not liked it so much, it likely would have frightened him witless.

But what *had* frightened him had been the sight of her bruises. He had hurt her badly; he could only hope she knew how deeply he regretted having had to do the like. He was only grateful he'd seen the mishap coming. And that led him back to wondering just what foul fiend had Anne in his sights. Or was it Anne? Surely an assassin couldn't have been so inept to have been targeting him, yet managing to find Anne each time.

He rubbed his eyes suddenly with the heels of his hands and rose. He would accomplish nothing by just sitting and stewing. 'Twas a sure sign of his muddled state that he'd even been caught doing the like. But perhaps he could be forgiven it, given the day he'd had.

Of course, it might have begun more pleasantly if he hadn't been suffering from another miserable night's half-sleep in the chair. He'd retreated to the lists at dawn only to find them a mud pit that even a sow wouldn't find to her liking. If the lists had been unpleasant, his return to the keep had been even more so. He'd been assaulted by his father's steward immediately upon his return to the hall, even before he could snatch a morning meal. That had taken far longer than he'd wished, but he'd had no choice but to make decisions about foodstuffs and the like. And if that hadn't been trouble enough, he'd heard himself agreeing to take on his father's court of justice tasks.

Though now that he'd had a chance to sit and think for a bit, he could see that overseeing such a thing might prove to be very interesting. Perhaps there was some soul aggrieved enough to think to punish them all by hurting Anne. Aye, that would be worth a day's time.

But now all he wanted to do was seek a bit of peace and quiet. His siblings were above and likely needing a report from him, but after he had finished with them, he would see if Anne wasn't amenable to spending the rest of the afternoon in his sire's solar. She was likely growing weary of the bedchamber.

He made his way upstairs and walked quietly down the passageway. The guards were at their posts, though they looked less than happy to see him. A sense of foreboding immediately assailed him.

"What?" he demanded as he neared them. "Is my family within?"

"Aye," one of the guards said hesitantly. "Most of them."

Robin threw open the door before the man could say more. After all, it was their responsibility to keep murderers from entering. He hadn't instructed them to forbid anyone from leaving.

It took him but a moment to ascertain that everyone was within—except Nicholas and Anne.

"I'll kill him," Robin growled. He looked at Miles. "You couldn't stop him?"

"Anne wanted to go," Miles said.

Amanda rose, gathered up a handful of cloth, and shoved it at Robin. "Take this to her."

Robin yelped as he grabbed hold of a fistful of needle. "Saints, wench, what are you trying to slay me with?"

"Believe me, brother, if I were trying to slay you, I wouldn't limit myself to a paltry needle."

Robin started to glare at her, then he caught the look on her face. Her heart wasn't in her slander and Robin felt an unaccustomed sense of fondness for his sister. He frowned anyway, though, so she wouldn't see it. There was no telling what she might do with the knowledge of such a weakness.

"She wanted to go?" he asked.

Amanda shrugged with a sigh. "She was restless and Nicky offered to take her to Father's solar. He thought it was safe enough."

Miles came to stand next to Amanda. He put his arm around her and smiled faintly at Robin. "If you want my opinion, I think she wanted to look for you."

"Though why she'd want that is a mystery to all rational souls," Amanda added.

Robin scowled. Well, at least Amanda hadn't completely lost herself amongst those foreign feelings of kindness she'd been having toward him. That was somewhat reassuring.

"Oh, Amanda," Miles said, giving her a slight shake, "you are a cruel wench."

"And you're a mindless twit," Amanda said, turning a frown on her younger brother. "What know you of what Anne wants?"

"I have eyes," Miles said placidly. "A woman does not spend a goodly part of her time watching the door if she isn't waiting for a man to come through it."

"She could have been waiting for a meal," Amanda said tartly.

"You have not a shred of romance in your soul," Miles returned with a bit of a laugh.

"No time for it," Amanda said. She looked at Robin. "Well? What are you standing there gaping at? Off with you and seek out your lady before Nicholas escapes with her."

"Right," Robin growled, then turned and left the chamber. He looked at his guards. "No one enters or leaves without my permission. Use your blades if necessary, especially on my sister Amanda."

He received four fervent nods, though he could tell that at least one man was having second thoughts about the last. Even Robin would concede that his sister was beautiful. Perhaps they could prod her where it wouldn't mar her face.

He made his way quickly down to his father's solar, then burst inside. That the door wasn't bolted only increased his ire.

But just as a torrent of words were about to gush from his mouth, the scene before him and the possible significance of it reached his poor, overworked mind.

Nicholas was sitting in one of their father's chairs, reading some manuscript or another. Robin couldn't have cared less which one it was, or even that his brother was doing something so useful with his time. What struck him immediately was that Anne was not sitting in his brother's lap. Nor was she sitting in the chair next to him. Robin's relief was followed immediately by concern that she wasn't where she should have been.

And then he spotted her in the alcove, sitting on one of the benches there and looking out the window. He would have chastised her for sitting in such a perilous place, but even he had to admit that since the solar was on the second floor, it was unlikely that she would be harmed with anything put through the window. And she looked so contemplative that he couldn't begrudge her her post.

But he could begrudge Nicholas the company. He caught his brother's eye and motioned to the door.

"I'm comfortable here," Nicholas said.

"You'll be less so very shortly if you don't go," Robin informed him. "Get out."

Nicholas sighed, returned the manuscript to its trunk, and left, without further comment or protest.

That seen to, Robin bolted the door and then turned to Anne. She hadn't turned to look at him and that made him nervous. He cursed under his breath as he threw her sewing into a chair, snatched up a blanket, and crossed over to her. Apparently she hadn't the good sense to keep warm, else she would have been sitting next to the fire. 'Twas a wonder she had survived as long as she had without him looking after her.

He wrapped the blanket around her shoulders, sat down next to her, then hesitated. Casting caution and his pride to the wind, he gently slid his fingers under her hair and pulled it free of the blanket.

"Why are you sitting here in the chill?" he asked, his voice rough despite his efforts to gentle it.

"I love the rain," she said, still not looking at him. "It softens things so, don't you think?"

He snorted. "Try sleeping out in it for weeks at a time and see how you feel about it."

She looked at him over her shoulder and smiled faintly. "Always the sensible one."

"Always the dreamer," he returned.

She shrugged, turning back to her contemplation of the garden below her. "Life is easier thusly."

He sucked on his teeth, wondering what to say now. The first foray into conversation hadn't gone exactly as he would have liked. There was certainly no warm welcome for him in her words. Had he imagined the cessation of war between them the night before?

And why had Miles thought she had gone seeking him? She had likely been hiding from him. Well, best to know now, before he was disappointed later.

"I left you in the bedchamber" he began.

"I was restless."

"And your life meant so little to you that you couldn't endure a bit of that in exchange for safety?"

"I took Nicky with me."

"And how was he to save you? Talk your assailant to death?"

She did turn then and to his surprise, Robin found her smiling at him. "He can wield a sword, Robin. Surely not as well as you can, but he isn't past all hope."

Robin grunted. "Then you haven't been watching him in the lists of late, if that is what you believe."

"Oh, Robin," she said with a shake of her head.

Robin rubbed his arms. "Could we seek out the fire, at least? 'Tis bloody cold here."

She shook her head. "Let me look out a bit longer, if you please."

He sighed. "As you will." But he rose and fetched her another blanket. No sense in not saving her from herself. He returned and laid it over her legs.

"Thank you," she said.

"It was nothing I wouldn't do—"

"—for your mount, I know," she finished.

"What a stubborn baggage you are, and I was going to say 'Twas nothing I wouldn't do for my sister." *Or for you*, he added silently.

"She would no doubt appreciate it, as do I. Here, come take your mind off the matter. See you the mist yonder?" she asked, pointing over the castle walls.

"Aye."

"Don't you find it beautiful?" she asked. "'Tis full of all manner of ghostly shapes, don't you think?"

Robin knew she had turned her head to look at him, but he couldn't pull his eyes away from the scene before him. By the saints, he wished he could see nothing but promise in that drizzle. Unfortunately, the sight struck him so strongly with a memory, he couldn't pull himself away from it.

"Will you know what I see?" he asked slowly, not intending it as a question. "I see Coyners in France in October, two years past. I see bloody ground before me and the mist obscuring the fallen men around me. I hear the screams of my fellows and of the enemy, screams of the horses, battle cries echoing in the air." He took a deep breath and let it out slowly, finding himself hesitating to say more.

And then he felt a hand come to rest atop his. He took a deep breath and continued on.

"I taste fear in my mouth, I smell blood and death about me, I hear the whistles of arrows and blades. The rain soaks me to the skin, chills me, makes the ground beneath me slippery and treacherous." He smiled bitterly. "I killed a score of men that day, in the rain, and watched the drizzle wash away their blood from my sword and my clothes."

"Oh, Robin, I'm so sorry."

He shook his head. But as he looked in her eyes, he prayed he would see something there that would ease the heaviness in his heart. He wanted her to know what he'd seen and how desperately he'd wished in his innermost heart that she would want him home, that she would want him next to her, that she would be proud of what he had become.

Tears spilled over onto her cheeks. Robin shook his head.

"I didn't say that to grieve you."

"You fool," she said with a groan. "I know that."

He looked down at his interlaced fingers and saw that his knuckles were white. Anne's slender fingers were resting atop them.

"I'm sorry, Robin."

"There's nothing to be sorry about," he said with a sigh. "War is war. There is no glorifying it. 'Tis a bloody business."

"Are you returning soon?"

Now, if that wasn't a question to be answered carefully he didn't know what would be. He didn't dare look at her. Did she want him to go back to France, or did she want him to stay? He could scarce bear the thought of knowing.

But a coward he wasn't, so he took his courage in hand and looked her full in the face. "I'm not sure."

"Your father needs you here, Robin."

Ah, of course. His father would need him. He sighed. There was no mention of how she needed him, but he knew he couldn't have expected the like.

"He's been terribly lonely without you."

Robin pursed his lips. "He has plenty of other sons."

She didn't reply.

Robin couldn't move; he could scarce believe what he'd just said. It was out, his worst demon. He looked away, unable to meet her gaze. So his sire had been the baron of Ayre, a powerful man in his day. Robin would have torn the blood out of his own veins if it would have meant Rhys de Piaget's blood flowed through them. It was possibly the one thing he wanted the most, and the one thing he knew he could never have.

Save Anne, that was.

"You are his firstborn, Robin," Anne said gently. "He loves you very much."

"He may tolerate me," Robin said stiffly, "but you know as well as I that I am not his firstborn. Miles has that honor. My sire was a miserable whoreson." He slanted a look her way, wondering if she would agree with him or not.

She merely smiled gently. "Was he? Perhaps when you're a better frame of mind, I'll give you my thoughts on it."

"There is no thinking to do on it, Anne. You cannot change the facts."

Her smiled turned amused. "You are an impossible lad, aren't you, Robin? I don't think I've ever met a more stubborn soul."

"I am not a lad. I'm a man full grown. Your disrespect is, at the very least, highly insulting."

She leaned back against the stone wall, but she didn't take her hand away from his. Robin didn't dare move, for fear he would frighten her away. She stared out over the courtyard again.

"Don't you remember how we loved the rain when we were small?"

He forced the tension out of himself. Aye, he remembered well. Rainy days had been his favorite, the only time he had had full days of leisure. He had passed them with Anne as a rule, finding that her sweetness was much preferable to Nicholas's teasing or the other lads' sharp, judging eyes. They had spent hours in this very spot, playing chess or simply talking softly as Rhys carried on with the business of the keep. Robin had boasted of the fine warrior he would become and she had remained silent, listening to him raptly. She had been such a shy, dreamy child and he had been her protector, her champion. He'd taught her to play chess on the same bench they now occupied, allowing her to win time and time again, merely to hear her laugh at him.

Aye, he had loved her dearly.

He had never allowed her back after his humiliation. She'd tried to come, knocking on his door softly, begging him to let her in. In time, the knocking had ceased and he had been alone to squelch his tears with harsh young pride.

"Do you remember how you used to lie using my legs as your pillow and pay me to sing to you?"

He blinked away his hard memories and looked at her. "What?"

"Don't you remember?"

"I remember no such thing. I never had time for such foolishness. And even if I'd had the time, I certainly wouldn't have been forced to pay you."

She smiled sadly. "Your memory is short, my lord." She rose and limped slowly over to the fire. Robin watched her take up her sewing trinkets and sit down on a chair near the hearth. She bent over her work; all Robin could see was the glint of firelight on her pale hair.

He leaned his head against the wall. Pay her?

Ah, of course. Now that he thought on it, he remembered very well. He'd never considered her request for his aid a payment at all. She'd begged him to take her to Mass each morn, as she couldn't bear the teasing of the pages. Morning after morning he had escorted her there, keeping his arm around her to shield her from prying eyes and taunts. He'd never understood why the pages teased her so. Perhaps she hadn't possessed Amanda's striking beauty, but she'd been a comely child. Shy but comely. Children were cruel and Anne had suffered because of it.

Well, Mass was over for the day, but perhaps he could serve her in other ways. He'd meant to see her work her leg anyway. Perhaps taking her on a stroll through the passageways would be exercise enough. He could keep her safe. The walk would do her good and it would certain keep him from babbling anything else foolish for an hour or so. Aye, this was something he could do for her and succeed.

He rose and walked across the chamber purposefully. He stopped before her and held out his hand. "Let us walk."

She paused in her work and looked up at him. "I beg your pardon?"

He took her sewing and put it aside, then held out his hand again. "Come walk, my lady."

"Freedom?" she asked, looking as if he'd promised her something far more desirable than a bit of painful exercise.

"Aye," he said, pulling her to her feet. Then he thought better of his haste and looked about him for what he would need. He strode over to a trunk and opened it.

"What seek you now?" Anne asked.

"This," he said, pulling out a cloak his mother had worn several years past. He drew the cloak around her shoulders, pulling the hood up over her head and covering her glorious hair. He looked down and was surprised to see her face fall.

"What is it?" he asked.

"Nothing," she said quietly.

He was tempted to give her reaction more thought, then thought better of it. He would get her out the door whilst she was still amenable to the idea. He led her to the door, opened it, then looked out to see that the passageway was empty. He turned and looked at Anne. She seemed to have lost much of her enthusiasm for the prospect, but perhaps she had begun to realize that it wouldn't be all pleasure. He took her hand and pulled her out of the solar behind him.

"We'll go slowly at first. I don't know why you've let yourself favor that leg, Anne, but you shouldn't. The less you use it, the more it will pain you."

She jerked her hand away. "If my limp distresses you so, begone then."

He looked at her in surprise. "You need to work your leg, Anne. I'm here to see you do it properly."

"Very well, then," she said flatly. "Do what you will. It matters not to me."

Women. Would he ever understand them? Perhaps it was only Anne who baffled him. The women at court he could understand. They wanted him, ready, in their beds. They couldn't have cared less about his chivalry or lack thereof. He pleasured them well and they were left with a tale to tell their solar companions the next day.

But Anne was different. Robin couldn't understand her and he suspected he never would. He likely never had. From the looks of things, she couldn't bear his touch. And his generous offer to help her regain her strength had obviously displeased her.

He was tempted to sit down until his poor head stopped aching.

Saints, he'd never felt so unsure of himself. At least with women at court he knew how to comport himself. A single lifting of one eyebrow was all it usually took to have his bed warmed. He lifted his eyebrow seldom indeed, though.

He didn't want to speculate on why.

He walked the corridor with Anne and cursed under his breath. Damnation, he wasn't adept at gentle wooing. Demanding, aye; taking, surely; but wooing? Nay. He'd never had to.

She stumbled and he instantly caught her around the waist. Once she was steady, he tucked her hand under his arm. She jerked it free so hard, she almost went sprawling. Robin turned to her and put his hands on her shoulders to keep her upright. Before he could speak, she'd yanked her hood back.

"Begone from my sight, you heartless swine," she spat.

Robin felt his jaw slide down. "By the saints, Anne, what in the bloody hell have I done to you *now?*"

"You hypocrite. You cover my face so no one will see me, yet you hold on to me as if we were lovers. Find some wench more foolish than I to ply your unsavoury trade upon."

She turned on her heel and limped away. Robin stood, rooted to the spot. Hypocrite? *Hypocrite?* Damn her, the only reason he had kept her covered was to keep her safe! As for walking as lovers would, the woman had no idea what that meant. Perhaps he would do well to show her, that she never mistook a gallant touch for anything else again.

A shaft of pale light fell over her as she passed by a stairwell.

And he could have sworn there was a faint jingling sound in the distance.

"Anne!" he gasped, leaping forward.

She was so startled, she tripped and went down. A crossbow clattered down the stairs and came to rest at her feet. Robin skidded to a halt next to her. He gaped down at the weapon, still cocked, then looked up the stairwell.

"Guards!" he thundered suddenly. He looked down at Anne, torn. He could either go up the stairs himself after the murderer and leave Anne alone, or he could take her to his sire's chamber and lock her in, and never let her out again.

He looked at Anne and found that she wasn't moving. He cursed, waving a fond farewell to any hope of seeing who had attempted to harm her. He knelt next to her and gently drew her up.

"Open your eyes," he commanded. "Anne, look at me!"

She threw her arms around him and clung to him. Robin was too unsettled to be surprised. He looked up as several of his guardsmen thumped down the steps and came to a teetering halt before him.

"Did you see anyone?" Robin asked.

"Nay, my lord," his captain said. "Just the normal servants and guardsmen."

Robin took Anne in his arms and rose to his feet. "Anyone you would remember?"

He watched them think, then frowned at four shaking heads. Well, he supposed he couldn't fault them overmuch. There were servants and men-at-arms aplenty in the keep, and the passageways were certainly not off-limits to them. Robin sighed, bid his men follow him as he carried Anne up the steps and down to his sire's chamber.

His siblings rose almost as one as he entered. He ignored them and sought the fire, sinking down into a chair with Anne still in his arms.

"Anne, you're safe," he said quietly. "I'll not leave you again, I swear it." He wasn't sure how he would manage that, or if it would even be safe to keep her at his side. But for now, it was the best he could say to her.

"W-who is d-doing this?" she said, her teeth chattering.

"I don't know, but I'll find out."

"What happened?" Miles demanded from Robin's side.

"Aye," Nicholas said, coming to stand before him, "what mischief has been wrought? And why weren't you more careful?"

Robin explained and answered and thought he might go mad if his siblings didn't give him peace. And just as he thought he might have satisfied their poking and prodding, Anne tried to push out of his arms.

"I can't sit with you like this," she said, trying to escape.

"You've been sitting with me like this for a goodly while already; you'll survive a bit longer. Besides, I'm powerfully rattled. You'll need to hold on to me, very tightly, lest I break down and sob."

"Don't mock me!"

"Aye, don't mock her," Amanda added, cuffing Robin smartly on the ear.

Robin threw his sister a glare before he turned back to his lady. "I'm not mocking you. Can't you feel how I tremble?"

He wasn't about to tell her that fear was only part of the reason he trembled. By the saints, when was the last time he'd held her in his arms? When he'd been ten-and-four? At nine, Anne had hardly been the woman of his dreams.

"Robin, why does someone want me dead?"

"I don't know." By the saints, he wished he did.

She nodded, then sucked in her breath as she tried to stretch. Robin realized that he had her leg pinned against him, paining her. He sighed and rose with her in his arms. He carried her to the bed and laid her down. He covered her with a blanket, then turned back to his family, prepared to clear them from the chamber.

They didn't want to go, he could see that, but he couldn't stomach any more of their questions. He also thought he might get Anne back in his arms if they were alone and that wasn't something to be taken lightly. Besides, Nick and the twins could head up a search of the keep while Miles kept the girls safe. He himself had enough to do with his father's court to hold on the morrow. What else could he possibly find more important to do with his time that day than woo?

Then something else occurred to him. He looked at Anne. "I covered you up to keep you safe, not because I was ashamed of you."

"Robin—"

"Understood?"

She sighed. "Aye."

He knew she didn't believe him, but damn it, he didn't care. She would believe him if it were the very last thing she ever did. He'd see to it personally. He hadn't earned the reputation for being ruthless for naught.

He straightened and threw his siblings out. Nicholas, however, seemed loth to leave. Robin considered. He needed to plan a strategy, but he found that somehow it was the last thing he had the stomach for.

Just how was it a battle-roughened knight with flawed manners went about wooing a delicate lady? Nicholas would surely know. Nicholas could charm an abbess out of her clothes.

Robin hesitated at the doorway and frowned. He'd be damned if he'd ask his *younger* brother for advice. Nicholas would likely offer it to him with a straight face, then go off and howl over it until he was ill. Robin didn't need his suggestions anyway. Hell, it wasn't as if he didn't know Anne already. They'd been raised together. She liked . . . well, she liked . . . He sighed. He had no idea what she liked.

He straightened. It would just take him a bit to remember it. After all, he hadn't had much to do with her for the past ten years. A girl's tastes changed. But he'd go to hell before he'd admit his ignorance to Nicholas. The last thing he needed was to be faced with that irritating smirk at every turn.

His brother stood and approached him. Without thinking, Robin threw a fist into his brother's belly. Nicholas doubled over with a cough.

"What'd I do?" he gasped, straightening.

"Stop your smirking, you arrogant whoreson," Robin growled, hauling him outside into the passageway. He glared at his guardsmen for good measure, then pushed his brother in the direction of the steps. "You know exactly what you've done."

"You're daft! What do I have to smirk over?"

Robin gave him another shove. "I can woo her without your suggestions, fool."

"Woo her?" Nicholas spun around to look at him. "Woo her?"

There was the smirk. Robin was easily as irritated by it as he knew he would be.

"If it were me . . ." Nicholas began.

"It isn't, so shut up."

"I would prepare a bit of fine verse about her beauty," Nicholas continued, backing up as he spoke. "But perhaps rhyming isn't one of your skills."

Robin clenched his fists and wondered if clouting his brother strongly on the head might rid the dolt—and the rest of England, poor isle—of his own skills in the like.

"A ballad, then," Nicholas said. "Can you play the lute?"

Robin gritted his teeth. His brother knew he had no skill with minstrelsy, nor much else that didn't involve a blade and an opponent in which to stick it.

"Dancing?" Nicholas asked doubtfully.

How he continued to think so deeply and continue walking, Robin surely didn't know. It had to have come from all that time spent capering about great halls to music. A damned unmanly pursuit, to his mind.

Nicholas sighed heavily. "I don't know how you'll manage it, Rob—"

"Go!" Robin bellowed.

Nicholas winked, turned, and loped down the stairs. But Robin knew he couldn't be so fortunate as to escape one final barb.

"Brush her hair," came the faint suggestion. "Even you could manage that."

Robin blew out his breath, rolled his eyes heavenward, and turned back toward his bedchamber.

21

Maude pressed herself against the door of the garderobe and tried to catch her breath. The smell didn't help her in that effort, but she wasn't used to much finer, given the state of her sire's hall, so she made do. And as she took very deep breaths to calm her racing heart, she decided something.

Weapons of war were not her forte.

It had been a good hour since her failed attempt on Fenwyck's get, an hour in which she had wondered if now her own life might be the forfeit. Lady Edith's words had rung in her head with such force, she thought she might faint from the fear they inspired.

A clean death is much more dignified, don't you think? And in this intrigue we're engaged in, disobedience would merit the like.

You won't disobey again, will you, Maude?

Maude put her hand over her racing heart and closed her eyes. She would die if Edith discovered what she'd done, she was certain of that. There was no mercy in that woman's soul, despite her pretty tones.

But damn her, what did she expect? For Maude to stand there, doing nothing, watching Robin fall tinder that blond witch's spell?

If only she hadn't dropped the bloody bow before she'd managed to get it around the corner.

Well, at least the guards hadn't marked her. She was both flattered that she was able to escape notice so neatly and insulted that she was able to escape notice so neatly. Many a man had thought her memorable.

Many.

She took one final, cleansing breath and opened the door. The passageway was refreshingly cool and pleasant and she felt quite calm as she made her way along it.

To the kitchens, of course. There was no sense in lingering about in a place where there were no witnesses to any mayhem that might be combined against her.

Especially by Edith of Sedgwick.

Maude shuddered and quickened her pace.

22

Anne shifted in her chair, then forced herself to turn her attentions back to her stitching. She had much to be grateful for, she knew, not the least of which was the fact that she was in Gwen's solar and not her bedchamber. Things indeed could have been much worse. She looked up and smiled at the sight of her companions. Miles was sitting next to her, reading. The twins were playing chess in the corner. Amanda was laying out for them all an enormous list of Robin's flaws and Isabelle was chiding her for the like.

It was, on the whole, a most typical morning.

Or it would have been, had she not feared for her life every step she took outside the lord's bedchamber.

She wondered if Robin felt the like when he went into battle. It was odd to think that someone else moved and breathed with the thought of another soul's death consuming them. Nay, battle was not for her. She very much suspected she wouldn't have the stamina for it.

A movement startled her and she looked to her left. The only other occupant of the chamber was Edith of Sedgwick. Anne had been faintly surprised at Robin's having allowed Edith to join them in the solar, but no doubt he had his reasons. She suspected that Robin felt sorry for the girl. After all, she'd had to endure Sedgwick for several years. That and the fact that she hadn't been able to escape her brother's foul presence even at Artane was likely enough reason to pity her.

Anne watched her and wondered about her. They were of an age, and

Anne wondered why it was Edith had never found herself a husband—or, more to the point, why Edith's sire had never found a husband for her. She wasn't uncomely and she wasn't unpleasant to have speech with. Though Anne had to admit that there was something in Edith's eyes that she couldn't dismiss.

A coldness.

Edith caught her staring and Anne looked away quickly. She took up her stitchery again and made an effort to look busy. She could only be grateful that it was almost sunset and time to cease working. She'd passed far too much of the day in speculation and that was never good for a body. What she needed to do was force Robin to sit and have speech with her. He'd passed the evening with her the night before, but there had been little in the way of conversation. He had brought the steward up and they had talked far into the evening about matters that would arise today in Artane's court. Anne had listened and remembered, that she might tell Rhys that Robin had done well—at least as far as her opinion went. His questions had been piercing and unrelenting. Anne had suspected the steward had been very much relieved when he'd been allowed to go.

The sudden jingle of a bracelet almost wrenched a scream from her.

"By the saints," she gasped. "What was that?"

Isabelle held up her arm. "Robby gave it to me." She looked at Anne, a puzzled expression on her face. "Haven't you seen it?"

Anne forced herself to take slow, even breaths. As she looked at Isabelle's wrist, an unruly, impossible thought assailed her.

Could Isabelle be behind this?

She shook her head sharply to clear it. Never had a more absurd notion come into her mind. There was nothing but deep affection between her and Artane's youngest daughter. Not only that, it was impossible to believe Isabelle capable of such malice. Nay, 'twas foolishness.

"It's beautiful," Anne managed.

"'Tis the second one he bought me," Isabelle said, twisting her wrist this way and that and watching the bracelet. "He said the first one was uglier, though, and perhaps 'twas a good thing he lost it."

Amanda snorted. "He can hardly hold a thought. It shouldn't surprise you that he couldn't manage to keep hold of your bracelet."

"How kind of him to find you another," Edith said, smiling. "He is a good brother."

"Aye," Isabelle said, giving Amanda a pointed look. "He is at that."

"You must wonder, however," Edith said, "where it was that he lost it."

Isabelle shrugged. "It matters not to me."

"I think," Edith said slowly, "that I've seen one like it."

"Have you?" Isabelle asked.

"The location escapes me," Edith said with a frown. She looked up and smiled brightly. "It doesn't matter, I suppose. 'Tis enough that Robin found you another."

"Aye," Isabelle agreed. "And I'm happy someone else besides me thinks so. Anne does, of course, but Amanda is truly impossible when it comes to Robin."

Anne watched Isabelle and Edith carry on an animated discussion of Robin's good points. Amanda snorted and muttered her way through the same list, leaving Miles chuckling now and again. But no one else in the chamber seemed to find anything unsettling about the girl. Anne shook her head. Perhaps she was the one who was going daft. Edith had likely had a miserable childhood. Perhaps 'twas only that which Anne saw lingering in her eyes.

The door opened suddenly and the lord in question himself stood there. Anne looked up at him and couldn't squelch a small tingle of pleasure at the sight. She resolutely pushed away any thoughts of how long she might enjoy such pleasure. For the moment she was home and Robin seemed determined to keep her well within his reach. She could hardly ask for more.

Edith stood suddenly, her sewing dropping to the floor. Anne watched as Robin retrieved it for her, then handed it to her. As Edith passed him out the door, she favored him with the same smile she gave to everyone. Anne couldn't help but think that it was tinged with something.

Triumph?

Anne clapped her hand to her forehead. By the saints, she was losing her wits. It had to be too much confinement. Perhaps Robin had learned something that day that might purchase her a bit of freedom.

"Miles, take the children back to our chamber," Robin said shortly.

"Children?" Amanda echoed. "Just who do you think—"

Anne found herself relieved of her sewing and drawn to her feet before she knew what Robin intended. He put his arm around her and led her to the door.

"Nick will be up later to see how you fare," Robin threw over his shoulder.

He paused, looked up and down the passageway, then pulled Anne out with him. She found herself tucked securely at his side as he made his way to the stairwell. She was surprised to watch him draw a dagger before he preceded her down.

"This is madness," she whispered.

His only reply was a grunt.

Once they had reached the lower floor, Robin again drew her close and walked with her down the passageway. His guards were outside the bed-chamber door.

"Anything?" Robin demanded.

"Nay, my lord," said one. "Nothing."

Robin sheathed his dagger, then led Anne inside the chamber. He led her to a chair, but Anne shook her head.

"I'll pace for a bit," she said. "I've been idle too long this day."

"Would that we could both take a turn about the lists," he said grimly. "I too have suffered too much confinement this day."

"Did you learn aught?" she asked, coining to stand next to him.

He knelt before the hearth and brought the embers back to life. "Aye, more than I ever wanted to know about the pettiness of mankind."

She smiled at his disgruntled tone. "You've sat with your sire often enough on these things, haven't you? It should have come as no surprise."

He scowled at her. "Aye, but it was never my own sorry self trying to mete out justice. By the saints, Anne, why can these souls not treat each other kindly?"

"Why indeed," she mused.

He opened his mouth to speak, then shut it and pursed his lips. "Is that a barb especially for me, Lady Anne?"

She shook her head with a smile. "For us both, my lord."

"After today," he said, "I vow I would be happy never to bicker again."

"Even with me?" she asked.

He paused. "Aye," he said. "Especially with you."

Damn him, would he never cease to take her off guard? She cleared her throat, desperate to redirect his attention. The very intensity in his eyes made her nervous.

"Could you say the like about Amanda?" she asked, grasping for something to distract him.

He looked up at her with a glint in his eye. "She is my sister. You, however, are not."

Before she could recapture the breath she'd lost hearing *that*, Robin had risen, dusted off his hands, then made himself comfortable in a chair. He looked up at her.

"Come here." He patted his knees.

"I beg your pardon?"

"Come sit here. Now."

"Absolutely not!"

He hooked a stool with his foot and dragged it in front of him. "Here then. I want you over here."

She lifted her eyebrows as far as they would go. It would have been more effective if she could lift only one as Robin and Nicholas could. She hoped her look was haughty enough as it was.

"Now why would I want to come over there when you haven't the manners to ask me politely?"

He leaned forward. "Because you don't want a chivalrous knight. I'm sure of it. Now, come you here while my humor is still sweet."

"Why?"

"Your place is to obey me, not question me. Did my mother teach you nothing?"

"She taught me to think for myself!"

"More's the pity."

She looked at him narrowly. "What are you going to do? Throttle me?"

"As I said before, you are not my sister. You're safe from that fate."

Anne considered, but before she could make up her mind just what he was about, he had risen, led her over to the stool, and very gently sat her upon it.

"My concession to chivalry tonight," he grumbled as he sat down behind her. "Are you close enough to the fire? Too close?"

"Fine, but what—"

He put his hand on top of her head to keep her from turning around. "I've never met a woman who could talk as much as you do. Your silence would please me greatly."

She opened her mouth to let fly a retort, then she felt his hands trying to remove her wimple and veil. She didn't wear them much, as a rule, but Robin had insisted that morning that she might have her hair covered and thereby retain some anonymity.

"Vexing contraptions," he grumbled.

"Robin," she said, swallowing hard, "what do you?"

He sighed so hard, he blew her veil over her face. "I plan to brush your hair," he said in annoyance. "If you could just let me be about my work!" He gave a hearty tug, and her headwear came off in his hand.

She felt his hand slide gently down her hair, his touch belying the gruffness of his tone. And speech deserted her. She heard Robin's chair scrape against the floor as he moved closer to her. She knew he was closer because his knees were touching the back of her arms.

She closed her eyes and swallowed convulsively the moment she felt the brush touch her scalp. By the saints, she could scarce believe she wasn't dreaming. Nay, that was his hand wielding the brush so hesitantly, as if he feared to hurt her. And he thought himself ruthless. It was perhaps well none of his men could see him at present or they would have had a different tale to tell.

She trembled as he pulled the hair gently back from her face.

"Hurt?"

"Nay," she whispered.

Once he was certain no tangles remained, he began to drag the brush through her hair with long, chill-inducing strokes.

She shivered.

His hand stopped. "Should I cease?"

"Aye, if you don't value your skin."

He snorted out a laugh. She looked over her shoulder at him, surprised. It had been years since she'd heard Robin do anything akin to it. But he only put his hand atop her head and turned it around again.

She closed her eyes and simply enjoyed. She waited for Robin to grow bored and stop, but he seemed perfectly content to do nothing but continue with his work. He brushed her hair, then he began to trail his fingers through it. Finally he merely skimmed over it with the flat of his hand.

"I can see why you cover your hair," he said quietly.

"Can you?" she asked. "It compares poorly with Amanda's and Isabelle's. Theirs is so rich and dark."

"And here I was thinking yours was like pale, spun gold," he said, sounding amused. "I thought you covered it not to shame them."

She couldn't stop herself from turning around to look at him in surprise. "You didn't."

He smiled and the sight of it was so beautiful, she could scarce look at him. "Anne," he said, with a slow shake of his head, "you do yourself too little credit."

"I have eyes that work perfectly well," she said tartly.

He took her hands in his. "As do I, and I know what I see. You've no reason for shame in their company, for you are indeed their equal."

She felt her jaw slide down, but could find nothing to say to that. Surely, he didn't think her beautiful.

"Well," he said, frowning a bit, "perhaps not Amanda's equal."

She shut her mouth with a snap. There, now he began to sound more rational.

"Her tongue sours some of her beauty, I think, whilst yours does not."

She watched as he brought her hands to his mouth and kissed them. A shiver that started in her poor, captive fingers worked its way down her arms and up to her head. She was certain her hair was beginning to stand on end. His smile faltered and he looked at her with a seriousness she had rarely seen him wear.

"Anne . . ."

Anne watched in astonishment as he leaned toward her. By the look on his face, she very much suspected that he intended to kiss her.

And *that* was enough to fair send her falling off her stool in surprise.

She watched one of his hands reach toward her and slide under her hair to touch the back of her neck. Robin bent his head, his eyes never leaving her face. She didn't dare breathe, didn't dare blink, didn't dare even think too hard lest she break the spell.

He was going to kiss her.

The moment she had waited for the whole of her life was about to commence.

"Anne," he whispered, his lips a hand's breadth from hers.

And then a fierce banging on the door almost sent him tumbling into her lap.

Anne caught him before he pitched fully into her arms. He straightened and blinked, as if he'd just been struck strongly on the head.

"Robby," a voice called, accompanied by more banging. "I've brought supper. Open up."

Robin blinked at Anne. He looked as dazed as she felt.

"I'm going to kill him," he managed. "I vow I'll do it this time."

The banging on the door continued. "Hurry. The trencher is heavy!"

Anne watched Robin heave himself to his feet. He stomped across the chamber and threw open the door.

Nicholas barged in, elbowing Robin in the belly to gain passage. Anne watched him shove supper into Robin's hands, then cross the chamber to her. She couldn't even smile. All she could do was look at him, mute.

"What have you done to the girl?" Nicholas exclaimed. "She looks positively bewildered."

"He brushed my hair," Anne whispered.

Nicholas sat down in Robin's chair and made himself comfortable. "I'm ready for a demonstration, then. Robby, come show me how 'tis done."

Nicholas was summarily hauled to his feet by his hair.

"State your business, then go," Robin growled, shoving his brother before he set supper down on the floor.

"And leave you alone with her? Never."

"Have you any tidings for me?" Robin barked.

"Nay."

"Then begone. We've no need of you."

"I disagree—"

Anne watched Robin propel Nicholas into the hall with all the efficiency of a shepherd's hound. The door was slammed shut and bolted. Robin turned slowly and looked at her. Anne could do nothing but stare back at him. She watched him take a deep breath, then put his shoulders back.

She had the feeling he would not be thwarted in his plans this time.

And that was enough to weaken her knees so greatly she wasn't sure she could stand.

He marched purposefully across the chamber toward her. He stopped before her, took her by the arms, and pulled her to her feet. Anne swayed, then put her hands on his chest to steady herself.

Robin wrapped one arm around her waist, then slid his hand under her head again to cup the back of her head.

"Oh," she said involuntarily. By the saints, she had never expected to have these kinds of tingles overcome her at the mere thought of kissing Robin of Artane.

She had certainly never felt the like when Nicholas had kissed her.

And then she had no more time for thinking. Robin bent his head, gathered her more closely to him, and captured her mouth with his. There was no other way to view it.

It was no polite kiss.

She shivered.

So did he.

She found herself slipping her arms up around his neck. It seemed the thing to do, because she was sure that way she would have a better chance of using him to keep from falling to her knees. She closed her eyes and gave herself up to the devastating sensations that rocked her to her very core. He kissed her again and again until she wondered if she would ever again take a normal breath.

And then, if that hadn't been overwhelming enough by itself, he kissed her deeply.

She lost all rational thought. All she could feel was Robin's hand in her hair, his mouth on hers—

She sincerely hoped his eyes were closed so he couldn't see her blush. Her mouth had never been investigated by anyone besides the barber surgeon when once she'd had a sore tooth and he'd been peering inside, not using his—

Robin kissed her mouth closed with a brief, hard kiss, then stepped back a pace. His chest was heaving. He looked flushed, which eased her mind greatly for she suspected that she looked the same.

He said nothing. He merely held her by the arms and stared at her with an intensity that fair burned her to cinders where she stood.

Then he blinked and cleared his throat.

"Dinner," he rasped.

"Aye," she managed.

"'Twill grow cold, else."

"Likely," she agreed.

But she ached like she had never ached before with the desire to go back into his arms and never leave them. By the saints, having a taste of what it could be like to be encircled in his embrace was overwhelming.

Never mind how it felt to be kissed by him.

She suspected that she would never be the same.

23

Robin waited impatiently for his squire to see to his mail. He shrugged his shoulders and rolled his neck, trying to work the kinks out of it. Too many more nights spent either in the chair or on the floor would be his undoing. It was one thing to know that naught but the ground was available; 'twas a far different thing to be sleeping ten paces from a bed, and a comfortable one at that, and knowing that all that kept him from it was good manners.

And it surely wasn't as if he possessed those in abundance.

Though after kissing Anne the night before, he was almost certain that lying abed with her would be a very bad idea indeed.

"Be quick, Jason," he whispered.

Anne slept still and Robin wished for her to remain that way until he could make his escape. He wasn't sure how she would view the events of the previous evening once she'd had a chance to digest them in her sleep.

He knew how he felt, though. And not only had he stolen that first mind-numbing kiss, he'd bested her twice in chess, which had led to many other simple tastes of her sweet lips. He hadn't dared kiss her again as he had at first. He was still reeling from it. And that was one of the reasons he had slept on the floor and not in her bed.

He held up his arms while Jason helped him into his surcoat, then belted his sword about his waist. He felt his heart begin to soften toward his squire, who was always so diligent about caring for his gear. He supposed perhaps it was a menial task for the future baron of Ayre, but the saints only knew he'd done his share of menial tasks as a squire.

Robin clapped Jason on the shoulder. "I'm in the mood for sport this morn, lad. Perhaps you'll care to provide me with it."

"Me?" Jason said, his surprise poorly hidden.

"Aye, you," Robin said with a half smile. "You're a fine enough swordsman. I should know, as I'm the one who has trained you."

"Of course, my lord."

Robin paused. It was on the tip of his tongue to tell Jason he was sorry for the terrible places he'd dragged him, all the battles, the endless sieges, the dangerous courts. It was a wonder Jason could still smile.

"Have you had such a poor life, Jason?"

Jason looked at him as if he'd never seen him before. "My lord, are you unwell?"

Well, perhaps that was answer enough. Robin turned Jason toward the door and gave him a gentle push. "Fetch Miles and return. He'll be capable of protecting Anne for a bit."

Jason trotted off dutifully. Robin sighed as he adjusted his sword at his side. Jason would leave soon enough to make his own way and Robin would be sorry for it. He was a good lad, likely all the better for not having grown to manhood at Ayre.

Not that it was such a foul place. After all, Ayre was his, because of his sire. Robin had never had any desire to live there, or to be its lord in truth. Jason's father, John, had been Alain of Ayre's youngest brother and had willingly taken on the task of seeing to Ayre.

John was a fine lord and Robin had never had any complaints about his care of the soil. Jason would likely make just as fine a lord when the time came. Robin smiled to himself. At least he knew if Jason displeased him, he could yet thrash the lad in the lists. It wasn't such a poor way to settle a dispute.

Robin looked at the bed. Anne slept still, surely. He hesitated, then moved to take hold of the bed curtains. Just a small peek to assure himself that she slept well. He couldn't be faulted for that, could he? He pulled the curtain back and looked down at her, her face scarce revealed by the dim light in the chamber.

She opened her eyes and he jumped in spite of himself.

"I thought you slept still," he managed.

She shook her head.

Robin forced himself not to shift uncomfortably. He'd kissed the woman before him senseless the night before and now he felt as callow as a young squire. Did she regret it? In how many ways had she found him lacking?

"I need to train this morn, to clear my head." *To give you time to decide if you want me or not*, he added silently.

She nodded.

"Miles will arrive presently."

"Thank you."

He nodded, then made his way out of the chamber before he did anything else foolish. He waited until his brother arrived, instructed him to stay out in the passageway until Anne had risen, then pushed Jason in front of him down to the great hall. Robin stopped for a cup of ale, grateful to be doing something besides sitting and stewing.

"My lord?"

Robin frowned at him, hoping to dissuade him from speaking.

"My lord," Jason said again, shifting uncomfortably, "ah, the lady Anne . . ."

"What about her?" Robin demanded.

Jason clasped his hands behind his back. "Ah," he began, looking completely miserable, "about her virtue, my lord. I hesitate to speak of this . . ."

Five years ago, Robin could have lifted Jason off the ground with one hand and held him suspended there while he shouted at him. Jason was now ten-and-six, and much heavier. And much braver, Robin thought grudgingly.

"She's a maid still," Robin grumbled.

"But, my lord, I know it has been many months since you have taken a woman—"

"Enough," Robin interrupted sharply. "It isn't my habit to despoil virtuous maidens, and you know it well."

Jason nodded, miserably. "But, my lord, when Fenwyck learns . . ."

"I'll see to him when the time comes, if that time comes. What you don't seem to understand, little lad, is that there is no safer place for her than my chamber with my sword before her. Unless you think you are more capable than I of protecting her?"

"Of course not, my lord. You are a master."

Robin grunted and set his cup down. "We'll go to the lists and I'll prove it to you again."

Jason trailed behind him obediently. Robin rolled his eyes at the number of times Jason cleared his throat as they walked out through the inner bailey and out the gate to the lists. Finally, he could stand it no longer. He whirled around.

"What?" he demanded.

Jason bumped into him, then jumped back and made a small bow. "Nothing, my lord."

"Stop quivering. I've yet to lay a hand on you, you pampered puss." It was true. He might have hardened his heart against others in his life, but he'd always harbored a soft spot for the young lad with bright blue eyes who had looked at him as if he could do no wrong. "Speak your mind freely, Jason. As I have the feeling you'll do anyway," he muttered.

Jason wiped his hands on his thighs. "My lord, I know you and the lady Anne haven't been close in years past—"

Robin grunted.

"But, well, have a care with her, won't you?" Jason asked, looking up at Robin earnestly.

"I gave you my word she would remain a maid."

"I speak of her heart, my lord," Jason said quietly.

Robin looked at his squire, seeing him in a different light. The lad was no longer a child, but a lad on the verge of manhood. Robin folded his arms over his chest and looked Jason over carefully.

"What would you know of her heart? Or any woman's heart, for that matter?"

Jason reddened. "I am not ignorant of the ways of men and women, my lord."

"Of course you aren't."

"I speak of matters of the heart, my lord, not of bedding." He paused and took a deep breath. "She loves you, my lord."

Robin pursed his lips, "Of course she doesn't. She wants a chivalrous lout with a sweet tongue and gentle manners."

Jason shook his head. "I must disagree. She may say that is what she wants, but her eyes tell a different story. She is quite easy to read if you look closely enough."

"And just what would you know of reading a woman, boy?"

"I know how Isabelle looks at me," Jason insisted. "And I know how I feel about her. 'Tis all in the eyes, my lord—"

"Isabelle!" Robin gasped, finding his tongue. "My sister Isabelle?"

Jason blushed to the roots of his hair. "A slip of the tongue, my lord."

Robin lunged and took Jason down to the dirt. "Isabelle," he repeated, incredulous. "Jason, she's a *child*!"

"Old enough to be betrothed," Jason insisted.

Robin couldn't decide if he were more shocked about Jason telling him that Anne loved him, or knowing the identity of the woman who held Jason's heart. How had this come about? They hadn't been home a month!

"But you hardly know her!"

"Ofttimes, it doesn't take long," Jason managed.

"Does my father know?"

"Saints, nay," Jason said quickly, shaking his head. "He'd likely have me strung up if he did."

"Have you touched her?" Robin demanded.

"I wouldn't dare!"

Robin grunted. "See that you don't, or you'll answer to me." He rolled off his squire and heaved himself to his feet. "Daft, Jason. That's what you are. She'll give you gray hairs before you earn your spurs." He hauled Jason to his feet.

"Will Lord Rhys give her to me, think you?"

"Why you'd want her is a mystery to me."

"She's beautiful. And kind. And I want to be braver and more gallant when I'm with her. Isn't that reason enough?"

Robin shook his head. "I suppose so, lad."

Jason walked next to him with his head bowed. "Would you speak kindly of me to him if he asked you of me?"

Robin took Jason by the back of the neck and shook him. "I'll see how you show this morn, Jason, before I decide what I'll tell your lady's father about you."

Robin was surprised he hadn't known about it sooner. Was he truly so unobservant, or was Jason better at hiding his feelings than Robin had given him credit for?

Robin watched Jason critically in the lists. The lad had become a fine warrior in the past ten years. Robin even felt himself begin to smile as he marked Jason using some of Robin's own techniques against him. Perhaps Isabelle could do worse than this lad.

It was a goodly while later that Robin finally called peace and put his hand on Jason's shoulder.

"Well done, Ayre. Your father will be most pleased with you."

"And yours?" Jason smiled. "Will he be pleased also?"

Robin frowned. "Little lad, you should rather be more concerned that I am pleased with you. My father is not your master, I am."

"My lord, I know you are pleased with me. And you do not hold my love's fate in your hands. I daresay you likely feel the same about my lord Fenwyck."

"Be silent," Robin hissed. "Think you I wish for everyone to hear your witless words? Moon all you like over my sister, but do not expect me to join you."

"Of course, my lord," Jason said quickly. "I meant it only in jest."

"And Fenwyck's opinion matters not to me," Robin added with a growl. "I could best him on any field."

"Aye, you could."

Robin looked up as Nicholas approached, grinning lazily like the idiot he was. Robin scowled at his brother.

"What do you want, dolt?"

Nicholas put one hand on Jason's shoulder and the other on Robin's. "You two are as chatty as two ladies-in-waiting. Discussing your lady-loves?"

Robin knocked his hand away. "We were discussing the best way to disembowel a grinning fool. Jason, perhaps you should test my theory on this fool here."

Nicholas only laughed and slung his arm around Jason's shoulder. "It sounds as if he has a fine ease of it, doesn't it, Jason?"

"I couldn't say, my lord," Jason answered, yawning. "My lord Robin thinks a dagger vertically down the belly is most effective. What say you?"

Nicholas grinned and winked at Robin. "You know, I think he kissed her last eve. I couldn't tell if she was pleased by his attentions or so ill she was dazed. Perhaps you'll come with me tonight and you can decide—"

Robin sheathed his sword and shoved his brother. "She was not displeased!"

Nicholas threw back his head and laughed heartily. "St. Michael's bones, Rob, you are a besotted pup."

Robin drew his sword with a curse. Nicholas grabbed Jason by the shoulders and put him between them. "Now, now, brother. You wouldn't want to disembowel your squire. Jason, what has put him in such a terrible temper? Could it be love?"

"This isn't amusing anymore," Robin snarled. "Release the boy and face me like a man, if you're capable of it. Or have too many evenings spent honing your skill with the lute left you unable to put your fingers to the hilt of your blade?"

Nicholas had shoved Jason aside and drawn his own sword before Robin could blink. Robin countered his brother's parries with thrusts of his own, ones that should have silenced Nicholas permanently, or at least warned him he was close to being so silenced. Nicholas wasn't paying Robin's warnings any heed, if his attack were any indication. In the back of his mind, Robin was vaguely impressed with his brother's detachment and precision. But he didn't spare it much thought. His mind was on fire and he went with the heat, not caring if he cut his sibling to ribbons before he came to himself.

It wasn't how he usually fought. He knew he had a warriorly reputation for recklessness, just as Nicholas did for being cold and methodical. But even in the heat of battle, while the blood was thundering in his ears and his fury was all-consuming, Robin never released that small part of his mind that was perfectly calm, perfectly rational, perfectly sane. It was the logic that controlled his strategy.

He couldn't find that calmness at present. He was embarrassed. He'd known Nicholas would make sport of him, but to keep harping, to speak loudly enough that others could hear—that he hadn't expected even from his hopelessly romantic sibling. Damn him, he should have had more respect! Whatever intimacies Robin shared with Anne were not fodder for conversation in the lists.

Not that he'd share them again. Bloody hell, if this was what kissing her earned him, he'd never come within two feet of her again!

"Robin!"

He heard Nicholas's warning shout and jerked back the moment before Nicholas's blade would have gone through his arm. As it was, there was a fine rent in his tunic sleeve.

"By the saints, Rob, what were you thinking about?" Nicholas exclaimed, dropping his sword and coming toward him. "I almost cut your head off."

Robin had no good answer for that. "Jason, come with me," he said, shrugging off Nicholas's hand. "Nick, see that the men attend to their work. This is not a day of leisure."

"And you will be?" Nicholas asked.

"Making certain that all is well inside," Robin said. He strode through the lists, wanting nothing more than to escape notice until he could regain his composure.

"Artane, a moment!"

Robin saw Baldwin coming toward him with a purposeful glint in his eye. He cursed and waved the man away. He had no time for him this day.

"Stop," Baldwin exclaimed. "Stand and face me!"

Robin paused and glared at him. "For what purpose? To best you again? Was last time not sufficient?"

Baldwin drew his sword with a flourish and a curse. Robin muttered under his breath and drew his own blade. Perfect. Could his day deteriorate any more than this?

He set his squire out of harm's way and drew his own blade the moment before Baldwin's reached him. He might have been distracted with Nicholas, but he suffered no such affliction now. Baldwin was furious and Robin supposed he couldn't blame the man. After all, he had humiliated his cousin badly on their first and only encounter. Perhaps Baldwin had listened to the recent laughter of Robin's family over and over again in his head until his temper was past being controlled. Robin smiled pleasantly as he easily deflected Baldwin's paltry attack. Perhaps all those years spent warring had been a benefit after all. He'd faced much worse than this and lived.

"I'll kill you," Baldwin snarled.

"You continue to say as much," Robin answered, "yet I live still. How is this possible?"

"I haven't," Baldwin said, grunting with exertion, "begun my labors in truth."

"Haven't you?" Robin asked. "Please alert me when that day comes. I'll want to be ready."

Baldwin only snarled a curse in answer. Robin watched him as they fought and a thought occurred to him. Was it possible Baldwin was behind the attacks on Anne? No sense in not finding out.

"Are you coward enough to attack a woman?" Robin asked suddenly.

Baldwin sneered. "I wouldn't spare one the effort. Why, when I've your death to think on?"

"Why indeed," Robin muttered. He found, suddenly, that he tired of this confrontation. Though he could surely understand his father's desire to keep Sedgwick in his sights, he wondered if that necessity hadn't passed. Should he remain at Artane, he would suggest to his sire that life would be more pleasant without Baldwin's smirk to endure each day. And 'twas a certainty Baldwin was no sterling swordsman.

Robin went on the attack and took as little time as possible to dispatch his foe. Baldwin's sword went flying, and he came at Robin with his fists. Robin sighed, tossed his blade at Jason, and showed Baldwin as quickly as possible that he knew how to use his hands as well as his weapons. When Baldwin tripped and went down heavily onto the field, Robin walked away without another word. He had had enough. Perhaps he would find another tunic and see how Anne fared.

It was his duty after all.

And he wasn't one to shirk duty.

It would also give him ample time to see if she looked on him with disgust. He could have sworn he'd felt her shiver the night before, but that could have been with revulsion.

By the saints, he didn't even trust his own instincts anymore.

"Jason."

"Aye, my lord," Jason said, handing Robin his blade.

"Help me off with this mail upstairs, then use the rest of the afternoon for your pleasure. You might train a bit more."

"Aye, I could."

"Or you could deliver a message to my sister Isabelle for me."

"If you required it of me, I daresay I could force myself to."

Robin smiled before he could stop himself. "Ah, Jason, I have ruined you for polite company."

Jason shook his head. "You have taught me much, my lord. I could not have asked for a finer master. And I would gladly accept any advice you could give me in the matter of wooing this headstrong wench of mine."

Robin had a hard time hiding his surprise. "Me? Rather you should ask my womanly brother."

"Nay, I would rather hear your words. Any man could win a woman with flattery. Isabelle is apparently unmoved by it. What else would you suggest?"

Robin gave it a good deal of thought until they made their way to Artane's bedchamber. Robin paused before the door. "Brush her hair for her," he said. "For the life of me I don't know why, but they all seem to like it."

"And kissing?"

"If you kiss my sister before she wears your ring, I'll disembowel you. Lengthwise across your belly. We decided that was a much more painful and prolonged death, didn't we?"

Jason gulped. Robin opened the door. "Come inside, Jason, and help me. Then you are free for the day."

Anne gasped the moment he entered. She rose and started toward him. "What happened to you?"

"Nothing," he said shortly.

"Nothing?" she echoed. "Your clothes are fair to falling off you and this is nothing?"

Robin ignored Anne as Jason pulled off his mail shirt. He pulled off his tunic as well. Then he looked at her.

And all his irritation over Nicholas's teasing vanished. Being the object of Nicholas's jests wasn't that painful. He could always thrash his younger brother if need be. And, besides, did any of that matter when he held Anne in his arms, felt her trembling mouth beneath his, touched her smooth skin and silky hair? Nicholas could laugh as long and as loudly as he liked. He had no woman of his own.

Robin caught Anne's empty hand and brought it to his lips. "I am well."

"You're unbloodied," she corrected. "Well is still undecided." She looked at Jason. "Who did this?"

Jason laid Robin's mail shirt over a trunk. "Nicholas, my lady."

"Is his skill so poor that he tripped and fell on you with his blade bared? Or was he mooning over some wench? Aye, I can see that readily enough."

Robin snorted. "As can I. Jason, I want a meal. See to it before you seek out my sister, would you?"

By the swiftness of his leave-taking, Robin suspected his squire had a mind to woo himself. Poor wretch.

Robin made himself comfortable in a chair before the fire and passed a goodly hour watching Anne surreptitiously as she sewed. There came a point, though, when he couldn't bear just the watching anymore. He leaned over and before he could give it more thought, kissed her softly.

She looked at him in surprise.

"What?" he asked. "Must I best you at chess before I kiss you?"

She looked at him in silence for so long, he began to grow uncomfortable.

"Anne, what is it?"

She shook her head. "I vow I do not know you."

"Don't you?"

"Why are you doing this to me?"

"Why not?" he said, tossing the words off casually. Saints, what was he supposed to say? *I'm wracking my poor head for ways to please you?*

"You bastard," she said through gritted teeth. She rose ungracefully to her feet and glared at him. "I'll not be sport for you."

Sport? He felt his temper rise swiftly, but before he could give vent to it, Anne had limped over to the alcove.

And then he could have sworn he heard a sniffle.

Ah, by the saints. He rolled his eyes as he heaved himself to his feet. He stepped up behind her and put his arms around her waist, dropping his chin to her shoulder.

"Anne, you aren't sport for me."

"Of course not," she said curtly. "Why would you even take sport of a cripple, much less anything else?"

"Cease with that talk," he exclaimed. "You know it angers me when you speak of yourself that way."

"How would I know?" she demanded. "You've hardly spoken to me since it happened, except to curse me."

"That isn't true."

"Aye, it is."

He stood there and considered her words. Was it true? Not at first. At first, they had recovered together. Ah, but then he'd tried to defend her honor and Baldwin had humiliated him. Had he spoken to her since? Unlikely. He put his hands on her shoulders and turned her around to face him.

"Anne . . ."

"Please don't hurt me," she wept "I couldn't bear it, Robin. I vow I couldn't."

"Anne, why would I hurt you?"

"You hurt me just by being here," she said. She pulled away from him and turned toward the window. "I beg you to go. Please."

Robin felt his heart still within him. "You want me to leave?"

"Aye," she said. "I want you to go."

Robin didn't want to, but he couldn't see what else to do. Anne wasn't turning to face him. So he turned and walked soundlessly from the chamber. He hardly noticed that he wasn't wearing his boots. He nodded to his men, then continued on down the passageway. At least Anne would be safe with his guards at her door.

Her weeping haunted him all the way down to the great hall.

The next day Robin still sat in a chair before the fire in the great hall and stared into the flames before him. He hadn't moved since the afternoon before and already it was afternoon again. Anne's words rang over and over in his head. She didn't want him. He'd come home for naught. She found him lacking. Hadn't she said as much? What else could she have meant by telling him if he stayed he would only hurt her?

Booted feet stopped next to him and a long frame settled into the chair facing him.

"Rob, what is it?"

Robin spared his brother a weary look before he turned back to the fire. "I regret there is no longer anything for you to laugh about," he said heavily. "Forgive me for not providing you with more sport."

"Now, Rob, how often do you provide me with something to tease you about? And I'm sorry about almost cutting you. You know I didn't do it purposely."

"I know." Robin sighed. "It was my fault. I was preoccupied."

"Speaking of your preoccupation, why aren't you with her?"

Robin met Nicholas's gray eyes. "She bid me leave her," he said flatly.

"Perhaps she needed a moment of privacy."

"She bid me go away, Nick. For longer than merely a moment of privacy. She said I hurt her merely by being near her. You tell me what that means if not that she cannot bear the sight of me."

Nicholas looked into the fire. Robin watched his brother's expression sober and his heart sank even further. So it was obvious to Nick too. Robin groaned inwardly. How could he have ever imagined that she would come to care for him? It was obvious that someone like Nicholas was what she wanted, a man with polish, a man who wouldn't hurt her with his rough edges.

Nicholas leaned forward with his forearms on his knees.

"If I told you something honestly, from my heart, would you hear me?"

How much worse could he hurt than he hurt at present? Robin nodded slowly.

"And you won't immediately discount my words as the ramblings of your younger, empty-headed sibling?"

"Difficult, but I'll try."

Nicholas didn't smile. "Robin, I've jested with you in the past about things, about women and your poor tastes, but you know I only did it because I love you so well. And I think you take yourself far too seriously." He smiled briefly. "'Tis a younger brother's duty to torment his elder sibling and, since you never let me forget that you are the saints only know how much my senior, I have ever repaid you by teasing you. But I'm in earnest now."

Robin didn't move. "Go on."

"I'm certain you would see this as well, were you able to step back a few paces and look at what has happened between you and Anne over the years. She loves you. She's loved you for as long as I can remember. And after our little morning at Baldwin's mercy, she loved you still. But what you don't know is that she never saw what happened—"

"And she'll never know of it," Robin growled. "If you say one word to her about it, I'll kill you."

Nicholas shrugged off the threat. "That isn't the point. What you don't understand is that she has no idea why one day you were welcoming her into your sickroom and the next you were casting her from it. She thinks it is something she did."

"Of course she doesn't. She's done nothing to me. Short of making me daft each chance she had."

"You're not listening to me, Robin. Anne doesn't trust you."

"But I'm not planning to hurt her. Can't she see that?"

"Based on what? How you've never wavered in your devotion before?"

"I never did," Robin snarled. "My feelings for her never changed."

Nicholas looked at him so long in silence, Robin felt like squirming. Then he realized what he had said and how far he'd laid open his heart to his brother.

"She irritates me as much as she did when she was eight," he said quickly, hoping he'd put enough gruffness in his voice.

Nicholas smiled gravely. "Did you just hear yourself?"

Robin scowled at him in silence.

"Rob, you just admitted to loving her, then you denied it. Is it any wonder Anne's frightened witless of letting you close to her? How would you feel if she told you she loved you, then immediately made light of it?" He put his hand on Robin's shoulder and shook him gently. "Don't be a fool, Robin. You love her and she loves you. Somewhere, deep in that hidden heart of yours is a place she needs to see. I don't expect any of the rest of us will ever see it, but Anne deserves to. Be as gruff as you like with her in public, but don't do it in private." He rose and looked down at Robin. "She's far less likely to hurt you than you are to hurt her. I'd certainly trust her with my heart."

Robin watched him walk away. He fought with himself until Nicholas reached the hall door.

"Don't you dare," Robin called after him.

Nicholas smiled and made him a small bow before he left the hall. Robin turned back to his contemplation of the fire and his brother's words. He had no trouble seeing the truth of the matter. How could Anne possibly have known why he pushed her away? For all she knew, he could have shunned her because of her limp.

He felt the room begin to spin. Had she actually thought such a thing? Pieces began to fall furiously into place. She thought no man would want her because she was crippled. And why shouldn't she think that? He had shunned her after her accident. It would have been easy enough to assume that was the reason why. She hadn't seen his humiliation at Baldwin's hands;

he'd threatened anyone who ever spoke about it so severely that it had likely become past history in everyone's mind but his. Robin put his head in his hands and groaned. It was his fault. His stupid, foolish pride had hurt the very last person he had wanted to.

He rose, needing to pace. Was it too late? Nay, it couldn't be. He wouldn't allow it. It would likely take time, but perhaps he could win her trust again. He could never offer her flowery words and prettily sung ballads. Perhaps she would take him as he was, flawed and rough. Perhaps she could gentle him. If anyone could, it would be Anne.

But first a bath and a change of clothes. He'd borrow something of Nicholas's, then present himself at his chamber and hope that Anne would unlock the door.

24

Anne sat in the alcove with her knees drawn up and hugged to her chest. It was a painful way to sit, but she didn't care. The pain in her thigh numbed the pain in her heart. She'd hardly moved from the spot since Robin had left her there. His sire's bedchamber was the very last place she wanted to be, but she remembered vividly the sound of a crossbow clattering at her feet. If nothing else, she was safe where she was.

But once the culprit was discovered, she would be out of the lord's chamber immediately, never to return.

She was past weeping. She hadn't wept the night before, which had almost surprised her. Either she was too tired for the like, or she had expected Robin's words. Or perhaps it was that Robin truly did not love her and thus her tears need not be spent over him. She could hardly believe he had kissed her as he had. Perhaps boredom had driven him to it, or that he wasn't free to bed several of Rhys's serving wenches in rapid succession. Well, he was welcome to them. She wanted no part of him.

She was also a very great liar.

She sighed and leaned her head back against the wall. More was the pity that she loved him. And despite his words, she couldn't help but believe he harbored some affection for her.

Unless he could truly kiss her as he had without his heart taking part in it.

Was that possible?

A soft knock sounded on the door, interrupting her thoughts. She groaned as she unfolded herself from the seat and made her way haltingly across the floor. The knocking continued until she gained the door and pulled back the bolt. She opened the door and flinched once she saw Robin standing there.

He looked as if he hadn't slept since he'd left the night before. Likely because he'd been ravishing as many of his father's serving wenches as possible. She pursed her lips and turned back toward the alcove, leaving the door open. He could come or go as he pleased. She didn't care.

She was very surprised, when she sat down, to find Robin hovering in front of her. He covered her with a blanket, then stood there with his hands clasped behind his back.

"Are you comfortable?"

She didn't look up.

"I'll build you a fire."

He walked away, not waiting for an answer. Anne looked out the window. She heard Robin tending the fire, then heard his sound of dismay when he saw the untouched food. She closed her eyes and listened to the sound of wine being poured into a cup and that cup being set on the stone of the hearth. Wine would have been good. It might have soothed the chill in her heart.

She heard Robin's firm footfall as he walked to her. He shuttered the windows.

"I've made you a place by the fire."

"I'm not interested in it."

Anne didn't protest when he picked her up in his arms. Why bother? He wouldn't listen to her anyway. Had he been capable of listening, he wouldn't have come back.

She saw the nest of furs and pillows and then found herself set atop it. A heavy chair had been set there to support her back.

"I'm not a cripple," she said stiffly as Robin arranged a pillow behind her back. "I need none of this."

"Anne, this has nothing to do with your leg. I would certainly be more comfortable sitting this way."

"You seem to have no trouble sleeping on the uncomfortable floor."

"I'm accustomed to sleeping on the ground. I even slept in a tree once. The floor seems as commodious as a stack of goosefeather mattresses. Well, perhaps not a stack. Saints, woman, must you be so contrary?"

She looked at him, ready to give as good as she got, only to find him looking at her kindly. It was enough to irritate her into silence. She turned her head and tried to ignore him.

It didn't last. He nagged her until she ate. And after she could barely breathe, which satisfied him, he put a cup of warm wine in her hands.

She drank it, merely to have him cease troubling her, then she rose and walked to the alcove. Her leg was slowly beginning to pain her less. Perhaps she could credit Robin and his endless walking her about the chamber for that.

"I would like to do something to please you," he said quietly.

It was difficult to hide her surprise. By the saints, life with this man would be more complicated than she could stomach. Perhaps she would truly be better off without him.

"As a penance," he added.

"For what?"

"For speaking foolishness last night."

She waited, but apparently that was the only detail she would have from him. He looked very unwilling to say any more and that left her to speculate on just what he'd said the night before that he found foolish. There was ample material there, so she took his words and put them aside for future contemplation. What she did understand, however, was that she might very well have him at her mercy.

"Take me outside," she said, without hesitation.

He scowled. "Nay."

"To the chapel then."

"And if I say you nay, the fate of my soul hangs in the balance."

She waited, listened to his sighs, but remained unmoved by them. Finally he grumbled and rose. "Very well."

She felt a surge of victory. "I'll fetch my cloak."

"You will not kneel at St. Christopher's shrine today."

Perhaps she had no more need of prayers, now that Robin was returned safely. And she suspected her supplications hadn't gone beyond the chapel ceiling anyway, for 'twas a certainty that her pleas for him to love only her had gone unanswered. She had no idea what jest her saint sought to work upon her, but she would have no more of it.

No more of Robin's kisses, either.

She made that decision as Robin put her cloak around her shoulders. Aye, she would have no more of that and if he offered, she would refuse. Perhaps she would extend the courtesy to Nicholas again, should he be so inclined.

Though she had to admit, and it galled her to do so, that Nicholas could not compare to Robin in that kissing business.

Damn Robin anyway.

She walked toward the door. Robin caught her by the arm before she managed it, and looked down at her gravely.

"Forgive me," he said.

"For what this time, Robin?"

He looked about him helplessly, as if he sought an answer lurking in the bed curtains, or perhaps lost behind a tapestry. That Robin of Artane was actually apologizing, albeit for nothing in particular, was something of great note. She began to wonder if that was what he had been thinking on the whole of the night. Perhaps she would do well to suggest he spend another night determining just what it was he'd done that merited such groveling.

A contrite and supplicating Robin was an interesting thing to see indeed.

"For many things," he said at length.

"When you can tell me what it is I should forgive you for, then I'll think about it. Until then, walk me to the chapel."

He began to mutter under his breath, and she suspected his mutterings included several uncomplimentary things about her. She supposed, however, that if he couldn't come up with anything decent to apologize for, he wouldn't be equal to the task of spilling the contents of his heart.

One thing was certain, he wasn't concentrating on her. Anne watched him as he swept the great hall with his gaze as they entered it. The trip to the chapel was made with even more care. Whatever else his faults might have been, at least he was capable of keeping her safe. She was grateful for it.

He led her into the chapel and sat down with her near the altar. Anne bowed her head and said her prayers.

When she was finished, she looked next to her. Robin sat with his hands folded in his lap and his eyes closed. His long, dark lashes fanned over his cheeks, reminding her of how long she'd always thought his eyelashes to be in his youth. He had been such a beautiful boy. And he had become a beautiful man. He had every bit of Rhys's handsomeness, along with a bit of ruggedness that was his alone.

And she felt her traitorous heart begin to soften yet again. She could hardly believe he had been sitting so quietly for so long. In his youth, Robin had always given the impression of being headed in a dozen different directions at once, even while standing still. Nicholas could be lazy. Robin had never known how. Anne frowned. He drove himself too hard trying to ever prove himself worthy. Of what, she didn't know. Had he no idea how very much Rhys loved him? Or Gwen? Anne could bring up hundreds of memories of Rhys bragging about his heir and what a fine man he had become. Robin likely wouldn't have believed the words if he'd heard them. As far as he was concerned, he was still proving himself. In truth, all he was doing was exhausting himself. He'd proved himself years ago.

Anne reached up and before she thought better of it, tucked a lock of hair behind his ear. Robin opened his eyes and slid a look her way.

"Did you think me napping?"

She couldn't help but smile. "I confess I did."

Robin reached for her hand and held it between both his own. "Nay, Anne. I've much to be grateful for. I was giving thanks and had only reached the middle of my list. I believe I stopped just after being grateful for Anne of Fenwyck's beautiful green eyes and before her fiery spirit. Perhaps I will save the rest of your virtues for another time."

"Nay, finish. It won't take long."

"'Tis fortunate for you that I know you are not in earnest. The saints only know how I might have to repay you for that slight to my lady."

His lady? She looked down at her hand between his work-roughened hands and shook her head. Ah, that she could actually believe his words. It would have been a sweet thing indeed.

He squeezed her hand. "Let us go back. All this piousness has left me with a powerful hunger."

Anne let him pull her to her feet and followed him from the chapel. He kept his arm around her as they left the building and started across the courtyard. Anne tried to ignore the stares they received. Perhaps it wasn't seemly . . .

"Are you so ashamed of me then?"

She looked up at him. "Of course not."

"Then why do you pull away?"

"What will they think?"

"They will realize I'm keeping you warm. And if they're very quick, they'll realize I'm being noble and chivalrous."

"Indeed."

He pursed his lips. "I am making an effort, Anne. Credit me with that."

"Is it so difficult, then?" she asked.

"What? To walk with you so politely when the barbarian in me thinks it would be more to my taste to haul you into my arms and stalk off with you? Aye, 'tis very difficult."

"Kind of you, then, to make the effort."

He snorted as he drew her closer and led her up the stairs. Anne couldn't stop a sigh of relief when the hall door was shut behind her. She hadn't felt unsafe outside with Robin there beside her, but she couldn't deny that knowing she was behind heavy doors was a reassuring feeling.

Then she caught sight of Amanda standing before the hearth, tapping her foot purposefully, and wondered if she might not have been safer outside.

Amanda pulled Anne away the moment they reached the fire.

"Amanda," Robin rumbled dangerously.

"Go find my foster sister some wine," Amanda threw at him. "She's chilled."

Anne soon found herself sitting before a roaring fire and squirming under Amanda's sharp glance.

"Has he touched you?"

"Amanda!"

"Has he?" Amanda demanded. "By the saints, I'll take my blade to him if he has."

"Amanda, he's been perfectly—"

"—chivalrous? I don't believe that for a moment, sister. Robin isn't capable of it. Now, you leave him to me. I'll tell him just what will happen if he doesn't comport himself properly."

"Amanda, I'm certain—"

"Aye, I am too. I've lost count of the number of his bastards—"

Anne gasped as Amanda was hauled up to her feet. All she saw then was Robin's back as he dragged his sister away. Anne watched as Robin backed her up against the back wall of the hall. The sound of him slapping his palms against the stone echoed in the chamber. But she heard nothing after that. And when Robin and Amanda came back over to the fire, Amanda was wearing the expression she usually wore after Rhys had chastened her for something, Robin sat down in the chair opposite Anne and glared up at his sister.

"You may pour us wine."

"I'm not pouring you anything, you arrogant cur—"

Amanda shrieked as Robin jerked her over his knees. He held her there with two heavy forearms over her shoulders and lower back.

"I fear I didn't hear you," he said pleasantly. "What was that?"

"Miserable whoreson!"

Anne jumped as Robin gave his sister a healthy whack across her backside.

"You were saying?" he said.

"Damn you, Robin, let me up!"

"That is *my lord Artane* to you, you disobedient shrew. Now, will you comport yourself as a lady, or do I beat decorum into you?"

"You, my lord Artane, are a mannerless pig!"

Anne hastily covered her mouth with her hand to hide her smile.

"Robin, release her!" Nicholas vaulted over the table and stood over his brother, bristling with anger.

"I'm teaching her how to behave herself. Sit you down, lest you force me to teach you as well."

"You might try," Nicholas scoffed.

"Nicky," Anne said warningly, catching a full view of the dangerous glitter in Robin's eyes. "I daresay now is not the time to push him."

Nicholas leaned over the back of Anne's chair. "Haven't you kissed him today, Anne? Surely that would sweeten his mood."

"Cease," Anne said, feeling herself beginning to blush uncomfortably. Never mind that she fully intended never to kiss Robin again. She had very vivid memories of past experiences with the like. "My lord Artane does not wish to be teased today."

"Then let us certainly honor his wishes," Nicholas said, inclining his head. "Go ahead and beat the wench, Rob."

"Nicholas!" Amanda wailed. "Robin, release me."

"If you can behave, aye, I might."

"I won't say another bloody word about your scores of bastards. Now, let me up!"

Nicholas reached over and pulled Amanda away. "Saints, Amanda, use your wits! Does it not occur to you that Anne might not want to hear about that?"

Anne waved away his words. "Nay, 'tis nothing." By the saints, this was the last thing she wanted to discuss! A quick look at Robin's face told her that he likely felt the same way.

"It would certainly mean something to me," Nicholas said. "Amanda, exert yourself to be less thoughtless in the future."

"If you two are finished babbling," Robin growled, "you may go. And, Amanda, remember the feel of my hand on your backside. It will be there as often as is needed to teach you the manners Father never did."

"Ha," Amanda said scornfully, but she kept herself well out of Robin's reach. "Take me back upstairs, Nicholas. I fear what I might do if left here to retaliate."

Anne looked into the fire until she and Robin were alone. She couldn't look at him.

"Anne?"

She continued to look at the flames. "Aye?"

"I have something to apologize for."

"What?"

He sighed. "My lack of discretion in the past."

"It matters not."

"I would hope it would. It would certainly matter to me. If you had taken a lover, don't you think I would hunt him down and geld him?"

She looked at him reluctantly and decided that, given the look in his eye, he might have. She pursed her lips. "And what am I to do with all your past lovers, my lord? Take blades to them?"

"There are far fewer than I'm credited with and 'tis best if you forget them. I certainly have."

"Ah, but have they forgotten you?"

He winced. "You say the damndest things, Anne."

She only looked at him.

"All right, damn you," he snapped. "I'm quite certain that whatever sorry nights I spent in anyone's bed has completely escaped the poor wench's memory. You've no need to fear anyone coming to regale you with tales of my prowess. Satisfied?"

"And why would that bother me anyway?" she asked politely.

His mouth worked silently for the space of several breaths, during which time Anne began to wonder if she had misjudged him. He was seemingly concerned that she not be assaulted by any of his former lovers, concerned that she believe their number to be fewer than he was credited with, and now he could not muster up a decent answer as to why it should trouble her.

And, most notably, he had apologized. More than once.

He spluttered a moment or two more, then cursed as he stood abruptly. "We shouldn't be here. It isn't safe. Come with me upstairs to Father's solar. We'll have supper."

Anne soon found her hand in his. More was the pity that she was starting to become accustomed to the like. She sighed and followed Robin up the stairs and down the passageway to Rhys's solar.

Supper arrived soon enough and with it Robin's siblings. Anne sat silently during the meal, bemused by Robin's apologies. She found herself watching him with new eyes. His grumbles, she noted, were directed at those who had somehow either touched his heart or awakened his ire. He was, to be sure, gruff and impossible, but she suspected that beneath those growls lay a great deal of love for his family.

It was a highly enlightening meal.

It was also a very typical one, except that Robin threw a bite of everything he planned to eat to the dogs first. Anne wasn't allowed to eat until he'd tried it then on himself. Other than that, supper was a normal affair. Amanda and Robin bickered. Nicholas tried to keep the peace and finished off supper by challenging Robin to a wrestle. And for once in his life, Robin refused. Anne had never seen him do the like and she wondered what it could possibly mean.

Robin excused them and led her to his sire's bedchamber. He sat her in a chair and took the stool before her.

"Comfortable?"

When the alternative was the bed, aye, she was comfortable enough. And then the thought of the bed brought the thought of bedding to mind and Anne began to blush.

"I never should have said aught about any of it," he said, "but it was something to apologize for."

"So it was," she agreed.

He looked at her in silence for a moment, then rose and held out his hands. "Let me plait your hair for you, then I'll put you to bed. Too much apologizing is exhausting. You'll no doubt need your rest to listen for another round of it on the morrow."

"More apologies?" she asked with a smile. "How delightful."

He scowled at her as he lowered her to the stool. He sat behind her and began to brush her hair. Anne closed her eyes and savored it. He would have made a fine maid. He plaited her hair deftly, then sat back. Anne stood and turned to look down at him.

"Thank you," she said.

He nodded solemnly. "Off to bed with you, then. And don't fret over me. I'll be perfectly fine here in the chair or on the floor."

She pursed her lips. "You said you had no trouble sleeping on the floor."

"That was before I exerted myself brushing your hair."

"Then don't sleep on the floor," she said, then she bit her tongue. She should have been glad of his discomfort, but somehow she found she couldn't be.

He looked at her in surprise. "Truly?"

"Well, you could sleep in your clothes," she said pointedly.

"Couldn't," he said, shaking his head. "Too uncomfortable."

"Robin—"

"The bed is large and I give you my word of honor you will remain untouched." He cleared his throat. "You needn't strip, if you'd rather not."

Anne could hardly believe he wasn't putting up a larger fight about sleeping next to her, but perhaps he was weary of the floor. She frowned at him.

"Douse the candle and close your eyes. Far away from me, if you please."

He did so and Anne took off her gown while she had the chance. She crawled into bed in just her shift and prayed it was enough to protect her modesty.

Anne listened as Robin's clothes fell to the floor with soft thumps and she prayed he had clung to some sense of decorum and left something on. The bed creaked as he slid in from the opposite side. She took a deep breath.

"Robin?"

"Aye."

"Are you wearing anything?"

"Naught but my sweet smile."

"Robin . . ."

"Your virtue is safe. I vow it."

"Oh, Robin—"

"Hush, Anne. Go to sleep."

Well, she'd made the offer after all, and 'twas likely too late to toss him from her bed. She closed her eyes and prayed she hadn't made a very large mistake.

One thing was certain, she would not sleep at all.

25

A brisk knocking on the door roused Anne from a deep slumber. She pulled the bed curtain aside, but the chamber was still dark. It had to be surely the middle of the night. Why would someone be knocking in the middle of the night? Had war come to Artane?

"By the saints," she said, starting to get up. Then she realized several things almost at once.

She was abed with Robin.

She had apparently fallen asleep in spite of her fears she never would.

And someone was at the door who would, unless she did something very quickly, enter and discover that she was abed with Robin and had fallen asleep where likely no maid with any virtue would have dared.

She clutched the blanket to her chin. "Robin," she whispered frantically. "Someone knocks!"

"Tell 'em to go away," he mumbled, burying his head under a pillow.

She jerked the blanket off him. "Go answer it, you fool!"

He groaned and rolled from the bed. Anne heard the hiss of a candle being lit, then saw much more of Robin than she'd ever intended. Robin padded to the door, rubbing one eye sleepily with his hand. It was then that Anne realized she had never seen a naked man before. Boys, aye, but a man? Never.

Especially one in that condition.

She could only assume he was, well, not at rest as it were. But perhaps the condition came naturally to him, for he made no mention of it. Indeed, he seemed not to notice it.

He grumbled as he pulled back the bolt and jerked open the door. "What?" he demanded.

There were so many gasps, Anne hardly knew where to start in identifying them.

First there was hers, when she watched Robin's sire push his way inside the bedchamber, torch in hand.

Then there was Robin's, when he realized his father had come home, and at least a fortnight early at that.

Then there was Rhys's when he caught sight of not only his son in his naked glory, but Anne peeking from within the bed curtains.

And if Rhys's gasp had been loud, Geoffrey of Fenwyck's was deafening. He strode into the chamber, ripped open the bed curtains the rest of the way, and glared at her. Anne clutched the blankets to her throat. She half wondered if her father would take a mind to beat her.

But apparently he had other prey in mind,

"You whoreson!" he bellowed, turning and launching himself at Robin.

Anne fell out of bed, then struggled to her feet, pulling the blanket out and wrapping it around her.

"Father!" she shouted, praying her father wouldn't throttle Robin. He had his hands around Robin's throat and had slammed him back up against the wall. "Cease! He's done nothing—"

"Nothing?" her sire bellowed. "*Nothing?*" He released Robin and whirled on Rhys. "Artane, I vow I'll kill him if it's the last thing I do!"

Rhys said nothing. He didn't have to say anything. He looked first at her and she saw him absolve her of any part in the current situation. Then his steely gray eyes slid to his son. Anne had to admire Robin's calm in the face of what would surely be a wrath he had never seen from his father before. Rhys's eyes missed no detail. Robin stood panting against the wall with his hands by his side, not attempting to shield his nakedness. Anne watched his father look down. Robin flushed and rubbed his throat.

"Think you I would be in this condition had I just bedded her?" he asked defensively.

"Think you it makes one wit of difference if she is a virgin or not?" Fenwyck bellowed. "You fool, what possessed you to do this thing!"

"I had a very good reason—"

Anne's father roared. Anne clapped her hands over her ears, praying her sire wouldn't do anything she would regret, such as kill Robin.

"My lord," Robin began.

"Silence!" Geoffrey drew his sword, but Rhys put his hand out.

"My friend, kill him and you kill your daughter's husband."

"Husband!" Geoffrey gasped. "How can you possibly entertain the notion that I would give my child to this bold, honorless whoreson!"

"Because he could very well be the father of your grandchild," Rhys said calmly.

Anne stole a look at Robin, then wished she hadn't. His expression was grimmer, if possible, than his father's. She didn't want to speculate on his thoughts.

"Geoffrey, come with me to my solar," Rhys said. "We'll reason together there."

"I'll go nowhere—"

"My solar," Rhys bellowed suddenly. "It serves us nothing to stand here arguing."

Anne found herself in her father's sights once more before he cursed his way from the chamber and slammed the door behind him. She hoisted the blanket up a bit higher and turned her sights to Robin's sire.

And then she wished she hadn't.

She had never seen him look so grim before. If it had been possible, she would have given anything to have disappeared before him rather than see the censure in his eyes.

"I would suggest you two retreat to separate chambers to dress," he said evenly, "but I can see 'tis too late for that. Robin, I will expect you in my solar immediately. Do not keep me waiting. Unreasonable delays will not soothe my temper and I assure you, you do not wish to increase my ire this night." He turned, then paused. He looked back over his shoulder at Robin. "I expected more from you than this."

With that, Rhys left the chamber, closing the door softly behind him. Anne looked at Robin, but he wouldn't meet her eyes.

"Robin," she began.

He shook his head, once, then walked over to his trunk. He pulled on his clothes silently. Anne limped over to the fire, heavily favoring her right leg, and pulled her dress over her head. By the saints, this was a disaster.

"Robin. . ."

He didn't look at her, or acknowledge that he'd heard her. He simply pulled on his boots, belted his tunic, and left.

Anne stood in the middle of the chamber and wrapped her arms around herself. She had done nothing wrong. There was no reason for the shame that coursed through her. Robin had just been protecting her, though she had to admit that sleeping in the same bed with him had been very ill-advised. Her generosity had certainly been unwise, though she had hardly expected her sire and his to return home and assume they'd lain together.

Though what else were they to think?

Anne sighed and considered her next action. She could remain where she was and wait for her fate to come to her, or she could go to meet it. She hadn't been invited to Rhys's solar, but there was no reason she couldn't eavesdrop and find out what was going to happen.

And possibly keep her father from killing the man she loved.

She opened the chamber door and saw Robin's guards still there. They looked at her with expressionless faces and she could only speculate on what they were thinking. She lifted her chin and pushed her way past them. They fell into step behind her and she stopped and looked at them.

"I'm out for an intrigue," she said, "and do not need a cluster of knights clomping along behind me."

One of the men made her a low, creaking bow. "My lady, we are bid guard you by my lord. We cannot fail him."

"And my sire is liable to kill him unless I make exceedingly great and silent haste," she returned.

They did look at each other then, and a pair of them shifted uncomfortably.

"One man," she said, looking at their apparent leader. "You. But come silently."

It was only after she was creeping along the passageway that she realized how bold she had been in ordering Robin's men about. She shook her head. A pity she had found her tongue when it likely wouldn't serve her.

She paused before Rhys's solar door and motioned Robin's man behind her. The door was shut, but that was remedied easily enough. The growling going on inside would likely cover whatever sound she might make disturbing the sanctuary. She pushed the door open only far enough to hear what was being said.

"I overlooked your indiscretions in the past," Rhys was saying, in a voice so cold that it sent chills down Anne's spine, "but this is no common slut you've bedded."

"I didn't bed her!"

"You've kept her a virtual prisoner in your chamber for how long? A fortnight—"

"I had to!" Robin exclaimed. "She's fair lost her life four times. Did you not see my guard outside? Did you not think to wonder why they were there?"

"Likely to protect you from prying eyes!" Fenwyck bellowed. "Enough of this, Rhys. I'll have him in the lists!"

Robin's snort almost made Anne smile, if she could have managed it given the circumstances. At least Robin had no lack of respect for his own skill, and her father's lack of it in his eyes.

"Would you have done aught differently?" Robin demanded. "Would you not have done whatever you could to keep her safe?"

"My actions are not under discussion; yours are."

"I had no choice!"

"You were naked in her bed!" Rhys thundered. "A fortnight in my chamber, Robin. Think you any sane man would believe you haven't touched her?"

"Believe what you will," Robin snapped. "I'm no liar."

"And I say you're a bloody wretch who deserves to be hanged!" Fenwyck bellowed. "Rhys, I demand retribution!"

"You'll have it," Rhys replied, in that same, cold voice he'd used at first. "The wedding will take place immediately."

"You cannot force me to wed," Robin growled.

"I can and I will."

"I will make the choice myself!"

There was silence and Anne felt coldness steal over her heart.

Apparently that choice would not be her.

"To say I am disappointed in you, Robin," Rhys said quietly, "does not come close to describing the feelings that plague me at the moment. You will wed with the woman I choose for you and you will do it when I say you will. Or you will forfeit your inheritance."

Anne clapped her hand over her mouth to stifle her gasp. Surely Rhys could not be in earnest. What would Robin do without land?

And then Robin laughed. It was the most humorless laugh she had ever heard.

"That would please you well enough, wouldn't it?" he said, laughing again. "Give it all to Miles, Father. Give him the title, your lands, your gold. Give it to your son of the flesh. Give him Anne while you're at it, for I bloody well won't be told what to do by you or by anyone else!"

"Aye," Rhys said hotly, "you will. You will wed Anne as soon as the priest can be roused."

"I will wed when and where I choose," Robin snarled. "If you would but listen—"

"To what?" Rhys demanded. "What pitiful excuse can you make for your actions? By the bloody saints, Robin, she was in your bed! Hell, it wasn't your bed, it was *my* bed. I should beat you for that alone!"

"There was nowhere else!" Robin shouted.

"Enough," Rhys said curtly. "You'll wed within the hour. Go to the chapel and give yourself over to prayer—"

"You take your pious demands and go to hell!" Booted feet crossed the chamber with heavy stomps.

"Robin—"

"And why are you home so early?" Robin demanded, apparently stopping just short of the doorway.

"We met Hardwiche on the road," Rhys said shortly.

"And how did you know Anne was in my chamber?"

"A servant told us as we came into the hall," Rhys said impatiently. "Now, as for you—"

Anne pulled back into the shadows of an alcove a heartbeat before Robin jerked the door open, then slammed it shut behind him. She was too stunned by the events of the middle of the night to do aught but watch as Rhys left the solar hard on Robin's heels, or her own sire who followed right behind.

She was still as stone, wondering if she would ever again breathe a normal breath.

So, Robin didn't love her. What else was she to divine from his words? If he'd wanted her, he would have taken her no matter the means.

And then she gasped as her father suddenly reappeared before her. She had never seen him angrier. It took every ounce of courage she had to face him and not cower, but she did it.

"Did he force you?" Fenwyck demanded.

What would it serve her to explain anything to him? In his present mood, he likely wouldn't believe her anyway.

"Nay," she said simply.

He clapped his hand to his head. "Then you went to his bed willingly? You foolish girl, what were you thinking?" He grasped her by the arm and jerked her down the passageway.

"My lord!" Robin's guardsman said in alarm.

Geoffrey snarled a curse at him and continued to pull Anne along. "I suppose the only thing good to come of this is you will be wed after all. To Artane's get, since he's ruined you for anyone else." He grunted in disgust. "I suppose I can trust him with my lands, though I daresay I shouldn't. I couldn't trust him with my daughter. Perhaps he has more sense with soil than he does with women."

Anne listened to her father cite a listing of both Robin's flaws and good points, but she couldn't agree with any of them. She knew one thing and one thing alone:

Robin of Artane did not wish to wed her.

But she suspected he would have to.

Her sire opened the door to Rhys's chamber and pushed her inside. "Stay here," he grumbled. "I don't like this, but obviously 'tis the only thing to be done. Do whatever it is you have to to make yourself presentable. And do it quickly. I don't want the bastard changing his mind before we get to the chapel."

And with that, he shut the door, leaving Anne to her thoughts.

And they were not pleasant ones. She had wanted to stay at Artane. She had prayed she would stay at Artane. She had hardly dared hope that she might remain there as Robin's bride.

She had never envisioned having all of it come about because of a sword in Robin's back.

The humiliation of it was almost more than she could bear. Anne found herself envisioning the day that would stretch before her and she almost sat down on the floor and wept. If Robin appeared at the altar, he would do so by means of his father's guard forcing him there. How would Rhys wring any acceptance of the marriage from his son without bloodshed? Even if they could get him to the chapel, Robin would likely cut down half his sire's garrison to be free of the place.

Free of her.

Had he felt any affection for her over the past fortnight, had there been anything tender growing in his breast, it was gone now. By the saints, the thought of him repudiating her at the altar was almost more than she could take.

But that was hardly her fault.

Anne felt her chin lift the slightest bit. No one had asked her opinion on the matter. Never mind that inquiring about such a thing never would have crossed her father's thoughts even had he been drowning in his cups. No one had asked if she wanted to wed Robin, if she had any affection for him, if she thought she could stomach the rest of her life spent in his company.

If she was going to wed anyone, she would at least wed someone who wanted her—for her dowry if nothing else.

She turned and headed toward the bedchamber door. She wasn't powerless to decide her fate. She would leave the keep, hopefully unnoticed in the confusion. Perhaps there was a place for her at court until her sire's temper cooled. Then she would have another look at his choices for her mate and she would wed one of them based on his lust for her lands. Lust was lust, perhaps, where a husband was concerned. She threw open the door, fully prepared to escape.

And she came face-to-face with her sire leaning against the far wall with his arms folded over his chest. Robin's guards were conspicuously absent.

There would be no escape.

But before she could say anything, the lady Gwennelyn came down the passageway and swept her back inside the bedchamber. The next thing Anne knew, she was ensconced in her foster mother's tender embrace.

"Sweet Anne," Gwen said, pulling back and smiling ruefully, "what folly has Robin pulled you into?"

"What folly?" Anne asked, feeling suddenly very near to tears. "This farce of a marriage?"

Gwen shook her head with a gentle smile. "Love, 'tis no farce. Things will settle themselves in time, I daresay."

"He is unhappy—"

"As are you, I imagine," Gwen said. "I doubt this is how you would have wished your wedding day to go."

"It wasn't as it seemed," Anne said.

"Aye, I know," Gwen said. "Nicholas gave me the entire tale and I don't fault either you or Robin for your actions. Indeed, he could have done nothing else with his most precious of treasures."

"His horse was safely in the stables at all times," Anne said grimly.

Gwen laughed softly. "Ah, my Anne, you know I speak of you. Robin has his father's stubbornness and 'twill likely take him a goodly amount of time to come to his senses. If you're patient, you'll no doubt be rewarded."

Anne didn't want to tell Gwen that she had lost all her wits when it came to Gwen's firstborn son, so she remained silent. And she said nothing when Gwen combed out her hair and found a simple circlet to place over a sheer veil. She supposed she looked bridal. She knew herself that she was certainly virginal.

But she suspected no one else would believe it.

She couldn't find anything to say as Gwen walked with her to the chapel a goodly while later. She wasn't looking forward to seeing Robin, for she could only imagine what had transpired in his sorry life over the past pair of hours.

She hoped it hadn't included bloodshed.

Of any but his, of course.

26

Edith woke to the sound of screeching. Actually, she'd been awake for longer than she would have liked, as there had seemingly been a great deal of shouting. She had been almost certain she had dreamed the like.

"Oof," she said, as she felt something collapse onto her sleeping pallet. She sat up and pushed the offender off.

"Oh, Lady Edith," Maude gasped. "You must awake!"

"I already am," Edith said curtly, not daring to hope that the other two women in the chamber hadn't been awakened too. It could have been worse.

The entire community of Gwen's castle ladies could have been sleeping in their accustomed chamber. The ones who had been left behind were either too deaf to hear Maude's squeals, or too stupid to understand what they meant. She looked at the girl in the faint light of dawn and was unsurprised to see a look of complete panic.

She sighed. "What is it now, Maude?"

"Lord Rhys has returned!"

"How lovely, but you needn't alert the entire keep to the fact."

"He's found them in his bed together!"

Edith paused. Now, that was a tidbit she couldn't have hoped for. "How interesting. How did he happen upon that?"

"I told him, but that isn't the worst of it!"

Edith could scarce wait to hear more. She yawned. "Go on, Maude. And hurry so I can return to my slumber."

"They're set to wed!"

Edith smothered her yawn abruptly. "Robin and Anne? How do you know?"

"I heard it myself!" Maude wailed. "I'll never have him now."

"Well, men take lovers—"

"I'll not be his mistress!"

Edith refrained from pointing out to the twit that his mistress was what she had already been, though perhaps that was giving a single night of lust too lofty a title.

"I fear, little one," Edith said sympathetically, "that there is nothing you can do."

"I'll stop the wedding!"

"How?"

"I'll kill the priest!"

Edith sighed.

"Kill *her* then."

Edith felt a tingle of alarm go through her. Not yet. That wasn't her plan. Torment Anne, aye. Make her life a misery and thereby torment Robin, aye. But kill her?

That would come last.

Once all the rest had been seen to.

Edith put a restraining hand on Maude's arm, and held her trembling limb still. "You've naught to fear," she said soothingly. "I daresay Robin will not allow this to happen." *And if he does, all the better for my plan. To lose a love would be painful. To lose a wife, perhaps a wife with child?*

It was almost enough to send shivers down *her* spine.

"Think you?" Maude asked, lifting up her tearstained face. "Think you truly?"

"I'm certain of it. Now, off with you and make no mischief. I will see to it all."

Maude nodded, less happily than Edith would have liked, but at least she was seemingly in agreement. Edith laid back once Maude had left the chamber and gave herself over to contemplation of this new turn of events. Perhaps Maude's attention could be turned to the other children.

A handful of dead lads and lasses.

She smiled. What a lovely wedding gift that would be.

She rose to dress. If she wanted to be at the wedding, she would have to make haste.

27

Robin continued to walk blindly down the passageway, ignoring his father's continuing commands that he stop. Well, at least he couldn't hear Fenwyck behind him bellowing out any more threats of death and dismemberment by means of a very blunt sword and other painful implements. Had he been in different straits, he might have found Anne's sire to be quite imaginative.

But he wasn't in different straits.

So he continued to walk, lest he be completely unmanned by breaking down and sobbing. By the saints, all that he had struggled for the whole of his sorry life had been ruined.

His father found him lacking.

There were simply no words to describe how badly that hurt, how deep the agony went. Robin couldn't breathe. He could only walk and hope that when he stopped, the pain would stop. He had no idea where he was going. All he wanted to do was escape from his father's condemning glance.

An eternity later, he found himself in the chapel. It wasn't where he wanted to go, but it was where his feet seemed bent on taking him. He strode to the front and sat on a bench near St. Christopher's shrine. He stared at the likeness grimly, wondering why Anne had bothered with all her prayers there, kneeling on that cold floor. What had they served her? To acquire a husband whose fondest desire was to run from the scorn in his father's eyes?

And from that sprang his second greatest hurt: the scorn he would no doubt see in Anne's eyes.

Should he ever have the courage to look in them again, that was.

She'd seen him in his fully flawed glory that morn. She'd watched him be reduced to a lad of seven or eight summers by the censure in his father's voice, watched him do nothing but stand there and whimper at his father's chastisement. If he'd been a man, he would have hauled Anne into his arms, told his father to go to hell, and arranged for the wedding himself.

Instead, he'd let himself be ordered about like a whipped whore's bastard and trudged off to his father's solar to receive his due. By the bloody saints, he was a man full grown! He hardly had need to listen to his father's lectures. He'd known immediately that marriage was the only course of action. In truth, he'd known that before he joined Anne in her bed. He was beginning to wonder if he'd known it before he'd locked her in his father's bedchamber with him alone as company.

He dropped his face into his hands and groaned. This was not how he would have had it. He should have courted her. He should have swallowed his pride and asked Nicholas for ways to woo her. He should have humbled himself and gone to her sire to ask for her hand. Perhaps he himself wasn't much to rejoice over, but his inheritance was vast and his skill with the sword unmatched. He suspected that he might even manage to keep her lands producing as they should if given the time to prove himself on that sort of battlefield.

And if nothing else, he should have gone down on his knees before Fenwyck and assured the man that Anne was loved and would be treasured above all else.

Not that Fenwyck would believe him now.

Nor, he suspected, would Anne.

He shook his head in disbelief. It was barely dawn, yet his entire life had been changed already. Anne's too. It wasn't how she deserved to be wed—with swords at their backs.

Her ring.

Robin jumped to his feet. That at least he could provide her. And perhaps that small token might salvage at least some portion of the morn for her. She might not believe that he loved her, but surely the ring would say something, wouldn't it?

He started toward the back of the sanctuary, then froze. His father stood leaning against the door, his face fixed in an uncompromising frown.

Well, damn him, it wasn't as if Robin planned to escape. He started toward the door and almost immediately found himself facing a drawn blade.

"Oh, by all the bloody saints," Robin said in disgust.

But his sire didn't move. His adopted sire, Robin corrected himself. The man whose approval meant everything to him didn't move. The condemnation. Robin saw in Rhys's eyes was almost enough to break his heart.

Had he had a heart to be broken, that is. Robin turned and resumed his seat on the bench. And as he did so, he felt his heart chill and harden. Perhaps this was for the best. Perhaps wanting to please his sire had been a foolish dream. Indeed, he suspected it was. He was likely well rid of it.

In fact, perhaps he was well rid of his desire to please Anne as well. Aye, he thought as he sat on the bloody uncomfortable bench at the front of the chapel just a handful of paces from where she had knelt the saints only knew how many times praying for him, perhaps all the events of the morn had come about for a reason. What had possessed him to believe that giving his heart to anyone would serve him?

Nay, 'twas best that he keep it protected. He would do as his father willed and wed with Anne.

And then he would be off once again to do his manly labors.

In France, perhaps.

After all, a man was expected to do his duty, no matter where that duty took him. Aye, he would travel as far away as he could and put all his energies into warfare where they were best suited. It couldn't be construed as fleeing from his troubles. No one would suspect why he'd left. Anne would be free of her father's desires to see her wed. She would remain at Artane and she would be happy. Robin suspected that was what she wanted the most anyway. And if that were the case, her ring would be better off left in the bottom of his box.

It had been a foolish idea anyway.

He heard the door open behind him, heard voices and footsteps but made no effort to identify them. He looked up as the priest moved to stand behind the altar. He frowned. Surely the betrothal would take place inside the great hall, not the chapel. 'Twas the custom, was it not?

And then his father's scribe was ushered up to stand next to the priest. Robin smiled without humor. Well, it looked as if the betrothal agreement would be signed here before Mass. Perhaps his sire feared he would escape should he have had a bit of open ground between the hall and the chapel.

And then a heavy hand came to rest on his shoulder. Robin didn't look up, for he knew to whom the hand belonged.

"'Tis time," Rhys said.

Robin didn't look at his sire. He merely rose and took his place before the altar, standing stiffly. He could have sworn he felt Anne's presence before he heard her uneven steps coming down the aisle behind him. She came to a stop beside him. He hardly dared look at her and when he did, he wished he hadn't.

She was so pale, she looked as if she might faint. Robin wanted with all his heart to reach out to her—his earlier resolutions aside—but he didn't dare. If she pulled away or flinched at his touch, he wasn't sure how he would bear it.

So he kept his face resolutely forward and hardened his heart.

It was the only way to protect it.

And then he felt control of his own life slip through his fingers. The betrothal agreement was laid before him. He knew that 'twould be his father's right to list his holdings. He wouldn't have been surprised in the slightest if Rhys had retained all that Robin would have eventually inherited had things been different.

He lifted his chin. Rhys's lands didn't matter. He had his own lands, lands that he had inherited from Ayre. Those would have been more than sufficient to appease Anne's sire.

Then again those and the choicest of Rhys's own lands would likely have had the lout falling on the floor in a fit of rapture.

To his surprise, though, Rhys did not deny Robin anything that was due him. And when he heard no thump behind him, he assumed Fenwyck had known all along what Robin would bring to the union.

His true surprise, however, came from Fenwyck's recitation. He would have assumed that many of Geoffrey's holdings would have gone to his stepdaughter and her husband. Apparently Fenwyck either distrusted the lad entirely, or he thought Robin capable of managing his fiefs.

Either that or Robin was considered the lesser of two unpalatable alternatives.

Not that Robin cared about Fenwyck's lands. What Geoffrey didn't realize was that, despite his rich soil, the true prize was the woman who stood next to him, the woman who was starting to sway a bit.

Robin almost reached out and put his arm around her.

But that would have meant he loved her and that wasn't something he was going to admit to. Not now. Not when he planned to leave as quickly after the ceremony as possible—

"Robin, *turn*!"

The shout had him spinning almost before his brother's words registered in his poor abused head. He and Nick had protected each other for years with that simple command. It had been instinctive to obey.

And then he felt everything slow as if the pace of the world had ground to a halt. He found himself with his dagger in his hand. He watched in amazement as a body came flying down the aisle toward them with arm upraised.

And then he thought he heard the jingle of a bracelet.

Robin took a step forward, his rage and frustration overcoming him. He had looked for this soul for days, cursed his own inability to flush him out. Now that he had him in his sights, he would accept no defeat. He thrust upward with all the anger that lay simmering beneath his hurt.

The hooded figure cried out, gurgled out a curse, then fell toward Robin. Robin shoved the body away and watched him collapse to the floor, a wickedly long dagger still clutched in his hand. A bracelet encircled the assassin's wrist. Robin stared down at the figure, then looked at Anne.

There was a slash down the back of her skirt and blood splattered everywhere.

And then just as suddenly as events had slowed, they quickened until Robin could scarce keep up with what he needed to do. He took a step backward, grasped for Anne, and hauled her close. "Are you hurt?" he demanded frantically. "Did he cut you?"

She only shook her head and clung to him.

Robin wrapped his arms around her and held her head against his chest with her face turned away so she might not see. Nicholas knelt next to the body. He gingerly turned him over. Robin couldn't stop a gasp at the sight.

It wasn't a man.

It was a woman.

And one not unfamiliar to him.

The young woman looked up at Robin. "Failed to stop it," she managed, then gurgled her last breath.

There was absolute silence in the chapel. Robin looked about him and noted the expressions on the faces there. Shock for the most part. Even Fenwyck looked to be taken aback.

"A servant, Artane?" he managed.

"Aye," Rhys answered slowly. "But recently recommended and retained, though."

Robin wondered if now would be a good time to mention that Maude was a lord's daughter. Or that Robin had a very personal, intimate acquaintance with her.

Not that it was something he remembered with fondness. Looking back on it now, he wondered how he had ever found himself in her bed. She was greedy, grasping, and tenacious.

Or had been, rather.

Aye, even with shorn hair, she was unmistakable. Robin watched Nicholas close Maude's eyes, then look up at him. Robin knew his brother knew. Though he likely could have counted on Nicholas's silence, there was little point in it. The tale would come out eventually. He might have been a coward that morn, but he would be such no longer. 'Twas a man's right and privilege to be truthful, no matter the cost.

He could only hope the cost wouldn't come too dear this time.

"She's no servant," Robin said heavily.

All eyes turned to him and Robin wished heartily that he could sink into the floor. Even Anne pulled back to look at him. Robin looked away from the crowd, avoided Anne's eyes, and settled on staring over the altar only to meet the condemning gaze of the priest.

Bloody hell.

"One of your lovers, perhaps?" Geoffrey said, his voice laced with scorn.

Damn the man. "Aye," Robin said shortly.

"Maude of Canfield," Nicholas supplied. "It would seem, Rob, that she wasn't overfond of the thought of your nuptials."

"Well," Rhys said grimly, "at least we have our assailant."

I'm thrilled, Robin thought sourly. What impeccable timing.

"And she's blond," Geoffrey added, no less scornfully. "We know where your tastes run—"

"Enough," Robin said, glaring at his future father-in-law. "My past is my own and no affair of yours. You insult your daughter and I'll have no more of it."

"I intended to insult you," Geoffrey said curtly.

"Then do so in the lists. I've no stomach for a fight with words." Robin turned to the priest. "Wed us. Now."

"But," the priest said, gesturing to the cooling corpse behind Robin.

"Now," Robin growled. "We'll forgo Mass today."

"Perhaps that's wise," the priest agreed. "Especially in light of . . . well . . ."

"Oh, by the saints, cease with your babbling!" Fenwyck bellowed. "Get on with the bloody ceremony!"

Robin gritted his teeth and wondered if clouting his lady wife's father in the nose could possibly worsen the events of the day. There he stood with blood on his hands and clothes with a dead lover at his heels.

And then he heard someone begin to be violently ill.

He turned to see Isabelle being heartily sick. Miles was trying to help, but turning very green very quickly. The twins had clapped hands over their mouths and Amanda's eyes were beginning to roll upward in her head. Robin watched as Nicholas caught her before she slumped to the ground.

And Anne began to weep.

At least they wouldn't have to stand there and listen to any more recitations of holdings. Robin signed the contract with a curse, then shoved the quill into Anne's shaking hands. He doubted anyone would recognize her name as her own, nor would they believe it hadn't been signed under duress. Nevertheless, the contract was made before witnesses and 'twas legitimate. Never mind that several of the witnesses were too far gone in various states of incapacitation to be useful.

"The blessing," the priest began.

"I doubt it will help," Robin said grimly. He put his hands on Anne's shoulders, ignoring the blood that covered him, and kissed her very briefly. He pulled back, fully prepared to bolt and make for France.

Then he noticed his bride.

She was looking at him.

He couldn't tell if her expression revealed abject horror or complete misery.

Or was that wry amusement?

The sight of her stunned him so, 'twas as if he'd never before seen her. And as he looked at her, and realized that she was indeed his, he began to question the idea of France.

It was, after all, a very nasty place to be in winter.

He considered. He could remain at Artane. The lists were fine. He could ensconce himself there for great stretches of time. At least that way he could look on Anne from afar now and again.

The lists. Aye, that was the place for him. Soon, before he began to entertain any other foolish thoughts.

Such as being Anne's husband in truth.

He reached out and swept her up into his arms before anyone, mainly Anne, could protest. Without comment, he turned and stepped over Maude's body and approached his mother.

"See to Anne, will you?" he asked.

"And where do you think you're going?" Fenwyck demanded.

"To the lists."

"Go if you like," Rhys said, "but your mother won't be here to tend Anne."

Robin blinked. "She won't?"

"I won't?" Gwen echoed.

"You won't," Rhys said shortly. "We're leaving."

"But we just returned home," Gwen protested.

"Fenwyck has invited us for a lengthy stay," Rhys said.

"I have?" Geoffrey said, looking less than delighted about the prospect. "I don't remember that."

"Children," Rhys said, "collect your things. We'll leave within the hour."

Robin let Anne slip down to the ground and she took a step away from him with more enthusiasm than he would have liked.

"You're leaving?" she asked Gwen, sounding quite horrified by the prospect. "Now?"

"Not a bad idea," Geoffrey said, coming to stand behind his daughter. "No use in staying for the bedding anyway, especially given that she isn't a virg—"

Robin let his fist fly. He watched himself plow that fist into his father-in-law's face and wondered absently at the wisdom of it. Fenwyck lay sprawled on the floor, apparently too stunned by the blow to move. Robin smiled in grim satisfaction.

"Speak disparagingly of my wife again," he said, wishing Fenwyck would heave himself to his feet so he could brawl with him truly and repay the lout for several annoying things said to Anne, "and you'll not find me so lenient."

Fenwyck groaned, but did not move.

Robin sighed regretfully, then took Anne's hand. "Come, Anne. Let us leave the rabble to their plans."

He didn't wait for her to agree or disagree, he merely pulled her behind him out the chapel.

"Cheeky bastard!" came the sudden bellow from behind them. "I'll kill him yet myself!"

Robin grunted. "At least he isn't permanently damaged."

Anne choked, a soft sound that made Robin wonder if she were laughing. He looked down at her, but she had bowed her head and he could not see.

He slowed his pace to match Anne's once they were down the steps and a goodly distance from the chapel. He released her hand, then stole a look at her to see how she would react.

She merely clasped her hands in front of her and continued to stare at the ground.

Ah, so perhaps she truly could not bear him. Robin frowned to cover his consternation. He shouldn't have been surprised. Perhaps the best thing he could do was keep his distance from her. He would resurrect his plan to return to France—

Which he now couldn't do, given that his sire was leaving again.

He cursed his father under his breath. Had the man anticipated Robin's thoughts and thwarted them before Robin could act? Damn him.

Robin waited as Anne mounted the steps to the great hall, then he opened the door for her and crossed with her to the hearth.

"I will don my mail and train," he said.

She only nodded. She didn't meet his gaze.

"What chamber will you have?"

She did look up at him then. "What?"

"Well, I didn't suppose you would want to continue in my sire's. 'Tis the finest, of course, but after this morning . . ."

"But I thought," she began, then bit her lip and fell silent.

Robin wasn't sure how to react to that. Did she expect to share a chamber with him? He took a deep breath.

"Mine is comfortable, but I daresay Amanda's is cleaner. You can have whichever you choose."

"Of course," she said quietly.

Robin scowled. Damn her anyway, what did she want him to say? *Come share my bed?* She was his wife, after all, though he hardly dared claim his rights.

"Father's then," he said in exasperation. "You can decide later on a more permanent solution."

He looked down at her. There was blood spattered on her hands. Her gown sported an enormous rent in the back and he had likely been the one to muss her hair clutching her to him as he had.

Before he could think better of it, he reached out and put his fingers under her chin. He lifted her face and looked at her. She was pale and teary-eyed and lovely. It was all he could do not to drop to his knees and apologize right there for having ruined her wedding day.

But for all he knew, she was ready to weep because she found herself his wife.

So, he slowly dropped his hand and took a step backward, never taking his eyes from her. And when he could bear it no more, he turned and walked away. He heard his squire trailing dutifully along behind him and prayed Jason would keep himself silent. He also hoped for men in the lists, for he was in sore need of something to take his mind off the sorry state of affairs in his life.

The only good thing had been that at least now they knew who had been trying to hurt Anne. Robin shook his head as he made ready to wage mock war. Maude of Canfield. Who would have thought a simple dalliance would lead to such trouble?

But Fenwyck had been right. Maude was blond. There was a reason for that and Robin hoped Anne wouldn't think overlong on what that reason might be. It would likely horrify her more than the day of her nuptials had.

28

Anne stood near the fire in Rhys and Gwen's chamber and watched the flames twist and dance. It was mesmerizing and she wondered how long she had been standing there, unseeing. She finally pulled herself away and sat. She wasn't sure she could face thinking on the events of the day, but she knew she had little choice. It was necessary to resolve a handful of things in her mind and putting that off wouldn't serve her.

She leaned her head back against the chair and sighed. One good thing to come of the day was that her assailant was dispatched. Anne looked down at her hands. Washing them had made them clean again, but she suspected it would take her longer than that to rid the memory of blood on them from her mind. Or the horror of knowing how close she had come to having Maude of Canfield's dagger in her back. Bless Robin for his quickness.

Yet at the same time, she couldn't help but pity the girl. How miserable she must have been to have found herself driven to such lengths. Anne wondered if she had loved Robin so deeply, or merely been furious that he had left her in his wake, as it were. Perhaps a little of both. All Anne knew was that at least now she might walk freely about the keep without having to look over her shoulder. Maude had perhaps earned her reward for her actions, and there was surely nothing Anne could do about it but to put it behind her and look forward.

It was in the looking forward, though, that she found her most vexing concern. Perhaps it did her no good to think on it, but she couldn't help but wonder if Robin would ever make her his wife in truth. He certainly hadn't sounded as if that were in his plans.

She smiled to herself. How greedy she had become. A month ago, it would have sufficed her merely to remain at Artane by whatever means available. Now that she was wed, she found she wanted more than just a place to lay her head. And it was Robin's fault. Had he never kissed her, never held her in his arms, never even for a brief moment become her safe haven, she never would have wanted more.

But she did.

She closed her eyes with a sigh. Perhaps there would come a time when he would be so starved for company that he would seek her out. Rhys, Gwen, their youngest children, and her sire were already departed, so he would not have them to converse with. She suspected, though, that Robin was very thankful her sire had gone, even though he had departed complaining loudly about the condition of his nose. Anne couldn't help a small smile over that. She couldn't deny that he had deserved it. And she couldn't help but have warm feelings toward Robin for having done the deed.

If that wasn't defending her abused honor, she didn't know what was.

But that was something she would think on later.

Amanda, Nicholas, and Miles had not gone with their parents. They were instead making for one of Nicholas's holdings nearby. The three of them got on perfectly and Anne almost envied them their companionship. They would likely enjoy themselves immensely.

She wondered if she would enjoy the next few days.

Not to mention the rest of her life.

The door opened behind her and Anne leaped up out of habit.

"Only me," Nicholas said with a smile. "You can be at ease now, remember?"

"It has been a less than leisurely day, my lord."

He shook his head. "Leave it to Robin to do things any way but the most simple. At least you can cease worrying about your safety. That should bring you some comfort. Well, as comfortable as you can be given that you're now Robin's wife."

"Nicky, I cannot jest about that," Anne said. "Truly, I cannot."

Nicholas dropped onto a trunk a pile of things contained in a sack. "Rob's gear," he said, then crossed the chamber to take Anne's hands. "Give him time. He's a bit thickheaded."

"I daresay time is what I have the most of," she said with a sigh.

Nicholas kissed her very chastely on the forehead. "Don't leave him out in the lists all day. It's raining and he'll mold. Either that or he'll rust, and think on the complaining you'll need endure."

"I'm sure he'll come in eventually."

"And I'm just as certain he won't. The lad is possessed."

"By something foul, to be sure," Amanda said, coming into the chamber.

"Perhaps he'll find sense," Miles said, trailing her, "now that he's wed his ladylove."

Anne snorted. "I doubt I'm that."

Miles only nodded knowingly. "That and more, I daresay." He slung his arm around Amanda. "Think on us while you're residing here in comfort."

Anne looked at Nicholas. "You're for Wyckham?"

"Aye," Nicholas said. "I've a few repairs to make—"

"It has no roof," Amanda put in, wrinkling her nose. "Nor a decent garderobe, I'll wager."

Nicholas only smiled pleasantly. "Sunshine and a goodly amount of exercise taken while trudging to the forest to see to your unmentionable needs, sister. What more could you ask for?"

"A goosefeather mattress and a decent meal or two."

"Which we will not have if Amanda's at the fire," Miles said affectionately. "The cooking will obviously fall to me."

"The saints preserve us," Amanda said, looking green again.

"I'll cook," Nicholas said with a sigh. "I'll put on the roof. I'll build you a cesspit to be the envy of all in the north, Amanda. Will that suit you?"

"I'll see your work, then judge."

Anne laughed in spite of herself. "And here I was envying you your little holiday together. Off with you, and pray send me word now and then that all three still breathe."

Nicholas made her a bow, then pulled his brother away. "Come with me, Miles, and let us see to our lady's baggage. I vow she intends to reside in comfort judging by the weight of it."

"I will not live in a tent," Amanda called after them. Then she turned to Anne and hugged her tightly. "I'm so sorry, Anne."

Anne shook her head. "Nay, all is well."

Amanda pulled back and raised her eyebrow. "You were wed with my father's sword bared, Robin's dead lover cooling at your feet, and Isabelle heaving her porridge into St. Gertrude's shrine. I imagine you could have wished for a better start to this than that."

"'Tisn't the start that matters so much," Anne said, praying that was true. "'Tis the finish that's important."

Amanda looked unconvinced. "Well, you have him, whether you will it or no. I wish you good luck of him. If he mistreats you, send word and I'll come thrash him for it."

"He won't."

"He's a clod, Anne. I know you love him, but I vow I can't understand why."

"Are you trying to help?" Anne asked in exasperation.

"Well, aye—"

"You aren't. Go. Enjoy your sunshine and bitter air. I'll pray it doesn't rain overmuch. Did you bring a cloak?"

"Nicky brought me one home from France. It will serve me well enough."

"Then off with you."

Amanda hugged her tightly, then ran from the chamber in a flurry of skirts. Anne followed her, closed the door, and started to bolt it. Then she realized there was no need. But to think how close she had come to death. If Robin hadn't turned so quickly. If he hadn't saved her life . . .

She turned away from that thought and from what she'd seen that morn.

Robin had wed her and given her the gift of Artane to enjoy for the rest of her life. Perhaps that would be enough.

She turned, leaned back against the door, and surveyed her domain. Gwen had bid her make free use of the chamber and vowed they would be gone for at least half a year. Anne suspected it wouldn't be that long, but still there was no sense in not making the chamber hers for the time she would have it. Once the unremarkable task of unpacking had been accomplished, she could turn her mind to other things.

Namely, how she would survive a life with Robin of Artane if he intended to spend all his time in the lists.

And then she would worry about why he apparently preferred the sport of his fellows to her company and what that boded for her marriage to him.

She pushed away from the door and turned her mind to her task. Her clothes had been brought for her and laid upon the bed. It took her little time to put them away, for she had left much behind at Fenwyck. Not as much as her sire would have liked at the time, but enough that she had precious little here to call her own.

Robin's gear was not much more. Anne opened his sack and put his clothes into his father's trunk. He had no trinkets as such and she came close to folding up the rough linen bag when she realized there was something else inside it. She reached down and pulled out a battered wooden box.

And she wondered just what it might contain.

Her conscience warred with her curiosity. She shouldn't look. These were Robin's private things, things he likely wouldn't want anyone perusing.

But then again, they might give her some insight, some hint into the contents of his heart. Wasn't that reason enough to paw through them like a thief?

She got to her feet, quickly bolted the door, then retreated to the alcove. There was precious little light from the gray sky outside, so she fetched a candle. She set it a goodly ways away from the box, lest she set the contents on fire, took a deep breath and opened the lid.

Laying on top of everything else were four things she recognized immediately. Ribbons she herself had fashioned for Robin at various times in his life. The sight shocked her so, she could barely lift them out.

She looked at the first, a wide ribbon she had embroidered for Robin during his illness. She remembered vividly sitting by his side and listening to him tease her about her clumsy attempts. But it had been gentle teasing and he had accepted her finished gift with a grave smile and a hug that had almost broken her ribs. He had vowed he would never be without it. Later she had been certain he had been lying. Now, she knew he had been telling the truth.

The next three had been fashioned by more skillful hands. She had given them to him at his knighting, at his first tournament, when he had gone off on the crusade. To her knowledge, Robin had never worn any of them. But the ribbons before her told her a different tale.

She could hardly believe he had kept them.

She took the favor she had given him at his knighting and trailed her finger over his crest, over the black lion rampant with the aqua eyes. There were no scars on that one, though she could see even now where the knot had been tied to hold it around his arm.

The next ribbon was the one she had given him at the first tourney he'd attended after his knighting. She looked at one end of the ribbon. Those were not her stitches mending the thing and she could only surmise that Robin had done the honors himself. And that could only mean that somehow it had been cut from him. Perhaps he had it after all.

She took the last ribbon in her hands. There was hardly anything left of it. She remembered well how she had snuck into his chamber and left it for him on his pillow on the night before he'd left for the crusade. It looked as if he'd worn it continuously—or so she told herself. His clumsy stitches were all over it. The crest was unraveling and the ribbon was in shreds. But it was clean, as if it had been cared for tenderly.

Anne set the ribbons carefully aside, still so stunned by the finding of them in Robin's box that she could scarce see for the tears that threatened to spill down her cheeks.

She brushed them aside, though, for she had more to look at and little time in which to do it.

There was a letter there and she opened it without hesitation. And she found herself weeping in earnest at the words Gwen had written there, words of encouragement, words of love. It was no wonder Robin had kept it close.

She put it aside and pulled out a heavy silver ring, stamped with his crest. She remembered when Rhys had given it to him, though to her knowledge, Robin had never worn it.

She paused. Why was that?

She supposed that perhaps he might not wear it because it certainly couldn't be comfortable to wield a sword with a ring on his hand.

Or did it go deeper than that?

She held the ring up to the candlelight and looked at it thoughtfully. Did Robin not wear it because he didn't feel he had earned the right? His words in Rhys's solar came back to her. *Give it all to Miles, Father. Give him the title, your lands, your gold. Give it to your son of the flesh. Give him Anne while you're at it.*

Was that truly what he thought? She shook her head, marveling at his stupidity. Rhys could not possibly love a son more than he loved Robin.

Nor could a son possibly look any more like his sire than Robin did Rhys. She wasn't sure how such a thing might have come about, but there was little doubt in her mind over it.

She shook her head and put aside the ring. Perhaps one day she would have the answer to that mystery, as would Robin, and he would be at peace.

Nestled in the bottom of the box was a heavy gem and Anne recognized it at once. Rhys had given it to Robin, desiring him to bind it into a sword. No doubt that gift resided herein for the same reason the ring did. She could almost hear Robin saying it.

This should go to a son of his flesh.

Anne stared out the window. Could Robin be Rhys's in truth? That would mean that Gwen and Rhys had lain together while Gwen was married to Alain of Ayre. How would Robin react if he were to learn he was actually Rhys's bastard son? By the saints, she didn't want to see the shouting match that would ensue from that. Nay, perhaps 'twas best she keep her suspicions to herself. Perhaps Rhys himself didn't know. Though how he could doubt it, she couldn't imagine. But souls were ofttimes blind— Rhys and Robin being perfect examples of the same.

She put aside the stone, read another pair of letters from Robin's parents, then paused. The last thing remaining was something wrapped in a bit of cloth. Slowly, she unwrapped the cloth and caught her breath.

It was a ring. Anne held it up to the light. It was the most beautiful green stone she had ever seen. The gold was so fair, it looked to be silver.

It was sized to fit a woman's hand.

Anne was so tempted to try it all that the impulse fair felled her on the spot.

But what if she tried it on and it didn't fit?

Or worse, it did?

She curled her fingers around it, brought it to her chest, and closed her eyes. By the saints, this had been a poor idea. What had she been thinking to grope through his things? She deserved this. Nothing good ever came of eavesdropping and she could now add to that rummaging through one's husband's private things. She was a fool and she deserved the pain she'd just brought upon herself.

All the same, now she had come this far, there was no sense in not finishing the deed. She took the ring and slid it onto her finger, the finger that should have worn a betrothal ring.

It was too big.

But not by much. Better too big than too small, she conceded. Should such a thing have been for her, could it have been easier to have it made smaller or larger?

A pity she knew nothing of goldsmithing.

Before she could wallow any longer in her foolishness, she rewrapped the ring and placed everything back in the box as it had been—or as closely as she could remember. Perhaps if Robin thought she had been meddling, then he would shout at her and she could question him.

She placed the ribbons back carefully on the top and took small comfort in that. He had saved what she had given him. That was enough for her at present.

He had also wed her and saved her life, and the latter more than once. There were many reasons to have kind feelings for him. She put his box in his trunk, shut the lid, and sat down upon it to give the morning's events further consideration.

Robin had surely been wounded by his father's doubt of him. Now that she looked back on what he'd said, he hadn't disparaged her. She suspected he'd felt a goodly amount of shame at his father's rebuke, especially given the fact that Robin hadn't been allowed to explain himself. He would have taken that as a personal affront and she could only imagine how that would have angered him.

Or hurt him.

She turned that thought over in her mind for a goodly while. Aye, perhaps that was it. Perhaps he felt he'd been embarrassed in front of her and that distressed him. The thought of Robin of Artane being embarrassed on her account was so ridiculous she felt her cheeks begin to burn. She could hardly believe she was actually considering such a thing. By the saints, she was a simpleton. Her opinion could not possibly matter to him. His sire's, aye, but not hers.

She looked back over the events of the past fortnight, though, and she had to concede that he might have some affection for her. She suspected that if he'd been toying with her, he would have bedded her, not simply asked for a virginal kiss or two.

And there was her wedding to consider. Anne sighed deeply. It certainly wasn't how she had envisioned it, though now she wondered how she could have imagined anything else. Robin had defended her, wed her, and clouted her father in the nose all within moments of each other.

Only Robin could have done the like.

And there was the look he'd given her once he'd deposited her inside the hall. She'd known he expected an answer of some sort regarding where she would sleep, but for the life of her she'd had none to give. She had assumed she would sleep with him, though she'd certainly avoided thinking on consummating their marriage.

She frowned. Was it that he had no intention of doing the like?

She sighed and shook her head. There was nothing to be done but see to dinner, drag Robin in from the lists, and hope that things sorted themselves out in time. With everyone gone, they would have no one to distract them. It might happen that they would be so desperate for conversation that they might speak to each other and then who knew what might happen?

Anne rose and left the bedchamber. She saw to supper, blessing Gwen for having taught her so well that the servants honored her requests without question. At least in this aspect of being Robin's wife she would succeed.

She put her cloak on and made her way out to the lists. It was dark and a substantial rain was falling. Anne walked carefully over the slippery ground, holding her skirts up well out of the mud. She'd changed her gown for something less blood-spattered and it was almost all she had to wear unless she filched something of Gwen's.

And then without warning, she ran bodily into someone.

She jerked back with a cry only to find herself facing Edith of Sedgwick. Anne looked at her in surprise.

"Edith?" she asked. "Are you unwell?"

Edith only stared at her in such an unsettling manner that Anne almost turned and ran. The woman was dripping wet, as if she'd been standing out in the rain for the whole of the afternoon. Her face was haggard, her eyes empty, and her cloak askew on her shoulders. Indeed, she looked as if she'd suffered a great tragedy of some kind.

"Edith," Anne repeated. "Are you unwell?"

Edith shivered once, violently, then blinked and looked at Anne.

Or looked through her, rather.

Without another word, Edith stepped around her and started back toward the great hall. Anne didn't wait to watch and assure herself the other woman had reached her goal. She hiked up her skirts and hastened to the lists as quickly as she could. Would that Rhys and Gwen had taken Edith along with them.

She saw the light of a torch in the distance and felt relief flood her at the sight. It took her little time to join Jason under a wooden shelter that rested against the outside of the inner bailey wall. He was shivering and the torchlight flickered as a result. He made her a low bow.

"My lady," he said, straightening and frowning at her. "What do you outside in this weather?"

She shook off the unease that Edith had inspired in her. "What do you think I'm doing?" she asked dryly. "Someone has to fetch him in for supper." She looked out into the gloom. "Where is he?"

It looked as if all the men had gone in, for there was no one there. And then she caught sight of a figure running in the distance, keeping close to the wall. She'd seen Robin running about in such a fashion more than once, but usually only after he'd finished off his own men and there was no sport left for him. But that had generally been in dry weather. She could hardly believe he was doing such a thing when the chances of him landing face-down in the mud were very good indeed.

"He won't come in," Jason said, sounding as if he very much wished Robin would.

Anne glanced at Jason to find he looked miserably uncomfortable, and it looked as if his discomfort didn't come completely from the rain. "What ails you, Jason?" she asked.

"I'm sorry," he said hesitantly. "I know it isn't my place to apologize for my master, but he should be inside with you. I tried to speak to him about it, but he flicked my ear most vigorously and bid me be silent."

Anne looked at Jason for a moment, then turned to watch Robin thoughtfully. A day ago she might have been terribly hurt to think he would rather be in the lists than at her side. She likely would have either cursed him and hardened her heart, or she would have retreated to her chamber and wept.

But now things were different. She'd had a peek into his heart. She suspected that Robin was doing his damndest to outrun his demons.

Well, he could run until he dropped, but it wouldn't change a thing for him. Perhaps in time he would come to realize that. But it was his realization to make. All she could do until then was try to keep him fed so he would have the strength to keep running.

She watched him continue to make his way around the lists toward her and Jason. He came to a halt before her, then leaned over with his hands on his thighs and sucked in great gulps of air.

"What . . . do you . . . here?" he wheezed. "You'll catch . . . your death."

Anne pursed her lips, unimpressed. "Come inside and eat."

He straightened. "I'm not . . . finished."

"You are for the moment. You are welcome to return after I've seen you fed."

He looked at her, his eyes inscrutable in the torchlight. His hair was dripping into his eyes and his surcoat clung to his chain mail. Anne wondered if Nicholas had it aright and Robin would actually rust. What she did know, however, was that Robin looked a bit like a drowned rodent of some sort and he was the one who would catch his death if he didn't come inside and warm up.

The other thing she noticed was that he wasn't arguing with her. He was merely watching her as if he couldn't understand why she was there. Was he so surprised, then, that she would come to fetch him? That made her pause. Perhaps she would be unwise to act on her newfound knowledge of him. Would she be better served to be aloof?

She shook her head, wondering if perhaps standing outside was beginning to turn her common sense to mush. She would not resort to foolish games. She would treat Robin with respect and courtesy. If he at some point decided to unveil his heart to her, she would accept it gracefully.

And if he never did the like, she would accept that as well—though perhaps not as gracefully.

It was enough to know he had kept her ribbons. He had cared for her gently over the past fortnight. He had wed her that morn. She suspected that not even his father could have forced him had Robin been truly determined not to.

But she wouldn't make the first move. That was for Robin to do.

He pushed his hair back from his face and frowned. "A small meal. Then I'll return."

And then, miracle of miracles, he offered her his arm. Anne accepted, ignoring the water that began to pool in her sleeve and the way her slippers squished in the mud. She had won a victory and she had nothing to complain about.

"A meal." Jason sighed happily from behind them.

Anne smothered her smile and walked on.

29

Edith of Sedgwick stood in the tower chamber, perfectly still despite her garments, which were soaked through to her skin. She would not shiver. It was a weakness and she would tolerate no weakness, neither in herself nor others.

Perhaps 'twas a good thing Maude was dead.

She had watched Lord Rhys carry the body off with him on his journeys. She imagined that Canfield wouldn't care much about his daughter's death. She'd been a plague to him for quite some time. And no one would blame Robin. It had been a matter of defense.

Which led her thoughts in a new direction.

Having a legitimate reason for murder was never a poor thing.

The door opened and slammed shut behind her, sending her candle flame flickering wildly.

"Can you believe it?" a voice exclaimed.

Edith closed her eyes and reached down deep inside herself for patience. It was all she could do not to turn on her brother. Was he such a fool he couldn't see how Maude's death had fouled her plans?

"He took all his bloody children with him!" Baldwin exclaimed.

Edith had cursed over that bit of misfortune as well. First Maude running amok and now Artane having taken Edith's other potential victims with him.

It had not been a productive day.

"And why did he leave the eldest three behind?" Baldwin demanded. "How does that serve me?"

"They didn't stay," Edith said. "Off to Wyckham, I believe."

"How am I to wed with Amanda, now that Robin has wed with Anne?" Baldwin spoke as if he hadn't heard her, which, knowing him, he likely hadn't.

Edith pursed her lips. "Mayhap you can—"

"My prey," Baldwin interrupted, looking as baffled as if a fox had suddenly slipped from under his nose. "They're gone!"

"Surely you can track them."

He blinked, then began to pace—never a good sign. Edith sighed and waited for him to spew some other bit of rot.

"I'll track them," he announced suddenly.

"You'll need help," Edith suggested.

"Ah," he said, nodding, "of course. That can be hired." He resumed his pacing. "I'll see to Rhys and the brood he has with him, then turn my sights to Wyckham."

Edith sincerely doubted he would find Rhys and his brood unattended enough for slaying. They would likely ensconce themselves in Fenwyck for a goodly time. And Rhys was no fool. He'd been a mercenary himself in his day, and his family was full of spies for the French king. If anyone could escape Baldwin's clumsy attempts at murder, it would be Rhys. Likely half-asleep and well into his cups even.

But seeking lads to aid him would keep Baldwin occupied and that was not something to be dismissed lightly. Edith listened to him plot and scheme, encouraged him when needed, then watched him leave all in a bluster.

And then she turned her attentions back to her own dilemma.

Her own plans were ruined.

Ruined.

Someone would have to pay for that.

She suspected she would have little trouble deciding upon whom.

30

Joanna of Segrave swept into Artane's great hall at sunrise, happy to be off her horse and more than happy to be at her journey's end. She pointed her cook toward the kitchen entrance and sent him off with instructions to make the best of things. Though Gwen and Rhys set a fine enough table, Joanna was not prepared to settle for anything marginal at supper. She had work to do and no time to worry about trivialities such as the condition of her daughter's larder.

The hall was oddly quiet and it puzzled her until she made her way to the lord's table. One weary soul slept with his face mashed against the wood. His squire kept him company, his own head lolling back against his chair, his mouth wide open to accommodate his snores.

Joanna lifted the first's head by his hair and was greeted by the sight of bleary gray eyes.

"Are you drunk?" she asked bluntly.

"Grandmère," the man said with a sweet smile. "How lovely . . ."

Joanna let his head resume its resting place with a none-too-gentle thump. "Robin, where is your bride?"

"Hmmm," Robin said, smacking his lips a time or two and then drifting back off to slumber.

Joanna slapped the table with both hands hard enough to make Robin's squire choke on his snorts and throw himself suddenly to his feet. Robin only continued to sleep on blissfully. Joanna fixed Jason with a steely glance.

"Have you answers for this, lad?"

"He trained until but a few hours ago, my lady," Jason said, snapping to attention.

"And his bride?"

"She allowed it."

Apparently there was more to the tale than she could divine at first glance. Joanna looked at Robin's squire, then at Robin, then she considered.

Once she had heard Robin had returned to Artane, she had immediately decided to take up her journey north. 'Twas far past time the boy was wed and she had been determined to see it happen. Though she had never taken part in such matchmaking in the past, she had decided perhaps it was a new vocation to pursue. She had been blessed with a love match in her youth and had mourned her late husband for years. She had watched her daughter have her own long years of difficulty while waiting for her marriage to Rhys de Piaget to come about. Joanna had waited for Robin to come to his senses for too long.

She had encountered her daughter the evening before on the road to Fenwyck and a hasty retelling of the past fortnight's events had left Joanna no less determined to see Robin happily settled. Anne deserved to be properly wooed and it was a certainty that Robin didn't have the skill to do it on his own. It was a grandmère's duty to see to that education, especially when that grandmère was so immeasurably suited to the task.

It was for that reason that she had brought a score of souls possessing various talents related to the art of life at court. If Robin couldn't learn to behave with those bodies as his instructors, then the boy was truly hopeless and Joanna would have no choice but to leave him to his own devices.

And pity Anne for it.

And if she waited much longer to begin her labors, she would have no great-grandchildren to fuss over before she found herself in her own grave. The time for action had come.

"A bucket of water, young Ayre," Joanna commanded.

Jason's eyes widened quite dramatically. "But, my lady—"

"You're a quick lad to see my purpose," Joanna said. "Be even quicker about fetching me what I need."

Jason gulped and nodded, though it was done none-too-enthusiastically. Joanna watched him fight his way through the gaggle of souls who currently sought to gain entrance into the hall at the same time. She looked over her little flock and was pleased with what she saw. These were various and sundry souls who had wound up at her keep for equally various and sundry reasons, not the least of which was her fondness of all things refined. That and, she supposed, the quality of the meals her kitchen had consistently produced since shortly after she had become mistress of Segrave. Whatever the true reason, she had amassed a following of impressive proportions and each man a master at his craft.

And now young Robin was about to have their expertise distilled upon his poor, unchivalrous self.

Whether he willed it or no.

The noise in the hall had become almost impossible to speak and be heard over. No matter. She had no intention of shouting to wake her grandson. She waited patiently until Jason returned with his heavy bucket of water. Then she gestured pointedly at Robin.

"Douse him," she commanded.

Jason looked as miserable as if she'd commanded him to plunge a blade through Robin's heart. "But, Lady Joanna . . ."

"I'll tell him 'twas my idea."

"Forgive me, my lady, but that won't matter."

Joanna searched her wits for something that would motivate the lad, short of having her guards poke him with their swords. She'd known countless men over the years who had been swayed by their bellies, but she suspected Robin inspired a loyalty in Jason that not even a decent meal could influence.

That, she decided, was a point in Robin's favor.

She tried another course. "Jason, the sooner he wakes, the sooner he can be taught the ways to win over his lady."

"My lady?"

"Chivalry training, Jason. I've brought his teachers with me."

Jason looked over his shoulder and his eyes widened. "Them?" he squeaked.

"And none other," she said. "Now, wake him please, and let's get on with this."

Jason shook his head, took a deep breath, and pulled back the bucket. "He won't like it, my lady."

"They never do, my lad."

Jason closed his eyes, blurted out a heartfelt prayer, then he took a deep breath and let fly the water. Robin leaped to his feet with a howl. Joanna found the bucket thrust into her hands and Jason under the table before she could protest. Robin had his sword drawn and looked as if he planned to kill the first person he clapped eyes on. But since that person was her, she merely smiled pleasantly at him.

"A good morrow to you, grandson," she said, setting the bucket down on the table.

He stood there and spluttered for several moments, then realization apparently began to dawn. She watched his fury battle with his respect for her. It was very engaging and she did her best not to laugh at him. Finally, he swallowed his ire and made her a low bow.

"Grandmère," he said. "Forgive me for not being at my best this morn to greet you."

She waved away his words. "'Tis nothing, Robin, my love."

"How lovely of you to visit," he continued.

"I'm not here to loiter without a purpose," she said. "I've come to work."

"Work?" he echoed in horror. "You?"

"Aye," she said calmly. "I've a task to see accomplished."

"And that would be?"

She waved expansively to her little flock behind her. "Why, your civilizing, of course."

He was speechless. Joanna smiled in satisfaction

Perhaps this wouldn't be as difficult as she feared.

31

Robin stood behind his father's table and stared in horror at the souls that now filled his father's hall. Minstrels and various other artistic sorts, the lot of them. If Robin hadn't been so weary, he would have fled to his father's solar and bolted himself inside for the duration. Not even a man of the staunchest courage could face that rabble and not feel a bit anxious.

"Ah," his grandmother said in satisfaction, "there is your lady. Anne, my dear, how fare you?"

Robin looked to his left to see Anne coming down the last pair of steps into the great hall. He wondered absently how much of the proceeding madness she had been privy to. And he realized in an instant just how laughable he appeared, standing there drenched and gaping.

"Lady Joanna," Anne said, coming around the table and taking his grandmother's hands. "How lovely to see you. I see you brought your courtiers."

Joanna laughed. "You flatter an old woman, love. I'm hardly holding court, but you know I can't bear to be away from my little pleasures for long."

"I'm sure we'll enjoy them as well," Anne said.

No doubt, Robin thought sourly. Anne wasn't the one Joanna intended to torment with the louts. He could well imagine what his grandmother had in mind for him, for he had spent a goodly amount of time at her hall and seen the goings-on there. But he'd be damned if she would turn him into one of the perfumed peacocks strutting before him now.

Though he had the feeling, judging by the look in his grandmother's eye, that that was precisely what she had in mind.

He suspected that he had just lost control of his own fate.

"You'll need chambers," Anne said. "You are welcome to take Lord Rhys's finest, of course—"

"She is not," Robin said, turning to look at Anne in astonishment. He turned to look at his grandmother. "The girls' chamber is in fine shape."

Joanna only waved a hand negligently. "As you will, Robin. We can see ourselves settled. Perhaps you have things to see to?"

Robin felt her pointed gaze sweep him from head to toe. He scowled at her. By the saints, he wasn't the one who had put himself in this drenched state!

"I need to train," Robin said.

"Didn't you just finish training?" Joanna asked.

Robin frowned. She would have him cornered if he weren't careful. "A man cannot train too much," he said firmly. She could hardly argue with that.

"Surely," his grandmother said just as firmly, "there are many things you must see to *inside* the hall. Though you would no doubt know much more about the manly workings of a keep than I."

Robin snorted before he could help himself. His grandmother had managed Segrave alone for well over a score of years—and managed to keep herself free of the various suitors who considered her a fine widowly prize. Hell, she could likely run the entire realm without perspiring. At over three score years, she was a formidable woman with an iron will.

But Robin was, after all, her grandson and a goodly amount of that wily blood flowed through his veins as well. He leaned on the table and gave her his most disarming smile. He didn't use it much, but he knew it was effective.

"I should at least see to my men," he said. "I won't neglect you, Grandmère."

"It isn't me I'm concerned with," she said, leaning on her side of the table and putting her still very beautiful visage close to his. She lowered her voice to a whisper. "You are freshly wed, my boy, are you not?"

He scowled at her. "'Tis a marriage fraught with complications, my lady."

"Then you'd best be at the unraveling of them straightway, don't you think?"

"When I think, Grandmère, I always find myself in trouble."

His grandmother laughed, put her arm around his neck, and kissed him on the cheek. "Ah, Robin, my love, I have missed you. Go be about your play, then come indulge me in a bit of conversation. I can see we've much to discuss."

And he could see by the purposeful glint in her eye— her sweet words aside—that his reprieve would be short-lived at best. So he grunted at her, fixed his squire with a pointed look, then started around the end of the table.

Only to come face-to-face with his bride.

It wasn't that he had forgotten she was there. It was, well, it was that he had forgotten that she was his. Yet as he stood there like a half-wit and gaped at her, he wondered how he could have lost sight of such a thing.

She looked disgustingly well-rested. Serene even. She certainly didn't look like a maid who had spent her wedding night alone, sobbing into her pillow because of it.

"You slept well?" he asked, because he could think of nothing else to say.

"Well enough," she replied, looking up at him solemnly. "You, my lord, have table marks still in your cheek."

He scrambled for an explanation. "I didn't want to wake you," he said, feeling very quick on his feet considering the amount of sleep he'd had.

Anne only smiled a small, gentle smile in return. "I'll have a meal ready for you after you've finished in the lists, if you like."

Robin frowned at her. Was she seeking to feed him to death? He wondered, absently, why she wasn't shouting at him for having left her alone. Unless, of course, she was relieved about that. Though she didn't look all that relieved. She looked, well, serene.

It was enough to set his teeth on edge.

A meal from his lady, then tortures from his grandmother to endure. It wasn't much of a day to look forward to. Mayhap he would be better off to hide in bed.

But nay, Anne would fetch him. For all he knew, his grandmother's minstrels would come fetch him and he wasn't sure he could bear the humiliation of that.

The lists. He clung to that thought with his last shreds of dignity. He grunted at his lady as he set her aside and walked away. He heard Jason fall into step behind him. Joanna's gaggle of artists scattered before him like frail leaves blown by a fierce wind.

"Ah, Anne my love, how good it is to see you," came floating along behind him and Robin suppressed a shudder. The saints only knew what havoc his grandmother would combine upon his wife.

He paused at the door, wondering if he should perhaps separate the two for the morn. He looked over his shoulder and cursed. Too late. His grandmother had already swept his wife up and was propelling her toward the stairs. He had no doubts they would barricade themselves in one of the solars for the saints only knew what kind of conversation. He stroked his chin thoughtfully. With any luck at all, it might be conversation that included him. Favorably.

Then again, it might not.

He might have had Anne's hand, true, but he wasn't certain he had her heart.

Was it too late to win that?

He looked about him at the supposed masters of various arts and found himself scowling in spite of himself. He was to find himself aided by these? Peacocks, the lot of them.

He left the hall before he did them any damage. After all, they might have a suggestion or two he could use. It was possible.

But he doubted it was very likely.

With one thing and another, it was late in the afternoon before he managed to get himself inside the hall again. Preparations were just being made for supper and Robin looked forward to a hearty meal. Things certainly smelled good. Perhaps one of his grandmother's lads had been hard at work. Robin followed his nose, which led him in a straight path back to the kitchen, only to find his way blocked by a stout figure of a man holding a cooking implement of some kind as if he intended to do damage with it. Robin stopped and folded his arms across his chest in his most intimidating pose.

"Move," he said without preamble.

The cook bristled. "The lady Joanna commands that you attend her in the lord's solar."

Robin pursed his lips, but decided that it was passing unfair to cut down a man who thought so highly of a wooden spoon, and likely wielded it with the same enthusiasm. Who knew what he would find at his place if he offended the man? He'd heard of souls receiving very unpalatable servings at his grandmother's table for naught but a look askance. Who knew what sorts of nasty tidbits bloodshed might bring him?

So Robin, who never backed away from a fight or found himself intimidated by another soul, stepped back and conceded the battle. He could do nothing less for the sake of his poor belly.

He made his way to his father's solar, sighing heavily with every few paces. He paused before the door, took a deep breath, and prayed he could control his temper. He suspected that even though he had forborne slaying his grandmother's cook, he might not have that counted in his favor if he decimated the rest of her entourage.

He opened the door and peeked inside.

It was worse than he had feared.

His sire would have come undone had he been privy to this sight. Every available surface was covered with either cloth, baubles, or his grandmother's *artistes*. And, worse yet, all eyes were turned his way.

Robin toyed with the idea of escape, but he suspected that the delicate souls before him were no doubt very fleet of foot. The humiliation of being chased down by his grandmother's minstrels and such was just more than Robin could contemplate. So he took another deep breath, let it out slowly, then entered the chamber.

The door was shut behind him and bolted. Immediately.

"Ah, Robin," his grandmother said, smiling what he could only assume

she believed to be a disarming smile at him. "We have been anxiously
awaiting your arrival."

"No doubt," Robin said as sternly as possible. Best to begin as he intended to finish—with some shred of dignity remaining him.

"Our first task," she continued just as pleasantly, "is to see you properly
groomed and dressed." She gestured expansively to a tub set before the
hearth. "In there, if you please."

Robin grumbled but didn't argue. There was little harm to be found in
a bath now and then, despite what some thought about the perils of soaking
in water. And Robin had to admit that there was something almost comforting about having his grandmother wash his hair for him— something
he was certain she hadn't done in years.

But once his head was free of the soap and he had shaken the water out
of his ears, he noticed the murmuring going on directly behind him.

"I say we cut it."

"Nay," another said thoughtfully, "'tis goodly hair."

"Unfashionably long, though."

"Perhaps it could be trimmed here and there," offered another.

"Nay, cut away a goodly amount," insisted the first. "Don't you agree,
my lady?"

"I defer to your expertise, Reynaud," Joanna said blithely. "Lads, be
prepared to hold him down if he fights."

Robin struggled to turn around and fix his would-be assaulters with a
glare. "I don't want my hair cut."

The three looked at him as if he were a new breed of vermin they must
needs eradicate or face a lifetime of misery otherwise.

"Cut it," Joanna commanded.

"I like it long!" Robin exclaimed.

One of the three came at him with a knife and Robin looked about him
frantically for a weapon. He caught sight of his gear—safely tucked behind
his grandmother's slender form. And then he found himself ringed by a
collection of men whom he likely could have dispatched with his bare hands
alone.

Then again, maybe not. He looked at them and found in the group a
lad or two with a glint in his eye that spoke of ample time spent in places
much less civilized than Segrave's great hall. Robin sank back into the tub
in a wary crouch.

"Very well, then," he said. "But I'll not have my head bared as these
fools in court do." He clutched the sides of the tub. "Not too short," he
repeated.

The knife began its foul work and Robin closed his eyes. There was no
sense in watching his poor hair falling about him in ignominious heaps.

After that torture was over, he was instructed to rise. He didn't dare touch his head for fear of what he wouldn't find there any longer. So he dried himself off, then allowed himself to be dressed. The clothing was fine—even he had to admit that, though he did it in the sternest manner possible. There was no sense in allowing his grandmother to think she could do with him as she liked.

But then some lout or other approached him with footwear. Robin gaped at the toes of the dainty shoes.

"What is that foul protrusion?" he demanded, pointing a shaking finger at the same.

"The latest fashion from Paris," the shoe bearer said, fondling the toe with a rapturous sigh. "Lovely, isn't it?"

It was without a doubt the silliest thing Robin had ever seen and he could hardly believe these dolts intended that he should wear the like on his feet. His were manly feet that demanded boots that could withstand mud and dung and all manner of manly elements. He sincerely doubted that he could cross the rushes in these without falling straightway upon his arse. And, given his luck of late, he would likely impale his eye upon the toe of his shoe in the process!

"Absolutely not," Robin said, folding his arms.

Several daggers appeared out of voluminous sleeves and his grandmother cleared her throat meaningfully.

"Damnation," Robin snarled as he surrendered his feet to a humiliation they had never before had to endure. It did not bode well for the rest of the evening.

But when two seamstresses materialized from the crowd and came at him with baubles, needles, and thread, Robin knew action had to be taken.

"You will not," he said to the two women, giving them his most formidable glare, "attach those to my clothes. Absolutely not. Never. I refuse and resist."

"Tie him down," his grandmother said with a sigh.

"What?" Robin screeched. He listened to himself and could hardly believe the sound was coming from him. He never screeched. He bellowed. He snarled. He commanded legions with a mere shout alone. Yet look what pointy-toed shoes and shorn hair had reduced him to.

And then before he could reconcile himself to the fact that his grandmother had indeed been in earnest, he found himself overpowered, overwhelmed, and overcome. The wave of mankind receded and Robin found himself in a chair. Tied to it, actually, and completely unable to move. He glared at his grandmother.

"If you think—"

"I think you wish to win your lady," his grandmother said shortly, "and we are here to help you do it. The sooner your lessons are done, the sooner she will be yours. Is that not what you want?"

Robin scowled, but said nothing. He gave his grandmother a short nod and closed his eyes as he felt his clothing being attacked. Perhaps she had it aright and what he needed to win Anne was a little civilizing. Perhaps she would see him dressed as a fine lord and take a liking to him.

Assuming she didn't laugh herself into a faint first.

"Feathers now," Joanna instructed. "And don't be shy, mistresses. He has many appearances of less-than-lordly stature to make up for."

Robin snarled out a curse, but that was the best he could do.

The saints only knew what Anne would think when she saw him.

32

Anne sat at a table in the healer's house and contemplated two things. One was that she actually had the freedom to sit in peace without wondering when a stray knife might find itself between her ribs. The other was the sight of the herbs lying in bunches before her. She recognized most of them, but that wasn't because she'd studied them diligently. She'd had them used on her so often during her convalescence that she could recognize most by smell alone.

That was not necessarily a pleasant skill to have.

"Rose," Master Erneis said, gesturing with a slender finger.

"Aye," Anne said absently. "I know."

"Good for several things, though I daresay the lady Gwennelyn has them for beauty alone. These come from well-established plants."

"They were laid along with the stone for the keep," Anne said.

"Long before my time," he offered. "I daresay Mistress Berengaria saw them planted though."

Anne smiled at his tone of reverence. She couldn't help but agree with him. Berengaria had been Artane's first healer, and the one who had seen Anne through her troubles. There had been a great many times when Anne had wondered if Berengaria had been adding something extra to her brews, though Anne couldn't have said what. Her hands had been steady, her knowledge of herblore ample, and her gentleness a soothing balm. Anne had grieved mightily when Berengaria had found Erneis and brought him to Artane to train him in her skills so she might make her way in the world, but it hadn't been for Anne to say who should go or stay.

Master Erneis, however, seemed even now to labor under the woman's shadow. Anne couldn't fault his knowledge, though, or his skill. But he was, after all, just a man. Anne wondered mightily if Berengaria might have possessed a few skills that no simple healer should have.

"My lady?"

Anne blinked, then shook her head. "Forgive me. My mind wanders." She turned her attentions fully back to the table. Now that she was the lady of Artane, if only for a little while, it would behoove her to know more about the healing arts. That was why she had ignored her discomfort over the idea, forced herself to cross that courtyard with its smooth stone, and presented herself at the healer's house for a lesson.

Even though the smell was less than pleasant.

The door opened behind her and Anne couldn't help but feel a bit of relief over a possible reprieve. She looked behind her only to find Edith standing there. And in spite of herself, she shivered.

"Cold, my lady?" Erneis asked.

Anne shook her head. "Hungry perhaps. I should likely see to dinner inside. Thank you for your aid—"

She would have said more, but she caught a flash of silver and turned just in time to see Edith producing a blade from somewhere on her person. Anne shrieked, then watched the blade as it flew.

It pinned a rat to the floor.

Edith look at her with puzzlement. "My lady?"

"Nothing," Anne rasped. "I'm overwrought."

"I'll walk back with you—"

Anne held up her hand. "Nay, Edith, but I thank you most kindly for the offer. I wouldn't want to interrupt your business here."

And with that, she moved as quickly as possible to the door and out into the fresh air. Once there, she lifted her face and looked into the late afternoon sky.

By the saints, she didn't trust that woman.

"Lady Anne?"

Anne blinked, then saw Jason standing before her. She smiled in relief. Now that Jason was there, all would be well. Anne took his arm.

"The saints be praised," she said with feeling as they walked slowly. "Would that you had come hours ago while I was captive in the solar."

"Captive, my lady?"

"Joanna bade me stay until she had finished her work with your master. I vow if I'd had to put another stitch in a tunic, I would have gone mad. 'Tis only recently that I've escaped her."

Jason cleared his throat, a bit uncomfortably to her ears. "I daresay, my lady, that my lord has the same feeling."

Anne looked at him and smiled. "A difficult afternoon for him?"

"If he appears for supper, 'twill be nothing short of a miracle," Jason predicted.

"What could the lady Joanna possibly have done to him?" Anne asked in surprise.

"I couldn't begin to describe it," Jason said. "I'll leave it to you to see the results."

Anne kept her curiosity under control and ascended the steps carefully to the great hall. She watched her feet as she crossed to the hearth, lest she trip and take Jason down with her. He stopped and she stopped with him. She raised her head.

It was all she could do not to gasp.

Well, it was certainly Robin, but it was a Robin she had never seen before. She now understood what Jason had meant by stitches in tunics.

Never in her life had she seen a shirt so adorned with buttons, ribbons, and—this she could hardly believe— feathers. Anne looked down and marveled at the pointed toes of his shoes. She could scarce believe Joanna had convinced him to put them on. She worked her way up past the hose, back up past the bedecked tunic, and up to meet Robin's scowl. She couldn't tell if he was resigned or furious. She suspected it might be a bit of both.

Then there was his hair. It was substantially shorter, and Robin continually pulled on it, as if by doing so he could restore some of its length. One thing it did was reveal his ears, which she was certain she had never seen.

They were, she had to admit on closer inspection, perhaps ears that were better left under hair. They resembled his mother's a great deal and such substantial protrusions were her bane.

And then a most startling realization struck her.

He was wooing her.

His grandmother had laid out in great detail her plans to civilize Robin, once she had poked and prodded enough to learn that Anne wasn't praying for an annulment. Anne had listened politely, certain Robin would never, *ever* allow himself to be dressed up like a pampered lord at court.

Yet apparently he had.

For her.

Had she ever had any desire to laugh, it disappeared at the dangerous glint in his eye. She suspected that if she even came close to any expression of mirth, she would never be forgiven for it. So she put on the most serious look she could muster and moved to stand near him.

And then she sneezed.

Robin's look of irritation had turned to faint alarm. She watched him sniff about his person anxiously. He wrinkled his nose at what he found, but shrugged it off. He turned to her and made her a low bow, sending another waft of perfume her way.

She sneezed thrice in rapid, uncomfortable succession.

"Something in the hearth," she said quickly, waving her hand in front of her face. "Bad wood."

Robin's look of dismay didn't diminish much, but at least he wasn't making any more sniffing forays in his immediate vicinity.

And then the hall began to fill with garrison knights and the like, come to partake of their evening meal. Anne watched them catch sight of Robin and prayed—for their sakes—that they did not giggle.

Robin's men, who either had been trained very well or were so battle-hardened that they were no longer surprised by anything, marched in and took their places happily at one of the lower tables. Rhys's men, ones who were either less well-trained in keeping their thoughts to themselves or had just rotated in for their yearly service, stopped so suddenly in the middle of the hall that they formed a knot of men who were suddenly staggering about, trying to keep their feet.

Robin's expression darkened considerably.

The gaping turned to grinning on some faces and Anne had the feeling those men would pay dearly for their sport at Robin's expense. Robin gave her a curt nod before he strode across the rushes and stopped but a hand's breadth before the foremost man.

"Something amuses you?" Robin demanded.

"Nay, my lord," the man said, but he was unsuccessful in wiping the smile completely from his face.

Robin looked at the rest of the men gathered there. "Anyone else unable to repress their chuckles? Ah, I see a few lads here who find something to tickle them."

"The feathers on your tunic, my lord," one of the men said with a guffaw.

Robin found that man, put his arm around his shoulders, and led him to the other lower table. He beckoned to the other men and bade them sit as well.

Anne suppressed a shudder.

"Enjoy your meal," Robin said, patting the shoulder of the first man he'd seated. "Then meet me in the lists."

There was a small chorus of ready ayes. Robin walked back to the hearth, a satisfied smile on his face. He made Anne a low bow.

"My lady?"

She could hardly contain her surprise. "You aren't going to kill them?"

Robin shot his grandmother a quick look and Anne turned in time to see her sharp shake of the head. He sighed.

"Apparently not. But fortunately my sire has a fine healer. I imagine he'll be busy with much stitching tonight."

"Robin," Lady Joanna warned.

"Maiming, Grandmère," Robin growled. "I promised no death, did I not? But that doesn't mean they can't be taught a lesson in respect."

Clearly someone had informed the most outspoken of the lads of Robin's reputation because there was a groan and thump as one man fell backward off the bench and cracked his head soundly against the floor under the rushes. Robin merely raised his eyebrow and offered Anne his arm.

She took it, wondering absently just how Robin intended to teach anyone any lessons in the lists while wearing those shoes. He barely made it to the table without pitching forward half a dozen times.

She soon found herself on his right while his grandmother sat on his left. As she smothered a sneeze and began fanning away as surreptitiously as possible Robin's perfume, she suspected that this might be one of the longest meals of both their lives.

"Ah, food," he said as the dishes appeared before him. He placed his trencher directly before him and began piling a goodly amount of food atop it.

"Robin," his grandmother whispered fiercely, "what do you?"

Robin's sigh fair blew over his wine goblet. "I'm eating. I'm allowed to do that, am I not?"

He pulled off a huge piece of the trencher as well, and managed to get it most of the way to his mouth before aged, bony fingers came to rest on his arm. *Rest* was, perhaps, not the word for it. Anne watched in fascination as Joanna slapped her fingers on Robin's arm and jerked it down.

Anne watched Robin turn to look at his grandmother. Joanna was making motions that he should replace the bread. Robin shook his head forcefully enough to send several feathers on his shirt flapping. His grandmother whispered something to him in urgent undertones. Robin cursed, then put the bread back on the table and made an attempt to rejoin it with the mangled trencher.

His grandmother began to sigh.

"What have I done now?" Robin demanded.

"Share your trencher with Anne, Robin," Joanna exclaimed. "By the saints, boy, where have you been dining the past few years? At a trough?"

Robin grunted, but said nothing.

Anne soon found the trencher closer to her than it had been, but not by much. Robin almost managed to eat something, but he was again thwarted.

"The best pieces go to her."

"Grandmère, I am fair starved to faintness!" Robin exclaimed.

"That doesn't matter."

"It matters to me!"

"What should matter to you, grandson, are your manners!"

Robin growled, then snatched a goblet and drank before he could be stopped.

"Wipe off where you've sipped, then offer it to your lady."

Robin took the cloth that covered the table, wiped the rim of the cup, then began to wipe the rest.

"Best remove all my traces," he grumbled. He then offered it to Anne with a scowl. "It would seem, my lady, that 'tis only *now* the cup is fit to drink from."

Anne raised the cup to her lips, then couldn't control the hearty sneeze she left lingering in said cup. Robin pursed his lips at her, then looked at his grandmother.

"What now, O Wisest of Advisors?"

A sharp slap to the back of his head left him hunching down over his half of the trencher. Anne couldn't blame him. Between the perfume that emanated from his person and the feather that seemed to be protruding from his shoulder and lingering beneath her nose, it was all she could do to down anything at all for her sneezes. She had to admit it was with a sense of relief that the end of the meal came. Robin seemed to be just as relieved. He shoved his chair back from the table without hesitation the very moment he was allowed to.

"Jason!" he bellowed. "My boots!"

He stood, ripped off the tunic he wore, scattering feathers, buttons, and assorted other baubles across the table and floor. Several of Joanna's following gasped in horror and leaped up to rescue their work. Robin sat down, jerked off his shoes, and flung them across the great hall as well. Anne could have sworn one of Joanna's lads began to weep.

Robin stood up with a purposeful clearing of his throat. Mail was brought and donned. He turned and Anne found her hand grasped in his. He leaned over, then was stopped by his grandmother's hand on his shoulder.

"You don't kiss," she said.

Robin turned and gaped at her. "What?"

"Isn't that so, Stephen?" she asked one of her lads.

"Aye, my lady," Stephen said, bounding over enthusiastically. "'Tis a new thing at court, but very well thought of, to my mind. The gentleman bends over the lady's hand and feigns as if he kisses it. It leaves less spittle on her fingers, which might give her a distaste of him before he can pursue his suit with her."

Robin's jaw had gone slack. "What's the point then?"

"'Tis all in the art, my lord. The art of wooing."

Robin looked at him, then looked at Anne. She had never seen a more perplexed look on a body's face. "He's daft," he said, then released Anne's hand and backed away. He looked at Stephen. "I'm for the lists where when a man comes at you with a blade, he means it! By the saints, I do not understand this wooing business!"

And with that, he vaulted over the table and strode across the great hall.

"Out," he said to his previously selected evening's entertainment. "I've business with you all outside. In the lists," he threw over his shoulder at his grandmother pointedly. "Where men are men and do manly things!"

The door banged shut behind him to be opened rather less enthusiastically by the men who followed him out. Anne watched them, then looked at Stephen and Joanna who were shaking their heads.

"I can wield a sword," Stephen protested. "And very well, if I might say so."

"Of course you can," Joanna said. "You've merely chosen to spend your energies of late in studying the finer points of courtly manners. There is no shame in that."

"Look at what he did to that tunic!" one of Joanna's seamstresses said, holding out the offended garment.

"And the shoes!" the apparent keeper of the footwear said with a great deal of distress. "He caught me between the eyes with one of these!"

"He's a barbarian," another man said with a shudder.

"Aye," Anne said happily.

"This will never do," Joanna said with disapproval. "We'll have to work on him again tomorrow, my friends. A good night's rest and up early before he escapes off to the saints only know where."

"He'll never submit again," a man said, a man who was sporting a very swollen and abused eye.

Anne could only assume he had tried to subdue Robin the first time.

"He will," Joanna said, looking at Anne. "If he wants the prize, he will."

Anne shook her head as she excused herself and made her way upstairs to Rhys and Gwen's bedchamber. Her bedchamber, she supposed, though it was certainly not meant to be hers alone. Robin had likely had enough civilizing for his lifetime and she would only be surprised if she ever saw him anywhere else besides the lists.

But as she made ready for bed, she couldn't stop either a final sneeze or a smile over his efforts that day.

Feathers and buttons indeed.

33

Robin awoke in his father's solar, but couldn't force himself to open his eyes yet. He remained rolled in a blanket on the floor and gave serious consideration as to whether or not all these machinations were worth it. Surely most men did not go through such tortures to woo their brides.

Nay, he thought with a snort, most men wed with women they scarce knew, much less loved, and the question of wooing did not enter into things. His was a different tale entirely.

He didn't begrudge Anne her due. After all, she'd had to endure his poor manners for years. And he'd ruined her wedding day with the unfortunate incident in the chapel, though he wasn't going to take responsibility for Isabelle losing her breakfast so abruptly.

In truth, though, he could scarce believe the events that had transpired on Artane's holiest ground. He should have been more vigilant. He should have taken more time to investigate, though in fairness to himself, he had looked the servants over carefully several times. He had never seen Maude, of that he was certain.

Or had he, and just not realized who she was?

He had to concede that perhaps that was possible. He flexed his hands. Killing a woman—now that was something he had never had included in his lengthy list of deeds before. He sighed heavily. It wasn't something he would have done, or could have done, had he known who it was who threw herself at Anne. How could he? No woman had ever felt even a blow from him, or the flat of his hand. Well, save Amanda, and he had only taken his brotherly due of a friendly swipe or two at her backside.

Nay, women were God's most precious gift to man. He believed it fully. He had never betrayed that belief.

He sincerely hoped Anne would understand. It was not how he would have had her day proceed. He would do much to make it up to her.

But even with all that on his conscience and a fairly strong desire to redeem himself before his lady, he wasn't sure he could bear another day of civilizing. Thrashing the lads in the lists the evening before had been satisfying enough, but he hadn't been at his best and he blamed his grandmother for it. The anxiety he'd felt whilst trying not to trip in those damned shoes before supper had drained his strength. He would surely not be wearing anything else so foolish on his feet.

He opened his eyes, then yelped in surprise. His grandmother sat in a chair next to him. Indeed, she was fair sitting upon him and he could scarce believe he hadn't heard her come in.

"You," he said, sitting up and willing his heart to stop pounding, "are a wily old woman."

She only smiled, a feral smile that set the hairs on his arms to standing. The saints only knew what she had in store for him today.

"Am I?" she asked pleasantly.

"Aye, you are, but you can cease with your plans for the day. I've business to attend to."

"Your business is taken care of," she said smoothly.

"What?" he exclaimed. "How could you possibly—"

"Know how to run a keep?" she finished. "I can do many things, whelp, not the least of which is keeping your father's lovely hall from falling into ruin for the whole of a single day."

Robin pursed his lips. "I have things only I can see to."

"I think not. I've put one of my lads in charge of your business. Things will proceed perfectly well without you attending to them for one day. Besides, you have other things to concentrate on today."

Robin wondered if it would be a mark against him to lock his grandmother in one of the guard tower upper chambers, far away from the keep proper, of course, where he could not hear her foul cursing of him. He could leave her there only so long as necessary—say until she tired of her current schemes and vowed to return home quietly.

"Dancing," Joanna stated firmly.

Robin shook his head. "I will not—"

"Aye, you will."

"Grandmère, I've business to attend to that cannot be entrusted to one of your frilly fools!"

She looked at him. Robin could see her thoughts whirling in her head and it gave him a bit of an unsettled stomach.

By the saints, she was a dangerous woman.

She nodded briefly. "Very well, then. Finish it by matins."

"Impossible. This afternoon, at the earliest."

"Noon, and not a moment longer, lest I be forced to drag you in by your ear."

Robin had several very vivid memories of his elegant grandmother doing just that in his youth, so he rubbed his ear protectively and glared at her. "I cannot possibly—"

"Learn to dance? Of course you can. Even your grandsire, God rest his soul and his cloddish feet, could sketch out a few steps after some instruction."

Robin paused. "How much instruction?"

His grandmother ignored the question and that convinced him that he was facing another day of complete misery.

"Noon," she said, rising. "Do not be late."

Robin watched her leave the chamber and as he looked at the door, another thought occurred to him.

He was almost certain he'd bolted it behind him the night before.

He scowled. Either he had slept like the dead because he'd been overwhelmed by his own perfumed stench, or his grandmother knew things she shouldn't and possessed skills no woman of her age should.

He didn't want to speculate on which it was, for either alternative was unpalatable.

He rose. Best use his time wisely whilst he had command of his fate.

He finished training at noon. He'd toyed with the idea of remaining out in the lists for yet awhile, just to see if his grandmother would actually make good on her threats. The other reason he'd been tempted was that Baldwin of Sedgwick had not deigned to grace them with his presence that morn and such had pleased Robin enormously. He had learned from one of his father's men that Baldwin had departed for points unknown the night before, which likely should have given him pause. But Baldwin was like unto cesspit odor, ever present and only disappearing long enough to catch a body unawares when it returned in its full glory. Robin suspected his cousin would blow back into the keep soon enough. For now, Robin was merely enjoying the respite.

Unfortunately his respite from his grandmother's torture was now over. There was no point in avoiding what she wanted him to do. He trudged back to the keep grimly, wondering just how well he would fare with her lessons in dancing. He'd danced a time or two over the course of his score-and-four years, but it had never been a pleasant event—either for him or the ladies so cursed to have him partner them.

Perhaps he had inherited his grandfather's cloddish feet.

Joanna was standing at the top of the steps leading up to the great hall, tapping her foot impatiently.

"I am not late," Robin growled at her.

She bestowed a smile upon him. "Indeed you are not. I was just preparing my feet for a vigorous lesson today."

"My feet would be much happier to find themselves propped up on a table where they could enjoy the music without having to participate."

Joanna took his arm and drew him into the hall. "Never fear, grandson. They'll find this much to their liking. First, though, we must put them in something more suited to dancing. Booted feet never a happy maid made."

He scowled at her. Had she invented that fiendish statement on her own, or was it something handed down from generation to generation of women bent on torturing their men with such frivolous behaviors? Even he, though, could see the logic of it. Better to step on Anne's feet in something besides his boots.

Robin found himself led over to the hearth where he was pushed into a chair, his boots removed and flimsy slippers placed up on his feet.

"Dancing slippers," one of his grandmother's peacocks sighed rapturously.

"Perfect," Robin muttered under his breath. Indeed, he muttered several things as his grandmother's little group of minstrels tuned their instruments and did whatever minstrels did to prepare themselves for a hearty round of torture. Robin had no musical gifts, nor much of an ear for it, so it all sounded like screeching to him.

He looked about the great hall and was somewhat relieved to find it empty. Well, save his grandmother's entourage. But there were no servants, no men-at-arms to see his humiliation. He lifted an eyebrow. Perhaps he had given his grandmother too little credit. She might have been bent on humiliating him privately, but at least she had made some little effort to save his pride publicly.

And then his grandmother cleared her throat.

The musicians ceased and all eyes turned to her. Robin looked at her as well. He knew she would likely pull his ear if he didn't.

She gestured expansively toward a cluster of souls near the middle of the floor in the great hall.

"Behold your dancing master," she said. "Wulfgar."

The gaggle parted. Robin felt his jaw go slack. He could scarce believe what he was seeing.

The man standing there cracking his knuckles enthusiastically was taller than Robin by no doubt half a head, and perhaps even broader through the chest and arms. He looked more suited to lifting mailed knights over his head and heaving them great distances than he did capering about to music.

"He will, of course, expect your full cooperation," Joanna said happily.

Robin rose with a sigh. He could take the man, of course, for he had no doubts of his own skill. But it would be a messy business and there would be a great deal to clean up off the hall floor afterwards. Besides, if a lout this size could learn to dance, perhaps Robin would find himself not unable as well.

He found himself relieved of his weapons suddenly and he submitted.

Then he crossed the great hall, folded his arms across his chest, and gave his dancing master his most formidable glare.

"Get on with it," he commanded.

The man made him a bow. "As you will, my lord. And as you can see, if I am able to move about so gracefully, so should you be likewise able."

"My thoughts exactly."

"Think of it as a battle, my lord," Wulfgar continued in a gravelly voice that sounded more accustomed to bellowing orders than gently instructing prancing steps, "and think of your body as your troops."

Robin stroked his chin. War? Aye, this was something he could understand.

"Your goal, my lord, is to negotiate the battlefield as delicately as possible, guard your lady as you go, and reach your goal."

"Which would be the finish of the song?" Robin asked darkly.

Wulfgar laughed, a hearty laugh that made Robin think of tankards of ale shared in wayside inns after a successful siege. He felt immediately warm and comfortable and even managed a smile.

"Aye, my lord," Wulfgar said. "There is that as well. Now, let us begin."

Well, at least he wasn't required to clasp hands with the man as if they'd been lovers. Wulfgar maintained a perfect warriorly distance as he showed Robin what he needed to do.

Even so, Robin suspected it would be a very long afternoon.

But he was no coward. And if Wulfgar the Large could do the like, so could he.

Though he had to admit, once a small rest was called for, that this dancing business was much more difficult to do correctly than he had dared believe before. He stood there, panting, his head spinning with dancing strategies, patterns, and tactics.

By the saints, 'twas enough to give a man pains in his head.

Not to mention his feet.

Robin walked gingerly to the high table only to see a sight that simultaneously brought a flush to his face and a chill to his veins.

Anne was sitting on the bottom step, her elbows on her knees, her chin on her fists, watching him.

Robin came to a dead halt. How bloody long had she been observing him? He wasn't sure if he should shout at her or ask her if she thought him skilled. He shut his mouth with a snap and scowled.

And then another thought occurred to him. Would Anne be able to do any of these steps with her leg? He'd learned many intricate caperings that morning. Would she be equal to them?

But before he could decide anything, he caught sight of his grandmother hastening to Anne's side.

"He learned well, didn't he?" she asked.

Anne smiled. "Aye, Lady Joanna. He's very skilled."

Robin paused and considered. Kind words from his lady. There was something in that.

"Come, my dear," Joanna said, raising Anne to her feet. "Come try a turn or two with him."

Robin wanted to bid his grandmother be silent, but perhaps she knew better than he what Anne could do where this dancing was concerned.

He found himself suddenly with his lady's hand in his and his mind completely free of all the things he'd recently learned.

Damnation.

When it was clear to everyone including Anne that he was hopelessly lost, Joanna bid the screechers of song and pluckers of lute strings cease. Wulfgar was summoned again to the center of the hall. Robin took Anne's right side and Wulfgar took her left and Robin watched his dancing master as they rehearsed their steps again. And as they did, Robin realized how ingenious his grandmother had been in her choice of things for him to learn. He did a great deal of foolish prancing about, but Anne was required to do little but walk a bit and look lovely. The dancing steps she took were graceful and she seemed to enjoy them, but he suspected they wouldn't tax her overmuch.

And when he was finally released from his tortures and allowed to take his place at high table, he escorted his lady there and sat with a happy sigh. He was vastly relieved to be off his feet.

Until, that was, his grandmother approached purposefully.

"We'll dance again tonight," she announced. "That Robin might trot out his hard-won skills."

Robin scowled, but realized he had no recourse. Besides, a sliding glance Anne's way revealed that she didn't look opposed to the idea.

Dancing.

He only hoped it was the last of the tortures his grandmother had in mind for him.

34

Anne sat in the alcove of Gwen's solar and enjoyed a bit of peace and quiet. She'd pulled the curtain across to give herself privacy, something she rarely did lest she offend everyone else in the chamber. But Artane's ladies had been dispatched to various locations unknown, Joanna was off marshalling her last reserves of patience by indulging in a nap, and the saints only knew where Robin was. She'd seen Jason earlier and he told her, as he headed toward the kitchens where any sensible boy of ten-and-six went when given leave, that he was enjoying a day of liberty and had no idea where his master was.

Anne could only hope Robin wasn't in the village, bedding as many willing wenches as possible.

Now, with her precious privacy, she could give herself over freely to the contemplation of her situation. She stared out the window and smiled to herself. Who would have thought that Robin of Artane, of all people, would have put himself through such travails just to please her? Her father would certainly have been surprised by it, Amanda appalled, and Nicholas—well, Nicholas would have laughed himself to death, and that would have sparked several battles between the two so perhaps 'twas best Robin had made his forays into fine-lorddom by himself.

The curtain moved suddenly as if set to flapping by a stiff breeze. Anne jumped in spite of herself. Then she heard the voices in the chamber and relaxed. Her attacker was dead and her husband was on the other side of the cloth. She was safe.

"Very well," Robin said heavily. "Let us have this over with."

"My lord," said a voice whose beauty just in speaking made Anne catch her breath, "skill with the lute cannot be acquired if 'having it over with' is all you are willing to dedicate to its mastery."

"And how could skill with the lute possibly serve me?" Robin demanded. "It certainly won't save my neck—or my lady's if that romantic notion suits you better, ah, you, um, Master Lutenist."

"Geoffrey, my lord."

"Ah," Robin groaned, "not another one."

Anne smiled. There was no mystery regarding Robin's feelings for her sire. She settled back to listen, wondering greatly how it would all play out.

She sincerely hoped Robin wouldn't decapitate the minstrel. He had a beautiful voice and for that alone he should be forgiven his part in Lady Joanna's scheme.

"Two lutes?" Robin complained. "By the saints, man, have you no mercy? There'll be no rest for me at all if you've two of those bloody things."

"One for me," Geoffrey said smoothly, "and one for you, my lord. Now, if you'll be so kind as to take the instrument. Hold it thusly, there you have it. Well done, my lord!"

"Leave off, will you?" Robin said crossly. "Even I can manage to hold it. 'Tis the playing of it that I'll never manage."

"If you can wield a sword, you can play the lute," Geoffrey promised.

"Hrmph," Robin grunted. "Is that what you say to all the half-wits who find themselves in your vile clutches?"

Geoffrey laughed and it sounded more like a waterfall than a man's voice. Anne was half tempted to peek around the curtain and make certain her husband wasn't about to be enspelled by a faery or sprite from the woods. Surely no mortal man possessed such a beautiful voice. Joanna had very fine taste indeed.

"We will learn a ballad first, my lord," Geoffrey said. "But two chords and easy ones at that. Here, watch you my fingers and place yours precisely so on your strings."

Anne heard one strum of the lute and assumed, perhaps a little unkindly, that it hadn't been Robin to produce that sound. His next words confirmed it.

"Bloody hell, man, how do you expect me to fit my lumps of fingers on these spiderwebs!"

"Perseverance and patience, my lord. Perseverance and patience."

Neither of which, Anne learned as the morning wore on, Robin possessed in much of an abundance. Robin's cursing drowned out any hope of hearing anything else Geoffrey might have had to say.

"Take a deep breath, my lord," Geoffrey said, loudly enough to be heard over Robin's slander.

Robin, blessedly, was silent.

"One more time," Geoffrey cajoled. "For your lady, my lord."

Robin heaved a huge sigh of what sounded like immense frustration, then produced what might have been construed as a chord. There was an accompanying twang of a string struck improperly and, of course, the ever-present curse to follow, but at least it was an improvement.

"Well done, my lord!" Geoffrey exclaimed.

Robin was silent. Then he strummed again. It was quite a bit better that time; Anne wished desperately she could have seen his face.

"That wasn't completely hopeless, was it?" Robin asked, with something akin to surprise in his voice.

"You've made great strides, my lord. You will make a fine lutenist if you've the mind to try."

Robin snorted. "Nay, my brother plays much better than I ever could. There is no point."

"Ah, but who would your lady prefer to hear? Your brother, my lord, or you?"

There was a goodly bit of silence. Then Robin spoke.

"Another chord or two, if you please, Geoffrey. I'm certain a handful of minutes at this each day could only improve my swordplay."

"No doubt, my lord."

Anne leaned back against the wall and listened raptly to Robin's efforts to master something that was completely beyond his normal experience. She was almost sorry when Geoffrey told him he thought that perhaps they should cease with their lute lessons, lest Robin learn too much in the first day and overwhelm his lady with his skill.

"Then I'll be off," Robin said, sounding rather relieved.

"Ah, but what of verse?" Geoffrey said quickly. "Surely you don't want to neglect that."

"Don't I?"

"You don't, my lord."

There was a very heavy sigh and a thump, as if Robin had resumed his seat with extreme reluctance. "Very well. May as well plunge the dagger into the hilt while you've already begun your work."

"Well done, my lord," Geoffrey said. "I daresay you'll find this quite easy as well."

"If you say so," Robin said doubtfully. "What first?"

"First you decide upon a subject for your verse. I daresay you would likely have the most to say about your lady, aye?"

"Aye," Robin said.

And Anne could have sworn she heard a bit of wistfulness in that aye. Then again she could have been imagining it. With Robin, one just never knew. It could have been indigestion from all that dancing after last night's supper. She hadn't seen him about that morn. Either he had found the guard tower to be a fine place to hide, or his feet were still smarting from all their hard work learning the task his dancing master had set before him and he'd been abed recovering. Anne had to smile over that. Poor Robin. He couldn't help but be relieved when his grandmother turned her attentions to some other of Rhys and Gwen's offspring.

"Now, if you were to say something about your lady, what would it be?"

"She is the most profoundly stubborn woman I've ever met."

Geoffrey's little gasp of astonishment only told Anne that he hadn't spent all that much time with Robin yet. She pursed her lips. She could scarce bear the waiting until Robin truly found his tongue where she was concerned.

"But, my lord," Geoffrey said, sounding rather aghast, "you must say something complimentary about her."

"That was a compliment. Tenacity is a fine quality."

There was a bit of silence. Then Geoffrey apparently gathered the shreds of his innocence about him enough to recover his powers of speech.

"Try something else, my lord."

"Well," Robin said slowly, "she has more courage than any bruised and bloodied lout I've ever fought with. She's braved her own demons and come away the victor, time and time again. Aye," he said, sounding more enthusiastic, "the courage of half a score of the most sliced, bludgeoned, and maimed men I've had the pleasure of hoisting a sword with—"

"My lord, you cannot sing of bloody battles and your lady in the same breath."

"Why not?" Robin demanded. "Bravery's nothing to scorn, man. I daresay you could think of worse souls to guard your back than my Anne."

My Anne.

Anne blinked back tears. It was the most unpolished verse she'd ever listened to and she'd even heard a lay or two composed about her own poor self. But it was without doubt the most moving.

"Her eyes, my lord," Geoffrey pleaded. "Say something about her eyes."

"Well, she has two—"

"The color!" Geoffrey exclaimed. "Praise the color! Compare it to beryls, seacoasts, rare and exquisite jewels. Use your imagination!"

There was silence for a goodly amount of time—time during which Anne wondered if Robin was reaching for his blade. Then he cleared his throat.

"Her eyes . . ." he began slowly, "well, the color of her eyes is akin to . . . hmmm . . ." He trailed off and there was a bit more silence, then a foot stomped in triumph. "Akin to sage, aye, *sage* after it's sat in the sun too long."

There was a slap and Anne could only assume it was Geoffrey clapping his hand to his own forehead. Aye, that was definitely a groan and it was not coming from her husband.

"I told you," Robin said defensively, "that I've no head for poetry."

"The lute," Geoffrey said weakly. "We'll pursue the lute. You can sing other men's songs."

"Are we finished now?" Robin asked hopefully.

"Aye," Geoffrey said. "I doubt either of us can face any more today."

Anne heard the door open, followed by Robin's curse.

"Grandmère, no more today," he said firmly.

"You've lessons in bowing, grandson. Come with me."

"Nay," Robin said tightly, "I will not. Bowing will not win my lady."

"And mucking about in your boots will?" Joanna asked tartly.

"Perhaps not, but being the best damn bloody swordsman in England just might!" Robin returned hotly. "So I go, my lady, to continue to seek after that goal in the lists! With your permission?"

The door slammed shut and Anne could only assume that Robin hadn't waited for his grandmother to say him aye. She rose, groaned as she did so, and swayed. She caught herself with her hand on the opposite wall. Within a heartbeat, the curtain had been pulled back and Joanna stood there, a worried frown on her face.

"Are you unwell——"

The door burst open and Anne saw nothing but a blur as the curtain was jerked closed.

"Aye?" Joanna said.

"I've come to a decision," Robin announced. "You and my lady will present yourselves in the lists posthaste. I will woo her *my* way, Grandmère, and that will begin by demonstrating my prowess on the field. Fetch Anne, if you please, and come immediately where you may watch and admire."

Joanna was silent for a moment or two, then she cleared her throat. "As you will, grandson. I'll find your lady and bring her."

The door slammed shut and the curtain began to open. Before Anne could say anything, Joanna had spun around as the door was flung open yet again.

"See that she dresses warmly. And have one of your frilly lads make himself useful by bringing her a blanket or two."

The door slammed shut again and Anne sighed in relief. Joanna pulled back the curtain. She shook her head at Anne.

"Impossible lad."

"Of course," Anne said with a smile. "But I'm fond of him that way."

"Of course you are, my dear." Joanna took her hands and smiled. "Can you bear the chill outside, Anne? I daresay heads will roll if we neglect his commands."

Anne nodded to Geoffrey as she crossed the chamber. He, though, only stared at her in surprise. Anne was momentarily tempted to check her clothes and hair, then forced herself to assume the best, not the worst.

"Aye?" she said.

"You are his lady wife?" Geoffrey asked incredulously.

"Aye," Anne said.

"And he could find nothing to say but that your eyes were the color of sage?"

"What?" Joanna exclaimed.

"Apparently so," Anne said cheerfully.

Geoffrey shook his head. "*I* will compose his verses for him, for I have a great deal to say about your loveliness, my lady. Your lord has little imagination."

"Minstrelsy is not where his gifts lie," Anne conceded. "But he does the best he can."

Joanna snorted. "You're a besotted goose, Anne, and I pray Robin is someday grateful for it. Now, come and let us have this over with. I don't fancy an afternoon sitting in the mud, but there you have it. What we won't do to humor a man."

Anne walked with Robin's grandmother down to the great hall, then stopped her before the door.

"Are you disappointed?" she asked.

"Disappointed?" Joanna asked. "In Robin? Nay, he's cooperated much longer than I thought he would. He must love you greatly to have endured such tortures."

Anne smiled faintly. "He has submitted very well, for whatever reason. The one thing I'm sorry for, though, is the clothing. It was passing fine and he was handsome in it."

Joanna snorted. "It grieves me as well, but what use does he have for fine clothes when he ruins them in the rain anyway? I vow, Anne, you'll never be free of the mud and such he'll bring in on his boots."

"I think his manners may have improved," Anne offered.

"My dear," Joanna said, putting her arm around Anne and giving her a squeeze, "this was merely to bring him to his senses, for I was certain he would never arrive there on his own. You deserved to be wooed. It is Robin's right and his duty to woo you, and all the better if he does it as it pleases him. If I have in some small, insignificant way pushed him to do it sooner than his stubbornness might have allowed otherwise, then I am content."

Anne couldn't help a small laugh. "You are devious, my lady."

"From whom do you think Robin inherited that trait, if not me?" Joanna asked, with one eyebrow raised. "Now, come my girl, and let us be away before he comes to fetch us. Whatever other flaws he might have, he is at the very least a powerfully fine swordsman. I wouldn't want to force him to prove it by prodding us where he wants us."

Anne nodded and went to fetch her cloak. She made her way as quickly as possible down to the hall. Joanna was waiting for her at the door to the great hall, swathed in furs and followed by several lads carrying fine chairs, blankets, and foodstuffs. Anne was only surprised not to see someone else toting supplies to build a pavilion.

"If we must be there," Joanna said crisply as Anne approached, "we may as well be comfortable."

Anne had no intentions of arguing. She walked with Robin's grandmother out to the lists, doing her best to keep her skirts well out of the mud. Hopefully her father would have some sense and send her the rest of her clothing. It wasn't all that much, but she possessed another gown or two and that might come in handy if she were required to present herself at the lists for any more admiring.

After all, Robin was wooing her *his* way.

And if that wasn't enough to bring a smile to her face, she didn't know what was.

Robin was tromping about, looking irritated until he saw them arrive. Anne watched him gape at the trappings that accompanied them, then shrugged his shoulders. Anne soon found herself seated in a comfortable chair, her feet propped up on a padded stool, her person covered in blankets and furs, and her elbow near a small table covered with foodstuffs and a cup of warm wine.

And she began to wonder if inviting Joanna north more often might be a very good idea.

"Primitive," Joanna said with a shake of her head, "but I daresay we'll survive it for a bit. Comfortable, my dear?"

Anne nodded happily, remembering all the hours she had spent watching Robin in the lists while trying to be inconspicuous. That had generally entailed crouching against the wall or making use of some uncomfortable bench or other. She suspected that with this kind of luxury surrounding her, she could watch Robin all day.

Which was, she suspected, his intention.

She looked at the field and blinked at what she saw. There was Robin on her left, standing by himself, cracking his knuckles and flexing his arms over his head. Facing him was the rest of Artane's garrison, made up of his own men and his father's. She frowned. Did he intend to fight them in a bunch?

She realized, an hour later, that he had planned to dispatch them one by one. She also realized, that same hour later, that such a thing was not beyond his reach.

Swords went flying. Men cried peace. Lads who were freshly knighted were humbled with quick strokes. Men who wore their years of experience solidly on their shoulders were eventually forced to concede victory.

And through it all, Anne could scarce take her eyes off her husband. Her wine went undrunk, delicacies went unnibbled, and substantial meals were brushed aside in annoyance.

By the saints, he was beautiful.

She could only shake her head in amazement that such a man was hers, even in name only. Perhaps had she known the true extent of Robin's prowess, she might have been less free with her tongue at his expense. His strength was unflagging. He fought man after man without so much as a pause. His wits were unmatched, for she watched him never be drawn into any devious scheme to rid him of his blade. And his skill was unequaled, for no man bested him in that very long afternoon.

And when the line of challengers was no more, she watched him throw his sword up into the air and laugh for the sheer sport of it.

She suspected that she might never recover from the sight of *that*.

He caught his sword, turned, and strode over to them purposefully. He shoved his blade into the mud at his grandmother's feet and looked at her, his chest heaving.

"*That*, Grandmère," he said haughtily, "is what I do best. Can you find fault with it?"

"Of course not, Robin, my love," his grandmother said, looking at him serenely. "I never could."

Robin scowled, then turned his attentions to Anne.

"And you, lady? What think you?"

Anne swallowed with difficulty. "I think you, my lord, are . . ."

"Well?" he demanded.

"Magnificent," she finished, wondering if she looked as lustful as she felt. By the saints, 'twas all she could do not to leap to her feet, throw her arms around his sweaty self, and bid him take her right there.

Robin blinked in surprise, but recovered quickly enough.

"A word I might have chosen myself," he said. "Now, come, my ladies, and let us sup. You'll need your strength for the morrow."

"We will?" Joanna asked hesitantly.

"I've plans for you after my business is finished in the morn."

"Plans?" Anne asked.

"I will see you both in my father's solar at noon. Do not be late."

"Will you entertain us with the lute?" Joanna sounded rather hopeful.

"Ha," Robin said scornfully. "Tales of battle, Grandmère! Bloodshed! Victories!"

Joanna frowned.

"It will be very exciting," Robin promised.

Anne couldn't imagine anything more exciting than what she'd just witnessed, but she could be patient and see.

With Robin, one just never knew.

35

Edith stood just inside the outer gates and watched the little party begin to make its way back up to the keep. She could scarce believe the luxury in which Joanna of Segrave wallowed. By the saints, even a visit to the lists necessitated trappings Edith had never enjoyed during the whole of her life.

Perhaps striking at the old woman first would gain Robin's attention.

Edith wiped her hands on her hose, then looked down and cursed softly. The blood was too stale for wiping; 'twould take a proper washing to remove it and she would have to find water outside. She could not retrieve her clothes from their hiding place in the stable and enter the hall with blood-ied hands.

She'd been out hunting.

It honed her considerable skills.

But rabbits were poor sport and not wily enough to truly give her plea-sure. Nay, for that, she needed a creature with greater wits. And greater wits meant the use of more of her own for the chase. Not that the chase need be hurried, though. She had no need of haste. She was, after all, a very patient woman.

There would be time enough for all her plans. Maude's death had been a surprise, but perhaps 'twas nothing the wench hadn't deserved. Edith had told her to stay far away from the wedding, though she'd suspected Maude would have found it too powerful a lure to resist. She'd disobeyed.

Death had been what she deserved.

But that was behind Edith. Now, her own plans deserved her full atten-tion. Hunting that day had given her new ideas to consider. For was it not all the game of stalking the quarry, flushing it out, then killing swiftly and without hesitation?

She very much suspected it was.

But first, clean hands.

It would throw her prey off the scent.

36

Robin leaped up the steps, then strode down the passageway to his father's solar. He'd had a fine day so far, what with great success in the lists, nothing broken, stolen, or in an uproar in the keep, and now an afternoon of freedom in which to tell his favorite stories. Life improved with each day that passed.

Anne smiled at him a great deal these days.

Robin suspected it boded well for their marriage.

He burst into his father's solar and was highly pleased to see both his lady and his errant grandmother sitting before him, apparently prepared and waiting for him to astonish them with tales of his prowess in battle. Robin rubbed his hands together with great energy.

"Where shall we begin?" he asked, slamming the door shut behind him with his foot.

"With a large cup of something strong," his grandmother answered without hesitation. She blinked at him innocently. "To soothe our delicate constitutions, of course."

Robin snorted. He'd seen his grandmother flay more than one hapless suitor alive with naught but her sharp tongue. *Delicate* was not one of the words he would have chosen for her.

But he was in a fine mood, Anne looked happy to see him, and he did have the whole of the afternoon and evening to trot out his favorite battle tales for their inspection and admiration. Filling his grandmother's goblet now and again was small payment for such pleasure.

So he filled, saw to the fire, and moved a chair or two aside so as to have the most possible room for pacing, for he knew the sheer exhilaration of relating such breathtaking tales would drive him to movement. He looked to make certain his ladies were attending him, then rolled his shoulders, shook out his hands, and stomped his feet a time or two.

"Let's begin in Spain, shall we?" he asked.

His grandmother sighed.

Anne smiled, though, so Robin took that as encouragement enough. And as he stole another look at her, he remembered telling her what a bloody business it was, and that almost gave him pause. For there was a very dark side to it, and dreams of it troubled his sleep quite often. There was a part of him that would have been glad never to engage in it again.

But there was also the glory and the toil and the satisfaction of an enemy routed, a victory won, a wrong righted. He put his shoulders back. 'Twas of that he would speak, for there were those tales aplenty.

"Now," he said, "I will tell you of a skirmish Nick and I had in a little town just outside Madrid. We likely shouldn't even have been there, but the weather was fine, the wine excellent, and we heard there was a bit of gold in the deed for us as well."

It was also where Robin had found the stone for Anne's ring, but that he would tell her later, when he'd found the proper time to give it to her.

"Did you really need the gold?" Anne asked.

Robin blinked. "Well, aye. Always."

She looked at him in confusion. "But, Robin, you have lands aplenty."

"Aye, but this was gold I'd *earned*. By my own sweat."

"And you don't protecting your holdings?"

It was going to be a very long afternoon if this was the kind of response he was going to get. He frowned at her.

"'Tis a different matter entirely. I was just another hired sword, not Artane's son."

She looked at him for a moment in silence, then she smiled a bit. "I see."

And as he watched his grandmother take a hearty draught of her wine, he suspected she did as well.

"Damned foolish, if you ask me," she said tartly, "but men will be men. Be about your work, grandson. These old ears of mine can only stand so much talk of battle in one day."

Yet they could stand hours on end of string plucking and screeching, Robin thought with a grumble. He scowled at his grandmother for good measure, then took up his tale again.

"We were in Spain," he continued.

And once he was finished with that small skirmish, he moved to larger battles. He told his tales with complete accuracy, for there was no need to embellish or augment his part in them. His deeds spoke for themselves and he related them with as much humility as he could manage.

Then he told of humorous things, of arrogant knights shamed, foolish lords humbled, and crafty innkeepers outsmarted.

And when he'd finished that, he turned to the most glorious of battles and the most daring of escapades.

The afternoon passed into evening.

Robin paused in his pacing to gauge the effect his most exciting tale yet had upon the women. He looked at his grandmother to find that her head was resting against the back of the chair and she was sound asleep. Every now and again a delicate snort would come from her lips.

His lady wife was not asleep—not yet. He watched her smother an impressive yawn, then watched as she realized she was being observed.

"Interesting," she said, nodding. "Breathtaking. Truly." She smiled encouragingly.

Robin pursed his lips, hoping that she could see that he didn't much believe her enthusiasm.

On the other hand, he had to concede that she was smiling at him and listening with a pleasant, if sleepy, expression on her face. He couldn't complain about that.

He sighed and pulled up a stool in front of her. Perhaps he'd regaled the pair with enough tales of bloodshed and the like. He had a moment of peace with his lady; he might be wise to use it. His grandmother was snoring peacefully, albeit daintily, so their self-appointed chaperon wouldn't be looking at him pointedly if he made some unacceptable social blunder. He looked at his lady and was faintly surprised at the ease he felt in her company. Surely she had seen him at his worst—bedecked with feathers and all manner of baubles—yet she hadn't laughed at him. He'd stepped on her toes enough for a score of dancers, yet still she seemed to endure his presence well enough.

Yet now that he had her, he hardly knew what to do with her. More stories of battle seemed a bit inappropriate, even for him. He racked his pitiful brain, praying for some small bit of inspiration. He watched Anne shift in the chair and suddenly it occurred to him how he could amuse her. Or at least show her that he had thought of her over the years. After all, wasn't the avenging of your lady's honor a noble thing? Perhaps it was time she knew it.

"Anne," he said.

"Aye?"

"Do you remember Peter of Canfield?"

She paused, then a look of perfect stillness descended upon her face. "Aye," she answered carefully.

And remember him she should. Never mind that he was Maude's brother and Maude was someone he would rather avoid talking about. Peter had once trapped Anne in a stable and taunted her until she was hysterical. Robin hadn't been privy to it, though he'd heard tell of it through one of the little twins who had witnessed the event. Robin had thrashed Peter several times in the lists afterwards, but it had never seemed quite enough. Fortunately, another opportunity had presented itself.

"I saw him," he began, "in a tourney three years ago in France."

She didn't reply.

"It might interest you to know that I bested him in the joust and held him for ransom. I took, of course, all his gold, his horse, and his mail."

"Of course."

"But I left him his tent."

She smiled faintly. "Good of you."

"Aye, it was. And whilst he slept in that tent in the midst of the lists, for he could find no one to help him move it, as his squire and sundries were too thrashed by my lads to aid him, I crept in and took what clothes I had left him."

"You didn't."

"I did," Robin said pleasantly. "Not a stitch remained him."

She waited expectantly.

"Now, the stands the next day were quite crowded with a great number of France's finest nobles. I, being the diligent soul I am, had noised about that there would be a great bit of entertainment that morn and 'twould serve all in the area to arrive early to see it."

She laughed. "Oh, Robin."

He couldn't help a smile himself. "As you might imagine, the lists were full when Peter came stumbling from his tent, naked. He was laughed off the field and out of France. He hasn't dared show himself at another gathering since."

Anne shook her head. "You are incorrigible."

"Well," he said mildly, "I do what I can for the cause of truth and right. Now, perhaps it would amuse you to hear the fate of Rolond of Berkhamshire. I remember him being such a fine, upstanding young lad in his youth."

Actually Rolond had been one of the worst. Robin could still remember hearing him call Anne ugly time and time again. Well, at least she was still smiling now. She hadn't been then.

"My memory fails me on his character," Anne said, "but I'll accept your word for it. What havoc did you wreak upon his hapless soul?"

"I was at court briefly a year or so ago," Robin began, "flattering and courting the king as was expected, when I happened to learn that Rolond and his substantial wife, Alice, were there. And let us not forget his mistress, Martha, who was placed in a nearby chamber."

She caught her breath. "You didn't."

Robin smiled modestly. "It was purely by chance that I saw Rolond go into his mistress's chamber. Fearing for his eternal soul, I hurriedly sought out a servant to inform his wife of the deep sin into which her husband was about to fall face-first."

Anne was watching him with a smile. "How thoughtful of you."

"Aye," he said, "it was. Now, as it happened, the servant wasted little time in passing on the tidings. It seemed just a moment that I spent hiding in an alcove—just to see that no stone was left unturned, of course—before Lady Berkhamshire came thundering down the hall with the fury of an avenging angel. She didn't bother to knock; she merely burst into the chamber. She rescued her mate from the clutches of that fallen woman, dragging him out with his hose down around his knees and his hands continuing to clutch what had surely been his mistress's ample bosom only moments before."

"You *didn't*!"

He smiled. "I can only take credit for being a spy and a teller of tales. Lady Berkhamshire provided the amusing sport. And the last I heard, dear Lord Berkhamshire hasn't seen the outside of his walls since. It would seem his wife rules with an iron hand."

Anne leaned her head back against the chair and smiled at him. "You are a terrible troublemaker, Lord Artane."

"I have several more stories that I think you would find just as amusing, should you wish for me to trot them out for your inspection."

"My lord, you are so gallant."

He felt his smile falter. "It won't last."

"I wouldn't want it to."

He sighed. "I'm not fond of playing the gushing lord at court, Anne. As you should have noticed by now."

"Robin, what makes you think that is what I want? I never could stomach a man with affected manners and no substance underneath them. I can't imagine why they're so popular."

He tried not to show his surprise. "But surely you want a chivalrous knight. Every woman wants a chivalrous knight."

"Chivalry hasn't served me before, except from one lad in my youth. I haven't had much use for it since." She met his gaze unflinchingly. "There is more to love than chivalry, Robin."

He could hardly believe she'd said the like, but there was no hint of jest in her face. And what was this business of a chivalrous lad in her youth? She couldn't be possibly talking about him. Could she?

Robin looked down at her hands folded in her lap. Then, before he could think better of it, he reached for one and held it between his own. It wasn't as if he hadn't held her hand before. But he'd never held her hand knowing that she was his, that it was his privilege to enjoy such simple joys of marriage. He took a deep breath.

"Anne, I've much to beg pardon for."

"Again?" she asked in surprise.

Robin scowled. He wasn't all that encouraged by that, but then again, he had many regrets so perhaps he deserved to writhe in penitent agony for a bit. He stole a look at his grandmother to make certain she slept on, then looked back at his lady.

"I have," he said, mustering up all his reserves of courage, "treated you badly."

"Have you?" she asked. "When?"

She tried to raise one eyebrow, but both went up. He watched her prop one up with her finger and he almost managed a smile.

"You mock me," he said reproachfully.

"You're groveling. 'Tis most unsettling."

"Anne, I'm in earnest. I was a dolt in my youth and a fool in my manhood."

She cocked her head to one side and smiled faintly. "Perhaps I do want to hear this. Go on, if you please."

She was not giving him or his confession the consideration it warranted. He glared at her and wondered if an apology counted if given whilst the giver was powerfully tempted to throttle the receiver.

"I can stop," he growled.

She shook her head, still smiling just the smallest bit. "Nay, Robin, I daresay I will be glad of it when you've finished. But you aren't the only one at fault."

He grunted. "You can take your turn after I've had done. I'd best babble whilst I can stomach it."

"Then by all means, proceed, my lord."

He scowled at her again, just out of habit, then plunged ahead before his pride managed to close his mouth.

"I turned away from you in our youth—"

"Why did you, Robin?"

Damn her, he was never going to finish this if she didn't stop interrupting him. "It isn't important—"

"I think it's very important," she said. She looked at him expectantly. "Why did you?"

He was up on his feet pacing before he knew what his body intended. He realized just as suddenly that it would be uncomfortable for Anne to chase him and wring the truth from him, so he returned to stand before her. He looked at his grandmother.

Still sleeping.

He looked about him, hoping to find some corner that might be more private for the blurting out of his darkest secret.

There was nowhere else save the alcove; it had no light but perhaps that was just as well. Robin pulled Anne to her feet, waited until he sensed she had put weight on her leg, and found it to be sturdy beneath her, then he led her over and sat with her on one of the benches. There in the shadows, he took her hand and held it tightly between his own. She said nothing, but he felt her clasp his hand. Robin took a deep breath, then felt his heart begin to pound and his limbs begin to tingle. By the saints, he never felt the like even before the worst of battles! He could scarce believe that relating such a simple, foolish event could cause him this kind of distress.

And then he felt Anne lean her head on his shoulder.

"Robin, perhaps 'tis too close still," she whispered. "If it grieves you this much, I'll not demand the tale."

He shook his head. "Nay," he began, and his voice cracked. He cleared his throat. "Nay," he said again, "you deserve to know. I was a fool then and I'll not repeat the mistake now." He blew out his breath. "'Twas one morning near the healer's house. You had walked across the courtyard to the hall. I should have accompanied you. I don't know now why I didn't."

"You'd been abed with the fever, Robin. 'Twas a wonder you hadn't died."

Her hand fluttered between his briefly, then was still.

"Aye, well, whatever the reason," he continued, "I watched you and saw the . . . um . . . the—"

"You may say it, Robin. It won't grieve me."

"'Twas teasing, Anne," he said, feeling a surge of anger over the memory. "Lads who should have known better. One lad in particular."

"Baldwin."

Robin gritted his teeth. "Father had pulled you into the house. I called to Baldwin, for I could not let his slurs go unavenged."

"Oh, Robin," she said softly. "I didn't know."

"Aye, well, there wasn't much to know. He thrashed me soundly for my cheek, then broke two of Nick's fingers as his reward for a challenge." He paused, then took another deep breath. "He left me wallowing in the mud."

Anne was silent. Robin waited for her to say something, but perhaps the shame of it was enough to make her wish she had wed elsewhere. He never should have told her—

"Is that all?"

Robin blinked. "Is that all?" he demanded.

He felt her lift her head. "Aye. Is that all?"

"He laughed at me!"

"Robin, he laughed at everyone," she said, sounding mightily confused.

"He humiliated me before every lad in the keep!"

"But," she asked, still sounding as if she simply could not fathom the depths of his shame, "what has that to do with your shunning me?"

"He humiliated me!"

"And you punished me for it?"

"Anne, damn you," Robin growled, "I wasn't going to see you laugh at me as well!"

He could see the faint outline of her face. She was shaking her head.

"I thought *I* had done something," she said softly.

"I didn't want to give you the chance to do anything," Robin said grimly.

"All this time, all these years wasted because of Baldwin. By the saints, Robin, we have made a great jumble of things."

"We?" he demanded. "I was the fool."

"I could have asked you what troubled you."

He gritted his teeth. "You did, Anne. More than once."

She smiled. He could hardly believe the sight, but there it was. "Very well," she said gently, "you were the fool. I forgive you for it. Now you may apologize for staying away so long. I assume 'twas for much the same reason." Then he felt her stiffen. "I mean . . . well, what I meant to say was that you likely had a very good reason for being gone." She paused. "I doubt it included me."

Robin was tempted to ask her how she could think something so foolish, but he knew precisely where she had come by the notion. He'd given her ample reason over the years to believe just that. He stood up, then pulled her to her feet and wrapped his arms around her. He rested his cheek against her soft hair and closed his eyes.

And he came very close to weeping.

"Anne," he said, wincing at the crack in his voice. Saints, but she would think him a whimpering fool if he did not regain some control over himself. "Anne," he tried again, "there was not a day that passed that I did not think of you."

He felt her breath catch, then heard a sniffle. He could only hope that she wasn't weeping because the tidings were ill ones to her ears.

"I should have wed you the moment I won my spurs," he said quietly. "I should have come home, demanded the right from your father, and wed you then. I've wasted five years and I've never been sorrier for anything in my life."

He paused, struck by an unwholesome thought.

"Unless," he said hesitantly, "unless you would have found that distasteful."

"Robin de Piaget, you are a fool."

She was weeping. Her arms were around him and she clung to him as if he were all that kept her upright.

Or as if he were very dear to her.

He chose to believe the latter. He gathered her even closer to him and wrapped his arms securely about her. He wanted to tell her that he loved her. He wanted with equal intensity to sweep her up into his arms and carry her to his bedchamber where he was almost certain they could come to an agreement on a few other things.

She was, after all, his wife.

There was a snort, a cough, and a delicate stamping of feet. "Children, children," Joanna called, "where have you gone?"

"Damn her," Anne muttered.

Robin snorted. "I couldn't agree more." He cleared his throat purposefully. "We can see ourselves to bed, Grandmère."

"Absolutely not," Joanna said. "Bring Anne back, Robin lad. She needs her rest. I'm sure you'll find somewhere comfortable to sleep. Come out of there. 'Tis far too drafty for her."

Robin found himself obeying out of habit, then he dug his heels in a few paces from his grandmother. He looked at Anne to find that she was looking anywhere but at him.

"We *are* wed," Robin pointed out.

"Is she properly wooed?" Joanna demanded.

"Well—"

"I think not," Joanna said. She rose, took Anne by the hand, and started toward the door. "I'll sleep with Anne tonight, just to keep her safe. Best practice your dancing a bit before you retire, love."

Anne looked back at Robin with wide eyes, but apparently she was unable to free herself. Robin scowled as he watched her be dragged off. The door was shut firmly.

Robin gritted his teeth.

He sat down with a curse, stretched out his legs, and scowled. What were the penalties for separating one's love from one's grandmother using a blade?

He suspected that the list of his sins was long enough, so perhaps he would refrain. But this would be the last time his grandmother thwarted his plans. It looked as if the only way he would have Anne to himself would be to liberate her from his grandmother's vile clutches.

He stroked his chin and wondered if the weather might be tolerable enough for a small outing on the morrow.

37

Anne woke to a brisk knocking. She blinked, sat up, and shook her head. Ah, nay, not that again.

And then she realized she was abed with Robin's grandmother, Robin had bedded down the saints only knew where, and her father and his were likely indulging in blissful slumber safely tucked away at Fenwyck. Could it be ruffians having overrun the keep? It certainly didn't sound like that sort of frantic pounding.

Anne yawned as the pounding continued. Lady Joanna slept like the dead and Anne would have had a fear for her had she not snored with such great enthusiasm. She rose quietly, pulled her cloak around her, and went to the door.

"Aye?" she asked, pulling it open.

Robin stood there, looking purposeful. "Dress, lady. We've plans for the day."

She stifled a yawn. "We do?"

"Aye, and they do not include my grandmother, so endeavor not to wake her."

Anne felt a shiver go through her, and she suspected it wasn't fear. It was certainly enough to wake her fully. "Just us?"

Robin scowled. "Is that such an unappealing thought?"

"Oh, nay," she managed.

He grunted. "Then make haste, Anne. And dress warmly. I'll wait for you below."

He pulled the door shut quietly and Anne remained there, staring at it as if she hadn't seen it before. Robin of Artane had just told her he planned to have her to himself for the whole of the day.

Alone.

Unchaperoned.

Never mind that he was her husband. Never mind that he'd spent the past handful of days enduring numerous tortures in an effort to please her. That he wanted to be alone with her, with *her* mind you, was something she wasn't quite sure she could digest.

The door opened suddenly and Robin peered in.

"Don't hear you moving," he said.

And then he gave her the briefest of smiles before he shut the door again.

Anne wondered if she might manage to clothe herself before she fell over in a faint. Alone and facing his smiles at the same time?

By the saints, this was unexpected.

She shook her head to clear it, then went in search of clothes. With no idea of what Robin had in mind, she dressed as sensibly as she could. She could only hope his idea of a day of pleasure did not include a lengthy stay in the lists, though she wore her boots just in case.

Once she was dressed, she took a deep breath, put her shoulders back, and opened the door. No sense in dawdling. Robin would come to fetch her otherwise.

Though she had to admit the thought of that wasn't unappealing either.

She shut the door behind her, then looked up and squeaked. Robin himself was leaning against the opposite wall with his arms folded over his chest and a frown on his face. Apparently the lists did not figure into his plans for the day, for she could see no mail on him. He pushed away from the wall and straightened. Anne looked up at him and felt somehow very small and fragile. She tried a smile.

"Will this suit?" she asked, holding up a bit of her gown for his inspection.

"Aye," he said, taking her hand. "Perfectly." He lifted her hand to his lips, then stopped and scowled. "Do I kiss?" he asked, sounding rather irritated, "or do I not? I vow my grandmother's peacocks have left me positively bewildered."

Well, there was no point in beginning to bite her tongue now. She'd spent the whole of her life sharpening it on the man before her, so she'd best continue as she'd begun. He might begin to worry if she didn't speak her mind.

"Kiss," she stated.

"Think you?"

"Definitely."

And so he did.

Anne felt tingles start on the back of her hand and work their way down her arm and up the back of her scalp. She shivered.

And he smiled.

"Think what those silly lads at court are missing," he said.

"As well as their ladies."

"Though I would kill anyone who took such a liberty with you," he added.

"You are barbaric, my lord."

"But do I suit?" he asked.

"Perfectly," she answered, without hesitation.

Robin stared at her for a moment or two in silence, looked over her head at the door behind her, then scowled.

"Damn her anyway," he grumbled.

And with that, he took Anne's hand and pulled her down the passageway with him. She hardly dared speculate on why he was having such unkind feelings toward his grandmother, but it seemed to have something to do with her inhabiting his bedchamber.

Or perhaps 'twas that she was inhabiting his bed.

That was almost too lustful a thought to contemplate, even given her recently lustful state of mind. But since Robin was in truth her husband, and since she had more courage than any bruised and bloodied lout he'd ever fought with—his words and not hers, though she had found them very much to her liking—there was no sense in not being honest about her feelings toward him.

For indeed, his kiss had been exceptionally memorable.

As were his confessions of the night before. She could hardly believe that such a simple confrontation with Baldwin had been what had ruined so much of their lives. Looking back on it now, she could understand Robin's actions completely. From the time she'd known him, she'd known he wished to prove himself worthy of Rhys's affection. The possibility of failure, and the accompanying disgrace, had driven him far past where it should have in the lists.

And it wouldn't have made any difference to Robin if he had been just recently recovered from a fever. That he'd been humiliated before the other lads would have devastated him.

But to think 'twas her opinion that had mattered so much to him.

The witless oaf.

She sighed as she stepped down the last step behind him into the great hall. Much as she grieved for their loss, she grieved as well for the suffering it had caused him. And for what? To prove himself superior to Baldwin? That had never been in question. To prove his worthiness to Rhys? Never had a son been more beloved of a father. To prove himself to her?

Rather that he had not shunned her.

But that was behind them. He took her hand in his as they crossed the great hall and Anne felt as if the years gone before had never been, so great was her pleasure in the present moment. Robin was hers, she was his, and nothing else mattered.

She even suspected he and his father would again see eye-to-eye before the winter was out. She had no doubts Rhys had been angry with him, but she very much suspected Rhys had pushed Robin to the altar simply because he had known it was what Robin wanted deep in his heart.

Hadn't Robin said he should have wed her earlier during their conversings the night before?

And for her, there was no question where her heart lay. Nay, she would
thank Rhys when next she saw him, and flick her husband smartly on the
ear if he didn't do the same.

They left the great hall and Robin slowed his pace to match hers as
they descended the steps to the courtyard. In spite of all her fine thoughts,
she couldn't help but wonder if Robin regretted her limp. She looked up
at him.

"I'm sorry," she said.

"For what?" he asked gravely.

She sighed. "For going so slowly."

He shook his head. "You've no need to apologize for it. It gives me
ample time to enjoy the beauty before me."

"Well, your father's keep is marvelous."

"I spoke of you," he said, "though I must admit Artane is a fine place as
well. But you," he said, looking at her intently, "aye, you are a pleasure to
look on at length."

She could hardly believe the change in him, but she wasn't about to
argue. She smiled up at him. "Robin de Piaget, are you wooing me?"

"Aye," he said cheerfully. "Do you like it?"

"Very much," she admitted.

He squeezed her hand, then led her across the courtyard to where a
cluster of men waited. Robin stopped, looked at her, and frowned thoughtfully.

"I've wondered what would be more comfortable," he said slowly,
"but I couldn't decide. Do you prefer your own mount, or shall you ride
with me?"

"I could bear my own," she answered.

"And the other?"

"I could bear that as well, if you like," she said.

"I'll endeavor not to drop you," he added.

"My thanks, I'm sure."

"We'll bring your mount just in case." He nodded at his men. "They'll
come too, of course."

"Of course." She looked at the men, but they were busying themselves
seeing to their gear. They were men Anne had seen before with Robin, and
she suspected by looking at them that they were a handful of the fiercest of
the lads he had brought from France with him.

"'Twould be foolhardy to take you from the keep without some men to
guard you."

"Though you would be enough," she said.

"Likely so, but I fear I may become distracted and not be able to give my surroundings my full attention."

Fortunately it was cold outside, so the crisp air saw to the fire in her cheeks, else she would have been tempted to fan herself.

"The lads will disappear," he continued. "You'll never know they're there."

She looked up at him and frowned. "They're accustomed to this sort of thing?"

"If by *this sort of thing*, you mean secret trysts with lovers, then nay," he said, returning her frown. "I daresay they're more accustomed to scouting out the enemy. It would hardly serve them to show themselves before they've discovered anything, now would it?"

She made a solemn, silent vow never again to presuppose anything about her husband. She suspected that her guesses would never be close to the mark anyway. She sighed.

"Forgive me. I have misjudged you."

"'Tis never wise to believe rumor."

"I can see that now."

He leaned closer to her. "I have far less experience than I've been credited with," he whispered.

She looked up at him in surprise. "In truth?"

"In truth."

"But . . ."

"You've little experience with women at court if you think all their boasts are truthful. What else are they to say when I come to my bed, find them there waiting, and boot them out with not so much as a kiss for their trouble?"

"Except the fair-haired lasses, of course," she said, wondering if he would now clout her in the nose for repeating her father's words.

He looked at her narrowly. "Your cheek is astonishing."

"And how dull you would find it otherwise." She squeezed his hand. "Let us leave your lovers, however few they may be and whatever their hair color, in the past, my lord."

"Gladly," he muttered as he led her to his mount, then swung up into the saddle. It was a low saddle, however, and she could easily see where she might fit before him on his horse's withers. She could only hope it would not be as uncomfortable as it looked.

One of Robin's men lifted her up and he settled her sideways across his thighs. He took up his reins and clucked at his horse.

"Painful?" he asked.

"That depends on the length of the journey," she said.

"Will you last to the shore?" he asked.

"The shore?" She looked at him with surprise. "Truly?"

"I thought it might please you."

"You thought well," she said happily. "Aye, 'twill be a pleasure to walk there. I've missed it this year."

He was silent as they made their way down to the outer gates and away from the keep. Anne grew used to the motion of his horse and the feel of his arms around her. She even found herself leaning her head against his shoulder.

"You know," he said slowly, "I have no other keep so close to the sea. Well, save one in France and 'tis unfit for habitation."

She thought on that for a bit, wondering what it was he was telling her. "And?"

"Well, I suppose my sire won't cast us outside the gates, but we may have to spend time in other places not so near the sea. Will that grieve you?"

She looked at him. "Does it matter?"

"Of course," he said, looking puzzled. "I don't wish for you to be unhappy."

"Robin, I daresay the place doesn't matter so much as the company."

He grunted thoughtfully, but said nothing more. Anne watched the land before her fall away to the sea and marveled not only at the beauty of it, but the delight of watching the like from the shelter of her husband's arms. Her husband. She could scarce accustom herself to the idea of calling him that, yet it seemed as if it always should have been so.

Once they had reached the shore, Robin bid his mount stop, then he swung down. The beast was perfectly still until Robin had held up his arms and pulled Anne into them. She looked around and was surprised to see none of his men.

"They're still here?" she asked.

He nodded. "Aye. Scouting and such. 'Tis what they're most adept at, and it pleases them as well."

"And that matters to you?"

He smiled dryly. "Though many would say a mere command should be enough to sway a man, I've found that such commands serve me better if given to men whose talents already lie with what they're required to do. I've the luxury of my own guard and the means with which to pay them very well. I chose men who suited my purposes and whom my purposes suited."

"And they are fond of you, I suppose," she said.

He shrugged. "I doubt they lie awake at night thinking on it, but I suppose they are fond enough." He straightened her cloak over her shoulders, then took her hand. "Their purpose, however, is to be forgotten today, so let us do so. I brought you here to have you to myself."

She shook her head and smiled as he took her hand. "I don't know that I'll ever accustom myself to hearing such things from you."

He sighed. "I suppose another apology—"

"Nay," she said with a laugh, "no more of those. I vow I'm not recovered from the ones I've already received."

He paused. "Perhaps, my lady, we should begin again."

"How mean you that?" she asked.

"Mayhap it would serve us to begin afresh, as if we had never met and had nothing of our past burdening us."

"Is that possible?" she mused.

"Is it worth the time to try?"

If such a thing were truly possible, she couldn't see how it could hurt. So she nodded. "Aye, I daresay it is."

He looked at her thoughtfully for a moment or two, then released her hand and shooed her away. "Go walk."

"I beg your pardon?"

"Go walk," he repeated. "Down the strand."

"By myself?"

"You'll be perfectly safe, if that's your worry. Besides, you never know who you'll encounter on a lonely strand in the north."

She hesitated. "The sand is not the easiest thing to walk on."

He frowned immediately. "Will it pain you?"

"It will shame me."

He rolled his eyes so forcefully, she feared they might stick up in his head.

"By the saints, Anne," he said, sounding mightily annoyed, "it matters not to me. Is there nothing I can do to convince you of that?"

She smiled. "I vow you just did." She took a pace backward and gave him a little wave. "I'm off to encounter handsome, dangerous strangers."

He grunted and folded his arms over his chest. Anne turned and began to walk north. The sand here was smooth and fine. If it hadn't been so bitterly cold from the sea air, she would have taken off her boots. A pity there was no sun, else the sand might have been warm. She looked up into the gray sky, heavy with clouds, and wondered if she might get a soaking before the day was through.

She heard the thunder of horses' hooves and turned to see Robin coming toward her with her mount trailing behind him. He gave her a wide berth, then swung his beasts around, stopped them, and dropped to the ground. He strode toward her and stopped a pace or two away.

And Anne wondered what she would have done had she not known him. Likely dropped to the sand in a swoon.

The wind blew his dark hair away from his face, leaving his rugged features fully revealed. His eyes were the color of the clouds. She was certain she had never seen a more handsome man, and she had certainly seen an enormous number of men over the course of her years.

And then he smiled gravely and made her a low bow.

"Fairest lady, I saw you walking along the shore and I trow my heart stopped within me, my mind seized upon your loveliness as if upon an elusive dream, and I could do nothing but stop and plead for your name that I might ever carry it in my heart."

He blinked, then a look of complete consternation came over his features, as if he could scarce believe the words had come from his mouth. "By the saints," he said in amazement, "I've been corrupted by peacocks!"

Anne laughed before she could stop herself.

He scowled. "Ah, a saucy wench, I see. Mayhap you do not realize who you are laughing at."

"Doubtless I don't," she said, managing to reduce her mirth to a mere smile. "Though you look passing fierce."

"And you look passing fair," he returned. He looked her over, then frowned. "You've a hitch in your step, I see."

She didn't let her smile falter, though it was not easily done. "Aye."

"An old battle wound?"

"You could call it that."

He grunted. "Have them myself. Perhaps later we'll compare them. For now, I think I should acquaint you with my own sweet self, so you can see if I'm to your liking."

She listened to him dismiss her leg, and wondered if it might be just as easy for her to do the like herself. And why not? There was little she could do to change it.

Or to change the past, she realized with a start.

Perhaps Robin had matters aright. Could they not leave the painful things behind and begin afresh? If he could overlook her flaw, could she not overlook his foolishness?

She suspected she could.

She slipped her hands up the opposite sleeves of her cloak and waited patiently for Robin to begin his game.

"Robin de Piaget at your service," he said with a little bow. "Handy with a blade, not handy with the lute, and perfectly incapable of rendering a decent rhyme."

She laughed softly. "Indeed."

"And I don't dance. Well," he amended, "not very well."

"Is that so?"

"Aye," he said. "But I've several good points you might be interested in."

"Then, by all means, trot them out and let me have a look at them."

"Well," he said, stroking his chin thoughtfully, "I've a pair of lovely gray eyes."

"You do indeed."

"I'm reasonable—"

"Are you?"

"Tolerant," he continued archly, "kind to a fault and ever pleasant to all."

"That is quite a list of virtues," she remarked.

"I've only begun. Let me know if the list grows too long for you and I'll fetch you a seat."

"How thoughtful of you."

"Add that to my list."

She looked up at him and smiled as he continued to enumerate in great detail all the things he was. And as she listened to him extol his virtues as if he were a stallion someone intended to sell, she realized that he did indeed have many fine characteristics. Had he been presented to her as a potential suitor, would she not have dropped to her knees and kissed her father's feet in gratitude?

She suspected she would have indeed.

"But," he said, "I've neglected to tell you the most important thing about myself, the thing I've carried in my heart the longest and the secret that few know." He looked down at her solemnly.

"And what would that great secret be, my lord?"

He paused. He looked at her for a moment or two in silence, then he held out his hands for hers. She pulled her hands free of her cloak and put her hands in his. His palms were callused, his fingers rough from work. But all she noticed truly was that his hands were warm and that they held hers gently. She looked up and found that his expression was a very tender one.

For Robin, that is.

"It is that I love you," he said quietly.

"Oh," she said, blinking. She cast about for something to say, but all she could do was stare up at him in complete surprise. She had expected him to reveal that he loved children, or had a soft place in his heart for hounds.

He waited.

And then he began to scowl.

"Well?" he demanded.

"I'm still recovering from that, my lord. Pray tell me you've no more revelations of that kind."

"It would be passing kind of you to reveal something of yourself! Something of that ilk!" he said heatedly.

She looked at him in surprise. "Well, of course I love you, you great oaf."

He spluttered for a moment, then glared at her. "Prettily spoken."

"Oh, Robin," she said, with a laugh. She went into his arms and hugged him tightly. "Surely you've always known it."

He shook his head. "Nay, Anne. I hoped it. And I told myself what a goodly life I would have, had I but your love in it."

She looked up at him. "And now that you have it?"

He smiled. "Today, my lady, knowing that you care for me only leads me to believe I could do anything you willed of me."

"You've already done that."

"What?" he asked. "Brought you to the shore and given you my heart?"

"Aye," she said, "that."

"And taken yours in return?"

She pulled her head back to look up at him. "That as well."

One of his eyebrows went up. "Is there aught else you would demand of me whilst I am baring my soul?"

"A kiss?"

"A fine idea."

"I thought so as well."

"If my lady will permit?"

"I suspect I will begin to demand if you don't cease with your babbling."

He smiled, then gathered her closer. "As my lady wishes," he said, lowering his head to hers.

And at that precise moment, it began to rain.

And it wasn't a pleasant, gentle rain.

The heavens opened and a torrent descended.

Robin clapped his hand to his head. "We are doomed!" he exclaimed.

And then the winds began to blow.

"Complain later," she said, holding her hands over her head. "Find us shelter now!"

He cursed. "Can you ride?"

"Gladly!"

He put her up into her saddle, then swung up into his own. "To the forest, then," he called over the wind. "Follow me!"

It was only then that Anne realized he had shortened her stirrups for her. And to her great surprise, it was far easier to ride with her knees bent so far than it was with them scarce bent at all. She had little trouble keeping Robin's pace and each time he looked over his shoulder to see how she fared, she urged him on until they were flying across the ground. Laughter tore from her; she was powerless to stop it.

She saw Robin's guard keeping pace with them, a short distance away, of course, and just the sight of it relieved her. Not that she had any reason to fear, but it never hurt to have extra men about.

The forest was a goodly distance from the shore, and perhaps that was too lofty a title for it. There were trees, true, but 'twas nothing as tall as she'd seen near Fenwyck, nor as dense as she'd heard tell of in the north. But it would provide them at least a little relief from the storm and for that she was grateful. Once they were under the shelter of the trees, Robin swung down off his horse and held up his hands for her. She was out of breath from the exhilaration of riding so swiftly, and from her laughter.

He pulled her under a tree, then Anne found herself backed up against it with Robin in her arms.

"By the saints," he said breathlessly, "you are beautiful." His eyes were bright, his hair was blown all about, and he was staring at her so intensely, Anne wondered if she might begin to melt. "I can hardly believe," he whispered, "that you are mine."

And then he bent his head to kiss her.

Anne was powerfully glad she had something to lean against. She closed her eyes as he buried his hands in her hair and tilted her face up. And when his mouth came down on hers, she couldn't stop a shiver, or the abrupt loss of her breath.

And then her surroundings faded until all she could feel was Robin's mouth on hers and his strong arms about her. She gave herself up completely to his kiss.

And then she completely lost her sense of time passing. All she knew was that she simply could not have enough of Robin's mouth on hers.

And she wasn't at all sure that kissing was going to satisfy the longing he was stirring inside her. That wasn't a bad thing. He was, after all, her husband.

Slowly, she became aware of her surroundings. The rain continued to fall, pattering on the last autumn leaves above them. The wind continued to blow, wiping her hair and his. And then she noticed that Robin was dripping on her.

He tore his mouth away, then leaned his forehead against her, drawing in ragged breaths.

"Are you unwell?" she asked, her own breathing equally ragged.

"Ask me in an hour or so, when I've recovered."

She saw the twinkle in his eye and frowned at him. "Are you jesting at my expense?" she asked, wiping the rain from her face.

"Nay, my love," he whispered, kissing her again softly. "I'm giving you an honest answer. The saints be praised we have somewhere dry to sit here, for I doubt I have the strength to walk." He looked about him, then smiled at her. "Will you have something to eat?"

She smiled dryly. Robin's concern for the filling of his belly was nothing if not predictable. Perhaps he had suffered from too many polite meals at his grandmother's table. "As you will, Robin."

"Then sit you there on that log and I'll fetch my saddlebags. My grandmother's cook was persuaded to pack us something tasty."

"Using your gentle influence again, my lord?"

He snorted. "A drawn sword, rather. He was most unwilling to rise when asked."

She shuddered. "Then let us pray 'tis edible."

"Oh, it is," he said, coming to sit next to her. "I know this, for I watched him sample everything before he packed it away. There should be no mystery as to his size."

Anne watched him as they ate, and found herself surprised by his ready smiles and hearty laughter. It had been years since she'd seen the like and she realized then how much she had missed it. Robin looked as if he'd shed a handful of years and a heavy load of care.

He looked up from his consumption of a tart and smiled at her. "What is it?"

She shook her head, smiling as well. "Nothing, really."

He hesitated. "Did I eat too much?"

She put her arm around his neck and leaned over to kiss him softly. "Nay, Robin. I was just looking at you."

"And finding me to your liking, apparently."

"Apparently," she agreed.

He reached up and held her hand that rested on his shoulder. "You know, Anne, my grandmother could find somewhere else to sleep."

"She could indeed."

He paused. "Should she?"

"What do you think?"

"I already know what I think," he said. "What I'm interested in are your thoughts."

She chewed on her lip for a moment or two, then cast aside any semblance of reticence. There was no point in it. "I think," she said slowly, "that she would be passing comfortable any number of other places."

Robin was on his feet before she had finished her words. "Then let us be off," he said. "Best see her settled early, so she has no complaints." He pulled her to her feet, then released her to go fetch his saddlebags. Anne watched, then noticed something on the ground near where they'd sat. She walked over and picked it up.

"This must have fallen out," she said, handing the scrap of parchment to him. "Words of love from Cook?"

"Wooing ideas from my grandmother, no doubt," Robin said with a snort. He unfolded the paper, then went perfectly still.

The sight of the change in him from lover to warrior set Anne's hair on end.

She didn't think she wanted to know what had caused it.

38

Robin stood in the shelter of the trees and considered. He'd passed a marvelous day up to that point. Anne had seemingly found the contents of his heart bearable and his kiss tolerable. The rain had been a less than pleasant occurrence, but it had been remedied easily enough. He had looked forward to returning to the keep and passing the rest of his day closeted in his father's bedchamber with his wife, consummating their marriage. He had thought it an afternoon to relish.

He suspected that this new development, though, just might be enough to ruin that.

Robin looked down at the note and suppressed a shudder at the words written there.

I know where you sleep and you'll die there. I'll not rest until the keep is mine.

Anne ripped the note from his hands before he could stop her. He watched her still completely as she read the words. Then she looked up at him in horror.

"It isn't over."

"Nay, my love. Apparently not."

She threw herself into his arms and he gathered her close. He gritted his teeth in frustration. Perhaps thinking Maude had been behind the attacks had been naive. But if not Maude, then who? Who would want Artane badly enough to kill for it?

He latched onto one name with strength borne of certainty.

Baldwin of Sedgwick.

He whistled out a bird call and within moments, his guard was surrounding them. Robin read them the note, but said nothing else. He wouldn't need to. They would understand that their duty was to look after Anne, for he'd spoken to them of it more than once in the past.

He looked back at his lady. "Can you ride?"

She nodded without hesitation.

He put her up into his saddle, then swung up behind her.

"Are we going home?" she asked.

"Briefly."

"Robin, what will we do?"

"Kill the bastard," Robin growled. He reached for the reins and kicked his horse into a gallop.

Half an hour later, he thundered into the inner bailey and dropped to the ground. He held up his arms for his lady, then set her on her feet. He bellowed for the acting captain of his father's guard.

"Sedgwick?" Robin demanded.

"Haven't seen him since yesterday, my lord," the man said, looking at him with wide eyes.

That brought Robin up short. If Baldwin had been gone a pair of days now, how could he have placed the note in their saddlebag?

He cursed, then pulled Anne along with him up the steps to the great hall. He found his grandmother loitering near the fire and collected her on his way up the stairs. Perhaps if they reasoned together, they might identify who had done this.

He looked at Anne as she followed him, with his guards trailing hard on her heels. He smiled grimly.

"How fare you?"

She shook her head. "I cannot possibly spend the rest of my life this way. We will lose our minds."

He nodded, agreeing completely.

He went into his father's bedchamber with sword drawn and a guard with a torch going before him. He searched the chamber thoroughly, then ushered Anne and his grandmother in. Once he'd started a fire and seated them to his liking, he handed his grandmother the note.

"What do you think?" he asked.

His grandmother peered at it, then pursed her lips. "An annoyance," she said dismissively.

"Whilst such a thing is indeed true, it is not so easily ignored," Robin said.

"Anne told me a bit of the happenings before my arrival," Joanna conceded. "I thought, however, that such troubles ended in the chapel."

Anne shivered. "Aye, so thought we as well." She looked at Robin. "Think you 'tis but a jest?"

Robin sat, rubbed his hands over his face, and sighed deeply. "As much as I would like to believe thusly, I cannot risk my fate or yours on such a hope."

"But it could have been a servant," Joanna protested.

Robin scowled. "One who speaks French instead of peasant's English?"

"Mine do," Joanna said, then she blinked. "Think you it could have been—"

Robin shook his head. "These attacks began long before you arrived."

"But those were directed at me," Anne said. "Surely this isn't the same person."

"Perhaps," he said slowly, "they thought to strike at me through you."

"But what sense does that make?" she protested.

"How is it best to wound a man?" he asked with a grim smile. "Strike first at what he loves best."

"Oh," Anne said softly. "I see."

Joanna clapped her hands. "The saints be praised," she said happily. "'Twas obviously all that civilizing, grandson, which has brought you to such a realization."

Robin glared at his grandmother. "The note," he said. "Let us think on that more, for 'tis our best clue. Now, I agree it couldn't be a servant—"

"Maude was a servant," Anne interrupted.

Robin turned his glare on her. "Meaning there could be another lord's daughter hiding in the kitchen with my death on her mind?"

"'Tis possible," she offered.

He grunted. "Any other suggestions?"

"A scribe," Joanna said. "A priest. Another nobleman. Someone who can fashion his letters without mistakes."

"Well, I suppose that eliminates Sedgwick," Robin said with a snort.

"It could be those Lowlanders," Anne offered. "The border shifts so often and your sire always finds himself in the midst of whatever skirmish is happening. He has ever had troubles with them."

"Aye," Robin agreed, nodding slowly, "but what use would they have for the keep? Steal one of Father's daughters, aye, but his hall? They would find themselves routed within days."

"It could have been anyone, Robin," Anne said helplessly. "Men come and go through your sire's gates in droves. It could have been anyone who resented you."

"But how many of those men want Artane?"

"How many don't?" she returned with a half smile. "Robin, this is a marvelous hall."

"Maybe 'tis someone you offended dispensing justice," Joanna said suddenly. "How many souls did you anger that day, my love?"

Robin pursed his lips. "I dealt as fairly as I knew how, Grandmère."

She shrugged her shoulders. "Men are complicated creatures. I would look to my rolls were I you. And while you are about your business, Anne and I will remain here cozily. Send up the minstrels when you go, love."

Robin had no intentions of being dismissed so easily. He stood, pulled his grandmother up, and embraced her heartily. "I love you, Grandmère," he said, kissing both her cheeks, "and I appreciate all you've done for my sorry self. I'm quite certain Anne will benefit the rest of her life from the courtly skills your lads have endeavored to teach me. But you're in my marriage bed and I want you out of it."

"But—"

"'Tis best you pack up your lads and head home."

"But—"

"'Twill be much safer. Anne and I will come for a visit once this is all sorted out."

"Nay," Joanna said, shaking her head. "I am of no value to any assailant, my lad. I'll just keep myself tucked up nicely in your sire's chamber."

"And if someone enters?" Robin demanded. "What then?"

His grandmother smiled, but it wasn't a very pleasant smile.

"Do you actually think," she said, leaning forward and looking at him intently, "that I've lived this long, survived as many kings, and fended off as many undesirable suitors as I have without having learned a bit of this and that?"

"Well . . ."

"Think you my lads are for ornament only?"

"Aye, Grandmère. That is what I think."

"Then you haven't looked very closely at them." She sat back and smiled indulgently. "See to yourself, Robin, and leave me to my little comforts. I'll be safe enough here."

Robin considered. And he watched his grandmother consider as well, though he suspected the older woman was fairly sure of the outcome. After all, she was the one acquainted with her lads' skills. Finally, Robin sighed.

"Very well, Grandmère. The victory is yours."

"I'll think on a plan whilst I'm enduring my confinement," she said, tapping her finger against the arm of her chair. "We'll root out this fiend soon enough."

"May you have better luck than I've had," Robin said, inclining his head." He looked at Anne. "We had best pack, then, my lady."

"We're leaving?" Anne asked.

"For the moment. I'll not be a prisoner in my own hall."

"But where will we go?" she asked.

"Where I am most accustomed to sleeping."

"In a tent?" Joanna asked, aghast.

"Aye," Robin said, satisfied by the prospect. "Anne loves the shore, and I am very fond of my life. We'll stay out in the open, well beyond the range of any bows, and see if our assailant has the spine to come against us in a fair fight."

Joanna sighed. "I would say it isn't safe, but if anyone has the skill to protect Anne, it would be you, love." She patted his cheek. "Off with you, then. Unless," she said, with a calculating look, "unless you would like me to prepare the marriage bed—"

"Nay," Robin exclaimed, only to realize Anne had done the same thing. He wondered if he was as red in the face as his wife had suddenly become.

Joanna pursed her lips. "Robin, should you not send for your sire?"

He shook his head. "I want him and the children safely out of the way. This is a personal attack on me, not him. I'll see to it." He paused and looked at her. "Be careful, Grandmère."

"I always am."

"And you, my lady," Robin said, turning to Anne and pulling her to her feet, "will remain with me and I apologize in advance for the tedium you will endure."

"I'll be with you. How tedious could that possibly be?"

He only smiled grimly and hoped she wouldn't do him bodily harm when she realized the truth of the matter.

It was barely past noon when Robin found himself standing in the courtyard, watching his gear be packed into a wagon. He looked at the men doing it. They were all sworn to his service, those lads, and there wasn't a one of them he wouldn't trust with his life.

I know where you sleep.

He couldn't stop thinking about the note. He could scarce believe what he'd read, but as he still held the blighted scrap of paper in his hand, he couldn't deny that it was true.

And to think he'd believed Maude behind it all.

What a fool he'd been.

He gave more thought to what he'd just discussed with his grandmother. Was it possible it could have been one of her servants? He couldn't believe that. This all had begun long before they'd arrived.

I know where you'll sleep, and you'll die there.

All the more reason not to retreat to the safety of the keep. 'Twas obvious that someone inside had his death on his mind. All the more reason not to bolt himself inside his chamber and remain there. What would that serve him? To remain a virtual prisoner there?

Nay, he would sit idle. And he would not spend another day looking over his shoulder as he walked down a passageway.

I'll not rest until the keep is mine.

Not if he could help it. He had no choice but to draw out the fiend, face him on his own terms, then slay him.

For he would not give up anything that was his, not Anne, not the keep, nor his own life.

Which was why he was watching his gear be loaded into a wagon. He had given the matter quick, hard thought, and come to a decision. He would take Anne far from the keep, surround her with his men, and see if their assailant had the bollocks to come against them.

For Robin was itching for a fight.

And his lads were equally as eager.

He looked about him and wondered if Baldwin had returned. Was it possible his cousin was behind this? No doubt Baldwin wouldn't scorn Artane were it offered to him. But to obtain it by murder?

He seriously doubted his cousin had the imagination for such a thing. Nay, Baldwin's means of obtaining anything would be to lower his head and charge Robin. A note would likely be beyond the lout's capabilities.

But if not Baldwin, then who?

Robin shook his head. He wasn't sure how well he could investigate inside the keep if he were out of it, but he couldn't see any other option. The safest place for Anne was outside the keep. Perhaps then he could scrutinize whoever tried to come near them.

He dragged his hand through his hair. Someone wanted the keep. Someone wanted him dead. He could scarce believe it.

At least the latter was something he was accustomed to, for he certainly had made his share of enemies over the years. But he was wary and deft with a blade, so the ending of his life never concerned him much. Now, he had begun to feel differently. He had souls depending on him.

One soul, he corrected himself. He looked behind him to see her standing at the top of the steps up to the great hall. She'd come and gone a time or two, always accompanied by a pair of his lads, of course. He was relieved to see her coming outside again.

The weak autumn sunlight fell down upon her pale hair and upon the deep green of her cloak. Robin shook his head in wonder. Was it possible that she had grown more beautiful because he loved her, or had his love made her more beautiful? He surely didn't know.

With any luck he'd have a lifetime in which to come to a conclusion about it.

He turned back to supervising his packing.

39

Anne stood in the courtyard, heartily regretting her rash words about being happy with Robin wherever he was and whatever he was doing. The task of packing up enough gear and seeing to the keep in his absence, albeit a not very distant absence, was chafing to say the very least. Packing themselves up hadn't taken very long, but then had come preparations for meals, the gathering of documents for Robin to study, and the grilling of each of his men. He took none but his own lads, and they were apparently accustomed to moving on in a hurry.

He had left his father's steward in charge and Anne watched the man carefully as Robin laid out for him what his duties would be. And when he'd warned the man that there was trouble afoot in the keep, he hadn't blinked. A glance at his scribblings left her in no doubt that this was not the assassin.

Even the priest had not escaped Robin's scrutiny. His hand was passing fair, but not the neat, precise characters in the note. Anne had begun to wonder if it might not be a woman's hand they were looking at. Though few women of her acquaintance could write, she certainly could, as could all Gwen's family.

And what of Gwen's ladies?

But that thought was so ridiculous, she immediately pushed it aside. She'd never sat in the same solar with anyone who would have wanted Artane for their own. Even Edith couldn't possibly be interested. Edith would likely rather wed with Robin than slay him.

Wouldn't she?

Anne shook her head as she stood waiting for Robin in the courtyard. Perhaps it was a passing nobleman whom Robin had recently offended. That was entirely possible. Perhaps, given the time, they would find out who it was.

Then they could retreat to a warm bedchamber, for much as Anne loved the sea, she suspected it would be a bloody cold fortnight spent there.

It was late afternoon before Robin's great tent was pitched. A fire had been lit before it and Anne found herself huddled next to it, shivering. They had already eaten, which should have warmed her, but the bitter wind from the north had stolen all her heat. She looked up as Robin threw himself down next to her.

"By the saints," he said with a scowl, "you wouldn't think a simple removal half a league from the hall would be this much trouble, would you?"

She shook her head with a smile. "I fear I've never done the like, so I've nothing to compare it to."

"Trust me," he said grimly, "'tis usually far simpler than this. But at least we'll be safe." He looked at her. "Your lips are blue, lady."

"I'm nigh onto freezing."

He frowned. "I vow, Anne, I hadn't thought on that overmuch. I fear I was far too worried that we have a safe place to sleep."

"I'll manage," she said. "I would rather wake numb from cold than numb from lack of life."

He reached for her hand and laced his fingers with hers. "I'm sorry," he said simply. "Truly this wasn't how I would have had any of this proceed."

"And how would you have had it proceed, my lord?" she asked with a smile. "In a commonplace fashion with no death, destruction, or keep-snatching hanging over us?"

"It would have been passing pleasant to have a quiet little Mass said over our heads, then retire to our quiet little bedchamber for a pair of weeks where meals could have been delivered to us without us worrying about dying from ingesting them."

She shrugged. "Dull."

"Pleasant," Robin insisted.

"I suppose we'll have to make do with what we have, then," she said, "since the other is not an option."

"I promise, my lady, that there will come a time when our lives are quite peaceful."

Anne only hoped they both lived that long. She looked at Robin and found him staring thoughtfully out at the sea. She followed suit, and it wasn't long before the ceaseless roar of the waves coming into shore had lulled her into a half sleep. It was not without alarm that she came to herself. Would Robin's men be just as soothed, and neglect what they were supposed to be seeing to?

And then another gust of arctic wind blew across the sand and Anne blinked. Perhaps they would be safe, as long as the wind blew. For all she knew, their assailant wouldn't have the courage to venture out in such weather.

A pity they themselves had been driven to the like.

"Anne?"

She looked at him and smiled reflexively at the sight. She suspected she would be hard-pressed to ever accustom herself to the fact that Robin was hers. Even harder still would be to realize that he was hers and apparently was content with that fact.

"I have something for you," he said, reaching inside his cloak and pulling forth a box.

His box.

Anne recognized it immediately and prayed she would have the skill for a goodly bit of subterfuge. It wouldn't do for Robin to think she had ransacked his things while he'd been about his business.

She watched him lift the lid, then shield the contents from the wind. But she didn't miss the ribbons he carefully held onto, as if he treasured them in truth. He dug about for a moment or two, then pulled forth something wrapped in a bit of cloth.

And Anne forced herself not to decide beforehand what it all might mean.

Robin replaced his ribbons, shut the lid, and tucked the box inside the tent. Then he carefully unwrapped the ring and held it to the firelight. Anne bit her lip. 'Twas still the same ring she had seen before and wondered about its purpose.

Robin buffed it for a moment with the cloth, then looked at her and smiled gravely.

"I wanted to give this to you in the chapel, but I would have had to cross swords with my father for the chance to fetch it from my chamber." He looked at the ring and his smile turned wistful. "Hard as it might be to believe, I've had this almost five years."

"As a token for some fair maid?" she asked before she could bite her tongue.

He looked at her, amused. "'Tis your wedding ring, Anne, and it was ever meant to be such. Why else would the stone match your eyes, or the gold match your hair?"

"Oh," she said, but very little sound came out.

"You remember I told you about that first little skirmish in Spain?"

She didn't dare answer nay, so she nodded.

"I walked Nick through one of the worst rainstorms I've ever seen simply because I'd heard tell of a goldsmith whose skill was unsurpassed living near Madrid. The gem he had as well, though I would have searched for that had he not had something to suit."

"Indeed," she managed.

"It may be too large," he said, frowning down at it. "I vow I could not remember what size might suit you, so I used my smallest finger for a model, then had the man decrease the size even more." He looked up at her and smiled. "Will you have it?"

Her hand was shaking as she held it out. Ah, how she had misjudged him. She watched as he took her hand and tried the ring on several fingers. The only place with which it met any success was on her thumb. Robin frowned.

"That won't do," he said, looking at her hand as if he could will her fingers to plumpen.

Anne curled her fingers into her palm. "It will suit for the moment."

"I could bind a bit of cloth to it, to make it fit elsewhere."

Anne hesitated to let him have it back, but she supposed he wasn't going to change his mind about giving it to her. After all, he'd had it fashioned with her in mind.

As amazing a thing as that was.

She heard a rip and groaned silently as she watched him continue to take his dagger to the hem of his tunic. He looked up at her from under his eyebrows and smiled.

"Sorry," he said. "I vow I'll mend it myself."

She pursed her lips. "That I doubt."

"I'm capable."

"You're also wed," she said dryly.

He laughed. "You would think you'd just sentenced yourself to a lifetime of mending my clothing."

"I have."

"I'll be more careful."

She'd seen Robin's clothing and she suspected a little more care wouldn't be enough to save her from hours of mending. But somehow, when he'd adjusted her ring to his liking, a bit of mending didn't sound like such an onerous task when she would have his ring on her finger to look at as she did the like.

He slipped his ring onto her finger, then took her hand in his and ran his finger over her ring.

And then he looked at her.

And she wondered if it was the fire to have warmed her so suddenly.

"There is," he said slowly, "other business we might see to as well this night."

"By the saints, Robin," she said with half a laugh, "you make it sound as if you're preparing for a clandestine conflict with some band of mercenaries."

He scowled at her. "I've never had a wife before. I'm not exactly certain how one goes about this . . . um—"

"Business?" she supplied.

He shut his mouth and scowled a bit more.

"Deflowering?" she offered.

He pursed his lips. "You've passed too much time with my sister, I can see that."

She only smiled. "If my father could see us now, he might think again about his assumptions."

Robin shook his head with a short laugh. "Saints, Anne, but our lives have been a tangle thus far."

She watched him rub his thumb over the back of her hand and smiled at the sight. It was all the more miraculous because she wore his ring. "How would you have had it go, my lord? If you had had the ordering of the day's events?"

"First," he said, looking at her with a dry smile, "I wouldn't have found myself in your bed before I wed you. A maid should never be subjected to a man's snores before she's already wed with him and 'tis too late to change her mind."

"I doubt I would have done that," she said,

"I was, frankly, astonished you came to the chapel at all," he continued. "Given the circumstances."

"It wasn't fully under my own sails," she admitted.

"And it should have been you and I there with the only sword bared mine as I laid it at your feet and pledged to protect you with my name and my body," he said, his smile turning grave. "I would change it if I could, my lady."

"But you cannot, so do not try. But you can entertain me with how things could have proceeded from there."

"A fine meal," he said, taking her hand in both his own. "A bit of dancing, perhaps."

"Which you are remarkably skilled at," she said with a smile.

"For a warrior with cloddish feet," he agreed. "And such compliments would have been met with ones of my own in which I praised your beauty and your own skill with the steps. And whilst all the rest of our family danced and made merry, we would have escaped to a tent made ready by the sea, surrounded by my guards that we might have had a great amount of privacy to be about our—"

"Business," she finished.

"Of course."

She looked behind them. "The tent is here, I see. And such a sturdy one."

He smiled. "I had it fetched once I arrived here. I had left much gear behind at Nick's hall in France, but subsequently saw that I might have a need for it."

"Then you planned to stay," she said softly.

"How could I leave?" he asked. "You were here."

She could only look at him, silently. He returned her look, but a corner of his mouth twitched.

"We have our tent," he said, with a little nod in its direction.

"So we do."

"It might be warmer inside," he offered. "Buried under blankets and furs and such."

She could hardly argue with that. Besides, the thought of being warm distracted her from the thought that she was surely on the verge of becoming Robin's wife in truth and that was a thought she had so often denied herself, it was almost painful to allow herself to entertain it.

Robin produced a candle, lit it in the fire, then entered the tent, pulling her inside with him. He set the candle on a stool, then straightened and looked at her.

"Does it suit?"

"'Tis passing large, this tent of yours," she said, looking around her in surprise. "Luxurious, even."

"You didn't think I would shelter you in anything less, did you?"

She reached out and fingered one of the heavy cloth walls. "Substantial."

He smiled. "No one will see inside, my lady. We have our privacy."

"And our furs and blankets as well," she said. She looked at him and wondered just what she was supposed to do next. And then she looked at Robin and saw him truly. The gentleness in his expression was almost her undoing. She reached up and touched his cheek. "I can scarce believe I am here with you," she whispered. "That you have wed me."

"And who else could I have wed?" he asked, just as softly. He reached out and touched her cheek in return. "I loved you the moment I first clapped eyes on you—"

"When you put a worm down my gown—"

"And every moment since," he finished with a smile.

"Even when you didn't?" she asked gently.

"Every moment since," he repeated. "Especially during the moments in which I tried to convince myself I didn't. But I knew in my heart that my life would only be sweet if I had but one thing."

"One thing?"

He nodded. "If I had you." He tucked her hair behind her ears. "Not a day passed that you didn't consume my thoughts, neither did a night pass in which you did not haunt my dreams."

"I wish I had known," she said wistfully.

"Well, you know now," he said, "and if you'll give me time, I'll remind you every day from this moment on."

"And how will you do that, my lord?" she asked.

He took her hands and put them up around his neck, then drew her closer to him. "I'll tell you," he said, bending his head to kiss her. "I'll tell you a thousand ways every day, with every look, every word and every touch."

"When you're not grumbling at me," she breathed.

"Well," he said with a smile, "I have a reputation to maintain. Wouldn't want the lads to think I'd gone soft. But," he said, raising one eyebrow, "that will only be during the daytime."

"Is there any other time?"

"There is the night, my love. And during the nights, I will show you that I love you."

"Will you?" she managed.

"Perhaps not a thousand ways each night," he conceded, "but certainly enough that there will be no doubt in your heart that it could have been no one but you for me." He kissed her softly. "No one but you, Anne."

She looked up at him.

"Show me," she said simply.

"I will."

And he did.

40

Robin opened his eyes and came fully awake. It took him a moment or two, however, to understand why he was so warm and why he felt sand beneath his back instead of a finely stuffed goosefeather mattress.

He was warm because his wife was sprawled over him like a blanket and his back was paining him because he was sleeping on the shore.

He did have to admit, though, that there were a pair of positive details that came immediately to mind. One, he was still alive, which meant he had survived the night. Two was that he was deliciously warm despite his and his lady's lack of any clothing whatsoever.

There was, he decided, something to be said for life in a tent.

His candle had burned down to its final hour, but the light was enough that he could see Anne's eyelids flutter and open. She smiled a sleepy smile at him.

"Oh," she said with a yawn, "it's you."

He laughed in spite of himself. "Aye, my lady, 'tis me. The lout you fell asleep with last night."

"Did we sleep?" she asked pleasantly. "I surely don't remember much of that."

Nor did he, and he was certain that they hadn't slept all that long. He reached out and brushed his lady's hair back from her face and wondered if he slept still. Surely that she was his was naught but the stuff of dreams.

"You know," he said with a start, "I think I might make a poet yet."

"Think you?"

"I'm thinking very poetic thoughts about you, my love."

"A pity I've no paper and ink, else I would take them down. Geoffrey the Lutenist would be most impressed."

He blinked, then looked at her in surprise. "He told you?" Then another thought occurred to him and he felt his eyes narrow. "You were in the alcove."

"I stand so accused."

"Anne!"

She only smiled and leaned closer to kiss him. "It was a marvelous gift, that morning," she said. "And I think you a perfectly fine bard. Too much gushing sours the song, don't you think?"

"What I think, my lady," he said, "is that you've insulted my fine minstrelsy skills. I have no choice but to demand reparation and satisfaction of you."

"Oh, please do," she said with a lazy smile. "Demand all you like."

He started to do just that, then hesitated. "Perhaps I am too bold," he said softly. He had worried, at first, that he might not only crush his lady, but injure her leg. He had been exceedingly careful, though he had to admit that his enthusiasm had overcome him a time or two.

She only smiled and shook her head. "I am well. Truly."

"Truly?"

"Aye. Be about your work, my lord. I would think we had yet a bit of night left and I vow I am still unconvinced completely that you love me."

He paused and looked at her. "You aren't truly, are you? Unconvinced?"

She smiled and pulled his head down to hers. "Leave your thoughts behind, Robin, and love me. 'Tis what you promised me. Remember?"

He could scarce forget. And so he loved her and as he did so, he could hardly contain his joy. By the saints, he had been blessed more than he deserved, for in Anne he had certain found his match, not only in wits but in spirit.

And then he found he could not think at all.

It was a great while later that he finally forced himself to lift up the bottom of the tent the slightest bit to determine if it were indeed daylight outside. He looked at his lady.

"I suppose we should rise," he said reluctantly.

"You still look very tired," she said. "You'll likely need a small rest after supper."

"Think you?"

"I'm almost certain of it."

He pulled away, then paused and looked at her. "Did I please you?"

"Which time?" she asked politely.

"Well," he grumbled, "we won't discuss the first time."

"Passing unpleasant," she agreed.

"It has improved since then, hasn't it?"

"Greatly."

"Then I did please you?"

"I'll tell you once I've discovered if I can walk again," she said, sitting up with a groan.

"Ah, Anne," he said, dragging his hand through his hair. "I feared you would suffer because of it."

"Robin," she said, flicking him smartly on the ear, "I meant it in jest. As a compliment," she added.

He blinked at her and wondered why he had ever thought Anne of Fenwyck to be shy and reticent.

"What?" she asked with a smile. "Do I offend you?"

"Saints, nay," he said, with feeling. "I prize your honesty."

"You may regret that someday."

He pursed his lips. "You've bludgeoned me with sharp words regularly over the course of my life, my love. I daresay I would suffer from the lack of it if you ceased. Please, speak your mind freely."

She laughed. "Are these the words of love I can look forward to during daylight?"

"Those and more," he grunted. Then he looked at her appraisingly. "'Tis barely dawn. Are you prepared for words, or would more deeds suit you better?"

She wasted no time returning to the comfort of warm coverings. "Deeds," she said. "Especially if they can be wrought under cover."

Robin blew out the candle. Anne of Fenwyck, lately of Artane, was his and he would miss no opportunity to show her that he was grateful for the like.

The dawn could wait a bit longer.

It was well past first light before he emerged from his tent, drawing his lady out behind him. He bid her wait for him whilst he looked about them and determined that all his guards were still at their posts. He called to his captain, who with Jason had pitched what would serve as a mess tent and garrison hall a goodly distance away. Jason emerged, rubbing his eyes, but looking none the worse for the wear. Robin beckoned to him. Jason looked about him, then dashed for their tent.

"Well?" Robin asked. "Any movement?"

"None, my lord," Jason said. "The men have been taking watches all night and nothing unusual occurred."

"And all are still accounted for?"

"Aye, my lord." Jason made Anne a bow. "My lady."

"My lord Ayre," she said in return.

Jason looked at Robin and smiled hesitantly. "You passed the night well, my lord?"

Robin snorted, put his hand on the back of Jason's neck, and shook him. "'Tis no affair of yours, my lad, but aye, we survived."

"The lady Anne looks lovely this morn," Jason said.

Robin looked at her and tried to frown. Her hair, which was ever tidy, looked as if she'd rolled from her bed without thought of comb or braid. Perhaps that came from his burying his hands in it too often.

And then there was her mouth, which looked as if it had been kissed thoroughly—and more than just once, at that.

Indeed, if Robin had to tell the tale true, it looked as if the woman had been thoroughly bedded the night before and had just risen to stretch before returning for more of the same.

And that was enough to make him seriously consider a small nap. After all, 'twas his duty to see his marriage well consummated.

"—justice rolls?"

"Eh?" Robin asked, realizing that Jason was talking to him. "What was that?"

"The justice rolls," Jason said again, looking at Robin with wide eyes. "Do you want them, my lord?"

He could think of several things he wanted much more than scribblings from his day of dispensing justice, but perhaps 'twas best he be about his business whilst he had the wits to concentrate on it. Besides, the sooner he managed to unravel the mystery of the note, the sooner he could pack up his gear and return to his father's bedchamber and his father's soft, comfortable goosefeather mattress.

And that left him looking at Anne purposefully.

"The rolls, my lord?" Jason said pointedly.

Damn the boy. Robin glared at his squire. "Fetch them," he growled. "I'll look them over right away."

Jason bolted and Anne laughed. Robin turned his glare on her. "Something amuses you?"

"You look at me as if I'm a tasty leg of mutton you've a mind to gnaw on."

"'Tis a compliment," he said archly.

She smiled up at him. "I know. And I would kiss you for it, but your squire returns."

"So?"

"You've a reputation to maintain, my lord."

"It is but my squire."

"There is that," she agreed.

"Now, were it my captain, or another nobleman," he said slowly, "*then* I would no doubt be forced to forgo such sweet attentions until a more appropriate time."

"But it is just Jason," she said.

"He can be intimidated." He lifted one eyebrow. "Well?"

She wrapped her arms around his neck, stood on her toes, and kissed him full on the mouth. Robin made a grab for her before she could pull away, and clutched her to him. And then he wondered at his own stupidity, for though it might have just been his squire gaping at him, there was his own distraction to worry about.

"No more," he gasped, when she pulled away. "By the saints, my mind is mush."

Anne only smiled serenely. "Poor lad. Shall I sit by you and aid you?"

"The saints preserve me," he said with feeling. "Jason, I hope you brought wine. Cold wine. Cold something. Quickly."

Anne laughed and Robin smiled at the sound. He stole a look at his lady and couldn't help the lightening of his heart either. She was beautiful and content and he could scarce believe he'd been fool enough to have let so long pass before he wed her.

At least he was a fool no longer.

He could only hope he would live long enough to enjoy that.

And it was with that thought that he set to work pouring through the scribe's notes, looking for something amiss. Jason fed the fire and Anne read over his shoulder. And he thought he might expire from the tedium of it all. He simply could not believe that disputes over livestock and water could anger a man enough to drive him to murder his liege-lord.

Though he supposed he'd seen men murdered for less.

Indeed, he'd fought for men who had less reason for war than that. It was entirely possible that he had angered someone during his day of sitting in his father's chair. But he couldn't believe he could have inspired murder.

Though he'd certainly inspired the like in Maude of Canfield.

He shuddered and pushed himself to his feet. He needed to pace and whilst he could not go far, he could at least roam about the fire for a bit and see if that didn't provide him better answers than sitting idle.

Maude had wanted Anne dead, and he could almost understand that. Even when he'd looked on Maude with a bit of favor, he'd wondered if there was something amiss in her mind. He'd feared she would call their marriage banns herself after the first time he'd shared a trencher with her. But for her to ensconce herself in Artane as a servant for the sole purpose of harming Anne?

Unlikely.

It had to be someone else, someone with enough wits to plan a murder. Robin began to wonder if Maude had been but a pawn in the fiend's scheme. But that would mean that the true murderer had known of his association with Maude.

Which meant it had to be someone who had at least visited Canfield.

Or someone who had overheard gossip at Artane.

Robin paused and looked down at his lady. She sat near the fire with her lame leg stretched out before her and the other knee bent so she could rest her chin atop it. Her hair glinted in the sunlight as it lay spread about her shoulders. The light also caressed her fair skin, coloring its paleness with a golden hue. Robin felt his heart clench within him. He couldn't lose her. There was a part of him that almost wished he'd never had her, either in his bed or in his heart. He certainly could have spared himself grief that way.

Ah, but what he would have missed. He walked over to her, then knelt before her. He looked into her pale green eyes and couldn't stop himself from leaning forward and kissing her softly.

"I love you," he whispered. "By the saints, Anne, I vow I do."

She reached up and touched his cheek, her eyes full of tears. "I love you as well," she said quietly. "So much, it almost pains me to look at you."

"Then we are both in sorry shape, lady, for those are my thoughts exactly."

"Then what shall we do?" she asked wistfully.

"We shall live," he said. "Very long lives."

"I hope so," she said. "I hope so."

Robin looked at her a moment longer, memorizing her smile and the love he saw in her eyes. Then he rose and looked for his squire. The sooner he was about his work, the sooner he would solve his mystery.

But when he saw Jason and who accompanied him, he began to wonder if the solving might come sooner than later.

"Who," Robin said curtly as Jason came to a halt before him, "is this with you?"

"Reynaud of Agin," the man said with a low bow. "Lately of Segrave, thanks to the lady Joanna's generosity."

One of his grandmother's peacocks. Perfect. And Robin suspected he was the one who had been in charge of the pointy-toed shoes. It was hard to tell one from another, but Robin had seen more of this dolt than he'd cared to.

"I bring word from said lady," Reynaud said, with another bow. "Here."

A scroll was presented with a flourish. Robin read it quickly, scowled, and looked up into the sky. He noted that it was blue, which was odd for the time of year. Usually the coast was wreathed in fog, but he wasn't ungrateful for a bit of sunshine.

Fog could, of course, easily hide an assassin.

Robin made a decision. He shoved the scroll at Reynaud.

"Tell her I agree," he said shortly.

"As you will, my lord," the man said with an expansive bow that almost caused him to impale an eye on his own ridiculous footgear. "I'll return immediately."

"Do that," Robin suggested. He watched until the man had summited the last rise of sand before he turned and went to sit next to his wife.

"Well?" she asked.

"My grandmother has a plan."

"Of course she does."

"It includes dancing."

Anne laughed. "Of course it does."

He scowled at her. "I'm not certain I like it."

"I could expect nothing less from you."

"She thinks to invite the surrounding nobles to a celebration in our honor."

"And will she interrogate them at the hall door, or invite them to the dungeon where she may use the hot irons?" Anne asked politely.

Robin grunted. "The saints preserve us."

"It might work."

"It might end both our lives."

"Teach me to use a knife," Anne suggested.

He looked at her and wondered if he could possibly do such a thing. Sweet Anne with a knife in her hand? He shook his head. Now, his sister was very handy with several lengths of blade and he had no trouble envisioning her plunging any number of said blades into any number of assailants. But Amanda had a steely side to her he could not credit Anne with.

"I can do it," she added.

Robin looked at her a bit longer and considered. Perhaps he misjudged her. She certainly looked determined enough. And he could see the advantages of her at least knowing enough to protect herself.

"Could you kill?" he asked softly.

She returned his look unflinchingly. "If it meant protecting you. Or a child. Aye, I could."

"You could not hesitate," he warned. "Hesitate and you would be lost."

"Teach me."

"I don't want to."

"But you need to."

He moved as close to her as he possibly could, then put his arm around her shoulders. It wasn't enough. He carefully lifted her into his lap and wrapped both arms around her. He closed his eyes and buried his face in her hair.

"Ah, Anne," he whispered. "I don't know how—"

"You'll manage," she said. "I'll help you."

He held her until the harshness of the idea trickled out of his soul. The waves rolled in one after another and the sound of it soothed him until he almost managed to think about it without wincing. And when he thought he could speak again, he sighed.

"Very well," he said wearily.

Anne pulled back and smiled at him. "You sound tired, my lord."

He managed a half smile. "Think you I could do with a rest?"

"A true rest, Robin," she said gently. "Put your head in my lap and sleep for a bit. I'll keep watch."

"I'll not lose you, Anne. I vow I won't."

"Rest, Robin."

"For a moment or two," he conceded.

He made her comfortable, then stretched out and put his head in her lap. His drawn sword lay by his side under his hand. He closed his eyes and sighed. He wouldn't sleep, but he would rest. He smiled faintly.

"A rest will likely serve me," he said quietly.

"Will it?"

"With any luck, my labors during the night will again be very heavy."

"Taxing," she agreed. "Surely."

He opened one eye. "Think you?"

She closed his eye with her hand, but not before he saw her dry smile. "I think a great many things about your labors, my lord, but some of them I'll save for later. You would not sleep did I tell you of them now."

"I pleased you."

"Aye, Robin. You did."

He took her hand and held it between both his own.

And he counted the hours until he could again use something besides mere words to tell his lady wife just how deeply he loved her.

And perhaps whilst he was about his work, he would remind himself just how far he was willing to go to keep her safe.

He pitied the fool who had raised a sword against them.

41

Anne stood with her back to the hearth and forced herself to keep her hands down by her sides. That in itself was something of a battle. There was, of course, the pleasure of actually warming her hands against a blaze that had the might to restore some bit of warmth to her fingers. Though she certainly had not lacked for heat during the nights of the past se'nnight, the days had taken their toll.

Then there was the matter of the blade strapped to her forearm, under her sleeve where no one would mark it.

She felt decidedly, and uncomfortably, like a mercenary.

And a very unskilled one at that.

There was some comfort, though, in having Robin standing immediately at her left. He had told her repeatedly that he would not leave her side and should they be attacked, he could readily defend them both. She knew she should have taken comfort in that. After all, he was a swordsman without peer.

But even Robin couldn't see a crossbow bolt coming at them from across the hall.

She closed her eyes and prayed briefly for safety. Perhaps St. Christopher had been attending her devotions at his feet all those years and Robin would survive the eve intact. And once everyone retreated to their beds, she and Robin would retreat to the priest's chamber. The man hadn't been overly enthusiastic about the idea, but Robin had ignored his hesitancy. Robin had been adamant they would not find themselves trapped inside his sire's chamber.

"Anne, you remember Lord MacTavish, do you not?" Robin said pleasantly. "Arrived just this moment from his hall in the north."

One of Rhys's most troublesome neighbors, Anne noted as she smiled and nodded.

"A pleasure, my lord."

MacTavish grunted. "Best get a babe soon," he said curtly. "Artane's an old man."

And with that, he stomped off, bellowing for drink.

"Well," Robin said under his breath, "we can remove him from our list of suspects."

"Too obvious?"

"Too gluttonous. He already had sauce on his shirt. I doubt he'd interrupt his supper long enough for murder."

Anne smiled and shifted. As she did so, the weight of the blade against
her arm caught her attention and sobered her instantly. By the saints, this
was no matter for jesting. She had little doubt that the murderer would
come, to prove his prowess if nothing else. How could she possibly expect
to protect herself with a knife stuck up her sleeve? She could scarce draw it
without trembling. Perhaps Robin had it aright; she likely couldn't kill.
She would hesitate, and then all would be lost.

As if he knew her thoughts, Robin put his arm around her and gave her
a firm squeeze. He looked down at her gravely, but said no word. Anne took
a deep breath, put her shoulders back, and nodded.

She would do what she had to if the time came.

Robin leaned over and put his mouth next to her ear. "I've plans for you."

"Do you?" she murmured.

"Later. We'll stuff a bit of cloth in the priest's ears. No sense in upset-
ting the man."

That he believed there would indeed be a later was reassuring. And even
though she knew he was making light to ease her, she couldn't help a pang
of sorrow over what she stood to lose.

To have Robin for so short a time, then have him taken from her?

And should they survive this, she would never survive it if he went off
to war again.

"Stop thinking," Robin whispered. "'Tis deafening."

"As you will, my lord."

"We've frillies about, my lady, listening and remembering. There are
guards aplenty. Even my grandmother carries a very sharp needle or two and
the saints only know what else. All will be well."

She looked up at him and tried to smile. "You'll not leave my side?"

"Not for a moment," he promised.

"I would be hard-pressed to guard your back otherwise."

He gave her a half smile, but she saw in his eyes that he was relieved at
her words. There was love there too, in his glance, and she promised herself
a goodly amount of time to contemplate that mystery once the assassin was
caught and dealt with.

Joanna crossed the floor of the great hall, several of her lads in tow. She
kissed Anne, then looked up at Robin.

"It would seem that all our guests have arrived, grandson. Shall we
begin the celebration?"

"With some bit of talk?" Robin asked grimly.

"Of course. The lord must welcome his guests."

Robin looked as if he'd been commanded to clean the cesspit single-handedly. He sighed deeply, took Anne's hand, and led her to the lord's table. Anne forced herself not to look behind them anxiously. Robin's captain and two other of his guardsmen were there, as well as Jason. Indeed, the entire great hall was ringed by either Robin's men or Joanna's, though the latter were certainly more recognizable in their brightly colored clothing.

"Honored guests," Robin said loudly, raising his cup in salute, "I bid you welcome to the celebration of my wedding. Eat your fill, drink until you're sated, and enjoy the fine minstrels who wish nothing more than to please your ears."

Anne watched him and realized that he hadn't tasted his wine. Perhaps others might have believed it, for he brought the cup to his lips, but he did not drink.

And then Robin began to talk to those around him. Indeed, he talked so much, he had no time to eat. Anne watched him cast a bit of everything placed before them to the dogs. When none fell to the floor in a fit, she reached for some supper.

Robin caught her hand and held it in both his own, continuing to speak to the lord next to him.

Perhaps he feared a slow poison.

She wondered if she would survive the night without something to eat.

"Bread," Joanna said from her right. "Perfectly delicious and beneficial."

Anne looked at her gratefully. "Nothing added?"

"None. My cook confirms it."

She didn't need to hear more. It was a poor meal when compared to the feast before them, but at least she wouldn't die from the enjoyment of it.

She sincerely hoped she could say the same for the dancing.

The minstrels performed throughout the meal, but when they truly began to play with enthusiasm, Anne knew the time had come for her and Robin to present themselves to the guests. Joanna had informed them that 'twas their duty to perform one dance by themselves for the company.

Men moved to the exits from the hall as Robin led her around the high table. The other tables had been pushed aside to allow room enough for movement. Robin looked at her once as the music began and she knew he shared her thoughts.

Let this not be our last.

Robin did not falter in his steps and she admired that absently, storing up the memory to praise him for later. Even with that, she sensed that his mind was elsewhere and she decided that that too should be praised at her earliest opportunity.

But no one moved.

No twang of a bowstring was heard above the lute.

No body launched itself over a table with blade bared.

Anne almost wondered if perhaps they had made a mistake. Could the missive have been a poor jest? She looked about her. There was no one there from Canfield come to avenge Maude's death. Not even Baldwin had returned to torment them.

It was almost unsettling.

And then the dancing began in earnest.

Robin remained by her side despite the number of requests for his presence with some other nobleman's wife or daughter. He demurred, he stalled, and he pointedly refused. Anne hoped he didn't offend half the countryside, but she wasn't about to relinquish him so he could flatter someone else.

The music stopped and she found herself facing her lord. He took her hands and looked down at her solemnly.

"Safe so far," he said.

"Aye," she agreed. "Perhaps 'twas all a—"

And at that moment, 'twas as if the gates of Hell themselves had loosed a foul commotion.

There was a melee at the door to the great hall. Anne lost count of the men who became embroiled in it. All she knew was when the sea of bodies parted, three souls stumbled out into the midst of the great hall and collapsed.

Nicholas, Amanda, and Miles.

Robin grasped her hand and pulled. She stumbled several times as she struggled to keep up with his furious strides. He knelt down next to his siblings.

"What befell you?" he demanded.

Amanda was crying so desperately, she couldn't speak. Neither Nicholas nor Miles looked to be capable of answers either. They looked as if they'd just escaped a war. All three were covered with blood and it looked as if a good deal of that blood was their own.

"Robin," Anne said, tugging on Robin's sleeve, "they need care. I'll take them to Master Erneis."

He hesitated, then nodded. "I'll send my guard." He frowned deeply. "I should likely see to the settling of our guests."

"Aye," she said, "you should. Perhaps someone will reveal something in the confusion."

He took her hand and kissed it in his usual fashion. "I'll follow you as quickly as I can."

"I will be well. Watch your own back."

He nodded, then motioned to his men. Anne soon found herself surrounded again by his fierce lads and she felt a measure of relief in that.

It took a goodly amount of time to gather up the three wounded ones and herd them out to the healer's quarters. Anne saw them inside, leaving Robin's men without. There was no room for them and she suspected they might serve her better if they kept watch outside.

Nicholas's wounds were the gravest and Anne winced as she aided in stitching them closed. Amanda's sobs had subsided to mere trembling and sniffles. She sat at Nicholas's head, alternately wringing her hands and dragging her sleeve across her face.

"Just a scratch," Nicholas croaked.

Anne looked at Amanda. "What befell you?"

Amanda shook her head. "I cannot speak of it yet. See to Nicholas and tend him well."

Anne looked at Master Erneis and prayed he would manage the feat. She couldn't deny his skill, but she couldn't help either wishing for a bit of Berengaria's special potions that had ever worked so well. But Erneis was clever enough and 'twas a certainty he was used to wounds from a skirmish, so Anne felt somewhat relieved by that.

Then again, Sir Montgomery had been felled by a lesser wound than any of the ones Nicholas bore.

Anne pushed that thought aside.

She looked at Miles, who lay on a pallet, awaiting his turn patiently. Anne began to cut his tunic from him.

"Can you speak?" she asked.

"Always," he said with a weak smile.

"Then give me the tale. What happened?"

"Ruffians," he said with a cough. "They set upon us from the trees."

"What possessed you to leave the keep anyway?" Anne asked in surprise. "I thought you'd gone for a lengthy stay. And where were Nicky's guards?"

Miles groaned as she pulled cloth from under his back. "We rode ahead, leaving the men behind to bring our gear. And all was because of the missive you sent."

"We sent?" Anne asked.

"We assumed Robin had been in his cups when he wrote it," Amanda put in hollowly. "The scrawl was almost illegible."

"Many words . . . mis . . . spelled," Miles said, through gritted teeth.

"We sent no missive," Anne said in surprise.

Amanda looked at her and blinked for several moments in silence. "But," she said finally, "it said you needed us immediately."

"It was a lie," Anne said, feeling a chill go down her spine. "We never . . ."

She felt a breeze blow over the back of her neck.

As if someone had entered Master Erneis's inner chamber.

Anne jumped to her feet and spun around.

Edith of Sedgwick stood there, come from nowhere.

"I thought you would need aid," Edith said calmly.

But Anne saw much more than that in the woman's eyes. Indeed, the coldness there sent shivers through her that she suspected no fire could warm.

She knew, she *knew* she was looking in the eyes of death.

Anne's mouth was completely dry. She tried to swallow, but 'twas futile.

"We could have used aid a handful of hours ago," Amanda said wearily.

Anne wanted to bid Amanda be silent, but she could form no words. All she could do was stare into Edith's eyes and see her own life extinguished there.

"Ruffians abound," Edith said, in that quiet, composed voice that made Anne want to scream. "Travel is very dangerous."

Miles snorted. "Deadly, I'd say."

"Deadly, then," Edith conceded with a shrug.

And then she slipped her hand inside her cloak. Anne watched in horror and realized that now was the time she should be reaching for her own dagger.

But she found, to her dismay, that she couldn't.

All she could do was stare death in the face and wait, powerless and terrified.

The door behind Edith opened and slammed shut. Booted feet stomped several times and a rubbing of hands followed.

"Bloody *frigid* place," Robin groused. "Excuse me, Edith. I should see how the little ones have fared."

Anne watched Edith remove her hand from under her cloak. Edith looked at Robin and smiled, a friendly smile that anyone would have been happy to receive.

"Your guards were kind enough to let me pass," Edith said. "I thought to be of some use, but apparently all is well here."

"My thanks," Robin said, patting her briefly on the shoulder. "You'll likely want to return to the hall. Take one of my men for your protection."

Anne wanted to blurt out that the man would be putting his life in jeopardy, but all she could do was gape at Edith. Speech was beyond her.

Robin turned away to look over his siblings. Anne found herself facing Edith once more.

Edith smiled.

It was the most terrible thing Anne had ever seen.

"My lady," Edith whispered, then she turned and left the chamber.

Anne stood there and shook.

But once the door was closed, she turned and threw herself at Robin. He staggered in surprise, then regained his balance and pulled her close.

"What?" he asked, looking baffled. "What is it?"

"It's her," Anne hissed. She pointed back at the door. *"Her!"*

"Who?" he asked, blinking stupidly.

"Edith, you fool!"

He looked at her as if he'd never seen her before. "What are you babbling about, Anne?"

"Edith!" Anne whispered frantically. "She's the murderer!"

Robin's jaw slid down. "Surely you jest."

"I do nothing of the sort!"

"Anne, it's *Edith*," he said, as if her very name guaranteed her purity and goodness.

"She's behind it!"

He groaned and pulled her close, wrapping his arms around her. "Anne, I believe that you believe such a thing," he said quietly. "I believe you've had a hellish fortnight—"

"Which have no doubt seemed like a hellish pair of years with you as company—" Amanda put in.

Anne held on to her husband before he could pull away and retaliate.

"A hellish *fortnight*," he stressed, "and perhaps that has you overwrought."

"I am not overwrought."

He pulled back and looked down at her gravely. "Anne, what has Edith to gain by hurting me?"

"Maybe she just wants me dead so she can have you," Anne said, starting to shake.

"Why she'd want him is a mystery," Amanda muttered.

Robin looked heavenward and blew out his breath. And in that small gesture that he had made countless times over the course of his life, Anne found comfort. Robin was obviously digging deep inside himself for the patience to endure his sister's barbs. At least there was something still the same in a world where everything had just changed. It was almost enough to lead her to believe there might be hope for the righting of their lives. But that wouldn't come truly until Robin saw the truth she had seen.

"You're wrong," she said bluntly to him.

He scowled at her. Slowly, though, his scowl turned into a thoughtful frown. "What will you have me do?"

"Tell your guards not to let her in again."

He looked at her for a moment in silence, then nodded. "As you will, my lady. But I still cannot believe such evil of her."

"Time will tell," Anne said grimly.

Robin hugged her briefly. "Aye, it will. Now, let us unravel this tangle here." He kept his arm around her and turned to face his siblings. "The tale, if you please."

Anne soon found herself sitting on a stool while Robin paced and listened. But she could hardly concentrate. No matter what Robin thought, she knew what she had seen.

And she had seen her own failing in the face of that. She'd had a weapon, yet been powerless to use it. Perhaps 'twas time she enlisted Amanda's aid in the like. She suspected by the condition of her foster sister's clothes that defending herself with a blade or two had not been beyond her abilities. Anne herself could attest to Amanda's ready tongue and flat of hand, for Amanda had defended her honor many a time against pages who were cheeky enough to voice their insults.

"Where is the missive?" Robin asked.

Amanda produced a crumpled, bloody bit of paper and handed it to Robin. Robin smoothed it out and stared at it.

"I did not send this."

Miles laughed a half laugh. "I told Amanda you spelled with more skill than that, but she was convinced."

Robin scowled at his sister, then looked at his brother. "Who delivered it?"

"No one we knew."

"Then why did you believe it?"

Miles pointed to the back of the letter. "Your seal, brother."

Robin flashed a look at Anne, then looked back at his siblings. "Who set upon you?"

"Hired ruffians," Miles said promptly. "But a goodly amount of them. Perhaps a dozen."

"How many slain?"

"Eight, perhaps. Fortunately for us, Nick's guard arrived as we were almost overcome. The rest of our assailants fled as they heard the men approach." Miles smiled at Amanda. "Our sister was most fierce. I daresay they believed to find a swooning maid when they realized that her hose and tunic were a ruse. Instead they found themselves facing a mightily wielded dagger."

"Dispatch any?" Robin asked his sister.

She looked at him bleakly. "Aye. One."

Robin was silent a moment or two, then he crossed the chamber, bent down, and put his arms around his sister.

"I'm sorry," he said quietly. "That never comes without a price."

Amanda looked as if she might burst into tears. Anne watched her take a deep breath and then let it out raggedly.

"Aye," she agreed. "It didn't."

Robin kissed her forehead, then rose and looked down at her. "You seem to have earned your share of marks." Amanda managed a tremulous smile. "Apparently I need more practice with a blade, for words certainly didn't defend me as well as they usually do."

Anne watched as Master Erneis turned his attentions to Amanda and realized that her fierceness had indeed not come without cost. Though her wounds were not grave, she did have a hurt or two that would require needle and thread. Perhaps skill with a blade came more dearly than Anne had counted.

"To continue our sorry tale," Miles said, taking a deep drink of the healer's draught, "after the rest fled, we gathered ourselves and the guard up and rode hard for the keep. 'Twas all we could do to get past your men." He looked at Robin. "I assume you've had further troubles?"

Robin produced his own note and handed it to his brother.

"What's it say?" Nicholas asked weakly.

"Someone has Rob's death on their minds," Miles said mildly. He looked at Nicholas and shrugged. "The usual."

Anne reached for Robin's hand, a single name burning in her mind.

"Anne, my love," he said, "Edith doesn't want me."

"You don't know that—"

"Her sire has suitors for her," Robin insisted.

"But you didn't see her—"

"She was likely as disturbed by these events as we are."

"I am unconvinced."

He sighed. "I will keep watch for her."

"And for Sedgwick as well," Miles put in. "He surely has no love for you."

"There are many who have no love for me," Robin said grimly. "And we've little to fear from Baldwin, as he hadn't deigned to grace us with his august presence of late."

Anne felt the entire chamber still. Even the healer ceased with his ministrations and looked up at Robin. They remained thusly for several moments, no one moving, no one scarce breathing.

"You don't think . . ." Miles whispered.

"It couldn't be," Amanda said, shaking her head.

"Well," Nicholas croaked, "the spelling of the note . . . was indeed dreadful."

Anne looked up at Robin in surprise. "Think you 'tis possible?"

"I think," he said slowly, "that any decision we make right now will be the wrong one. We've all suffered too many hurts of late to reason clearly." He looked at his siblings and managed something of a smile. "Rest this night and we'll think on the tangle tomorrow. I've no doubt things will look much clearer in the light of day."

"I doubt it," Miles said quietly. "But I could do with some rest. Unless you'd have me stand guard?"

"My guards are without. Nick's can be sent for. We'll be perfectly safe here."

"But what of your grandmother?" Anne asked. "And Jason? He was left inside to keep watch over her."

Robin hesitated. "She is not incautious."

"But she might not be looking in the right direction."

He sighed. "Very well. I'll have word sent to her."

"Better that you lock Edith in the dungeon," Anne said with a shiver.

"And then how are we to know if she's behind it?" Robin asked with a smile.

"The attacks would cease."

"Better that they continue," he said, suddenly looking very intent. "Aye, there is great sense in that. Perhaps we have been going about this in the wrong manner."

"How?" she asked. "By protecting ourselves?"

"Exactly," he said. "Perhaps I would do better to make myself an easy mark and see who comes to take me."

"You cannot be serious," she said.

"He is," Miles said. "Look at that fiendish light that has entered his eyes." He shook his head. "It never bodes well."

Anne looked up at her husband and saw that Miles had it aright. And she very much suspected that there would be absolutely nothing she could do to dissuade him from whatever witless plan he was brewing up in his head.

And if he intended to find himself dead on the morrow, there was naught she could do but hold on to him well that night. She pushed him toward the door.

"Send your grandmother's message," she commanded.

He blinked, then went to the door to do just that. Anne turned to her foster brothers and sister.

"You three rest."

There were three nods of varying degrees to answer her. Then she turned to Master Erneis.

"Have you a place Robin can rest in peace?" There were beds aplenty in the chamber they stood in, but there was no privacy to be had. And given that she had other things in mind for her husband besides sleep, those beds out in the open simply wouldn't do.

"Aye, my pallet in there," he said, pointing across the chamber. "You can draw the curtain if you wish to block out the light."

"You'll keep watch over my family?" Robin asked wearily. "Wake me if aught goes amiss."

"Aye to both, my lord."

Robin looked at him and shivered. "Forgive me, Master Erneis, but I've passed too much of my life in these chambers of yours. Know 'tis with great reluctance that I deprive you of your bed."

Anne pulled Robin along before he could think better of it.

Erneis's little chamber wasn't as luxuriously private as Robin's tent, but it would do. Anne pulled the curtain across and wrapped her arms around him. He looked down at her with a frown.

"No sleep?" he asked.

"Later."

He pulled her close to him and hugged her tightly. "All will be well, Anne. I vow it."

"But in case it isn't, come you here and endeavor not to make too much noise."

She felt him smile against her mouth.

"Ah, Anne, I do love you."

"Then show me," she said as she pulled him down to the pallet with her. "'Tis the night, after all."

"And I do keep my promises."

"Then promise me you won't do anything foolish."

"I don't know if 'tis fair to wring a promise from a man whilst he is abed with his lady wife."

"Promise me, Robin," she said, pulling his head down to hers and kissing him thoroughly. "Promise me."

He only groaned in answer and she supposed that was assurance enough. She shuddered to think what he might have in mind, and she only hoped it wouldn't be foolhardy enough to end his life. For even though she couldn't have said who was behind the attack on Nicholas, Amanda, and Miles, she had no doubts who had written the note Robin had found. But there was one thing she didn't understand, and it was the one thing that left doubt in her mind over her assumption.

Why would Edith want Artane?

And if she did want Artane, why would she want Robin dead?

"Anne, stop thinking," Robin whispered.

"I can't—"

"Aye, you can. Here, let me help you."

Well, she couldn't deny that he was persuasive and very distracting. And perhaps Robin had it aright and things would look clearer in the morning. There was no sense in not making best use of the night while she had it.

42

Five days later Robin stood on the steps leading up to the great hall and chafed at the sight greeting his eyes. It had taken him this long to politely invite all his guests to leave, and that had been accomplished only after several days of expensive entertainment and sustenance. He'd even gone so far as to have a private little bit of jousting for their enjoyment, knowing full well 'twas outlawed save for tournaments the king might call for his own sport.

He'd never had a more unpleasant day on the field.

He had come to realize that there was much more to being lord of a keep than he'd suspected before and it had mostly to do with endeavoring not to humiliate his potential allies in the lists. He had, of course, come away the victor in the end, for he would not fail just to appease someone else's pride, but it had been an exhausting bit of exercise, for he'd dragged each and every match he'd been party to out far longer than he would have liked.

And then there was having to continually keep half his attention focused on Anne and his grandmother in the stands.

Not to mention looking out for himself so he didn't find the addition of an arrow lodged between his ribs.

So it was with great enthusiasm and relief that he had watched the last of his neighbors depart through the front gates. If he could only move his grandmother and her entourage along with the same alacrity, he might be able to turn his attentions back to his original plan.

Becoming easy prey.

He felt a hand slip into his and he didn't even have to look to see who it was. He smiled in spite of himself. By the saints, what he had almost missed through his own stubbornness.

"I don't suppose it will serve me to tell you yet again that I do not like this."

He looked at his lady and felt his heart ache within. It seemed he couldn't look at her anymore without immediately wondering how it would be to lose her.

Or to lose himself and thereby never have her again.

"You can tell me," he said calmly, "but nay, it will not serve you."

"Bloody stubborn man."

He winced at the genuine worry in her eyes. "Anne, what else can I do?"

She sighed. "Nothing other than this."

"I will be careful."

She held up her arm and he could see the blade inside her sleeve. "I could guard your back."

"Let us pray you will have no need, but I would be glad of it just the same."

Though after having seen what killing a man, albeit in defense, had done to his sister, Robin wasn't at all sure he wanted Anne anywhere near a murderer. Amanda was still trembling almost a se'nnight later.

He stared out over the courtyard and wondered a great many things. Who could have put his seal on a missive without his having noticed it?

Unless it was his father's seal.

Robin turned that thought over in his head. He doubted his sire would have left such a thing behind, but 'twas possible. It was also possible it could have been removed from his sire's solar at any point over the last fortnight, by any number of people.

Baldwin, for instance.

But why would Baldwin want to hurt Robin's family? Before he could give that more thought, his own words came back to him with the force of a dozen fists.

How is it best to wound a man? Strike first at what he loves best.

He blew out his breath slowly. Perhaps Baldwin was behind the attack. Robin was beginning to believe it more all the time. Baldwin had, after all, been absent for over a fortnight, he would have had ample time to filch something from Rhys's solar, and he certainly had no love for Nicholas or Miles. And 'twas also a certainty that Baldwin couldn't spell to spare his own life. Robin would have been surprised if the man could have signed his own name.

Why he would have wanted to injure Amanda was a mystery, but hadn't Miles said the ruffians had been surprised to find her there? Perhaps Baldwin had wanted to slay Robin's brothers and keep Amanda for himself.

Which certainly would have guaranteed him Artane in time.

Assuming Amanda wouldn't have murdered him in his own bed.

Aye, Robin thought with a nod, 'twas entirely possible that Baldwin was behind the entire thing. He could have had Robin's note written by someone else and slipped into the foodstuffs at precisely the right moment. He would have been away from the keep at the time, which would have removed suspicion from him.

The more Robin thought about it, the easier the thought rested with him. He could understand Baldwin's motives, indeed he could sympathize with him. It would have chafed Baldwin sorely to have had Robin as his liege-lord, and that only if Baldwin had survived his uncle and his uncle's infant son. And Sedgwick's liege-lord was precisely what Robin would become on his father's death. Not that Robin wanted Sedgwick, but it was his, after all. Baldwin had nothing. Why not seek for Artane itself if he were planning on a little murder?

The door opened behind him and Robin spun, his blade halfway from its sheath. His grandmother held up her hands in surrender.

"Only me, love, come to bid you farewell. If you're certain—"

"I am," Robin said quickly, replacing his sword. "Lovely to see you, Grandmère. Have a pleasant journey home."

Joanna pursed her lips and frowned at him, then turned to Anne. His wife at least received a sunny smile.

"I'm so pleased to see you so well settled, my love," she said, giving Anne a kiss. "I wish you good fortune of this one. A little more polish and he'll be quite presentable."

"Goodbye, Grandmère," Robin said pointedly.

Anne only laughed as Joanna flicked Robin smartly on the ear before she descended the steps. Her lads made her comfortable in a spacious wagon, then the company set off—not as quickly as Robin would have liked, but they did leave eventually. And once they were gone, Robin turned to Anne.

"I'm going to the lists."

"I'll come."

He hesitated. "I would rather see you safely guarded inside."

"I'm sure you would," she said, but she didn't move.

"Anne . . ."

"Robin, I'm not leaving you alone." She looked up at him and there were tears welling up in her eyes. "Think you I could bear a single day without you?" she asked. "Have you thought of that?"

"Continually," he said, pulling her close and wrapping his arms around her. "Every moment of every day, that is the thought that haunts me and breaks my heart." He squeezed her gently, then pulled back far enough to look down at her seriously. "But I want an entire lifetime with you, Anne. We'll not have that unless I end this. Today."

"I'm coming with you."

He hesitated, then relented. "You'll sit by the wall. With my guards—"

"No guards."

He blinked. "But—"

"You said yourself it wouldn't serve you to have guards. I'll not need them either."

"But—"

"Robin, how else will anyone come against you?"

He knew she was right, but he could hardly stomach the thought of her sitting half a field away from him without anyone near her. As fond as she was of her little blade, he knew it would scarce serve her if someone came at her truly.

But surely Baldwin wouldn't have a go at Anne if Robin were there, standing mostly empty-handed. He had seriously considered leaving his sword behind as well. It would be just too tempting a target for Sedgwick to resist.

Robin took Anne's face in his hands, kissed her softly, then took her hand.

"Come along, then," he said. "Let us have this finished."

He slowed his pace down the steps to hers almost without thinking. But it was something else he could certainly repay Baldwin for, for it had been Baldwin to dare her to ride that stallion in her youth. Robin set his jaw. Baldwin would have no more power to work any more harm in their lives. Robin would see to that himself.

The short journey to the lists seemed to take nothing less than an eternity. With every step, Robin wondered if it would be the last he'd take with his love. By the time he had reached the inner bailey wall, he realized how useless such thoughts were to him. He would either survive or he wouldn't. Brooding about it wouldn't change anything.

Best, then, that he not fail.

He paused at a little bench set against the wall. He looked down at his lady, saw the weak sun glinting on her fair hair and her pale visage as she lifted it to him. He took her in his arms and kissed her with all the passion he had in him, so that she might never forget just how deeply he loved her.

"I will not fail us," he said hoarsely. "Anne, I vow it with my life."

She only shook her head and clutched him tightly to her. And then, just as suddenly, she stepped away from him.

"I'll be waiting for you," she said quietly.

Robin nodded and unbuckled his sword belt.

"Robin," she gasped.

He drew the blade and handed it to her, then dropped the scabbard onto the bench. He smiled gamely.

"If I'm to be prey, may as well be easy prey."

"Robin, nay—"

"Think you I am only skilled with a blade?" he asked.

"You are skilled with many things, my lord," she said briskly, "but no doubt your sword might serve you?"

"I'll return for it." He sat her—and rather unwilling she was about it—on the bench, stepped back, and made her a low bow. "Until later, my lady."

He took one last look at her, gingerly holding his sword over her knees with her hand on its hilt, and prayed he wasn't making the biggest mistake of his life, leaving her there alone. For himself, he couldn't think of anything more sensible. If Baldwin were truly behind all this, then seeing Robin in such a defenseless position would be too much temptation to resist.

And so Robin turned and walked out to the middle of the lists. He turned, faced the road that led between the inner and outer gates, and folded his arms across his chest.

And he waited.

There was no movement and very little sound. Perhaps things seemed quiet after such commotion over the past few days. Robin had instructed the outer guards to let no one who did not belong to the keep to enter and no one at all to leave. That way if Baldwin did return, he would be let pass and would no doubt quickly come to the lists to take his pleasure.

And if it were someone from within the keep, they would be hard-pressed to bolt.

He continued to wait.

He looked over at Anne. She had taken his sword and propped it up against the bench. Perhaps she tired of the delay. He couldn't blame her. He was half tempted to sit down and have a little rest himself.

And then he saw movement near the gates.

Baldwin of Sedgwick.

Robin smiled. Perhaps this would go as he planned after all. He tapped his foot impatiently and watched his cousin hesitate. Robin held wide his arms to show he bore no weapon.

Baldwin, as expected, took the bait. He turned his horse and walked it across the lists. He came to a halt some thirty paces away. Robin didn't wait for him to speak.

"Finished with your labors at Wyckham?" Robin asked pleasantly.

Baldwin's jaw went slack and that told Robin immediately all he needed to know. Baldwin shut his mouth with a snap and scowled.

"I was on an errand—"

"To procure ruffians?" Robin smiled politely. "I understand my sister dispatched one of them quite handily. Best scout a little harder next time for mercenaries, cousin. Those don't look to have earned their gold."

Baldwin's mouth worked for several moments, but he seemed incapable of producing intelligent speech. Then he gathered his wits about him.

"You whoreson," he spat.

Robin only smiled. "My mother was not a whore, my lad. I wouldn't want to hazard a guess about yours, however."

Baldwin roared and spurred his horse forward. Robin sidestepped him and turned. Baldwin wheeled his mount around and looked at Robin, apparently weighing the benefits of making another pass. He made no move, however, so Robin could only assume he'd thought better of the impulse. Robin contemplated drawing the knife tucked in his belt. That might infuriate Baldwin enough to force him to act and who knew what sort of sport that might provide him with.

"My mother was a lady," Baldwin snarled. "And at least I know who my father was."

Robin blinked, then shrugged. It was obviously meant as an insult, but he couldn't for the life of him divine why he should be offended by it. He looked at his cousin who was currently drawing his sword with a great flourish, and wondered if he might have an answer or two before he dispatched the cretin.

"You wanted my siblings dead?" Robin asked.

"The lads," Baldwin said. "And you, of course."

"Of course. But my sister too? Passing unsporting of you, I'd say."

"I didn't want *her* dead," Baldwin said, sounding disgruntled. "Damned idiots didn't realize she was a she. I have other plans for her."

"You wouldn't survive the night in her bed," Robin assured him. "She's very handy with a blade."

"A woman can't wield a blade if she's been beaten enough," Baldwin said.

Robin couldn't even contemplate the like and he would be damned before he saw Amanda in the clutches of a wretch like the one facing him.

"Well," he said, "there's no need to worry about that, for you'll not get close enough to touch her, much less feel the bite of her blade." Robin cocked his head to one side and looked at Baldwin. "I am confused about one thing, though."

"More than that, I'd say," Baldwin snorted.

"Why Maude? Why Anne?"

"Maude was a sniveling twit," Baldwin said in disgust. "She was here to torment you until I could kill you."

"And she happened to dislike Anne?" Robin asked. "A little extra trouble for your trouble?"

"Aye," Baldwin said with a nod.

Robin was unsurprised. The only thing that did surprise him was the fact that he hadn't seen it from the start. The saints only knew where Baldwin had dredged Maude up from, but he could understand Baldwin's desire to make him miserable.

And damn him if it hadn't been quite effective.

But now it could be over and Robin could scarce wait to begin. He held open his arms. "Here I am, Baldwin. Do your worst and let's have this at an end."

Baldwin balked. "You have no sword."

"Don't need one."

Baldwin's expression darkened considerably. "I'll not fight you that way. There is no honor in it."

"Yet there is honor in poisoning a child," Robin said slowly. "And pushing a woman down the stairs."

"That was Maude's work. Mine is to kill you and I'll not do it unless you face me truly!"

Robin sighed. This was just his luck—to be fighting an imbecile with ideals. Robin wondered if it would be worth his time to return and fetch his sword, or if he should just take his knife and throw it through Baldwin's eye. Though it was tempting to do just that, he realized with a start that he found it just as unsporting as Baldwin likely would.

By the saints, he was losing his wits.

"Well," he said with a goodly bit of disappointment in his voice, "I had hoped you would find yourself with bollocks equal to taking me on, but if you've misplaced them—"

Baldwin charged. And as Robin flung himself out of Baldwin's way, he realized he'd found Baldwin's sore point. Apparently it wasn't his parentage, his sister, or his honor. That it was what rested inside his hose shouldn't have come as much of a surprise.

Baldwin's horse seemingly had as little fondness for Robin as Baldwin did, for Robin found himself diving and rolling to avoid the slashing hooves. He heaved himself to his feet and flung his dagger before his own arrogance did him in.

His knife lodged in Baldwin's leg. Sedgwick leaned over to jerk it free at the precise moment his mount reared yet again. Baldwin went crashing to the ground. Robin stood there, sucking in air, and waited for his enemy to rise to his feet. Baldwin jerked Robin's knife free and threw it at him with all his strength. Robin heard the blade whistle past his ear and wondered if he might have given his cousin too little credit. He spotted his dagger and dove for it, feeling somewhat grateful he'd been cavalier enough to have left his mail behind, for the lack of it certainly aided him in quick movements.

He came up with his dagger in time to see Baldwin bearing down on him. Robin rolled aside as Baldwin's sword went ferociously point-down in the dirt.

"Nicely done," Robin said brightly. "Think you you'll ever manage to stick it in my flesh?"

Baldwin howled with fury and Robin barely made his feet before Baldwin was swinging his blade with mighty strokes. It was as Robin scarce avoided being decapitated that he began to contemplate the merits of perhaps returning to his lady for his blade. Baldwin dropped his sword suddenly and hunched over, gasping for breath.

"You aren't going to faint, are you?" Robin demanded.

Baldwin only waved him away.

Robin sighed. No sense in not taking advantage of Baldwin's generosity. He sighed and turned to retrieve his sword only to stop dead in his tracks.

It was at that precise moment that he realized he had made a terrible miscalculation.

Edith stood next to Anne some thirty paces behind him.

She had a knife to Anne's throat and Robin's sword in her other hand. Anne was so pale, Robin thought she might faint. She stood, still as stone. Edith glared at Baldwin.

"Finish him," she commanded.

"He doesn't have his sword," Baldwin wheezed. "I'll not do it unless I do it fairly."

And just when Robin thought things couldn't deteriorate any further, he looked behind Edith to see his siblings shuffling across the field. Perfect.

"Stop," he shouted. "Edith has a knife!"

The trio came to a teetering halt. Edith dragged Anne to the side so she could see both Robin and his siblings.

"Come no closer," she shouted. "I'll kill her if you do!" She looked at Robin and then threw his sword toward him. "There," she said. "Take your blade."

Robin looked at her, trying to judge her trustworthiness. As if having a blade across his love's neck wasn't indication enough of that! But he wasn't about to discount the aid his sword would provide him. He retrieved it carefully, then backed away slowly. He didn't dare look at Anne.

"Baldwin," Edith commanded. "Finish him."

Robin continued to back up until he had both Baldwin and Edith in his sights. Baldwin had apparently recovered his breath. He was scratching his head, scowling.

"I've been thinking," he began.

"The saints preserve us," Edith said with a sigh.

"What good will it do me to kill him?" he asked, pointing at Robin, "when Miles is Artane's son of the flesh? He's the one I should be doing in. Robin means nothing."

"Robin means everything!" Edith exclaimed. "Dispatch him, you half-wit!"

Baldwin continued to stare at her. "You really want me to kill him? I thought you wanted him for yourself."

"I want his keep," Edith said. "The grave can have him for all I care."

"I don't know why he matters anyway," Baldwin groused. "He's not Artane's son anyway."

"Baldwin, you imbecile," Edith said in disgust, "of *course* he's Artane's son. Have you not two good eyes in your head?" She pointed back at Robin's siblings. "Look you at Miles, then look at Robin. They could be demon twins for all they resemble each other! And look you at Nicholas. Artane's image, only with fair hair!"

Baldwin looked. Robin found himself looking as well. It was true Miles and Nicholas looked powerfully alike, save the color of the hair, but Robin had assumed it was because . . . well, he had no idea why. It had just been so.

"What are you saying?" Baldwin demanded. "That Robin is Rhys's son?"

Edith clapped her hand to her forehead. "Aye! Sired on Gwennelyn of Segrave. I overheard her speaking of it to Lord Rhys when first I came here."

Robin gaped at her and felt his sword slide down to rest point-down in the dirt. "You did?"

Edith glared at him, then slowly she began to smile. It was a very chilling smile. "Aye. Didn't you know? Ah, apparently not. Then allow me to share the truth. Rhys sired both you and Nicholas, apparently within hours of each other on the night before your mother wed with Alain of Ayre. Did you never wonder why Ayre wanted so little to do with you before his untimely demise? I daresay he couldn't stomach looking at you and seeing his enemy staring back at him through your eyes."

Robin could scarce believe it. He looked at Anne and found that even she was looking at him with compassion.

"You knew?" he asked hoarsely.

"I suspected."

Robin vowed three things in that moment. One, he would finish Baldwin. Two, he would rescue Anne and throw Edith in the dungeon. And three, when next he saw his sire, he would kill him.

With his dullest blade.

His sire. Robin snorted. The man deserved to be disemboweled in the most painful way possible.

He glared at Anne. "Think you *he* knows?"

"Doubtful," Anne managed. "Or it could be that he already thinks of you as his, so heredity doesn't mat—"

Edith pushed her blade against Anne's throat and she ceased speaking immediately.

"Enough," Edith snapped. "Baldwin, be about your business. Once he's dead, you've four more here to see to."

"I don't want to," Baldwin said. "Look you; he won't even raise his blade against me."

Robin wished for nothing more than ten minutes to stagger about the lists like a drunken man, reeling from the impact of what he'd just learned. Hadn't he always wondered why he and Nick looked so much alike? Hadn't he marveled that he and Miles resembled each other so greatly when they only shared a mother in common?

"Now!" Edith commanded.

Robin promised himself a good think later. For now, he had to finish Baldwin and free Anne, likely within the same moment. He suspected if he killed Baldwin and couldn't reach Anne within the same heartbeat, Edith would finish her with that blade across her beautiful white neck.

And the thought of that almost paralyzed him.

He turned to Baldwin. "Very well," he said, raising his blade. "I'll give you the fight you want."

"At least you'll die a man," Baldwin sneered.

"One could hope," Robin said with a sigh.

And then it was begun. Robin pushed aside thoughts of how much rested on what he did at present, of how many lives depended on his showing there. His sword hilt was slippery in his hands and his legs felt unsteady beneath him. And he had to admit that during the first few clashes of his blade against Baldwin's he thought he might not manage it. He found himself falling back and it wasn't a matter of strategy. His blade felt heavy and awkward. His mind was clouded with shock and dismay.

And his cousin was beginning to wear the look of contempt he'd worn during every encounter in Robin's youth.

And for a moment, Robin wondered if he would fail.

Their swords came together with a mighty clash, the blades slipped down until they were locked at the hilt. Baldwin's face was a hand's breadth from his. His breath almost knocked Robin over by itself.

"Pitiful whelp," Baldwin sneered. "Shall I leave you wallowing in the mud again?"

Robin felt the humiliation of that moment wash over him again as freshly as if it had just happened. He almost went down on his knees.

"Robin."

Anne's quiet voice carried across the field. Robin looked at her and saw the trust in her eyes. She was standing with a blade across her neck, her life resting on his performance, and still she could look at him as if she thought he couldn't fail.

Robin turned and looked at his cousin and as he did, he remembered who he was.

The best bloody swordsman on English soil.

After all, all that de Piaget blood was apparently flowing through his veins and his father was a bloody good swordsman himself.

Damn him to hell.

Robin shoved Baldwin away from him. "No mud for me today," Robin said simply. "As you can see, fool, the ground is dry. But I suppose I couldn't expect someone of your few wits to appreciate the difference."

Baldwin charged and Robin fended off his attack easily. Indeed, he wondered why he'd had so much trouble with Sedgwick in the first place. The man was nowhere near his equal.

"Make haste!" Edith exclaimed.

"I'm trying!" Baldwin bellowed, increasing the fury of his attack.

Robin clucked his tongue as he easily kept his cousin at bay. "I fear those clumsy strokes simply will not win the day for you. Perhaps if you had trained a bit harder in your youth."

"Finish him!" Edith shouted.

Baldwin turned and spat at his sister. Robin didn't waste any time with thoughts of a fair fight. Perhaps he could finish Baldwin quickly and that would cause Edith to at least drop her guard for a moment. That would be enough to rescue Anne. It would have to be enough.

He suspected it might be all he would have.

Robin stepped up behind Baldwin, ready to plunge his blade through Baldwin's heart when he turned.

Only Baldwin didn't turn.

Robin watched in amazement as Edith shoved Anne away from her and slapped her brother as hard as she could across his face. Then she jerked him around and pushed him toward Robin.

"Take him," she demanded.

Baldwin stumbled, thanks to another great push, then spun aside the moment before he would have skewered himself on Robin's uplifted blade.

Edith, however, was apparently not so graceful.

Robin watched in horror as she tripped and fell.

Full onto his sword.

It came thrusting out her back, through her dress, bloodred and glinting dully in the sunlight.

Robin released his sword before he knew that was what he intended. Edith lay facedown on the ground, unmoving. Robin knelt down next to her, then rolled her on her side. She looked up at him.

"I . . . wanted . . . Artane," she breathed.

Then her eyes stared at nothing.

"You bastard!" Baldwin roared.

Robin looked up in time to see Baldwin looming over him, his sword bared and raised. Robin realized with a sickening flash that he would not have time to pull his sword from Edith's body and wield it quickly enough to fend off Baldwin's attack, nor would his only other weapon—the pitiful dagger that found itself dropped somewhere behind him in the dirt—have been sufficient for the task.

And then Baldwin stopped. With his sword upraised, he turned in surprise. Robin leaped to his feet, looking about him frantically for his dagger.

But it was unnecessary.

Anne stood there, trembling but holding her ground. Baldwin looked at her, then his sword slipped from his hand. He slowly began to fall toward her. She jumped backward awkwardly in time to have him fall at her feet.

There was a blade buried to the hilt in his back.

Robin stepped over Edith's remains and dragged Anne a few paces away, then hauled her in his arms.

"Are you hurt?" he asked frantically.

She shook her head and clung to him, trembling.

"By the saints, a man could not ask for a finer woman to guard his back," Robin said, with feeling. "He would have killed me, else."

"M-my p-p-pleasure." Her teeth were chattering. "D-don't ask m-me to d-do it ag-gain."

He laughed in spite of himself. "Pray that we never have another need, lady, but 'twas very well done."

He stood there with his love in his arms and felt a great wave of relief wash over him. They were safe. He closed his eyes and rested his cheek atop Anne's head.

"'Tis finished," he whispered.

Anne nodded. "Edith planned it, Robin. She told me as much."

"I should have listened to you."

"You should have listened to me about a great many things."

He pulled back and scowled down at her. "Did you truly know?"

"About your sire? Aye."

"And you didn't tell me?"

"Would you have listened?"

"Of course not," Robin said. He looked up as the rest of their little group shuffled over to them. He met Nicholas's gaze and received an answering look of irritation. "I'll kill him," Robin growled.

"I'll help," Nicholas said. "Give me time to heal, so we may do a thorough job of it."

"Think you *he* knows?" Robin demanded of Anne. "And how is this possible?"

"The usual way, I suspect," Nicholas said dryly. "And if you don't know what that is, you're in more trouble than I thought."

"I know very well *how* 'twas accomplished," Robin snapped. "I just want to know for a certainty *when*."

"Hmmm," Nicholas said. "We might just discover that I am the eldest."

"Ha," Robin said, but the very thought of that pierced him to the quick. He looked at Nicholas. "Think you?"

"That would be a question for your father," Anne said. She was smiling, damn her. "Why don't you ask him?"

"I fully intend to," Robin growled.

She waited. "Well, go ahead."

He cursed her, but she only continued to smile.

"Go on," she said, pointing behind him. "There he is."

Robin turned around to see none other than Rhys de Piaget, the bloody bastard, standing behind him, looking rather green. Robin decided words could be had later in abundance, as well as questions as to why Rhys found himself at that very moment standing in Artane's bailey. Now was the time for action. He launched himself at his sire, determined to throttle the life from the man.

"You knew!" Robin bellowed, taking his father down to the dirt. "You *knew* and you never said anything!"

"Robin!" his mother exclaimed. "Release him!"

Robin clutched his sire about the throat and pounded his head against the dirt a time or two for good measure. "Damn you!" he shouted.

And then, quite suddenly, he found himself on his back with Rhys's substantial self pinning him there. Robin snarled out a curse or two, but realized that his father—damn him to hell a thousand times—was still every bit his equal in size and strength.

And no wonder.

What with him being his sire and all.

Robin glared at his mother. "You knew as well!"

And damn *her* if she didn't look just as sheepish as her husband.

"Why didn't you tell me!" Robin demanded. "Damn you both!"

He had to curse, for he realized, with a start, that if he didn't continue to snarl and bellow, he quite likely would break down and sob. All the years he had spent cursing the fact that he was Alain of Ayre's son and not Rhys de Piaget's. All the times he had turned himself inside out to prove he was worthy of being Rhys's adopted heir. All that time and energy and effort. And for what?

Well, he had to concede that it had served him well, but he'd be damned if he'd admit it.

Rhys rolled off him and hauled Robin to his feet. He frowned.

"I wasn't sure—"

"*Merde*," Robin snarled.

"Very well," Rhys returned hotly, "I wanted it desperately and then by the time I was quite sure and I dared discuss the matter with your mother, you were already my heir anyway and what purpose would it have served?"

"I would have known I was yours!" Robin bellowed, then he realized he sounded like a child of five summers. He glared at his sire. "It would have been nice to have known."

"It makes no difference," Rhys insisted.

"It makes a difference to me!"

"It makes you a bastard!" Rhys exclaimed, then he shut his mouth with a snap and glared at Robin.

Robin felt his jaw slide down. And then he heard someone begin to laugh. He looked over at Nicholas and watched as his brother shuffled over and flung his arm around Robin's shoulders.

"Ah," he said with a last weak chuckle, "what a special kinship we have, Rob. Bastards both."

"I should thrash the both of you for your cheek," Rhys said sternly. "This is hardly talk for the field."

Robin could only stare at first his sire—his true sire, no less—then at his mother.

"I am having the most difficult time taking this in," he said finally. He looked for his wife. "And you?"

Anne smiled as she came and stood at his other side and put her arm around his waist.

"I love you whatever and whoever you are."

Robin grunted, then looked at his mother. "You could have told me. And how was this accomplished? Do you not think I deserve to know?"

"We could discuss it inside," Rhys said pointedly.

"Nay," Robin said. "I was married with a corpse at my heels, I may as well learn my parentage with a pair of them cooling behind me. Please, give me the tale."

Rhys looked at Gwen. "Well, wife. Go ahead. Give him the tale."

"Coward," she said fondly.

He grunted, then put his arm around her. "I wed her in my heart the night before she was forced to marry Alain of Ayre."

"Are you certain he's the elder?" Nicholas asked pleasantly.

Robin elbowed his brother in the ribs. "Continue, if you please."

"Aye, I'm quite certain," Rhys said, glaring at Nicholas, "for unlike you two randy stallions, I was a virgin before I took my lady to my bed."

Robin gaped at his sire. "You weren't."

"I certainly was."

"How did you manage that?" Nicholas asked in admiration.

"I loved Gwen from my youth and vowed if I could not have her, I would have no one." He looked at Robin. "And so I made her mine. And then those bloody Fitzgeralds filled me full of drink and when next I woke, your mother was wed to another and I was abed with," he looked at Nicholas, "um, well, your dam. And I knew nothing more of her until she died and we found you."

"Well," Robin said, blinking.

"Aye," Nicholas said, sounding just as surprised.

"And I don't regret either," Rhys growled, "and if you care to face me over blades to satisfy yourselves, I'll be happy to oblige you."

"You could have told us," Nicholas pointed out. "I already knew I was a bastard."

Rhys shook his head. "I could not have loved you more, even if I had not sired either of you. I saw no point."

"And now we know?" Robin asked.

"Will you have the entire isle know you're a bastard?"

"That depends," Miles put in. "Do I inherit all now?"

Robin gaped at his brother until he realized Miles was not in earnest. Rhys only glared at his other son, then looked at Amanda. He sobered.

"I fear, daughter, that I have no such startling revelations for you."

Nicholas put his arm around Amanda and pulled her over to lean on her. "It looks as if you and I are the only ones unrelated, sister dear."

"The saints have looked on me kindly then," she said, scowling up at him.

Nicholas only laughed and kissed her forehead. "You love me and you know it well." He looked at his sire. "Well, if you've no more interesting tidbits for us, I'm returning to bed." He made Robin a shaky bow. "My gratitude, brother, for ridding the keep of our foul murderers. I'll hear the entire tale when I'm more myself. Amanda, let me lean on you and help me back to the healer's house. Too much excitement in one day has completely sapped my strength."

Robin watched his brother, his very real brother mind you, slowly and painfully make his way back to the inner bailey. He looked at his mother to find her looking at him with something akin to compassion.

"Are you so very angry?" she asked quietly.

He sighed. "I'll survive it."

"We didn't think it would serve you."

Robin looked at his sire. "And you? What's your excuse?"

"I don't need an excuse. I'm your father and I can still thrash you on any field."

Robin found himself pulled suddenly into his sire's arms and crushed in an embrace from which he wasn't sure he would emerge intact.

"I'm proud you're mine," Rhys said hoarsely. "No matter how the deed came about in the beginning."

Robin slapped his father's back several times, then pulled away. "Then I may still stretch forth my greedy hands for all your lands and gold when you die?"

Rhys looked at Gwen. "This is your fault, this greed of his. I never had such lust for land."

"Ha," Gwen said, poking him firmly in the chest with her finger. "'Tis a flaw that runs entirely in *your* family."

"Why are you home?" Robin interrupted.

"Thugs tried to slay me on a little outing," Rhys said. "I caught one, beat Sedgwick's name from him, and we returned home as quickly as we could. Would have been here sooner if we hadn't been swarmed by your grandmother's bloody artistes."

"I didn't need aid," Robin said stiffly.

"Never thought you would," Rhys returned. "I just didn't want to miss out on a chance to watch you thrash Baldwin. If ever anyone deserved it, 'twas him."

"But Edith," Gwen said, with a shake of her head. "Tragic, truly."

"Not if you'd been here the past month," Robin said grimly. He looked at his sire. "Well, since you're here, Anne and I will be off."

"We will?" Anne asked.

"Aye," Robin said shortly. "To the shore."

"We're not staying," Rhys said.

"We aren't?" Gwen asked, sounding very unenthusiastic about another journey.

"Your mother requires our presence," Rhys said, sounding equally as unenthusiastic about another journey—especially if it seemed to include Segrave as a destination. "Once she learns of what we've just discussed—and I've no doubt she'll hear of it before we've a chance to tell her—I will never have another decent meal at her table. Besides," he said, reaching out to clap Robin on the shoulder, "my son is perfectly capable of seeing to my hall." He smiled at Gwen. "Think you?"

"Damn," Miles muttered. "So much for my inheriting everything."

Robin made a few gruff noises to cover something he couldn't identify as either relief of joy, then he embraced his father, embraced his mother, and looked at his wife.

"I'm still for the shore, lady. What say you?"

"As you will," she said, but she looked as if the prospect didn't displease her.

Robin smiled his sunniest smile at her, then realized that he had more to do than run off without another thought. He turned and looked at the fallen siblings behind him. He shook his head, then went to pull his sword from Edith's body. He laid her on her back and closed her eyes. A shadow fell over him and he looked to find his sire kneeling across from him.

"A troubled girl," Rhys said quietly.

"She wanted Artane," Robin said. "Nothing but Artane."

"Can you blame her?" Rhys asked with a faint smile.

"I don't know that I'd kill for it," Robin answered with just as faint a smile. "'Tis but a pile of stones, after all."

"Home is a different place entirely," Rhys agreed.

Robin looked at Anne and suddenly felt everything in his world shift. It settled into a peaceful, serene place and he knew without a doubt that as long as he had her by his side, the place most certainly didn't matter.

But she did love the shore.

And Artane was right there on the coast.

Robin clapped his father on the shoulder. "I'll take your keep, Papa," he said.

"And my gold, no doubt," Rhys groused.

"I won't spend it all whilst you're away."

"We aren't leaving quite yet," Rhys said. "I've a mind to talk to my steward and see what havoc you've wreaked. I understand there was a fair gathering here the past se'nnight. Is there perchance aught left in my larder?"

Robin rose. "I'll see you about it tomorrow. I've other business to attend to this day."

"Don't mind this," Rhys said dryly, gesturing expansively before him. "I'll see to it."

"Consider it a wedding gift to me," Robin said.

"I already gave you a bloody wedding gift and as you remember it was almost everything I have!"

"Damn," Miles grumbled loudly.

Robin smiled at his brother, gathered up his lady, and began to make his way across the lists.

"They look happy," came his father's voice.

"Are they happy?" his mother asked from behind them.

"Aye, and their 'happiness' has ruined my sleep for almost a se'nnight," Miles complained loudly. "Let us be grateful they're making for Robin's tent where they won't keep the rest of us awake tonight."

Robin looked at Anne and felt himself begin to blush. "Sorry," he whispered.

She only put her arm around his waist and hugged him. "They'll survive it." She looked up at him and smiled. "Are you happy?"

"Deliriously. Giddy, even, now that I have the peace to enjoy it. And for that I thank you kindly."

"'Twas nothing."

"Nay, my love, 'twas a very great thing requiring much skill and courage."

"You would have done the same for me. Indeed, I'll wager you were trying."

Robin shivered once. "It was a passing close thing, Anne. I about fell over in a faint when I saw her standing with her blade across your throat." He looked at her. "You may tell me again that I was wrong, if you like."

She shook her head with a smile. "I'll just savor it in silence."

He snorted, but couldn't help a smile. "I love you," he said as they made their way to the stables. "And I you."

Robin walked up the way to the inner bailey with his lady wife at his side and smiled to himself. He could scarce believe that not two months earlier he had come home expecting to bolt from it the first chance he got.

Now it looked as if he might never have to leave. And as he listened to the distant roar of the waves and smelled the tang of sea air trickling through the bailey, he couldn't imagine anything else. He had a marvelous hall to watch over and a beautiful, courageous woman who loved it as much as he did. And she loved him as well. He looked at his lady wife and smiled.

Life without her? Never.

Eternity with her?

Aye, and then some.

He shook his head with a smile and continued on his way.

Epilogue

The woman stood at the door of the healer's house and stared out over the courtyard, eyeing the dirt and flat-laid stone. Her mind spun with the things she had learned that morn of herbs and such. She had found a goodly work to do, and an unexpected one at that. But it behooved her to learn a bit of healing, given that she was at least for the moment looked to as Artane's lady. It had been a morn of many surprises.

For she had learned yet another thing that would surely change her life's course.

She was to bear a child come spring.

She looked at the distance separating her from the great hall and, judging the distance to be not unmanageable, released the doorframe and carefully descended the steps to the stone path that led to the great hall.

The weak autumn sunlight glinted off her pale hair and off the gold embroidery adorning her dark green cloak. The latter was a gift from her love, for green was one of his preferred colors.

"How fares the fairest flower in Artane's garden this morn?"

The voice from behind her startled her, and she turned quickly to look at who spoke. And then she smiled.

"I doubt I am the fairest flower in the garden," she said, but the saying of it did not pain her.

"You are the fairest flower in *my* garden," her lord said, putting his arm about her shoulders and pulling her close. "Is not my opinion the one that matters the most?"

She had no argument for that, so she merely smiled in reply and walked with him to the great hall. He matched his mounting of the steps to her pace, then opened the door for her with a low bow.

"After you, my lady."

"How gallant you are, my lord."

"You'll avoid letting on about that to anyone else, of course."

"Of course. Your reputation is at stake."

He merely grunted and saw her inside the hall.

And once there, Anne of Artane looked about her and felt a joy sweep through her that she was certain would never dim. There, clustered by the hearth, were the souls she loved best. All Artane's children were there, laughing and talking about things that pleased them. Missing were Artane's lord and lady, but that was nothing unusual these days. They had taken to traveling about and Anne couldn't begrudge them their freedom for a bit. They could be called back readily enough for the welcoming of their first grandchild.

She realized, as she stood with her hand in her husband's, that the scene before her would not always be as it was now. Nicholas would wed, as would Amanda and Isabelle. Miles would seek his own way and she suspected that even the little lads would find things to pull them away from home.

Home. Even the very word made her heart swell within her breast and forced tears to her eyes. It was more than she ever could have hoped for.

But should everyone in the scene before her leave, it would not diminish her happiness, nor make her any less content with her life. For her home was not before her, nor was it in the stones that surrounded her.

Her home was standing beside her, holding her hand under his cloak and wearing a gruff expression that belied the caressing of her fingers.

Whatever else happened, whatever souls came and went from the keep, if Robin was beside her, she would still have that still, quiet place she had longed for the whole of her life.

"You're weeping again." Robin looked down at her and frowned.

"I'm happy."

He shook his head and pursed his lips. "I vow, my love, that I will never understand joy of that ilk. But if you're happy, then I cannot complain."

She suspected that he would understand it very well indeed someday, but she kept that to herself. This was not the place for tender conversings. She would save that discourse for the privacy of their own chamber. And then she would give him the tidings of his coming child and see if that didn't give him reason to weep a tear or two of joy.

But for now, the joy was hers and she would nestle it close to her heart and savor it. She turned and slipped her arms around Robin's waist and laid her head on his chest. She closed her eyes and sighed.

Strong arms came around her and a cheek came to rest gently on her head.

"Does something ail you, my love?"

"Nay," she whispered.

"And the reason for your sweet arms about me?"

She sighed and smiled. "No reason. Other than happiness because I'm home."

"Home," he repeated, and his arms tightened around her. "Aye, my love. You are there, indeed."

Anne smiled.

Aye, she was there, indeed.

family lineage in the books of

Lynn Kurland

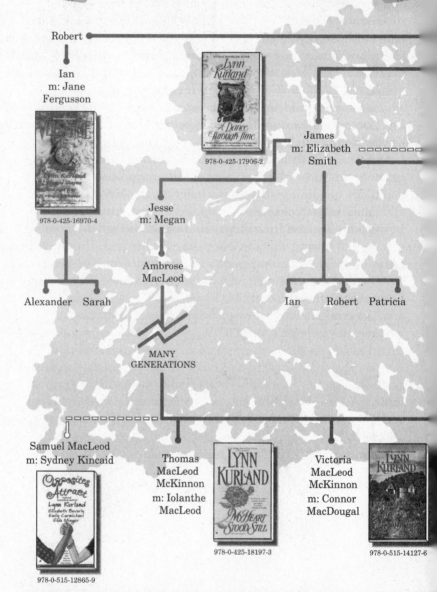

Robert

Ian
m: Jane
Fergusson

978-0-425-16970-4

978-0-425-17906-2

Jesse
m: Megan

James
m: Elizabeth
Smith

Ambrose
MacLeod

Alexander   Sarah

Ian   Robert   Patricia

MANY
GENERATIONS

Samuel MacLeod
m: Sydney Kincaid

Thomas
MacLeod
McKinnon
m: Iolanthe
MacLeod

Victoria
MacLeod
McKinnon
m: Connor
MacDougal

978-0-515-12865-9

978-0-425-18197-3

978-0-515-14127-6

MACLEOD

Douglas

978-0-425-19202-3

978-0-515-14470-3

Patrick
m: Madelyn Phillips

Sunshine
Phillips
m: Robert Cameron

Alexander Smith
m: Margaret of
Falconberg

Zachary
Smith
m: Mary
de Piaget

Julianna Nelson
m: William
de Piaget

978-0-425-18237-6

978-0-515-14624-0

978-0-515-13151-2

oel   Frances   Amery

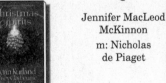

Megan MacLeod
McKinnon
m: Gideon de Piaget

978-0-515-12174-2

Jennifer MacLeod
McKinnon
m: Nicholas
de Piaget

978-0-515-14296-9

PA-4860

family lineage in the books of
Lynn Kurland

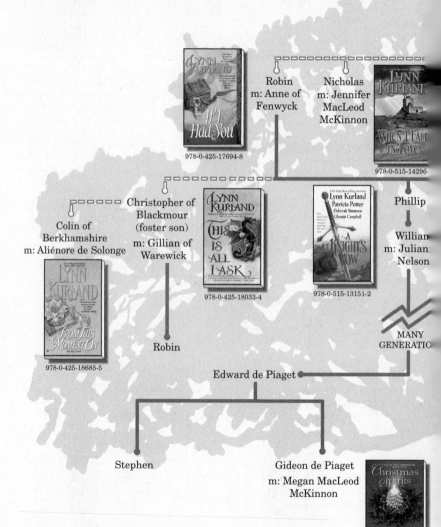

Robin
m: Anne of
Fenwyck

978-0-425-17694-8

Nicholas
m: Jennifer
MacLeod
McKinnon

978-0-515-14296

Colin of
Berkhamshire
m: Aliénore de Solonge

978-0-425-18685-5

Christopher of
Blackmour
(foster son)
m: Gillian of
Warewick

Robin

978-0-425-18033-4

978-0-515-13151-2

Phillip

William
m: Julian
Nelson

MANY
GENERATIO

Edward de Piaget

Stephen

Gideon de Piaget
m: Megan MacLeod
McKinnon

978-0-515-12174-2

DE PIAGET

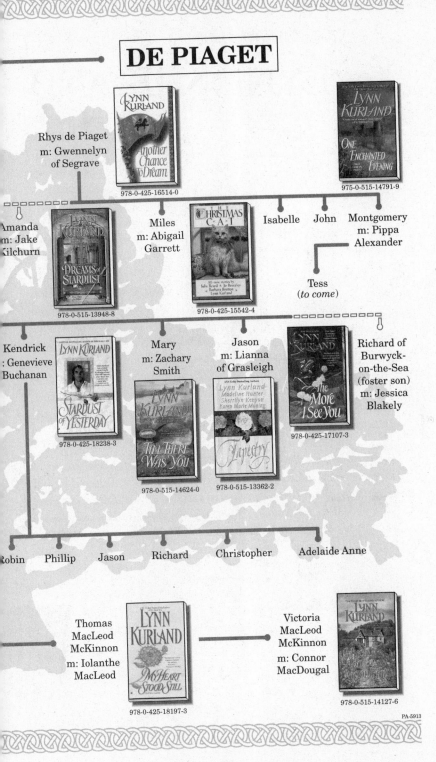

Rhys de Piaget
m: Gwennelyn
of Segrave

978-0-425-16514-0

975-0-515-14791-9

Amanda
m: Jake
Kilchurn

Miles
m: Abigail
Garrett

Isabelle John Montgomery
m: Pippa
Alexander

Tess
(*to come*)

978-0-515-13948-8

978-0-425-15542-4

Kendrick
: Genevieve
Buchanan

Mary
m: Zachary
Smith

Jason
m: Lianna
of Grasleigh

Richard of
Burwyck-
on-the-Sea
(foster son)
m: Jessica
Blakely

978-0-425-18238-3

978-0-425-17107-3

978-0-515-14624-0

978-0-515-13362-2

Robin Phillip Jason Richard Christopher Adelaide Anne

Thomas
MacLeod
McKinnon
m: Iolanthe
MacLeod

Victoria
MacLeod
McKinnon
m: Connor
MacDougal

978-0-425-18197-3

978-0-515-14127-6

PA-5913